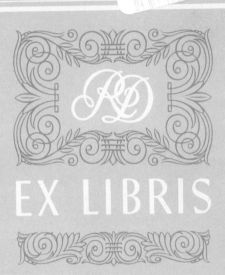

EX LIBRIS

READER'S DIGEST
Condensed
BOOKS

READER'S DIGEST

Condensed Books

Volume 1 · 1957 Winter Selections

THE READER'S DIGEST ASSOCIATION
Pleasantville, N. Y.

The condensations in this book have been created by The Reader's Digest Association, Incorporated, and are used by permission of and special arrangement with the publishers holding the respective copyrights.

With the exception of actual personages identified as such, the characters and incidents in the fictional selections in this volume are entirely the product of the authors' imagination and have no relation to any person or event in real life.

• • •

The Reader's Digest Association, Incorporated, wishes to draw further attention to the following notice by Richard Powell, author of *The Philadelphian:*

"The people and events in this story are imaginary. I have, however, used some names which have been well known in Philadelphia history for a few of my characters. The names given to my characters are in no way intended to, and to the best of my knowledge, after investigation, do not, identify any living person as being involved or a participant in any actual or supposed event or series of events similar to those described in this book. If there is any resemblance between my characters and actual people it is entirely coincidental and unintended. A check of many types of directories, including local telephone directories, the *Social Register, Who's Who* and *Poor's Register of Directors and Executives* indicates that the full names of these imaginary people do not match any of the names listed therein.

"On the other hand, any resemblance between the Philadelphia way of life, and the way of life depicted in this book, is intentional."

Contents

CAFÉ DE

CIDRE
BIÈRE
VINS

Illustrations by Harry Beckhoff

BON VOYAGE

A condensation of the book by

MARRIJANE AND
JOSEPH HAYES

Bon Voyage is a blithe account of an American dream come true. Katie and Harry Willard of Terre Haute, Indiana, were newlyweds when they started saving for a trip to Paris. By the time they set sail they had company: Amy, a beautiful daughter of marriageable age; Elliott, a world-weary teen-ager; and Skipper, a twelve-year-old dynamo.

Rocketing about Europe, the Willards managed to do everything that good tourists should, and in the process they learned a lot — about history, food, architecture. But they learned even more about romance, as the game is played in the Continental manner.

If you haven't already got a penny bank labeled "Family Trip," chances are you will have when you finish this tender, merry novel by the author of *The Desperate Hours,* in collaboration with his wife.

CHAPTER 1

THERE's nothing like a picture to bring things back to you — especially when it's in color and especially when it's a moving picture and especially when it's of you. That's how come I'm sitting here late at night, dictating this into a tape recorder. Last evening we were sitting in the living room with the projector whirring away, maybe a little nervous about what we were going to see, when my son Elliott finally got the contraption focused and then *voilà*, up there on that white sheet was the whole darn Willard family staring back at itself. (*Voilà* is one of those words that I picked up last summer, but I'm careful where I use it because I wouldn't want anyone to think I was showing off just because I spent a few weeks in France.)

Well, anyway, these were home movies, and I expect they were as good — or as bad — as most home movies. I certainly don't make any claims to being a photographer; fact is, I'm in the general contracting business. My son Elliott took most of the pictures. He was always right there and ready every time something happened. I began to suspect, while I watched the movies, that Elliott took a kind of backhanded delight in being right there just when one might have wished to heaven he'd stayed home in

Terre Haute, Indiana, where he claimed he wanted to stay in the beginning. You see, this camera had a telescopic lens fitted on it — which can make a man look pretty foolish through its sneaky little eye.

Elliott has got just one trouble — he's eighteen. Just to take an example — while we were sitting there waiting for a shot of the family in front of the Arch of Triumph in Paris — well, what we saw was a split-second view of the Arch and then a long, lingering view of a good-looking French girl climbing out of one of those low-slung French taxis. Elliott's interest began down around the ankles and then moved up. About the time the camera reached her face, this girl happened to catch sight of Elliott, I guess, and she let go with a dazzling smile, and that picture jumped up and down like the poor boy's heart was trying to batter the camera to bits.

When my daughter Amy's turn came, you could recognize her shots without any trouble because they all had a sort of excited jiggle. During the trip, Amy didn't relish taking pictures anyway; she preferred to be *in* them. When you're twenty-one and as pretty as Amy, that's only natural, isn't it?

Maybe I better go back and tell you how this whole thing started — this trip, I mean.

Back in 1933, when we hadn't been married long, my wife, Katie, and I saw a newsreel of a parade in Paris, and in the background was the Eiffel Tower. So I made the historic remark about how it'd be nice to climb that tower someday. That did it. Next thing I know, the house was cluttered up with travel folders and photographs of ships and I began to examine the bankbook and, well, it just didn't make sense, but I got pretty excited. Anything seems possible when you're twenty-some years old and been married less than two years.

What happened next caused the travel folders to be put away. We didn't talk about Paris while Katie was pregnant; we had too many other exciting things to talk about. But if you imagine she forgot, you just don't know my wife. Why, when she was sitting up in the hospital bed, with Amy no bigger than a doll in her arms, she said to me, "Amy will love Paris, won't she?"

Three years later Elliott put in an appearance. The Christmas he was seven — well, *you* know what he built with his Erector Set, right there under the Christmas tree. It sort of leaned to one side, but there was no mistaking what it was meant to be.

In the years that followed, we kept the family savings account chalked up on the kitchen blackboard. While I was in the Army during the war, we added a comma to it; and after I was released from service and started into business for myself it looked like maybe we could swing it when, well, Katie didn't really believe it herself at first, but it was true. And once Skipper arrived, you couldn't really be disappointed. Skipper is twelve years old and no matter how he behaves now (every once in a while, that is) he was about the most lovable baby you ever saw. The comma disappeared from the blackboard, but we put it back just as soon as we could, and one day Katie convinced me that for the last three years it hadn't actually been the money that kept us home, but my business — which was true. I'd been working hard to build it up and plowing money back into it in order to make more money. As Katie said, "What's the point, Harry? We don't know how much longer we'll all be together now." So Katie announced to the children, "We're sailing in June." After all that time, it was hard to believe.

You had to believe it, though, when you found yourself packed in a taxi in New York City, heading toward the Hudson River. When a ship's horn blasted, not too far away, Amy let out a shrill blast of her own: *"Listen! Did you ever hear anything so thrilling in your life?"*

Elliott swung around and fixed Amy with a disgusted expression. "Do you want them to hear you back in Indiana?"

Skipper whipped around too. "That whistle doesn't sound very big," he said. "I thought you told me the *Queen Mary* was a *big* ship. Why, heck, Amy can make more noise than that without even trying."

Amy was saying, "You can tease me all you want. I don't care about anything, I'm so happy!" She made it sound like a song.

Then, directly ahead, I saw it. The *Queen Mary* was a mighty big ship. I don't mind admitting it just about took my breath away.

I turned to see whether Katie had seen it — and she had. She was all doubled down, peering out the windshield up front, and she was *young*. She was twenty-one again, and her eyes looked like somebody'd just handed her the *Queen Mary* for a present. There are times when a man feels lucky and proud and humble all at the same time. That was one of those times. Katie was going to Europe, the way she always wanted to go, and I was taking her!

The taxi stopped at the pier entrance, and we spilled out on both sides; but Elliott managed to disentangle himself completely, like he didn't really want to be considered part of our group. Even after we turned our luggage over to a porter and started up inside in the elevator, Elliott stood kind of turned away, as if he didn't really know any of us. "What's the matter with Elliott?" I whispered to Katie.

"He still doesn't want to go, dear," Katie said. "It's that girl. You know. Ruth Hendricks."

Ruth Hendricks was a skinny little child back home who wore tight blue jeans and had black bangs. She called everybody chum. Including me. Well, if Elliott thought that he was going to throw a wet blanket on things just because of a chit of a girl with black bangs —

The elevator stopped. Then the door in back of me slid open, and everybody started to push and I stumbled backwards, with my hat slipping sideways, before I got my balance and was able to take Katie's arm. Amy and Elliott glided past, walking fast, and Elliott said, out of the corner of his mouth, "Great start, Pop."

"There it is, Harry," Katie said as we started past the gang-planks. "See? Where it says Cabin Class Passengers Only."

The way she was holding my arm, her excitement kind of rippled through our arms together. I said, "It'll be fun to roam around the boat before she sails. Thank the Lord we don't know anyone in New York so there won't be any of those bon-voyage parties."

"Hmmm," Katie replied. "You can't tell, dear. Some well-meaning relative might — "

I felt a shiver inside. "I thought your parents wrote they couldn't make it for the sailing," I said.

"They may want to surprise us. Please, Harry, act surprised and happy when we get to the cabin. You always complain about parties and then have a better time than anyone else."

I started to say, not if it was one of her parents' parties, but I didn't. I wasn't going to throw a pall on things for Katie.

We lined up at the cabin-class gangplank and, just as Elliott joined us, I caught sight of Amy. Her face was lifted up, and she was talking to someone I'd never laid eyes on before. He was almost as tall as I am, and he had reddish hair, crew cut.

When we were all on board Amy introduced us to him. His name was Nick O'Mara. He said, "Please don't blame your daughter for speaking to me. I spoke first."

Just the way he said it, I put him down in my book — too smooth. I'm not prejudiced and usually I like people, but I just didn't care for this boy's manner, or the way he'd picked up Amy or, for that matter, the way she kept hanging onto every word he said; and pretty soon Katie and I left them talking and headed for our cabins.

What Katie had said about my always complaining about parties and then having a better time than anyone else — that's absolutely true. That may be because I don't drink much: Katie and I don't circulate in the martini circuit back home. Anyway, by the time I'd had a drink at that bon-voyage party, it didn't look so bad, in its own peculiar way. Our two cabins were jam-packed with Katie's parents and a lot of people I'd never seen before, and everybody rushed over and kissed Katie, and she looked all flushed and happy.

Everybody began talking at full tilt, and it seemed they all had been to Europe at least once, and some of them had practically lived their entire lives there. A little fellow who had on one of those narrow suits that's cut short in the sleeves and has hardly any lapels at all but is supposed to be the best kind of suit you can buy came up to me and said, "Great girl, Katherine. Have you known her long?"

"A few years," I said.

"Are you from Greenwich? I've never seen you around there."

"I'm from Terre Haute," I said. "My name's Willard."

"You don't say?" he said. "So *you're* the one." He peered at me with his eyes half closed. "You don't tell me."

Well, there wasn't much I could say to that, so I didn't. I was beginning to feel the need of fresh air, but when I started to leave the room a woman stepped right into my path. She wasn't young and she wasn't old and she had a sly look on her face, like you and she knew a secret. She held an unlighted cigarette between her fingers.

"You're Harry Willard," she said, and she made it sound like some sort of guilty secret between us. I nodded, and she said, "Spark me, Harry. Please." So I fumbled around for a match, and she pushed back the veil on her hat a little and I lit her cigarette. She drew in smoke, very deep, and let it out through her nose, all the time keeping her eyes on mine. "I've been watching you, Harry, ever since you came in. You saw me."

I couldn't remember seeing her watching me. "Well, maybe I did notice," I said, and she smiled in a satisfied way.

"I'm Frieda Harrington," she said. "Now you must tell me what you were thinking about, standing off there by yourself and watching all of us. Tell me what you thought the first time you looked at me. The very first thing that came to your mind!"

Now I don't like to insult a woman, so I said: "The first thing? It was . . . what kind of perfume is that she's got on?"

Her voice grew low and husky. "You like my perfume, Harry?"

Well, I hadn't intended her to take it just that way. "What I meant was . . . there's only one thing in the world I'm allergic to, and that's perfume. It makes me sneeze."

She drew herself up like she was about to explode and then she whirled around on her high heels; and as she went away I heard her say, "Katherine did marry a backwoods boy, didn't she."

I sneezed. The way I let go, I bet the captain up on the bridge sent a sailor down below to see which engine blew a gasket. Then I got another glass of champagne and pushed my way into the passageway.

Right here I better explain about how Katie came to marry me. She came out to Terre Haute one summer to visit a girl who'd gone to high school with us and then gone East to Smith, the same college Katie was going to. To tell you the truth, when I met Katie she didn't impress me very much. She had this way of talking, all bright and in a rush and with all the right words; and besides, she seemed so *sure* of herself, the way she danced, and played tennis, and all that. And Katie thought I was too tall, too thin, too standoffish. The funny thing is, she was convinced I was too sure of myself, because, she said, I was so relaxed and quiet all the time. Well, one night a bunch of us were out on what I called a weeny roast and Katie called a wiener roast, and somehow we got involved in a silly argument about how you pronounce it.

Finally Katie and I were kneeling there, practically yelling at each other across the campfire; and I remember the way her face looked, lit up by that fire and angry and lovely, and I kept getting madder and madder, and so did she, until somebody said this was a private feud, and then they all went off and left us alone, and I got up and marched around the campfire and I said that I hardly ever lost my temper like that and I didn't like it and Katie stood up, her eyes blazing, and right then I took her into my arms and I kissed her, and she kissed me, too. And that was just about it. I knew then, just like that, that I was going to live the rest of my life with this girl, only I didn't know how. I was just an ordinary carpenter in those days and, it being the Depression, there wasn't a lot of building.

After she went back East, I waited a few miserable weeks, till I couldn't stand it any longer, and then I hopped a train to Connecticut and found her house and, after walking around the block about sixty times, I worked up enough courage to go to the door and knock. Katie came to the door, and the first thing she did, she burst into tears. She introduced me to her folks, and then she and I went out in her roadster, and I remember telling her about all the things I'd been thinking about on the train — the better ways there were to build houses, and the new materials that so far builders around Terre Haute hadn't taken advantage of, all sorts of things that I didn't even know I knew. And at the end Katie said, "If you're asking me to marry you, Harry, you don't have to promise me anything." Then, of course, her folks

raised about seven kinds of Cain and her father made me feel
pretty bad about all I'd be depriving her of, only Katie stood right
up to them. She said she was in love and that was enough; but
when her father gave her away, I had to feel sorry for the old boy,
no matter how happy I was myself, because he looked like he was
climbing up the guillotine.

So when Frieda Harrington called me a backwoods boy it all
came flooding back to me.

I started down the corridor, not exactly knowing or caring where
I was going, and there was Elliott slouched on a big leather couch
near the elevators, looking glum and bleak. I said to myself,
You've got to help the poor kid: this wasn't the spirit you started
a vacation in. Here he was, just out of high school, not knowing
what he wanted to do, trying to decide whether to go into the
Army or wait till he'd had some time in college — all the problems
kids his age are facing these days.

I sat down beside him and I thought, What can I say to the boy
anyway? So I said, "Uhh," because "Uhh" is what I invariably
say when I'm on the brink of trying to hold a serious conversation
with Elliott.

There was a pause and then he said, "Pop, is it too late for me
to get off this boat?"

"Ell, what would you do if I said no?"

"I'd hop the next train for home. You mean I *can?*"

That's the kind of a fix Elliott can put you in. "No, I don't mean
anything of the sort!" I said. "Look, Ell, the ship's crawling
with pretty girls. Why don't you find yourself one?"

"Pop, you just don't understand anything."

That's a sort of theme song with Elliott, and it made me forget
my tact and all my good intentions, too.

"Listen, Elliott," I said, "you listen to me. Nothing — nobody
— is going to spoil this vacation for your mother. So you cheer up;
because if you pull any of this long-face hocus-pocus after we sail,
I'll throw you overboard!"

Then I turned around and went down the stairs. That was
the way things always seemed to go with Elliott and me. Katie
said it was his age but sometimes I got to feeling it might be my

fault. For instance, I was all burned up because I'd been called a hick, and how could a man be sure he exploded at his kid because of what the kid actually did or because he was all worked up about something else to begin with? It's questions like that that plague a man.

Then I began to think about the things I was supposed to do, like arranging for a table in the dining room, so I found the mess steward's table, got in line and waited. I could see the deck from where I stood, and I saw Amy pass by, still talking to that young Nick O'Mara. I can't explain the way I began to feel. Back home the house was always filled with boys dating Amy, and I always got a kick out of it. But I knew those boys and their folks. This young fellow, who walked along like he owned the ship, he didn't seem like Amy's kind. Too sophisticated. Too smooth. Only that wasn't fair. Here I was finding fault with somebody just because he didn't act the way the people I knew acted. That made me as prejudiced as those people who thought I was a hick. But I reckon I sensed even then that this young fellow might threaten the family somehow.

I was still a couple of passengers away from the mess steward when a gong sounded. Then a steward came in from the deck, beating the gong and saying something about visitors going ashore. Right back of the steward marched Skipper, keeping step with him, and every time the man struck the gong, Skipper said, "Booooooong-booooooong." People were pointing and smiling and the steward was ignoring it completely. Back of me, a woman's voice cooed, "Isn't he *darling*? Isn't he *cute*?"

And a man's voice grunted, "Little demon. Why'd anybody in their senses want to take a kid along to Europe?"

So, after that remark, I arranged for the children to eat at an early mess and for Katie and me to eat later. I felt better, even if it did mean eating supper later than I like.

Back in the cabin, I found Katie and her folks in a huddle, and everyone else gone. And I could tell from the way Katie looked up when I came in that she and her folks had been talking about her sister, Elsie, who lived in Paris.

Katie knew how I felt about her younger sister. What I felt

was this: if a thirty-year-old woman decides to live in Paris and decides not to marry, well, people should let her alone. If she wanted to be a Bohemian, let her be one. Katie's folks were always trying to get her to come home and I knew they'd been asking Katie to help from the way Katie's father wheeled around and lifted his voice and said, "Why, here's Harry back among the living!" He didn't fool me though, because I knew darn well he wasn't *that* glad to see me.

He took my arm and patted me on the back. "Harry, did you arrange for the deck chairs? And what about the bath steward?"

"What about him?"

Katie's father started for the door. "Don't worry, I'll arrange it all." He kissed Katie, shook my hand and went out.

Then Katie's mother began to kiss Katie, both almost crying, and then Katie's mother turned toward me and said, "Take care of her, Harry. Take care of our little girl."

When she said that, it gave me a funny sort of feeling that Katie was a little girl and that I'd better take care of her. It was about the first time Katie's mother had seemed human, so I gave the old girl a kiss on the cheek.

After her mother was gone, Katie started straightening up, the way she would at home. Then she said just what I knew she was going to say: "I think everyone had a good time, don't you?" After you've lived a certain length of time with a woman, it's kind of astonishing the way you get to know just what she's going to say, like after a party, for instance.

"Just fine," I told her. "Now let's get up on deck."

So we went up on deck, where the wind was blowing and the ship's horn bellowing like a bull caught in a barbed-wire fence and everybody was laughing or crying, but all having a fine time.

Just then Amy materialized in back of us, her arm looped through young O'Mara's. "Nick's been to Europe six times!" she cried. "His mother lives in London — she's a famous actress! And she's married to an Englishman now, and her last husband was a White Russian!"

I was saying to myself, I was right, I was right from the beginning. "Mighty interesting life you've had, Mr. O'Mara," I said.

"Nicholas is an architect!" Amy cried.

"Well, not exactly, Amy," the young man said. "I've just finished my graduate work at Yale."

"With honors, and offers from all sides. And his sketches won some very important prize," Amy said. "And he's going over now to visit his mother!"

"Well," I heard Katie say, "we certainly do know all about you now, don't we, Mr. O'Mara?"

O'Mara said, "I know a lot about all of you too, Mrs. Willard."

"I'll bet you do," Katie said, narrowing her eyes just a fraction at Amy.

Then, all of a sudden, we realized that the ship was moving. I grabbed Katie's arm and Amy let go with a shrill squeal.

"Nick!" And she was off toward the front of the ship.

"See you again, I trust," Nick said.

"It looks that way," I said. "It sure looks that way, O'Mara."

When they'd gone, Katie said, "Harry, what have you got against that boy? I never saw you act that way before."

"I had a hunch about that fellow right from the start. Broken home! Actresses! I thought he had a crazy background."

"What does it matter, dear? Amy isn't marrying the boy."

"I'll say she's not marrying him!"

Just then Skipper came running. He stopped a few yards away and stood there, looking up at us.

"You weren't in the room!" he said accusingly. "Where have you been?"

"I was helping the steward clear the ship," I told him. *"Booooong-booooong!"* But about halfway through the second *booooong*, I stopped because Skipper's lower lip was trembling. So I stooped down and straightened his tie and said, "You ought to know we'd be on the ship somewhere, son. We wouldn't get off without you, you know."

"Well," Skipper said, "you ought to tell a guy where you're going, that's all. This is a darn big place."

He leaned over the railing and waved to everybody back on the dock. He said, "They got a whole city on here. Post office, barbershop, swimming pool. They even got a gym." I moved over to stand beside him, and he said, without looking around, "I wasn't worried, if that's what you think. I knew you were around here someplace. Hey, we're turning!"

Everybody seemed to realize it at the same time and everybody on our side ran over to the other side of the deck. Katie took my arm and said, "Don't look now, but isn't that someone we know up on the promenade deck?"

Whenever anyone says don't look now, I'm just like the next fellow, I look. And there, up on the next deck, was Elliott. He was smoking with a man-of-the-world air, and next to him was a girl with pale-olive skin and jet-black hair, tight to her head; the wind was whipping her long flowing dress around her slender body. You looked at her and you thought of harems, jewels and incense — things like that. At least I did.

Katie said, "There's a girl won't call you chum, chum."

That girl was too much. I thought of our porch at home, and Amy dashing out with one of the boys from Rose Polytechnical, and Skipper playing Run Sheep Run on the street corner, and Elliott taking the family car for a date with that Ruth Whosis. "Katie," I heard myself say, "you don't suppose we have made a mistake, do you?"

"Well," Katie said, "it's a long swim now."

CHAPTER 2

THAT NIGHT at dinner I saw that the eating arrangements I'd made hadn't worked out just exactly as I'd expected. I'd neglected to ask for a table for two, so we got a table for six, and that meant eating three meals a day with strangers. Their name was Hendrickson, all four of them, and they didn't stay strangers for long, because Mrs. Hendrickson was one of those women who talk just about all the time. She told us her whole life that night at the table, and let us know how kind it was of the senior Hendricksons to give the junior Hendricksons this trip for their honeymoon.

By about the fourth meal, it really hurt me the way Mrs. Hendrickson affected those two young people. They'd only been married for two days and you wished they'd found some little rustic cabin alongside a lake somewhere and let the senior Hendricksons go gallivanting off by themselves. The girl was small, with dark eyes that kept getting brighter all through the trip, but not with joy; and the boy was nice-looking, with a crew cut but with one of those chins that just isn't there. Maybe that was the trouble. Anyway, at the end of every meal, Mrs. Hendrickson would announce the schedule for the rest of the day, the two kids would just look at each other once, and Mrs. Hendrickson would stand up like some kind of queen, and off they'd go, all four of them, to enjoy the honeymoon.

Katie's father had bought wine for us. So about the third evening I ordered it. Then I started to talk. Right through that dinner, I talked so fast that Mrs. Hendrickson couldn't have gotten a word in with a shoehorn. I told those people just about everything that ever happened to me, and a lot of things that had never happened to anybody. Pretty soon I saw young Mrs. Hendrickson glance over at her husband and I saw him begin to grin, and then I felt a kick under the table, which was young Mr. Hendrickson's foot searching for young Mrs. Hendrickson's. At the end of that meal I said, "Mr. Hendrickson, how about a game of bridge?"

Mr. Hendrickson said, "I'll take you on, Mr. Willard. Yessir. Mrs. Willard and I against you and my wife."

That was something I hadn't bargained for, but young Mrs. Hendrickson leaped up and took her husband's hand and they started out on the double, mumbling something about a walk in the moonlight, so that made me feel a little better.

At first I thought that Mrs. Hendrickson was trying to get her revenge on me, but after a few hands of bridge I decided she simply didn't know how to play. She would bid anything just to make me be the dummy. I was dummy nine tenths of the time and this gave me a chance to walk around, which I appreciated.

It was while I was dummy for about the hundredth time that I happened to stroll out on deck to look at the moon. I looked up and, on the deck above me, I saw two people kissing. I mean,

they were *kissing*. This made me feel fine because I jumped to the conclusion that it was the young honeymooners.

Only it was my daughter Amy and O'Mara. They happened to look down and I knew they'd seen me, and O'Mara dragged Amy back away from the railing.

Well, after the game was over I said to Katie, as we walked to our stateroom, "Katie, what have you told Amy about things?"

"What sort of things, darling?"

"You know what I'm talking about."

"Well, let's see. I've always answered every question honestly. Well," she hedged, "as honestly as I could, at any rate. Am I imagining it, or has the ship begun to rock?"

"What I'm trying to get at —" I began.

"I know what you're trying to get at, Harry. What have *you* discussed with Elliott? Did you see him tonight — still another girl? That viking he played ping-pong with all afternoon. If you ask me, Elliott's in need of more instruction than Amy."

"You're not answering my question."

"Harry, Amy told me not three months ago that she'd never met a young man who stirred her in the slightest. You don't suppose we've been too strict with her, do you?"

"No, I do not!"

"Please don't bark like that. Darling, you're tired."

"Yep."

So we went to bed.

NEXT MORNING the ship had definitely begun to roll.

Skipper swooped down on the deck chairs like a tropical monsoon as soon as I reached mine after leaving Katie in the cabin writing letters. "How do you like this!" he yelled at the top of his lungs. "Boy, is this a neat tub!" He swayed with his arms stretched out. "Feel the way she pitches? Makes you feel good inside, doesn't it?"

Skipper's swaying didn't make *me* feel good inside. I stood up and then wished I hadn't. I walked around the deck and kind of got hold of myself in front of a door that said *Library*. I ducked in, thinking maybe I'd find a mystery novel, and I was trying to locate one without stooping when I saw Amy.

She was sitting bent over a table with what looked like the entire *Encyclopaedia Britannica* stacked around her; now and then she scribbled on a pad beside her. I eased around till I could see over her shoulder. On the page she was studying were the words ANCIENT ARCHITECTURE.

Easy, I told myself. Take it easy now. This is worse than you thought. I'd never known Amy to bone up on a man's subject before.

She looked around then and she said, "Hi, Pop. What happened to you?" I sank down into a chair next to her. "You've got it, too. So does Nick. He's been across so many times but he can hardly move this morning. Isn't that funny?"

"Hilarious." Then I decided that the worst thing I could do would be to start criticizing O'Mara, so I said, "He seems like a nice boy. I like him." That was a barefaced lie, but there are times in life when it's better to lie.

"You do?" Amy said. "Nick doesn't like you at all. Not you

specifically, I mean. Just people *like* you. Dull, respectable people
with families. He says — oh, let it ride."

"I'm kind of interested," I said.

"Well, he says people like you are either hypocrites, just pretending they're happy, or else they're deluding themselves. Say,
you do look bad. Shouldn't you see the doctor?"

"I never felt better. I suppose you've never met anyone like
Nick before, have you?"

"No. You have to know Nick to understand him."

"No, thanks," I said before I could catch myself.

Amy closed the book in front of her with a bang. "I knew you
hated him. You don't understand, that's all. He's been pushed
around ever since he was an infant. Schools in Paris and London
and Switzerland. His father lives in New York and gives him
money and just pushes him off! And his mother — married three
times!" Amy stood up. "Nick's a lonely boy, Pop. Even if you can't
understand it, since we've all been so lucky. Sometimes Nick
breaks my heart. I wish I'd never met him, and that's the truth!"

She ran out of the library. Now I've bungled it, I thought.
She's probably tearing straight to his stateroom right now. I sat
there for a long time, trying to make up my mind what to do,
and that's when it came over me that I'd neglected my kids. First
Elliott and now Amy had told me that I didn't understand, and
I began to wonder if it might not be true. Now was the time, now
when I had the leisure that I'd never really had before, to spend
more time with them, get to understand them.

Somehow Elliott and I, we'd lost contact. I would find him and
spend the rest of the day with him and as much time from then
on as Elliott wanted to spend with me.

After another turn around the deck that almost turned the
trick as far as my stomach was concerned, I found Elliott playing
deck tennis. His opponent was the viking Katie had mentioned.
She was all over the court, and Elliott didn't look happy. When
he saw me he stopped dead and the viking's return hit him
smack in the eye. But even that didn't seem to bother him. You
never saw a boy so glad to see his old man. He just told the viking
he'd see her later, family business, walked off and left her standing

there on her bare legs. He hustled me off down the deck, breathing hard. "That gal," he said, "is just a mass of wires and motors inside. Boy, you came along just in the nick of time. I can't escape her."

"You could say no," I said.

"She doesn't know the meaning of the word. Come on, Pop, I'll change clothes. But we gotta get the lead out, because she comes right down to the stateroom and drags me out."

In the cabin Elliott started to change, in a big hurry, and I sat down and said, "Ell, how'd you like to send a cable to Ruth?"

"What's there to say in a cable?"

"Well, you could say you miss her."

"She's probably so squiffed at me for going off, she's playing pattycake with Harold Shoemaker, just to show she doesn't care. Well, if that's the way she wants it, I can play pattycake, too."

"Your mother thinks I should talk to you about that, Ell. You'll meet a lot of young women on this trip. And, uhh, well — "

"You've sure got me pegged, Pop." He put on a sports shirt that practically screamed. "How do you like it?"

"We're not talking about clothes, Ell. Now, to handle yourself with these young women you're going to meet — "

"Pop, I'd like to talk to you, but I'm already late. You see, that little East Indian gal, Shamra, she takes a turn around the deck every day about this time. Good-by, Pop."

So there I sat, right where I usually wound up when I tackled Elliott, about midway between frustration and relief.

THE LAST NIGHT, before dinner, Katie said: "Whether you know it or not, Harry, this trip has knocked five years off your age."

Katie was right: all of a sudden I was in the gayest, friskiest mood. "By the time I get home, I expect to be about twenty-two years old again, Katie," I said.

She reminded me of that while we were dancing later, just as Elliott danced by with his East Indian girl; he winked at me and did a fancy, slow turn around the edge of the floor. I'd have my talk with Elliott later, probably after we got home. As for Amy, she danced for a while, and then she and O'Mara disappeared out on the deck. She'll kiss him good-by and that's that. Shipboard romance. Inevitable. Get it over with.

"You even dance better than usual," Katie said.

I danced her right off the floor then and we went out on deck. It wasn't a very good place for kissing, whatever the books say about a ship being a romantic place. There was always somebody strolling by, pretending not to look; and also, as Katie said, "They'll swear you're kissing somebody else's wife, Harry."

"I can't help it if they have that kind of minds on this ship," I told her.

Katie looked at me. She said, "Harry, I love you. I really do. I sometimes think it's a miracle, you and I. I honestly do."

CHAPTER 3

I T WAS just before we landed at Southampton that Katie told me about Amy. Katie said she hoped she wasn't betraying a confidence but that she and I had this understanding that we'd tell each other everything about the children. Anyway, she said that Amy had confessed to her that she was glad the sea voyage was over because she wouldn't be seeing Nick O'Mara again. She had found out something about herself on that trip. Amy, Katie said, had discovered that she had a passionate nature.

"Do you mean this O'Mara character — what happened?"

"Oh, nothing happened, Harry. Amy wouldn't let anything happen and she doesn't think Nick really wanted anything to happen. She doesn't know what he does want."

"Well, I do. I think I'll have a little talk with this O'Mara kid." I started to stand up.

"Harry, sit down." She pulled me back. "That's the reason they're so quiet today, walking round and round the deck and not saying a word. It's kind of touching. Amy says the boy's so mixed up he doesn't know what he wants out of life. He doesn't believe in marriage. Says he's seen too much of it with his mother. I feel sorry for the boy. So does Amy."

Well, anyway, I thought, this was the end of the line and this was the end of O'Mara.

THE BOAT TRAIN to London had a lot of little compartments, and we had one to ourselves. Outside the windows, little towns sailed by. It was the end of the day, men were coming home from work, women were cooking supper in the kitchens, and even if the houses did look different, with that old look that everything had — even so, life went on about the same here as anywhere. Times like that, you feel close to everybody, like there aren't really any strangers, only millions and millions of people like yourself.

Amy was slumped down on the seat opposite me, staring out the window. Looking at her made me feel sort of sad. On the dock, Katie had whispered that O'Mara's mother hadn't shown up to meet him, but that she'd had a car waiting for him to drive to London. Katie said, "Parents like that ought to be shot!" and I agreed; I'd happened to catch sight of O'Mara looking at us as we walked down the dock toward the boat train and his face had looked very young and forlorn. Still, it was a relief to think of the rest of the trip without worry about the boy and Amy.

It wasn't quite dark when I saw Amy come to life. She placed her forehead against the window, with her nose mashed to one side, so I looked out, too, and there, waiting for the train to pass, was a little open red car, and sitting on its hood was Nick O'Mara, waving a long piece of red silk back and forth.

"My scarf," Amy said. "He forgot to give back my scarf."

Well, that little car must have traveled like the wind because, every other crossing or so, there it'd be, with O'Mara waving that scarf. Pretty soon Amy was smiling, and I was cursing O'Mara to myself. But when I saw Amy happy again, I felt glad. That doesn't make sense, I know it, but that's the way it was. I just plain wanted to see Amy smile, even if it meant we'd have to see O'Mara again.

I happened to glance at Katie then and she caught my eye and she reached over Skipper, who was sleeping with his head on her shoulder. She took my hand. *"C'est la vie,"* she said softly.

"What?"

"C'est la vie," she said again. "That's life, Harry."

When we reached our hotel in London, Amy found the flowers: an enormous bouquet with a note attached and her name on the envelope. It didn't take a mind reader to know who'd sent them.

I WON'T say we saw everything in London, but I will say we wore out five good pairs of legs trying. We saw Piccadilly Circus, and Westminster Abbey, and the Houses of Parliament, and Buckingham Palace. But what I got the biggest kick out of was looking at the people, and the shops, and all. You had to get used to the idea of how old everything was, let the idea of all those centuries sink inside you, and then you could get a bang out of just strolling along. People weren't friendly the way they are in Terre Haute, but once in a while one of them would nod, friendlylike, and you'd feel right at home. Some of the men wore bowler hats and some even wore tweed suits although it was July, but I figure that's a man's privilege, to dress any way he wants to; and that's what we've got in common with the British, is freedom.

One morning we went to Madame Tussaud's, where they have those wax dummies of famous people in history and modern people, too, like Danny Kaye and Bob Hope. On the stairs there is this man wearing a guard's uniform, and Elliott, who was acting pretty bored with the whole thing, went up to him and asked where he'd find the chamber of horrors. The guard didn't answer because he was a dummy, too, with nice friendly blue eyes that stared right back into yours. Well, I saw Elliott's face turn red. That held him for a while.

You had the feeling that all these wax figures were really living. There was Lincoln and Teddy Roosevelt and Truman and Ike, all looking right back at you like maybe the next minute they'd speak up. There's this woman called Sleeping Beauty, and you'd swear she's breathing. After a while, it looks like they're all breathing.

So I wasn't really surprised to see someone I knew in there among the figures, standing still and quiet with his eyes open, the way they all did. I nudged Amy and she looked and let out a squeal. The figure came to life then and it was Nick O'Mara. He ran over and shushed Amy, who was mumbling that if the guards saw him they'd boot him out. Then he said to me, "I was in the lobby of your hotel this morning, Mr. Willard. I heard you ask about this place, so I took a chance." After that he and Amy wandered around pretty much on their own.

"I thought Amy said she didn't want to see him again," I whispered to Katie.

"He had to return her scarf," Katie said.

After that, Nick was unofficially included in the sight-seeing for the day, and I'll say this for the boy: he knew his architecture. He could tell you who'd designed a church and who'd redesigned it and which part was old and which was new. He gave me a better idea of just what work and sweat and love went into those buildings — not like the buildings I was used to putting up, all in a rush, the most important thing not the beauty but the cost. It was a day well spent, letting Nick show us around. Although I can't say I felt any better about him — not when it came to Amy.

That night, when she was getting ready to go to the theater with Nick, she said, "You still don't like him, do you, Pop?"

"I'm crazy about him. He's a great architect."

"He's not, you know. He may never be. He has knowledge and ideas, but what's it worth if he won't do anything about it?" She was pacing and she was furious. "He expects to start at the top! He could get a job in some architect's office and learn the practical side, but he says he doesn't feel like it. He's spoiled, and weak, and plain awful. He can't believe in anything or anybody! I wish I'd never met him!"

There wasn't much I could say to that; if I agreed, she'd climb down my throat; and if I didn't agree I'd be taking O'Mara's part. So I let her pace a while, talking.

"He asked me if I wanted him to get a job so he'd settle down and be just an anonymous nobody like everybody else. And I said as far as I was concerned, he might as well stop making all those handsome drawings and just live off his father and forget about being anything because he was too weak! And I told him that I didn't want to see him again, and here he is fifteen minutes late!"

"Slow down, Amy," I said. "Back up now, girl. You don't have to see him tonight, if you don't want to."

"That's the most terrible part of all. I do. I can't help it. He's gentle and considerate. And he's so alone." She kind of collapsed onto the bed, where she sat and looked up at me. "I guess my feeling about him is just something I'll have to fight through by

myself. And get over. Because that's what I intend to do, Pop —
get over it!"

"If you want to start tonight — "

"But I can't do that. He has the tickets! Besides, I'm all dressed.
Oh, don't worry, he won't even so much as hold my hand. He
knows the rules now. I can't help the way he makes me feel when
I'm with him, but I couldn't fall in love with a character like that!
I'd be ashamed of myself!"

The phone rang. It was Nick. I told him Amy would be right
down. And out she swept, tossing a kiss over her shoulder.

It was a few nights later that Nick invited us to see his mother
in the play she was in and then to go backstage to meet her. Amy
told me she was the toast of London, even if she was an American;
and on the stage she looked like a girl to me, maybe twenty-two
years old. Afterwards, we went back to her dressing room, Katie
and Amy and me; Elliott was "baby sitting" with Skipper back at
the hotel. Nick knocked on the door and it opened and she just
swooped down on us. She was wearing this negligee, all very
elegant with gold in it, only it looked a little worn and splotched
with make-up, and she hugged Nick and snatched our hands and
held on, and all the while she was talking away, "Nick, my baby,
you came, wasn't I hideous, one of my worst performances in this
dreadful farce, and you've brought them, Mrs. Willard, precious,
and Mr. Willard, so handsome and tall, isn't he the tallest thing,
and this must be Amy, Amy, you're a raving beauty, you charmer,
I've heard about you, come in, those dreadful people keep staring
at us, close the door, dahling, dammit where are the drinks, do sit
down, oh, what a nice, nice family, and so American, so down-to-
earth, Nick, how did you do it, you dahling boy, wait till I wriggle
out of this and dress, wasn't it a shameful performance, that Sir
Richard loused things up with that cannon-ball voice of his, a
shambles, dammit now I've busted a strap!"

Miss Charlotte Hatfield, as Nick's mother was known, had removed her stage make-up and put on some other that looked just
about as heavy, and she'd put on a dress, off in one corner with all
those people pouring in. Pretty soon that little room was jammed

with people, and Nick's mother, cocktail glass in hand, fixed her eyes on me. "Now tell me, dahling, you're from Terre Haute, that's Illinois, isn't it, dahling, I'm in love with Amy, she's so genuine, so straightforward, I'll tell you what we'll do, we'll get supper, I've sent Amy and my dahling for a table at the Ivy, you'll love it there, enchanting, here, splash a little more in, you're a drinking man, I can tell by your beautiful eyes, if only I were going to Paris, now tell me where you're off to after Paris."

"We'ell," I said, "we're going to drive down to the Riviera. The AAA made up a map — "

"Did they? I didn't know they did things like that, you mean they have members all over France?"

"I don't know about members," I said, "but — "

"I would have sworn you didn't have the problem, you look so healthy, dahling, but what about wine, you'll never make it through France, I'd better come with you, this is a horrible play, I'll get my barrister to break the contract, hey, listen everybody, I've made a decision, listen, will you, Mr. Willard has convinced me, I'm going to Paris!"

Nobody was paying any attention, so she reached over to the bar and picked up a tall glass and threw it on the floor. Everybody stopped yammering, and Miss Hatfield leaped up on a chair and started in again. "Dahlings, shush, please, I'm off to Paris, so please finish your drinks and go home, I love you all, go home now, dahlings, shoo, all of you, shoooo."

Everybody started edging to the door, so pretty soon we were standing on the street beside Charlotte's car, and by the time the fresh air hit me I knew I shouldn't have had that last drink. Nick's mother got in next to Katie, who said something about Harry not being able to drive a right-hand-drive car like this, in a big city. Well, sometimes my stubborn streak comes out. So I slid under the wheel. I had quite a time fiddling with the gearshift lever which came right out of the dashboard, but finally I got it into gear and gave her some gas, and we started backing up, fast. Somebody screamed and Charlotte burst out, "This is going to be great sport, give it the gun, Harry!" I managed to get the thing in first gear, and we shot forward like a bat out of hell and auto-

matically I swerved it over to the right side of the street, and a taxi
turned the corner and came straight at us. Katie was yelling,
"Harry!" and Charlotte was shouting, "Use your horn, Harry,
you've got as good a horn as he has!" She reached past Katie and
beat on the horn, and a funny little beep-beep came out. But that
taxi knew his rights and he kept coming. Then just at the last
second I remembered and whipped back over to the left side.

I was sobering up pretty fast now, although not fast enough.
Somebody said something about slowing down and I said I v.
going as slow as the car would go and I heard Katie yelling to stop
and let her out, she'd walk. So I stomped around and found the
brake and kicked it down to the floor and we all like to went
through the windshield. A lot of horns started, and then came a
high whistle. I started up again and the horns stopped, but that
high thin whistle didn't. "Turn left here, Harry, left . . . I *think* the
Ivy is down this street, but I must be wrong because this is a one-
way street and aren't we going the wrong way?" Somehow I
made another turn and then Charlotte yelled, "Stop!" I stopped
but a fellow behind me didn't. When he hit us, we went sailing up
over the curb right in front of a restaurant.

I stepped out of the car to apologize, and about then that whistle
that I'd kept hearing came closer and there, running pell-mell
down the street, was one of those London bobbies. He asked who
— puff — owned that — puff — car, he'd been — puff — chasing for
— puff — miles.

Nick and Amy came rushing from the restaurant and pushed
through the crowd, and Nick's mother started murmuring to the
bobby, who was busy writing down license numbers and things,
and while she was talking to him a man slipped up and lifted his
camera and asked Miss Hatfield please to move in a little closer,
and then he flashed a picture, and everybody in the crowd clapped
and Nick's mother laughed and waved her hands, saying, "Shoo,
please, the show's over, let's get inside, come, dahlings, I never had
so much fun in my entire life, oh, Mr. Willard, I love you dearly,
but I do see why you're going to have to let Alcoholics Anonymous
help you through France, here's our table, now where's a drink?"

"Alcoholics Anonymous?" Katie said, blinking.

"Miss Hatfield," I said, "listen. AAA means the Automobile Association of America."

"Waiter," Charlotte cried, "bring this man some milk, he's had enough, now he's trying to cover up, you shouldn't be so defensive, Mr. Willard, some of my best friends belong to your organization, here we are, bottoms up, dahlings, oh, Willards, I love you, we're going to have ourselves a wing-ding in Paris!"

WELL, next morning — our last one in London — this picture came out in the paper, and underneath it said that the world-renowned actress, Miss Charlotte Hatfield, last night was involved in a slight motorcar accident. Pictured with her were her son, Nicholas O'Mara, and his fiancée, Miss Amelia Willard, of the United States.

The way I put it to Katie was, if that picture'd come out in the Terre Haute papers we'd just naturally have to consider that Amy *was* engaged, but hardly anybody in Terre Haute reads the London papers. Katie just kept shaking her head every once in a while on our way from London to the airport.

CHAPTER 4

IT WAS fun looking down from the plane on the English country-side, all neat and in a pattern, with the fields and hedgerows and narrow little roads; but this would be a good chance, I had told myself, to study a few basic French phrases, so I started on that. I didn't get very far in the book, only to *Please: S'il vous plaît,* pronounced *Seel voo pleh,* and *Je ne comprends pas,* pronounced *Zhuh nuh kohn-prawng pah,* which means *I don't understand.* Then the stewardess came along and served lunch, with wine, and by the time she came back and took the tray the sign came on that said *Fasten seat belts.* All I could do was hope *Zhuh nuh kohn-prawng pah* would carry me through any situation that I might encounter during my visit to France.

"Harry, look! Children. Elliott, Amy, Skip — look now!" Katie's face was plastered against the window and she was straining at her seat belt. It did me good just to watch her face.

"There it is!" Amy said, from across the aisle, and then Skipper and Elliott unfastened their belts and charged over to her side of the plane and gawked out the window, and there was a faint moisture around Katie's eyes while the plane kept getting lower and lower over the rooftops of Paris. Way off in the distance I got one fast little glimpse of the Eiffel Tower.

Going through customs, I couldn't understand a single word anyone said to me, and those Frenchmen, they get mighty excited over the slightest little thing. Our porter kept asking me some question over and over, and I tried to explain, in English, that we'd like to go to the waiting room because my wife's sister was going to meet us there. I stood there bobbing my head and shrugging my shoulders and waving my arms around and pointing and Katie said, "Harry, you look exactly like a Frenchman, if only you were speaking French."

And then there was her sister, Elsie, waving and yelling *yoo-hoo* and *àllo*. She grabbed Katie and Katie grabbed her and there was a hullabaloo of hugging and kissing and laughing and crying, and our porter shrugged his shoulders and said something which I took to mean, "Emotional people, these Americans." Anyway, the French people around us all laughed and nodded.

I remembered Elsie as a harum-scarum kid, with her hair flying; but this Elsie was dressed the way women dress in magazines, neat and trim and slender, and she spoke to the porter in fast French. We all got into her little car, and Elsie drove us to our hotel.

Even my ride through London the night before hadn't prepared me for Paris. Elsie started down that street at fifty miles an hour and plunged into spaces that didn't even exist until we were through them. After London, where everybody seems to have some slight regard for human life, Paris is a jungle. If you've ever wondered about all those changes the French are always making in their gov-

ernments, you'd come to understand them in just a short drive
through Paris. It sure explains what anarchy means. In front of
the hotel, Elsie edged into a parking place that really wasn't there
and, as we went inside, Katie whispered, "Harry, you've met Elsie
before. Are you sure this is Elsie?"

Well, it seems this was not Elsie. Her name was now Elise.
She'd always detested her name, it sounded so cowlike, she told
us as we went up to our floor in the hotel's old-fashioned open-
grilled elevator. When we reached our rooms, high above the rooftops of Paris, she said a friend of hers was stopping by to meet us.
He was a novelist, and his first book had just come out in America
and the reviews were calling him the new F. Scott Fitzgerald,
wasn't it marvelous? He lived in Paris; he couldn't bear to return
to the States, because he found the atmosphere over there destruc-
tive to his talent. While she went on about him, Katie looked
across at me and nodded as if to say her sister was in love, wasn't
it wonderful?

Well, when this Arthur Pope came in he just happened to be
the kind of man sets my teeth on edge. He was big and smooth and
just a little too pleased to meet us. His grip was a little too tight and
his smile was a little too bright; and he had a habit of smoothing
his mustache, first one side and then the other. His reviews had
just arrived by air mail, he said, and Elise insisted we all have
a look. The book was about people living in Europe because the
life there was free. One reviewer said, "His first novel is destined
for popular success in the homeland he has spurned." Pretty soon
Pope shook hands all around again, and went out, saying he'd see
Elise later.

After he left, there was a lot of palaver between the girls about
Katie's parents and how disappointed they were that Elise didn't
write more often; and then Elise got a hard look around her lips
and said she wrote as often as she had time. I signaled to Katie to
lay off. After all, Elise's life was none of Katie's business and we
hadn't come to Paris on a mission.

Katie said, after her sister'd gone, "I don't think she's happy.
The poor child." Then she asked whether I'd noticed the hungry
look Elise got in her eyes when she looked at Skipper and the other

kids and I said Elise did look hungry, but only like she didn't eat enough because she was worried about her figure; which, I said, wasn't much compared to Katie's because Katie looked like she'd lived some, not like she was posing for a magazine. This put Katie in a better frame of mind.

When we went downstairs, nobody had to ask where we were going because there was only one place to go our first afternoon in Paris. But riding up in that little open-grilled elevator in the Tower gives you the sense of height and uncertainty even before you start to move, and Katie said she didn't want to spoil anyone's fun, but she thought she'd get off at the first landing if we didn't mind. So I stepped out with her. That black steel did look a mite fragile and you could feel a kind of sway, even here. Anyway it was good to be alone with Katie for a while.

Then I happened to glance up and my heart like to jumped out of my chest. Elliott, with that camera at his eye, was perched way up on top of us, kind of hanging out from the black steel, holding on by his legs! In the movie Elliott was taking, I look like I just about went crazy. I started waving my arms and yelling for him to get back, but Elliott just kept leaning farther out to get a better shot. And then he started pointing down below and I saw that little red sports car down on the street, and a figure striding from the car to the entrance of the Tower; in the sun Nick's red hair glowed like a beacon.

Elliott must have told Amy because there was one helluva mix-up then, with Nick coming up and Amy going down to meet him. Pretty soon they burst out of the elevator on our landing. Amy was angry, and Nick looked tired, with circles under his eyes. He needed a shave. I asked him if he had a pleasant trip and he said no, he'd driven all night, come across on the ferry and when he got to Paris he knew we'd probably be here, so he tore down here without even getting a shave, and now she wouldn't even speak to him! I asked if he'd seen the morning paper, and he said he'd left London before it was on the street. I showed him the clipping I had in my pocket. His eyes popped and he took Amy's shoulder and turned her to him and said he didn't know anything about this, he was sorry, it was all his mother's fault.

"I'll make them print a retraction! Why are you so sore at me? You and I know we're not going to be married!"

Then Amy looked at him, with her eyes narrowing, and said, quietly, "That's right. You don't believe in marriage, do you?"

With that she turned and pushed into the elevator just as the gate was closing and Nick went tearing after her and forced the gate open while the French guard started yelling, and then they disappeared, going down.

"You don't suppose Amy imagines she's in love with that pip-squeak, do you?" I said to Katie.

"Well," Katie said, "all I wish is that Nick had never told her he didn't believe in marriage. You know how Amy's always been about anything she couldn't have."

And right then and there, I got an idea that Katie called brilliant. We decided that what we'd do would be to let Amy see just as much of Nick and his mother as possible; we'd even throw them together. Then it wouldn't take Amy long to realize that she couldn't risk marrying a kid with Nick's crazy background and, as Katie said, she'd go back home with a bittersweet memory but no real regrets.

So we were feeling pretty good by the time Skipper and Elliott came down. Elliott said he had the whole thing on film, and it was pretty dramatic, too. He said he'd about decided that he ought to be a big-shot director in Hollywood.

"Well, Ell," I said, "you try any more of that daredevil trick stuff and you'll be a splotch on a Paris sidewalk," and then Skipper said *he'd* like to have a picture of *that*.

THAT NIGHT we met our first French-man. What I mean to say is, we met the first Frenchman we could talk with, be-cause he spoke English. We were going out to dinner with Elise and we expected she'd have that writer fellow, Pope, along, but instead the man was named Jacques Sarignac. He had a shock of dark hair and brown eyes that sort of snapped at you, and I liked him right away because when he said he was "charmed" to meet us, he said it in a way that didn't make a man's hackles rise. He sounded like he meant it. Jacques drove us through the Bois de Boulogne, and we ate outside in a fancy place right smack in the middle of the park. Right away Elliott and Elise got involved in a conversation about American movies. Elise wanted to know, did all the young people in America carry switch-blade knives and were most of them organized in gangs and did they all hate their parents the way the films made it seem? And Elliott said none of the kids he knew were like that, but he supposed since the movies showed this it might be true in other parts of the country.

Then Skipper wanted to know whether you could get into the sewers because he'd seen a movie where a policeman kept trailing the hero all through the sewers of Paris. Jacques said but of course, it would be his pleasure to take Skipper if Skipper's *maman* would give permission. I noticed Katie'd been studying Jacques pretty hard, and when she said, "If Skipper will promise to mind you, yes," I knew she'd taken to him. Well, everything seemed to be sailing along, so I proposed a toast. I lifted my glass and I said, "To Aunt Elise, also known as Elsie, and to her children when that time comes."

Katie looked at me in an odd sort of way, and Elise looked startled, and she blushed. Then Jacques lifted his glass and drained it as much as to say, *"I'll drink to that!"* Elise made some remark in French and refused to drink, and Jacques laughed, kind of shortlike, and he made some remark. The rest of us just sat there while Jacques and Elise carried on this private feud in French. It went on like that all the way back to the hotel.

When we got there Jacques shook hands and said good night and, with a tiny last look at Elise, who was glaring, strolled out of the lobby. Then Katie asked me to take the kids up to the room; she and Elise would sit in the lobby a while, she said. When she came into our room she was crying.

"Hey," I said. "Hey, our first night in Paris. What's going on?"

"She's not happy, Harry. Oh Harry, she's such a child. She wants to be free. Freedom's more important to Elsie than anything in the world. Jacques wants Elsie to marry him and have children and all that, but Elsie won't. As I said, it's a sort of principle with her."

"Nuts!"

"Harry, if only you wouldn't get so excited — "

"I always get excited when you cry! I didn't come to Paris to see you cry!"

"I've stopped crying, Harry. Let's get to bed."

So we got into bed and Katie told me everything Elise had told her — how Jacques was just too conventional and bourgeois, coming from a farm in the north of France, still a small-town type even if he was successful in the automobile business in Paris. Katie said Elise had made up her mind to tell Jacques her decision tomorrow when they took Skipper down to the sewers. Then Katie said, "It's sad, isn't it, when you think about the dreams you have as a child and what they turn into."

Well, that was an innocent enough remark, but it set me to wondering, thinking about Katie and her sister back there in Connecticut as girls, dreaming about the men they were going to marry and the kind of life they were going to have. Back home whenever I'd hint that maybe Katie had some regrets, she'd laugh at what she called my "inferiority complex" and say that she wouldn't trade our house for a castle in Spain. Only I guess I couldn't help wondering there, just for a second, whether Katie, if she had a choice, would trade places with her sister.

OUR REAL sight-seeing began next day. Elise picked up Skipper; and the rest of us, with Nick, went to Notre Dame Cathedral.

Nick knew more about that Cathedral than any guide you'd ever hire. He explained how it was begun in the twelfth century, and how it took five whole generations to build, with people devoting their entire lifetimes to it, and about the Cathedral's twenty-two chapels, and how the Gothic arch works, with no steel framing, just stones on stones making a perfect arch that seems to go way to nowhere and kind of takes your breath away. Listening to Nick, you could see all those years and all that labor and it made you wonder about those people who did the building. It made a man feel humble and little, yet proud at the same time. While Nick talked, Amy took his arm and she looked up into his face, like she was realizing how little she really did know him.

Then we left Amy and Nick, and outside the Cathedral Katie bought some of those ugly little miniature gargoyles that, Nick had explained, were exact reproductions of the ones up on the Cathedral, which the people in the Middle Ages believed frightened evil spirits away from their church. After that, we saw the

little chapel that the kings of France had used, Sainte Chapelle, with its stained-glass windows, with colors that you can't describe and that no photograph ever captures. And we went to the Conciergerie, a dungeonlike place, where Marie Antoinette had been kept during the Revolution, in a little cell with a door so low she'd have to stoop down to get in and out, so she'd feel less like a queen. Then we took a cab up to the Sacré-Coeur church, on top of a hill; from there you can see the city of Paris better than any other way, I guess.

I went outside to take some pictures, shooting down along the high steps to the little narrow street below, with shops and sidewalk cafés, and waiters standing there chatting; and *voilà!* there was Amy coming up the steps, with Nick stepping fast to keep up with her. Suddenly he grabbed her, not very gently either, and kissed her. Amy kind of struggled, and then she was kissing him hard, reckless and kind of wild. In a minute or two, she came walking by, as fast as before, her face flushed and her eyes bright and angry, and went inside the church. Nick came up to me and leaned against the stone railing and looked me in the eye and said, "Is your daughter crazy?"

"It's possible," I said.

"Back where you come from, does a girl have to be engaged before she'll let a boy kiss her?"

"Nope," I said. "I reckon there's just about as much kissing goes on in Terre Haute as in Paris."

"She likes me to kiss her. I can tell that. But she won't let me. Amy's put a price tag on herself. A pretty high price, too. Marriage."

"Young fellow," I said, "you start that sort of talk and I'm going to kick you all the way down those steps."

"Listen, Mr. Willard. I'm not interested in marrying anybody. I don't believe in marriage. It starts out fine, but after a while the people stop loving and then they find somebody else and get a divorce and start all over again. It's a trap."

"You don't think there's anything in it for you?"

"No, sir. I happen to look a little more deeply than most people. And I make up my own mind. If your daughter thinks she's going to change it — "

"She doesn't want to change it, dammit!"

"If she thinks she's going to change it by playing hard to get and if you came abroad to get a husband for — "

"The last thing in the world I want is — "

"Count me out! I only started talking to you because I thought you might be able to explain Amy, but I should have known you don't know the first thing about anybody in your family because that's the safest way to be — deaf and dumb and blind. That way people like you can pretend that you love them all, because it's a nice safe habit. And it gives you that phony feeling of importance to think they all love you back, but the truth of the matter is none of you people know the first damn thing about love! None of you!"

Then he whipped around and he went stumbling down those steep steps and disappeared. I had the impression that he was about to bust into tears, like a little boy. That's the reason that I wasn't angry: I figured this kid was about as hungry for love as any human being I'd ever seen.

I followed him down the steps and there he was, having a drink at one of the little tables that were all around. I went over and sat down, feeling as helpless as if he was one of my own kids. He was drinking a brandy, called a *fine,* pronounced *feen.* So I had one, too, and we sat there, not talking. After that, we walked back up those steps and found Katie and Amy. Amy looked at the two of us like she didn't know which one she hated more, and we all drove back to the hotel in a taxi.

When we got to the hotel Skipper and Elise told us what had happened to him that day in the Paris sewers. A guard took them in a group of tourists down under the streets, where it's like a big cave with a lot of tunnels going off on the sides, and he warned them, in French, that everyone had to stay with the group. Elise said she made a point of translating this warning for Skipper, but Skipper said he didn't remember it.

Anyway, Skipper claimed that he had to go to the bathroom and he decided he'd slip down a side sewer, knowing he could always get back to the group because they had lights. Well, that's what he did and pretty soon Elise asked Jacques if Skipper seemed to be enjoying himself — and Jacques said the child was with her, and she said he was not with her, and the guide asked if there was anything wrong, and Elise said there was a boy lost, and then she started yelling Skipper, Skipper, and pretty soon the guard was yelling Skeeper, Skeeper, and everyone was flashing lights around. Skipper said he could hear them calling, but when he went toward the voices they started coming from behind him and he started in that direction, only then they were coming around a corner. He started yelling and Elise heard him, so she cried, *Attention!* and then everybody in the group decided the voice came from a different direction and little flashlights started out in all directions with the guard screaming for them all to stand perfectly still.

"Uncle Jacques rescued me," Skipper said. "I was crying." Elise said he wasn't crying nearly so much as she was. So in all the excitement she never did talk to Jacques about her decision that day.

Katie said, "We must thank Jacques. Where is he?"

Elise said he was still in the sewers, helping the guards find all those other people who'd gone off to look for Skipper. And she said, "It was the most amusing thing. Everyone thought Skipper was ours. Imagine! Oh, Skip, don't forget, we're going on that cruise on the river tomorrow. *Au revoir.*"

After she was gone, Skipper said, "She's not as bad as she seemed

at first. I mean, I like her. She told one old dame that I was her son, hers and Jacques'!"

THE NEXT few days, by some miracle, passed without any incident; we spent them like any other tourists in Paris. It was Elliott who said, "I bet this would be some place without all the tourists." And he said *tourists* in that same way that everybody I know who has ever been to Europe says the word, like it meant criminals or something. There was hardly a tourist anywhere who didn't think there were too many tourists in Europe that summer.

Every morning Katie went shopping; she'd stagger back to the hotel loaded down with presents for people back home. The closets started to bulge, and the packets of traveler's checks to un-bulge.

One night we went to this theater famous for its horror plays. It's called the Grand-Guignol, and it's just a little bit of a place, stuck off down an alleyway, and inside it looks like it might once have been a stable.

The program said the play that night was supposed to be set in a small town in America, so that sounded interesting and we settled back and pretty soon the lights went out, and some weird music started, and there stood a big Negro, in a sort of eerie greenish light. Then the stage lights went on and we were looking at a little country jail, like the ones they used to have around Terre Haute when I was a kid. A couple of men dressed like deputy sheriffs came stomping on, one of them eating a chicken leg and the other one chewing tobacco. For a few minutes there I felt a little homesick. But then all hell broke loose. There was a siren, and a couple of other men grabbed the Negro and threw him down on the floor and three of them held him while the fourth one stomped on his arm. Well, I'm not going to go into all they did to that poor colored man, but it was pretty bad. The fact is, it was so bad you didn't want to sit and watch. Then they brought in a sexy-looking girl and she took one look at this colored man and started to wail, and then she turned around and spit in the face of the deputy, and he hauled off and landed one right on her mouth and she crumpled down on the floor, and then there was more weird music, and with that the curtain came down and that was the end of the first act.

Elliott allowed as how it was an unusual play, and I said if this was a Frenchman's idea of life in America, no wonder the world was in the mess it was in. The second act was worse. This time it was the woman who was beat up. They were trying to make her tell them something, so they whipped the clothes practically off her back. They must have got all their ideas about America from the covers of those twenty-five-cent paperback books in the drug-stores back home. I could tell Katie was getting pretty fed up.

"Well," I said, "I don't care how it ends," so we left and I don't know to this day how that play came out.

One afternoon, Nick and our kids went to Fontainebleau, and Katie went with Elise to Elise's hairdresser, so I was all alone. I decided to take a walk, and after strolling a while I sat down in one of those cafés and had a *fine*. A girl at the next table kept smiling at me in a sort of inviting way, until I had to get up and go out. Then she followed me a block or so down the street. Going into the hotel, I took a look at myself in the plate glass, trying to figure out what a young kid like that could see in me, but not feeling unhappy that it'd happened, if you want to know the truth.

I hadn't been in the room more than half an hour when Katie came in. She crossed to the mirror and took off her hat, and I could almost feel my chin hit my Adam's apple. She saw my face and whirled around. "You don't like it!" she cried.

I couldn't speak. I just stared. She kept pushing at her hair, what was left of it. It was short and swirled around her head, with a few wisps on her forehead; she just didn't look like Katie any more.

"It's the latest thing," she said, in a sort of little voice. "It's what they call an Italian cut. Elise said it would change my whole per-sonality."

I gurgled something.

"It'll grow out. My hair grows fast, Harry." She slumped into a chair. "You don't like it."

"Sure, I do," I lied. "It's . . . cute. It's a crew cut, that's what it is. If it's what you want, Katie — "

"I do think it's attractive. And different. I honestly do."

I said it was different, all right, and she said there was nothing made her angrier than having me agree with her when I didn't mean it, I said it looked very Italian and movie-starrish and she was a knockout and a lulu, and then she really did blow her lid. She said I must be seething to say those things.

Well, it went on like that through the next day. I don't know why that doggone haircut affected me the way it did. I reckon I'm a conservative and don't like to see things change. Also, I didn't care for the way those Frenchmen began to eye Katie on the street.

Then, the following afternoon, Nick's mother hit Paris like a tornado. "I rang you up first thing, dahlings, because you must come over to tea, at once, I won't take no for an answer, I'm at the George V, just around the corner, shall we say fifteen minutes, your lovely daughter, she's sitting right here, a picture, fifteen minutes, not a second longer, toodle-loo dahlings."

Well, it turned out that when Charlotte said tea, she meant tea — at least for me. When we came in, she planted a kiss smack on my cheek, saying, "You don't mind watching others drink, do you, you're exactly as I remembered you, so *distingué,* and dahling Katie, how Paree does agree with you, you're blossoming, you've turned back the clock, you were divine to come, we'll just whisper what we'll have to drink, what would you like, dahling?"

Katie looked at me, her eyes just flickering at the teapot in front of me, and said, "May I have a double martini?"

In a way I was glad. I've always said Katie should try more than one drink sometime, and I was curious to see what would happen. Every time I reached for a glass instead of a teacup, Charlotte would shake her head and beg me not to, because, she said, she didn't want me to have a relapse like that night in London. There was no use trying to explain that the AAA was not the same as AA because she just wouldn't listen.

"... horrible trip, horrible, bumpety-bump all the way, I think they stole the plane from the Wright Brothers or someone, but we're all here, now dahlings I must ask you both a great favor, please, just a trifle more for me, Nick, I need Dutch courage, to Le Corbusier, dear old Le Corbusier, what a divine architect, you've heard of him dahlings, Nicholas adores him, Nicholas and I want to show your daughter the last word in modern architecture, it's a church at Ronchamp, Nicholas wants your Amy to share his enthusiasm and I'm to be chaperon, I'm very strict, if there's anything I loathe it's loose living so you may depend on me, dahlings, say it's agreeable, put poor Nicholas out of his misery!"

Nick sat listening, with his face set and his eyes hard. He said, "Here are some pictures if you want to see them."

The pictures showed a white structure that looked like a cross between a barn and a ship. There was a big white pillarlike thing that looked like a silo, and a roof that kind of swooped up at one end to a point, like a prow of a ship. Nick said it was built of concrete and it allowed the architect to create a building without any straight or parallel lines, like sculpture. It was a revolutionary idea, yet the townspeople and the priests were pleased, and now people from all over the world went to see it. You could tell from the little throb in Nick's voice that this meant something to him that maybe I couldn't understand but that I had to respect.

"Dahlings, it's no distance at all, whist, you'll hardly know we're gone, we leave the first crack of day, about eleven o'clock, you can't refuse him, it's too close to Nick's heart, you can't."

Katie said, "How long is whist-you'll-hardly-know-we're-gone?" Then she helped herself to another martini.

"If we left before eleven, we'd be back the following evening."

Katie swallowed, and then she said, "It seems a long church to go to see a way."

Amy's eyes popped at that, and Katie blinked in my direction as if to ask what everyone was staring at.

"Then it's settled!" Charlotte cried and swooped over and gave me a kiss on the cheek again, saying what a good boy I was to sit there while everyone else was drinking, it showed immense will power. "I'll have the hotel pack a picnic lunch, cold breast of guinea hen, oh, I'm so happy to be able to do this for you, my dahling Nicholas!"

Amy stood up. "Now that it's all settled, did it ever occur to anyone to ask me?" And she stalked out of the room with her head in the air and slammed the door.

Nick took a step after her, then stopped and looked at me, as though I'd slammed the door in his face. "What'd she do that for?" Then to his mother, "You didn't give me a chance to ask her!" Then to Katie, "Mrs. Willard, if Amy had half your good manners and poise, I wouldn't be on the verge of insanity!"

He went out then, fast, and Katie said, "He didn't thank for me to wait him."

Charlotte Hatfield started in again. "Did you ever see it to fail, I always get the blame, the mantle of guilt always falls on these shoulders, dahlings, sit here and cheer me, I get lonely this time of evening, don't fret about the children, all lovers quarrel, don't you agree, Mrs. Willard?"

"Harry and I ever quarrel," Katie said. "I mean *never*." And she stood up and walked to the door. "We're past all that. Harry and I are getting too old."

Well, I had to bite my tongue then. I took Katie's arm and turned her in the right direction as we came out of the Hotel George V. She said, "Maybe you could get a crew cut, Harry."

That did it. "What do you mean, old? What made you say that?"

"I hate the taste of martinis. Why did you let me drink that jelly glassful?"

I was sore. "You act like you really want a fight."

"I do hope it was good tea, Harry. Considering the way you detest tea."

CHAPTER 5

ONE OF those travel books had said that we couldn't leave Paris without having dinner at the Reine Pédauque, so that night that's what Katie and I did. The headwaiter sat us down at a table with about eighteen glasses on it, all shapes and sizes, and then

another waiter, with a bunch of grapes embroidered on his vest, set up one of the glasses and poured some wine into it. Katie said that the wine came with the meal for the same price, a different wine for every course. I decided we'd made a mistake, because Katie'd already had those martinis, but I didn't want to say anything and have her call me old again, or worse, so I tasted my wine and it was great. Then about three waiters started bringing the food, course after course, and every time you looked up there was a fresh glass of wine, usually some other color from the last glass.

Funny thing about that wine: it didn't clap you on the back the way whiskey sometimes will; it kind of climbed up in you and gave you a hug and made you feel warm, with a glow. We were both glowing so much that we had to pass up dessert. Katie explained to the waiter that she had to watch her weight, and the waiter got very grave and said this was against nature, that madame, of all people, had no reason to watch her weight, her weight was superb, as m'sieur would verify, would I not? I said her weight suited me fine and the waiter nodded and then, when we were standing up to go and passing out the tips, he said, "May I wish madame and m'sieur a most happy honeymoon in Paris?"

When we were out on the street, Katie burst out laughing; she leaned against the building and laughed in great whoops.

"Look," I said, "it's the same line he uses with all Americans."

"Harry, that's not the truth. He thought we were on our honeymoon and that's what we are, whether you like it or not!"

Then she started to walk, and I said did she want to take a taxi and she said no, why take a taxi when you can swim?

I said, "I'm floating."

Then Katie said, "Come on, I'll beat you to the corner, Harry. I wasn't on the swimming team at Smith for nothing!" and she started to run. By the time I started to run after her, she was way down there, with her hat in one hand and her skirt up over her knees, and she *ran*. It looked like I was chasing her, and that's the idea some people got, because they started a hullabaloo on the corner and by the time I got there, there was this gendarme coming out of nowhere. He stood with his fists on his hips, looking at me as I puffed up to the corner. There was Katie with a crowd around her, all jabbering away, and when the gendarme started in talking to me, I didn't have to understand French to know what he was asking. I tried showing him my wedding ring, which made him shake his head as if that didn't make my shenanigans any better. Then Katie moved in between us and she stood on her tiptoes and kissed me; then she stepped back, smiling, and took my arm. At that the crowd of people smiled and the gendarme shrugged. A woman's voice said, *"Jeu d'amour américain"* and at that everybody got a big laugh, except me. So we got into a taxi and Katie kissed me again.

"Hey," I said.

"I love you, Harry," she said, clinging to me. "We haven't said that for a long time, have we? I love you, love you, love you!"

We were almost to the hotel when the cab came to a dead stop; the street was blocked off and behind the barricade a group of people were watching something in the center of the street. A gendarme motioned for the cab driver to back up and the driver muttered something about the Bastille.

Katie said, "Harry, they're dancing in the street; tomorrow's Bastille Day! Listen to the music! Let's dance. Tip the man, come on, darling."

We edged our way through the crowd and watched for a minute or two. The band was playing "Night and Day." There were all sorts of people dancing — kids and young lovers and tourists and old women and dignified middle-aged men and sailors in white uniforms with their red pompons bouncing, and everybody seemed to be having a fine time, so we started dancing, too. The music got faster with the next tune and I tried a few little steps that I just made up, and Katie went swinging right along, so I made up a few more. I enjoyed dancing like that; it wasn't a bit like those dances at the country club back home. In Paris that night there were banners streaming up above in the wind and a lot of voices laughing and the band wasn't anything to write home about but it was gay.

Between numbers, one of those sailors came up and made a little bow at Katie, and when the music started, he grabbed her and whirled her away, with her smiling at me over his shoulder. Then an elderly woman, wearing a shawl over her head, made a little bow to me, so I had a dance with her. She could dance, too. She was a gay little woman with crackling black eyes that still had the devil in them and the only words of English she knew were, "Is it not a pretty moon?" Whenever she said it, she looked up at the sky, where there wasn't even the suggestion of a moon, and then she'd chuckle: she knew it was a joke.

Then I happened to spot Katie and she was jitterbugging. She looked kind of startled at first, but then she began to follow the sailor's feet and, by golly, if she didn't jitterbug better'n anyone I ever saw. Her eyes were bright and her short hair was flying around and she looked like a kid. After that, an elderly gentleman in a Homburg hat made a bow in front of her and they danced, stiff and dignified, and I started twirling around with a girl about fifteen years old who had a sort of fixed happy smile on her face, like she didn't know who she was dancing with but she was pleased with the world.

I was with Katie again, and all of a sudden it came over me how lucky we were, how alive we were, with all that life beating around us. Everything that came before was only a sort of preparation for this, Katie and me holding each other in the middle of the street in Paris. Then I realized that Paris really had little or nothing to do with it. What it was, was life with a capital L, and we were realizing it, not just slipping along from day to day, with habit taking the edge off the things we felt; no sir, we were living it and knowing it, right up to the hilt. I knew it couldn't always be like that, not only because of the habits that we'd just naturally fall

back into once we were home, but because we were getting older and time was rushing by. It wasn't a bad feeling, though, because it made that night more precious somehow.

Katie must have been reading my thoughts because she said, "I didn't mean what I said about our getting old, Harry. I don't feel a bit old tonight."

I ran my hand through her hair, which was soft and beautiful, and I said, "I like it, Katie. I really like it."

She didn't answer, only put her forehead against my chest and we danced till the music ended.

WHEN Amy came back from her jaunt with Nick and his mother, she acted very subdued, and she didn't volunteer any information, just answered Katie's questions. Yes, she'd had a good time, and yes, Nick and his mother were just fine. Then she went into the bathroom to take a shower. It didn't take second sight to see something had happened to Amy.

Around noon the next day, Amy ran into me in the lobby and said, "Pop, can we eat together? I'm famished."

We found a small café, and right away Amy started talking about everything under the sun. I got to thinking while we chatted away, how strange it was — Amy was almost a woman and yet how many times had she and I, just the two of us, sat down and had lunch together, or a cup of coffee, or anything? Why didn't I think sometime to invite her to meet me downtown in Terre Haute for lunch? Here she was a woman with maybe a serious problem, and did it take *that* to make us sit down together and talk?

Finally Amy said, "It was lovely, Pop. That chapel. It has a feeling. You should see Nick's drawings of it. He climbed up on the hill and made some sketches that really catch it. They make it all clear, what the architect was after." Then suddenly she said, "Pop, do we have to hang around Paris three more days? Couldn't we just pack up this afternoon and get in the car you've rented and head south? Couldn't we, Pop?"

Well, I explained, Elise was having a party this afternoon for that writer fellow, Arthur Pope, and she would be pretty disappointed if we didn't show up, and Katie had some plans, too.

"Never mind. Skip it," she said.

"Look, Amy — "

So then she told me about Nick. She told me how it came to her, up on the hill with him, that he was hopeless. "Really hopeless, Pop."

So it was over, just the way Katie and I'd hoped it would be. It was just like a load lifting. But at the same time I didn't like that look in Amy's eyes. "Why?" I asked, finally.

"Because he's a spoiled mixed-up child." She smiled then, probably because of the way I looked, and reached across the table and took my hand. "I'm mixed up, too, Pop."

"I think you've got it all figured out pretty well."

"Well, it's not simple. On Bastille night in the village they had dancing in the square, and I danced with every male in town, even the mayor. And do you want to know what Nick did? He found himself a French girl and took her off by himself. When they came back he was furious. And so was she. And then he dragged me away from the crowd. As soon as he let go of me I smacked him, Pop, and then he got hold of my arms and tried to explain how I was ruining every other girl in the world for him. He went tramping off through the hills then. And I never wanted anything so much in my life as to go after him. Sometimes I wish I had." She stopped and lit a cigarette. Then she gave me a flimsy smile and said, "I'm sorry I bent your ear like this."

"Amy," I said, "I can get the car right after lunch. We can be in the château country tomorrow."

Amy shook her head. "I guess it wouldn't work, Pop. I can't run off and leave it dangling."

It was a woman talking, not Amy, not this child. Walking back to the hotel, she finished her story. The morning she and Nick and his mother were to leave the village, they were having break-fast on the outdoor terrace of their little inn, and Nick started talking about what he might do — which was, go back to New York, after all, take one of the three jobs he had been offered and see what he could do with it.

"Then his mother kissed him and gushed and cooed. But no sooner did she say how marvelous she thought his scheme was than he lost interest. Nick resents his mother so much, he'll do anything to cross her. Anything. Now he thinks he might drive down to the Riviera to her villa. He says he feels like swimming in the Mediterranean."

"Good Lord," I said.

Amy laughed, a short little laugh. "Thanks for listening, Pop. It's good talking to you. We ought to do it more often."

And we went into the hotel. . . .

I DIDN'T want to go to the cocktail party in the first place. Even getting ready was something in itself. Katie allowed herself about two hours and studied herself in the mirror and changed her clothes twice before she was satisfied, and she said she wished I'd stop pacing up and down while she brushed her hair because I made her nervous. So I wasn't in exactly a party mood when we reached Elise's apartment, which was the whole second floor of a pink stucco house in Neuilly. As Katie and I walked up the driveway, she said, "Now, Harry, try to relax and get over the idea people are staring at you, or waiting for you to trip over the rug or spill your drink. You don't know how charming you can be if you'll just unbend a little."

We went into the front hall, and Katie tripped on the first step of the stairway and I caught her arm. "You'd better relax a little, too," I said.

When we knocked, a man in a purple vest opened the door, another door popped open and Elise stuck her head and one bare shoulder out and said to sit down, she'd be right out, ask Philippe for a drink. Then she pulled her head in and closed the door.

"We're early," Katie said, like the world was coming to an end.

"Don't fret, dear," Elise called out. "I did say five thirty, so people would start arriving by seven. There won't be much of a crowd, because hardly anyone's in Paris. All the lucky ones are vacationing on the Côte d'Azur."

Well, everybody who wasn't vacationing on the Côte d'Azur, which means the Riviera, was in Elise's apartment in less than an hour. That place was packed to the rafters, with everybody talking at once and in a different language. The joint was jumping. Katie wandered over to where I was looking out a window and yelled, "Why don't you mingle, Harry? They're just people!"

"They don't look like people!" I yelled back at her.

That party was quite a collection. Several of the men had beards, one a great long one that had a streak of gray right down the middle of it, like it'd been painted on — which it probably had — and at least two had goatees, one of them a brilliant red. Most of the women had on skintight dresses with their shoulders bare, but there were some mannish-looking women, and some woman-ish-looking men. The place reeked of perfume. All I could do was wait for the sneezes to begin. I drank a martini and felt a little better, but not much.

"Is there anything I can get you, Harry?" Elise was moving through the crush with that cool dignified look that still didn't seem like the Elsie I'd met years ago. I said I didn't think so unless she could give me a bourbon instead of these martinis everyone was drinking, and she said, "But naturally, Harry." She took my arm and led me out to the kitchen and gave me a bottle of bourbon and a glass. "You don't approve of me, do you, Harry?"

"Approve? Sure I approve." I poured myself a stiff drink. "And what does it matter what I think anyway?"

"Do you want to know something, Harry? I often wish you had never come to Paris."

"That's nice," I said. "We'll only be here three more days."

Just then two dogs came romping into the kitchen and Elise bent down and hugged them and cooed at them. "I love them dearly," she said. "But I'll trade them both for Skipper."

I looked at the dogs. They were French poodles all trimmed up, like they'd just come home from a beauty parlor.

I said, "No deal, Elise. They're nice enough dogs, but Skippers aren't easy to come by."

Elise's eyes looked sort of unhappy. She turned on her high heels and clicked back to the party. By the time I came in she was slithering around again, with that cool little half-smile on her face. I saw Arthur Pope push through to her and kiss her on the ear and whisper something and she smiled and nodded.

"Shall we drink to the guest of honor?" I turned around and there was Jacques. "I have read his book. It reveals the struggle between the conventional American mind and the freedom-loving French. It is — how you say? — bogus?"

"You're prejudiced, Jacques," I said.

"I admit its excellence but I recognize its emptiness. Even a poor automobile salesman may be permitted to comment on literature, eh?"

She's told him, I thought. Elise has made up her mind. It's Pope and the free Paris life and she has told Jacques. He must have read my mind because he said, "We are civilized men, eh? If a woman decide, she decide. We no longer carry the club, strike her over the head, drag her to our cave. You do not object to the handsome Hungarian who is charming your wife in corner. He kiss the hand, he make love with his eyes. You no object."

"I no object," I said.

He shrugged and strolled off, and I started looking for Katie. Sure enough, she was backed into a corner by this fellow. Making love with his eyes? Hah! Katie'd handle him.

I could see she was trying to push past him, all smiles but with that strained look she gets when she wants to do something and somebody won't let her. Then I caught sight of the man's face. It was about the handsomest face I'd ever seen. He had dark hair and eyes, and he was as tall as I am. He moved as Katie did, one hand casually touching her bare arm, talking all the time.

I didn't like it. I wasn't jealous, I never get jealous, but I didn't like it. And also, Katie never looked lovelier. I was not angry, just miserable: Katie seemed to fit right into Elise's kind of life. We should have stayed home in Terre Haute. This Paris business was all a mistake.

There was an argument going on now; people were sitting on the floor and arguing about marriage. Someone said that French wives now wanted to be like American wives, with careers as well as families and husbands, and they were consequently growing unhappy and nervous like the American women. Then an elderly lady who looked like somebody's grandmother but was drunk said, But American men didn't know how to make love. They treated their women like queens, and lavished electric dishwashers on them, but only the European male understood love.

This Hungarian fellow was lighting a cigarette and he passed it over to Katie and she took it, and he said, "Perhaps we shall educate the so-charming madame by the time she leaves us."

I heard a woman's voice from way across the room: "What about Mister Willard? What does he have to say?"

"Hogwash," I said. "All you folks do is talk. Love isn't something you talk about."

They whooped and hollered and clapped then, and they all stood up, like that finished it. A little fat man came over and shook my hand.

"Did you ever drink absinthe?" he asked.

"No," I said, "but I'm willing to try anything."

He went away and Katie was standing at my side. "Harry, help me," she said. "I can't get away from that man."

"You don't want to get away," I said, and Katie frowned and whispered, "Harry, let's go home."

"Home? Home's thousands of miles away. Enjoy yourself. You're in Paris. They'll teach you a few things."

"Harry, you stop this. What's come over you? I never saw you like this before."

The Hungarian was standing there with a drink for Katie. He was smiling. His name was Rudolph Muschak, he said, and he was enjoying my sparkling wife. She was so charming, so fresh. And he looped one arm all the way around Katie's waist.

"You're kind of fresh yourself, Rudolph," I said.

"It's late, Harry!" Katie said, pushing at Rudolph's hand.

"It's the shank of the evening," I said.

"I have heard it said that American husbands are narrow-minded and possessive. Madame Willard has warned me of your violent temper. But now I meet you, I see she exaggerate."

"Did she tell you I was once a professional wrestler?"

"Wrestler, what is this wrestler? You are pulling my leg."

"Brother," I said, "when I pull your leg, you'll know it."

That really did make Katie angry. She turned around and walked away. I could feel my right fist all tight and ready, but I kept saying to myself, If you sock him, she'll never forgive you. You know how Katie is about scenes in public.

Rudolph started through the crowd after Katie, and then the fat little man came back with a tiny little glass with some green liquid in it. He explained to me how you sipped absinthe, very slow, one glass should last a couple of hours. That wasn't what I needed right then so I downed the stuff in one gulp.

"Is there more where that came from?" I asked.

All of a sudden my head felt clear and empty and the next thing I knew all that racket kind of faded away, and it was quiet. Too quiet. The strangest thing was happening to my legs. They were weaving and waving like a couple of skinny snakes doing a hootchy-kootchy dance. So I went outside on a little balcony. The fat fellow came back and handed me another little glass and eased away.

It was right about then I discovered this gay little house down in the back yard, painted red and yellow and blue. I thought it was a kid's playhouse, and I couldn't believe my eyes when somebody opened a door and Elise's French poodles went inside. It made me mad, thinking of that house for dogs, not kids, and so I hauled off and threw my absinthe glass with all my might and it hit the glass windows of that house. The dogs started barking and yipping and the glass kept falling and tinkling, and there was a hullabaloo in back of me, and pretty soon there were so many people on that little balcony that I was sure it was going to fall off the house, so I went inside and Katie was sitting on the sofa and on the floor at her feet was that Hungarian fellow, looking up in her eyes. I knew right then that I'd better get out of there.

I never would admit it to Katie afterwards, but I don't remember leaving that party. The next thing I remember is sitting at a table in this little bar they call a bistro and staring down at something in a glass that looked like it was made of old lemon peels and then looking up into the bright black eyes of Jacques Sarignac.

HE SAID, "One is not savage, is one?" And then he started talking about the consequences if one behaved today like our ancestors, dragging a woman by the hair. I said the women didn't have enough hair. Jacques said the American was closer to the original man; the Frenchman had so many centuries of culture behind him that he could only smile and behave like a gentleman.

"Let's get one thing straight," I said. "I'm not jealous."

Jacques said, "You are purple with jealousy. It is delightful. I approve. It makes one to realize his inferiority."

"Jacques," I said, "is there a law against assault and battery in France? With intent to murder?"

"We have a more civilized viewpoint: if woman is the cause, violence is to be expected."

"I think I'll go take a poke at Rudolph if you'll *pardonnez moi,*" I said.

Jacques pulled me back down to my chair saying I should not try to prove anything by violence, that kindness formed the path to a woman's heart. "You see, m'sieur, what every woman wants is a home, security, *les enfants.*"

"What every woman wants is freedom, lovers, romance."

"But a woman needs a husband, and as many *enfants* as nature will provide."

"Grow up," I said.

"He tells me to grow up. Hah!" Jacques was getting pretty worked up all of a sudden. "This American, he tells me not to be naive!"

"You've been giving me advice ever since we sat down here," I said. "I don't see why you're getting so excited."

Jacques stood up. He had a gleam in his eye. "I am excited because, m'sieur, you have convinced me! A man, if he is a man, must act! *À bas civilization!* I shall say, 'Elise, *ma chérie,* tomorrow you will go with me to my family's farm as you have so repeatedly promised. If you refuse, I shall drag you by the hair through the streets of Paris to *la gare!* You, m'sieur, have shown me the way."

"Don't put it on my head," I said.

"You, *mon ami,* and your wife and charming children are invited. It is a family celebration. Have you been to Normandy? No? You have not seen France. You will come?"

"Sure we'll come," I said.

"*Au revoir* then, till the train of the ninth hour!"

And off he went. I was feeling pretty sober now, knowing just what I had to do. I had to go back to the hotel, tell Katie I was sorry to be late and not once mention the Hungarian. After all, any civilized man would be pleased if his wife proved attractive to another man. Only a stupid American would behave as though an innocent little flirtation meant the end of the world.

On the way up in the elevator I knew Katie was going to be angry at me for leaving the party and for coming home late. I'd point out how really funny it was, her being sore at me, and Katie'd see the point. We'd have a good laugh, and that'd be the end of it.

Well, when I got to our rooms, the place was empty. It stayed empty. After a while I began to worry about Katie. I began to imagine all the places she could be and all the people she could be with. Well, not all the people, either, just one person. I stalked up and down the sitting room and smoked about fifteen cigarettes. I was beginning to get hungry. From the window, I could see the light spilling out from the front of the hotel and every once in a while the doorman opening the door of a taxi. Finally a taxi stopped and Katie stepped out. Then a tall man stepped out, paid the driver and made a little bow to the doorway, where Katie'd disappeared.

I don't know what did happen to me then. Something snapped inside. That's the only way I can describe it.

But when Katie came into the room, I was sitting slumped in a chair. I looked up and yawned like I'd been dozing. Katie took off her hat and shook her hair and asked if I was all right.

"All right?" I asked. "Of course I'm all right."

"I telephoned the hotel three times. You weren't in."

"I've been out on the town, in gay old Paree."

"You're — isn't that astonishing? — you're boiling, aren't you? That's really hilarious, Harry."

"That's me," I said. "Good old hilarious Harry. Always there to come home to."

"Harry, I want you to listen to me." She threw her hat to the sofa, and that was a danger signal, but I didn't really care. "Why didn't you lend a hand back there? You could see I needed you to get rid of that leech."

"Now, Katie," I said, "is that any way to talk about a man who's just taken you out for the evening?"

"Harry, if you don't climb down off that high horse — "

"I'll have supper sent up. How about some Hungarian goulash?"

"Harry!"

She stomped into the bedroom and I could hear her opening and shutting drawers — the second danger signal.

I pressed the little button that called the waiter and then Katie came bursting out of the bedroom, breathing fire.

"Harry, you listen. You ought to know how I feel about those handsome Joes who go around making passes at every woman they meet."

"Where'd he make passes?" I asked. "In the taxi?"

"I was speaking figuratively. Rudolph didn't make a pass."

"Oh, *Rudolph* didn't, didn't he?"

"I couldn't help learning his name, could I? I've been with the man for hours."

"Did I ask you where you've been? Did I once?"

Just then the waiter came. He stood by the door with his pencil poised and I said, "Two Hungarian goulash, medium rare."

The waiter studied the menu and then he shook his head. I pointed at something or other and held up two fingers.

When he was gone, Katie sat down and took her shoes off and she started rubbing her feet. "If that man brings goulash, Harry, I promise you I'll dump it out the window."

"I don't see what you're so charged up about," I said. "I've been a perfect little gentleman, under the circumstances."

"Under what circumstances? What about the circumstances of your leaving me high and dry at my sister's party! What about the circumstances of my chasing you all over Paris, because Rudolph said he knew where Jacques would go and that's what I've been doing, walking, from bar to bar, all up and down the Champs Élysées, and my feet are killing me!"

"Bistro," I said. "They don't call them bars. Well, just so you enjoyed yourself, that's all. That's what we came here for, so everybody'd have a good time. Each in his own way, of course."

"Harry, if you don't stop this ... !"

"If you lived here, like Elise, think of all the fun you could have." It was like I was wound up: listening to myself, I couldn't believe what I was hearing. "Maybe this is the life for you, Katie."

"If you keep on like this, I'm going to throw something."

"Can I get you something? Do you want something heavy?"

"Oh Harry, don't you see? Rudolph was playing a game; he really had no idea where you and Jacques would go. It was all a trick so he could be alone with me. Finally I called a taxi. Rudolph hopped in with me and then, going through the park — " She broke off and looked at me, with her eyes flashing, and I waited. "Harry, get that expression off your face! Yes, he kissed me. You might as well know. I slapped him. And then I told the driver to take me to the hotel, *tout de suite,* and I left a perfectly good new glove in the taxi, and if you don't get that expression off your face, I'm going to slap *it!*"

I knew I should grin or maybe kiss her. But I heard myself say, "I thought you said he didn't make a pass. What do you call a pass, Katie? I'm kind of curious." And that's the way I sounded, too — curious but detached. Katie stood up, with her shoe in her hand. I said, "No man can kiss a woman who doesn't want to be kissed, can he?"

Well, that did it. That gold-colored, high-heeled shoe sailed through the air, straight at my eye, so I ducked and it went right out the window. Katie was breathing hard, with her feet planted wide apart, and we stood there and stared at each other, waiting to hear the shoe break a glass down below, or hit somebody who'd yell bloody murder. There wasn't a sound. I stuck my head out the window, but I couldn't see anything.

"I hope you're satisfied," Katie hissed.

I said, "I hope they don't throw us out of the joint."

Katie stooped over and picked up the other shoe and threw that one out the window. I watched it sail.

"Well, that one lit in a tree," I said.

Then Katie went into the bedroom and I lit a cigarette and called myself a few names and decided I'd better wait a little before I tried to straighten things out. Then Elliott came in.

He walked over to me and reached under his jacket and brought

out a high-heeled gold shoe. He looked at me, in a kind of be-
fuddled way, and said, "It's Mother's, isn't it?"

"It doesn't look like your mother's to me," I told him.

"It's got a Ben Becker label, and that's where she buys her shoes
in Terre Haute. I found it in the gutter in front of the hotel."

"Go throw it away, and don't mention it to your mother. She
has a headache." I looked out the window at the tree across the
street. The other shoe was still hanging there.

"I hope it doesn't blow up a storm tonight," I said.

CHAPTER 6

IT GAVE me a jolt when I saw, in the movie of the trip, the shot
that Elliott took the next morning, a long moving shot of the
Paris rooftops, dropping down to Katie's shoe hanging in the
branches by its heel. But I never volunteered any explanation to
Elliott because, until a kid's grown up and married, he wouldn't
ever be able to understand how a woman who loved her husband
could throw a shoe at him.

If you'd seen Katie's face that morning, you might've doubted
that she *did* love her husband. It had been a cold night and the
day promised to be colder, and I'm not referring to the weather.

She wasn't too pleased at joining Jacques and Elise on the trip
to Normandy, and she wanted to let me know it and at the same
time not let the kids know it. She was talkative and acting mighty
gay. She always has the idea this fools the kids, but the truth is,
it always makes one of them whisper to me, "What's eating Mother
today, Pop?" Which is what Skipper asked us as we went into
the railroad station. "She's getting tired of *croissants* for breakfast," I said.

Jacques didn't drag Elise into the waiting room by her hair,
but she looked like she was being dragged. He was exuberant and
friendly, shaking our hands. "The sisters, they look alike, I see it
now," he said. "They have the same two expressions, yes?"

I looked at Katie and Elise. "Yep," I said. "The Gold Dust
Twins. They both got up on the wrong side of different beds."

There was a hoot and a clack and a clatter and we all piled onto the train, taking one of those little compartments. Jacques sat looking out the window, watching the rich farmland country get lusher and richer-looking, with its vineyards and its expanses of grain fields and meadows with fat healthy-looking cattle. He looked like a man who was going home, and I knew that feeling. You could tell that it was a prosperous part of the country. You'd see sleek, handsome horses, not plow horses but thoroughbreds, looking proud and strong and confident. If there's anything I love next to people it's a horse, so I sat there and feasted my eyes. Jacques caught my eye once and nodded; he knew what I was thinking.

The train kept making stops, alongside neat little towns, with white stations, and cobblestone streets curving between rows of stone houses, and finally Jacques herded us all off at one of these little towns. We got into a high old-fashioned bus with wooden seats, and we chugged and bumped over the countryside, down little dirt roads between apple trees, fields of poppies that looked like red lakes, and the sweet-smelling vineyards. A light came into Jacques' eyes when we stopped in the center of a village, with the church on one side with organ music coming from it and a big statue in the center of the square. A big old black car was standing there waiting. The driver looked like Jacques, only younger, and he and Jacques hugged and smiled and clapped each other on the back. Jacques introduced his brother, and we piled into the car and whipped out of town to the Sarignac farm.

It was a big place, with three stone houses grouped around the farmyard, looking like they'd been standing there for centuries. The barns and stables were enormous. People poured out of the houses, and they all started hugging Jacques and bowing and smiling at us. I couldn't understand what they said, but they sure did make a man feel welcome. They ushered us into the main house, which had rough hand-hewn beams on the ceiling, and we all sat down and stared at each other. There was an enormous man in a stiff-looking black suit, smoking a pipe; and a woman who must have been his wife, almost as big as he was, kind of smiling at us; and then there were all the others who I guessed were Jacques' relatives. It was uncomfortable at first, just sitting there

in the stiff furniture staring at each other and not being able to talk
except through Jacques, but pretty soon Jacques' father broke out
the applejack. "Calvados," Jacques explained as the womenfolk
served us all. Then more people started pouring in, in cars and on
bikes, all marching in and bowing and listening to Jacques translating the same things over and over. Elise sat off in one corner with
a look of distaste on her face, and Jacques kept glancing over at
her, looking like everything had gone wrong and he wished he was
back in Paris and hadn't dragged her along, by the hair or otherwise.

Then another car pulled in and right away you could tell that
somebody important had arrived. Jacques' father stomped outside
and ushered in a little old lady, in a long black dress with lace at
her collar. She had a small wrinkled face and keen little eyes that
snapped at you, and she was about as dignified a woman as I'd ever
seen, even if her hands were kind of rough-looking and she was a
little stooped. When Jacques introduced us she just nodded, till
she came to Elise. She looked Elise up and down and said something to Jacques in French and he said something to Elise. Elise
turned around slowly, like one of those models, and the old lady
looked her over from head to heel, and then said something else
(it was my guess the old lady had said she was too skinny), and
Elise snapped something in return, which caused the old lady to
lift her brows and smile a little, enjoying what Elise had said back
to her. Then she took Elise's hands and turned them over and examined them, and I noticed the enormous ring the old lady was
wearing. It sparkled in the sunlight. She looked into Elise's face,
with her eyes crackling, and she shook her head. Well, Elise threw
her head up in the air and sat down.

Pretty soon we all went outside where long tables had been set
up under the trees and we sat down to eat. Each course was itself
a full meal, and after about three or four along came a fish for each
person, each one big enough to serve maybe three people. All the
time they kept passing artichokes and salads that smelled of garlic
and there was pea soup with sausages, and mussels in garlic sauce,
and eggs stuffed with shrimps, and I don't know what all. Every
time I thought the meal was over, the women'd come staggering

out with more platters. We must've sat there eating for over an hour. Then suddenly everybody started getting up and stretching. I was stuffed. Jacques said, "It is customary to delay two hours before the main course. I hope you are not too hungry."

Jacques' father showed me through the barns and stables. He kept puffing away at his pipe and pointing to his prize cows and horses, and I kept nodding and trying to indicate that I thought he had quite a little old farm, yes, sir. Then he broke out his accordion and started to play, perched up on a chair under a tree. So I reached in my pocket and brought out my harmonica. Pretty soon everybody was crowding around, and Jacques' father kept going from one tune to another, with me managing to keep up with him. After a bit he took off his tie and his stiff collar and tossed them to the grass, so I took off my tie and my jacket and the big man took off his. It turned into quite a party, all in all.

Skipper was off with the kids, riding a horse cart, all of them yelling and shouting. Elliott and some of the young people were playing like kids; one young girl about Elliott's age was real pretty and bright-looking, and when Elliott started showing them how to have a three-legged race, it gave him an excuse to tie his ankle to her ankle. When he sprawled with her on the grass, everyone laughed and clapped and shouted — all except a dark-looking boy who glowered and looked like he'd enjoy taking a swing at Elliott.

I could see Katie standing inside the window of the kitchen, so I *pardonnez-moi'd* myself and walked over to the window. Katie had an apron on and she looked more like herself than she had in days. She was washing dishes. I reached in and ran my hand through her hair and she laughed, and that's all there was to it, but it meant we were both sorry and it meant a lot of other things, too.

Feeling about a million times lighter, I went back to Jacques' father and I started in on "On the Banks of the Wabash," which he'd never heard before. But he joined right in when I hit the chorus the second time, so I began to think up other songs like "Swanee River" and "A Pretty Girl Is Like a Melody" and "Old Black Joe" and we had us a big time. A lot of people gathered around and a girl who looked to be about Amy's age asked for

"Stardust," saying just that one word in English, so I played that, wondering how she'd come to know it. Skipper came tearing back then, saying I should see the bullet holes in the barn where an American paratrooper had hidden during the war. So then I knew how this girl, who must have been a very small child at the time, came to know American songs.

When everybody started drifting back to the tables, Elise appeared. She was dripping wet, from head to foot, and her hair was plastered around her face, and her Paris dress was clinging to her and covered with mud. But she carried her head high. I noticed Jacques' grandmother studying her but you couldn't tell what she was thinking. Nobody said anything, even after Elise disappeared into the house. Then Jacques came over the hill, carrying a stick and swinging it at the flowers and weeds, like he was hot under the collar. He came over to the table and sat down. Skipper piped up. He wanted to know what had happened to Aunt Elise. Jacques said, "She fell into the river. She slip. It is true I was angry, yes, but she slip."

Then everybody started to eat and to talk hastily about other things and in about ten minutes Elise came back out of the house. Her hair was all natural and blowing, and she wore one of those peasant skirts and a white blouse and no stockings and flat-heeled shoes. She looked like the Elsie I remembered, and about ten years younger. Jacques' grandmother moved over and sat down on the bench next to her. Then, Elise looked straight across the table at Jacques, and she stuck out her tongue. Only she did it in such a way that there was a smile behind it. Everyone whooped and laughed and Jacques' face was the color of one of those ripe apples on his father's trees.

That meal reminded me of a family reunion back home, only none of the food here was like that. We had long loaves of bread, crusted hard on the outside, and Burgundy beef and roast suckling pig with chestnuts and about the best cheese I ever sank a tooth into and cold roast duck in red wine, and tarts and cakes with wild strawberries, and a lot of other kinds of fruit. It all reminded me of a painting I saw once that always stuck in my mind. It was by a Dutchman, I think, named Breughel, and it showed people eating

and kids running around and all, with wheat fields in the background. It always seemed to me to say more about people and what they really like to do and be than anything I ever saw.

Afterwards, telling everyone good-by and trying to thank them for the day when you just couldn't thank people for a thing like that even if you knew the language, I felt time rushing by. I can't explain it, but in the midst of all that gaiety and laughter, I could feel time going right past my ears, like a wind.

Back on the train, meandering through the dark fields back to Paris, I realized something else had happened that day. Jacques and Elise were sitting across from me, with Skipper nestled sound asleep against her. I happened to glance down at her hand, and there was that big ring that I'd seen earlier on the wrinkled hand of Jacques' grandmother. I looked at Elise, who smiled; and then Jacques whispered, *"Merci, merci beaucoup."* I didn't know what he had to thank me for. But then I got to thinking, looking at Katie next to me, that maybe somehow all of us did have something to do with what happened between Jacques and Elise. It came over me again, that sense of time rushing by, and I was sorry the day was over.

O**N OUR WAY** from Paris to the Riviera, we stopped at Versailles, and traipsed all over the palace and gardens. We stopped at Chartres to see the Cathedral and then scooted on down into the château country, full of places right out of a fairy tale. Some of those châteaux have upwards of three hundred rooms, all elegant. You wondered how a man could ever sit down and kick off his armor and really relax in a place like that.

Amy had her heart set on seeing some caves that had some of the oldest paintings known to man on the walls and ceilings. "Nick O'Mara's idea," Elliott said. We all piled out and went in. Well, it was worth it. Prehistoric cavemen had painted pictures right on the walls and ceilings there — horses and ponies and wild bulls that looked like they were alive and moving. It gave you a queer feeling, thinking of all those thousands of years. We bought a booklet called *The Caves of Lascaux,* and Elliott studied it for hours as we drove along.

We stopped at Carcassonne, which is the only truly medieval city in France, with a wall still intact around it; and then we rolled on into Provence. Katie said, "Look! Look, Amy! It's Van Gogh country!"

And that's just what it was. Amy has two or three pictures by Van Gogh hanging in her room, and they never meant very much to me till I saw Provence; but with the sun glaring down on the fields and the poplars, by golly if it didn't bring those pictures to life. Or maybe it's the other way around. Anyway, it sets a fellow to thinking, the way a man can come along and see a place in his own way and put it down on canvas in paint and then, years later, another man can drive along and look at those same fields and feel he can see them clearer and better, just because that artist painted them a certain way.

My favorite place of the trip, though, was the coast between Toulon and St.-Raphaël, where the red rocks jut up in crags from the bluest water I ever saw. I could have stayed there longer, but everybody was eager to get to the Riviera.

I had an idea when we hit Cannes that I wasn't going to like it. Maybe it was because of the way Elliott kept looking out the windows at girls in those bathing suits that just aren't there; maybe it was because no sooner'd we pull up in front of our hotel than I saw that little red sports car again. Or maybe it was because of that note that was waiting for Katie at the hotel desk:

Dear Madame Willard:

Is it not a beautiful coincidence that I have been urged to Cannes on business so that we may continue our conversation which was begun so charming in Paris? With deep admiration,

Rudolph

CHAPTER 7

CANNES, Nice and Monte Carlo — that's what most folks refer to as the glamorous Riviera. It's a great place if you like to dress up to your ears at night and undress to practically nothing during the day. It's an international sort of place, too; you can hear almost any language on the streets and beaches — Chinese, Italian, Hindustani, Brooklyn — but the language that really talks is an American dollar bill. As a matter of fact, a dollar bill just makes a little squeaky sound and not even a twenty-dollar bill comes right out and hollers. One of the reasons I remember the Riviera is, that's where I had to cable my bank in Terre Haute for more money. I didn't mention this to anybody; they were all having too good a time.

The first few days were nice and peaceful. I didn't see a lot of Nick and Amy, but enough so that I noticed that Nick was awfully quiet. He seemed to be studying all of us.

First pop out of the box, Elliott took up with this little French girl on the beach, wearing one of those Bikini things. She was always with Elliott; he even dated her evenings. As for Skipper, he badgered me into shelling out ten dollars, and he went trotting off and came back to my bench on the sidewalk with a pair of binoculars. One peak through them — you could practically see Spain — and I knew they must've been worth maybe two hundred dollars. They had a name stamped on them, in gold letters, *Property of Samuel P. Goodwin,* but Skipper said he didn't believe he bought them from Mr. Goodwin, because the man looked more like an Arab. So we went on a hunt for this Arab, and Skipper spotted him just about the same time the Arab spotted Skipper, and that was that. He must have rubbed his magic lamp, because he just plain went up in smoke.

Then there was Katie and that Rudolph. If I'd let it, that could have ruined everything. I decided to ignore Rudolph.

"You can talk about ignoring him," Katie said. "I can't. He appears out of nowhere as soon as I set foot out of this hotel."

"Rudolph told me he'd never met a woman like you before, Katie. The more you try to avoid him the more he'll chase after you."

"You . . . you talked to him about all this?"

"Katie," I said, "that's the way things are done over here. You don't want me to paste him one, do you?"

"If you do that, Harry, I'll never forgive you."

"Katie," I said, "I won't make a fool of myself again. I know you don't give a hang about this so-and-so. If only he wasn't so damn pleasant about it, smiling and talking to me like I'm some bystander or something. He makes it all seem innocent, somehow."

"What Rudolph has in mind isn't innocent, Harry."

ONE DAY we lunched with Charlotte Hatfield, who had rented a villa near Nice. It was pink and it was perched up on a hillside overlooking the sea. No sooner were we out of the car than she came plunging down the steps and took Amy in her arms and then Katie, and she even kissed me.

"Dahlings, you really came, isn't it magnificent here, oh, Mr. Willard as tall as ever, so strong and silent and *distingué,* my dahling Amy, *ma petite,* no wonder poor Nicholas has the shakes, come in, oh Nicholas, yoo-hoo, come out, Nicholas baby, he's pouting, Amy, why is he pouting, have you been cruel to my boy, have an *apéritif,* only not you, Mr. Willard, tea for you, and I do hope you've been behaving yourself. . . ."

When the drinks came, Nick passed them, his face set and the muscles in his jaw jumping. Charlotte kept going all the time: ". . . now we can settle down to some serious talk, let us all sip our lovely drinks and discuss the marriage arrangements, it's obvious of course that you'll want it to be in Terre Haute, Illinois, and frankly — "

We all sat up straight at that and Nick clutched his glass so I thought it'd shatter in his fist.

"Mother," he said, "if I've told you once, I've told you a thousand

times, Amy and I are not going to be married, in Terre Haute, *Indiana,* or anywhere else."

"Nicholas! There is no need to get vehement — "

Nick whirled to face his mother. "Get it straight. I-have-not-proposed-to-Amy, I-am-not-going-to-propose-to-Amy, and-Amy-and-I-are-not-going-to-be-married! What do you think of that?"

Well, Charlotte was too much of an actress to take that sitting down. So she stood up. "You'll have to get used to Nicholas' violent moods, dahlings, he's so emotional, I worry about him, I suspect he's fundamentally unstable, I'm only warning you, you're all so calm and collected and poised, now, Nicholas, my pet, let's sit down while we discuss matters in a rational manner."

For a second I thought Nick was going to pick his mother up and throw her over the parapet. But he walked over to Amy and said, "I'm sorry, I didn't know she was up to this. Tell your father, Amy — have we so much as mentioned the word marriage?"

"Nicholas!" Charlotte cried. "Don't you know how to handle anything, my poor pet, can't you do anything delicately, one doesn't discuss these matters, I begged you to leave me alone with the Willards today, but no, no, no, you insisted on staying, if you have any sense at all you will grasp this chance at security, this opportunity for marriage with a simple, lovely, Midwestern child who will trust you and love you, you will beg this child to be your wife!"

Now Amy stood up. I thought she was going to explode, but she didn't. She took Charlotte's hand and she said, smooth as silk, "Thank you for asking me, Charlotte. I can't remember when I've spent a more revealing half-hour."

And she turned on her heel and went down the steps.

"Nicholas!" Charlotte screamed. "Nicholas, go after her, run, child, you have been a boor and unforgivable, but she loves you, I can see it in her eyes, she loves you and she is hurt, oh run, what are you waiting for, you weak-kneed little wretch!"

Nick picked up a bottle of gin and went into the house, without glancing at any of us.

Charlotte slumped back into her chair. "You raise them and

you never know, I've done all I could, to see him throw away his one chance at a decent life, the travail that boy has put me through, popping in, popping out of my life, nothing ever enough!"

Katie cleared her throat and we both stood up and managed to say good-by. In the car, we didn't say a word for a long time. But finally Katie blurted out: "I don't understand her or Nick or any of it, even Amy."

"Don't try," I said. "Relax and just drift, darling."

So we drifted back to the hotel, and Katie remembered a little shop where she'd spotted a wedding gift for Elise, so she got out and I went back to the rooms alone. I found Amy in a Bikini bathing suit Charlotte had bought for her in Paris. Elliott was doubled up laughing. "Pop, look at her," he said. "She's a mess."

Well, I looked at Amy and she looked back, just daring me to cross her. All the time we'd been in Cannes, she'd been soaking up the sun in a conventional bathing suit, so most of her was tan now; only there were parts of her that were white, and those parts were exposed by the little pieces of nothing that made up that Bikini. She was a sight, but I knew better than to say that. So all I said was, "Where are you going, Amy?" and she said she was going for a swim and she threw on a beach robe and stomped out.

"Son," I said, "this promises to be one of those days. I'm going to catch forty winks so I'll have the strength to face the rest of it."

Only it didn't work out that way, naturally. No sooner'd my head hit the pillow in the bedroom than the telephone shrilled like a wounded animal and I heard Elliott talking in the sitting room, fast and excited. Then, in a few minutes I heard hushed voices in the sitting room. Even before I got up and went in, I knew the day was going along just about the way it had started. Sure enough, when I came in, Elliott stopped talking and turned to look at me, with his face the color of a half-ripe tomato, splotched green and red. Sitting primly on the sofa was the little French girl I'd seen around with Elliott. Standing at her side, with one hand on her slim shoulder, was a big Frenchwoman. The woman's name was Madame Clébert, Elliott spluttered, and then he began to quiver all over.

Madame Clébert was enough to make anyone quiver. She had bright black eyes, stood like a ramrod, and was bursting with righteous wrath. "M'sieur," she exploded, "m'sieur, it cannot be done! The rich *Américain* cannot come and do this thing!"

"What thing?" I asked, beginning to glare at Elliott.

"It may seem lightness and nothingness to you, in your country, m'sieur, but you will find that it is a costly business here."

"What isn't?"

"Hah, he laughs, he makes *américain* joke, eh? It is not so amusing, m'sieur. You will find. The police, they take interest in protecting the virtue of my daughter."

It didn't take much clairvoyance to tumble to what she was up to. All it took was looking at her, and at her daughter, sitting there half embarrassed and half determined, avoiding Elliott's eyes.

"If the rich *Américain* wishes the scandal" — she went on; a shrug — "he will have the scandal" — bigger shrug — "but if he wishes to close the matter without scandal, we can do so with quick dispatch!" — biggest shrug of all.

I lit a cigarette, thinking hard. "Madame," I said, "what is the price of the virtue of your daughter?"

Madame Clébert drew herself up, with her mind clicking in back of her snapping eyes. "There is no such price!"

"How much?" I said again.

"If m'sieur comprehends that there is no price for virtue, we leave this matter entirely in his generous hands."

I sat down and crossed my legs. The fact is, I was beginning to enjoy this. "Son," I said, "what did you have to do with the virtue of this woman's daughter?"

Elliott didn't move. "Absolutely nothing," he said.

Madame made a great huge shrug then, smiling as if she didn't believe him and knew that I would not believe him, either. Then it hit me — out of nowhere. I uncrossed my legs. "Madame," I said, "my son will marry your daughter."

"Marry?"

"As a matter of fact, Madame Clébert," I went on, "I've been worried we wouldn't ever find a wife for this boy. Your daughter is an answer to a father's prayer."

"M'sieur jokes."

"Jokes, heck. Sit down, take the load off your feet, my wife'll be here in a minute. You might as well meet the whole family."

For the first time the girl spoke. "Mama, he speaks of the marriage?"

"He sure does," I said. "Elliott, phone down for champagne. We'll celebrate." I nodded pleasantly at Madame Clébert.

"The m'sieur," she said then, "he is — how you say? — comical man, no? Hah hah, he make joke."

"Hah hah," I said. "He sure does." Then I walked over to the girl and I reached down and opened her mouth and examined her teeth. "How old did you say this girl is?" I asked.

"Old? Old?"

"Is she strong?" I asked.

"Strong?" Her voice sounded a little weak.

"For the farm," I said. "We need strong women on our farm. Does she know anything about cattle?"

"Cattle?"

"Well, never mind. If she's not strong enough, we'll put her in charge of the hogs."

"M'sieur . . . is . . . ?"

"Here's the champagne! I'll open it myself, waiter." And I grabbed a bottle and knocked it against the marble top of the table, breaking the head off. The wine went fizzing and bubbling all over the wall and the floor. I walked over to the woman and shoved the broken bottle at her.

She was backing toward the door. *"Fou!"* she kept yelling, *"ce m'sieur, il est fou!"*

The waiter decided not to stay. He went out the door, forgetting to make his little bow.

"Fou Américain!" the woman shouted. And she started making motions to her daughter, who stood up and went walking around me in a big half circle.

"Fou to you, too, madame," I said.

The girl broke into a run and the woman backed out and closed the door. I turned to Elliott. *"Fou* to you, too," I said.

Elliott wiped his brow. *"Fou* means insane, Pop."

"Then she sure picked the right word. Come on, get some towels and help me wipe up this mess before your mother starts asking questions." While he was in the bathroom, I called, "And next time stick to dates with girls who have bangs and call me chum."

AFTER THAT episode, I began to think about Amy out there on that beach in her Bikini, so I went outside and walked along the sidewalk that runs all along the shore. I didn't find Amy, but I found Skipper. He was on a bench, with his binoculars. He said, "Amy's having herself a big time out there, Pop. You want to look?"

"No, thanks," I said. "Out where?"

"In a little motorboat out there with Nick. They're kissing."

"I didn't let you buy those glasses for this, Skipper."

He looked through the binoculars again. "Now they're not kissing any more. They're arguing. Amy looks sore. . . . Now she hit him! Wow! Pop, Amy hit him!"

I grabbed for the glasses, and found the boat. I saw Amy stand up, getting poised for a dive, with Nick reaching for her. It was like watching a silent movie. Amy turned around to Nick, and she said something, and then she dived in and started to swim for shore. Nick stood up in the boat, yelling at her, but Amy kept right on swimming. All I could do was watch. I wasn't even surprised. I couldn't be surprised any more. I saw Nick go over to the wheel of the boat and fiddle with the controls, and then he whipped the boat around and came alongside Amy. He cut off the motor and leaned over the side, reaching for her, but Amy just swam away from him, and then he ran back and started the motor and headed for her again. People along the shore line saw the commotion, and soon there was a good-sized crowd standing there watching Amy swim and Nick try to pick her up.

"I've got to hand it to Amy," Skipper said. "She's not good for much else but she can sure swim. Pop, it's my turn."

I handed him the glasses and started walking down the beach to where Amy was heading. She reached the shallow part, stood up and walked in, breathing hard, her chest heaving, but her head high. Nick yanked the boat around and then he headed straight into the shore. That little boat came like a bat out of hell, and ran up on the beach so hard the whole bottom must've caved in. Nick flew through the air and landed face down on the sand. I ran over to Amy, and walked her back to the hotel so fast Skipper could hardly keep up.

Inside the sitting room, she said, "Pop, I was never so ashamed in my life." Her teeth were chattering. "Let's go home."

"We're leaving tomorrow. Tonight if you say so, Amy."

She gave me a kind of faded half-smile and went into the bedroom, saying over her shoulder, "Tomorrow will be fine, Pop."

I SHOULD have known better than to take Katie to the Monte Carlo Casino that night. But it was our last night and she had her heart set on it.

We both dolled up in our best bib and tucker — which means my ten-year-old double-breasted tux and Katie's gown she'd bought in Paris — and we went. Nick was there, alone, at the roulette table: betting and betting and losing and losing. We watched for a while, getting used to the hubbub and the glitter, watching the little ball click round and round and stop. Nick looked at me kind of funny once in a while, almost like he was thinking of something insulting to say but he never said it. He made me nervous. I wondered what had happened on that boat with Amy, but I didn't want to discuss it tonight. Then in popped Rudolph. Katie, who was sitting down by that time, glanced at me in a kind of disgusted way when he came over and included himself in, not quite shoving me aside to stand behind Katie, but it amounted to that. He bent down and whispered into her ear, all the time smiling and cheerful; then he moved some of her plaques around on the board and, wouldn't you know, she wins.

Pretty soon I noticed that Rudolph wasn't exactly keeping his mind on the game. I happened to see his hand sort of drift down against Katie's bare shoulder. It made me go all hollow inside. But I decided to ignore it. Then the next thing, he was standing there with one hand resting right smack on her shoulder. Katie reached up and shoved the hand off like a fly or something, but

Rudolph simply smiled down at her in a pleased way. So Katie stood up, pushing back her chair and catching him in the shins with it, and she strolled over to another table where they were playing baccarat. Rudolph strolled alongside. Meantime, I was getting hollower inside and my collar was getting tighter and tighter. Rudolph pushed in next to Katie, explaining the game to her in whispers. His left arm was all the way around her now. His eye happened to catch mine right then and by gosh if he didn't smile, like we were old buddies or something.

That did it. I didn't even know I'd moved till I saw Rudolph sprawled out on the floor. I wouldn't have believed what happened if it hadn't been for the pain that started in my right knuckles and then spread up my arm. It was the best pain I ever

felt, though I knew I'd done just the thing Katie would hate. People came running, and hollering in about seventy different languages, and next thing I knew I was being half ushered and half pushed by two men through a couple of fancy rooms, and outside, and then a couple of policemen grabbed me and walked along with me in between, neither one of them touching me.

I thought that I was going to be tossed in the clink, and I wondered how I'd ever get out of it, since I couldn't speak the language. But mostly, I was thinking of Katie and how she must be feeling. Those policemen marched fast down some stone steps and around a couple of curves, with the Casino all bright and gay in back of us. It was still worth it. If I end up on a chain gang in Monaco, I kept telling myself, it was worth it.

They took me into a little beat-up café, with hardly anybody inside, and then out on a dim little alleylike street. There were a couple of French gendarmes standing around there, and there was a confab between the Monaco police and the gendarmes with all four of them glancing over at me once in a while. I lit a cigarette and watched my hands trembling.

A pair of headlights turned down the alley then; a car stopped, and I heard a familiar voice speaking French. Then Nick stepped into the light and came over to me. "It's all right, Mr. Willard," he said. "Come with me."

I climbed into the car and Nick reached out his hand, which was filled with franc notes, and one of the policemen grabbed them and tapped his cap and then turned to his friends and started dividing them up as we headed back to Cannes.

"They don't like bad publicity in Monaco," Nick explained. "So they turn undesirable characters over to the French police that way. The café's on the border, you see. The front door's in Monaco and the back door's in France. It's done all the time. I sent Mrs. Willard to the hotel in a taxi. I've got some questions I want to ask you."

"Nick," I said, "I've got a few I want to ask you, too."

"Why did you sock him?" Nick demanded.

"Because he's had it coming for a long time."

"You did it because you're in love with your wife, didn't you?" Nick was staring straight ahead. "How long have you been married?" he asked.

"Twenty-two years," I said.

"Twenty-two years. To the same woman. And you're in love."

"You're darn right I am," I said. "Now what about your telling me what happened on that boat?"

"Well, it all goes a long way back. You see, I've never met anyone like you or Amy before. And while you were on your way down here from Paris, I began to think I was really in love, Mr. Willard. The way you are. But when I saw Amy again, I didn't know how to handle it. Mr. Willard, I don't want to be engaged. It frightens me. And with a girl like Amy—"

"*Are* you engaged?" I asked.

"No. And now Amy doesn't want to be."

"Because of what happened on the boat?"

"That and a lot of other things. Do you know what Amy said to me once? She said it might be better if I loved my mother, rather than hated her. I didn't even know I hated her. But the more I thought about it, the more I knew Amy was right. And then I saw the way you and Mrs. Willard get along and I began to see all Mother's missed, and pretty soon I wasn't hating her. I was pitying her. It's all happened too fast, Mr. Willard. My head's going around and I guess I shouldn't be talking to you like this, but I haven't ever had anyone I could talk to before." He twisted his face away. "Why couldn't I have had an old man like you?"

He slowed down then, pulling up in front of our hotel. The beach looked white and still in the moonlight. "Go ahead and spill the rest, Nick," I said. "I'm not in any hurry to face the music I've got to face up there."

A ghost of a smile crossed Nick's lips, and he said, "You've got a right to know what happened on the boat. Well, Amy was in a funny mood this afternoon. I think she'd decided that, since you're going back to Paris tomorrow, we might as well . . . have something, even if it was only —" He broke off and shook his head. "And I was a little sore at everything, so I said to myself, so what, why not?"

He stopped and fumbled for a cigarette. "I'm the great so-what kid, Mr. Willard." He took a deep pull and exhaled. "Matter of pride. So when she came out on the boat with me, I made a fool of myself. And while I was kissing her, she changed her mind. I asked her why she came looking for me if she didn't intend —" He swallowed. "Well, she slapped me and dove into the water, and I was so mad because I thought she was going to drown I nearly died. And after she made it, I smashed up the boat."

"You sure did, Nick. What're you going to do now?" I asked.

"I'm taking the morning plane to Paris. Then New York, and a job." He opened the door of the car and got out. "You take care of Amy, Mr. Willard. Take care of her."

And he went striding down the street, his shoulders hunched and his hands jammed down in his pockets.

I went up to the rooms, and I don't mind admitting my heels dragged. Sure enough, there was the whole family sitting there. I could tell from the calm expression on Katie's face just how put out she was. But right then all I could think of was Amy.

"Amy," I said, "Nick's taking the morning plane to Paris."

She lifted her brows. "You don't say? I'm sleepy." She yawned and strolled toward the bedroom. "I had a long swim. It makes me tired." And she closed the door after herself.

"Did they arrest you, Pop?" Skipper asked.

"Why aren't you in bed?" I said.

Elliott piped up. "You laid him flat, eh, Pop?"

"How much did they fine you, Pop?" Skipper asked.

"Katie," I said, "you told the kids!"

Katie came over and took my arm. Her voice was hushed. "Naturally I told them, darling." She was smiling. "There may have been other ways of doing it, Harry, but that was your way."

"Children!" I shouted. "Get to bed!"

And when they'd gone, I still stared at Katie. She was smiling, with that devilish look I'd seen in her eyes when she was dancing in the street. Finally she said, "It was your way, Harry, and that's all that matters. If it's your way, I love it, darling." She was hugging my arm tight. "Just think — tomorrow morning we'll be on our way home. Won't it be great to be back in Terre Haute again?"

THE EXOTIC Riviera looked a lot nicer in the early morning when we turned away from the beach and up into the hills, going back to Paris. To get a picture of the part of the country we hadn't seen, we followed the Rhone River north, and turned off into the hills at Lyons, toward Vichy. For almost a whole day we traveled through the rolling country, where the mimosa grows so close together and so lush it's like riding a boat through waves of yellow.

It was a funny thing, but once we got into Paris we all had the same feeling: that it wasn't a strange place at all. We walked along the Champs Élysées again, all of us, under the chestnut trees, knowing we were leaving in the morning and that this was good-by. Something was coming to an end, and we all knew it and really didn't want to talk about it.

The next day we went up to Normandy, on the same train as before, and it was like coming home, because Jacques and his family, in the midst of all the preparations for a wedding, took us right in. Elsie looked fifteen years younger; she looked like a child.

Elsie and Jacques were already married, Katie explained to me in our big bare room that night.

"They've been married at the civil ceremony, but tomorrow is the religious ceremony. Meantime, they can't be alone together. You do like Elsie now, don't you, Harry? Because you should look as though you really love her tomorrow when you give her away."

"When I *what?*"

"Oh, Harry, you don't even have to rehearse it. Just do what Jacques tells you in the morning. You only have to learn a few little phrases. I've got them all written down here in my notebook."

Well, I stayed up most of the night, studying those phrases in the light of a candle in our bedroom. And next day I marched down that aisle and acted like I was Elsie's father, and everybody said I did fine. It was worth it, too, when I saw Jacques and Elsie kissing each other afterwards. That wasn't a nervous peck on the lips, the way most grooms kiss a bride in America. This was France, and that was a *kiss*.

THE PLANE from Paris to New York stopped over at Shannon Airport in Ireland, where we had a good big dinner, topped off by Irish coffee — which Katie swore was an old Irish custom but which I think is an invention of the air-line companies. It's a tall glass with Irish whisky in the bottom, then heavy black coffee poured over that, and whipped cream on the top. It's a good way to ruin coffee and it doesn't do a thing for that Irish whisky, either. What it did do, though, was to put you in a spending mood, and let me tell you that airport's no place to be in a spending mood. Katie said the prices were *unbelievable,* and that's just the way I'd found the prices all over Europe — unbelievable. However, I reckon no self-respecting man ever came

home from a vacation with money in his pocket. Katie fell in love
with some Irish linen, and Amy got excited over some Conne-
mara-marble bracelets — and Elliott found a sports jacket that,
without it, he couldn't grow up or something. For myself, I
thought I'd take some of that Irish whisky back to Terre Haute.
The only smart one was Skipper. He said, "If it's all the same to
you, Pop, I'll just take the money."

It had been dusk when we left Paris and it was still dusk when
we left Shannon and it stayed dusk all the way to New York, only
then it was called dawn. That's how fast that plane was traveling.
We put down at Iceland to refuel, and I slipped away to have a
cup of coffee in the airport. Elliott joined me at the counter.

"Pop," he said, "what would you say if I told you I think I'll
start college instead of enlisting? Because there's something I
want to study. Before this trip I never had anything I was really
interested in, but now I'd like to find out all there is to know about
history — not just battles and dates. Before all that. Way back in
the time that we don't know much about. As soon as we get back,
I'm going to find out what's the best college in the country for
archaeological study and I'm going to try to get in. Does this
sound nuts to you, Pop?"

"If that's what you know you want, son, I'm all for it."

"Well, that's it." He stood up from his stool. "You know what
got me started on this? Those caves at Lascaux. I can't get 'em
out of my mind." We were walking back to the plane now. "Did
you ever see anything so beautiful in your life, Pop? Did you?"
And then, just before we went up the steps, he sort of jabbed my
ribs with his fist. "You should have clobbered me a couple of times
back there, Pop. I just wanted to say thanks."

And then he went up the steps fast, and from behind he looked
like a man, not a boy. It gave me a funny feeling. And then it
came to me that we'd had our first talk. We'd sat down together,
like friends, and we'd talked.

On the plane over Pennsylvania and Ohio and Indiana, everybody got as excited as they had on the plane between London
and Paris — which is right and natural, because I wouldn't give

you a plugged nickel for a man who didn't get a kick out of seeing his own home.

And then, a few weeks later, after we'd had the rolls of film developed, we invited my sister over, and also that Ruth girl (who'd let her hair grow because Ell didn't like those bangs) and Elliott ran off the pictures. While the projector was clicking away, I couldn't help glancing around the room and thinking back on everything that had happened. I got that same funny sense of time that I'd had before. In a month or two Elliott would be moving on to college and, after that, the Army; Skipper was almost ready to graduate from grammar school and, after that, it was no time at all till he'd be on *his* way; and Amy'd already moved off in a sense: she was a woman sitting there. I remembered Katie dancing in the street on the eve of Bastille Day. Right then I was *aware*. I could look back and I could feel the present and I could see the future, too.

The last reel flickered through and the sheet was white and bright up there on the living-room wall and then Elliott flipped off the projector. In the darkness, everyone moved at once, and then someone flipped on the lights, and there was Ruth, making for the front door, her shoulders set and her face hot with jealousy, and Elliott after her. "Ruth's gone to buy herself a Bikini," Skipper said.

Katie said, *"Pardonnez-moi* while I make some lemonade."

Outside I heard a familiar sound. The purr of a motor. But not like the motors of any of the cars in our neighborhood. Then I saw Amy's face and right away I knew why the motor sounded so familiar. Amy looked like she couldn't move; she couldn't breathe, that was sure. Katie came to the kitchen door. "Harry, did someone stop in our driveway?"

"Yep," I said, "they sure did."

There was a knock at the door. Amy was too paralyzed to move, so Skipper leaped over and threw it open and then he started pounding Nick on the back, and Nick was stepping toward Amy, and I took a glance out the window and sure enough there was the little red car. When I turned back into the room, Amy and Nick had just stopped kissing and Katie was asking Skipper

to run down to the corner for some ice cream. So after Skipper'd
taken off, I walked over to Nick and we shook hands and I
told him we were all glad to see him and asked how long did
he plan to stay and he said he had to be back at the office in New
York on Monday morning and I looked at Amy then, and it was
like saying good-by, but not as bad as I'd always imagined it
would be.

Then I went out to the kitchen and told Katie to skip the lemonade and put on some coffee and I'd break out the Irish whisky
and whip us up some cream. Then I happened to glance at the
blackboard and, on top of the grocery list, in big white letters,
I read, HIM. $759.62. So I said, "Katie, what does HIM. mean?"
and she said, "Don't you remember that TV program we saw
night before last? You said you'd always had a secret hankering
to try to climb one of those mountains."

"A small one is what I said, Katie."

"Well," she said, "they have all sizes in the Himalayas."

"The Himalayas," I said. "Hmmm. That's near India, isn't it?
I've always wanted to see Bombay, too."

"Have you, darling? So have I. I've got some maps in the drawer
here, and the travel agent says — "

"Katie," I said, "what made you decide to visit in Terre Haute
that summer?"

"Oh, you know me, Harry. I've always liked to see distant
places."

Marrijane and
Joseph Hayes

MARRIJANE (Johnston) Hayes was born in Indianapolis
in 1920, a year and a half after Joseph Hayes was born in
the same city. Eighteen years later they met, married and
worked their way together through the University of
Indiana. In 1941 they came to New York, where he worked
as an editor at Samuel French, Inc., play publishers, and
began his writing career. He has written short stories,
television scripts, and a novel, *The Desperate Hours* (Condensed Books, Summer 1954), which he later adapted for
both stage and screen.

Although *Bon Voyage* is their first novel written in
collaboration, Joseph and Marrijane Hayes have been co-
authoring plays for more than ten years, and they plan to
write more novels together in the future. Parents of three
boys, ranging from one and a half to eleven, they now
divide their time between two homes, one in Connecticut
and one near Sarasota, Florida.

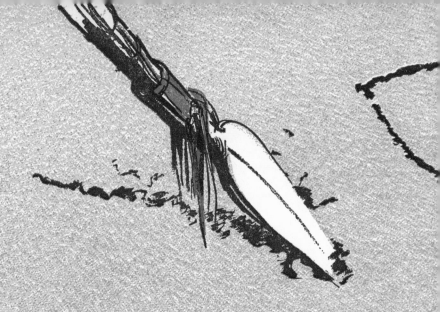

THE TRIBE

LOST

A condensation
of the book by NICHOLAS

Illustrations by Austin Briggs

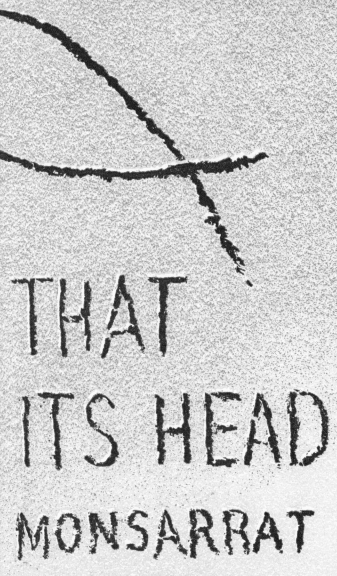

THAT
ITS HEAD
MONSARRAT

$\mathcal{IT}$ was an evil day for Pharamaul — a British Protectorate off the West Coast of Africa — when its young native chief returning from Oxford happened to travel on the same plane with Tulbach Browne.

For Browne, star reporter for a sensational London newspaper, was an expert in distortion and spite and did not hesitate in his dispatches to twist the young man's innocent words into inflammable declarations. Thus a chain reaction of unrest was started that tore to shreds the orderly fabric of British administration until it finally exploded in a fearful outburst of savagery.

Pharamaul is an imaginary island. This is a work of fiction. But so lifelike are the characters, so convincing is the situation, that the reader is caught up in a compelling drama that could occur anywhere in the world when a primitive people seizes self-rule before it is equipped to do so.

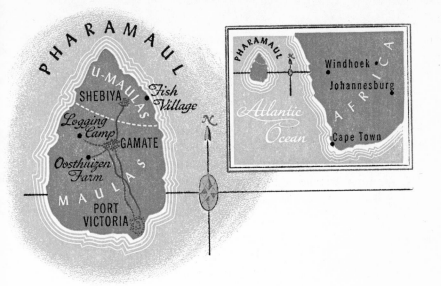

Chapter 1

THE PLANE, a shabby old Dakota, bumped twice in the noon-day heat, then settled down on its steady course. Windhoek was left behind, a dusty town set in arid scrub desert; presently the plane crossed the South-West African coast line, and headed out over a pale blue hazy sea — due west for Pharamaul.

The four passengers relaxed, stretching their legs, occasionally glancing out of the side windows. After the glaring heat and dust of the short inter-plane stop at Windhoek, the shadowless Atlantic below them looked gratefully cool.

TULBACH BROWNE of the *Daily Thresh,* seasoned traveler of a thousand flights, went through his usual take-off routine. He pressed his eardrums and swallowed until his throat was comfortable; popped two Dramamine tablets in his mouth and washed them down with a swig from a flask of whisky; exchanged his scuffed shoes for worn carpet slippers; and unbuckled his belt.

He was a small wizened man of forty-seven, with sandy hair and a look of permanent disdain. His face was ordinary, rather ugly, his body spare and average, his manner unimpressive. As a by-line correspondent for the *Daily Thresh,* syndicated most of the way round the world, he was in a class by himself. No one could so adroitly "interpret" the news, no one else could touch him at invective, innuendo, spite, and making plain truth into the cloudy lies that the *Daily Thresh* lived on.

Now he was going to Pharamaul, and he was irritated because it was probably a waste of time. The trip was really a fill-in after his South African tour: he had just "done" South Africa — seven days, three thousand miles, three stories — and his office had cabled him something about the local chief coming back to Pharamaul from Oxford to take over the tribal chieftainship. There might be a story there, particularly if something went wrong and he could flay the civil service, British administration, the snob color bar. Otherwise the time was likely to be wasted.

Two SEATS behind Tulbach Browne, the old guy who looked like a Colonial civil servant reached out a hand and drew towards him a shabby brief case. He was Andrew Macmillan, C.M.G., Resident Commissioner at Gamate, native capital of the Principality of Pharamaul, returning to duty after twelve weeks' leave in England. Twelve weeks' leave was a long time, Andrew Macmillan had discovered, when, after a fortnight in Oxfordshire with some distant relatives, and a week in London on his own, he realized that he was longing for nothing but to get back to Pharamaul. The Residency at Gamate was hot, damp, ant-infested; the work repetitive and often dull. His hunger for these things was ridiculous, yet it was a fact. Pharamaul, which he knew to its last dried-up watercourse, was his home, and only there could he be happy.

Macmillan was fifty-seven, solid, graying, severe. He had soldiered for a while, in the old days; then he had gone to Pharamaul as a young, energetic Assistant District Officer, and in Pharamaul he had stayed, for the next thirty-five years, climbing the administrative ladder, finally assuming the top job of Resident Commissioner. He knew the whole country — knew it, loathed it, and loved it. He knew the chief tribe, the Maulas, and he felt for them as a benevolent father feels whose backward sons will never quite grow up, never really leave the nursery.

It had been a hard, dedicated life, a life of endeavor, patience, and little reward. Now he was fifty-seven: he had three modest letters after his name, three more years of service to go. He had no children: his wife had died a decade earlier; he had only one home, and only one family — a hundred and twenty thousand of them. Perhaps the proof of that lay between his hands, in the papers he had drawn out of his brief case.

It was the manuscript of his book, the book that had occupied all his few spare moments for the last fifteen years, and was still a long way from completion. "The Principality of Pharamaul," he read on page one, as he had read a thousand times before, "came into official existence on the fifteenth day of April, 1842, by Royal Decree. A company of Her Majesty's Foot Guards having been brought in to quell an insurrection which threatened British trading interests, they stayed to ensure public order; and thereafter a Lieutenant-Governor was appointed (in the words of the proclamation) 'to re-establish the rule of law, inculcate the principles of good administration, and work towards such degree of self-determination as the inhabitants' best endeavors, and Her Majesty's Government, may from time to time decide.' " From that moment, Pharamaul was a British Protectorate under the Crown.

"Pharamaul (latitude 5° east, longitude 22° 50' south) is an island some three hundred miles long. . . ." Macmillan sat back, contented at last. He was going home. He would arrive in time to welcome a new chief, a youngster who had been fifteen years old the last time they had met; but a new chief was nothing to Pharamaul, and nothing to Macmillan either. He had seen them come, and seen them go.

Life went on — not good, not bad, but sufficient, and his own life with it. One day the Maulas would be able to look after themselves; but that day was a long way ahead, and in the meantime it was his appointed job to take care of them.

ACROSS the aisle from Andrew Macmillan — and sometimes eying him speculatively, like a lonely stranger in a bar — sat a young man who might have been anything. David Bracken, recent recruit to the Scheduled Territories Office, newly appointed to the Governor's staff of Pharamaul, had not so far settled in any recognizable mold. This was his first overseas job in government service, and he was not yet acclimatized to any of it. He was young, fair-haired, pleasant-looking, strongly built; his gray flannel suit became him.

From the career point of view, David Bracken had been caught out by the war, though he wasn't complaining about it and did not really mind. In 1943, when he should have been going to Oxford, he was landing at Salerno; on his twenty-first birthday, in 1945, he was celebrating peace in Paris. Now, a decade later, after three years of Oxford and unsuccessful attempts at the law and publishing, he was committed to the life of a civil servant; and because of an incipient dedication, a wish to work for something more than a set sum of money every month, he was undeniably glad that this was so.

Today, on his way to Pharamaul, he was hesitant, a little nervous, and happy. It would all be very new. He took out of his pocket a small white booklet labeled: *Scheduled Territories Office: Sub-Equatorial Territories,* and turned once more to a page he had scanned many times before. It was headed "Principality of Pharamaul," and it read:

Governor and Commander in Chief	Sir Elliott Vere-Toombs, K.B.E.
Aide-de-Camp	Captain H. G. Simpson, O.B.E., R.N.
Secretary (Political)	A. Purves-Brownrigg, C.M.G.
Secretary	L. M. Stevens
Secretary (designate)	D. Bracken, M.C.
Assistant Secretary	Miss N. Steuart
Resident Commissioner (Gamate)	A. Macmillan, C.M.G.
District Commissioner (Gamate)	G. L. T. Forsdick

Agricultural and Livestock Officer (Gamate)	H. J. Llewellyn
District Officer (Shebiya)	T. V. Ronald
Security	Captain K. Crump, M.C., Royal Pharamaul Police

He liked, especially, "Secretary (designate): D. Bracken, M.C." The total list was a lot of people to get to know, but *not* a lot of people to administer an island of thirty thousand square miles, and the lives of a hundred and twenty thousand people.

THE LAST passenger was Dinamaula, son of Simaula, grandson of Maula, Hereditary Chieftain of Pharamaul, Prince of Gamate, Son of the Fish, Keeper of the Golden Nail, Urn of the Royal Seed, Ruler and Kingbreaker, Lord of the Known World.

Dinamaula had left his home at Gamate when he was fifteen years old, in pursuit of a plan, proposed by the Administration and backed by his father, for educating him completely in England. He had been to a fine old school; he had been to Oxford, and had graduated with a passable law degree; now his father was dead, and he was returning to Pharamaul to claim his inheritance.

He was by now somewhat uncertain of the latter. Pharamaul he remembered as a rough featureless country, devoted for the most part to stringy scrub cattle and enormous flocks of goats. Gamate had been (and doubtless still was) an untidy straggle of mud huts, sprawling like dusty beehives across two valleys and sheltering over a hundred thousand people — and many more goats — and the people themselves he knew to be largely backward, unenterprising folk, degenerating in the northern parts to a simple, uncontrollable savagery.

His London friends did not understand about these people. When they argued about immediate self-government for Pharamaul, they were thinking of Dinamaula himself, not of the childlike peasant Maulas at Gamate, or the cruel, magic-ridden U-Maulas upcountry. Dinamaula *did* know about them; his eyes were fully, sometimes fearfully, open, and he wanted to do something about it, something about everything.

Dinamaula became aware that someone was standing above him; he looked up to find that one of his three fellow passengers — an oldish, smallish, nondescript man in a rumpled seersucker suit — had paused by his seat.

"Hallo!" said Tulbach Browne. "Just stretching my legs. Is this your first trip?"

Dinamaula smiled, recognizing in the stranger's look and tone the basic English lust to demonstrate broad-mindedness. This man would really have preferred to talk to one of the other two white passengers: therefore, he had chosen the only Negro.

"No," he answered. "I've flown before. Won't you sit down?"

Tulbach Browne eased himself into the vacant chair, and extended his hand. "I'm Tulbach Browne of the *Daily Thresh.*"

"I'm happy to meet you," Dinamaula said formally. "Of course I know your name well. I am Chief Dinamaula."

"Chief." Tulbach Browne looked at him, instantly wary, instantly working. "You must be — you've been at Oxford."

Dinamaula inclined his head. "Yes." Normal words would not come. He said stiltedly, almost Biblically, "I am that man."

Tulbach Browne looked sideways at Dinamaula again. He saw now a tall, slim, good-looking Negro, with neat clothes, a lightish skin, an air of courage and breeding. It could be *real* material. He said, briskly, "This is a very lucky meeting," and set himself to stir, to probe, and to lay bare.

THE PLANE had suddenly tilted and jerked, and two of the passengers, who had been reading, looked up, and then caught each other's eye; and now, after four or five quick questions, they were suddenly in tune.

"You're replacing Morrison." Macmillan grinned. "He wasn't much good."

David Bracken smiled. "You're up at Gamate?"

"Yes. The Residency has always been there. That's where we do all the work."

"What's it like?"

"Hot. Dusty. Half asleep, except after the harvest — then they're drunk all the time. There's a lot of routine stuff — inspection of cattle, soil conservation, inoculation, trying to knock some sense into their thick heads."

"Are the Maulas — " David Bracken searched for the right word " — are they capable of managing their own affairs? Is there any sort of political advancement?"

Andrew Macmillan stared, then shook his head. "You've got to forget all that stuff. They're simply children and we look after them."

"But in the future?"

"The future is a long way ahead. It *may* come: there are one or two bright sparks already. But not now. *Now,* we teach them not to overgraze their lands, not to doctor themselves with dried toad skin and manure, not to kill a man because he takes someone else's wife, not to let rain water run to waste. It's a slow process. It's mostly 'not.' But we look after them."

AT ABOUT the same time, five seats behind them in the rear of the plane, Tulbach Browne was saying to Dinamaula, "That's an interesting idea of yours. I've always thought that modern methods of farming and water conservation could transform a backward economy almost overnight. The trouble is, of course, to get the officials moving. Do you anticipate a lot of obstruction?"

"That I do not know." Dinamaula smiled hesitantly. "You must remember that I've been away for seven years. I'm not in touch with what Government has been doing. And then, of course, my own people — not all of them can understand these things, not all of them are ready for such changes."

"You mean, there's a conservative element who would resist anything that might threaten their own position in the tribe."

"Conservative, yes. Backward, perhaps."

The warning sign, "Fasten your seat belts," glowed suddenly from up ahead. Tulbach Browne sat up, preparing to go back to his seat.

"I'd like to come up to Gamate and see you, as soon as you've settled in."

"You will be welcome," answered Dinamaula politely. "We live simply, of course. I hope you won't be disappointed."

LIKE COUNTLESS other parts of the inhabited globe, Pharamaul owed its entire existence, as a country, to Great Britain; otherwise, like India or the West Indies or enormous stretches of Africa, it would have remained a global nonentity, eternally torn by strife, weakened by disease and indolence, and condemned to remain in the jungle shadows for another three or four hundred years.

Pharamaul had been lucky, as the first paragraph of Andrew Macmillan's book had tried to indicate. Shortly after the accession of Queen Victoria British troops had been landed to protect white settlers from marauding bands of tribesmen. Soon it became clear that Great Britain, having arrived to pacify and discipline, would remain to educate and administer.

In time, in counterdominion to the loose rule imposed by the British, a black dynasty emerged in Pharamaul, impelled to power by a dominant tribe. They called themselves the Maulas, after their newest and strongest chief, a bloody ruffian called Maula. Maula the Great brought order to a troubled country: making laws which had to be kept, killing off all challengers to his rule, exiling the break-away, discontented tribe of U-Maulas (literally, "Not Maulas") to the miserable jungle that lay to the north of Gamate.

Then Maula came under the influence of a brilliant district commissioner called Hayes, fell in love with British rule and a garish photogravure of Queen Victoria, and survived to attend her Diamond Jubilee in 1897.

His son, Simaula, saw the crowning of King George V; his grandson, Dinamaula, had, as a wide-eyed young man of nineteen, viewed the coronation of Queen Elizabeth II from a modest seat half hidden behind a pillar in Westminster Abbey.

The country which this Dinamaula was now to rule had never become rich; but it had prospered wonderfully, when compared with the savagery and chaos from which it had sprung. Pacification had brought trade and settlers, and settlers had geared up the whole economy of the island. In Port Victoria, there was now a modern abattoir, to handle the cattle coming down from the Gamate plains; a big logging camp up north kept the Port Victoria sawmills busy most of the year round; a scheme for fish canning, on the coast near Shebiya's "Fish Village," was now moving towards actuality. Health, agriculture, water conservation, the rule of law — all had improved under a century of British rule.

Formal government sat at Port Victoria: the Governor's white stone mansion dominated the residential quarter, the Secretariat crouched in its shade. Field government was centered at Gamate, the native capital, two hundred miles away to the north, at the end of Pharamaul's only railway line. There sat a Resident Commissioner in whose charge were a hundred thousand souls, concentrated in one of the biggest "native villages" south of the equator.

Government of any sort faded north of Gamate, where the dry ranchlands gave place to jungle, and the Maulas to the U-Maulas. A single District Officer camped out at Shebiya, the U-Maula capital; his only link was a radio schedule, his only strength a white skin and a twelve-bore shotgun.

TULBACH BROWNE of the *Daily Thresh,* sweating in the humid cage that was Port Victoria's best hotel, had already, within twenty-four hours, filed his first Pharamaul story.

"Yesterday," he wrote, "I had the privilege of talking to one of the most remarkable young men ever to come out of Africa. He is Dinamaula, descendant of a long line of Maula strong men, a gifted African now returning from a brilliant career at Oxford to assume the chieftainship of the Principality of Pharamaul.

"He does so at a difficult moment, and his chieftainship is likely to be a mockery of the word.

"Will he succeed in his virile plans for the expansion, reform, and development of his beloved homeland? I do not know, and Dinamaula, for all his fresh enthusiasm and undoubted talent, does not know either. Will there be official obstruction to these blessings too long denied to a forgotten corner of a backward continent?

"'I do not know,' he told me. 'There are reactionary elements in the tribe, too,' he went on to warn in his attractive, musical voice, 'who may resist change.' His dark eyes flashed. 'But they will be taken care of.'

"It is typical of Pharamaul that I could not even take this lineal

descendant of a dynasty of chiefs to the local club for an evening
'sun-downer.' The club, like everything else in Port Victoria, is
rubber-stamped: 'White Men Only.'

"Dinamaula's plans are far-reaching, statesmanlike, eminently
wise. His chances of forcing them through, in the face of British
officials worried about nothing worse than their next pay increment, their next shipment of cheap gin from London, are slim
— slim as this young and gallant chief himself.

"Tomorrow: The Cocked Hat Brigade of Pharamaul."

Sir Elliott Vere-Toombs, K.B.E., Governor and Commander
in Chief of the Principality of Pharamaul, sat behind a leather-
topped desk at one end of his study. It was a large room, well-
proportioned and lofty, but, for all that, hot and humid.

Sir Elliott was sixty-one, a small spare man, with a high beaked
nose and a prim mouth; his dry wrinkled skin and bleached hair
proclaimed that heat was no stranger to him.

There was a knock, the door opened slowly, and a girl emerged.
Nicole Steuart, at the age of twenty-four the best-looking girl in
thirty thousand tropical square miles, was young and happy, and
interested in this odd, man-made world.

As she came forward, the Governor said, "Yes, Nicole?"

This was a Christian-name Secretariat: it was really too hot
for anything more formal.

"It's Mr. Bracken, Sir Elliott."

"Very well." He smiled a tired smile. "What's he like?"

Nicole Steuart smiled back. "All right. They're all the same
when they're new, aren't they?"

"What a very disillusioned remark! What are they *all* like?"

"Oh — young — keen — nervous — wanting to please."

Sir Elliott coughed, reminding himself that there was, or should
have been, a world of difference in status between Nicole Steuart
and David Bracken.

"I'll ring when I'm ready," he said formally. "I just want to
finish this dispatch."

Nicole withdrew, not at all abashed. The formal tone, she knew,
was part of the drill. She shut the door carefully behind her and

said to the waiting young man, "He's busy at the moment. Not for long, though. Won't you sit down?"

David Bracken, caught between the agonizing cross fires of a first interview with the Governor and the nearness of a girl whose fresh beauty, dark hair, and candid shapeliness had knocked him flat, answered foolishly, "Yes, please."

DAVID BRACKEN's interview with the Governor lasted an hour and was unexpectedly satisfactory to both sides. The Governor found that he liked this young man: he was a trifle more mature than the run-of-the-mill entry, less ready to take opinions on trust; but that was the way of the world nowadays. Bracken, on his side, was disarmed by a man who he knew had had a distinguished career (and, on one occasion in Bengal, a notably brave one), but who could still talk in simple and direct terms of a beginner's problems in administration. Sir Elliott Vere-Toombs had two rare qualities — honesty and devotion — which should never be sold short on any market.

Only once, across a chasm of thirty years, did they discover a measure of disagreement.

"Don't you think, sir," asked David Bracken at one point, when they had been discussing other parts of Africa, "that a place like Pharamaul is bound to fall into the pattern of the rest of this part of the world?"

"Of course." The Governor raised his eyebrows. "It *is* part of the pattern already."

"That means, then — self-determination."

"Self-determination? It depends what you mean by that very elastic term."

"I meant, like the Gold Coast, or perhaps parts of the Rhodesias, progress towards independence."

"My dear fellow," said the Governor, leaning back, "that is *not* what self-determination means to me."

"But, sir, you said they're part of the same pattern."

"Certainly. The whole of Africa is a pattern — a pattern of change, variety. What is appropriate in one part is unthinkable in another. You can't hurry the thing up, and you certainly can't apply an advanced program here just because, in some other totally different part of Africa, there are some Negroes who could knock spots off most lawyers or politicians in the outside world." He drew breath. "To give Pharamaul the same self-determination — " the Governor sniffed at the word " — as a country like Nigeria would ruin it overnight."

David Bracken smiled. It was the only thing to do. "Things will stay much as they are, then?"

"I hope so. The thing works." The Governor looked at him, alert for radical nonconformity, and yet aware that this young man was searching for an equitable formula for all the world — as he himself had searched, thirty years before. "They really are a backward lot, as you'll discover before long. Occasionally they throw up a first-class man: old Maula himself was a very considerable statesman, though a complete barbarian in many other ways, and Dinamaula may become the same sort of character, in good time. But basically, they are very simple people. We will have to help them, for a very long while."

"That was what Macmillan said on the plane."

"A wise man, Macmillan. Now let's see about your office, and things like that. My secretary will take you round."

DAVID BRACKEN closed the door behind him.

"Feeling better?" asked Nicole Steuart.

"Fine." He looked at the girl: she was as pretty as he remembered. "He — the Governor said you'd show me round."

Nicole Steuart nodded. "We'll do that. Where were you before this?"

"London." He perched on the arm of a chair and looked down at her. It was an agreeable view.

"Where before London?"

"Nowhere. I was new." He began to be nettled by this cool-looking girl who could survive a temperature of ninety plus to put him through the hoop. "What about you?"

"I'm new, too. I came out here on a holiday two years ago. I liked it." Nicole smiled at him.

"What did you like about it?"

"It's worth while. People need our help. We give it to them. No strings attached. It's something we've been doing for hundreds of years." She was very pretty, very serious.

"But do we do enough for them?"

"All we can."

"Things could move a good deal faster, surely?"

"I used to think that. Now I'm not so sure. Africa's a slow continent. Speed could ruin everything. When you've been here a bit longer, you'll understand that."

"You've only been here two years."

She smiled again, less warmly. "It's longer than two hours."

There was something between them already, not an antagonism, but a readiness to do battle. She's very pretty, he thought, but she has these opinions.

At the same moment, Nicole was thinking, a little incoherently: nice-looking, prejudiced, ready-made ideas, a bit priggish, but he's here for a long time. She stood up.

"You'd better meet the rest of the staff," she said.

They walked round. It was a somewhat confused process, not aided by the oppressive heat. David met a man called Stevens, a secretary at the same level as himself. He met a booming character whose cheerful, sweating face owed much to the climate, more to pink gin — Captain Simpson, the naval aide-de-camp. He met the Political Secretary, Aidan Purves-Brownrigg.

Holding out a slim hand, Purves-Brownrigg said, "So glad you got here safely," as if Bracken had hacked his way through a dozen enemy columns to Port Victoria. "Nicole, darling, you look ravishing. So cool, too."

Purves-Brownrigg himself looked pre-eminently cool: his dove-gray lightweight suit was immaculate, his fair hair a miracle of neatness. "Did you have a nice journey?" he asked David.

"Very," said Bracken. "I was on the same plane as Macmillan."

"Such a stalwart old character," said Purves-Brownrigg.

Bracken looked at him, not sure whether this was going to be tolerable. Why were people like this sent to represent Britain in rugged outposts like Pharamaul, when they were so much better off in Paris or Rio or Washington? He pulled himself up, aware

that this must be showing in his face. Then he nodded. "He seems
to know everything there is to know about Pharamaul."

"He's an encyclopedia. A hundred volumes."

"Why didn't you like him?" demanded Nicole, when this door
was shut in turn.

"Not my type," said David.

"I think men are really awful."

"I'm afraid I don't like lightweights. Let's leave it."

"All right." She was surprised, somewhat taken aback by an
unexpected crispness in his manner, and surprised also at the way
she reacted to it. Here was a young man who at least knew his
own mind. That was a change, anyway. "Aidan is very good company and he works hard. It's a pity to write him off because he
strikes you as frivolous."

"I won't do that. Whom haven't I seen?"

"That's the lot, I think. The rest are up at Gamate. You'll meet
the wives later on."

A FEW DAYS later, as he walked back to Port Victoria with
Purves-Brownrigg after a dinner at Government House, David
was forced to acknowledge that Nicole Steuart might have been
right about him. When all was said, he was entertaining company, discussing his co-workers with an unfaltering malice that
David knew could have been applied just as readily to himself.

"I like the old gentleman," said Purves-Brownrigg. (It was his
invariable term for the Governor.) "He's getting a bit past it, of
course. You wouldn't think, to look at him, that he once defied
the mob in Bengal, waving his stick, like Gordon at Khartoum,
till they all just melted away."

"I've never heard the details of that."

"Give the old gentleman time," said Purves-Brownrigg. "You'll
hear them. The Governess is the end, of course, so good-hearted
and forceful and boring. And that Mrs. Simpson! *What* those
sailors have to put up with! It'll be a happy release when the gallant
captain is made into an admiral and she can relax."

"Will Simpson be made an admiral?"

"They've got to keep their numbers up. Actually he's a rather pathetic old party — I like him. His great-great-uncle was one of Nelson's captains. He dreams of action the whole time, and all the action he gets is Mrs. Simpson."

"What about the Stevens?" asked David.

"Pathetic, aren't they? He's so hard-working, it makes me ill to watch him. And all those filthy children — four of them, all wearing each other's castoff clothes. And what she looks like, poor soul — that hair-do is obviously straight out of the Kennel Club Magazine — do this with your wire-haired terrier and win first prize."

"People can't help it if they're poor and ugly," said David.

"They can't help it," agreed Purves-Brownrigg. "But it should all be hidden away."

Chapter 2

IT WAS GOOD, thought Andrew Macmillan, to be back home in Gamate. The shabby old Residency had never felt more comfortable, more private, more welcoming. He had whipped through Port Victoria with the minimum of delay, and now, after fourteen hot and dusty hours in the wooden coach, he was home at last.

Dressed in his old clothes — khaki slacks and a khaki shirt — he sat at ease on the Residency's wide cool stoep, his feet up on a second chair. The Residency, set on a hillside overlooking Gamate, commanded a superb view: beyond the town itself, sprawled untidily over its two valleys, were fifty miles of pleasant green plain, and beyond that the encroaching bush, and the purple foothills of the U-Maula country.

Here, two hundred miles north of Port Victoria, at the end of the rickety, single-line railway, here was absolute peace; Macmillan's own kingdom, benignly ruled, benignly enjoyed.

He was aware of the shuffling of feet on the worn boards of the stoep. It could only be Johannes, his servant of more than a quarter of a century, Johannes who was as much a part of his life as anything else in Pharamaul.

"*Jah, barena,*" said Johannes.

Macmillan looked at him. Johannes was his own age, fifty-seven, but he seemed much older, as all Negroes did: on his spare flesh the white house coat hung limply, and the gray hair above the wrinkled face was now sparse and thin. His life is my life, thought Macmillan, we are both old — two old men of Gamate, bound to each other till the grave takes one, or both.

"Johannes," he said. "Dinner. Three *barenas*. Mr. Forsdick, Mr. Llewellyn, Captain Crump."

"Yes, *barena.*"

"What's in the larder?"

"Chicken, *barena*. Wife kill this morning."

"My chicken?"

"Wife's chicken, *barena.*"

"What happened to my chickens? Six of them?"

"All *barena's* chickens die, two, three weeks."

The squeeze was so obvious that Macmillan felt impelled to do battle. But then he relaxed again. He had been away for twelve weeks, after all. "What besides chicken?" he asked.

"Peaches, *barena*. Yellow *tin* peaches."

"All right. And soup?"

"No soup, *barena*. Tins no good. I throw away."

"Soup, damn you. Find one tin. Mushroom soup."

"Yes, *barena.*" Johannes stood waiting, shifting from one foot to the other, his old face creased and uncertain. He had a thing to say, and he must say it before he left.

"What is it, Johannes?"

"*Barena* have good holiday?"

"Fine, Johannes. But it's nice to be back."

The old black face broke suddenly into a smile. Johannes nodded, accepting a welcome cue. He said, with all the honesty in the world, "It's good to have you here again, *barena.*"

PRESENTLY Macmillan saw them approaching across the patchy burnt-brown lawn which was the playground of ticks and white ants: two men, dressed alike in khaki slacks, but wearing ties as a sign of evening formality. They were Forsdick, his District Commissioner in Gamate, and Llewellyn, the agricultural officer who covered the whole Maula territory.

Forsdick, who might one day succeed him, was fortyish, plump, red-faced, sweating; he walked heavily, as if his large ungainly body must be carefully steered from point to point. Llewellyn was the same as he had always been: a small swarthy Welshman, morose, overworked, single-minded in his pursuit of a thriving Pharamaul. What he knew about crops, cattle, water, and disease was phenomenal; what he knew about anything else was sometimes, for Macmillan, a matter of speculation. But perhaps that was the kind of agricultural officer one needed.

He opened the screened door as they reached the stoep.

Forsdick said, "Hallo, Andrew."

Llewellyn said, "Good evening, sir."

Macmillan motioned them past him. "Come in," he said. "Nice to see you. Where's Crump?"

"Glued to the radio," said Forsdick. "There's something coming through for us on the eight-o'clock police schedule — prefaced urgent and confidential."

"Government House in a flap again," said Llewellyn caustically. "Nothing else to do all day. They've probably lost the file on the New Year's Honors List."

Johannes shuffled in with the whisky, the beer, the ice, and the glasses, and Macmillan poured — a stiff peg for Forsdick, beer for Llewellyn. "They've got a new man to replace Morrison — chap named Bracken. Brand-new, but O.K. Cheers."

"Down the hatch."

They all drank.

"How was London?" asked Forsdick after a pause.

"Fine," answered Macmillan. He felt he had to add something. "Lots of traffic. I saw some shows."

"You can keep London," said Llewellyn, his singsong voice still on a somber key. "Like a circus, that place is."

That was enough about London. The long leave was over. London was past, swallowed up in the mist. Only Gamate was real.

"How are things here?" asked Macmillan.

Now they talked as they had talked on hundreds, even thousands of other evenings in the past: it was straight-cut shop, the kind of thing they talked best, the thing they really understood.

Gamate was much the same. The harvest was coming to an end, the taxes were starting to dribble in. There had been an epidemic of bluetongue disease up near the U-Maula border. Father Schwemmer, who ran the Gamate Mission, had been complaining about immorality. Finally, there had been a deputation that morning from the Council of Regents — the two uncles and one cousin of Dinamaula who had ruled the Maula tribe for the past year, ever since Dinamaula's father had died.

"How *are* those wicked uncles?" asked Macmillan, interested afresh.

"It was rather curious," said Forsdick slowly. "Of course, they're not going to quarrel about handing over control. But they said — " he wrinkled his brow, searching for the exact words " — they said they wanted to be sure there would be no great changes."

"Why should there be?" asked Macmillan.

"They wouldn't tell me. When I pressed the point, they got a bit vague, and then old Seralo started talking about the importance of carrying on the tribal customs, and at the end he said, 'We have heard talk of new things.' "

Macmillan shrugged. "I should say he was making that up. It's a natural line of thought. They're probably worrying about some racket they're running which Dinamaula will now take over."

Forsdick shook his head. "I don't know. It sounded as though they were on to something. You know the way they hear things."

In spite of himself, Macmillan was inclined to agree. The Maulas *did* hear things, by some scarcely credible grapevine which could, for example, carry news from Port Victoria to Gamate in a matter of hours. He was aware of uneasiness. It was as if he had suddenly sniffed the wind of the future and found borne upon it the faint scent of far-off trouble. He said, "When does Dinamaula arrive?"

"Tomorrow night," said Forsdick. "He's coming by truck from Port Victoria. . . . Here's Crump."

In silence they watched a jeep climbing steadily up the hill towards them. As it stopped, its dust cloud drifted gently away and was lost in the dusk. A khaki-clad figure sprang out and walked briskly towards them.

Captain Crump of the Royal Pharamaul Police was a burly,

cheerful Irishman who seemed to be laughing nearly all the time. He was young, strong, fond of his job, possessed of a total belief in the excellent native police force which he himself had built up. He had a young and pretty wife, a Military Cross from the last war, an assured future. What else should one do but laugh? Crump knew Gamate and the surrounding country, and the tribal feuds, and the good and the bad men nearly as well as did Macmillan himself, and the latter found him invaluable.

Now he saluted, a broad grin on his face, and said, "Sir!"

"Hallo, Keith," said Macmillan. "Nice to see you again. Have a drink?"

Crump laughed and said, "I will that!" Though he was in khaki like the three others, his khaki was different: immaculate tunic shirt, creased shorts, a belt and holster, puttees, polished bush boots. One of Crump's more printable Maula nicknames meant "The Shining Soldier."

Macmillan handed him the drink. "What was in the telegram?"

Crump took a folded pink flimsy from his tunic pocket. "It's about Dinamaula. He's been talking to the newspapers."

"Has he indeed?" said Forsdick. "What about?"

"Progress in Pharamaul," answered Crump. "He wants to improve everything." He fell silent as Andrew Macmillan, looking down at the pink telegram, started to speak.

"It's from G.H.," he said, "passing on a message from London. 'Urgent and Confidential,'" he read. "'Following telegram has been received from Secretary of State.' Begins:

"'This morning's *Daily Thresh* carries interview with Dinamaula by Tulbach Browne, now in Port Victoria. Dinamaula expressed dissatisfaction with slow progress in territory, government handling of Maula affairs, and said he was determined to introduce reforms whatever the opposition. There was also reference to reactionary tribal elements who would be taken care of. Following is quotation.

"'Quote Dinamaula's plans are far-reaching, statesmanlike, eminently wise. His chances of forcing them through, in the face of British officials worried about nothing worse than their next pay increment, their next shipment of cheap gin from London, are slim dash slim as this young and gallant chief himself. Unquote.

" 'Resident Commissioner, Gamate, should be instructed to interview Dinamaula and impress on him the necessity of working for an orderly change-over in tribal administration. In particular, criticism of government officials by chief-designate, and further publicity of this sort, should be avoided.' Telegram ends.

" 'Following for Macmillan. Please take action indicated in last paragraph and report urgently to me.' "

There was a brief silence after Macmillan had finished reading. He was frowning to himself. This was the trouble he had smelt from far away, the disturbing element moving towards Gamate.

"This was what Seralo meant," he said, "when he came to see you this morning with the other Regents. He told you they had heard talk of new things. This was it."

"Of course," said Crump, cheerfully, "you can't believe all you read in the papers. Dinamaula probably never said the half of it."

"Maybe not," said Macmillan. "But half is quite enough. You'll have to get your boys to work, Keith. Find out what's cooking."

By "boys" he meant not the uniformed police but the unofficial arm of Crump's small force — the talebearers, spies, informers who clung furtively to the edge of officialdom, who slipped into the office or the garden when the coast was clear at dusk.

"I'll do that," said Crump.

"And I want to see Dinamaula as soon as he arrives. Send a messenger down."

"Better make it a formal invitation, Andrew," said Forsdick gently. "He's the chief-designate, after all. Just arrived to take over. It's an important moment for Gamate. You can't just send the wagon for him, with a police corporal hanging onto the tailboard."

"All right." Macmillan grinned suddenly. He never minded this sort of correction from his staff. It was the *total* of knowledge and experience which was important. He winked at Crump. "Put on your medals and give him my compliments. But see that he gets here."

There was a shuffling sound behind them, and the dining room door opened slowly, creaking on its hinges. Johannes, in a clean white house coat, came forward, looking important and anxious.

"Soup on table, *barena,*" he said.

"Dinner is served," corrected Macmillan automatically.

"Dinner served," said Johannes. "Soup on table."

THE TRUCK, a tough, grimy old Chevrolet whose mileage indicator had long ago stuck at 86,000, roared northwards towards Gamate. In the front seat, Dinamaula gripped the door and stared at the unfolding ribbon of the road. By his side, his cousin Zuva Katsaula drove carelessly, his hands loose on the wheel. Already Dinamaula did not like this Zuva, whom he had not met for a long time. They had been together at Oxford, and then Zuva, a few months older than himself, had left the university and gone to London. There, it was clear, he had found strange companions. He had returned to Pharamaul a month earlier. Now they were going to Gamate together, but they were divided men.

Zuva was small, dapper, smiling, dressed in gray check trousers and a yellow coat with brown shoulder pads and curious lapels. "My zoot coat," he had said, when they had met at Port Victoria. "Pretty keen number, eh? Straight from Hollywood. Oh, baby!" Zuva had met Dinamaula at the airfield with four companions who formed a ragged shiftless bodyguard at his back. All wore dark spectacles, thick-soled shoes, black hats with wide brims. One had an empty shoulder holster strapped under his coat. When Zuva had told one of them to look after Dinamaula's luggage, the young man had answered, "O.K., Fingers!"

Dinamaula did not like it at all. He wanted no "Fingers" in Pharamaul, no zoot suits, no alien pattern of foolishness.

Certainly he wanted no such talk as Zuva had talked that night in Port Victoria, before they set out for Gamate.

On that night, Dinamaula had sat with Zuva and his circle of friends, in a squalid dive in downtown Port Victoria, drinking kaffir beer laced (illegally) with raw potato spirit. The talk had run in curious circles, as if they were each in turn taking pains to probe Dinamaula's spirit and feeling. But the thoughts behind the probing were all Zuva's thoughts — of that Dinamaula was sure.

Zuva had picked up, from somewhere, a kind of gangster independence of spirit, and had clothed it in the violent jargon of old movies, and the supple double talk of political Oxford. He had collected these immediate followers who thought the same way.

It was not Communism: indeed, it was scarcely a recognizable creed at all. It seemed to include no white men, nor any sense of tribal hierarchy either; it included only personal power for whoever could grasp it. The titles of the movement varied. So did the aims. So did the methods. It was a thing just beginning, they said. What did the new chief think of it?

They had sipped their heady beer, eying him across the chipped rims of their glasses. Dinamaula had thought for a long time, his face impassive in the lamplight. Then he said, "I have come back to be chief of my people. I will rule as my father ruled."

His words seemed to hang upon the air, unacceptable, doomed to be rejected.

"But there must be progress," said Zuva after a pause.

Dinamaula nodded. "Yes. But according to our accustomed pattern."

At that, a sigh had gone round the room, a fading of tension. Dinamaula knew then that he had failed to pass some test of theirs. They had found out exactly where he stood without greatly committing themselves. He was on one side, they on another.

Now he and Zuva sat side by side, driving together along the dusty road that led into the future. Dinamaula's own role was clear: he was to assume the chieftainship, the tribal mantle that had been awaiting him ever since he had been a small boy. Zuva's role was not clear, except that he wished to change things. There was a violent pattern of Maula scheming and treachery which he might well revive at any time.

Dinamaula sighed, eying the road winding into the hills, and the sun now beginning to dip towards the west. He wished to acquit himself well and honorably as chief, and this was likely to be very much harder than he had hoped.

It was a great night in Gamate; a night which, starting decorously enough with ceremonial greetings to the chief-designate, worked itself up to a wild Saturnalian pitch such as the town had not witnessed for many a year.

The Maulas were excited and happy, and happiness for them meant simple things — huge crowds thronging the hard-trodden tribal meeting place, the *aboura,* much talking underneath the thorn trees, much laughter and drinking and jostling, long speeches, long songs, long feasting. It was a great night; the harvest was nearly done, and their young chief had come back from far lands to be their father again.

First, for Dinamaula, there were the formal greetings, within the Gamate schoolhouse, out of sight of the crowd: a ceremonial welcome from the Regents and the headmen of the tribe. Seralo, the senior Regent and brother of Dinamaula's own father, was an old man now, past his best, and his head and lips trembled as he went through the prescribed forms of welcome. Next to him sat the second uncle, Katsaula, Zuva's father, a tall thin man of the middle years, grave and unsmiling, the historian of the tribe, known for his insistence upon the old customs. The third Regent, Puero, another cousin of Dinamaula's, was a fattish, gross man; his eyes, deepset in his creased flabby face, moved aside too quickly when they were met. This was the one with whom Zuva would talk, behind the reed screens, long after nightfall.

Solemnly, in turn, the Regents intoned the traditional phrases; when they were all done, Dinamaula took up the burden of answer.

"Old Uncle," he began, bowing to Seralo, "and you others, I thank you. I am happy to have returned from far countries. This is my home, and here I will stay."

Dinamaula saw Puero exchange a swift glance with Zuva, and wondered if that would be the beginning of secret things between them. Now, clearly, was the time to show what was in his mind.

Speaking gravely and slowly, he went on, "Remember I am the son of Simaula, and grandson of the great Maula. I will rule as they ruled. I will take thought for the people, and the cattle, and the crops. I will work with white Government, as in the past, to make the tribe prosperous, and to punish evildoers. But there will be no great changes." He looked at Puero, and then at Zuva. "It may be that we can improve upon the past, and learn from it, as our fathers did before us. But my mind is not hungry for power, nor for new things. I will rule as my father ruled. That is all."

Seralo, the oldest and the wisest, found words to round off the scene. "My son," he said, rising slowly to his feet, "you have spoken well, and we thank you. Now let us have no more of these heavy matters. The people are waiting outside, on the *aboura*. Show yourself to them."

Dinamaula was to remember that night for all the rest of his life. The scene outside was already fantastic: when he appeared on the rough stoep, the crowd on the *aboura* seemed to move towards him as though impelled by a giant hand. But the throng was orderly: the old men stood in the front ranks, and behind them the young warriors, singing and chanting, and then, behind them again, in accordance with the custom, the women waited in groups under the thorn trees, waving, calling in shrill tones to their welcome chief. When he raised his hand and spoke, it was to an electric silence; when he ceased speaking, a great shout of recognition and homage rose up under the sky.

He saw, with amusement and without annoyance, that there was a police truck standing a little to one side of the *aboura,* under a single thorn tree, with the black policemen smiling widely in his direction and the white policeman watching the scene at ease, free from care. At that moment, he wanted to unite all men, black and white, in one happy bond. He took the hand of the nearest old man in the front rank and pressed it, and gave the ceremonial greeting, *"Ahsula!"* — "Peace!"

The word was taken up. Other men pressed forward to clasp his hand in turn. *"Ahsula!"* called the younger men at the back. The women repeated it, in the further darkness, and then the children, making a jingle out of it — *"Ahsula,* Dinamaula! *Ahsula,* Dinamaula!" At his side, Seralo, his old face shaking with deep emotion, said, "Let them sing for you. Let them dance for you."

First the children sang, a song of peace and welcome, their piping voices sounding reedy-clear under the stars. Then the young men of his own age group danced a tribal dance, with stamping and mock killing. Then it was time to feast.

Seated under the thorn trees, Dinamaula and his party ate and
drank with lusty appetite. On a signal from Katsaula, a choir of
young women advanced, their hips swinging, their bright eyes
roving among the young men, and sang a lascivious song, yet a
song hallowed by custom. Then one of the young girls, not the
prettiest, advanced with a dish of olives and bent over his shoulder.

"My Lord," she said. "Take, eat."

"This is Miera," said Katsaula. "The daughter of my brother,
who died at the time of the bad sickness. She has been chosen."

"Chosen?" asked Dinamaula, alert. The girl was not comely, and her body, hot from the dancing, was acrid and shining with sweat. "How chosen?"

"Chosen for this honor," said Katsaula swiftly. He indicated the dish of olives. "She gives you the last food of the night, according to the custom."

The girl's wiry hair was plastered with ocher mud and her face was heavy and stupid. Something within him revolted — at the girl, at the greasy bowls of mutton, the fierce liquor, the whole noisy uproar that filled the *aboura*. Before, it had been decorous and honorable; now it was suddenly repellent in its crudity.

He said with difficulty, "Miera, I thank you," and took two olives. He saw Katsaula eying him askance, and he turned again to the girl, and said, "They have chosen you well."

But suddenly he could endure no more, and he stood up and nodded to Seralo, and said formally, "Old Uncle, I have journeyed far. It is time for sleep."

Sleep came to him on laggard steps. His hut was roomy and the couch of skins was soft, but the hot air of the night seemed to press heavily upon him. His brain was filled with many tangled thoughts: of what he wanted to do in Gamate, and what lay in his path. He thought with revulsion of the girl Miera, and of the clear intention that she was to be his bride. He wanted no girl such as Miera, stupid and uncouth and without grace. Many things he *did* want, for himself and for his people; but as he stared in despair at the laced reeds of the roof above his head, they eluded the cloudy confusion of his brain.

TULBACH BROWNE of the *Daily Thresh* sat deep in an old leather armchair in the smoking room of the Pharamaul Club, waiting for Lou Strogoff, the American consul. Tulbach Browne was bored, irritable, and out of sorts. He did not like Port Victoria, which was hot and dirty; but he had to stay. For the *Daily Thresh* had taken a fancy to the stories he was sending, and wanted plenty more of the same sort. He did not even like the Pharamaul Club, where he was now a temporary member. His fellow members were mostly large, hearty men, burned by the sun: planters, lumber executives, importers, rich and poor idlers, civil servants.

Tulbach Browne sat on, sipping his whisky sour, staring at the spotted mezzotint above the mantelpiece — inevitably, the "Death of Nelson." He had spent much of the past week in the club, but he had done other things, too. He had called on the Governor, asked him three questions about local administration, and one about Dinamaula, and had set it all down in "The Cocked Hat Brigade." He had written a blistering piece about the club itself, "The Gin Drinkers of Pharamaul," which would probably be in tomorrow's

Daily Thresh. He had written one about the humble and degraded blacks toiling inhuman hours for the white man; and he had met four friends of a man named Zuva Katsaula, a forward-thinking African who apparently headed a movement called the "Freedom for Pharamaul Party," and had written them up in glowing terms ("There Are Statesmen at the Bottom of the Pack"), as four of the only future saviors of the country.

But now he was bored again, waiting to go up to Gamate, waiting also for Lou Strogoff — and here *was* Lou Strogoff, that unlikely man who, after twenty years in Pharamaul, still admired the British-in-exile.

Lou Strogoff was an oldish, scholarly man, nearer sixty than fifty, soft-spoken and firm. As he came forward, greeting one or two friends on the way, he was smiling. "Still here?" he asked. "I thought you newspaper fellows never stopped so long in any country. Don't tell me you've fallen for Port Victoria?"

"No," said Tulbach Browne, somewhat sourly. "That has *not* happened. It's just that I've got one or two stories to cover, before going up to Gamate."

"The Cocked Hat Brigade again?" asked Strogoff innocently.

Browne stared. "How has that got back to you so quickly?"

"We have a very good intelligence system," answered Strogoff blandly. "It's modeled on the British."

They ordered drinks and sipped them slowly. The pine-paneled room was cool after the heat of the day. "Didn't you agree with the article?" asked Tulbach Browne presently.

Lou Strogoff smiled. "No, sir. I agree that the British *wear* cocked hats, I agree that the British *act* cocked hats, and sometimes *are* cocked hats. But I don't agree that it's wrong, for a place like this." He stared at his drink. "You're ruling a backward people here. You've got to make your Governor, and all the others, *look* like rulers. If that means cock's feathers, white uniforms, and plenty of dog, there's no harm in it. It suits Pharamaul."

"But it's treating the Maulas like children."

"Most of them *are* children."

"I'm surprised you feel like that," said Tulbach Browne. "I should have thought an American would have seen how silly it is."

"I used to think that way," agreed Strogoff amiably. "But when you've been here as long as I have — " His voice trailed off. "Give the Maulas democracy," he continued, "that is, full social and political equality, and you'll have the worst mess you can think of. In the first place, they wouldn't know what to do with it; in the second, the process of finding out would be very painful and completely chaotic; and thirdly, there are just enough smart operators among the Maulas to take advantage of the sudden grant of freedom and run it as a personal racket."

"Then we must teach them how to handle it properly."

"You *are* teaching them. But slowly. When I first came here, back in the mid-thirties, there were no Maulas at all on the town council. The idea would have been unthinkable. Now there are three; three, out of twenty-four. They're not particularly good, because they're so *very* conservative. They don't believe in drains, public washhouses, diphtheria immunization. However, they *are* learning. Anyway, Port Victoria isn't true Pharamaul. True Pharamaul is up north, in Gamate. There are only a few white men there, and they're different from the ones you see here."

"Local tin gods, I suppose," said Tulbach Browne sneeringly.

Strogoff looked at him. "It makes a good title for your next piece," he said quietly, "but it's not an accurate one. If they're white farmers, they run their places on a paternalistic basis which has worked very well for a couple of hundred years. If they're traders, they give a fair deal — otherwise they wouldn't last six months with the Maulas. And if they're officials, they do the damnedest job — combined father, mother, policeman, judge, and wet nurse, three hundred and sixty-five days a year, for less than we pay a second-rate salesman back home. I'm *for* this country, Mr. Browne, and the people that run it." He raised his hand and a white-coated servant advanced and collected their empty glasses. "When are you going up to Gamate?"

"In a couple of days. And I warn you, I'm not taking anything on trust. I'm going to see for myself."

"It's the best way," said Lou Strogoff equably. "If you can really use your eyes, the way God meant you to."

"How do you mean?"

"Not with rose-colored spectacles. Not with dirt-colored, either.
Not with spectacles at all, in fact. Just with the eyes."

Chapter 3

I N LONDON the Permanent Under-Secretary for the Scheduled
Territories sat at his desk, clearing up his papers before going
home. It was seven o'clock, and it had been a long and exacting
day, but not too long and exacting for Sir Hubert Godbold.

Godbold was one of the ablest civil servants in the country,
knowledgeable, tough, and untiring. He could have made a
fortune in industry; instead, he made £4500 a year (less £2061
income tax) as a senior civil servant, with some five years to go
before the retiring age. Now, as he sat at his nearly clear desk,
there was a knock at the door, and Crossley, one of his assistant
under-secretaries, came in, a sheaf of files under his arm.

"Sir," he said, "there's a P.Q. on Pharamaul."

"Oh." Godbold took the proffered papers and looked at the top
one, clipped onto the outside of the file. It was a foolscap sheet of
blue-gray draft paper; it was headed: "Parliamentary Question:
Principality of Pharamaul: Mr. Price-Canning."

"*That* man," said Godbold with feeling. "It's those damned
Daily Thresh articles, I suppose." He adjusted his spectacles and
read slowly, aloud: " 'Notice has been given of the following
Parliamentary Question, to be asked by Mr. Emrys Price-Canning
(Independent Liberal, South Oxford) next Tuesday, September
22nd: *"To ask the Secretary of State for the Scheduled Territories*
whether his attention has been drawn to various statements of
policy recently made by Dinamaula Maula, chief-designate of the
Maula Tribe in the Principality of Pharamaul; whether he is in
agreement with such statements; and whether he can give an
assurance that the plans outlined in these statements will not be
obstructed by government officials in the Principality itself." ' "

The Permanent Under-Secretary knew Price-Canning personally; there was hardly a senior civil servant who did not. The man
was everywhere: he spoke with fluent violence, and he was always
sure of favorable notice in the left-wing press. Price-Canning the

never-sleeping conscience of England, Price-Canning the soldiers' friend, Price-Canning the black man's shield and buckler — there was really no end to it.

Godbold considered the matter. The whole thing could blow over, because Pharamaul was in the main a prosperous, well-administered country, and Dinamaula, when they had had their farewell interview, had seemed sensible and coöperative. On the other hand, the *Daily Thresh* articles had attracted a lot of attention; and Tulbach Browne and Emrys Price-Canning, if they ever came into purposeful collaboration, could give the Scheduled Territories Office a very uncomfortable time.

It was Godbold's job to advise the Minister (who would have to answer the question in the House of Commons) on the best way of dealing with it. He knew his Minister, Lord Lorde, son of an aged marquis and probably Britain's most reassignable statesman; and he wanted to give him the best ammunition available. So astute a man was Godbold that, when Lord Lorde got up to answer the charges the following day, his notes contained such smooth and persuasive parries that the infuriated Price-Canning carried his invective too far and was suspended for his pains.

"Uproar in House," said the *Daily Thresh*. "M.P. Suspended. 'Bullying and Muzzling' in Pharamaul. See 'Rank Injustice' in *Spotlight,* page 4."

David Bracken was glad to be bidding a temporary good-by to Port Victoria. Though the long and uncomfortable journey to Gamate and on up to Shebiya was not in itself an attractive prospect, it was good to be making a start at exploring the country and meeting some of the people he was to administer.

When Nicole Steuart put her head round the door of his office, he realized that there was only one thing he was sorry to leave in Port Victoria. Smiling, she said, "Still busy?"

"No, I'm about finished," David said. "Come in."

Nicole sat down, with the grace and economy of movement which characterized almost everything she did. Conscious of his frank eyes upon her, she sat back and said coolly, "I suppose you're packed and everything?"

David nodded. "Yes. All ready. I hope that odd-looking train won't be too uncomfortable."

"It always has been whenever I've made the trip."

"When were you last in Gamate?"

"About six months ago. It doesn't change much." She continued, "There's been some sort of row in Parliament about Dinamaula."

"What kind of row?"

"Price-Canning was suspended for being rude." She frowned. "If the man really wants to help people like the Maulas, there are better ways of doing it."

"Oh, Price-Canning's all right. He focuses people's attention."

"On Price-Canning."

"Well, at least he stirs things up."

"That's not always the best thing to do with 'things.'"

He grinned again. "I know we don't agree," he said, falsely apologetic. "I'll *try* to see it your way. I'm new, you know. Still championing the underdog."

She looked at him, frowning once more. David Bracken could still annoy her enormously when he was in this satiric mood that had an element of priggishness about it. He really *did* believe that all black men were downtrodden, and all white men — except men like Price-Canning — usurpers or colonial despots. Nicole Steuart stood up. She had wanted to stay much longer, but it wasn't working out the way she had hoped.

"You'll get over it," she said briefly. "It usually takes people about six months."

THE MANY discomforts of that long train journey to Gamate were forgotten next day when David awoke to his first fabulous dawn in Africa. From the train window he looked towards the east, and the east was about to set Pharamaul on fire. As far as his eye could reach, the rolling plain stretched away to the horizon. The grasslands and rocky outcrops had a strange uncertain color — gray from the night, gold from the dawn. A pale sky was already drawing streaky orange light from the invisible sun.

As he watched, a conical hill on the horizon turned from black to purple. The dew and the spider webs on the grasslands started to gleam. A circle of huts came into view; gray, sleepy, motionless except for the first thin wisp of smoke. Then suddenly the golden edge of the sun swam up from the far horizon, and all the drab colors changed to the colors of hope and warmth — gray to silver, purple to blue, black to red. David stared entranced as the plains of Pharamaul rose instantly to the new day.

Presently the train ground to a stop at a rough siding — no more than a water tower for the thirsty engine, a clearing with a few huts and a single frame house. David threw on some clothes and climbed down from the train, glad to stretch his legs.

He walked forward to the engine. Black faces peered at him from masked windows; other figures climbed down stiffly. Away to the north, a thickening plume of gray smoke marked the south-bound train which would pass them at this point. From the caboose next to the engine, one of the train crew smiled at him and handed down a thick mug of coffee. Sipping it, watching the other train approaching, turning to stare at the sky and the limitless plain around him, listening to the veld dawn and the quickening bird song, David Bracken fell in love with Pharamaul.

That feeling was doubly confirmed, some hours later, in Gamate.

FORSDICK, the District Commissioner, met him at the station, sweating in the noonday heat, his khaki shirt wilting, his florid face a ruddy purple under the tan. "How do?" he said, advancing a solid hand. It was a long time since David had heard the homely, North-country phrase. "Did you have a good trip?"

"Fine," answered David.

"I'm Forsdick, District Commissioner. Macmillan's away up-country for today. Otherwise he'd have been here. I thought you'd like to come back home for a spot of lunch now, then we might go down to the office to have a look-see."

"I'd like that," answered David cordially.

Driving back through the dusty, winding track that served as Gamate's main street, Forsdick pointed out the town's meager features — the hospital, the mission, the hotel, the school. All round them as they drove were crowds of people, and huts close-pressed together, and wandering herds of goats. Their driver blew his horn almost continuously, while children skipped out of the way, and women turned to grin, and old men under the eave shadows raised their hands, palm outwards, in formal greeting.

Forsdick's bungalow was outside the main part of the town, halfway up the hill towards the Residency. Mrs. Forsdick met them at the door. She was a tall severe woman in a faded print dress, her complexion ruined by dry heat, her manner brusque. She had hardly greeted David before she turned on her husband.

"You'd better go and change your shirt, George," she said. "That one's not fit to be seen. I'm sure Mr. Bracken — " she smiled meaningly " — isn't used to things like that."

Forsdick went off with a muttered word of apology. When he came back, she said, "Lunch is just about ready. But I suppose you want a drink."

"Yes," said Forsdick. "Any complaints?"

Lunch, served in a shabby room furnished throughout in yellow pickled oak, turned out to be a very uncomfortable meal. It was clear that the Forsdicks loathed each other, and that their marriage was sustained on his side by alcohol, and on hers by continuous, ill-tempered nagging. Any topic that Forsdick raised was promptly squashed by his wife. When he got up to pour himself some more beer, she called out, "Steady on, George! You've got to work this afternoon, haven't you?"

"It's good weather for drinking," said David pacifically.

"Seems it's always good weather for that," said Mrs. Forsdick.

"Cheer up, old girl," said Forsdick, with heavy facetiousness. "Only two more years before our long leave."

"Where will you go for that?" asked David.

"To my wife's mother in Dorking," said Forsdick, and guffawed.

"George!" said Mrs. Forsdick in furious tones.

"I've never been to Dorking," said David, at a loss for a subject of conversation.

"You haven't lived," said Forsdick.

"George!" said his wife again.

Perhaps the most fearful thing about their exchanges was that they seemed to be nothing out of the ordinary. David, driving down to the office with Forsdick half an hour later, had expected some degree of embarrassment; instead, Forsdick merely said, "The old girl's on the rampage today," and went on to talk of other things. It was clear that the lunch they had just had was a part of the accepted pattern of their life.

There must, David decided, be something about life in Gamate to make up for it.

EXACTLY what there was in Gamate to charm the heart, subdue all restlessness, and erase all marital horrors was made clear to David during the next four days. He talked, watched, wandered at will through the curious town. He learned the importance of water in a dry land, the paramountcy of tradition to a people who wrote nothing down, whose only rule was a remembered rule. He learned the pattern of administration, the delicate balances of care and discipline that kept a backward people happy, the sense of hope and order that made people like Andrew Macmillan and Forsdick and Captain Crump and Llewellyn, the agricultural officer, content with their lot.

First there was Forsdick. "You can't live with this job without getting absorbed in details," he said one day. He waved his hand over his desk, where there must have been twenty or more files awaiting his attention; their titles stood out like dull inscriptions on a neglected tomb: *Cattle Culling: Local Orders and Reports; Office Administration: Grade II Clerks, Advancement; Maula Headmen: Minutes of Meetings.* "And when you get absorbed in the details," Forsdick went on, "you just can't see the over-all pattern. Luckily Macmillan carries the whole thing in his head."

"He must be a remarkable man," said David.

Forsdick agreed. "I only hope — " He looked uncomfortable for a moment. "One of these days, if all goes well, I'll be taking over from him. I only hope I can do it half as well."

"But you like the prospect?"

"Of course." There was a pause. "There is one thing wrong with this sort of life," he said candidly. "It's what the women have to put up with. They slave away for years on end — heat, dust, dirt, flies, ants, no one to talk to, no friends left in England when they go on leave. They wait patiently at home for chaps

like me to come back and tell them about a damned funny thing
that happened with a Grade One Sub-Translator in the office
that afternoon. By God, if I were a service wife in a place like
Gamate, I'd run amuck with an ax!"

David was astonished at the reactions behind that florid brow.
Suddenly he liked Forsdick very much. "What's the answer?" he
asked. "I mean, why do all of you stick to it?"

"The women stick to it because they signed on for it," answered
Forsdick. "At the age of eighteen, they waltz down the aisle with a
clean-limbed young genius who's just got his first job in the Scheduled Territories service and who's going to be the Governor of
Pharamaul, with a handle to his name, in record time. Twenty
years later, their husbands have moved up exactly two grades in the
service, and someone else has the handle and the Governorship.
We stick to it, because we like it. It's as simple as that. We make
our homes here, we get to know the country, we have a few good
friends — black and white — a few men we can trust, a few chiefs
and headmen who learn very slowly to trust us in turn. We like
the country and it becomes our life, and pretty soon we're unfitted
for anything else, and somehow it doesn't matter, because the life
here has everything we want and everything we deserve."

THEN THERE was Crump, the young Irish police captain. He was
a cheerful escort, and their tour of Gamate by jeep was an engaging
and sometimes hilarious affair. They made their way through
the teeming center of the town, pausing momentarily on the edge
of the tribal meeting ground, the *aboura,* while a procession of
chattering school children crossed it in a long straggling crocodile.

"What's going on?" asked David.

"It's a meeting of welcome for Dinamaula," answered Crump.
It was typical of him, thought David, that he automatically knew
the answer. "Have you heard them sing?"

"No."

"It really wrings your heart," said Crump unexpectedly. "Particularly at night, in the lamplight. They sing a song called
'Ekartha i Maula' — 'The Land of Maula Is My Home,' a sort of
children's national anthem. You feel they must all be angels, even

though you know very well that they're a bunch of little toughs who'll rifle the poor box just as soon as your back's turned."

Crump started up the jeep again, and they took the winding road that led out of the town and towards the Gamate dam. The small khaki car with the police pennant created a stir of interest wherever it went: the older men saluted Crump with open hand, the women turned to stare, the children tried to pat the jeep's side as it ground along in low gear. David had an impression of respect in all this notice — respect, and affection too. But when he spoke the thought, Crump only laughed.

"Oh, they're law-abiding enough, the older ones, at least. They behave themselves because it's expensive and uncomfortable if they don't. If it ever came to a showdown, more people would rally to our side than would dare to take a chance and get tough. At least," he added, frowning, "that's the situation at present."

David showed his surprise. "Could it alter?"

"Oh yes. They're like that, you know: quiet, logical, and friendly, until something — some silly thing that you and I wouldn't give tuppence for — gets under their skin. Then they change. Sometimes they change horribly. There's no warning at all. One day they're good, next day they're murdering, looting savages."

"Has that ever happened here?"

Crump nodded, giving his attention to a sharp turn in the road, with a frieze of goats blocking its edges. "Not recently. We had a big tax row, about five years ago. It started because some new receipt forms were printed on green paper — it's an unlucky color. I lost two of my chaps, torn to bits back there on the *aboura*. And there were some horrible things in the old days, before the present dynasty got properly settled in. The U-Maulas — that's the exiled lot, up north round Shebiya — are still pretty cruel."

They were now level with the mile-wide dam, and after a brief inspection they turned for home. The jeep descended slowly, braking for the sharp curves, skidding on the dry, corrugated track. Presently they were back on the other side of the *aboura*. Crump's sharp eyes, searching endlessly as they moved past huts and mealie patches, lighted on two men sitting close together under a thorn tree.

"That's Dinamaula's cousin Zuva and one of the Regents, Puero," he said. He blew an authoritative note on the horn, and the two men, a few yards away, raised their heads. They gave a perfunctory salute, and Crump returned it just as briefly.

"They're cooking something up," said Crump. "I don't know what it is, yet, but I'll find out one of these days. You saw that interview that Dinamaula gave to the newspapers. If they wanted to start building up on that, there could be plenty of trouble."

"Would Dinamaula join in?"

"Depends on how he's handled. Well, we'll see."

The jeep rolled on across the *aboura* and towards the hotel.

THE BAR of the Gamate Hotel was a sparsely furnished room with wickerwork tables and chairs, and a long open counter at one end; the "gang" who gathered there nightly were alike in many things — in dress, in thirst, in tenor of conversation. David, entering with Crump, recognized the Forsdicks sitting at one end of the bar — she grim, he flushed and talkative; standing next to them were Llewellyn and a huge blond man introduced as Oosthuizen, the only white farmer in the district.

"I'm South African originally," said Oosthuizen, in answer to David's query. "We've had our place here for nearly a hundred and fifty years. That's why we've been allowed to keep it, I suppose. All the rest was stolen by the British Government and given to the blacks." He grinned towards Llewellyn; it was evidently a long-standing joke between them. "But I'm not moving."

"We'll get you out, one of these days," said Llewellyn darkly.

"I've got five sons," said Oosthuizen, laughing. "The eldest is looking round for a girl already. I reckon you'll have to wait a bit."

David found a glass of beer thrust in his direction, and the man behind the bar held out his hand. "I'm Fellows," he said. "I run this place. Glad to see a new face."

Forsdick turned towards Crump. "Your wife coming in?"

"I hope so," said Crump coldly.

"So do I." Forsdick winked at David. "Wait till you see her. She's a honey!"

"My wife's having a baby," said Oosthuizen. "Or she'd be here."

The noise in the bar was considerable. All the tables were full, the men in dusty khaki, the women in slacks or creased print dresses. Another glass was pushed into David's hand.

"Who are these people, exactly?" he asked Crump.

"All sorts." Crump looked round the room. "Oosthuizen farms near here, of course. The people in the corner work on the railway; those others are down from the logging camp near Shebiya. Then there are all our own people and their wives, and the medical staff, and local traders. It's a friendly sort of place. We're all doing the same sort of job — running this part of the country as best we can."

"What about the Maulas themselves? Can they buy drink here?"

Crump shook his head. "No. They're not allowed alcohol. At least, that's the general rule. I don't mind the chief or the Regents buying an occasional bottle for themselves — Fellows knows that. But the ordinary tribespeople are barred."

"I should damn well think so!" said Oosthuizen, overhearing. "Natives can't take hard liquor — it just drives them crazy. I let my blacks break out once a year, at Christmas. It takes about a week to get them back into shape again."

Someone called to Oosthuizen, and he turned away.

"What's he like as an employer?" asked David in a low tone.

"First-class," answered Crump, "though you mightn't think it, to hear him talk. He employs about five hundred natives, all told — it's a very big farm. He looks after them well, houses them properly, gives them plots of land to farm on their own account. His wife doctors them, and keeps an eye on the women and the kids. It's like a big, spread-out family."

A very pretty dark girl appeared suddenly at his side and squeezed his arm. Crump exclaimed, "Molly, darling!" and introduced her as his wife. David found himself understanding Forsdick's patent interest in Mrs. Crump. In a drab and dusty town, among tired, run-of-the-mill women, she glowed like candlelight at dusk. He thought suddenly of Nicole.

"Darling," said Mrs. Crump presently. "I think you-know-who is going to make a move in my direction. What about it?"

Out of the corner of his eye, David saw that Forsdick was indeed looking towards them, and seemed on the point of joining their party. Crump stood back briskly from the counter.

"I've had my whack," he said. "Let's get going."

It was neatly done. By the time Forsdick had crossed the room, the Crumps had said good-by and were already through the outer door.

FATHER Schwemmer, the missionary, was weeding his garden when David called on him. He was a small man, not young, of brisk yet gentle manner; his hair was close-cropped, his rusty-brown cassock much in need of repair. Yellow dust lay thick on his cracked boots, and on the mission-house garden; the house itself, brick daubed with clay, was modest. Yet his eyes, as he raised them at David's step, were friendly and full of hope, and his handclasp warm.

"Mr. Bracken, sir," he said. "I was informed that you were in Gamate. Welcome to my house."

He was a German, he told David with curious formality, a member of an ancient Catholic teaching order.

"How long have you been here?" David asked.

"Thirty years, perhaps; time passes swiftly in Gamate. We are not rich, as you see." He smiled, a shy smile; and indeed, the life-time of poverty and faith was movingly apparent. Then he continued, "But the mission itself was established on this very piece of land, in the year 1782."

"Was it your order which brought Christianity to Pharamaul?"

The missionary shook his head. "I wish I could say that this was so. But it would not be true. It is also a very curious story. You do not know this country, Mr. Bracken? But you have seen maps?"

"Yes," answered David. "And of course I've read up on it."

"To the north of here — " Father Schwemmer pointed towards the U-Maula hills " — lies Shebiya. That is the other capital, the home of the exiles. Near it, on the coast, is a place marked 'Fish Village.' When the first missionary of our order arrived in Shebiya, he found traces of Christianity there already. There was a kind of — " he waved his hand " — a race memory of Christian teaching. There was a tradition handed down, a tradition going back into the very mists of time, the story of a Saviour who was the son of a virgin, and who was crucified, and whose followers were later persecuted for their faith. There was even something more. There was the fish that gave the village its name."

"I don't understand," said David.

"That first missionary attended one of their meetings — " he smiled " — their *nearly* Christian meetings. He found that one of their special rituals was to draw the outline of a fish in the sand, and then rub it out quickly. But that was not a new ritual; that was how the very early Christians used to recognize each other secretly. They would stand in the market place and draw the outline of a fish with their foot, so." He drew a fish on the sandy path with the toe of his cracked boot. "They would do it as if idly, and then rub it out." His foot moved, and the sand was smooth again. "That was their secret way of finding out if the man they spoke to was a Christian. They drew a fish, because the Greek word for fish was *ichthus,* and the Greek letters of that word stand for 'Jesus Christ the Son of God the Saviour.' "

David kept silent. The odd, potent story, related in precise accents by this shabby priest, had moved him very much.

"There have been many strange happenings in Africa," said Father Schwemmer, "and many wonderful things. But that is one of the strangest. It means that, perhaps in the first century after Christ, a wandering preacher, or an escaped slave, or a traveler who was a convert, or an apostle of whom we know nothing traveled all the way down Africa, and then took ship for Pharamaul and was cast ashore near Shebiya. There he taught the natives what he knew of the life of Our Lord, and taught them also to draw a fish — the secret sign of hope and redemption. And so the place where he landed was called Fish Village. It is still called that, after nineteen hundred years, and they still draw the fish when they come to worship, although I cannot say that it means the same as the fish that I would draw."

Silence fell between them when the missionary stopped speaking. With an effort David recalled himself to the twentieth century, to Father Schwemmer's parish. "Do you think," he asked, speaking carefully, "that we are doing all we can in Pharamaul? It's an old pattern of administration. Is it still the best?"

Father Schwemmer did not answer immediately. He was looking round him, first at the poorly tended mission house, then to the hills beyond. "Mr. Bracken," he said finally, "I cannot answer your question." He gestured round him. "In Pharamaul, in Gamate, all this seems natural and unchangeable. Up the hill, out of sight, the white man rules. Here, near my gate, the black man lives. The white man rules wisely, the black man obeys and lives a hard, dull life. But in New York, at the United Nations, men from other countries tell us that the pattern is evil, that the white man must go away and the black man must rule his own life."

Father Schwemmer paused, his eyes on the far hills. Finally he smiled. It was not a happy smile. "Perhaps somewhere between those two," he said, "with the white man *ready* to leave, the black man *ready* to rule, perhaps that is the fair answer. But the fair answer is for tomorrow, not today."

"We shall not be here tomorrow," said David, after a pause.
"No," said Father Schwemmer. "That is one thing certain. We shall not be here on that tomorrow. All we can do is to make today a day that leads towards it."

THE FORMAL meeting with Dinamaula and the three Regents was a constrained and queerly uneasy affair. When David walked into the schoolroom where they waited for him, he had the impression that they had been quarreling, or at least discussing something which had left them totally divided in thought. Old Seralo, the senior Regent, greeted him with quavering ceremonial; Katsaula used the single, prescribed word, *"Ahsula!"* Fat Puero smirked and held out his hand; Dinamaula himself, preoccupied and morose, said, "Nice to see you, Mr. Bracken," as one Oxford graduate to another.

Their exchanges were brief, pointed, and unreal. Even for an occasion which was, at best, a formal recognition of David's new appointment, it was an awkward session.

"Sir," began Seralo, bowing, "we are happy to welcome the new secretary. We hope you will be happy in our country."

"I'm sure that I shall be." David turned towards Dinamaula. "We were on the same plane, Chief," he said. "But I didn't know it was you."

Dinamaula grinned, a quick, mirthless grin in a guarded face. "I wondered who you thought it was."

"I was talking to Mr. Macmillan," said David, persisting on a point which seemed to contain the seeds of embarrassment. "We neither of us knew it was you."

"Yes," said Dinamaula. "I am sure of that."

After a moment of silence, Puero, the junior Regent, with the air of a careless man who has nothing to lose, said, "How long will you be staying in Gamate, Mr. Bracken?"

"I leave tomorrow," answered David. "I'm driving up to Shebiya with Captain Crump."

"Shebiya," said Seralo, and sighed.

"With Captain Crump," said Puero, faintly impudent.

"Mr. Bracken," said Katsaula, "Shebiya is very different from

Gamate. This is the capital of our country, and here we live quietly and work with Government. In Shebiya it is different. There is a man there, Gotwela, an exile — "

"My cousin," said Seralo sadly. "My own cousin."

"A man," continued Katsaula, "who does many strange things. He has the name of chief, Chief of the U-Maulas. You will meet him. He is not a Maula." Katsaula's tone was hard and unforgiving. "He has forsaken the tribe. Here, we obey the law and remember our fathers. In Shebiya it is different."

"I am sure," said Puero, smooth and sarcastic, "that Mr. Bracken knows how we obey the law. Gotwela also obeys the law." He seemed to be speaking from some inner compulsion to provoke and sting. "Otherwise, Government would punish him."

It was a moment of some discomfort, with which David was scarcely equipped to deal. "Of course, I've read a little about the U-Maulas," he said, trying for stiffness in his voice. "And I want to see as much of the country as I can."

Silence fell. Dinamaula was looking out of the window, Puero whistling between his teeth. Finally Seralo coughed and said, "Please take back our greetings to His Excellency the Governor."

David nodded.

"Our greetings and our loyalty," amended Katsaula.

"Certainly I will," said David.

"Tell him that all is well with the tribe, and with Gamate. Tell him that the harvest — "

"Old Uncle!" said Dinamaula, turning suddenly. "Remember I am soon to be chief."

There was an embarrassed silence.

"Greetings we send," said Dinamaula. David suddenly noticed that he was speaking under great tension. "Messages about the tribe and the future should wait till I am proclaimed as chief."

In the constrained silence that closed in again round the words, David thought swiftly. Now it was clear that his arrival had been preceded by some definitive family quarrel — Seralo's embarrassment, Katsaula's shocked surprise, and the look of sardonic toughness on Puero's face were all witness to this. The fact that Dinamaula had so far broken custom as to allow the quarrel to intrude upon a formal occasion pointed to its bitterness, a bitterness now amply reflected in his taut face. There could be no quick resolving of such a moment, David realized, nor would it be seemly for him to try for one. He stood up.

"I have to go, I'm afraid," he said awkwardly. "I'm glad that we could meet. I'll be back in Gamate in about a week."

It was a feeble leave-taking. David's last impression was of the derisive contempt in Puero's eyes. Behind the closed door, furious voices rose as soon as he left the room.

LATER, when David talked with Andrew Macmillan, he learned, among other things, the likely reason for the "family quarrel" that so nearly got out of hand.

"I had Dinamaula up here a couple of days ago," said Macmillan, after David had described the occasion in detail. "That was probably the start of it. I gave him a real flea in his ear."

"Oh," said David, surprised. The crude, schoolboyish phrases seemed somehow out of keeping with the job of Resident Commissioner, though this might not be so. "Why was that? What happened?"

"London was steamed up about that newspaper interview, as you know." The two of them were sitting at ease on the Residency stoep, drinking their coffee. The air was cool and peaceful, the garden deeply quiet in the dusk. "I got him up here," Macmillan went on, "told him we didn't like it. He started to argue the toss. Told *me* he'd say anything he liked, to any newspaperman he met." Macmillan grinned. "I hit the roof."

"But *did* he say all those things?" asked David.

"That's the silly part of it. He didn't. At least, he may have talked a bit about progress and development — no harm in that, either — but he didn't say anything as definite or as tough as Tulbach Browne made out. I believe him there, of course: most of those press boys are liars through and through. But then Dinamaula said that, although he hadn't talked exactly that way, he saw no harm in it. He 'stood on his right' to plan future development and discuss it freely with anyone. That was when I administered the rocket."

"How did he take it?"

"Turned sulky," said Macmillan. "Got up and left. I suppose he told the Regents and that was what the row was about."

"But how?" asked David, puzzled. "Why should they disagree?"

Andrew Macmillan shifted his weight. He seemed old and tired, and yet all-competent still.

"It's a bit complicated," he said. "If Dinamaula came back and said that he'd been reprimanded by me and explained why, the Regents would take sides automatically. Seralo and Katsaula, the traditionalists, would be very shocked, and tell Dinamaula he'd got what was coming to him. Puero's a progressive and tricky. He'd try to persuade him he was badly treated, and egg him on to do the same thing again, only more so. Then there's young Zuva, who is something else again. Maybe he doesn't know himself what he's playing with, but it's a damned dangerous movement that he's trying to get under way. He wants the black man in, and the white man out — *now*. Perhaps the nearest thing to it would be to say that it's the Pharamaul version of Mau Mau."

A chill wind seemed to invade the garden as Macmillan finished speaking, an uneasy breath of fear and evil. The syllables "Mau Mau" seemed to float in the air round them.

"There's always something, isn't there?" Macmillan said unexpectedly. "This country has had a pretty rough history, one way and another, like the mainland. It's quiet for twenty years, and then everything flames up, and then it turns quiet again. The thing to do," he said reflectively, "is to enjoy the quiet times, and make the most of them, and be ready for the crisis when it comes."

"*Are* we ready?" asked David, still under the spell of foreboding.

Macmillan jerked his head in derision. "As ready as we can be," he answered, almost contemptuously, "with the staff I've got to run thirty thousand square miles, a hundred and twenty thousand people. Work it out for yourself. If it's spread any thinner, anywhere in the world, I'd like to hear about it." He laughed, still not seeming to take it seriously. "The funny thing is, it *is* spread thin all over the world, and it still works. I don't know how we do it." Macmillan grinned. "But that's what we're paid for. Let's have a drink, and then bed. You've got an early start to make tomorrow."

"I'm really looking forward to it."

Macmillan nodded. "It's rough country. Some of it nearly jungle, in fact. Gotwela, the chief, is a real ruffian. If Zuva," he said, and his voice seemed distant and detached, "if Zuva really wants to start that bloody business, he'll join up with Gotwela. That's the character who *really* wants to murder every white man in Pharamaul."

THE JEEP, heavily laden, crawling like some brown industrious beetle from hill to small hill, made its slow way northwards. It left the Gamate plains, traversed the encroaching bush, climbed steadily, then forsook the flat grasslands altogether for the heavy-pressing jungle that guarded the approaches to U-Maula country.

Besides David Bracken and Crump, the jeep held their luggage and a sack of mail, and tools such as pickaxes and spades, and a forty-gallon drum of fresh water. It carried extra petrol, and a two-way radio set, and finally a black police corporal who clung to this piled freight like a child to a bucking pony.

Their journey took more than five hours: they stopped many times — to refill their boiling radiator, to eat and stretch their legs, to take the midday police schedule on the radio.

Crump, as usual, proved himself a cheerful companion, though at the start of their journey he seemed preoccupied, even morose. "I never like leaving Molly behind at Gamate," he had volunteered suddenly.

Later, when they were well within U-Maula territory, and had stopped to check their guns, David had asked, "How often do you make this journey?"

"About once a month," answered Crump. "We've got a police post up at Shebiya — a corporal and four of the chaps. This lad behind — " he jerked his head towards their passenger " — is the relief. He'll do a month up there."

"Will there be anything for him to do?"

Crump shrugged. "You never know. It's been quiet now for

a long time. Of course, there's always stock theft, and a murder or two, and a bit of rape on the side." He grinned. "You can't expect it to be like an English village. But Gotwela has the thing pretty well sewn up. When he cracks the whip, they jump. Saves us a lot of trouble."

"If you can trust *him*."

"I wouldn't trust him a short yard on a bright sunny day," said Crump crisply. "He's a crook, a murderer, and a very cruel man. But he rules the U-Maulas, and we rule him, and so the thing works. It wouldn't look too good on paper, but here it's just about all right — at the moment."

"You said that before," commented David presently. "Do you mean that things could really change so quickly?"

"This is Africa," answered Crump, releasing and then snapping home the magazine of his pistol. "Anything can happen. I always do this — " he patted the smooth, oily stock of the Luger " — because I might have to use it in a hurry. Gotwela keeps a tight rein but some of his lads are still trigger-happy. They're likely to take a pot shot at whatever they see moving. If it turns out to be a police jeep, so much the better. You could hardly ask for a nicer target, could you?"

THE TREMENDOUS, quivering salute which the corporal in charge of the police post tore off, as soon as he caught sight of Crump, seemed to argue a welcome level of morale, in this corner of Shebiya at least. But that level was not maintained elsewhere. The town was nearly deserted when they drove through it, although it was late afternoon, the traditional time of meeting and gossip. Instead of movement and life, there was a brooding quietness: no men rose to greet them, no women turned to laugh, no children touched the jeep as it passed. Only in the police post, with its flag flapping taut at the masthead, its neat pathways whitewashed along their borders, was there order, discipline, and grinning welcome.

Crump spent some time inside the post, while David, glad to stretch his legs, stood by the jeep. A few men passed him, without greeting or glance. Then a wagon drawn by a span of six gaunt oxen creaked by them, stopping a little way ahead, blocking the road. Its driver, a small wizened man, remained hunched over the reins, his long whip lying idly across the backs of his team.

Crump came out of the police post, looking pleased, stepping briskly, smart in his freshly laundered bush tunic. He glanced at the ox wagon, still blocking their way. He leant over and blew a long blast on the jeep's horn. The driver did not stir. After a moment, Crump called something over his shoulder and two black policemen came running down the pathway.

Crump pointed. The two policemen began to shout at the driver, and one of them, gesturing, made as if to climb up to his seat. The driver, motionless until the last moment, raised his long whip and brought it down, very slowly, almost derisively, on the backs of his two leading oxen. The ox wagon started forward again, moving with sarcastic deliberation out of their path.

"They try it on," said Crump briefly, as he climbed into his place again. "Then they give way, as slowly as they can. Shebiya is like that."

"But suppose he didn't get out of the way," asked David, disturbed by the incident.

"He'd come up before Tom Ronald, at the next summary court. Tom would tell him that he mustn't block the roads with his wagon, and would caution him not to do it again. That's all."

"But wouldn't it be better to put it on a legal basis? Arrest the man for obstruction to teach him a lesson?"

Crump shook his head. "No. That's what he really wanted, in a way, so we don't give it him. If we'd hauled him in, on the spot, my chaps would have had all the bother of moving the wagon themselves. Then the driver would have complained that one of his oxen had gone lame, through being handled by a ham-handed policeman, or that one of the wagon wheels had been forced over a big stone, and he was going to sue Government for a hundred pounds." Crump grinned, throwing it all away.

"What were the policemen saying, anyway?"

"They were calling the driver, among other things, a stupid, lazy lout," said Crump succinctly. "Must have given them a lot of pleasure. He's their uncle."

THE MAN who strolled towards them as the jeep drew up before the frame bungalow was Tom Ronald, the District Officer. He was young — twenty-two or -three — cheerful, and thickset, with a fair skin and curly hair: an ex-footballer, thought David, probably given to hearty reminiscence. He was not surprised when Tom Ronald's first words of greeting turned out to be, "What ho, chaps! Glad you got here in one piece. I bet you're about ready to wet the old whistle!"

As the conversation continued, David found that Tom Ronald was not really as simple as he sounded. Behind the "What ho!" and the "Cheers, chaps!" and the residual schoolboy inanity lay something strong and tough and competent.

Tom Ronald certainly knew his territory, and what was going on in it. While David listened to his account, he looked round the room in which they sat. It was something like the Forsdicks' sitting room, the furniture supplied from stock by the Office of Works, the woodwork painted throughout in that morbid hue known as Government Beige. Outside, the sun bore fiercely down on straggling flower beds, and a lawn marred by bare brown patches. Then his ear was caught by something that Tom Ronald was saying.

"I think we've got a new secret society in Shebiya," he remarked offhandedly. "There have been a lot of meetings lately, and some drilling, out on the hillside. Something to do with fish. They call themselves the Fish Men. Don't know if there's anything in it."

Crump nodded. "My chaps at the police post were saying the same thing. But there's always been that fish emblem in Pharamaul, hasn't there? One of the old Maula titles is 'Son of the Fish,' after all."

Ronald looked doubtful. "Maybe. But that's a religious thing. This seems to be different. Now they've started drawing fishes all over the place. Like a political emblem. We had half a dozen new people in the village last week. They also called themselves Fish Men. But *they'd* trekked up from Port Victoria."

Crump echoed the last words, "Port Victoria?" in a tone of the utmost surprise, and David felt his stomach give a sudden, uneasy heave. The word "fish" recalled his conversation with Father

Schwemmer, and the dark barbaric world which the latter had conjured from the past. He recalled also Andrew Macmillan, talking of Mau Mau. He felt the foreboding twinge gripping him again as Crump said, "You'd better keep your eye on that. Zuva, down in Port Victoria, is about ready to start something. I don't want him joining up with the U-Maulas. We're likely to have quite enough trouble with Dinamaula in Gamate, as it is."

"What's the gen there?" asked Tom Ronald. "Isn't he going to behave like mother's best boy?"

"No," said Crump. "That's the short answer, and it's the only one I can give you, at the moment. But you might let me know if Puero, the Regent, ever shows up here. He's another one who's feeling the spring."

An agreeable feminine voice behind them asked, "Who's feeling the spring?" and they all stood up as Tom Ronald's wife entered the room.

Cynthia Ronald was a surprise. David had had a picture in his mind, a picture drawn from Tom Ronald's own appearance. Since Tom had turned out to be a football type, his wife was likely to be a female football type to match — a wind-blown blonde with her hair done up in a scarf. Cynthia Ronald, in fact, was tall, dark, and attractive in a distinctly indoor way. When she placed her slim hands on Tom Ronald's shoulders, it was as if she were rehearsing the prelude to an embrace which would take place immediately their visitors were out of the house. David Bracken found her disturbing: she was so extremely attractive and so clearly absorbed in her husband that no spectator could remain entirely free of jealousy.

She said, "Hallo, Keith," to Crump, and then to David, "Thank God for a new face!" Then she perched on the arm of her husband's chair, and said, "Break it up, boys. The world will keep till tomorrow."

Later, after a surprisingly good dinner, they all played Animal Grab with an ancient, dog-eared pack of cards, till it was time to go to bed. No wonder Tom Ronald, as he had proclaimed several times already, liked his isolated assignment in Shebiya. On these terms, it hardly counted as isolation.

THEY STAYED for three days in Shebiya: days of exploration, inquiry, and a certain tension. The town itself was not much more than a clearing in the jungle. The rough road by which they had come led south to Gamate; another road led past Tom Ronald's house and eastwards to Fish Village on the coast; a third, smaller track wandered westward, to no particular place, and then petered out in a solid, impenetrable wall of vegetation.

Together, Crump and David Bracken sampled all that Shebiya had to offer. They had a day's good shooting in the hills. They spent an afternoon in the dusty Shebiya courtroom, where they heard eleven cases tried by Tom Ronald, unaccustomedly severe and stern. They visited the mission house, a dilapidated shack which clearly needed an early call from Father Schwemmer. On its outer walls, the fish emblem now blossomed in uneasy variety — sometimes daubed with paint, sometimes smeared in charcoal, here and there scored with a knife.

Their last call in Shebiya, on the eve of their departure, was a formal visit to Gotwela, chief of the U-Maulas. It was as well that they had kept this call until last; otherwise, thought David, it might well have spoilt their stay.

Gotwela, when at last he appeared, after a mortifying delay, in the doorway of his hut, proved to be a gross, dirty, ruffianly man of undoubted presence. He was tall, yet his enormous paunch and fat bare thighs gave him an illusion of squat ungainliness. He wore the *simbara,* the ceremonial lion skin which, outmoded in Gamate, still served as a mark of eminence in Shebiya. As he emerged into the sunlight, blinking under heavy brows, he staggered slightly, and free-flowing sweat started from his face and neck. Gotwela, David diagnosed, had a severe hangover.

It seemed, however, that he kept some state, on a savage plane that was not reassuring. A tall lithe warrior, also wearing the *simbara* and carrying a polished spear, preceded Gotwela's appearance; two others, similarly armed, ranged themselves at his side as soon as he took his stand. The strange, crudely arrayed group of four faced the two white men for some moments, without speech and without movement, and the tall, gross figure in the center, swaying gently, pouring with sweat, frowning under iron

brows, was a figure of menace. Then Crump spoke. *"Ahsula!"* he
said formally. "I am glad to see you, Chief."

Gotwela raised his hand, and his bodyguard, copying him, lifted
their spears. The broad blades caught the sun, flashing as if in
warrant of their murderous intent. Gotwela, insolently detached,
looked beyond Crump, noting the jeep and its attendant policeman. He smiled, widening his thick, cruel lips with sardonic

slowness. Then he spoke in turn, in a throaty voice.

"*Ahsula!* . . . Captain Crump . . . We are honored by this visit."

The three men of the bodyguard grounded their spears on the dusty forecourt of the hut, then looked intently ahead of them.

"I am glad to see you well, Chief," answered Crump curtly. "This is Mr. Bracken, a new officer of Government. I have brought him with me to see Shebiya."

Gotwela nodded briefly, but he did not answer. The bodyguard still stared ahead, oblivious of the sun, the flies, the voice of the police captain. Only their spears were taut and ready. Foolishly, David tried to calculate how long it would take him to reach the jeep, if those spears began to tremble and to lift.

He heard Crump speak again, "I hope that all is well here, Chief."

"All is well." Gotwela's voice, deep and coarse, seemed to say to Crump, directly, "All was well before you came. All will be well as soon as you have gone."

"The cattle?" asked Crump.

"The cattle are well."

"The crops?"

"The crops are gathered."

"The rain?"

"We have been fortunate."

There was a pause. Crump frowned. "What is this of the fish?" he asked brusquely.

Gotwela stared back at him, cool, unsurprised. "Fish?" he repeated, and shook his head. "I know no fish."

Unexpectedly, Crump moved. With the polished toe of his boot he drew the fish emblem in the sandy soil — two curved lines, coming to a point at one end, crossing at the other. Then he gestured downwards. "That is the fish I speak of."

David saw that the three men of the bodyguard were no longer looking ahead: they were staring down at what Crump had drawn in the sand, and their eyes had lost their veil of blankness. From them he looked again at Gotwela, but Gotwela was giving no ground. He faced Crump unblinkingly, his heavy head erect, his gross body solid as rock. He said again, "I know no fish."

Crump sighed, not at a loss, but as if he realized that this road was barred and he must find another one. He said curtly, "I am watching this fish," and turned away.

The ugly riddle seemed to be rearing up monstrously behind David's back, as he walked down the pathway towards the jeep. But no weapon smote him deep between the shoulder blades, no spear cleft his skull; only Crump's voice saying, in one breath, "*Ahsula!* Farewell," and in another, a few paces on, "Bloody old murderer! He knows all about it," seemed to tell of their defeat.

Not until the jeep began to move and they were fifty yards away did David, shamefacedly, realize his utter relief.

CYNTHIA RONALD was playing croquet by herself on the patchy brown lawn, when David Bracken came out to say good-by to her. It was an inane occupation for a pretty girl, David thought, as he drew near and found himself admiring her figure once more; and then he thought again, and the fact that she was playing this vicarage-garden game, thousands of miles from its natural setting in rural England, was somehow attractive and endearing. Exile in Shebiya, even exile with the man you loved, must need something like croquet to restore it to normality. He smiled as she glanced up, and said, "You look very expert. It's about time for me to go, I'm afraid."

"It's been wonderful having you." She let the mallet fall to the ground, and faced him. "We love it here, but it's nice to see some- one new for a change."

"Don't you ever get lonely?"

"Now and again. But there's lots to do. And we have visitors quite often. Father Schwemmer and Keith Crump turn up every month or so. Andrew Macmillan sometimes. Now there's you." She smiled. "And of course I have a nice husband."

"It boils down to that, doesn't it?"

"Pretty well."

David thought of Nicole and of seeing her again quite soon, and he said suddenly, "It's about time I got married myself."

"You do that," said Cynthia Ronald immediately. "It's the very best thing you can do. And then you can bring her here to see us."

The police jeep drew up at the front gate, and Crump waved to him, signaling his readiness. At the same moment, Tom Ronald came down the steps of his bungalow.

Linking her arm through her husband's, Cynthia Ronald said, "Darling, isn't it wonderful? David's going to get married and bring his wife up to see us."

"Good show!" said Tom Ronald.

"Wait a minute," laughed David. "I haven't asked her yet."

"Ask her," said Ronald. "Soon as you can. I recommend it."

"It's all very well for you two."

"Yes," said Cynthia Ronald, "it's all *very* well."

When, after cheerful good-bys, the jeep moved off down the road, David's last sight of them was as they stood arm in arm, in the middle of their lawn, waving farewell. They seemed so natural a pair, so naturally happy, that Shebiya itself shed its gloom as long as they were within view, and became, briefly, a secure and contented place.

But that illusion did not survive even the beginning of the return journey. By the time the jeep had traversed the sullen town and was grinding downhill through close-pressing trees, security

and contentment had ebbed to nothing. Tom Ronald and his
wife lost stature alarmingly, shrinking down to the level of
hostages, left behind in dubious country, and barely, guiltily
remembered from behind the barricade of safety.

Chapter 4

W HEN Tulbach Browne arrived in Gamate, he did not immediately make contact with Dinamaula. Being an experienced newspaperman, he first wanted to see the place where
he lived, the Maulas whom he ruled, and the white men who, in a
truer sense, ruled the Maulas and Dinamaula himself. Armed
thus, and with his prejudices sharpened, he hoped to come upon
the young chief with a dozen barbed inquiries that would tie his
series of stories up into one neat, poisonous bundle.

His headquarters was now the Gamate Hotel, and from there
he foraged diligently, intent on the murder of fact. He went everywhere — in the hotel, on the *aboura,* touring the outlying districts,
calling at the Residency, hanging round the tribal office. He had
a hired car at his disposal, and in the first week, which included
a sudden dart back to Port Victoria in order to file a confidential
dispatch to his paper, Tulbach Browne's taxi bill was £125.

The piece he did on "Gamate's Tin Gods" was alone worth the
money to the *Daily Thresh.* It stemmed from a half-hour talk with
Llewellyn, the agricultural officer, and a longer call on Andrew
Macmillan up at the Residency.

Macmillan had received Tulbach Browne, as he did all his
visitors, sitting on the stoep that overlooked the Residency garden
and the broad vista of Gamate that lay below it. He would scarcely
have received him at this hospitable level had it not been for the
tradition of welcome that was an essential part of Gamate and
innumerable places like it. Tulbach Browne was part of a moving
frieze of guests, as inevitable as the ants in the garden outside.

"Well," said Browne jovially, "I suppose there was a lot of excitement when Dinamaula got back here?"

"There was the usual party," answered Macmillan, rather
wearily. "Dinamaula was a good excuse for it."

"I see you take a rather detached view of the whole thing," said Browne. The phrases "Blasé overlord" and "Godlike eminence" swam briefly before his eyes. He continued, "But a new chief is something special, after all."

"Certainly he's something special, and I don't take a detached view at all." Macmillan felt himself nettled, realized that it was possibly dangerous, and took a pull at his self-control. "It's part of my job to see that that sort of occasion doesn't get out of hand."

"You mean, they're allowed to celebrate, as long as the party doesn't get too rough?"

"Yes," said Macmillan. "Like London on Boat-race night."

Tulbach Browne steered away from the reasonable comparison. "It must be very satisfying," he commented, "to be able to organize people's lives so completely." He saw Macmillan opening his mouth to protest, and he chipped in quickly, "Ah well, it's over and done with, anyway. Have you seen Dinamaula yourself?"

"Yes. I had him up here. I wanted to talk to him about his interview with you."

"Yes?"

"I didn't like it."

"Why not?"

"I thought he went too far."

"Did you tell him so?"

"Yes."

"You mean you read the riot act?"

"Yes."

Tulbach Browne sighed. This was so much better than he had hoped that he was inclined to leave it at that. But he wanted one more phrase, if possible, to complete this particular section.

"How did Dinamaula take it?" he asked.

Macmillan laughed. "Ask him. I'm not a mind reader."

"Doesn't it matter to you, then?"

"No," said Macmillan, and then corrected himself. "It matters, of course, but it's not really important. There are certain rules in a territory like this. They have to be obeyed, whether a man is a chief or a herdboy."

"That's what you told Dinamaula? Toe the line, or else?"

"There's no 'or else,' it's just 'toe the line,' as far as I'm concerned." Macmillan, passing his hand over his face, became conscious of three things — that he was tired as he had never been before, that he had spoken far too emphatically about something that had really had a softer outline altogether, and above all that he was not doing well with a man whom he *must* regard as an adversary.

Tulbach Browne was aware of nothing but pleasure. He had come in search of a peg on which to hang his "Tin Gods of Gamate" article, an article he had planned to write ever since he had heard of Macmillan's name and reputation. Instead of a single peg, he already had a whole row of them. Smoothly, without perceptible intent, he turned the conversation. "I was talking to Llewellyn, your agricultural man, a bit earlier. He was saying that he had a lot of trouble persuading the Maulas to thin out their herds, to go for quality rather than quantity."

Macmillan, glad to be on what seemed safer ground, nodded. "They have this idea," he said, "that the more head of cattle a man has, and the more goats and sheep running about the place, the richer he is. We have to show them that a hundred prime head of cattle, on a rich pasture, is a much bigger asset than five hundred half-starved animals, trying to live off grazing land that has been cropped nearly bare."

"How do you *show* them?" asked Tulbach Browne equably.

"We limit the number of head of cattle a man can own."

"But it's their capital, isn't it? It's their savings, the only thing they can own. Can you force them to accept that limitation?"

"Certainly."

"So it's 'toe the line,' even where farming is concerned?"

Macmillan suddenly awoke — too late — to the tenor of the conversation. "It's for their own good," he said.

"Very likely," said Tulbach Browne. "But would you tell an English farmer that he could only own a hundred cows? Or an English investor that he could only save a thousand pounds?"

"This isn't England," said Macmillan.

"No," said Tulbach Browne. "By God, it isn't!"

For the second time, Macmillan had the sense of having been

fundamentally outwitted. He knew that the thing was unfair: that one set of rules — in England — did not fit another set of people — here in Pharamaul. He knew it, and yet when he tried to explain it, he sounded either pompous or brutal. But he tried once more, aware of making a special effort, aware of an unaccustomed pleading in his voice.

"This *isn't* England," he repeated. "Give an Englishman an entirely free hand, and he won't make a fool of himself; he knows enough not to abuse his freedom. Do the same thing here, and God knows what would happen. They're just not ready to run their own lives."

"Perhaps not from your point of view," said Tulbach Browne. "But it's just possible," he went on ironically, "that a man like Dinamaula might be qualified to lead his people towards self-government. He might be the man destined to take the next step."

Macmillan shook his head. "They're not ready for it. I hope that no one tries to tell them that they are."

"Meaning me?"

Suddenly Macmillan became conscious of his position, his age, and his authority, and he felt grimly resentful of this man. "Yes, meaning you," he snapped. "You don't know what you're stirring up, and you don't know what you're talking about. If you write about the Maulas as though they could take charge of their own affairs tomorrow, if you talk to them on those lines, if you try to persuade them that they can do without *us* — " he tapped his chest " — it'll be the worst day's work you've ever done."

"I'm a reporter," said Tulbach Browne austerely.

"I wish that were true," said Macmillan bitterly. "But I think you're something more. I think you're a promoter. You want to promote a story here, regardless of what it costs. I tell you — " he had stopped being surprised at himself and was riding high and reckless, conscious only of the triumphant clarity of his thoughts " — you're playing with something you know nothing about. Let it alone. It works. Leave it that way."

"Sounds like 'Anything for a quiet life,'" answered Tulbach Browne. "Is that your motto?"

Macmillan smiled, unable to hold his mood. "Look," he said,

"we're getting in too deep, and obviously we don't agree. How about another drink?"

"Not for me," said Tulbach Browne, rising. "I've got to work." He sounded like a prim man fallen among sinners. "Thanks for the interview."

NEXT STOP, the Gamate Hotel. Tulbach Browne found himself at home there, and from at least three people he drew a notable dividend towards the contribution he was seeking in Pharamaul.

First there was David Bracken, on his way down from Shebiya, spending by chance a single evening in Gamate. David knew Tulbach Browne well by reputation; he was wary of him. But his care did not save him from providing Tulbach Browne with one spectacular, infinitely quotable phrase.

They had been talking, naturally, of Shebiya, and the inconclusive visit with Gotwela. The latter, David commented, was not a reassuring figure.

"What's he really like?" asked Tulbach Browne. "He's the local chief, isn't he?"

"Gotwela's the local chief," David answered, "in a slightly undercover way. He rules the U-Maulas. We work with Gotwela. It seems to be effective."

"And Gotwela himself?"

"Large. Tough. Not exactly civilized."

Tulbach Browne smiled. "You make him sound rather odd."

"He's all that," agreed David carelessly. "In fact, when you first meet him, he's like something out of the zoo."

THEN, also in the Gamate bar, there was the District Commissioner, George Forsdick: Forsdick (by ill chance) flushed with whisky, at his most unreliable.

"The trouble with you chaps," said Forsdick, sticking a solid thumb into Tulbach Browne's brittle chest, "is that you write such a lot of tripe. I expect you're paid damn well for it," he continued, slurringly, "but that doesn't cut much ice with us chaps on the spot. *We* know the sort of game you're playing."

"What game is that?" Tulbach Browne inquired.

"Looking for a scandal. Writing a lot of tripe."

"Dear me," observed Tulbach Browne pleasantly, "you don't seem to like the press."

"You wrote a lot of tripe about Dinamaula."

"What is your opinion of him?"

"Dinamaula," answered Forsdick, with rare, unfortunate, distinct enunciation, "is getting too big for his boots." His thumb jabbed Tulbach Browne's breastbone again. "In the interests of truth," he said, "that's not quite true."

"Why not?"

"Because," said Forsdick, struggling with sudden mountainous laughter, "he doesn't wear boots. So if you're writing some more tripe about Dinamaula, don't mention boots. Just a barefoot boy," he said, with a kind of drunken poetry in his voice, "getting too big for the boots he hasn't got."

LOOKING back on it — as Tulbach Browne did, with rare delight, many times afterwards — it seemed to him that it was that moment of that evening in the Gamate Hotel which somehow gave the signal for everything in Pharamaul to go wonderfully, irrevocably wrong. He knew, with true instinct, that the story he had come to find was now very near to him.

Forsdick had turned away, and Browne looked about him, seeking a bridge between promise and outcome. At that moment Fellows, the landlord, pushed a drink across the counter and said, "Compliments of the District Commissioner."

"Thanks," said Tulbach Browne automatically, his hand curling round the glass. He looked negligently about the room. "Pretty crowded tonight. Does Dinamaula ever come in here?"

Oosthuizen happened to be a short way down the bar, and he overheard this. "Dinamaula?" he repeated uncomprehendingly.

"The new chief. He's been in Gamate quite a few days."

"He doesn't come in here," said Fellows simply.

"Why not?"

Fellows shrugged. "He just doesn't, that's all. He can come round to the hatch at the side door, any time he likes, and I'll serve him, quick enough. The D.C. has said that's all right."

"But why not here?" persisted Browne. "That means a color bar."

"All right," said Oosthuizen, suddenly much larger and nearer. "It means a color bar. What the hell do you know about it? Have you ever seen a black with a couple of hard drinks inside him? Man, he'd have your guts to darn his socks with."

"I still say," said Tulbach Browne patiently, "that, in British territory, there shouldn't be a color bar. Dinamaula should be as free to come into this room as I am."

"You can't have that," said Fellows stoutly. "And it's no good covering it up with a lot of talk about democracy, and what they do in London. Dinamaula's black, Mr. Browne. This is a hotel for whites. He *can't* come in here."

Tulbach Browne turned aside, smiling. To himself he murmured, "What'll you bet? What'll you bet?" Aloud, he said, cheerfully, dismissively, "Time I bought us all a drink."

Dinamaula lay in the oppressive twilight of his hut, thinking the dire thoughts of solitude, knowing, in his own mind, how far he was from the picture of a young chief claiming his inheritance. He carried within his breast a stone of unrest, hatred, disappointment. Ever since he arrived in Gamate, his inheritance had seemed shoddy and not worth the burden of assumption. Ever since he had seen Andrew Macmillan, up at the Residency, it had all turned to bitter pantomime. Even now, a week after the interview, he lay in darkness, thinking the thoughts of mutiny and despair. He was still thinking such thoughts when Tulbach Browne sent a message, asking, with expressions of respect and hesitation, if he might be allowed to talk to the chief.

"As a matter of fact," said Tulbach Browne, nodding sagely, "Macmillan told me himself that he'd read you the riot act — whatever that means. Said he told you that you'd have to toe the line. Did he really say that?"

"Yes," said Dinamaula somberly, "that was what he said."

"But it's extraordinary. After all, you're the chief."

"He is a strong man," said Dinamaula.

"Or he thinks he is. He's not the only one, either. I was in the

Gamate Hotel, a couple of days ago. You know, they've got some funny ideas there. They actually told me," said Tulbach Browne carefully, "that you couldn't go in there and have a drink."

Dinamaula was silent.

"Now that, to me," said Browne, looking at his fingernails, "is an extraordinary idea. Here we are, in British territory, you are *in your own town,* and there are people actually boasting that the Gamate Hotel is reserved for whites only."

"It is the custom," answered Dinamaula briefly.

"Well, I think it's a rotten one."

"Nonetheless, it has come to be accepted."

"By you?"

"I have only just returned to Gamate."

"It might be a good moment," said Tulbach Browne, "to make a few changes."

Dinamaula knew where Browne's questions were leading, and he felt dangerously stirred by the knowledge. It was part of his vulnerability. He was sad and lonely; his self-esteem had been laid raw; here was a fellow human being, a white man, who treated him as he had often been treated in England. He felt himself carried along on a wave of predestined action. There was a step to be taken, a step that would show Macmillan, and people like him, that "chief" was a fact, not a word. But he hesitated, needing persuasion. He said slowly, "Why are you so interested in all this?"

Browne shrugged his shoulders. "I'm interested, like a lot of other people, in what goes on in the world. Here's an open color bar operating in a British protectorate. It needs putting right."

"How?"

"Come with me to the Gamate Hotel."

It was about noon, and there were not many people in the bar of the Gamate Hotel, when Dinamaula followed Tulbach Browne through the doorway and up to the counter. Dinamaula was trembling, and he walked behind Tulbach Browne as if the other's determined, bustling figure could draw a veil over his presence. But though he was trembling, he was not sorry to be there.

Fellows, from his station behind the bar, saw them coming:

Fellows and Llewellyn, the agricultural officer, and Oosthuizen, the farmer. Their reactions were characteristic. Llewellyn grew noncommittally watchful; Oosthuizen stiffened and stared. Fellows reddened, and the hand swabbing down the bar hesitated and then clenched in sudden tension. There were half a dozen other people at the tables; slowly awakening to the incredible, they nudged each other, and ceased to speak, and waited.

There was a deep silence as Browne said, "Two beers, please."

Fellows, now a fiery red, shook his head.

"Sorry, Mr. Browne. I can't serve you."

"Why not?" asked Browne, civilly enough.

"You know why not," said Fellows curtly.

Round them the silence grew into a pall of expectancy.

"I want two beers," said Tulbach Browne in even tones. "One for me, one for my friend. I'm staying in the hotel. You can't refuse to serve me."

"I'll serve you," said Fellows. "But I can't serve the chief."

"Why not?" repeated Tulbach Browne.

"You know bloody well why not!" This time it was Oosthuizen, solid and formidable, who broke in to take up the argument. "Because he's not allowed in here. That's why not!"

A man at a table behind them called, "Throw them both out!"

Dinamaula plucked gently at Tulbach Browne's arm. "Let us go," he said. He was now unexpectedly calm, free from anger, free from shame. He had known it would be like this. He did not mind — though perhaps he would mind later.

"We're not going before we get a drink," said Tulbach Browne.

Fellows shook his head once more. "I can't serve you in the bar." His tone grew pleading. "But there's a nice private room. Just through the curtain. I'll serve you both there, right away."

"Let's get this thing quite definite," Browne said. "I've ordered two drinks. You say you won't serve them here, but you *will* serve them in a private room, out of sight. Why?"

In the silence that followed, an unexpected voice intervened. It was Llewellyn. "Chief," he called.

Dinamaula turned towards him politely. "Yes, Mr. Llewellyn?"

"I don't think you ought to do this."

"You're too bloody right!" said Oosthuizen belligerently.

Llewellyn tapped his fingers on the bar. "Let's keep it decent," he said, with an authority odd in so small a man. He looked at Dinamaula again. "Mr. Fellows is quite right, and you know he is. It's not the custom here. If Mr. Browne wants to drink with you, he should take you through into the private room."

Tulbach Browne shook his head, denying all this out of hand. "I want two beers," he said. "Here and now. Do I get them?"

Ranged side by side, the black man and the white man waited. Then, after a long prickling silence, Fellows said, "No."

Dinamaula touched his arm again, and this time Browne was ready. He said, "All right, then," and turned slowly away from the bar and made for the door, holding Dinamaula lightly by the elbow to guide him out. As they walked through the door, conversation broke out in full spate behind them.

They walked in silence a few paces from the hotel, to the southern edge of the *aboura,* before they said good-by.

"Sorry about all that," said Tulbach Browne at length.

"It is no matter," answered Dinamaula. His eyes were downcast, as the rawness of defeat and shame started to flood in again. "It was what we both expected. It is the custom."

Tulbach Browne looked across the *aboura,* narrowing his eyes against the fierce midday sun. A man came out of the Gamate Hotel, looked at them for a moment, and then strode off. From the opposite side of the *aboura,* a woman left one hut and went into another. Tulbach Browne was reminded of something.

"I've heard talk about your marrying some girl named Miera."

Dinamaula shook his head. "No. I shall not marry Miera."

"But you *will* marry?" prompted Tulbach Browne.

"I hope so."

"Anyone special in mind?"

Dinamaula was thinking of other things, things further away, things rounded and far more happy — Oxford — London. Aware only of pain and loneliness, voicing the thin fabric of a random thought, he said, "No one special. As a matter of fact, I'd like to marry a white girl."

Chapter 5

For DAVID BRACKEN, his return to the Secretariat, after the strange world of Shebiya and the U-Maula country, was like coming home to a Christmas fireside.

The Governor was out when David inquired for him. "But I know he wanted to see you," said his secretary, with an overtone of threat in her voice. David was vaguely disquieted.

Stevens, the First Secretary, seemed preoccupied — indeed, rather sad; he said rather fussily, "You seem to have had some excitements with the press. There have been a lot of telegrams. You'll see them all on the file."

"Tulbach Browne was hanging about in Gamate. I believe he saw Andrew Macmillan and Dinamaula."

"So we gathered," said Stevens.

"Was there anything in the papers about that?"

"Yes. It's all on the file."

Captain Simpson, the naval aide, was, by contrast, very cheerful. His voice when he said, "Pretty rough country up there, I remember," had a manly ring that seemed to come from another world altogether. Then it was the turn of the Social Secretary, who looked at David's dusty clothes with cold dislike and said, "Garden party on November sixth, Mr. Bracken."

"Garden party?" asked David, surprised.

"Yes," said the Social Secretary. "His Excellency gives two every year. This is the spring garden party."

"What do we wear?"

"Morning dress," answered the Social Secretary, in acid disdain. "Or a short black coat would do." She did not sound as if it would do at all. "Four p.m. till six."

"How very formal," said David.

"It is the spring garden party," said the Social Secretary.

Then David looked in on Aidan Purves-Brownrigg, who greeted him with considerable fervor. "My dear fellow," he said, "we've been inundated with furious telegrams from London! What have you and Andrew been saying to that odious Tulbach Browne?"

David's heart sank. "Nothing special," he answered. "Why?"

"The *Daily Thresh* has been full of it," said Aidan. "At least two poisonous articles, each one worse than the last. Making out Andrew as an absolute monster. And you sounded like Caligula, at the very least."

"Me?" said David, confused. "I don't understand."

Eagerly Aidan Purves-Brownrigg went into details, exhibiting in the process a formidable memory for exact quotation. The first of Browne's two articles about affairs in Gamate had been "Gamate's Tin Gods," which dealt mainly with Andrew Macmillan and the cattle question; the second, a long piece called "Toe-the-line Democracy," which recorded interviews with Forsdick, and David himself.

"The first one was bad enough," observed Aidan. "Browne said that Dinamaula was treated like a child, and so were all his people. But in the second he really went to town. He said Forsdick had insulted him, and threatened the freedom of the press, and sneered at Dinamaula for being poor and backward."

"Good Lord!" said David.

Aidan grinned. "And *you,* of course, were particularly quotable."

David felt his stomach drop. "What about me?"

"Don't you remember what you said about Gotwela?"

"No. Not exactly."

"Tulbach Browne did. 'I thought that Gamate could show me no more surprises,'" intoned Aidan, from his copious memory. "'I was wrong. It was my misfortune, later that night, to hear Gotwela, one of the oldest and most respected of the local chiefs, described by Mr. Bracken, a junior British official, as being "like something out of the zoo." I felt, at the moment, that I had had enough of so-called official circles in Gamate.'"

"But Gotwela's not a respected chief at all!" said David in anguish. "He's a complete thug!"

"What does that matter?" asked Aidan. "Tulbach Browne made him sound like the old Prince Consort, and he made *you* sound like a boorish clot. That's all that the story needed."

"What did the Governor say about that?"

"I thought the old gentleman would have a heart attack," said

Aidan frankly. "He's better now, of course. I told him it was all the result of unscrupulous reporting, which it is, of course. But all the same," he looked at David, suddenly much more serious and more competent, "I think we'd better close the ranks."

"How do you mean?" asked David.

"No more stray interviews with that criminal Browne. No more friendly drinks with the press. From long experience," he said, "in such plague spots as Egypt and Persia and Trieste, I should say that here in Pharamaul a page of particularly sordid history is about to be written. Politicians will burst their buttons, pressmen will fuse their typewriters, heads will roll. We must all stick together."

"We're so handicapped," said David after a pause.

Aidan smiled. "As long as you realize the fact and believe that, handicapped or not, we can still win because we're *right,* all is not lost. Now, isn't it about time you saw Nicole?"

"How is she?" asked David.

"Never better. And thirsting for you, I shouldn't wonder. Waste no more time."

NICOLE was indeed waiting for him, in her shabby, sun-plagued office, looking cool, looking lovely. It was difficult for David, seeing her after a ten-day separation, not to stride forward and take her in his arms. Instead, daunted by her coolness and his own sense of inadequacy, he said, "Hallo! I just got back."

She was smiling, slightly breathless, but more ready with words than he was. "You got back at least half an hour ago. I have spies all over the building. It's not very flattering."

"I had to go round the office." He sat down on the edge of her desk, lighting a cigarette, his hand unsteady. "Aidan was telling me about the *Daily Thresh* articles. I seem to have made rather a fool of myself. I should have been on my guard."

"But you didn't *know*. How was Gamate, otherwise?"

"Wonderful. All that I expected. The journey up was like discovering the whole of Africa in a few hours."

Nicole nodded. "That's the way I remember it. And Shebiya?"

"It's a funny thing about that place," answered David after a pause. "It gave me the shivers at first — I saw a cannibal behind every tree. But we stayed with the Ronalds. Obviously *they* didn't have that feeling. They were entirely happy, completely satisfied with living in Shebiya."

"I think they'd be happy anywhere," said Nicole, smiling.

"I suppose so. But I got the idea that *I* could be happy there, too. It needn't be a frightening place at all, once one got over the strangeness, because there's so much worth-while work to be done." He looked at her. "Could you be happy there?"

Nicole felt herself coloring slightly. "I hadn't thought of it. . . . Yes, I suppose one *could* be happy in Shebiya."

With you — anywhere, David thought. Aloud, his voice unnaturally gruff, he said, "But I *didn't* like Gotwela."

"So I read." She gestured towards a file on her desk. "There was another telegram in this morning. Browne again."

"Oh no!" said David. "What is it this time?"

"About not getting a drink in the Gamate Hotel. Apparently he took Dinamaula into the bar, and they refused to serve him. 'Color bar in British hotel on British soil.' Emrys Price-Canning is in full cry in Parliament again."

David frowned and ground out his cigarette deliberately.

After a moment, she said gently, "It *wouldn't* be a good idea to have mixed drinking in Gamate, would it? Even if the Maulas were allowed alcohol?"

A few weeks in Pharamaul had given David the beginnings of the same feeling, but he was not yet ready to acknowledge it. Instead, he said, "It's very complicated. . . ."

He had a sudden conviction that there were many better things to think about, at this moment. "Let's forget the whole thing for now. Will you have dinner with me?"

"Certainly," said Nicole.

"Where can we go?"

"There are two or three places, all rather bad. Or I could cook for you myself."

"How do you feel about that?" asked David.

"Perfectly happy," answered Nicole, with composure. "Seven o'clock. If you like, you can contribute a bottle of wine."

"I'll do that," he said, with secret, serious joy. "Red or white?"

"Red for me."

"Red for me, too."

WILLIAM EWART O'BRIEN, the editor and proprietor of the weekly *Times of Pharamaul,* was engaged in an intricate game of solitaire when Tulbach Browne was announced. He was in his late sixties, neat, spare and spruce. Sitting in his drab Port Victoria office, hoping something significant would happen before the *Times* went to press in four hours, he welcomed the relief from boredom promised by Tulbach Browne's visit. He knew Tulbach Browne as a foreign correspondent of undoubted fame and patent skill, and he rose, with courtly grace, as his caller came in.

"My dear Mr. Browne," he intoned impressively, "this is indeed an honor! Our little backwater here is not often honored by a visit from one of the great men of the newspaper world!"

It was a friendly greeting, even a moving one. Tulbach Browne decided to play it straight. He wanted one single thing from this funny old relic, and he was going to get it.

"Well, sir!" he answered, on a hearty note. "I don't know about 'great men.' I suppose you must be just about the senior editor south of the equator, yourself. I've been wanting to pay you a visit."

They talked in this agreeable strain for some minutes, Tulbach Browne waiting for an appropriate moment to put the suggestion that was going to round out his current blitz on Pharamaul. His private aim was simple. Having just cabled the "Marriage to White Girl" story to the *Daily Thresh,* he wanted to put it squarely on the local map as well. That way, it would not be buried. It would be here in black and white, for all to see in their own newspaper; and it would surely lead to other stories.

He made his move. "I've just been filing a story," he said importantly. "A big story — in fact, the biggest I've found here yet. Perhaps you'd care to read it." He grinned, with oily bonhomie. "Take a look at it later on. You might like to use it yourself."

"I should be glad to read it, but I'm afraid — " O'Brien began warily.

Tulbach Browne waved an expansive hand. "It's all yours — if you like it," he said. "I've no objection to your running it under my by-line with my compliments. It will be in tomorrow morning's *Daily Thresh* in London. If you decide to run it, people will be able to read it in Pharamaul at just about the same time." He looked at the other man narrowly. "Why, you'll scoop the whole of Africa! Not for the first time, I'm sure. But you'll do it again. And it's a *very* big story."

WHEN Tulbach Browne was gone, William Ewart O'Brien read the story. He read it slowly, with increasing excitement, from the first sentence: "Tonight in Pharamaul, speculation is mounting about the white bride whom Dinamaula has declared he will bring back to the dusty, teeming village in the heart of his kingdom," down to the last one: "Whoever the girl may be, she promises a new, spectacular page in Pharamaul history."

He read it with appalled, interior satisfaction. He was on the inside now, right in the middle, possessed of the greatest scoop in the history of the paper. He believed it utterly, in all its shameful detail, its promise of embarrassment and clamor. He believed it because it was signed by Tulbach Browne.

Such a story — he wavered only for a moment — could have only one headline, in forty-eight-point Roman, the largest type ever used on the front page of the *Times of Pharamaul:* CHIEF DINAMAULA TO MARRY WHITE WOMAN.

THE FIRST time that Pharamaul Airlines had had to lay on extra flights to cope with a sudden rush of traffic had been in 1947, when a false rumor of a gold strike had brought prospectors scurrying half across the world. The second occasion was the *Daily Thresh* account of Dinamaula's marriage plans.

The story attracted visitors from many corners of the world, intrigued by this exotic news item which promised so many things to so many different men. Commercial travelers came, drawn by the magnet of a new name upon the map. Political observers came, eager to observe. Above all, beyond all, several members of the world's press arrived, to join Tulbach Browne upon his noisome battlefield. They were not a fair cross section, because this was not really a fair story. It was a story best exploited by men of marginal integrity; and these were the sort of people, representing the sort of newspapers, eternally attracted by such tainted game.

It was in the shabby, run-down bar of the Hotel Bristol that the press contingent first gathered after their arrival, greeting Tulbach Browne with a wary, thin-spread camaraderie as false as porcelain teeth. Among them were Axel Hallmarck of *Clang,* an American news magazine, and Pikkie Joubert of the South African News Service.

Clang differed from the *Daily Thresh* only in that its weekly publication schedule gave it more time to polish the apple of discord and serve it up as a simmering deep-dish pie. It was inevitable that *Clang* should send a man to Pharamaul, since the story promised a rich mixture of sex, misfortune, ill will, and British mismanagement. Axel Hallmarck was their man. He was spry and slim, with wiry crew-cut hair and a nominally creaseless nylon suit. He was young, ambitious, and energetic. He could write, *Clang*-style. He was almost certain to make good.

Tulbach Browne, who heard all the bad news, had heard of Axel Hallmarck. He was prepared to acknowledge him, as a likely fellow operator.

Pikkie Joubert was in a different category. He was no star: he was a run-of-the-mill wire-service reporter. The South African News Service, which covered Southern Africa and was relayed also to London, would report the Dinamaula story straight; that is, as a news story that affected very many people, black and white, between the Gold Coast and Cape Town. Its reporting would not be slanted, save in one particular: it would take it for granted that most people in South Africa would dislike the idea of a mixed marriage, and it might add to that the parallel idea that a mixed marriage had become possible in Pharamaul only because of some inherent weakness in British Colonial administration.

PIKKIE JOUBERT was making heavy weather of his interview with Aidan Purves-Brownrigg. Joubert was a big man, slow-moving, slow-thinking; Aidan Purves-Brownrigg was the precise opposite of all those things.

"What will be the outcome," asked Joubert laboriously, after they had talked without profit for some minutes, "of a mixed marriage such as this?"

"Coffee-colored triplets, I shouldn't be in the least surprised." Aidan smiled winningly. "The Maulas are a very fertile race."

Pikkie Joubert shook his head. "I did not mean that, understand me. What will be the effect on the country?"

"Distinctly odd. I should think the Maulas would be shocked to ribbons. It means the lowering of all their standards."

"Lowering?" said Joubert. "What do you mean, man? He's marrying a white girl, isn't he?"

"I mean that the older Maulas, who control things, have very exaggerated ideas of racial purity. The tribe is sacrosanct. A thing like this cuts right across all their established rules."

"Hell, I don't mind about the bloody natives!" exclaimed Joubert disgustedly. "What about *our* standards?"

"It's contrary to tradition there, too, of course."

"What are you doing about it?"

"Directly, at the moment, nothing. There are lots of reasons. Firstly, I doubt if the story is true. Secondly, we couldn't forbid such a marriage, though naturally we would discourage it."

"Of course you can forbid it! It's mixed, man, *mixed!*"

Aidan shook his head. "But it's not *illegal*. I agree with you that it would be a bad idea, although — " he smiled " — my reasons for saying that might not be the same as yours. From our point of view, it would be bad because it topples over — " he gestured with elegant, slim hands " — every basic custom of this country, all the traditions that have worked very well for hundreds of years. *We* wouldn't like it. The Maulas wouldn't like it. That *may* be enough to discourage it. But we can't forbid it, in so many words."

Joubert hunched his shoulders contemptuously. "We do things better, where I come from."

"You do them differently," answered Aidan briefly.

FULL twenty years divided Captain Simpson, the naval aide-de-camp, and Axel Hallmarck of *Clang;* twenty years, two wars, a lifetime of discipline, and a fathomless diversity of accent. They got on extremely well.

They discussed Nelson, the Boer War, Pearl Harbor, Communism, television, and the color bar. Axel Hallmarck asked sympathetic questions about life in Port Victoria, home leave in England, current social obligations, and the duty-free importation of liquor. Captain Simpson confided that his wife was "not really terribly keen" about Pharamaul. Axel Hallmarck agreed that it must have a good many drawbacks, and then asked if there was likely to be trouble over Dinamaula.

Captain Simpson said that whatever trouble there was would be taken care of, without the least difficulty. Dinamaula was "just feeling his oats."

Axel Hallmarck asked if the use of force was contemplated and Captain Simpson said, "I suppose so, old boy — if necessary."

Axel Hallmarck, laughing, said that in that case it would probably come as quite a relief to see a bit of action.

Captain Simpson said, "You're telling me, old boy! This place is like a bloody mausoleum. Now, how about a gin?"

People always got on extremely well with *Clang* correspondents, until later, when they read the current issue.

WITH a curious, twilight sense of doom, Andrew Macmillan read over the last sentence he had written in his history of Pharamaul, beginning the account of the big tax troubles.

"The center of unrest," he had written, "was the town of Gamate itself, already uneasy owing to the prolonged absence of Chief Simaula, who was visiting the outlying tribes."

Andrew Macmillan let his pen fall on the desk, and sat back. What he had just written was altogether too apt to the present. His hand rose automatically to cover his eyes. He was, as usual, desperately tired; he had a sense of defeat and inadequacy such as he had not felt in twenty years, a sense of defeat even before the battle was joined. Certainly Gamate today was full of rumor, full of uneasiness; certainly Dinamaula, like his father, Simaula, was absenting himself indefinitely somewhere outside the town, and the fact was causing all sorts of gossip and unrest. There were many things likely to set a spark to trouble: wild talk about the chief's marriage, vivid speculation on the arrival in Gamate of the press contingent. This was no time for the Resident Commissioner to loosen his grip. But that was what was happening.

He wished he had been able to see Dinamaula, and clear up at least one aspect of the problem — his marriage. But Dinamaula had first sent noncommittal messages of delay. Then he had been ill. Then he had left town, ostensibly to visit some of his cattle posts in the surrounding ranchland.

If it had been twenty years ago, if it had been ten years ago, he would have taken all this in his stride, dealt with it in a few sentences, a few brusque summonses to the tribal leaders, a quarter of an hour's forthright speaking on the *aboura*. Now, faced by vague and grotesque fears, he felt powerless to cope with them. Perhaps he had been too long in the Territory. Perhaps, at fifty-seven, he was too old and worn out. Perhaps history in Africa had moved on, leaving him bobbing foolishly in its wake, using old methods, mouthing old phrases, when the call was imperative for the new, the experimental, the bold and dramatic.

He wanted nothing more than to put through a priority call to Port Victoria, and say to the Governor, "Sir, I resign." Instead, he had to cope with Dinamaula (as soon as he could get a grip on that elusive character); he had to curb the riot of rumor that was running through Gamate like a rabid dog, leaving in its train hysteria, convulsive fear, and fleeting, unreasonable joy.

Chapter 6

C APTAIN CRUMP of the Royal Pharamaul Police sat at his desk, rough-typing a report for Andrew Macmillan. He typed slowly, in accordance with his thoughts, which were slow, concise, and heavy with contrasting items of intelligence.

"ONE," he wrote: *"The chief-designate.* Dinamaula has left Gamate to visit cattle posts to the southwest. He is alone, except for Mr. Llewellyn, who chances to be touring in the same area. . . ."

Under a yellow, low-hanging moon, the handful of men sat round the campfire. Behind the men a clump of trees stood sentinel beside the well of Baraula. The royal herd of Dinamaula, a gray shadow in the background, was at long last quiet; round the camp-fire, as the embers settled and the moon lifted above the rim of the far horizon, three men talked: Dinamaula, soon to be chief of the Maulas; Llewellyn, the agricultural officer, present at the cattle well by the true working of chance, and old Paulus, hereditary chief herdboy of this one of several royal herds.

Of the three men, one of them, Paulus, was contented, because his chief had come to see the state of the cattle, and the state of the cattle was good. Another, Llewellyn, was uncomfortable, because he had blundered by accident upon this meeting, and his orders now were to stay where he was until it was ended. The third, Dinamaula, was unhappy, puzzled, and angry.

The chance that had brought Llewellyn to the well of Baraula seemed to Dinamaula no chance at all but a matter of calculation, a continuation of the mistrustful, official spying which had so en-raged him during the last few weeks.

Dinamaula himself had come to this place — a half-dried water pan eighty miles from Gamate — to be alone — alone and traceless under the sky of his own country, alone as a chief might expect to be alone, if he wished it so.

But on the third day of his private wandering, Llewellyn, the agricultural officer — the man, moreover, who had been a close witness of his shame in the bar of the Gamate Hotel — had driven up to the camp at the edge of the water pan and hailed him as a friend, and then talked secretly on the radio. It had meant the end of privacy, of the dignity of a chief visiting his royal herds; the end, indeed, of his freedom to talk and think as a chief.

Paulus, the old man who had been an old man before Dinamaula was born, bent his head towards his chief, oblivious of tension, oblivious of any shadow on their meeting.

"Then there was the second year of the great drought," he said, intent on his careful account. "A hundred and a hundred and a half hundred of cattle died that year. But still the herd is good. It has increased — " the old man held up four sticklike, trembling fingers " — fourfold since the days of your honored father, whom God loved as we still love him."

Llewellyn, a small dark figure across the fire, stirred and spoke. "How big is the herd now, Paulus?" he asked.

The old man frowned, in deep concentration. "This herd," he said finally, "is seven hundreds."

"There are other royal herds besides the herd of Baraula," said Llewellyn, slowly framing the laborious Maula words. "There are five others, indeed. How big are they?"

The old man spread his hands, so that they caught the flickering firelight. "They are of many sizes," he answered slowly. "At the Pula well, let us say six hundreds. At the Batwela, eight. At the Batwansa, six. At the dry place, Espensa, four hundreds. At the Saksaula, best well of all, nine hundreds."

Llewellyn felt his fingers moving childishly as he completed the sum. That meant four thousand head of cattle, in good condition, on grazing land that could well support them. Say that they would fetch, in open market, an average of twenty pounds a head. That was eighty thousand pounds, and all, by tradition and by law, belonging to the chief himself, to Dinamaula.

Across the campfire, a harsh voice interrupted him suddenly.

"I make it eighty thousand pounds, Mr. Llewellyn," said Dinamaula. "Do you agree?"

Llewellyn grinned in the darkness. There were no flies on this young fellow — and that, alone, could be good for the Maulas, if sharp wits could somehow be turned to proper account.

"You beat me to it, Chief," he answered cheerfully. "But then, you were last in school, by a good few years."

"I am no longer in school," said Dinamaula gratingly. He longed to strike at the other man, good man though he was, friend though he might be. "And I have eighty thousand pounds. Can you add *that* together, also?"

"I don't know what you mean." Llewellyn was taken aback.

"I mean that I am no longer a child, to be spied on and — and followed." Dinamaula was suddenly enraged, as he stumbled over the words. It seemed that he could not even rebuke an agricultural officer without being conscious of their dividing color. "This is my country," he said hotly, gesturing in the half-darkness. "These are my herds, these are my subjects. If you had been here," he went on, conscious even as he said it of a childish boastfulness, "when I arrived at this well of Baraula, you would have seen how a chief is greeted in Pharamaul. That old man — " he pointed " — fell on his knees and touched my feet with his forehead. That is how an old man greets his chief."

After an uneasy pause, Llewellyn said, "I know that you have loyal tribesmen. And there is no question of spying or following."

"You were talking about me on the radio."

"I made a routine report on the police schedule," answered Llewellyn, somewhat sharply. "I mentioned that I had met you here, at the Baraula well. I would naturally mention it. The Resident Commissioner would expect me to."

Dinamaula smiled sourly. "What else does he expect?"

"He expects to see you as soon as you get back."

At that there was a pause. Paulus and the herdboys, content to be excluded from such company, had fallen back into the shadows of their exchange. But when the silence lengthened, and a faraway birdcall emphasized the unnatural stillness, one of the herdboys threw a handful of dry sticks onto the fire. It blazed up and showed their faces in sudden clarity. Dinamaula's was brooding and sullen. Llewellyn's was watchful. Opposite them, old Paulus, deaf to all overtones, seemed proud and content — proud to be with his chief, content that black man and white could talk in this fashion round a campfire.

Dinamaula asked suddenly, "Why does he want to see me?"

"There is talk of your marriage. There is talk of certain changes for the tribe. You have said many things to the newspapers. Mr. Macmillan wants to discuss all this with you."

"Is he angry?" asked Dinamaula, in spite of himself.

Llewellyn shook his head. "He is disturbed. He wants to talk to you. Chief," he said suddenly, appealingly, "when you talk about marriage in the way you did, it is not a good thing that you immediately go away from Gamate."

"I am visiting my herds," said Dinamaula. "I came here, and I am going to the other wells also, to talk of such things. I wish to discuss old matters, not new matters that bring trouble and insults."

"Insults?"

"Yes, insults. If I wish to marry, that is my own affair. If I wish to choose a wife in England, that is my own affair also."

After a moment, Llewellyn answered, "You know that that is not so. Think what you're doing, man!" he burst out, forgetting the formal pattern of their talk. Then he stood up. "I'll turn in. I'm sorry that we don't agree."

"You wish to talk on the radio?" asked Dinamaula ironically.

"No," said Llewellyn. "I want to think."

"Whatever you *think,*" said Dinamaula, with insulting emphasis, "I am not coming back until I choose to."

"TWO," wrote Crump, continuing his weekly report: *"Port Victoria.* A meeting of the 'Maula Freedom Party' was addressed by Zuva Katsaula. It was attended by about 220 persons, including Mr. Tulbach Browne, *Daily Thresh* correspondent. . . ."

The hall, a converted garage with boarded-up windows, a rickety platform set on trestles, and rows of wooden benches, was hot, and smelt acridly of sweat and tobacco. Overhead was a long paper streamer, which read: MAULA FREEDOM PARTY, the three words being divided by the fish sign.

Tulbach Browne, who had been led to a conspicuous seat in the front row, was there by arrangement with Zuva Katsaula. There were no women present, and the men were a kaleidoscope of downtown Port Victoria; clerks in flashy suits and zoot ties, laborers in jeans, other men in blankets and barefooted.

When there was a stir at the door, Browne was first surprised by the bodyguard which took up a position flanking the doorway, staring at the crowd under lowered lids, their hands in their coat pockets. There were four of them, dressed almost identically in tightly cuffed black trousers, American-style check coats, and red bow ties. When Zuva, after a suitable pause, strutted into the hall and strode towards the platform, the bodyguard lounged like lurcher dogs at his heels.

Tulbach Browne's second surprise was Zuva's quality as a speaker — his quality, and his elusive skill. As he stood before them, good-looking, slick, self-assured, one could feel the audience settling back, prepared to allow this young man to do their thinking, talking, and acting for them. His theme was a "new deal" for Pharamaul, a new deal that was to include "a fundamental change in Pharamaul's social structure."

If anyone in the hall had been hoping for a message of political encouragement, they got it in abundance. If anyone had been looking for sedition or the threat of force, they would have been disappointed. Tulbach Browne, noticing the infinite skill with which Zuva avoided the word or the phrase that might trip him, found himself lost in speculation long before the end.

Indeed, when Zuva, pausing towards the close of the meeting, looked down at him and said, "We have a special friend here tonight, a white friend from England . . ." it was some moments before Browne realized that he was expected to rise and speak.

"I cannot make speeches," he said when he arose, "and with this man in the same room — " he gestured towards Zuva " — I would not try." There was a stir of laughter and hand clapping. "All I want to say is that I will think a great deal about all that I have heard tonight. I would like to add that, whatever you decide to do, I can assure you that you have a lot of friends in England."

He sat down to a full burst of clapping. Zuva, smiling broadly, rose again.

"You have all heard," he said, "this promise of active help, from a man who is a great power in his own country. We have many other friends who will also help us in our struggle for freedom. Soon I am going to talk with our brothers to the north. I would like to take with me a vote of confidence from this meeting."

With his two hands, he sketched the sign of the fish in the air, like a benediction. "You know what that means," he concluded. "We are all sons of the fish. Give me your vote, and I will give you power in your own country."

The applause that filled the hall was the hungriest, crudest, most wholehearted that Tulbach Browne had ever heard.

"THREE," wrote Crump, squaring his shoulders for what he knew was the most diverse and complicated part of his report: *"Gamate.* A tribal *aboura,* attended by nearly two thousand Maulas, was addressed by Seralo and Puero (first and third Regents). The press (who attended) seem to have been advising Puero. . . ."

Though it was high noon, the hottest and most humid hour of Gamate's lowering day, the throng on the *aboura* was vast. Proceedings began decorously enough with old Seralo raising his hand in greeting. Puero sat in the shade behind him, a fat watchful man with friends and enemies within reach of the *aboura*.

"*Ahsula!*" began Seralo, wavering, and yet impressive on account of his age and his great wisdom.

The old men in front, and the young behind them, called back "*Ahsula!*" in their turn.

"*Ahsula!*" repeated Seralo. "I am glad to see you, in the name of the Regents of this tribe. I have some matters to speak of."

The throng settled itself to listen. "First," Seralo began, when all was still, "I would speak of our chief. Soon will come a day when my task is done, and Chief Dinamaula will rule in my place. That day — " he paused " — will be three weeks from this day."

There was an answering murmur from the crowd, but behind Seralo, fat Puero suddenly smirked and looked about him, catching here and there the eye of a friend on the *aboura*.

Old Seralo could not see the face of his young brother Regent.

"It will be a time for rejoicing," he went on, "not a time for drunkenness. Let us take care that the honor of the tribe is not stained."

There was a murmur of agreement from some of the older men. From those at the back, it came near to laughter.

"I say these things," went on Seralo, "because it is not seemly to see, as we have seen in the past few weeks, men stumbling and falling, full of their beer, empty of their sense. Often it is not beer," he went on sternly, "but *bariaana.*" He used the Maula term for the vicious home-brew, of fermented bread and fruit, which was forbidden by law. "Let it be beer, and beer only," said Seralo, with ancient authority.

Again there was a murmur of mingled agreement and derision. Then suddenly there came a cruder interruption. From among the young men, a grinning youth called out, "You say let it never be *bariaana*. But you Regents and the chief can get the white man's strong liquor, at the hotel, on any day that you choose."

There was a hiss of disapproval from the older men. The young man drew back, well pleased with himself. As Seralo was about to reply, in rebuke of this grave breach of custom, Puero advanced to his side. "The chief," he said, in a voice of anger and contempt, "*cannot* get the white man's strong liquor at the hotel."

There was now no division or doubt in the sound that came from the *aboura*. It was a growl of anger, long continued, rising from every heart. There was no man there who did not know their chief had been shamed, when he went into the hotel.

Seralo, gazing in cold disdain at Puero, took a step forward and called out to the still-murmuring *aboura,* "Let us not talk of foolish things. What was done in the hotel was done in accordance with the custom. You know that. Let us not be led aside."

"The day may come," countered Puero, unhesitating, as if he had prepared his words for many hours, "when the custom will be changed, and the hotel will be a meeting place for the tribe — and *only* for the tribe. Let us not be afraid." His voice was strong and bold; one forgot his fat body and gross mouth, and heard only the words of boldness. "Why should we be afraid? This is our own country. If there is a law that we hate, let us change the law. If there is a custom that offends, let us do away with it. If — " Puero paused, for effect and for breath " — if the chief wishes to do a certain thing, let us support him. If the chief, Dinamaula, wishes a certain marriage — "

The rest was drowned in furious clamor and movement. Suddenly the younger men at the back were shouting and surging forward; the older men stared at Puero in anger and astonishment. Finally, old Seralo was heard, above the disorder. "I am ashamed before the tribe," he said, quavering, "that such things should be said. The marriage of the chief is not a thing to be thrown from mouth to mouth. But since this man — " he pointed to Puero, while on the *aboura* stillness fell again at the insulting word and gesture " — talks so freely of it, I will say this. A marriage such as we have heard spoken of is against the custom. I do not say it is forbidden. I say it is not seemly." The silence on the *aboura* was now deep and full of meaning. "The chief should marry one of his own race. Anything else would be an impurity. That is all I have to say," said Seralo, his voice falling sadly, as was the way with old men overwhelmed by new things. "The *aboura* is ended."

But before Seralo could step back, Puero called out, "Hear this! A new chief who is ruled by the old men, or by Government, is no chief at all. Indeed," he said, on a last note of sly, mocking inquiry, "where is our chief today?"

Then he turned and passed within the doorway at his back, while behind him on the *aboura* astonished voices broke out in violent speech, and Seralo put his hand up to his heart, and sat down as if he had taken a mortal blow.

"FOUR," wrote Crump, squaring off his report on what seemed a satisfactory note of finality: "*Shebiya*. There is nothing to report from this area."

In the deep fronded silence, among the dripping trees which made the clearing in the forest a cavern of secrecy, two men advanced to their meeting, preserving each his barbarous self-esteem. When Gotwela, chief of the U-Maulas, looked at Zuva Katsaula, the man from the south, he restrained with an effort his contempt for a black man who used the white man's clothes to assume a white man's skin. When Zuva looked at Gotwela, he saw a savage, still bound hand and foot to the jungle. Yet each had a service to seek from the other.

"*Ahsula!*" said Zuva formally, when the guards had withdrawn and the two of them sat alone within the shadow of the royal hut. "I have made a long and secret journey to see you."

"You are welcome," growled Gotwela in answer. His huge sweating body, clad only in the *simbara,* the ceremonial lion skin, swayed backwards until it found the support of the reed wall. "Your messengers came before you, with much talk of new things. I am interested in these new things. Tell me of Gamate."

Zuva told him of Gamate, and of Port Victoria also, while the sun dipped towards the horizon, and the dank interlaced trees grew darker and more secret. The story he told was of the new creed that was driving like a flame through many parts of Phara-maul. Of course, Gotwela knew of the fish, said Zuva, looking at the great greasy body of the man who was to be his ally. Indeed, the story of the fish had started, in ancient days, in this very village of Shebiya. There would come a moment when the fish men of Port Victoria and Gamate and Shebiya would all join hands. When did Gotwela think that this moment would come?

"Certainly we know of the fish," said Gotwela sarcastically. "Indeed, we take an oath on the fish." He grinned suddenly, and then laughed aloud. "Do you understand me?"

"I understand you," said Zuva. His own messengers, men with keen eyes and furtive tongues, had spoken of this matter. "But it may be that our fish is not the same as yours."

Gotwela shook his heavy head angrily. "There is only one fish," he answered roughly. "It is the sign of freedom, the sign of blood-shed. We are ready to strike. Are you ready?"

"When next I come, that will be the moment to strike," an-swered Zuva. "I swear it."

Gotwela's eyes narrowed. "You will take the oath of the fish?"

Zuva swallowed. He knew something, by rumor, of this U-Maula initiation, by which the inner circle bound themselves by actions so loathsome and degraded that they were forever exiled beyond the pale of normal living, and doomed or dedicated to a path of hatred and violence. Truly, he was not ready to take such an oath. But he needed allies, and the oath-taking might secure them. "Let it be as you will," he said finally. "I am prepared."

THE GOVERNMENT House Garden Party pursued its well-estab-lished course. At one end of the lawn, under the oak trees, the band played mournful and patriotic airs. Under the pillared portico, the Governor, in dazzling white uniform topped by a plumed helmet, held his court. He was supported by Lady Vere-Toombs, splendid in huge hat and ankle-length lace dress.

A receiving line formed automatically. First came the dean of the diplomatic corps, the French commercial counselor, a wizened cynical man with the look and pace of an ancient tortoise, followed by his wife, a dead-pan blonde who affected the airs of Paris. Next, smiling gently, came Lou Strogoff, the American consul. Next, the honorary representative for Poland — courtly, trembling with ague, and clad in an ancient frock coat.

Hard on the heels of the diplomatic corps came the twenty-four town councilors of Port Victoria — twenty-one white, three black — in robes of russet brown and chains of gold. The line moved forward slowly, trying not to keep in step with the band, which presently abandoned "Greensleeves" and embarked on "Body and Soul" with crushing nonchalance.

There was over all the wide garden and the static throng a leisurely dignity. The Governor, freed at last from the receiving line, moved among his guests, smiling easily. His staff, impeccably tail-coated, kept one eye on his beckoning finger, the other on guests who in past years had proved awkward, or argumentative, or dull. The household servants, in their yellow robes, their scarlet tarbooshes, their tasseled sashes of office, moved about also from group to group, serving cooling drinks and sandwiches with deferential skill.

This was the Garden Party — formal, unchanging, dictated by tradition and protocol. Yet, in a sense, this year's party was entirely and disturbingly new. First, there was the situation in Pharamaul, of which no single guest could be unaware. And then there were this year's *new people* — chiefly the members of the press. It was a downright shame that they had to be invited, thought the Social Secretary. Everyone knew what they thought about Pharamaul, what they had said about it, what they were trying to stir up. They didn't even know how to behave. They were laughing at everything. They would go away and write awful things about it. They would spoil it all.

Aidan Purves-Brownrigg, David Bracken, and Nicole Steuart met almost guiltily under a tree at the farther side of the main lawn. Such a respite was something that they were specifically not entitled to enjoy; their orders were to watch the Governor at all times, in case he might need help or relief, and otherwise to Mix With the Guests. But after an hour, both these things had palled and they found themselves together. The three of them were by far the most distinguished group. David wore a black morning coat, Aidan a pearl-gray one with a high stock; Nicole looked completely ravishing in a formal dress of pale blue.

"*So* nice of you to come," said Aidan ridiculously, as they drew furtively together. "I *know* how busy you are. Don't you think the lemonade is absolutely stunning?"

Nicole giggled, then looked about her nervously. "We really shouldn't be doing this," she said. "You know we're not meant to talk to each other."

"If that's the worst thing you children have on your conscience," said Aidan cheerfully, "then you needn't worry."

It seemed natural for Nicole and David to catch each other's eye at that moment. Looking at her, admiring her face and her figure, David realized anew how far they were beyond the edge of love, how deeply bound to each other. Perhaps it was time for that feeling to be declared.

David was interrupted in his daydream by Aidan's remarking, "I just caught Lady Vere-Toombs' eye, from over there."

"But she's about fifty yards away," protested David.

"It's her favorite range," said Aidan, "and still one hundred percent lethal." He began to sidle away, calling over his shoulder, "Bless you, children. Behave yourselves."

Alone, happy in isolation, Nicole and David looked at each other. "Hallo," said David. "You're looking really lovely."

"You're looking very smart, too."

"Blue suits you."

"Black suits *you*."

"Will you marry me?"

After all, it was as easy as that.

THE LAST guests caught the Governor's eye, bade him farewell, and made for the main gates. The staff rallied around a table spread with derelict coffee cups and plates of biscuits. The very last guest of all, Miss Sproule, social editor for the *Times of Pharamaul,* noticed a curious fact as she got into her car: on the main gateposts, under the Royal coat of arms, some child or vandal had chalked a crisscross pattern vaguely resembling a fish.

Sir Elliott Vere-Toombs, approaching his staff with a gallant smile, took off his plumed helmet and smoothed his hair. "I think it all went off very well, don't you?" he said cheerfully. "It's always a dreadful bore, of course, but people *do* appreciate it."

Chapter 7

Andrew Macmillan was dozing in his chair when the telephone rang. Caught between sleeping and waking, his heart gave an uneasy leap at the harsh sound. He looked at the clock on the mantelpiece. It was ten o'clock, and through the undrawn curtains he could see that full darkness had come to the Residency garden. The phone rang again, and he reached out for it.

He heard a voice say, "Andrew? Keith Crump here." Without the label, he might not have recognized it; Crump's voice was taut, and he seemed to be breathing fast. Behind the voice was the staccato tapping of a typewriter, and behind that a vague murmuring, like the sound of a crowd over the rim of a hill.

"What is it, Keith? Where are you?"

"Down at the tax office. I'd have called you earlier, but things blew up suddenly."

"What things?" asked Macmillan harshly.

Crump reacted to the harshness. His voice became more controlled, measurably more formal. "There's been a bit of a riot down here, sir. I think it's O.K. now, but we had a sticky session for a time."

"What happened?"

"You know there was another big *aboura* this afternoon, and a hot debate over Dinamaula and his marriage. It ended with Dinamaula making a personal appearance and being greeted with a thunder of applause and homage."

"Yes; go on," commanded Macmillan.

"It was later that the trouble started. They overturned some wagons and set fire to a couple belonging to a headman who spoke against the marriage this afternoon. Those young chaps who call themselves the Dinamaula Regiment started the fighting. A headman was knifed in the groin. He's in poor shape. And one of my chaps got beaten up pretty badly."

"Why the hell didn't you call me?"

"Sir, it blew up so suddenly. And — " Crump's voice took on a small edge of pride " — we got it under control after a bit."

"Is it really quiet now?" asked Macmillan after a pause. "Do you want me to come down?"

"There's no need for that, Andrew, but I think you'll have to give them a pep talk, fairly soon. Otherwise it's going to happen again."

"I'll talk to them," answered Andrew Macmillan grimly. He leant back in his chair, no longer sleepy, no longer rendered indecisive by doubt of his own capacity. This was something he could surely deal with. "Get on to George Forsdick, first thing in the morning, or now, if he's still awake. I want Seralo to call an *aboura* — my official *aboura* — for tomorrow afternoon. Five o'clock. All the Regents are to be there, and the headmen."

"What about Dinamaula?" Now Crump sounded cheerful and confident, catching Macmillan's forceful change of mood.

"He is officially invited to attend."

"I doubt if he'll come. There's a lot of talk that he's not going to say or do anything, until he's confirmed as chief. Then he'll really go into action. It's a bit vague at the edges, but I get the impression of a plan of campaign. Could be something he has worked out for himself; or it could be those press chaps."

"I'll fix Dinamaula," said Macmillan brusquely. *"And* the press, if I have to. A few deportation orders would work wonders."

"All right," said Crump. He paused. "There's just one thing." His voice was careful. "The people are in a funny mood, Andrew. So are the Regents. So is Dinamaula. It might be a mistake to get too tough."

"The mistake so far," said Andrew Macmillan coldly, "is that we haven't been tough enough. We'll change all that tomorrow. And Master Dinamaula and I are going to have a very instructive meeting, if things don't go exactly as I want them."

A SILENCE altogether too decorous, too perfect, greeted Andrew Macmillan as he stepped forward from the shadow of the balcony overlooking the *aboura* and showed himself to the assembly. This

formal appearance was something which he organized very rarely
— once a year at Christmastime, and occasionally when there was
some special proclamation to be made, like the King's death or
the birth of an heir to the throne. All the stage dressing was correct.
Behind him, on one line of chairs, sat the three Regents — Seralo,
Katsaula, and Puero — and the chosen headmen of the Maulas;
level with them on the other side were George Forsdick, Llewellyn,
and Captain Crump.

Below them the huge crowd was ranged in rank according to
custom; older men in front, young men behind them, women and
children on the outskirts. There were policemen posted like senti-
nels at the rim of the *aboura*. There was a small knot of press
correspondents, including a movie-camera crew which had driven
in from Port Victoria. There were, in fact, all the trappings of
authority; the Resident Commissioner had only to speak, and
many hundreds of men and women would listen attentively. But
Andrew Macmillan felt, as soon as he stepped forward, a sullen,
rocklike wall of hate.

He had certain things to say that afternoon, and the mood of
the people counted for nothing with him. The people he was
addressing were Maulas — Maulas whom he had known and
loved for thirty years, Maulas whom he distrusted profoundly,
Maulas whom he laughed at, Maulas who, a few hours ago, had
been engaged, many of them, in a bloody riot on this very *aboura*.
(The stabbed headman had died during the night.)

He had these things to say, as part of his duty as Resident Commissioner, and as part of his conviction as a man. He was going to
tell the assembled Maulas what they were going to do next, without alternatives and without equivocation. If, divining this, they
had already turned sullen, that was no bar to plain speaking.

"*Ahsula!*" began Andrew Macmillan formally, his hand touching the pedestal of the microphone, his tall tough body standing
trim and erect before the crowd. His deep voice, magnified many
times by the public-address system, rolled across the width of the
aboura, while the absolute stillness continued. "*Ahsula!* I bring
you loving greetings from your mother the Queen."

He spoke in the Maula tongue. To most of the vast throng who heard his greeting, "your mother the Queen" meant Queen Victoria, their true mother, enshrined perpetually in love and honor.

The murmur of homage for the name of the great Queen was the last sound that greeted Macmillan. Thereafter his words — heavy, cold, and grim — fell like stones upon a vast silence, the stillness of hatred.

"I have some matters to speak of," he began formally. "Listen, and take heed. There is great unrest in Gamate. There is much foolish talk. Last night there was fighting against the forces of Government, and a headman was killed. His killing shames the whole tribe. Those taking part in the fighting will be punished. If the man who did the killing is caught, he will be hanged."

Looking about him, as the silence grew in intensity, he declared, raising his voice, "There are many other heavy matters. Taxes are being paid too slowly. Cattle are being withheld from inspection. If you have complaints to make against any man or any law," he continued, "state them according to the custom. Tell your chiefs and headmen. They will tell the Regents in council. The Regents will tell me. I will listen, and deal justly."

He spread his feet slightly and put his hands on his hips. His tall body seemed to grow in stature and toughness. "But I will not listen to foolishness," he said harshly. "There is to be no more violence in Gamate, no more foolish talk. That is the way of women. You are men. Behave like men."

Now his whole bearing took on an air of forceful contempt. "Soon you will have a new chief at the head of the tribe. He is not here today — " Macmillan's tone was ironical " — but he knows well what is in my mind. Now remember that a new chief in Gamate does not mean new things, nor any great changes. Nothing will be done that is against the custom. That I tell you plainly, so that there may be no more doubt."

A thousand pairs of eyes gazed back at him as he spoke. All knew that he talked of the chief's marriage, and that his words were heavy. But the heaviest were still to come. "It may be," he went on slowly, "that the idea of a new chief, and new prospects, is too unsettling, and divides the tribe. I will consider that matter. If it seems to me that the tribe is deeply divided, and the moment for change is not yet come, I will ask your mother the Queen to wait some time before the new chief is proclaimed."

He paused for a long moment, his bleak face stern and unbending. Then he said, "That is all. The *aboura* is ended."

Flanked by Crump and Forsdick, Macmillan turned, and walked towards his car. A few of the older men raised their woven beehive hats as he passed, but not a sound could be heard. When he reached the edge of the *aboura,* he saw the pressmen breaking ranks, as if at a signal, and begin weaving swiftly through the crowd towards the Regents, while all round them the whole concourse came to sullen, murmuring life again.

THAT NIGHT it was George Forsdick who telephoned him, towards midnight. Macmillan had been waiting for the call; nonetheless, the sound of the telephone shrilling through the silent house startled him painfully. He put his hand on his hammering heart, glad that there was no one to witness his weakness.

Forsdick's voice was urgent as Macmillan lifted the receiver. "I'm at the tax office, Andrew. They've fired some huts near the *aboura*. It's under control now. But I think you'd better come down. The police are having a tough time breaking up the fighting."

"Hasn't Crump got enough men?"

"Yes. He had them all standing to, like you said. But part of the Dinamaula Regiment drew them off with a diversion, and then another gang set light to the huts."

Macmillan heard an odd fading note in Forsdick's voice, as if he had turned his head away. Then it came back again, in full strength. "Now that's funny," said Forsdick, puzzled. "I thought I heard a shot and now it's suddenly gone absolutely quiet outside."

"I'll come down," said Macmillan, with foreboding. "Wait for me by the tax-office door."

In the unearthly stillness that had settled over Gamate, Macmillan's headlights picked out a few shadowy figures, but they melted soundlessly into cover as he passed. Near the tax office, a hut was still burning fiercely. All else was profoundly still.

Forsdick ran out as his car drew up at the tax office.

"Someone's been shot," he said, his voice queerly constrained. "A Maula kid of about ten. Back there by the burning hut. Then they all ran away. That's what the sudden silence was."

"Who did the shooting?"

"Only Crump has a gun," said Forsdick.

Macmillan called out to his driver, "Turn the car. Point the lights *there*." As the car's headlights swiveled, he walked forward towards the knot of men which had suddenly come into view.

The headlights, and the flickering fire from the burning hut, showed a scene full of menace and ill omen. A Maula child, half naked, lay on the ground, in the ungainly stillness of death. Crump and a policeman were looking down at him. By their side was Tulbach Browne, and a photographer who, even as Macmillan approached, took a flashlight photograph of the scene.

"Keith," called out Macmillan as he drew near.

Crump turned slowly. His face was stricken. It was the first time that Macmillan had ever seen him less than cheerful, less than lively, and the change was mortal. "He did it himself." Crump's voice was constricted. "He was in the crowd when we charged. He must have reached up and tried to take the gun from my holster. It went off as he pulled it out."

"Are you sure?" asked Macmillan harshly.

"Certain," said Crump. "I had a cane in my right hand. I never went near the gun. There wasn't any need."

There was a sudden movement nearby, and they all turned. A woman on the edge of the clearing, silhouetted by the burning hut, was shouting and seeking to evade the grasp of one of the policemen. Macmillan called out, "Let her through," and she shambled forward at an unsteady run, her voice breaking into piercing screams as she saw the body of the child. Then she threw herself down, in whimpering agony, by the side of the corpse.

In the deep foreboding silence, there came Tulbach Browne's stony voice, "It does seem a curious way to run a country."

WAITING for Dinamaula to arrive at the Residency, Andrew Macmillan found that he could concentrate on nothing, not even drinking coffee, or smoking a pipe. He knew what he wanted to say to the chief-designate, but the events of the previous night, and the general sense of guilt which, however unfairly, affected every white man in Gamate that morning — these things were working fatally against composure and control. When the police jeep stopped at the front gate, and Dinamaula, unattended, walked across the lawn towards him, he still did not know how best to treat this young man who was now divided from him by so many thoughts, and so much blood.

"You sent for me, Mr. Macmillan." Withdrawn and self-contained, Dinamaula spoke from the foot of the steps leading up to the stoep.

"Yes." Andrew Macmillan nodded. "I wanted to talk to you, Chief. I don't like the way things are going." Then, after a moment of silence, he said heavily, "Come in. We can talk better in here."

When they were indoors, sitting opposite each other in the worn armchairs, Dinamaula refused coffee and a cigarette, and appeared to be reconciled to unpleasant duty. Macmillan, vilely depressed by the previous night, had wished for a smoother beginning to their meeting. "I hoped to see you at my *aboura,*" he said after a moment.

"I was unable to be present," returned Dinamaula formally.

"You know what I said to the tribe?"

Dinamaula inclined his head. "I have been informed."

"Did you agree with it?"

Dinamaula looked almost theatrically surprised. "It is not for me to agree or disagree. I am not yet the chief. What the Resident Commissioner says in his *aboura* is not my affair."

"Chief," said Macmillan, leaning forward, "I knew your father. Two of your uncles were senior headmen. They were all fine men. We were able to work together for the good of the tribe. I hope to be able to work the same way with you."

"I hope so, too."

"Then what's it all about?" Macmillan tried to smile.

Dinamaula still wore the mask of wary, expressionless disinterest. "What is *what* all about?" he countered.

Macmillan sighed. "Let's begin at the beginning, then. There's a lot of unrest in the tribe. There have been two riots and two deaths already. There are a lot of rumors flying about. When you first arrived here, you talked a lot of hot air — " Dinamaula's eyes narrowed at the words, and then grew coldly negative again " — a lot of hot air about reforms. Later on you talked to the press about marrying a white girl. Those two things have led directly to all the trouble we're in now."

"I do not agree," said Dinamaula, with cool decision.

"Then what is the trouble?"

"Perhaps the tribe is disturbed by these — deaths."

"What caused the deaths?"

"A knife and a revolver," answered Dinamaula succinctly.

"I want you to answer some questions," said Macmillan; and Dinamaula inclined his head.

"What are these reforms that you have in mind?"

"Until I am proclaimed chief, I cannot say."

Macmillan was getting nowhere, and this cool young man was making the fact plain. He took a fresh grip, aware that he must take command now, or lose it altogether.

"Then there's the question of your marriage," he said, as if they were progressing easily from subject to subject. *"Are* you planning to marry a white woman? Who is she?"

"When I am chief," answered Dinamaula, "I will announce my marriage plans, and the reforms I have in mind."

"You will never be chief if you talk like that."

Dinamaula smiled faintly. "So you told my people. I understand that it was not well received."

"I don't give a damn how it was received!" returned Macmillan angrily. "I know what's best for this country. You are splitting the tribe from top to bottom."

"I shall know how to bind them together, when I am chief."

Macmillan sighed. Weariness assailed him, and a feeling that history was passing him by, and that his day was done, his hopes in ruins. Without looking at Dinamaula, he said, more gently, "Chief, please understand that I'm asking you to help me. I don't want to quarrel, I don't want to use force. The whole tribe is split. We haven't seen the last of this unrest — in fact we may only be at the beginning of it. I want you to use your influence on my side to smooth things out again."

"What influence have I, Mr. Macmillan?" Dinamaula's voice was faintly bitter — the first sign of his true thoughts. "You know what they call me in Gamate? The Resident Commissioner's dog. It will always be so, until I am proclaimed chief."

They looked at each other and Macmillan leant forward in his chair, squaring his heavy shoulders. "We're getting nowhere," he said curtly. "Perhaps I was a fool to hope that we would. You'd better understand this. I'm *not* giving you a free hand, either now or in the future. If there are to be any reforms, they'll be worked out by you and me together, and they *won't* come with a rush. The marriage, of course, is out of the question. Whatever you do or say, Gamate is my responsibility, and I have the last word. I'm going to run it *my* way."

Dinamaula rose. His bearing was suddenly icy, his face set. "I must ask you to excuse me," he said, with glacial formality. "I have to attend a funeral."

THAT NIGHT, and the night following, there was no more violence in Gamate. Then, on the third night, after a brooding, malevolent respite, rioting broke out again.

It started with a Maula girl-child, who was taken to the hospital with acute pleurisy. She reached the hospital too late, and died during the afternoon. Word instantly spread that the child had been poisoned, and that all Maula children would be so disposed of, one by one, till the entire tribe disappeared. Windows were broken at the hospital; a car taking some nurses to work was overturned and set on fire, and the girls manhandled. Thousands of people broke the curfew Crump had imposed, and the police, powerless to enforce it, were taunted and mocked intolerably.

Andrew Macmillan rang the Governor at midnight from the police station, after a tour of the huts in his car, and a brave, fruitless appeal for order. He had never before felt so feebly armed, so dependent on higher authority. The misfortunes and frustrations of the last thirty-six hours, taken together at the low ebb of his fifty-eighth year, seemed to have brought him to his knees.

Sir Elliott had been irritable, when first he was called from his bed to answer the telephone; during the past forty-eight hours the

Scheduled Territories Office had been plaguing him with cabled requests for information to combat a totally adverse press at home; and his staff had filled in the gaps with minutes, memoranda and draft cables. But as Andrew Macmillan painted his picture, in a few brisk foreboding words, the Governor awoke swiftly to crisis.

"I'm not surprised," he said presently, when Macmillan reached the end of his recital. "There's a good deal of unrest here, too, a decided undercurrent. What do you suggest, Andrew? I can't let you have any more men, I'm afraid."

"I've got enough men, sir," said Macmillan. "But we *must* somehow relieve the pressure locally. I'd like you to talk personally to Dinamaula. He's the key point in all this."

"Is he active?" asked the Governor.

"Not openly. But behind the scenes I think he's doing a lot of maneuvering and organizing."

"You must speak to the Regents, very strongly."

"I don't think it's the answer, sir," said Andrew. "Dinamaula himself needs to be taken out of this altogether."

"How do you mean, 'taken out'?"

"I'd like to send him down to you, sir. And I'd like him kept in Port Victoria, until things quiet down a bit."

There was a long silence on the wire. The Governor was thinking of the reaction five thousand miles away in London. Macmillan was thinking of immediate security. Even as he waited there was a long concerted howl from across the *aboura*.

The Governor spoke. "All right, Andrew. Send Dinamaula down to me. You can't spare Crump or Forsdick. Send him down with Llewellyn." Macmillan wondered at his decisive, knowledgeable control, and was deeply grateful for it.

"Write out a formal letter of instruction," came the Governor's voice. "Signed by you, on my behalf. Dinamaula is to come to Port Victoria, *forthwith* —" the unlikely word crackled over the wire " — forthwith, for personal consultation with me."

"Yes, sir," said Macmillan. "If he starts by one o'clock he should be there by breakfast time."

"The sooner the better," said the Governor. "Allow him twenty minutes to pack. Good night, Andrew."

"Good night, sir."

The line was already dead as Macmillan replaced the receiver.

LEAVING the engine of his truck still running, Llewellyn walked up the short path to the hut of Dinamaula, a single piece of paper in his hand. The hut stood well back from the *aboura,* but even here the angry tumult could be heard. A hanger-on — perhaps a guard — moved to intercept him as he approached. He said, "Get out of my way!" and then, calling more loudly, "Chief!"

"Who is it?" came Dinamaula's voice from within.

"Mr. Llewellyn," answered Llewellyn.

"Come in, please," said Dinamaula.

The hut was well lighted, with candles, and two flaring kerosene lamps. Inside were four people: Dinamaula, lying seemingly exhausted on his couch, Puero, lolling in a corner, and two pressmen — Axel Hallmarck and Tulbach Browne.

"I would like to speak to you alone," said Llewellyn.

"I am with my friends," said Dinamaula coldly.

"I have a message from the Resident Commissioner."

"I am with my friends," said Dinamaula again.

"Very well." Llewellyn proffered the piece of paper. "This is an order from the Governor," he said formally.

Dinamaula took the piece of paper. Puero, Tulbach Browne and Hallmarck leant across to read what was on it.

"This is completely unconstitutional," Tulbach Browne said.

Llewellyn was looking at Dinamaula, and only at Dinamaula. He saw a deep shadow cross the other man's face. "This comes as a surprise," he said. "I am not prepared for travel."

"I will give you time to pack," said Llewellyn, adding in the Maula tongue, "please make ready for the journey."

"Do not go," said Puero contemptuously. "This man — " he gestured crudely " — can wait till morning."

"We must start tonight," said Llewellyn evenly.

"Who says so?" asked Tulbach Browne.

"It is an order from the Governor," said Llewellyn.

A new voice now made itself heard. It was Axel Hallmarck, crisply inquisitive. "But what's it mean? Is he being deported?"

"He is going to Port Victoria to consult with the Governor."

"When will he come back?" asked Tulbach Browne.

Llewellyn said nothing.

Dinamaula rose to his feet. His face was tired. "I am ready to go," he said. Then he paused as if remembering something. "But I make a formal protest," he said, in a strange, almost theatrical voice, "against being ordered to leave my home in this irregular way." Then he brushed past Llewellyn, and with bent head walked through the door of the hut and towards the waiting truck.

As HE had feared, Macmillan's meeting with the Regents, which the Governor had ordered, ended in a deadlock. To Macmillan's appeal for help in quelling the mounting violence, the Regents presented a solid mutinous front. They would do nothing, they said, without their chief.

Why had he been spirited away in the night? When would he return? How could they hope to reassert the law, when Dinamaula was not at hand to lend them his authority?

"This is my last word," Macmillan said finally. "The chief will not return until I am satisfied that order has been restored in Gamate. I have asked you to help me. You have refused. If you will not rule for me, then I shall rule for myself. If it means the bringing of policemen, perhaps even of soldiers, then you have only yourselves to blame."

"You would bring soldiers?" asked Katsaula incredulously.

"I will bring order," answered Macmillan. He turned briskly on his heel and left the stoep. But within the house he sat down heavily in the nearest armchair, and put his head in his hands.

He knew that the meeting had failed, and that he himself had failed with it. He had talked of soldiers, but soldiers were failure in themselves, the defeat of reason and the rule of law. In using the threat of military force in his own town of Gamate he had sounded the defeat of his whole life.

TWO HUNDRED miles away in Port Victoria, the Governor and Commander in Chief of Pharamaul was also speaking his mind. He was briefing his staff, at the beginning of what might well be a critical phase in the affairs of Pharamaul; and his staff, all five of them, were united in his support.

Aidan Purves-Brownrigg contemplated the present company. For good or ill, this was the team which had to run Pharamaul. At the top there was the old gentleman, and himself. They both did their best, thought Aidan wryly, but it didn't seem terribly good. There was Captain Simpson, Royal Navy, a four-striper fish out of water among these land-borne dilemmas. There was David Bracken, in love with Nicole Steuart; and Nicole, in love with David. If they could just detach their minds from that particular subject, their contribution was not ineffective. Finally, there was Stevens, who *was* ineffective.

That was all there was, to deal with a hundred thousand Maulas — except for a handful of outlying players up at Gamate, who were making (at the moment) a monumental hash of the whole thing.

His somber thoughts were interrupted by the Governor, sitting trim and birdlike in the sticky heat.

"Some of you," said Sir Elliott, "will have seen the telegrams containing excerpts from the London press, dealing with what's going on in Gamate. They are highly critical, most of them — unfair, of course, and — er — highly critical. This is the sort of thing." His voice rising several tones higher, he read: " 'Chief Spirited Away From Gamate'; 'Dinamaula Hijacked, Leaves Under Protest'; 'Tribe Robbed of Chief on Eve of Coronation.' "

Not for the first time during the past few weeks, David was conscious of the ineffectiveness of what the Government team was doing in Pharamaul when contrasted with what the situation demanded. They had right on their side, but they never bothered to explain how and why, in clear and explicit terms. They were getting an atrocious press all over the world, and somehow they never caught up with it, never fought back at all.

"I saw Dinamaula yesterday, as you know," continued Sir Elliott. "I hoped that he would play, but he won't."

Play, thought Nicole. Now there's a funny word. . . . She had a sudden, irreverent vision of Dinamaula, in a loincloth, playing leapfrog with Sir Elliott Vere-Toombs, in cocked hat and spurs.

"Dinamaula won't play at all," repeated the Governor, as if he could scarcely believe what he was called upon to tell them. "He was very uncoöperative. And that brings me to my next point. Dinamaula *cannot* be allowed to return to Gamate at present. Andrew Macmillan rang me up last night, and again this morning, just a few minutes ago. Gamate is full of rumors about Dinamaula — that he's in prison down here, or going to be hanged — all sorts of things like that. There was some very bad rioting last night — the worst so far, in fact; a policeman was killed. Things are a great deal quieter this morning, but there are still gangs of people roaming about, shouting for Dinamaula. It's quite obvious that, if he went back to Gamate, he would continue to be the center of revolt — he couldn't help it. He must therefore stay here in Port Victoria. With that in view, I am issuing this Order-in-Council."

The Governor took up a sheet of stiff blue foolscap. He adjusted his spectacles and read: " 'In pursuance of the powers vested in me under Section Seventeen of — ' well, that's just the usual preamble ' — Be it therefore enacted as follows: ONE: A State of Emergency is declared within the Township of Gamate, and within a prescribed zone extending one hundred miles in any direction therefrom. Two: Chief-designate Dinamaula, by reason of his refusal to coöperate with the Resident Commissioner, Gamate, in matters affecting the future of the Maula tribe, is hereby prohibited from entering the prescribed zone affected by the State of Emergency. THREE: Chief-designate Dinamaula is hereby directed to reside within the metropolitan limits of Port Victoria, until the Governor in Council shall decree otherwise. That's all.' "

There was a silence. Once again, David Bracken was aware of a prickling uneasiness. There was a gap here, the same gap as before; the Government side was planning to do something pretty clear-cut and decisive, and again they weren't bothering to explain why.

"Sir," he said tentatively.

"Yes, David?" said the Governor, turning.

"Couldn't we issue a statement to the press about this? I think we ought to try to put our side of the thing across."

"Put it across?" repeated the Governor fastidiously. "What an odd notion. Our business is to restore order in Gamate. This — "

he tapped the Order-in-Council " — is how we are going about it."

David drew a deep breath. "We really *must* explain why Dina-maula is being barred from Gamate." He was aware of the others watching him, and especially of Nicole's face, gravely speculative, hearteningly lovely. "Unless we do so, in detail, it will look as if he's being bullied and badgered by us just because he won't obey orders, and the newspapers will automatically take his side."

"Ridiculous!" exclaimed the Governor. His blue eyes, a trifle frosty, formidably direct, regarded David steadily. "How could anyone in their right senses formulate such a view? I hope no member of my staff — " His voice trailed off, though he continued to stare at David with level persistence.

Across the room, Aidan spoke. "I think David's right, sir. We've got a case. We ought to state it more clearly."

"But will it do any good?" asked the Governor dubiously. "Whenever any one of us has tried to put our side of the case, as you call it, it's seemed to make things worse than they were before."

After a reflective silence, Aidan said, "I still think it's worth trying, sir. Shall I put up a draft?"

The Governor sighed, unconvinced. But a draft was something he understood, something manageable. "Very well," he said. "Let me have it as soon as you can." He glanced down at a memorandum on his blotter. There remained one more item. "That takes care of Dinamaula. It still leaves Gamate. I'm not quite satisfied that we're doing all we can to impress on the tribe the necessity of returning to normal. If the Regents won't coöperate, it's possible that their powers will have to be suspended and Andrew declared the sole Native Authority. I propose to go up to Gamate myself, in two days' time, and hold an *aboura* to explain matters to the tribe."

He looked round the room. Only Aidan had known in advance of this move; the faces of the others reflected their surprise.

"It will be a full-dress affair," said the Governor. "I shall want *you* to come with me — " he looked at Captain Simpson, indubitably a full-dress individual " — and you too, David. Uniforms, of course, and — er — swords. We'll leave by train tomorrow night. I think that's all," he said, looking round him, relaxing somewhat. "Thank you for coming along."

Chapter 8

FOR THE Governor of Pharamaul to hold a personal *aboura,* with full ceremony, was a very rare happening indeed. The most ancient memory of such an occasion was almost lost in the mists of legend: when the Great Maula himself had returned from a visit to their mother the Queen, bearing gifts, and had joined with the Governor at an *aboura* full of splendor, to mark the sixtieth year of the old Queen's reign. Now, it was freely said, the old Queen had turned angry, and had taken away their chief, and her special emissary the Governor was coming with soldiers to kill all who resisted, and to put on new taxes. It was no wonder that, all over the town, the old men talked with lowered voices, and the young men made secret plans.

"I don't like it," said Crump decisively. "It's not just gossip and rumor — it's something more definite."

"Cheer up, Keith!" said Forsdick. "Even if some of them do stay away from the *aboura,* there'll still be enough Maulas to make a show. That's all the old boy wants."

Crump shook his head. "I wish I could agree with you."

"All right," Forsdick said, subsiding in his chair with a freshly poured drink, "let's have it. What's on your mind?"

"It's talk, mostly," admitted Crump. "Downtown they are saying that this is a special *aboura,* for white Government only, and no Maulas are to attend. If they do attend, there'll be trouble."

"But that's just another rumor!" said Forsdick. "You know how many of *them* there've been lately."

"Maybe. But it *is* a fact that the Dinamaula Regiment have been drilling and practicing, up on the hill. They've marked out a space the same shape and size as the *aboura;* they run out and surround it as soon as the signal's given; and then they all turn *outwards.*"

"Odd," said Forsdick carelessly.

"It's bloody odd. If you put the two things together — the talk of a boycott, and the drill to keep people away from the *aboura* — it looks like a coördinated tribal resistance movement, with definite aims; and it adds up to a fair-sized flop, tomorrow."

"I wish Andrew would do something constructive about it," grumbled Forsdick. "I suppose I shouldn't say this," he continued, closely regarding his beer, "but the old boy rather seems to have lost his grip lately."

"It's been a very difficult situation altogether," said Crump non-committally.

"All it needs is a bit of organization!" Forsdick gestured expansively. "We've got to clear the press out of Gamate and then tell the Regents that they'll be out of a job unless they toe the line. Simple."

Crump smiled in spite of himself. "Simple! I'd like to hear something complicated. First, the press won't go. Why should they? Second, the Regents won't coöperate. Why should *they*? Thirdly, even if by a miracle both those things happened, you've still got a tribe in a state of continuous revolt, refusing to obey any sort of order unless Dinamaula comes back."

"And fourthly," said Forsdick obstinately, "we've got to give Dinamaula the sack, once and for all, and find a chief who will coöperate properly."

After a pause, Crump said, "I'm beginning to see why Andrew's job is so complicated."

WAITING on his stoep for the three Regents, whom he had summoned for a final appeal for coöperation, Andrew Macmillan talked to his headboy Johannes; talked to him, listened to his answers, and, with a strong sense of doom, feared for the future. It might be that the day of himself and of Johannes, his old servant, his old friend, was now over. They were both old men of Gamate, with a sense of tradition and order. History might have left them behind — history, and change, and a hungry search for freedom. None of those things was a bad thing, and it was true that someday Gamate would catch up with the rest of the world; but all his instinct, all his long training, told him that that day was not tomorrow, nor the next. It could not be, without disaster.

"What do they say about the *aboura* tomorrow, Johannes?"

Johannes considered carefully before replying. "They say, many people coming in to Gamate, *barena*. Coming from all around.

They say some young men are ready to kill, to stop people passing through to the *aboura*. Some people go back to their village already."

Macmillan sighed. It confirmed all that Crump had been telling him; there was to be an organized cordon enforcing a boycott.

"Have we no friends in Gamate?" he asked after a moment.

Johannes paused in his task of cleaning an ash tray. "Some friends, *barena*," he said gently. "But they have been led away by clever men. Some Maula men. Some white. They say, how can there be an *aboura* without the chief? They say, where is our chief? Is he in prison? Is he dead? They say, how can we trust Government, since our chief is stolen away when he should be declared chief before all the tribe?" Johannes shook his head, returning to his own thoughts. "The tribe is not happy, *barena*."

"But that is what the *aboura* is for," said Macmillan curtly. "So that the Governor can explain why Dinamaula has been taken away, and what will happen in the future."

"Yes, *barena*," said Johannes, dusting slowly. He put his head on one side, and turned towards the garden and the road leading down to Gamate. "Car coming now," he said.

Macmillan turned, looking over his shoulder. "That's the Regents," he said. "Bring coffee in five minutes."

BUT THE car did not bear the Regents, coming for their instructions; the car bore Captain Crump, bringing disgraceful news.

Crump stood before Andrew at the open door of the stoep, trim and taut in his freshly pressed khaki uniform. He said laconically, "The Regents are all ill."

It took a few moments for Macmillan to realize what the other man was talking about.

"Ill? What do you mean? I sent for them. Aren't they coming?"

"No." His principal communication made, Crump relaxed somewhat. "I tried Katsaula first. He really *is* ill, as you know. Then I went to Seralo's hut. He sent his best respects to the Resident Commissioner —" Crump's voice was ironic " — but he is too ill to come this evening. Then I called on Puero." Crump paused.

"Well?" asked Andrew, near to violent anger.

"He made *me* ill," said Crump contemptuously. "He was drunk. There were a couple of pressmen there. He said he couldn't come. I asked why not, and he lurched forward and was sick all over my boots. Then he said, 'You see now that I am ill,' and lay down again. I damned nearly hit him."

Suddenly Andrew Macmillan felt very old. "Well, I can't *make* them come," he said, after a long silence. "All I wanted to do was ask them to meet the Governor at the *aboura,* and to persuade the tribe to listen. Is there anything else we can do now?"

Crump thought: It's too late to do a damned thing — we should have handled this differently, from the very beginning. He knew in his heart that he had disagreed entirely with every phase of Andrew Macmillan's tactics; the latter had been tough with Dinamaula at that delicate moment when he should have been persuasive and friendly; then he had relented and cajoled, when the only course was a steady disciplinary pressure. But Crump could not say these things now, in this hour of inner decay; for now it was a salvage job — salvage of the *aboura* tomorrow, salvage of Macmillan himself.

"I don't think there's much to be done at the moment," he answered slowly. "As far as the *aboura* is concerned, we'll make our own arrangements, to keep it as free and open as possible. It ought to be all right, even if we don't get as many people as we expected."

THE GOVERNOR's party had been seen off in Port Victoria by the whole Secretariat staff, a police guard of honor, twenty-four town councilors, a troop of boy scouts, and the fire-brigade band. The Governor had inspected the guard of honor, shaken hands with the town councilors, nodded encouragement to the boy scouts, and taken formal farewell of his staff. The band had played "God Save the King," and "Will Ye No' Come Back Again."

David shared a compartment with Captain Simpson, the naval aide. They were late to bed that evening. Captain Simpson's traveling bar, encased in a wicker basket, had been in full operation. David's portable radio (a parting present from Nicole) had given them a series of soporific airs from Radio Port Victoria. The Governor, in tartan carpet slippers and a velvet smoking jacket, had paid them a visit and had talked long and learnedly of Pharamaul's curious bird life which they might be able to see the following day. When he had gone, Captain Simpson poured them both another monumental pink gin, and said, with massive deliberation, "Remarkable man, that. Of course, he's wasted in Pharamaul."

AT GAMATE station, the band played, and the policemen formed a guard of honor; Crump's tremendous salute was matched by Andrew Macmillan's grimly ceremonial greeting, while a handful of white bystanders clapped and smiled. But presently, driving through the town towards the Residency, where they were all to have breakfast, David was reminded of Shebiya. On the surface, Gamate seemed to be a lifeless town; behind the lifelessness was an atmosphere of close-pressing, sullen menace.

"Aye, it's quiet," Llewellyn agreed. "Much too quiet. The town's stiff with people, but they're all keeping indoors." He looked at the dashboard clock. "Seven o'clock — that means five hours to the opening of the *aboura*. At any other time the whole *aboura* ground would have been jam-packed with people already."

"What's it mean?"

"A fiasco," said Llewellyn. "You can see it coming a mile off."

At the same moment, two cars ahead of them, the Governor was looking round him with puzzled eyes.

"Seems extraordinarily quiet," he observed after a moment. "I suppose it's still a bit early in the day, what?"

Andrew Macmillan, beside him on the back seat of the ancient Residency limousine, stared steadfastly at the back of his chauffeur's cropped head. "It is quiet," he agreed. His hands, sweating in their white cotton gloves, were gripping the knees of his immaculate white dress trousers.

"But plenty of crowds later on, eh?" pursued the Governor.

"Sir," said Andrew, with difficulty, "there have been some developments. It's possible that most of the tribe will refuse to attend the *aboura*, unless Dinamaula is allowed back to Gamate."

"Oh come!" said the Governor stiffly. "That can scarcely be so, when my sole purpose in being here today is to explain why he must be kept away."

DAVID had changed into his uniform at the Forsdick house when the telephone rang. Forsdick took the call; he said first, "Forsdick," then, "Yes," then, "Yes, sir," many times, with increasing formality. With a final, "I'll tell Bracken straight away, sir," he put down the receiver and walked into the living room.

He looked at David. "That was the Governor," he said importantly. "There's a job for you."

"For me?" David adjusted his helmet. "What is it?"

"According to Crump," continued Forsdick, "the boycott *is* working, and it may not be worth while holding the *aboura*." He looked at his wrist watch. "It's half past ten already — an hour and a half to go. There still isn't a single soul down on the *aboura* ground. The Governor wants you to go down and scout around; you're to report back to the Residency on the tax-office telephone."

"All right," said David, feeling heroic and inadequate at the same time. "How do I get there?"

"Crump is driving by in the jeep," answered Forsdick. "He'll leave you at the tax office, while he takes a look round himself. All you have to do is keep in touch on the phone."

"How many people will there have to be," asked David, "before it's worth while holding the *aboura?*"

"The Governor is leaving that to you," answered Forsdick. "If there isn't a crowd, he won't come down."

THE SUN burned suddenly hot as David stepped down from the jeep in front of the ramshackle, forlorn tax office.

"The phone's in there," Crump said, putting the jeep into gear.

"Where will you be?" asked David.

Crump waved his hand vaguely. "Around . . . I want to see how my chaps are doing. I'll come back here in about half an hour. Good luck." And then, surprisingly, he added, "Lock yourself into the inner office if things get tough. I'll bail you out myself, for certain." Then he was gone.

David stood in isolation on the balcony of the tax office, at the top end of a three-hundred-foot square of bare brown earth beaten level by countless generations of Maulas, and now entirely deserted. Directly across the *aboura,* under the arid thorn trees, was a group of people; he could make out several pressmen — Tulbach Browne and Axel Hallmarck among them. There was the small brown figure of Father Schwemmer, and Oosthuizen's enormous bulk towering over them all. There was a handful of other white spectators, but only three black faces were visible: the tribal interpreter, and two of Crump's native policemen.

In front of him was the loudspeaker and the control panel of the public-address system. David stepped up to it, switched it on, and blew through the microphone. A subdued roar answered him. He switched off the microphone, retreated into the tax office, and picked up the telephone.

Captain Simpson answered his call, with a bare moment's delay. "Hallo," he said. "I just rang up to say that I'm here."

"That's good," came Captain Simpson's booming voice. "We were hoping you'd keep in touch. What's the form, old boy?"

"Not too encouraging," answered David. He looked once more beyond the dusty room to the *aboura*. Not a single human being stirred. "In fact, there's no one here at all, at the moment."

"I say!" said Captain Simpson. "That's a pretty bad show, isn't it? I must tell H.E."

"Do that." David looked at his watch. It was a little after eleven o'clock. "I'll ring again in a half-hour."

He replaced the receiver. The heat smote him as he went out into the sunlight again. Just in front of him, a scrawny goat was licking at one of the white-painted crosses on the *aboura*. After a moment David set out, determinedly, to traverse the empty ground towards the press correspondents. Tulbach Browne smiled a thin smile of welcome as he approached. A news cameraman took a few quick shots. Axel Hallmarck regarded him with sharp, weasel attention. David did not know what to say, and therefore said the first thing that came into his mind.

"*Ahsula!*" he said, and raised his hand in formal Maula salute.

There was a vague murmur in reply. After a pause, Tulbach Browne asked ironically, "What time is the meeting?"

"Twelve o'clock," answered David. He turned his head as a new sound made itself heard among the huts at the upper end of the *aboura*.

It was the police jeep returning; it paused at the tax office, then circled the *aboura,* making for David's easily recognizable figure. Crump was at the wheel, square and trim in his full-dress whites, and a policeman by his side. The jeep flew a small Union Jack from a metal staff welded to the top of the radiator; it seemed the only sensible and dependable thing within many miles.

The circle of correspondents opened as Crump, stepping briskly from the driving seat, strode towards them. He saluted David, indicating by the courtesy the necessity for putting on a show.

David returned the salute, with equal gravity and ceremony. "Any news?" he asked.

"Yes," answered Crump, in crisp tones. "The opposition have managed to put a pretty effective cordon round the *aboura,* preventing the tribe from getting through." He was speaking half to David, half to the correspondents who stood within earshot.

"What 'opposition'?" asked Tulbach Browne. "What kind of an effective cordon do you mean?"

Crump looked at him, his bearing stiff. "All the paths and approaches are guarded," he answered. "There's a rough element at work as well. It's impossible to break through."

"Does anyone *want* to break through?" asked Axel Hallmarck.

"Of course they do," answered Crump brusquely. "They're being kept away, sometimes forcibly."

David became aware of a general murmur of comment. He raised his voice, conscious of a public audience.

"It's obvious," he said, "that there's an organized boycott of the *aboura*. But apart from that, the people who actually want to attend are being kept away by the gangster element of the tribe."

"Can we quote you on 'gangster element'?" asked Tulbach Browne, faintly menacing.

"Yes," said David hardly. "There's a definite strong-arm organization — you can call them gangsters — who are keeping people away from the *aboura."*

Bang goes my career, he thought, nervous and reckless at the same time. But something in Crump's confident bearing made him totally unwilling to retract what he had said.

A new ally raised his voice nearby. "It's a bloody disgrace!" said

Oosthuizen, the big Dutch farmer, solid fury in his voice. "They're staying away from the Governor's *aboura* just because some bloody agitators tell them they ought to. They've been put up to every bloody trick in the book! And we've got to go on living here, when all you half-baked chumps are safe back in England!"

In the pause that followed this, David detached himself from the group, and spoke privately to Crump. "It's about time I reported again," he said. "Will you take me back to the tax office?"

The clock showed 11:50 as once more David dialed the private line to the Residency. This time the Governor himself answered. "Ah, David!" he said, on a confident note. "What news have you for us?"

"There's no one here, sir," answered David unwillingly. "The situation's the same as before. I'm afraid it's no good."

"No good?" repeated the Governor, as if he could scarcely believe his ears.

"No, sir. It's a complete boycott."

The wires fell silent between them for so long an interval that David had an idea that the Governor might have fainted dead away. But presently his voice came through again, as stiff and precise as ever. "Extraordinary business," he said. "I suppose we should make an announcement."

"Yes, sir," said David.

"You make it, there's a good fellow," said the Governor, as though struck with a thoroughly constructive idea. "Wait until twelve o'clock. Then just say that the *aboura* is canceled."

"When will you be leaving Gamate, sir?"

"Tonight," answered the Governor. "Informally."

"It's just about twelve o'clock," said David awkwardly. "I'd better make that announcement."

"Very well," said the Governor. "And thank you, David. You've really been awfully useful."

David turned away from the telephone. He looked at Keith Crump, now comfortably settled in an armchair.

"Poor old boy," said Crump, without a great deal of feeling. "Was he very depressed?"

"Difficult to tell," answered David. He felt in a sudden mood of formal, heroic determination. Someone had to make a good end to this fiasco. That someone had better be himself. "What's the Maula phrase," he asked, "for 'the *aboura* is canceled'?"

"That's easy," answered Crump, grinning. *"Aboura i faanga."*

"Aboura i faanga," said David.

"Fine," said Crump. "That's one you'd better memorize."

It must be, thought David, at least two minutes after twelve. He stepped out on the balcony into the bright midday sun. The *aboura* ground was still defiantly empty. At the lower end, the correspondents were all watching him. He switched on the microphone. There was no reason for delay.

"I have an official announcement to make." His echoing voice swept the deserted space. "The *aboura* is canceled. The *aboura* is canceled." Then he braced himself, enunciating with almost Parisian delicacy: *"Aboura i faanga. Aboura i faanga."*

On that night in Pharamaul, the focus of violence was naturally the town of Gamate. There, men had something to celebrate, and celebrate they did, with a wicked edge to their rejoicing which no sober thought could curb. The whole *aboura* was given over to riot; riot by torchlight, with shrieks, and savage dancing, and the burning of huts and buildings in a wild circle of flame.

On that night, the pressmen in Gamate worked late, and then ventured out in a body to see what was to be seen, and then returned to their hotel, eager to commit further morsels of public information to thirsty type. *On that night,* Katsaula lay deep in fever, and Seralo, the oldest of the Regents, turned his face to the wall, wishing to shut out forever the evil sounds that smote his old ears; and Puero, in drunken exultation, led the wildest of the young men in a roaring foray against the hut of a headman who had refused to join in the boycott, and burned him and his wife and his two children alive.

On that night in Pharamaul, the calmest and coolest man was probably the Governor and Commander in Chief, Sir Elliott Vere-Toombs, as he sat in his private railway carriage, sipping weak whisky and water, and leafing through a pile of telegrams, while the train made its slow way southwards to Port Victoria.

His thoughts were not especially troubled, and certainly not angry. He had no hard feelings about the day's events; the deliberate affront to his dignity was not really important, except insofar as it gave a clue to the grave state of affairs in Gamate. He took out his slim gold pencil and jotted down four short phrases, noting wryly the number of question marks. He wrote:

> Dinamaula to remain out
> Martial law? If necessary
> More police? Bring in troops?
> Macmillan, sick leave?

The Governor had left Andrew Macmillan, his Resident Commissioner, depressed and grimly apologetic. He was not at all sure about Macmillan, who had proved himself, in the past, a strong and capable man. But a strong man in decay was worse than any other sort of man, because his reputation promised something which he could not now deliver. He could not quite make up his mind about Andrew; he was glad that he had left David Bracken behind in Gamate, under the general heading of "liaison."

On that night in Pharamaul — but far to the north in Shebiya, in the U-Maula country — Tom Ronald, the District Officer, and Cynthia, his wife, were washing up the dishes after supper. It was the one night in the week that their houseboy, Samson, took off about four in the afternoon, and did not reappear until next morning. No hardship was involved thereby. Tom and Cynthia Ronald liked washing up. They liked anything they did together.

Cynthia Ronald soaped and rinsed, Tom Ronald dried. It was hot and steamy in the kitchen, hot and steamy outside; the only sounds were from the garden — sounds of frogs in the weed-covered pond at the lower end, sounds of crickets in the bushes, sounds of innumerable insects beating their hearts out against the screen door. Even though, a hundred yards away, the huts of Shebiya huddled close together and a thousand U-Maulas talked or drank or slept, yet the Ronalds' house seemed entirely isolated, a pinpoint of order and life in the middle of a vast malevolent wilderness.

But once again, they did not mind. They had love, mutual pleasure, and hope to sustain them.

"How are you feeling, old girl?" asked Tom Ronald, not for the first time that evening.

Cynthia was looking especially pretty, with an inner glow of contentment and happiness. "Perfect," she answered. "Don't fuss, darling."

"You've got to take care of yourself, you know."

"I know. Darling," she said, holding out a plate for him to dry, "it'll still take nearly *eight* more months."

"All the same," said Tom, "you don't want to overdo things."

"It's only the size of a medium bumblebee now. If that."

"But are you *sure* you oughtn't to rest? I'll finish this lot."

"Darling," said Cynthia, "I love you."

There was an agreeable silence between them. Tom Ronald walked to the screen door and looked out into the darkness of the garden. A few fires flickered in the trees beyond it; for the rest, Shebiya was invisibly curtained by the night. From the doorway, he said over his shoulder, "We ought really to take some leave. Get away from here for a bit."

"It's not a very good moment, is it?"

"No. We'll have to wait, I'm afraid."

"How was Gotwela this afternoon?"

"Bloody-minded, as usual." Tom Ronald sighed. "In fact, even more bloody-minded than usual. He actually had the sauce to ask me if I'd heard about the *aboura* in Gamate."

"What did you say?"

"Told him to shut up."

"Darling," said Cynthia, turning as she laid down the last dripping pan on the draining board, "Gotwela's not going to be difficult, is he?"

"He *is* difficult. They all are, at the moment. Probably it'll all pass off; usually does. But there's an undercurrent, all the time."

"When does Father Schwemmer get here?"

"Sometime next week. Why?"

"Perhaps they need a pep talk. He's so good with them, and you know how they love him."

On that night in Pharamaul, not all lovers were together. Tom and Cynthia Ronald might pass an evening of happy domesticity; but in a flat in the trim residential suburb of Port Victoria, Nicole Steuart was lonely and forlorn.

On that night, she missed David very much, even though he was away, according to plan, for less than forty-eight hours. She was comforted by the fact that, this time tomorrow, he would be back in Port Victoria again, back in her arms.

Hurry back! she thought, as she shed her light silk robe, and climbed into bed; hurry back, she thought, her long legs sliding to the foot of the bed, her hand on the switch of the bedside lamp. When the telephone rang, and she heard David's voice from far away, she thought for a moment that she must have already fallen asleep, and that this was a tantalizing dream.

"But darling!" she said, aghast, when she realized fully that it was David who was speaking. "Where are you? Why aren't you in the train?"

"I've got to stay here," David told her glumly. He was sitting in a narrow passageway between the Residency sitting room and the kitchen, trying not to disturb the household. Andrew had just shuffled wearily off to bed; Johannes had long ago shut the kitchen door behind him as he made for his quarters across the rear court-yard. David's voice sounded, to himself, unnaturally loud in the stillness. "The *aboura* didn't come off. No one turned up. H.E. wanted one of the staff to keep in direct touch with things here, so I'm staying on."

"Oh," said Nicole, inadequately.

Disappointed for many reasons, feeling lost and lonely, she turned to what was uppermost in her mind. "I was counting the hours, darling, I was counting the *miles.* You should have been more than halfway here, by now."

"Well, it proves one thing," said David.

"What?" asked Nicole.

"It's time we were married."

"Yes. It certainly proves that. Darling," Nicole said, relaxing, "don't go away for a long time. Tell me *everything* that's happened."

On that night in Pharamaul, in the same town of Port Victoria,
four men slipped furtively into the hallway of a house down by
the dock area. Zuva Katsaula identified himself to a man who
stood sentinel. Then, detaching himself from his bodyguard, he
climbed the stairs swiftly, alone, and knocked at the door of the
darkened landing above. A voice called, "Come in," and Dinamaula, his cousin, stood up as he entered.

"*Ahsula,*" said Dinamaula formally.

"*Ahsula,*" returned Zuva, on a conspiratorial note, as he came
forward. He jerked his head behind him. "I've left the boys downstairs. O.K.?"

"As you will," said Dinamaula. "I am free to receive visitors.
There are no restrictions."

Zuva, coming farther forward, looked round the room, the room
of the hereditary chieftain of Pharamaul. It was shabby and bare,
the bed was narrow and iron-framed, the tables and chairs were
fashioned of rickety split bamboo.

It was hard for Zuva to recognize Dinamaula, his cousin, Dinamaula whose title was Prince of Gamate, Ruler and Kingbreaker,
in the weary, defeated young man who stood before him.

But Zuva was not the man to acknowledge defeat, when the
situation called for something else. "Cheer up!" he said, with all
the confidence he could muster. "Things are really happening!
From now on, you don't have to worry at all."

"What things?" asked Dinamaula. His natural dignity was un-
diminished, but it was as if he did not know friend from foe, and
would never again trust either.

"The *aboura* in Gamate was a hell of a flop!" Zuva told him
gleefully. "The poor old Governor went up there, swords and
feathers and everything, and no one turned up at all! Man, that
must have been really something!"

"Tell me what took place," said Dinamaula, using the formal
Maula phrases, "today in the town of Gamate."

Zuva set to work to tell him, drawing freely on his imagination,
painting a derisive picture of authority mocked, tribal solidarity
triumphant, mutiny in the ascendant. For many a young man in
Dinamaula's place, it would have made a happy picture, promising

great hopes and great changes; for Dinamaula, it seemed to come as confirmation of his worst fears. His only comment at the end was, "I wonder what Mr. Macmillan thinks of all this."

"You don't have to worry about Macmillan, or anyone else," said Zuva. "I tell you, the whole tribe's behind you. All they want is a lead towards the next step."

"What lead?" Dinamaula's expression was blankly resigned. "I live in this room. I cannot talk to my people, I cannot succeed as chief. I have to report to the police, once every day. What lead can I give?"

Zuva looked at him. The aura of defeat was overwhelming, but still he persevered.

"All the people are ready," he maintained stoutly. "They are ready here in Port Victoria. They are waiting for you in Gamate. And in Shebiya — " he paused " — they have taken an oath to drive out the white man, and make you chief of all Pharamaul."

For the first time, Dinamaula looked at him with full attention. "I have heard of such an oath," he said quietly. "Gotwela may wish to drive out the white man. He does *not* wish to see me chief."

"That will follow," said Zuva uncertainly.

"It will not follow," said Dinamaula. "And the oath?" His eyes were steady and searching. "You have taken that oath?"

"Yes," answered Zuva.

"I have heard," said Dinamaula, "that the oath is an oath for animals and savages."

"It is an oath to bind friends," Zuva answered uneasily. "You need friends. Gotwela could be a friend. When you are back in the Chair of Rule in Gamate, we can decide such small details."

"I will never return to the Chair of Rule with such friends. I would not wish to do so. Above all," said Dinamaula, "I do not want to drive out the white man. Part of this country belongs by right to the white man, and to white Government. There would be no Pharamaul today without the white man."

"Or the black man."

"Or the black man. But the one does not drive out the other. They work together. There is no need for the oaths of animals, or talk of driving out."

Zuva stood up. "I do not agree," he said hardly. He could not gauge what had changed Dinamaula so greatly; a few days in solitude seemed to have turned him (in the Maula phrase) into a man with a white heart. "This is a class struggle," he declared. "The forces of reaction cannot stand in the way of progress."

"I also want progress," said Dinamaula. His tiredness was flooding into full possession. "I never wanted to drive out the white man. I wanted quicker progress in Pharamaul. I wanted to prepare my people for the time when the white men would shake our hands, and wish us well in our ruling."

"While you have been thinking these strange thoughts," said Zuva contemptuously, "your friends have been acting and fighting. In Shebiya, they have taken the solemn oath. In Gamate, they have refused to greet the Governor. And here in Port Victoria — " he smiled, as if conscious of playing a trump card " — here, there is actually, on this very evening, a strike."

"A strike?" repeated Dinamaula, surprised. "What strike is this? Where is the strike?"

"Where else," said Zuva, "but in the Pharamaul Club itself?"

On that night, in the Pharamaul Club in Port Victoria, things were going splendidly. It was Friday, and the occasion was the fortnightly club dance; everyone was there, as they always were, and everything was going with a swing, as it always did, fortnight after fortnight. The band, the Port Victoria Moonbeam Downbeats, played manfully, for hour after hour. They were colloquially known as the "Deadbeats," but it was generally conceded that they didn't play too badly.

The club bar was the habitual focus of all these fortnightly dances, and tonight gin, which had long been the essential fuel in Pharamaul, flowed across the counter in an uninterrupted spate. At the receiving end of this cataract were the masculine elite of the Pharamaul Club, who talked, argued, reordered drinks, shook dice, and sang merry songs. They sang "Tipperary," "Mademoiselle from Armentières," "Pack Up Your Troubles," and "Good Night, Sweetheart." They talked about England, Dinamaula, women, football, business, golf, and sex.

But that night — so cheerful, so secure, so traditional — was not, after all, to be like other nights. At one moment there were two Maula barmen and three aides, ready and adroit behind the bar; and then, almost before anyone noticed, there was no one behind the bar at all — no one serving, no one collecting dirty glasses, no one washing up.

Men hammered on the counter for quite a long time before they realized that there was nobody to hammer at. They sang and thumped out, "We want a drink!" to the tune of the Lohengrin Wedding March. Nothing happened. Presently, bereft, they straggled back to their tables on the dance floor, to their wives, daughters, business associates, enemies, only to be greeted by matching cries of woe.

From here also the tide had gone out, disgracefully, unbelievably. The bandstand was empty. The piano was shut, the cello leant coldly against the tenor saxophone. Farther out, extending the glacial ring, the tables were unattended. Not a waiter was in sight.

"But it's incredible!"

"They must have mistaken the time."

"Bloody Dinamaula!"

"But what I can't understand is, how they could *dare?*"

"One thing I do know, old boy, things can't go on like this."

Chapter 9

FIVE THOUSAND miles away, in London, inside the gloomy citadel of the Scheduled Territories Office, Crossley, the Assistant Under-Secretary, stood reading from some notes he had prepared for the Permanent Under-Secretary, Sir Hubert Godbold, who sat opposite him beyond the broad, scarlet-topped desk.

"Three more Parliamentary Questions on Pharamaul, sir. They boil down to this: First, how long are we going to keep Dinamaula away from Gamate? Second, when will he be proclaimed chief? Third, how long will the state of emergency continue?"

"M'm." Godbold ruminated. "Who's asking them, this time?"

"The first two are Price-Canning's. But the third one is from George Bellows." Bellows was a sedate Conservative back-bencher.

Godbold raised his eyebrows. "Bellows? I'm surprised. What's he getting interested in this for?"

Crossley pursed his lips somewhat primly. "Pharamaul has gone beyond the usual crackpot stage, sir. All sorts of people are involving themselves in it. And I think we all recognize that we're vulnerable. People generally don't like the ban on Dinamaula's movements. The press is dead against it, of course. They still maintain that we tricked him into leaving Gamate. I think that fairly soon we've got to say how long he's going to be kept away."

Godbold set his jaw. "He'll be kept away until things calm down. If they don't calm down, he'll be kept away — full stop. That's our policy, in two sentences."

He waited for comment from Crossley, but there was none.

"That being so," Godbold went on after a moment, "I think we'll give pretty short answers to those three Parliamentary Questions." He held out his hand, and Crossley passed him the single sheet of notes. " 'How long are we going to keep Dinamaula away from Gamate?' " he read out briskly. "As long as is considered necessary, for the maintenance of public order. 'When will he be proclaimed chief?' This is not an appropriate moment to forecast the date of such a development. 'How long will the state of emergency continue?' I would refer the honorable member to my answer to the first question."

Crossley, who had been noting down the replies, looked up as Godbold finished speaking. He was secretly appalled by the curtness of the replies, but this was one tide which he was not, at that moment, prepared to stem.

When the Assistant Under-Secretary had gone, with a markedly harassed expression, Godbold found his assured mood melting into anxiety. He did not think that his policy over Dinamaula, so far, was in the least "vulnerable" — that is, susceptible of defeat on valid grounds. But Crossley's "vulnerable" meant something quite different; it meant untenable in the face of determined criticism, unpopular, liable to lose friends. It meant that heads might roll, careers falter, strong men trip and fall, bringing lesser men, who chanced to be near them, crashing to the ground at the same time.

Godbold acknowledged to himself that the dictated replies were risky. But they were morally essential, and therefore had to be made. All that mattered was the *manner* of their delivery. Somehow he had to find a way, for the *nth* time, to stiffen the sinews of that forlorn old scarecrow, the Secretary of State for the Scheduled Territories Office, Lord Lorde.

THE FOLLOWING evening, Godbold listened to the debate in Commons from the customary civil-service vantage point: the modest cubbyhole at the southeast corner of the Chamber, to the right of the Speaker's chair and directly underneath the press gallery. During his first question, Price-Canning was, as usual, abusive, unfair and damnably clever. As usual Lord Lorde was ponderous and ineffective. Bellows' contribution was slight.

Full-dress debates were something which Godbold always enjoyed, whichever way they went, and however deep was his own involvement. There was really nothing like the House of Commons, the world's most civilized and most critical forum. Even the physical attributes of the Chamber contributed to the same sense of historic assessment; the splendid paneling, the unequaled acoustics, the opulent yet serviceable dark-green leather of the benches — these were the true trappings of consequence, the essential décor of the Mother of Parliaments.

Meanwhile, there was *this* particular debate. So far, it had gone as he had known it would go; the right wing had made comforting noises, the left had thundered and wailed about the rights of man. But, gauging the mood of the House, Godbold was uneasy.

Emrys Price-Canning, who had been conserving his energies for the final assault, would be the next member to catch the Speaker's eye.

Price-Canning started slowly, as he always did when he knew he was onto a good thing.

"The House has listened," he said, "with what I take leave to call cynical impatience, to those apologists for the Government who have tried to excuse what we are doing in Pharamaul. *They* say, there's a crisis in Pharamaul, and they have to take emergency measures and emergency powers. *They* say, Dinamaula is the cause of all this, and so Dinamaula has to be kept out of the way,

indefinitely. *They* say, just leave it to us, and to our lads on the spot, and everything will be all right." He drew an impatient breath, and gestured with a wide, sweeping, satirical motion. *"I* say, and I hope the House will follow me, that there's not a tittle of evidence to justify all this strong-arm stuff, and that if we do leave it to the lads on the spot we are automatically abdicating our right of directing Britain's colonial policy. There's another word for abdication, an ugly word, and that word is *cowardice!"*

In the slight pause that followed, the stir of reaction to the strong staccato thrust of "cowardice," Godbold pulled a pad towards him and scribbled three sentences. "Plenty of evidence of threats and violence affecting public order," he wrote. "Nine murders and countless riots already. Quite enough to justify emergency measures." Then he initialed it and, folding it over, passed it to a messenger to give to Lord Lorde.

Price-Canning was building towards his peroration, demanding that the Government admit its mistakes, bring back Dinamaula and make him chief. "And when we have the guts to do this — " he looked round him, and then directly at Lord Lorde " — I hope the right honorable gentleman opposite will have the grace to admit that he has been stampeded into hasty action, by three things: bad advice, rumors of disturbance, and rumors of a marriage which, if it reflects anything at all, reflects great credit on the womanhood of Britain."

It was typical of Price-Canning — colloquial, gross, and infinitely effective. When he sat down, flushed and trembling, the ground swell of "Hear! Hear!" seemed to sound, for the Government side, the knell of their policy.

Price-Canning, having bowed and withdrawn beyond the bar of the Chamber, was the center of a tight knot of people, whispering and conferring. It was, patently, a moment of balance.

Godbold was deeply worried, and he was not the only one to be so. As a stopgap speaker droned on, he noticed a single, silent, withdrawn figure, standing in the artificial twilight behind the Speaker's chair, listening with extreme concentration to the course of the debate. It was the Prime Minister.

It happened that the two of them were friends of long standing; indeed, they had been up at Oxford together, nearly forty years earlier. They dined together approximately once a month.

"Well, Hubert," said the P.M.

"Good evening, Prime Minister," returned Godbold. "An interesting debate."

"Fascinating."

Since they knew each other so well, there was an atmosphere of absolute truth and reality in their exchanges.

"This is going badly," said the Prime Minister. "Damned badly. You're absolutely sure of your facts?"

"Yes, sir. There's deep unrest in the tribe, and the possibility of more bloodshed. Dinamaula focuses it, whether innocently or not. He must be kept out."

"I thought your replies to the Parliamentary Questions were a little on the brusque side."

"Yes," conceded Godbold honestly. "We might have wrapped them up a bit. Or used a better tone. I left that to Lord Lorde. It didn't work."

"What do you want him to say now?"

"Just to stick to the brief. Be consistent and firm. He might even say — " Godbold paused, knowing that what he suggested now was almost certain to be passed on to Lord Lorde " — he might even start by saying he's sorry."

"Weak," said the P.M. "Dangerous."

"Worth taking a chance, though. If he could just — " Godbold gestured " — just sound perfectly frank, perfectly reasonable, but convinced that we *have* to do what we're doing in the interests of public order. Ask for a chance to prove that he's right."

"It might buy us a breathing space. But is time on our side? In Pharamaul?"

"We need a breathing space there, too."

The Prime Minister nodded and straightened up. "All right. I'll tell him. Come and see me tomorrow morning."

He walked, with a firm step, towards his place on the Front Bench, and then, passing his accustomed seat, sat down beside Lord Lorde, and fell into deep and earnest conversation with the Secretary of State.

To MANY members of the House of Commons, Lord Lorde's speech-in-reply was the best thing he had ever done. In any case, it was a big surprise, and to Godbold especially, deeply committed to success or defeat in this debate, it came as an astonishing relief. Evidently the Prime Minister must have spoken to some purpose.

Lord Lorde began by apologizing for the apparent brusqueness of his earlier answers.

This opening was so well done, with so genuine an air of contrition, that it had a remarkable effect on the House. They had not expected an honest admission of guilt, paving the way for an honest stand on principle. For the majority, it reopened a question on which they had already made up their minds. That, for the Government, was the first major gain of the evening.

There were many others, though it was not a long speech, nor as detailed and labored in rebuttal as most Ministerial efforts tended to be. It was simply an exercise in the art of persuasion. Lord Lorde dealt first with Price-Canning's own plea for a reversal of policy in Pharamaul.

"There is," he said, quoting almost verbatim the note which Godbold had passed on to him earlier, "ample evidence of threats and violence affecting public order. I need not remind the House that there have been nine murders, and countless riots, already. We must, on our side, regard this as quite enough to justify the emergency measures we have taken. In such an explosive situation, we have a clear duty to safeguard life and property. Part of that duty, regrettable though it may seem, has necessitated the detention of Dinamaula in Port Victoria. I should perhaps add that he is *not* being kept away because of the rumors of his intended marriage to a white girl, though it is perfectly true that the prospect of such a mixed marriage has shocked and divided the tribe. Dinamaula has been removed because his expressed opinions, and some of his actions, and some of the actions of his immediate followers, have contributed directly to tribal unrest. The Maulas are split. Their minds and loyalties are confused. It is our task now to compose and heal these differences, these confusions."

Concluding, the Minister said, "In this matter of Pharamaul, I would ask the House to reserve judgment, and give us a chance to prove we are right. I would ask them to help us by watching the position carefully, as we ourselves shall watch it."

It was at that point that the debate faded out, like a brief summer storm, on an astonishing note of anticlimax. Though earlier it had seemed a very near thing, at the end there was, throughout the Chamber, a patent willingness to suspend judgment, to wait and see. That was all Godbold had wanted — the breathing space he had prayed for.

THE WEATHER did not help much. Often, at this time of the year, it grew oppressive, discouraging all personal enterprise, from love-making to petty larceny. But now, as if to demonstrate which side was the side of the angels, it turned a little cooler; and Pharamaul, freed from a 95-degree noon temperature and a brutal humidity, gave itself afresh to the delights of popular demonstration. Throughout the length and breadth of the land, men stirred, and looked about them, and rose early to raise hell.

In Port Victoria, the native population was much heartened by the success of the strike at the club, and especially by its aftermath — acquiescence to the Maulas' demands for a ten-shilling increase in wages. It was on these ignoble terms that the Pharamaul Club got under way again. In the entire course of their adult lives, the members had never had to do without their club, and it was too late to start now.

As a strike, it had perceptible elements of humor; but in another part of the town, the dock area, there was a strike of another sort, with very different implications. It started with a water-front brawl, involving some sailors off a small South African coastal freighter, and a Maula stevedore. The Maula was shot through the head, and his killing sparked a murderous riot.

At dawn the following day, after a mass meeting at the dockside, every single Maula employed in the dock area walked off the job and vanished without trace into the town.

It all seemed so well organized that it fitted naturally and inevitably into the current mutinous pattern of Pharamaul. It was something for the police, something for the town council, above all, something for the Governor.

After an emergency meeting with his advisors, the Governor, as a first step, tried to find out who was behind it all. He failed utterly in this search; so did the police. Dinamaula disclaimed all knowledge; his cousin Zuva returned a blank, impertinent negative to all inquiries, while his "bodyguard" smirked and rolled their eyes. At the end, Zuva said, as if contributing something of value, "Perhaps they do not choose to work for murderers."

And one of the bodyguard, a short scarred man with a look of inward violence, said, "Perhaps they want their chief."

The harbor continued dead and forlorn, while the city merchants fumed and perishable cargo rotted on the quayside.

The Governor, after an abortive conference with the police, decided that there was nothing to be done. It must surely be better to wait and see if the thing would blow over, rather than to make himself and the police and the town councilors ridiculous by searching for men who did not seem to be there at all. And what he had to deal with was only a shadow of what now began to happen, two hundred miles to the northwards, in Gamate.

"They are killing our own brothers, in the town beside the sea" — so ran the message that sped from mouth to mouth, and from hut to hut in Gamate, an hour or so before Forsdick, the District Commissioner, read an urgent telegram beginning: "Disturbances in the dock area have led to a strike affecting port facilities." To Forsdick, a dock strike in Port Victoria seemed of precious little account; if that were the only thing they had to worry about down in Government House, he thought sourly, they could count themselves pretty well off. But to Gamate itself, already stretched to a fearful tension, plagued by rumors and strange visitors, the news from the south, presented as it was in terms of bloodshed and oppression, made glorious all that they dared to do. Any man in Pharamaul could now strike any blow, provided it was a strong blow against tyranny. Had they not been told by the men who wrote on machines that the whole world was watching them?

For David Bracken, the Governor's personal observer in Gamate, the focus was Keith Crump. Together they covered many miles each day, improvising, weaving new plans of action out of the confused air. Together they struck many blows, held many conferences, looked down on many dead men, watched much blood flow, and dodged many weapons.

David lived at the Residency, and his relationship with Macmillan was cordial and uncomplicated. But Macmillan seemed to have retreated into the shadows, from whence he witnessed, mutely impotent, the destruction of his whole working life. Tribal affairs were at a standstill; to take their place, a senseless destruction possessed all but a few Maulas. Stemming this, spearheading the counterthrust of order and discipline, Captain Crump of the Royal Pharamaul Police seemed like a lone heroic figure, molded for this single purpose from some indestructible fiber.

A dozen times each night, Crump, at the head of his police patrol, had to break up a riot, rescue hostages, defend a threatened strong point, give safe-conduct to a doctor or a nurse or a Government official. There came a time when, in one period of twenty-four hours, five huts were burned; Father Schwemmer's mission church was broken into, stripped, and defiled; some cattle, seized for unpaid taxes, were maimed and had to be destroyed; two men were shot by a sentry while trying to steal the key to the jail; a gang of simple-minded thugs breached the retaining wall of the Gamate dam, and let two months' rainfall escape in muddy chaos; and a wagon, overturned in reprisal for some fainthearted support from its owner, crushed to death the four children sleeping in its shadow.

All over the town every man's hand was against his neighbor's, every white skin was a lordly enemy, every black skin was suspect, for the first time within living memory. The careful cherishing of black by white that had been the rule for many generations was abandoned; in its place, a poisonous mistrust flourished, reaching its extreme form in many normal homes, where, when men and women sat down at table, they added to the knives and forks and spoons a new essential for the peaceful enjoyment of food — a revolver.

It was against such a background that Andrew Macmillan, the Resident Commissioner, made his last appeal to the three Regents of the Maulas.

As HE waited in the dusk — it was always dusk, there was no more true sunlight for him in Gamate — with a cup of coffee at his elbow, and David Bracken, ill at ease, in a chair opposite him, Macmillan knew the depth of his personal defeat. He no longer believed in what he was doing. Remote and lonely, he knew that he had failed both his own men and the Maulas.

There could be no more desolate end to any reign. It was the ultimate disgrace, the overthrow of a man's professional striving. But it was imminently at hand. He said, turning awkwardly and heavily in his chair, "More coffee, David?"

"No, thanks, Andrew." David, oppressed by the moment, summoned a warm response. "But that was very good coffee. I suppose these chaps should be here, any minute now."

"If they come at all."

"Oh, surely."

"Last time, they were all ill." Andrew lay back again, exhausted and spent. "When you get back," he said, his voice matching his defeated face, "tell H.E. something from me, will you?"

"Whatever you say." David reacted forebodingly to the fateful tone of voice. "But I hope you'll be telling him yourself."

"*You* tell him — when it's all over. Tell him that *originally* I was right about Dinamaula — he was trying to move too fast. Tell him to keep Seralo where he is, as senior Regent — the tribe will trust him. Tell him, after it's all over, that Dinamaula *could* come back as chief. In due course. With appropriate safeguards. At the moment, he's pure poison, from our point of view. But later on, he should make a perfectly good chief. *If* he doesn't go through with the marriage, of course."

Out of a deep disquiet, David said, "But couldn't you say something of the sort, now? Couldn't you tell the Regents what you think, hold out some sort of hope?"

Andrew shook his head. "No. There's a pattern to be gone through." Though exhausted still, Andrew Macmillan's voice seemed to be gaining strength. "Even if I can't quite understand it myself. I know, as clearly and strongly as anything in my life, that it would be fatal to reverse our policy at this moment, and bring Dinamaula back. Even apart from the marriage, he doesn't deserve it. He's not ready for it. Before that happens, more people have to be disciplined. More lessons have to be taught. Perhaps more people have to die." He was staring again at the shadowed garden, the loaded dusk of Gamate. "I don't know why I'm talking like this to you," Andrew said, his voice far removed from normal, "except that I trust you — trust you to sort it all out — and I don't think you'll take advantage of it. These things," he said, with latent energy, "are all for the future. They're not for tonight, and not for tomorrow. Tonight, and tomorrow, we have to play it out as it lies at the moment."

There was a noise behind them, and Johannes, Andrew's old servant, shuffled in on bare feet. His voice when he spoke was full of suppressed importance.

"*Barena,*" he said.

"Yes, Johannes?" said Macmillan.

"Three men come to see you, *barena.*"

"Three *men?*" repeated Macmillan reprovingly.

"The Regents of the tribe, *barena,*" said Johannes.

IT WAS not a short meeting, but its outcome was as short as a single word — the word "no."

Seralo, old, conservative, puzzled like Andrew Macmillan himself, conveyed this answer by a feeble indecision of manner; Katsaula, the formalist, by a blank refusal to act at all in circumstances so unorthodox. It was left to fat, gross Puero, clearly the man of the moment, to phrase the tribe's rejection of the rule of law, and this he did with crude and insolent relish.

After repetitive and futile argument Andrew turned once more to Seralo, sitting shrunken and forlorn by his side. "You know well what is in my mind, old man," he said, his tone somewhat gentler. "Will you not help me to bring back order?"

"I cannot," answered Seralo, on a querulous note. "The tribe will not listen to me."

"Will you not help me, Katsaula?" asked Andrew again.

"I will help you," answered Katsaula, with dignity, "on the day that Dinamaula, our chief, is anointed and enthroned, in accordance with the custom."

"That will not happen, for a long time. What about you, Puero?"

"There can be no order without the chief," said Puero, with uncouth emphasis. "He must return — that is the price of our help. But when Dinamaula returns, *he* will rule, not you. Therefore you will not need help. You will not be here."

David, who sat a little apart, was watching Andrew Macmillan at that moment; he saw a dull acceptance of Puero's insolence come down on the other man's face. He was no longer resisting. In a flash of intuition, David Bracken realized that it was he himself who must bring this wretched interview to an end. He stood up, his chair scraping loudly on the floor of the stoep. As the others turned towards him, "I think that's about as far as we can go," he said, with a determination he was scarcely feeling. "The Resident Commissioner has other matters to attend to."

"I — " began Andrew, and then stopped.

"But what is going to happen?" asked Puero, puzzled.

"You will be informed," answered David dismissively. "The meeting is ended."

The others had all risen. "But suppose," said Seralo uncertainly, "that there are more disturbances in Gamate?"

"We will bring order," answered David. "With or without your help. The meeting is ended." He felt an absurd sense of sureness and authority, as he sat down next to Andrew Macmillan again. Then he watched, with singular, childish pleasure, as the three Regents, after an uncertain pause, passed in procession through the door of the stoep and out into the Residency garden.

Presently, the lonely, withdrawn figure by his side stirred to life again, breaking the charged silence. "Thanks, David," said Macmillan. "I don't know what the hell's the matter with me tonight."

He sounded so spiritless, so utterly defeated, that David asked, "Are you feeling all right, Andrew?"

"I don't know what's the matter with me tonight," Andrew repeated. "Too much paper work, I suppose." His voice was taut.

"How about getting some sleep?" said David anxiously.

"You go off, if you like," answered Andrew, in the same measured, economical voice. "I've got some papers to look at. I won't be long. Do you want a nightcap?"

David, rising from his chair, shook his head. "I don't think so. Can I get you anything?"

"No, thanks. A bit later, maybe. Good night."

When David Bracken had gone to his room, Macmillan also rose and walked slowly into his study. On his desk was the loose-leaf manuscript of his book about Pharamaul. Opening the tattered, thumbed-over pages at random, he read thus, "The Governor of Pharamaul was much assailed by contemporary critics, in and out of Parliament, for his action in summoning troops to back up his authority; but at this distance of time, it is safe to say that the move was fully justified. We can see now that, in its task of maintaining order, the civil arm had failed, and had to be reinforced."

Andrew Macmillan sighed, deeply and painfully. Also on his desk was the red-tabbed file of that day's telegrams from Government House. The one on top — the latest to be received — was the one he was looking for. He read:

> I propose to proceed with plan for moving in troops at battalion strength from Kenya. They should be in Territory within four or five days. Dispositions will be discussed by commanding officer with you and Crump on arrival. Acknowledge.

Andrew Macmillan reached down and opened the top drawer of his desk, and took out his revolver. He said aloud, "I'm just going for a walk." The sentence, defiantly spoken, explained and excused the revolver, though it excused it only in a shameful context — the Resident Commissioner was going for an after-dinner stroll in his own territory of Gamate, and he had to take his revolver with him.

WHAT HAD started as a nearly innocent stroll, with only slight undertones of desolation and despair, quickly became a nightmare. The Residency garden was now wholly dark; beyond it, the rough bushland that sloped gently down towards the town of Gamate was unknown territory, full of traps and snares. As he buffeted his way onwards, tripping, pausing, Andrew Macmillan fell deeper into a desperate and futile expense of energy.

This was his evening walk, the reasonable man's respite from the cares of office; he was going to take his evening walk, even if he killed himself in the process. He forced his way on, panting, knowing that he had lost the path.

He came suddenly to a stop, this time not because of the rough impassable country, but because of the thought which had been troubling him. He had wrestled a long time with Pharamaul: first as a young man, full of hope and high resolve; then in his maturity, when his long efforts seemed to be returning a sober profit, and then as a man old in years and in responsibility. But the cutting truth was that, though he had wrestled, he had lost; Gamate, now become a murderous jungle like the jungle that hedged him in, had made no inch of progress under his rule, had returned no profit at all. Instead, it had swallowed him alive.

He stood exhausted in a stockade of tall coarse grass and impenetrable thornbush. His head began to swim and to pound. It was the old onset of death, the thing the doctor had talked about when he had had a minor heart attack some months before. Breathe deeply, the doctor had said. Breathe deeply, and lie down till it passes.

He could not lie down, nor sit down; in sober fact, he could not breathe either. Whatever it was, he must meet it standing up, on his own two feet, in the land of Pharamaul. The whole upper part of his body was leaden. Especially, his right hand weighed heavy. It was the revolver.

Knowing that he was doing wrong, sinning against instinct, not caring any more, deep in pain and defeat, he pressed the revolver against his stomach and squeezed the trigger, once and then again.

It was Johannes who discovered the body, for a body it had now become. Andrew Macmillan, sometime Resident Commissioner in the Principality of Pharamaul, had bled to death from two cavernous and fearful wounds.

Finding Macmillan's room empty when he brought the early-morning tea, the old servant had gone out alone to find his master. The faint light, growing stronger, revealed with desolate clarity the last walk of the Resident Commissioner. Johannes, his face a

brooding mask of pain and fear, followed it at a determined shuffle.

Here had the wandering *barena* stopped. Here, waist-high in *tambuki* grass, he had forced a pathway. Here he had stopped again, then plunged headlong into impenetrable bush. Here was a slashed clearing, heavy with ill omen. And here was the *barena*.

Andrew Macmillan lay where he had fallen, crouched over his gun, decently shielding his torn body from sight. Dew was on his back, and a misty shroud of cobweb.

Johannes said aloud, "Oh, *barena,* hear me now," and abandoned himself to bitter weeping.

"Macmillan died as he lived," tapped out Tulbach Browne later, "beating about the bush." But having written it, somewhat gaily, with frequent pauses for refreshment, he did not send it. The old baron who owned the *Daily Thresh,* and therefore owned Tulbach Browne, was against death; he had had two strokes already, and the subject had to be treated seriously.

Instead: "Let us not speak ill of the dead . . ." said the *Daily Thresh* leader, a day later. "But let us not glorify the legacy they leave behind them, either, if that legacy is an embarrassment and disgrace to us.

"The death of Mr. Macmillan affords an excellent opportunity to reverse the poisonous policy, pursued under the shoddy banner of colonialism, which will for all time be associated with his name."

It was the signal for disintegration. To many men, black and white alike, Andrew Macmillan had been a legendary figure, for two and three generations; indeed, there was no one in Gamate, young or old, whose life he had not touched. Now he was gone; it was as if a linchpin had been withdrawn from a wheel, or a span from a bridge.

During the two days between his death and his burial, in the dusty plot behind Father Schwemmer's mission house, an eerie stillness hung over Gamate. But it was the very last moment of such decent forbearance; indeed, it was among the procession of mourners themselves, streaming down the hill after the burial service, that the signal for revolt to catch ablaze again was given.

They started singing, softly at first, as if they were still affected by the somber occasion. But gradually the singing became louder, and somehow jovial; they seemed to be singing a song of freedom. By nightfall, they were openly rejoicing, drinking, boasting, shouting abuse at all who opposed them, and at all white men wherever they might be. There was no more need to obey, no more law. Law had died with the Resident Commissioner.

Forsdick, stepping into Macmillan's shoes, did his best, struggling manfully against the tide of ruin; Crump wore himself and his men to exhaustion. But the only effective answer to what was happening in Gamate was troops; and the troops, delayed by lack of transport, were still a full two days away from Gamate, when the first white man was killed.

OOSTHUIZEN, packing his wife and seven of their nine children into the cumbersome old station wagon, had no special foreboding as he bade them good-by. His family were taking their annual holiday, to be spent on the coast near Port Victoria. He himself, and his two older sons, would stay on as usual to manage the farm.

The next Saturday, the last day of Oosthuizen's life, started badly. It was the day of the week when by tradition his servants and farm laborers ceased work at midday, and gave themselves over to formal visiting and talk and beer drinking. But before dawn on Saturday morning, one of the farm's storehouses was broken into, and four cases of brandy were stolen and spirited away.

It would have been serious on any occasion; but with the countryside full of wandering Maulas looking for trouble, it could mean a disaster. Angry at the insubordination, Oosthuizen gave orders that work was to continue during all that Saturday afternoon; there was to be no customary holiday, no visiting from hut to hut, and no brewing of beer that night.

It was four o'clock on the same hot afternoon when Kleinbooi, the headman, woke Oosthuizen from his customary Saturday siesta. *"Barena,"* he began, "boys stop work, go back to compound."

"What!" shouted Oosthuizen. "What do you mean, they've stopped work? Just you tell them to get cracking again, or I'll come down with a *sjambok* and tell them myself."

Kleinbooi shook his head. "I tell them already, *barena*. They laugh at me. They drunk on the brandy."

Behind Kleinbooi, two other figures now appeared — Oosthuizen's two sons, Koos and Danie, seventeen and sixteen years old. They were both tow-haired, sun-bleached, barefooted, dressed alike in faded khaki shorts and shirts.

"What's the matter, Pa?" asked Koos, the elder.

"Some bloody nonsense," grumbled Oosthuizen. But he was alerted now. Huge and burly, he stood up, buttoning his rumpled trousers.

"What are you going to do, Pa?" asked Koos. He admired his father unstintingly; he knew that whatever he did would be utterly right. "Can we come with you?"

"No," answered Oosthuizen automatically.

"Oh, *Pa!*" protested Danie, immediately. "Go on, let us! We'll help you, eh?"

"All right," said his father. Soft heart, soft head, he thought to himself. Their mother would never have let them out of the house, at a time like this. But it's just a bit of bloody nonsense, anyway. I'll say two words, down at the compound, and they'll all go back to work. "But just you keep quiet," he cautioned. "Stay behind me, with Kleinbooi, eh, and don't get in my light."

"Be careful, *barena,*" he heard Kleinbooi say. "Much brandy. Boys very drunk."

The evening sun was still brilliant and fierce as the odd, almost patriarchal procession left the house. Oosthuizen was in the lead, huge and lumbering, his heavy boots stirring the dust as he strode determinedly down the garden path; his two sons followed, excited and awed, picking their way barefooted over the rough gravel; his servant, Kleinbooi, completed the Indian file of figures, padding along on calloused black feet, his face brooding and disturbed.

The sun fell, presently, on the outer wall of the main compound. But there it seemed to falter, and to lose its strength; for from within rose a confused and hideous sound, a roar made up of many odious notes — crude laughter, singing, stamping, the beat of drums, the banging of cooking pots, the cracked shouting of furious voices.

Oosthuizen did not falter. He gestured to the others to wait, and then he kicked open the heavy gate, and entered the compound.

It was a wild and ugly scene. The four cases of brandy, broken open and rifled, lay in the center; round them were fifty or sixty of his men, drinking, passing bottles from hand to hand, singing, dancing, shouting in obscene chorus.

Oosthuizen still did not falter, even in the face of a menace which he could closely gauge. He strode forward towards the middle of the compound and the brandy cases. When he came to a stop, he was surrounded by a hostile, graveyard stillness. Oosthuizen, unhesitating, pointed to the brandy cases, and said loudly and roughly, "Put those bottles back!"

No one moved. After a moment, he called over his shoulder: "Kleinbooi!"

Kleinbooi shuffled forward to Oosthuizen's side. *"Barena?"*

"Collect all the bottles. Take them away from those that have them." Oosthuizen suddenly turned, and pointed again, and shouted, "To start with, take *that* bottle away from *that* man!"

He was pointing to a tall Maula, a sweating, swaying, near-naked young man who held a bottle of brandy poised at shoulder height. As Kleinbooi stepped forward, the young man rolled impudent eyes towards him, and then unclasped his hand. The bottle crashed on the hard-beaten floor of the compound, and splintered to fragments. The brandy gushed out, spread momentarily over the hot earth, and was lost.

A roar of laughter rose throughout the compound. Oosthuizen suddenly saw red. He jumped forward towards the laughing Maula nearest to him, drew back his fist, and clubbed him savagely behind the ear. The man went down with an earth-shaking crash, insensible even before he reached the ground. In the startled silence, Oosthuizen shouted again, "I said, put back those bottles!"

As if in answer, a young, tough Maula shouldered his way through, his heavy chest gleaming, his reddened eyes fixed on Oosthuizen's face. He held in his hand, not a bottle, but a long-handled ax, raised already above the level of his neck. Advancing, he growled deep in his throat. The ax rose higher, arching backwards; the man was now within six feet of him, intent on murder. Oosthuizen drew out his revolver, took careful aim, and shot him through the head.

The next few moments should have been full of noise and shouting, but after the initial gasp of anger and dismay they passed in a deadly silence, full of concentrated violence.

Then a press of black bodies bore in upon Oosthuizen with weapons suddenly conjured from the air or the ground — hatchets, sticks, spears, jagged stones. He rose once above the mob, staggering, and shouted wildly to his two sons. "Run, Koosie!" he screamed. "Run. Both of you!" Then he went down again, under a torrent of blows. The two boys began to run and then, as if drawn back by a tightening cord, turned again, and started bravely towards their father. The crowd opened and received them with bloody claws.

It was all done in deadly silence, under the hot sun, with the spilt blood smoking like the flavor of sacrifice.

FAR AWAY in the secret northland, concealed in the forest which closed like a curtain behind their backs, three men met and conferred: Gotwela, chief of the U-Maulas, Puero, third Regent of the Maulas of Gamate, and Zuva Katsaula, cousin and blood brother to Dinamaula himself.

The three men met in secret, in the fronded clearing beside the chief's hut. There were things about each man that each disliked and mistrusted. Gotwela was gross, and a little drunk, and purely savage in his bearing. Puero was suspect because of his years spent as a Regent, under the license of white Government. Zuva was a dubious man, for all his oath-taking; he dressed as the white man dressed, he had traveled to their hated country, he talked of friends from outside.

Yet for all their dislike, their mistrust, their sly and brutish suspicion, they met by agreement, and talked for many hours. And what each man said was heartening, swelling music to the others. Puero talked of matters in Gamate. There, their brothers had risen, he said. The R.C., the Old Judge, had died and his rule was over forever. And another man, a known tyrant, a white farmer who used the whip, had been killed, together with his two sickly sons. Soon, others would die. It only needed a word.

"I have heard these things," said Gotwela.

Zuva, small and energetic, took up the tale. In his own town, far to the south, the white man's town of Port Victoria, all was in ruins. No one worked or went about their business. The merchants were at their wits' end; even the Governor himself walked in fear. It was the end of tyranny, brought about by Zuva himself and his strong army. It only needed a word, to drive the white man into the sea. Thus had he been driven out, from nearly all Africa. Why not from Pharamaul?

"I have heard some of these things also," said Gotwela. His thick lips curled. "But of Dinamaula, your great leader, I have heard nothing."

"Dinamaula," answered Zuva, "is a man no more. We need only

men." And then, as if prompting shy children, "What now?" he continued. "What more do we wait for? Let us strike, together. All three of us." He looked at Gotwela. "Do you agree?"

Gotwela spoke when he was ready, at the end of a long, insolent minute of silence. He spoke as a ruler, and they accepted it.

"I am ready," he declared. "We will strike."

Puero licked his lips. "You have a plan?"

Gotwela eyed him with irony and contempt, the chief eying a man who was not a chief. "I have a plan," he acknowledged. His voice was like the jungle that pressed in on them, a voice deep and threatening. "I have a plan, and I am ready."

Zuva watched Gotwela as he made his declaration; he was disgusted, and touched by misgiving. This man is a savage, he thought. Later there must be a pause, a sorting out of the civilized and the uncivilized. But later. "Then we are all ready," he said.

Gotwela touched the folds of his *simbara,* his royal lion's skin. He eyed Zuva and Puero from under heavy lowered lids. Zuva, the sly, blood-smelling hyena. Puero, the white man's jackal. Such company for a lion. . . . Later, there must be a pause, a pause for the disposal of allies. But later. He said, deep in his throat, "We will make our beginning, here, tonight."

Chapter 10

WHEN THE phone in the Residency rang late in the evening and David heard the faraway voice of Aidan Purves-Brownrigg, calling him from Port Victoria, he felt his spirits lift.

"It's nice to hear your voice," he said in answer to Aidan's greeting. "It's pretty bleak here. How are things at P.V.?"

"The strike's still on. We're all pretty busy. Nicole sent her love, before I forget."

"How about our friend D?" asked David guardedly.

"Won't talk at all. Won't say yes to anything, won't say no. Just says he wants to go home. It's driving the old gentleman completely mad. He asked me to ring you up, by the way, about the press. We've had pages of cabled reports from London, mostly editorial comment raving at us over the martial-law proclamation."

"If they could just take a look at things here!" David's voice was suddenly loud and truculent. "What about Oosthuizen and his kids? What more do they want? We're justified in imposing martial law, ten times over. I'd like to fly a few editors out to Gamate, and then see if they felt safe without it!"

"You sound a bit high-strung," said Aidan.

"I suppose I am," agreed David. He sighed deeply and resignedly. "It was so damned sad about Andrew. I feel as if he's still here. Incidentally, when do our khaki chums arrive?"

"In about twenty-four hours," answered Aidan.

"Good." Then, "What's this about the press, Aidan?"

"London is needling the old gentleman. He thinks we ought to hold a press conference. But the press are all at Gamate, aren't they?"

"Yes," said David. "The little loves."

"So you'd better hold it, yourself, up there."

"Me?" asked David, genuinely surprised. "But what about George Forsdick? He's the obvious person, surely?"

"No. The old gentleman thinks it should be someone on his own personal staff, speaking for him. Just give them a list of things that have gone wrong, here and in Gamate. Sum it all up, and then talk about the obvious dangers that lie in the future. Then say that the whole thing adds up to martial law, and nothing less. That's all we want you to do — just to put our side of the case."

"Well," said David, "I'll have a crack at it. Heaven knows what sort of questions they'll ask, though."

"You have been selected," Aidan said in a fair imitation of the Governor, "because of your singular discretion and iron self-control. Pray do not disappoint us."

Suddenly, David wanted to stop talking, and to be by himself, and to think. "Give my love to Nicole. How is she?"

"Pining." Aidan's voice was fading out, but the word was heart-warming, nonetheless.

David felt possessed by a secret exhilaration; for the first time since the war he had been given something important to do, not because he was the only available man, or the next in line, but because Authority had picked him out as the appropriate choice.

"Be with me, Nicole," he said aloud. "I want you to be proud of me, I want to deserve you. I *have* grown up a bit in the last few months. I *have* changed, and I think it's for the better."

And it seemed undeniably true at that moment as he surveyed the past and present. He had come to the island with nothing much more than a Military Cross to show for the vanished years, and a wish to liberate the blacks. Where was he now? He still had the M.C., honestly earned; but already he realized that most blacks, in Pharamaul at least, were not nearly ready for liberation, and might indeed be destroyed by it.

"Must remember to say that tomorrow," he muttered vaguely. He looked up at the grandfather clock at the end of the room. "Today, that is. Be with me, Nicole. I've got a hell of a job to do."

UNDER the lowering midday sun the pressmen arrived at the Residency. Now they were all gathered in Andrew's sitting room. They had listened with reasonable attention while David made the points which Aidan had suggested over the telephone. Some of them asked questions, without much intensity of purpose; the rest lounged about, fanning themselves against the fierce heat. Then, when the session seemed virtually over, Pikkie Joubert, the South African, suddenly looked up and remarked, "It certainly is a mess, eh? Seems like Macmillan picked the right moment to die."

David stiffened. He said, "I agree that it's a mess. The rest of that remark doesn't seem to me to make much sense."

Pikkie Joubert seemed surprised at the answer. "I meant that it's *his* mess, eh? Only he's not here to clear it up. It makes his career look a bit silly."

Conscious of anger, sorrow, and crude contempt all tumbling over each other in the race for self-expression, David answered: "Andrew Macmillan was a hard-working and devoted public servant. He gave his whole life to this country. No career like that should ever be called silly."

In the electric silence, Tulbach Browne's voice rose, annoyingly self-assured. "Oh, come now!" he said. "Don't let's lose our heads. Surely all he did was to sit on the safety valve?"

Suddenly David was furious. Caution went to the winds. He cast swiftly about him for a fitting rejoinder. It came, with fatal readiness. "He didn't sit on the safety valve. There wasn't such a thing as a safety valve in Gamate. There didn't have to be. Not until you people arrived."

Now there was no doubt that he had thrown a rock into the pool. For the first time in the history of public relations, an official spokesman had proclaimed his own exact version of the truth.

Tulbach Browne took up the challenge. "Then will you please tell us," he said, with great care, "what exactly the people in this room have done to raise the temperature, or however you like to phrase it, in Gamate?"

It was the pay-off question. Could he possibly give the exact answer to it — the one that he believed with all his heart?

The room — Andrew Macmillan's room — was silent and hot. They were all looking at him. He cleared his throat.

"It's difficult for me to be definite. It's the general effect, more than any special incident." That sounded feeble, and not what he really believed either, and he tried again, facing their cold eyes. "But I do think that there's one thing that you people have forgotten, or disregarded, and it's led to a lot of trouble. You've been treating the Maulas like sophisticated white men, when in fact they aren't a sophisticated people at all. They just don't function like people in America and England, white *or* black. They're a simple, fairly backward lot, and that's the way they should be thought about, and written about, and organized, and talked to."

After a pause, "Is that all?" inquired Tulbach Browne edgily.

"How do you mean?"

"Is that all we've done wrong?"

David stared back at him. The quality of menace in the other man's voice was something he wasn't going to take, from Tulbach Browne or anyone else. He decided to plunge, for good or ill.

"It's the general background," he returned crisply, "against which you've all been operating." Pencils were again busy: he did not mind. "Getting down to details, I'm absolutely certain, though I can't prove it, that you've been advising Dinamaula and the Regents on how they should go about getting what they want."

"You mean we've wandered outside the official pale, and started treating them like human beings?" asked Axel Hallmarck. "Even if we *have* advised them, what's wrong with that?"

"Because the direct result of that advice has been twelve murders, a paralyzing strike down at Port Victoria, and the whole Maula tribe in revolt." He turned his eyes now to Tulbach Browne. "And there's one thing that *you* did, which certainly caused a lot of trouble and unrest. That time in the Gamate hotel, when Dinamaula was refused a drink. You engineered the whole thing."

Tulbach Browne was very angry.

"All that you're doing," he said roughly, "is shifting the blame. You've all made a thorough hash of running this country, and so you say it's our fault when things get out of hand."

David shook his head again. "Not true. Things were going smoothly enough until you came along."

Axel Hallmarck jumped in. "What about Dinamaula, then? If it's all our fault, doesn't that let him out?"

"Of course not. He's the focus of the whole thing. He always has been. But —" David held Tulbach Browne's eyes for a long moment " — we'll never know, will we, what persuaded him to get out of line in the first place." Then, with deliberation, he said, "I think it's an unforgivable thing to come in here and stir things up, just to get a newspaper story."

The climax was obviously near.

"That's a hell of a thing to say," remarked Axel Hallmarck.

"I think it's absolutely true, nonetheless. And as well as being unforgivable, it's terribly dangerous, too."

"You talk," rasped Tulbach Browne, "as if the Maulas were apes or animals. Aren't they still human beings, even if they are the wrong color, from your point of view?"

"Certainly they're human beings. But they've not yet reached a Western level of civilization."

"You mean, they're inferior?"

Now they were all hammering it home, and David was ready to meet them.

"Yes, I do. I think that, man for man, at this moment of evolution, a Maula native is inferior to a white man."

"But that's not his fault, surely?"

"*Fault?* There's no fault. It's a historical accident, and it will be corrected in due course. But it is true *now*."

Suddenly, startling them all, demolishing the ugly tenseness, there was a resounding crash out on the stoep. It was the screen door, springing violently open, then slamming shut again.

Everyone in the room came to wary, acute attention; some of them rose to their feet. There were heavy footfalls, and then the sitting-room door swung open. But it was no ambush, no Maula assault with ax and knife and club. It was Keith Crump of the Royal Pharamaul Police. His left arm was in a rough sling; a glistening trail of blackened blood led down one side of his uniform tunic; he had a crude bandage round his head. He was far gone, in exhaustion and in wounds. But he could still hold himself erect, and stride like a soldier, and stand before them like a man.

David Bracken started forwards. "Keith. What's happened? Are you all right?"

Crump smiled, a tight smile in an exhausted face. "I'm all right," he answered. "A bit ragged round the edges, that's all."

David realized with unworthy joy that for him this was rescue. This canceled all other headlines.

Crump also was staring from face to face, working it out. He knew all the people present. With one exception, they were not his friends. "They've cut the road, just south of Shebiya," he said, on a firm controlled tone. "We were trying to get through, but we were ambushed. We lost two men, and I got hit myself. They've cut the road," he repeated. "It's just made for it, of course — thickest part of the bush — we'll need an army to get through. God knows what's happening up at Shebiya." He paused. "Sorry to interrupt, David. But I've got to see you, immediately."

THEY WERE speeding southwards in the police jeep; David Bracken at the wheel, and Keith Crump by his side, lying back on a pile of blankets. David drove, with tension and pleasure intermingled; it was a wild ride, with fear behind them and doubt ahead. Their departure had been swift, so swift that there had been no need for secrecy. When the press had left the Residency, Crump had said, "Got to see the Governor — got to work something out," and in a matter of minutes they were on the way. Since then the jeep had never been out of top gear and, no matter how vile the road, had never slowed below thirty miles an hour.

The shadows lengthened; evening drew a lowering canopy over their heads; soon it was time to switch on the lights. David took his eyes for a moment off the road. "How do you feel?" he asked.

"Stiff as hell. Otherwise all right."

"What happened?" asked David. "Up at Shebiya?"

"Bloody shambles," answered Crump. His voice came slowly, fighting the wind and the engine roar. "This morning, we called Tom Ronald as usual on the police schedule. Couldn't get any answer. I didn't like the sound of that, so I took four of my chaps, and started to drive up to Shebiya. All the way up, we kept trying to make radio contact. Still no answer. Then, a couple of miles south of the town, we were brought up short. Big tree lying right across the road. We all got out to look, scouting around, and suddenly all hell broke loose."

He was silent, for a full mile. "An ambush," explained Crump. "Very well laid on, too. Cross fire from rifles, a Sten gun somewhere, an old cannon blasting away. Two of my lads went down, for keeps. I got a bullet through this arm, and something else nicked me on the head. Nothing to do but turn tail and run."

"But what's it mean?" asked David.

"Murder," replied Crump briefly. "The town's cut off — which means that something's happened up there that they don't want us to know about."

"The Ronalds?"

"The Ronalds," answered Crump. "The late Ronalds. And the late Father Schwemmer, unless I'm much mistaken."

"Oh God!" said David. "Was he there as well?"

"Went up two days ago."

"But we must get through!" cried David, in anguish. His foot eased back off the accelerator. "What are we driving south for? We've got to go back and get through to them!"

"We're driving south," said Crump, in exhaustion and misery, "because we can't drive north. I haven't enough men to force that roadblock, even if I could leave Gamate without a single policeman, which I can't. So we're driving south to talk to the Governor. Now it's his problem. I've done the best I can, with all the strength God gave me. Either we collect a lot of soldiers, and fight back up the road to Shebiya — or we find some other way of getting through. And what the hell way *that* is, I wouldn't like to guess."

"The soldiers are due here tomorrow," said David.

"Good for them. Just in time for the ceremonial burial party."

There was now a vague yellow glow on the horizon ahead. "Port Victoria," said David. "Thank God!"

"I've asked you to come along," said the Governor, "because Keith Crump has just arrived — with some very bad news, I'm afraid — and I feel we ought all to know about it and decide on a plan." Opposite him, the clock on the ornate mahogany mantelpiece began to chime ten o'clock, and Sir Elliott Vere-Toombs waited, as if politely, for it to finish.

No one spoke. Crump, still pale and spent, but with his head wound freshly dressed and his arm in a neat sling, sat back on the couch. Aidan Purves-Brownrigg was beside him; in two other armchairs, David and Captain Simpson completed the semicircle. Nicole Steuart was installed at a small desk just behind the Governor. She too was pale and tense, just as she had been ever since David had had a brief word with her, before the meeting.

Then, she had put her hand to her mouth, said, "Oh darling. Those poor Ronalds," and wound her arms round his neck as if to ward off all evil.

The Governor raised his head again, looking at Keith Crump. "Just bring us up to date, Keith. Start from this morning."

Crump's account was succinct and precise. When he had finished, the Governor said, "Thank you, Keith. I think that's all quite clear. I'm sure you were right to — er — break off the action and go back to Gamate." He cleared his throat. "Before we consider ways and means, I'd like to complete the general picture for you."

Now it was the Governor's turn to report, and (somewhat to David's surprise) crisis had brought out tough qualities in him, qualities from an older, more effective past.

"This affair at Shebiya has come at a very bad time," he began, "when we were already stretched to the limit. The strike is still in operation down here in Port Victoria, but there's been very little further violence. We've recruited a civic guard, of sorts, from the Pharamaul Club."

David asked, "Sir, is there any more news of Dinamaula?"

"Not that I know of," answered the Governor. "He's still here, of course, but still proving stubborn, and quite uncommunicative." He looked at Crump. "Have your people anything to add to that?"

"Only one thing, sir," answered Crump. "Zuva Katsaula, his cousin, called on Dinamaula a few days ago. Then he disappeared. He's rumored to be up in Shebiya."

"So Dinamaula may well have planned this Shebiya affair?"

"It's possible."

The Governor nodded to himself. "Turning now to Gamate," he went on, gesturing towards Crump, "the main body of our police force still have a great deal of unrest and rioting to contend with up there. I take it that we cannot afford to weaken that concentration in any way?"

"No, sir," answered Crump. "Gamate is still very tricky. In fact, I took quite a chance this morning, detaching four men to go with me. And I lost two of them."

The Governor nodded. "Quite so. And that's the crux of our dilemma at the moment. Because — " he looked at each of them in turn " — the battalion coming from East Africa has again been delayed. They won't be here for at least another twenty-four hours. Then they have to disembark — another twelve hours or so."

"They're coming by *sea?*" asked David.

Captain Simpson, the naval aide, answered him. "Yes," he said weightily. "They've run into very heavy weather, rounding the Cape of Good Hope. I doubt if they'll even dock before tomorrow night."

"But sir," said Crump, in a taut voice, "can't they *fly* troops in from Kenya?"

Now it was Aidan's turn. "It's no good, Keith. All the troops that can be spared for Pharamaul are stuck in the transport, coming round by sea. They simply haven't any more to send. We're still completely on our own here, for the next thirty-six hours."

"And there you have it," said Sir Elliott. "Port Victoria is quiet, and possibly under control. Gamate is still highly explosive and dangerous. We have no one to spare to force a way through to Shebiya. Isn't that so, Keith?"

"We certainly can't spare enough men to break through," agreed Crump morosely. "It would take a small army. They're obviously well dug in. It'll mean a full-scale frontal attack, by a lot of men, properly armed. We can do it all right when the soldiers arrive. But in the meantime — "

"In the meantime," said the Governor, bridging the heavy silence, "Shebiya has already been cut off for over twelve hours. We really have no idea of what may be happening up there." The room suddenly seemed full of ideas, crude and bloody and tragic, of what could be happening up at Shebiya. "I'm afraid we'll just have to wait."

David caught Nicole's eyes on him, pleading for action. She was clearly in anguish, a woman in a man's cruel world mourning another woman who had been caught up in the same fearful web. He glanced sideways at Aidan, and saw a like reflection of horror and impotence. Sir Elliott was looking down at the blotter on his desk; Crump was lying back, exhausted.

Suddenly, inexplicably, Captain Simpson stood up. He was a tall man, and his bemedaled uniform was impressive; but now there was something in his bearing, something agleam in his ruddy face, that focused all eyes. He was standing at attention, his arms stiff by his side. He spoke throatily, as if under heavy stress. "Sir!" he intoned.

"Yes, Hereward?" said the Governor, taken aback.

"Sir, a cutting-out expedition."

"I beg your pardon?"

"A cutting-out expedition."

On the instant, there was throughout the room a general, deeply uncomfortable feeling that this was an unfortunate moment for the naval aide-de-camp to make a fool of himself. But in fact Captain Simpson was not making a fool of himself, nor anything like it, and he made the point clear within a few moments.

"What exactly have you in mind?" asked the Governor.

Captain Simpson had a lot in mind; indeed, as soon as he started to speak, words and phrases tumbled and burst forth, propelled by history, by the Royal Navy, by the dear twin ghosts of Nelson and of Sir Hereward Simpson, Vice-Admiral from 1816 to 1825. There were many different factors contributing to what Captain Simpson now said; but, strongest of all, he spoke from a deep need to acquit himself well, in face of dire peril — peril to others.

"Sir," he said, quickly, unevenly, "we can't get through to Shebiya by frontal land attack, but we *can* get through if we capture the village from the rear, while the people defending it are expecting us to come from an entirely different direction." His eyes glowed. "We can go round by sea, make our landing on the east coast, march through to the town, and be in full possession of it before they've really woken up to what's happening."

"You mean," said the Governor, narrowing his eyes, "we could make a landing at Fish Village, and take the forest track up to Shebiya? How far would that be?"

"Not more than thirty miles," said Crump, with awakening interest. "I know the ground, sir. It's a passable road."

"We could take the jeep," put in Captain Simpson. "Get through in about three hours."

"We could take troop carriers as well," added Crump. "I've got two of them available."

"Just a minute," said the Governor reprovingly. "What about a boat? We have nothing — "

"Sir, there's a boat in harbor at this moment which would just suit us." Simpson was pressing forward again, eager, knowledgeable. "She belongs to an American — a luxury cruising yacht, about a hundred and twenty feet long. And she'll do fifteen or sixteen knots. We could make the whole trip in about twelve hours."

"But she's not our boat," objected the Governor.

"She could be," answered Simpson stoutly. "In this sort of emergency, we could certainly commandeer her. Or we could arrange it through Lou Strogoff, the American consul. Or we could just ask the owner. He was very friendly yesterday. I'm sure he'd play with us, if only for the fun of it."

Now gradually the room was warming up again. Crump was on

the edge of the couch, staring sideways at Simpson as if entranced by the prospect he had opened up. Aidan was the next to speak.

"Granted that we could land at Fish Village, and — " he glanced up at Captain Simpson " — I think it's a wonderful idea, the *only* idea — what about men? We'd certainly be taking the U-Maulas by surprise, but we'll still need troops to do it."

Crump awoke to the last word, cutting in on Simpson. "We wouldn't need nearly so many troops, this way." He looked at the Governor. "You said it's pretty quiet here, sir, and we've always got the civic guard to fall back on. That means that, for a few days at least, we could spare perhaps fifty armed policemen. We've got Bren guns for them, in the armory here. If we could just achieve real surprise at the village, and then . . ."

He was seeing the whole course of the action in his professional mind's eye, and the others were catching the infection, and seeing it at the same time. Only Captain Simpson was frowning.

"Of course," he said, with odd formality, "this is primarily a naval operation. The troops are to be landed by sea transport, and then led into action, as if they were Marines."

"Oh," said Crump, getting the point. He frowned, and then grinned in relaxation. "I don't mind," he said, "as long as we get to Shebiya. It can be your show if you like, old boy."

"The landing is feasible?" the Governor asked Simpson.

"Yes, sir."

His eyes came round to Crump. "You could get your men through? The surprise element might well work?"

"Yes, sir. By God, yes!"

"Very well." Sir Elliott looked down at a piece of paper on which he had been writing, and then began to speak, half reading, half talking. "Captain Simpson in general charge of the whole operation. Keith Crump in field command of the police. David as second in command."

There was a slight question in his voice. David looked up and said, "Thank you, sir." Then he glanced at Nicole, and there was love in her eyes, as well as all the rest.

"There are three stages to be covered," went on Sir Elliott. "One, arrange about the boat. Two, arm yourselves and the policemen.

Three, get on board, with your transport, and start out." He looked at Simpson. "Number one is yours, of course. It's a bit late, I know, but can you get in touch with the owner of the boat?"

"I think so, sir," said Simpson. "He may still be at the club."

"I'll leave all that to you. Now for the police. Do you really feel up to this, Keith?"

"Yes, sir."

"How long will you need to collect your men?"

Crump considered. "I'll have to winkle them out, recall some of them from patrol, see about their arms, get them down to the docks, and load the vehicles. About six tomorrow morning, sir."

"Will it be light by then?"

"Barely, sir," said Captain Simpson. "But it doesn't matter, anyway. In fact, from the security angle, it would be better if we sailed before dawn."

"Very well," said the Governor again. "That really leaves only one more thing. David?"

"Yes, sir?" answered David, in doubt and some anxiety.

"Just behind you," said the Governor, with no change of expression, "is a cupboard. In the cupboard are glasses, soda water, ice, and a decanter of whisky. I suggest," he said, with a wonderful, heart-warming air of shedding a heavy load onto men whom he trusted implicitly, "that we all drink a quick health to the success of the expedition." As David rose, smiling, to obey, the Governor turned to Captain Simpson. "Wasn't it your great-great-great-uncle," he asked guilelessly, "who brought off this same sort of thing, a few miles north of Corunna, in 1797?"

At the low ebb of five o'clock in the morning David walked towards a cluster of lights at the end of the main jetty, where many figures were moving, and a donkey engine chugged busily, and the bows of a long white-painted ship emerged from the shadows like a trim ghost. He walked carefully, conspiratorially, conscious of fatigue, sadness, and a wisp of Nicole's perfume from his coat collar.

At the top of the gangplank, Simpson and Keith Crump were standing; Simpson was watching a troop-carrying truck being

manhandled aboard near the stern, Crump, white-bandaged, his
arm in a sling, was speaking to one of his sergeants, tapping meanwhile on a piece of paper. There was an open case containing a
dozen Bren guns at his feet.

They both turned as David stepped off the end of the gangplank onto the white-scrubbed wooden deck.

"How's it going?" David asked.

"Very well, so far," said Simpson rather grumpily. His manner
was preoccupied; he was the expert, the man of affairs surrounded
by amateurs and bohemians. "That's the last troop carrier. The
men are all aboard, except the ones loading."

"How do you feel, Keith?" asked David, turning to Crump.

"Better," said Crump. He was still pale, but his air was brisk and confident. "Much better."

"Anything I can do?"

"Don't think so. We'll sail in about half an hour."

"Forty minutes," said Captain Simpson.

"This is quite a boat," said David, looking round him. Stretching out into the shadows in the cold half-light, the boat looked elegantly luxurious. "What's she called?"

"*Wander Lust,*" answered Captain Simpson, with distaste.

"Where's the owner?" asked David.

"Up on the bridge," answered Simpson. "You might go up and say hallo to him. He's an engaging old boy, and mad keen about all this. He said 'yes' before I'd finished asking. But his wife, Mrs. Loganquist, is still asleep. I gather she hasn't been told what this is all about. We've got to reassure her when she gets up."

"Oh." David looked about him once more. Within view there were two troop carriers, and a jeep, securely lashed to the deck; a dozen Maula policemen in khaki uniforms; some piles of stores; one opened crate of Bren guns, and three still closed. "What are we meant to be doing, then?"

"Elephant hunting," said Simpson. "Very hazardous occupation. Even the beaters are armed to the teeth."

Up on the bridge, all was brilliance and light. The instruments gleamed, the glass was polished and dustless, the varnished wood-work immaculate. Just behind the wheel was a long-legged arm-chair, upholstered in light green nylon; and in it, playing idly with the controls, sat a small chubby man, middle-aged, cherubic, wearing a red baseball cap. At the sound of David's step, he turned.

"Hallo, there!" he said cordially. His spectacles gleamed an added welcome. "Glad to have you aboard."

"I'm David Bracken," said David, holding out his hand. "Secretary at Government House. Mr. Loganquist?"

"Mr. Loganquist," agreed the cheerful owner. "Friends call me Logey." He hopped down from his chair. "This is a wonderful assignment. I'm very grateful to the captain for suggesting it."

"We're very grateful to *you*. We had to have a boat, as you know, and this is exactly what we needed. She looks wonderful."

"Just took delivery, two months ago," said Mr. Loganquist.

"What sort of crew do you have, Mr. Loganquist?"

"Call me Logey. Crew of seven — skipper, engineer, bos'n, two deck hands, cook, steward. Steward's called Charlie, colored boy from Jamaica. Any time at all you want a drink," he added hospitably, "just ring the bell for Charlie."

"I'll do that," said David.

Mr. Loganquist took off his baseball cap. Above the pink cheru-bic face, his bald head gleamed like the whitest, largest egg in the world. "I guess I'll go lie down for half an hour, until we start. There's just one thing, Dave."

"What's that?"

Mr. Loganquist looked secretive, and shy at the same time. "Mrs. Loganquist — Ella — doesn't know what this is all about. I told her I was giving you boys a lift up the coast. You're on vacation, going on a big hunting trip. Understand?"

"Yes," said David. "I'll remember that."

"Hunting," repeated Mr. Loganquist. "Ella's not a strong woman. I don't want for her to have any sort of shock."

"We'll be very careful," David assured him.

As WITH that other voyage, which now seemed so long ago — his first voyage by rail from Port Victoria to Gamate — David Bracken was never to forget the voyage by sea from Port Victoria to Fish Village, two hundred miles up the east coast of Pharamaul. This one was also a journey into the unknown which had, all the time, a superb air of unreality.

The *Wander Lust* cast off and set sail a little before six o'clock. It was not yet dawn, though dawn trembled on the pale threshold to seawards; behind their backs, the town slept, bleary-eyed and tawdry, while ahead of them the clean and limitless horizon beckoned them to their voyage.

It grew light very gradually, as they cleared harbor. The sea was calm, with a light fluting breeze from the south; as with a million dawns, daylight seeped imperceptibly across the surface of the sea and the sky, bringing hope and warmth successively, transforming everything within view from black to pale gray, from pale gray to pinkish white, from pinkish white to a magical yellow gleam — the veritable gleam of sunrise.

Whatever lay ahead, hidden inland behind the northward coast line, it was good to be alive on such a morning. David stretched, felt his bristly chin, and walked a few paces to the ladder leading to the main saloon. When he entered, a young Negro in a smart white uniform poked his head out of the serving hatch, grinning a broad welcome. "Good morning, sir," he said.

"Good morning," answered David. "You're up very early."

"This is going to be a long day," observed the Negro steward unconnectedly. "Will it be breakfast, or a Scotch and soda?"

David blinked. It was not quite eight o'clock in the morning. But he did want a whisky and soda, more than anything else in the world, and there seemed no point in pretending otherwise.

"I *would* like a drink," he acknowledged.

"Where are you from?" he asked, when he received the glass.

"Jamaica," answered Charlie. "God's own banana paradise. Tell me," he went on, almost fiercely, "just what *are* those black rascals doing, upcountry?"

THE WHOLE of that day had the same inconsequent appeal as that eight a.m. whisky and soda; it was as if this preliminary stroke of immoderation set the tone of all that followed. At nine o'clock, Simpson and Crump came into the saloon, freshly shaved, briskly ready to lay the necessary plans for their landing; but they had scarcely settled down to discussion before their host and hostess put in an appearance.

Mr. Loganquist no longer wore a baseball cap, but he was as chubby, as cheerful as he had appeared earlier. Mrs. Loganquist was a tall, tough-looking blonde, a good twenty years younger than her husband; her tailored cream slacks, elaborate hair-do, and brilliant make-up seemed to improve on the sunrise by several degrees of light. Her first words were, "Hi! Good to see you all!" and her next a raucous, "*Charlie!* Set 'em up!"

Charlie appeared, beaming, with a tray bearing five gin slings. There appeared to be no choice, and no deviation possible. When they had all taken their glasses, Mrs. Loganquist raised hers, with a wide hospitable sweep of her arm.

"Glad you came aboard," she proclaimed, and drank deep. They all followed suit. Mrs. Loganquist set her glass down, and suddenly looked across at Captain Simpson. "What's the matter, Captain?" she asked. "Too early in the morning for you?"

"Not at all." Simpson, who had indeed been gazing at his hostess with startled attention, recovered swiftly, and smiled. "I was just enjoying my drink. It's really delicious."

"The English slay me," said Mrs. Loganquist to the world at large. "'Reallah delicious,'" she mimicked. "No one else can say it like that." She raised her frosted glass again. "Tell you what. Let's all have another round and then we'll catch us some fish."

Presently, spurred on by their host, they all went out on deck, into the midday sunshine; rods were broken out, lines baited with a magnificent variety of chromium spinners, plastic lures, and monstrous painted insects, and they settled down to fish. After half an hour, Mrs. Loganquist, obviously adept and skillful, struck hard into a fifty-pound tuna, played it briefly, and landed it in a flurry of foam, blood, and blue-green scales on the afterdeck.

Wander Lust plowed onwards, in steady power and pride; after lunch (watermelon, curried eggs, and crêpes suzettes) it was time for canasta. After some hours of play, punctuated by mint juleps, the game grew careless and disconnected; Mrs. Loganquist, a dashing performer, won seven pounds, exclaimed, "You're all such lousy players!" and threw her winnings through the nearest open porthole. With the air of a man who has said it many times before, Mr. Loganquist said, "Now, honey!"

Darkness came gradually, after a sunset of streaky, barbarous splendor which set the whole sea on fire. Presently the skipper stepped down into the saloon, surveyed the scene with sardonic approval, and said, "Folks, we've run a clear two hundred miles, by log. Must be getting mighty close. Yes, sir!"

They went out on deck to watch the nearing of the land, the mysterious growth of shadows, and the campfires of Fish Village come twinkling out of the darkness. Suddenly all three visitors were cold sober, watchful, and intent. As if impelled by some secret, well-remembered directive, they drew aside, under the lee of the bridge. There were details to discuss, and now it was amazingly easy to discuss them, and to plot their course, and to concentrate. The beguiling, necessary, and irresistible holiday was over.

"We'll lie offshore," said Simpson, speaking quietly, his voice in the darkness sounding cool and authoritative. "I'll take the launch and Crump and as many policemen as the boat will hold. We'll make our landing on the beach as quietly and quickly as we can, and put a cordon round the village so that no one can escape up the track to Shebiya. For all I know, this lot may be friendly, but we can't take any chances. Then — " he touched David on the arm " — I'll give you the signal by flashlight — one long and three short, the letter B — and you'll have this ship brought alongside the jetty. Then we'll unload our gear, and the rest of the policemen, and get on our way. Is that all clear?"

"Yes," answered Crump immediately. "But there's just one thing. I know the layout of the village, and the actual hut of the man we want to find, as soon as we can. He's the headman, an old chap called Pemboli. Nice old boy, much respected. *He* won't be bloody-minded, I can guarantee, and we might have to get him to make a speech." He looked at Simpson. "If you'll see to the outer cordon round the village, I'll go straight into the middle of it, with about six of my chaps, and nail Pemboli straight away."

"All right," agreed Simpson. "But if you get into trouble, fire three shots, close together, and we'll close in from outside."

"Thanks," said Crump equably. "And if *you* get into trouble, fire *four* shots, and we'll come running."

Suddenly, David found himself shivering. "But what if the people here — " he gestured towards the darkness " — are the same as the people up at Shebiya? They may be on guard, waiting for us."

"It's very unlikely," answered Crump. "There aren't more than fifty families at Fish Village, and they've always been a bit self-contained. Pemboli is quite an old autocrat, and a good friend of ours. Our principal worry is to make sure an odd straggler doesn't light out for Shebiya, and give the whole show away."

"But if we *do* run into trouble," said Simpson with a certain grimness, "you'll hear it, soon enough. Any sort of continuous firing will mean that there's real opposition. In that case, you must come in at full speed, and land the rest of the policemen. Make all the noise you can. Fire a few rockets — there are some up on the bridge. The more like an army you can sound, the better."

As it turned out, it was easy. Burning dimmed navigation lights, *Wander Lust* cut her engines and came to a gentle stop, a hundred yards from the shore; Simpson, Crump, and twenty armed policemen crowded into the launch, and sped for the beach, cutting a swath of rippling foam across the dark water. On the bridge, the skipper remarked, "Nice going." Mrs. Loganquist, wearing a blond mink coat thrown carelessly over her slacks, said it was a hell of a way to hunt elephants, even for the English. David stood apart, staring through binoculars at the secret, unknown coast.

There was a long pause, of fifteen or twenty minutes; then —
strong and clear against the flickering fires — a flashlight winked:
one long beam, then one, two, three short ones. David dropped his
glasses and turned to the skipper. "Let's go alongside," he said.

On the rough wooden jetty Crump was waiting, and two of his
men, ready to take their lines, and a tall old Maula, the headman
Pemboli. The latter bowed as David jumped ashore.

"I greet you," he said formally. "You are welcome to my village."

"Thank you, Chief," said David.

"Everything's all clear here," said Crump. "They know what's
happened up at Shebiya, and they don't want to get mixed up in
it. Pemboli had a local curfew imposed, long before we arrived."

Simpson's tall figure loomed up from the darkness at the end
of the jetty; light flickered momentarily on the Sten gun slung
over his shoulder. "Strictly according to plan," he said.

Beyond them was a ring of fires, and drifting smoke, and many
watchful figures — men, old women, small children aroused from
sleep. There was a deep gloom over everything, a water-front
murkiness interwoven with the acrid night smell of Africa. As
they began to unload the vehicles and the arms and the stores, men
crept towards them, and stood watching, and presently began to
help, carrying, hauling, coaxing heavy burdens away from the
policemen. It was as if there were some guilt which they had to
shrive, and this humble task was the only way to do it. Everything
was ashore, and loaded into the trucks, within half an hour.

To David's surprise, Mrs. Loganquist kissed him warmly, by
way of good-by. "Good hunting, honey," she said. "But take care
of yourselves, with all those wild animals."

She leant towards him, perfumed, slim, a tough wild animal
herself. She spoke softly. "I'm so glad you didn't tell Logey what
you're really doing. He has a heart condition."

Chapter 11

C APTAIN SIMPSON rode in the first car, the police jeep, with
Crump's senior sergeant, a gigantic gray-haired Maula, at the
wheel, and four armed men at his back, and a Union Jack flying

bravely on the radiator. Crump himself came next, in the biggest troop carrier, crammed to the roof with thirty men, a dozen drums of petrol and water, most of the stores, and all the ammunition. David Bracken brought up the rear with the remaining men, in the smaller troop carrier.

It was after midnight when the convoy left Fish Village; their advance was purposefully slow, timed so that they would reach Shebiya five hours later, at first light. But it would have been a slow journey anyway. The track through the untamed forest was narrow, winding, and villainously rutted. They drove towards Shebiya at a grinding ten miles an hour; and Shebiya was always with them, like the insects and the dust and the pitted road. For what lay ahead of them was part of their ordeal. They were not driving through hell towards a respite. They were driving through the sixth department of Hades towards the seventh.

By arrangement, the convoy halted at four o'clock, the three cars converging into a close-coupled unit as they came to a stop. David lifted his stiff arms from the wheel, scratched at an ankle bitten raw by mosquitoes, and jumped down onto the uneven track. Crump and Simpson were waiting for him as he walked forwards to the jeep, standing within the rim of the headlights.

"How far have we run?" Crump asked. "My mileage indicator hasn't been working for a long time."

"Twenty-four miles," answered Simpson. "About seven to go, and an hour's more darkness. The timing is just right."

"What's the plan?" asked David.

"We've got seven miles to go," repeated Simpson, "and we'll take them slowly." His tall figure in the headlights seemed to exude strength and efficiency. "After half an hour, we'll douse our lights, and move forward as quietly and slowly as possible. When we get there, we'll make one quick dash for it. You — " he looked at David " — will go straight to the police post. Find out what's happened to it. We had a corporal and four men there. If they're still alive, dig them out and take over the main square of the village. If they're not, stay where you are until we get back. You and I — " he was now looking at Crump " — will sprint straight through, and down the road to the roadblock. We'll take them in the rear, and by surprise. If they fight, we'll shoot it out. If they surrender, we'll bring them back to the police post, and join up with David. Then we'll see what's happened to the Ronalds."

"That all seems clear," said Crump. "But if this is to be our last stop, I think I'll get my chaps to check their weapons."

"All right," agreed Simpson. "But as quietly as you can."

From nearby a night bird screeched suddenly; farther off, a colony of baboons set up a sudden growling and chattering. Crump called his men from the cars, marshaled them by the side of the track, and went through a brief arms inspection. The clicking of bolts, the slapping of rifle stocks, the glint of light on polished barrels were reassuring elements in the murderous forest.

Standing apart from this military display, Simpson spoke suddenly. "Have you done anything like this before?"

"Yes," said David. "I have."

"Good. So have I. But it was a long time ago."

"Where?" asked David. He was preoccupied and afraid, but he felt that he ought to ask.

"China," answered Simpson surprisingly. "Pirates in the Yangtze Delta."

"Mine was Italy, near Salerno. Italian *neo-Fascisti*. But it's the same thing, really, isn't it?"

"Yes," said Simpson. "It's the very same thing."

SUDDENLY, swiftly, they plunged through the last uphill mile, towards the dawn that was to show them their target, and the clearing in the jungle that was Shebiya. The steady roar and rasp of the three engines seemed to fill the forest; the drivers crouched over the bucking wheels, the armed policemen peered out, ahead and to the side and behind them, their weapons cocked, their fingers ready. Then there was a break in the line of trees, a stretch of smoother track, and the convoy burst out into the open clearing.

The village awoke all round them — men, women, dogs, goats, children, all coming to astonished life; then, just as swiftly, it stiffened into immobility again. The men who came running from their huts with spears froze against their doorways. Light seeped through upon Shebiya, and with the light came guilty scruple much prudent second-guessing. David's car, the last of the three, veered off sideways towards the police post, while the jeep and the big troop carrier sped onwards, cutting a swath through the dew and the spiders' webs, like the first invaders of Africa.

David watched them go, continuing full tilt across the clearing and disappearing down the southern road; he felt the fear of loneliness, but he felt the tautness of anger and decision as well. He brought his truck to a sharp stop, wheels skidding in the yellow dust; his men tumbled down, and turned outwards, as they had been trained to do, daring any human to advance, or retreat, or play them false. But no one stirred. Especially, at the police post, no one stirred at all; no flag flew, no sentry came forward; the windows in the whitewashed huts were blank. There was a sweet smell of death all over the post, all over the village square.

He posted his guards round the clearing, took two men, and walked up the pathway, his Sten gun clenched in his hands. Whatever I find, he thought, it can only make me angrier, and then I can do *anything*.

THE TWO leading cars roared onwards, lumbering and bucking like small ships in a twisting sea. They ran a racketing mile, then another; their rendezvous could not be long delayed. Suddenly, at a sharp curve of the road, Simpson stood up, and pointed wildly, and shouted, *"There they are!"*

There they were. It was a rough encampment, grouped round the fallen tree straddling the road; perfectly sited for an attack from the south, foolishly open to the rear. There were guns — but they were pointing south, and the gunners were asleep. Simpson clambered down, waving his arm for the advance, sighting and then toppling with a single burst of fire two men who ran out of a hut by the roadside. Crump's big truck stopped, wheel to wheel beside the jeep. The armed policemen jumped out, shouting.

Other men jumped out — out of trenches, tents, leafy hideaways; men clad in blankets, scraps of forgotten uniforms, loincloths. They blundered forth in sleepy amazement, their eyes turning from the southerly road, where the attack *must* come, to the innocent approach from their own village, where the scourging enemy stood.

Simpson fired again, at a cluster of brave men trying to swing one of the Bren guns around, men who instantly died; Crump charged on foot at the head of his platoon, making for a clump of roughly built huts — the focus of the ambush, the headquarters. A fat man ran out, staring, a pistol in his hand.

"Puero!" shouted Crump. "Stop where you are!"

Puero, the slow-moving third Regent, faced him for a moment. Then he turned, his eyes squinting wildly. The nearest cover was the bush at the edge of the road, twenty full yards away. He made for it at a swift, snaking run, amazing for a man of his weight.

"Puero!" shouted Crump again.

There was no answer, only frenzied twisting. Crump fired, missed, and fired again. Puero dropped, some yards from safety.

From the same hut, another man, smaller, came running. It was Zuva Katsaula. He loosed off a wild burst, six shots that whined over their heads. Now it was Simpson's Maula driver who fired. Zuva screamed, dropped his gun, cradled a right arm shattered at the elbow. He looked across at the invaders, with pain, sleep, and fear clouding his eyes. He called, "I surrender! Prisoner of war!"

The road and the clearing were now full of men, blundering into captivity, their hands above their heads. The cordon of police herded them into a rough corral. There must have been four hundred of them, roused from sleep, shocked by the brief show of force, now fearful and leaderless.

"One missing," said Crump, glancing round him. "The one we want." He turned to the nearest of the prisoners, a thin trembling man. "Where is Gotwela?"

The man was silent. Crump's Sten gun lowered until it was pointing at the man's stomach. Crump was breathing heavily, with the effort of running, the pain of his wounded arm, the tension of his anger. "You know well that I will shoot," he said, in the Maula tongue. "Where is Gotwela?"

The man looked at the gun and then at his own stomach, but he would not speak. He has taken an oath, thought Crump; he has sworn himself to silence, like any other prisoner of war — like a Yank in Korea, like an Englishman in the Western Desert. This man's oath is vile and unspeakable, but it is the same sort of oath.

From behind him, from the ranks of the prisoners, came a high and wheedling voice, the voice of Zuva Katsaula. "Gotwela is in that tent," he said, pointing. "He was drunk last night. He sleeps still. I claim my rights under the Geneva Convention."

Simpson, as hard-breathing as Crump, but sweating and trembling from some inner force, raised his gun. He sighted the top of the tent, six feet from the ground, and fired a swift burst. It collapsed in a heap, the canvas smoldering. Then it heaved, and a man wormed his way out — a fat man, glistening with fresh sweat, naked save for the royal *simbara,* the lion skin, clasped loosely round his middle. It was Gotwela.

Gotwela blinked in the daylight, blinked at the guns and the new faces, scowled at his followers herded together and helpless. Then his gross features settled themselves into a sullen cast of indifference. A policeman came forward to pinion him.

His arms pulled roughly behind his back, Gotwela spoke at last. He raised his heavy head, and his eyes searched among the corralled prisoners, and at length found Zuva Katsaula. He called out, in deep throaty contempt, *"Hé,* hyena! Did you not tell me that all the Maulas were marching to join us at Shebiya?"

Zuva looked steadily at the sky and said nothing.

"You were right, hyena," said Gotwela. "But you did not tell me they were policemen."

"That's all!" said Simpson roughly. "Cut out the bloody cross talk! Now form up, and we'll all go back to the village."

The long column gradually took shape, drifting into straggling order; Zuva and Gotwela bound with straps, the rest with their hands clasped above their heads. They started to march back to Shebiya, a motley, shambling crowd, headed by the jeep, tailed by the troop carrier. The way grew hot as the sun rose, but the prisoners were sweating with more than heat. They were sweating an enormous guilt, over something they had been hiding, something which must now come to light. Brothers in hideous crime, they trudged back to be confounded by the facts.

DAVID BRACKEN met them at the outer gate of the police post: a gray-faced, shaken David, fresh from a view of hideous death.

Simpson, from the leading jeep, called out to him, "Well?"

David, who had been waiting for a long and lonely hour, looked at him. He looked at the Union Jack, the long dusty line of prisoners, the thin ring of policemen pushing and cursing. At his back, he felt penetratingly the police post, with its bloodstains, its corpses sprawled like unswept rubbish. He said, "Nothing much here. They've all been killed. All five. Probably two days ago. No one seems to know anything."

Simpson stepped down from the jeep. "Which way is the Ronalds' house?"

"There." David pointed. "But it's empty. I sent a policeman."

"Let's take another look at it." Simpson turned, called out to Crump, "We're going over to the District Officer's house."

Crump, preoccupied with the prisoners, raised his arm in brief acknowledgment. Leaving the transport and the guards, Simpson and David walked across the clearing to the Ronalds' house.

Silence hung over the small house like a pall — there was no movement, no sign of life, not even the corpses which both of them had feared. They stepped into the living room, and then into the dining room, Simpson leading the way. All was in perfect order.

The dining-room table was laid for three people, and the three people had clearly been snatched away from it without warning. Three side plates with crumbled bread and butter confronted their eyes, three dusty glasses of water, three sets of knives and forks, still waiting to be used. The three chairs were thrust back from the table. But nothing was in true disorder. It was merely an interrupted meal for three. The kitchen was equally deserted. On the center table was a dish of untouched, congealed curry.

"They certainly left in a hurry," said Simpson.

"GIVE ME a knife," said Simpson, without emphasis; and when the tall Maula sergeant handed him an open clasp knife, he brought the blade down to within an inch of Zuva's eye. The blade was steady, while the eye underneath it blinked wildly, and the pinioned man sought to writhe away. "I will take your eye, and then your tongue, and then your life," said Simpson, scarcely more than conversationally. "Tell me what happened to the Ronalds."

"I do not know," said Zuva. He was in an extremity of terror, as well he might be. "I have told you. I was not here."

"You were here," said Simpson.

"I took no part."

Simpson advanced the knife a fraction of an inch. "No part in what? Are they dead?"

Zuva squinted up at the knife, which was closing in, until it touched the very casing of the eyeball. Zuva screamed; a spray of sweat burst from his head and his neck. "I took no part," he panted. "It was true I was here, but I took no part."

"Are they dead?"

"Yes."

Simpson caught his breath, trembling, hearing the answer. From the circle of men watching — David, Crump, the sergeant, four or five policemen — came an echoing sigh; they had found what they came to Shebiya to find. There seemed nothing else to do now. Simpson stepped back a pace, balancing the knife in his hand. He stared at Zuva with a malevolent intensity. He said, "Now that you have talked, talk some more. Where are they?"

"In the forest."

"Whereabouts in the forest?"

Zuva hesitated. "It is difficult — " he began.

Don't give me that! Simpson suddenly roared. He dropped the clasp knife into his left hand, and with the right dealt Zuva a brutal slap on the side of his face. "Tell me everything," he shouted, "or I will kill you now!"

Zuva's head fell to one side; the heavy blow had numbed his wits. When he spoke, it was more slowly. "A half mile from here," he said. "To the north. There is a clearing, a meeting place."

"Who was killed there? Both the Ronalds?"

"Yes. And the priest."

"Who killed them?"

Zuva looked fearfully about him. "All the tribe."

Crump suddenly stepped forward. He wore the same expression as Simpson, tense, malignant, consumed by hatred and anger. He pushed Zuva roughly in the chest.

"I know all your secrets," he said grimly. "I know you have taken the oath, the filthy oath. But the oath will not save you. Look at the other people who have taken the oath. They are prisoners, and if they are murderers they will surely die. Some of them have died already. Puero has died like a dog. Who was the leader?"

Zuva looked past him, to where Gotwela sat on the rough ground. "That man was the leader," he said finally.

"How did they die?"

Zuva's eyes turned from the man he had betrayed, to the man who was questioning him. Suddenly, he was very small and very still. "I cannot describe — I cannot tell you in words. But Gotwela was the leader, all the time."

"What is this meeting place called, where they died?"

"Calavaree."

"What?" said Simpson, startled by the similarity to Calvary.

"Calavaree. It is something in the lore of the tribe. But that man was the leader."

"Gotwela!" called Simpson loudly.

Gotwela turned his head.

"Get up," ordered Simpson. "We are going on a short journey. You, too," he added to Zuva. He turned to Crump. "And all the prisoners, and any of the tribespeople you can round up. Form them into a column. They're all going to take a second look at what they've done. Gotwela!" he called again.

Gotwela, who was now standing slumped between his two guards, raised his eyes. They were empty, expressionless, doomed.

"You will lead us," said Simpson, "on the path to Calavaree."

It was not a clear path, the path to Calavaree; it lay uphill for the most part, a track wandering at will through the same kind of jungle foliage which had led them from Fish Village to Shebiya. The column that now filled it was a long one; Gotwela headed it, with Zuva a few paces behind him; then came their guards; then some other village notables — the headmen and the witch doctors; then the jeep, the focal turret of strength; then the long file of prisoners; then the police, grim-faced, baleful, inexorable.

It was a long column, and it moved slowly; partly because of the difficulty of the way; partly because Gotwela and Zuva at the head, and the tribespeople behind, walked with the slow steps of men keeping a reluctant rendezvous with death. They knew what Simpson, and Crump, and David Bracken, and the policemen did not yet know; they knew what they were going to find at the end of the journey.

The procession turned the last corner, and mounted the last slope of the hill. Gotwela slowed his stride, Zuva faltered and fell back another pace, trembling. Then they were in the open, the place of Calavaree. It was a cleared space of a hundred feet square, and they filtered out upon it like players on a huge operatic stage, gathered for the last act. For a moment, black and white alike, they were not looking at what it contained; and then the range shortened, the focus grew sharp, and they were all looking.

Three human bodies, and two animal, were in the clearing; dead for two days in burning heat, they had lost the sharp outlines of life, but they were still to be recognized. Two of them were Tom and Cynthia Ronald, lying staring at the sky. The third was Father Schwemmer. The two animals were goats.

The Ronalds were naked and, from the horrible mutilation of their bodies, it was clear that many men had taken part in their death, in a gruesome ritual. It was now clear also why Zuva, literally to save his life, had been unable to describe the hideous scene.

Father Schwemmer hung skeleton-thin from a cross, in the classic attitude of agony. On either side of his crude, yellowwood cross, seemingly according to some much older ritual, were two smaller crosses bearing, spread-eagled, two goats. The turf round the crosses had been marked out in the semblance of a huge fish, and brushwood burned in a long shallow trench, so that the fish emblem stood out, branded upon the living earth.

Crump, whey-faced, muttered The Saviour's name, in anguish. David's stomach heaved; he turned aside and vomited, and then faced the fearful sight again, with stony determination. Within the circle, Gotwela and Zuva stood like cast statues; at their backs, the U-Maulas formed a guilty ring, looking down at their feet.

Simpson, the leader, stood alone, nearest the crosses and the bodies. His face was working violently, with pity and horror; there were tears wet on his cheeks. When he had looked his full, he turned back from the crest of the hill; and then, as if cutting many corners, forgetting many laws, he pointed a shaking finger at Gotwela, and said, "Call your people."

"My people are here," answered Gotwela indifferently.

"Call *all* your people," said Simpson. His voice was shaking, but no one who heard it could have thought it the shaking of weakness. "There are many in the forest nearby." He looked beyond him at the ring of trees, where here and there a face or figure was to be seen, peering briefly from the shadows. "Call them."

"How shall I call them?" Gotwela protested on a surly note.

Simpson moved forward swiftly. With the blunt muzzle of his revolver he pried open Gotwela's mouth, and forced the gun within. "Call your people," he said again thickly, "while you still have a tongue to call with."

He withdrew the gun muzzle, wet and cloudy, and Gotwela swallowed. But he raised his voice, "Come out," he said, speaking towards the margin of the forest. "Draw near."

"Louder," said Simpson.

"COME OUT!" said Gotwela. He turned his head, shouting at the blank forest. "DRAW NEAR!"

He repeated it many times, an eerie sound of command against the wall of the trees; and presently men and women began to flock fearfully out of the forest, closing their ranks with the prisoners who were already there. Presently the whole clearing was filled with people, edging forwards, overrunning and obliterating the burnt marks of the fish, surrounding the bodies and the crosses. There must have been two thousand of them, staring, trembling, not uttering a sound. Captain Simpson looked towards Crump.

"Translate for me," he commanded. And then, turning to the main body of the people, "Look now at what you have done!"

Crump raised his voice, and repeated the words in the U-Maula tongue. Every eye was focused fearfully on the bodies.

"It is the fault of all of you," continued Simpson. David watched him, amazed; it was hard to identify this grim and avenging man with the hearty, gin-sipping naval aide he had known for the last few months. "You are vultures. You are all guilty. But the men most guilty are these two men."

There was utter silence as Crump repeated the words.

"All those who are guilty will be tried," said Simpson. "But these two, the leaders — " he gestured with his revolver " — will never be tried. The law is too slow for criminals such as these."

All eyes were upon him now. "You!" shouted Simpson suddenly, pointing at the nearest group of men. "Come here!"

Five or six men stepped forward, slowly and unwillingly.

"Cover them up," said Simpson, in the same loud voice, pointing at Tom and Cynthia Ronald. And as the men hesitated, not knowing how to obey, Simpson said, "Damn you! Take off your blankets. Cover these two." The bodies were quickly covered.

"Now take him down," said Simpson, pointing at the torn body of Father Schwemmer. The three shapes were ranged in the sunlight, decently hidden, restoring some order to the fearful scene. The air was the cleaner for it, but not yet clean enough.

In the silence, in the middle of the huge crowd, the click of Simpson's revolver was the loudest sound ever heard in the forest.

Simpson turned sideways to Crump. "You can take a walk, if you like," he said, as if he were talking in his sleep. "This is my show. If you hear a shot, it just means that my gun is in working order."

Crump looked at him levelly, preserving his own discipline, abdicating the rest. "I'm staying," he said. "You may be sorry afterwards. But you know what you're doing."

"I shall never be sorry," said Simpson, "as long as I live. David?"

"I'm staying," said David.

Simpson turned again. In the deadly silence, against the beating of a thousand hearts, he walked toward Gotwela and Zuva. "You are murderers," he said. "Kneel down."

Gotwela, sullen and resigned, obeyed without seeming to hear. Zuva also fell on his knees, but as he knelt he twisted his body round toward Simpson, and screamed at him, "You can't do this. It is contrary to all law. I demand a fair trial."

"A fair trial would condemn you to death, and you would be hanged," said Simpson, in the same sleepwalking voice. "Perhaps six months from now. But you are not going to live so long. You are too horrible. Turn round. Look up. Look at the cross."

Gotwela's head was sunk on his chest, and his huge body was

slack. By his side, Zuva still screamed and clasped his hands, and a babble of words poured from his lips. "Geneva Convention," he mouthed, as if reciting a charm. "Prisoners of war."

"Translate," said Simpson again, looking up at the sky. And then, to those watching in horror, "These two men, who were your leaders, are murderers. Remember this moment, because it is a moment of swift justice. You all know that they have killed a priest — " he pointed down at the blanketed corpses " — and the District Officer, and his wife. *Do any of you think that I will let them live?*"

Crump's voice as he translated was less taut, less filled with rage, but firm as a rock nonetheless.

"They are hereby condemned to death," said Simpson. "They are hereby executed." His head came down, the revolver came up. Crump was still translating as the two shots rang out.

Chapter 12

THE PLANE, a shabby old Dakota, bumped twice in the noonday heat, then settled down on its steady course, due east for Windhoek. Another trip, Pharamaul to the mainland, was under way.

But this time it was not a routine trip, the pilot mused; this was an official charter party, no less, with a secret take-off time and top Government priority; the plane reserved for Dinamaula, and the chap who was bear-leading him back to England. No other passengers allowed, no freight, above all no pressmen.

The pilot glanced behind him, through the open door into the main passenger space. Dinamaula, sitting by himself, was staring out of the window; the man in charge of him also sat alone, across the aisle, reading some papers.

Dinamaula had no thoughts, as he stared out of the plane window at the cloud-mottled gray surface of the South Atlantic; not even the bitter thoughts of an expatriate, not even the foreboding of a prisoner. This had been his mood for a long time now — a sort of emptiness of spirit and will — and he was carrying his vacuum with him into exile. He had come to Pharamaul with bright hope, stayed briefly and unhappily, and been ordered to leave. He was

numbed, not by pain or grief or anger, but by the abject nothingness that pervaded his spirit.

David Bracken had many thoughts, almost too many to contain
in one brain at one time. Though it had happened a full week
ago, the shock of Shebiya was still with him. Indeed, there had
been times during the past week when even the trusted Maula
policemen at Gamate, or the ancient servants at Government
House, were all lumped together in his mind as murderers, fiends,
deadly enemies. The task of acting as "Conducting Officer" to
Dinamaula had seemed deeply offensive for that very reason,
though now that the thing was in train, he simply wanted to dis-
charge it smoothly. He did not specially want to talk to Dinamaula.

The immediate past had been full of incident, and of work which
came as a relief from thought. The journey down from Shebiya,
where Simpson and Crump had been left to restore order and
separate the true criminals from their hapless followers, had been
swift; David had found Gamate sullen but quiet, resting firmly
upon a brusque military rule. For now there were soldiers everywhere: standing guard on Government buildings, clamping down
on meetings, enforcing strict curfew, patrolling at night — and
also shaving in the open air while stripped to the waist, peeling
potatoes, brewing tea, and spoiling all the children. On the night
of their arrival there had been one minor riot on the *aboura* ground,
swiftly quelled, followed by a vast, night-long roundup of prisoners
and suspects. After that, there had been nothing but good behavior,
the length and breadth of the town.

In Gamate, also, had been the assembled press; and to them,
David had given the first eyewitness account of what had happened
up at Shebiya. He had told his story simply, with nothing left
out, allowing the ghastly detail to have its effect. He did not say,
"I told you so," nor even infer it; there was no fun in being right,
when the cost was Cynthia Ronald and all the others. When he had
finished, the questions were few, and markedly subdued.

"Can we get any pictures?" asked a photographer. "People ought
to see this."

"I agree with you," said David. "But they've all been buried, and
the crosses have been burned. There's nothing left."

"Can *we* go up?" asked Tulbach Browne.

"No," answered David.

"Why not?" asked Axel Hallmarck.

Forsdick, the acting Resident Commissioner, sitting at David's side, answered for him. "The whole Shebiya area has been closed off," he said abruptly. "Military precaution. We're not allowing anyone in, till things are back to normal."

"That's pretty highhanded," said Tulbach Browne querulously. "How do we know — "

In a sudden blind rage, David broke in. "Can't you leave it alone, even now? The Ronalds and Father Schwemmer have been murdered, in this hideous way. The police are rounding up all the people responsible, and trying to make some sense out of the place. We don't want anyone to get in the way of that process."

AFTER Windhoek it grew hotter, and the plane bumped and lurched without respite as it weaved its swift way into the heart of Africa. Dinamaula still stared out of his window, preserving alike his silence and his indifference. Finally he put his hand over his brow, shutting out the sunlight, and tried to sleep.

David Bracken was staring at a piece of paper which he had drawn by chance out of his brief case. The paper was headed: "Chief-Designate Dinamaula: Arrangements for Transfer to London." It was the word "transfer" that had set him remembering again the final scene between Dinamaula and the Governor.

The Governor had not done well. He had talked round the subject of the current unrest in Gamate for some ten minutes; then suddenly he had gone off at a tangent, trying to connect Dinamaula directly with the shambles up at Shebiya.

"We have information," he said laboriously, "that your cousin Zuva called on you just before he left for Shebiya. Is that so?"

Dinamaula nodded carelessly. "Yes."

"What exactly did you tell him to do, when he reached Shebiya?"

"I told him nothing. I did not know he was going to Shebiya."

Sir Elliott sighed, fluttered some papers, tried again. "What about the strike, then, here in Port Victoria? That was obviously organized under your direction."

"No."

"Oh, come now! The ringleaders are known to have called on you, shortly before the strike started."

"I do not even know who the ringleaders are."

"Be that as it may," the Governor said, unexpectedly and nervously, "I have come to the conclusion that you are and have been directly connected with serious disturbances in various parts of Pharamaul, that you are a focus of intrigue and indiscipline, and that you cannot remain in this country. In pursuance, therefore, of the powers legally vested in me, you are hereby ordered to leave the Principality of Pharamaul forthwith, and you are not to return save with the express approval of Her Majesty's Government."

David, watching Dinamaula at that moment, saw an instant of absolute, hurt amazement; the mask slipped, showing them all a stricken man. Then Dinamaula said, with difficulty, "But my rights as chief? My inheritance?"

"They are in abeyance," said the Governor. "Indefinitely."

Behind Dinamaula's shocked face, David tried to see the dead bodies of Shebiya. He saw them, but not clearly; he tried to hate Dinamaula, but his hatred was not pure. Perhaps it was his own fault, because he realized, in spite of his hatred, that there were dappled shades of right and wrong in this matter, and that the only things in black and white were the people concerned.

"But can I never return?"

"I really have no idea," said the Governor, rising.

After that, it was simply office routine; and the routine had brought the two of them to this point of time and place, six thousand feet up, two hundred miles from Livingstone, on the crooked pathway to exile in England.

Like all air-line pilots whose routes took them anywhere near the Victoria Falls, a few miles south of Livingstone, this pilot circled the falls twice, at low altitude, before coming in to land. The view was the finest in Africa; trees, stray herds of game racing away from the plane's shadow, lush green vegetation, broad, slow-moving water — and then the sudden majestic cleft in the surface of the earth, down which the water plunged in a roaring curtain nearly a mile across. Both Dinamaula and David, who had moved across the plane to the seat behind him, watched entranced; no matter how many times one had seen this wonder, its massive power and torrential beauty made it freshly irresistible. Dinamaula looked at the scene with wide eyes, roused at last from his lethargy. David, gazing his fill, was struck by one crystal-clear resolve: that, in spite of everything, he would never leave Africa.

It was after they changed planes at Livingstone that the two of them started to talk. They started because it suddenly seemed foolish and artificial to do otherwise, and because they were now sitting side by side, in the big, comfortable BOAC plane, and silence at such close quarters was more awkward than speech.

David spoke first, remarking out of the blue, "I'd like to talk, unless you want to sleep."

Dinamaula was not surprised, and he spoke his own thoughts straight away. "I don't expect to sleep. I would like to talk, about anything at all. But I am not happy, and not very friendly."

David grinned. It was the kind of answer he had hoped for. "Fair enough. I've got one or two reservations myself."

"What are your reservations?" asked Dinamaula.

"Shebiya." There seemed no sense in not going straight to the point. "And before that, the riots at Gamate. And some of the things you said about running the country. What are yours?"

Dinamaula brooded, but his face was not sullen; it was simply young and hurt. "Being kicked out, at twelve hours' notice," he said briefly. "Being treated like a child. Being patronized. Mr. Bracken, can you tell me exactly where I went wrong?"

"You brought it on yourself, and I honestly can't express it in any other way," said David. "I'm not saying that your ideas aren't good ones, or that they wouldn't work out, but you tackled the whole thing in the wrong way, right from the beginning."

"I only wanted to improve things," said Dinamaula. "The whole place seemed so out of date, like a museum of the nineteenth century. I wanted to make it take a step forward."

"All right. So do we. But you've got to use the existing channels, you've got to fit your plans in with what's going on already. Andrew Macmillan, for example. You should never have got across him, the way you did."

"He annoyed me, from the very first day. It was ridiculous, intolerable. He always treated me like a schoolboy."

"Quite so. And what *you* did wrong was not to make allowances for him. He was an old-fashioned civil servant, near the end of his career. Don't forget he was old enough to be your father, almost your grandfather. Of course he was slow, he was schoolmasterish, he tried to discipline you. On the other hand, he did know the Territory from end to end, far better than you did, and he did have its interests at heart. And, you see, once you turned awkward and uncoöperative, he had to crack down. We all did."

Khartoum came, after the long, thousand-mile night haul over the desert and the foothills of Ethiopia. When the moon glinted, it glinted on the river Nile, a mile below them, its banks pricked here and there by nomad fires.

After Khartoum, the chips were down. "I had nothing to do with that horrible thing at Shebiya," said Dinamaula. "I only had a few vague hints about it from Zuva — nothing definite, nothing to go on. If I had known, of course I would have told you."

"We still think it was partly your fault — a chain reaction."

"I know you do. The strike at Port Victoria *was* my fault. I thought that was a good idea. And some of the riots at Gamate, too. I wanted to get my own back. But of course the people who did most of the planning at Gamate were the press."

"They were no friends of yours," said David hardly.

"Perhaps not. It was flattering, though."

"There'll be a lot of that in London, too. I honestly think it would be a mistake to get mixed up with them."

"Is that an official warning?"

"Sort of."

Cairo, at dawn, smelt like an ancient sewer; the stink hit them instantly, as soon as the plane was opened and a fat Egyptian official waddled in and began, with rare effrontery, to spray them with disinfectant. As they took off again, and rose above the Delta of the Nile, the new sun illumined a thousand streams and a thousand glistening mudbanks, and then suddenly the pure blue of the Mediterranean was the only thing in view.

"Pharamaul can't stand still," said Dinamaula. "No country in

Africa can. We both agree on that. But how is Pharamaul going to make any real progress in *any* direction if you block new ideas?"

"We don't," said David.

"You blocked *me*."

"Only because you wanted to move too fast. But of course, in the future, it *will* make progress. We mean it to."

"Do you think I will ever see that progress get under way?"

"I hope so."

"As chief?"

"I honestly don't know."

"I'd like to go back one day."

"There would have to be all sorts of safeguards."

"But even so. Tell them that, if you get the chance. I love that funny little country."

"So do I."

Rome on its seven hills was elegant, sunlit, and noisy — with planes taking off, motor scooters weaving across the macadam.

"Only a few more hours," said David. "Aren't you tired?"

Dinamaula smiled. "Not at all. After all, we've only been talking for twenty-six hours. You should belong to *my* tribe, Mr. Bracken. This would just be a preliminary chat."

High above the Alps, level with the crest of Mont Blanc gleaming like a snowy sheath on their left hand, Dinamaula suddenly said, "Of course, there never *was* an actual girl."

"Girl?" repeated David, who had been watching the white-encrusted hills and the wreaths of mist below.

"A white girl. The one I was supposed to be going to marry."

David turned, surprised at last. "Why on earth didn't you say so then?"

"I told you — Macmillan annoyed me. And also, I wanted to reserve my right to marry anyone I chose, black or white, *if* I wanted to. Why shouldn't I? There's no law against it. And don't you see? I wanted to feel *free* — free to marry, free to rule. After all, I was the chief. That is what a chief should be."

"You really should have told us there wasn't an actual girl."

"It wouldn't have made any difference."

London Airport was almost fogged in, with a cloud base at a

mere five hundred feet; they dropped through it, bumping and sideslipping. It would be raining in Whitehall, thought David; the murky gloom of the Scheduled Territories Office would be murkier still. He longed for Pharamaul, and dry sunshine, and his known friends, and Nicole.

Zipping up his overnight bag as they joined the disembarking queue in the aisle, he remarked idly, "I shall be getting married when I go back to Port Victoria."

Dinamaula asked, in a voice totally expressionless, "Are you going to marry a white girl?" and they both suddenly burst out laughing.

They were both still laughing when they got off the plane, and hurried past the barrier that held in check a surging mob of pressmen and photographers.

"Dinamaula was smiling bravely through his misery," commented the *Daily Thresh* next morning. "If there is any medal for men going into exile, he should have it tomorrow."

"The ineffable Mr. David Bracken," said the *New Nation's* most splenetic columnist, "stepped off the plane wearing a somewhat inane grin, which he did not trouble to conceal. It could have been a grin of triumph. Whatever prompted it, it was in execrable taste. Is it too much to ask that when minor Government officials are entrusted . . ."

SIR HUBERT GODBOLD strolled to the window, looked at the rain falling steadily on Whitehall, watched a bus recover from a skid as it rounded the sloping corner from Trafalgar Square, and then sat down at his desk again.

He shrugged, pulled some papers towards him, and began to focus his thoughts. He was seeing David Bracken within a few minutes, partly because he always saw anyone who came back to London as soon as they arrived, partly because he wanted to assimilate a few firsthand impressions.

He smiled a welcome as David entered. "Sit down, Bracken." He consulted his watch, and smiled a second time. "Now tell me about Dinamaula. What sort of journey did you have, and what sort of mood is he in?"

David glanced swiftly round the solid, high-pillared, luxurious room, and then back to Godbold again. The man behind the desk was wonderfully reassuring. He leant back in his chair, and began to answer.

"It was a good journey, sir. Better than I expected. Dinamaula was very quiet, perhaps rather sulky, when we left Pharamaul. But after Livingstone I started talking, and I suppose he felt like talking, too, because he came to life almost immediately."

"I'm glad you got him to talk. What was it all about?"

"Pretty well everything, sir. We were both perfectly frank."

David set to work to describe to Godbold those five thousand miles of conversation, with their revelations, surprises, and occasional disagreements. Godbold interrupted only once, towards the end, when David mentioned Dinamaula's marriage plans.

"You mean," queried Godbold, his eyebrows raised, "he made the positive statement that there was no white woman?"

"Yes, sir. He said he originally made the remark to show his independence, and that, when he was challenged on it later, he made up his mind not to back down. He was feeling by then as if he were being told to behave himself or take the consequences."

Godbold considered the information, his lips pursed, the lines on his forehead deep. David could almost feel the other man's powerful mind catching his up in great leaps, seeing beyond one peak to the next. "But it may still be an issue to the tribe," said Godbold finally, almost to himself. "It's still there, as a disturbing element in his personality, if he ever goes back."

"He might perhaps give guarantees on the point."

Godbold's eyes suddenly sharpened. "Did he say that?"

"Not quite. He said, or implied, that if there had to be certain safeguards governing his return, he would accept them."

Godbold smiled. "Your journey was not wasted. Go on."

"I think that's really about all, sir. He was quite candid about the mistakes he'd made, and about trying to move too fast. He agreed that there might have been faults on both sides — "

"Agreed?" Godbold's eyebrows rose alarmingly. "Did *you* propound such a proposition?"

"Proposition?" David was taken aback.

"That there were faults on *our* side?"

It was an awkward, even dangerous moment; in a single phrase, he might throw everything away. But it was also a moment to be honest; the man before him wanted a true account, and a true account included just such an element as this.

"I agreed with Dinamaula, sir," he answered slowly, "that if he had been handled differently, when he arrived — in spite of that silly newspaper story — all this later trouble might have been avoided. He agreed with *me* that he had gone about things the wrong way, giving the impression that he was going to put through a lot of radical reforms, no matter what the opposition."

Godbold's expression remained formidably critical. "I presume you made it clear that you were expressing a personal opinion."

"No, I didn't, sir. We were — " David floundered, and then recovered. "We were both trying to talk candidly, to tell the truth without scoring a lot of debating points. It was that sort of session."

Godbold was silent for perhaps two minutes; David stared at the carpet, aware that he had blundered; the picture in Godbold's mind — that of a junior official giving away points to the enemy — must be brutally clear. It came as another shock to hear Godbold saying, in a different voice, "Where did we go wrong — *who* went wrong — in our handling of Dinamaula, when he first arrived?"

David had a moment of pure panic; he wanted to say that he had changed his mind, that everything had been wonderful, that he had only been joking. But he raised his head to find Godbold looking at him with the same steady interest, and he took heart.

"I'm afraid it was Andrew Macmillan, principally, sir. Whatever he said to Dinamaula he must have put very bluntly and forcibly, giving Dinamaula no chance to explain or to withdraw. On the plane, Dinamaula said he was made to feel like a schoolboy. Andrew himself told me he had given Dinamaula a flea in his ear. That's surely wrong, in spite of the age difference. But I told Dinamaula that it was up to him to make allowances for Andrew as well, that he was old, and also very wise and very capable."

"What did Dinamaula say to that?"

"He said 'yes.' "

"What other mistake did we make?"

"I think they all stemmed from that, sir — treating him like a little boy, instead of the incoming chief. Then everything got out of hand very quickly, and Andrew tried the same sort of thing with the Regents and the tribe, and *they* wouldn't stand for it either. I don't want to seem to put all the blame onto Macmillan, sir. I think he was a wonderful man, and I wish to God he weren't dead. We *all* tried to deal with the thing in a rather — rather superior way, and it just didn't work. It was too serious."

"And too volatile?"

David nodded. "Yes. It just blew up in our faces. I think our Secretariat, and Andrew's people in Gamate, would have been good enough to handle that sort of crisis in ninety-nine cases out of a hundred. But the hundredth case was an exception, and we didn't measure up to it. Of course, it was the press who really put the lid on the whole thing. They made rings round us, right from the start. We should have taken a much stronger line with them."

Godbold shook his head. "If we were on firm enough ground, we should have been able to deal with them perfectly easily, without any 'strong line.' After all, you can't expect to operate in a vacuum. The press must be free to observe and to report."

"They did a lot more than that in Pharamaul, sir."

"Maybe so. In fact, certainly so. But the things we do and say, in a place like Pharamaul, ought to be proof against *all* criticism. If we are fair, if we are honest, and if we are steadfast."

Godbold rose and walked to the window. There was another long moment of silence, and then he turned, and spoke firmly and quickly, as if reflecting truth.

"We have these same problems all over Africa, as you know. There's no single answer to Africa. Out of any of our possessions or dependencies there, we can make, or try to make, one of three things: a black dominion, a black-and-white partnership, or a purified white enclave. I think we can write off the last alternative, as a matter of common sense. It goes directly against the historic trend. The black dominion is a perfectly feasible idea, if the people concerned are really ready for complete independence in a very difficult world. It's already emerging in Nigeria and on the Gold Coast. In my personal view the most promising of all — " he em-

phasized his words with a pointing finger " — is what they are trying to do in the Central African Federation. There's the beginning,
there, of a genuine black-white partnership, with both races sitting
down side by side to legislate and to govern. It's almost the only
one in the world, and God prosper it! If that Federation scheme is
a success, it may serve as a pattern for Africa as a whole, and that
would be a very proud thing indeed. But in all these changes, and
this is important when we think of Pharamaul, there is one thing
never to be forgotten, and that is the pace of Africa. It is a pace
which we have always had to follow. If we delay freedom, there is
an explosion. If we hurry it, there is disaster."

For the first time, David broke in. "But which is Pharamaul,
sir? There's already been an explosion — because of delay, I suppose. But they're not yet ready for anything like independence."

"I'll tell you what we're going to do in Pharamaul," answered
Godbold, glancing at his watch, "and then I'm afraid I must keep
my next appointment. We're going to forgive and forget, and *they*
are going to forgive and forget, and we'll move on to the next
step. It will involve more say for them in their own affairs, more
local self-administration. Specifically, we'll keep the Council of
Regents going, until a chief is ready to take over. That might well
be Dinamaula — it all depends on events. Forsdick will move up
as Resident Commissioner. I shall be reinforcing the Secretariat
with one or two people from here. It's possible that there will be
a new Governor, though that is strictly between ourselves at the
moment. And you," he said, smiling because he had so obviously
kept it till the end, "will take over at Shebiya, as District Officer."

In spite of himself, David started. The word "Shebiya" still
produced the old reaction, of horror and disgust and fear. Godbold
must have caught his glance, because he said instantly, "In some
ways, I realize, you have the hardest job of all, because you were
there, and saw the horrible things they did. But you too have got
to be part of forgive-and-forget. It will be quite easy for us to forgive
the Maulas, here in London; less easy in Gamate; and hardest of
all where you are going to be. But it must be done, because all of
Pharamaul has got to take the next step forward — and we have
got to grant them that step, and not have it forced out of us."

David swallowed. "I want to go to Shebiya, sir. There's nothing I'd like better. It's just that — surely they have to be punished?"

"Some of them must be punished," agreed Godbold. "But then we've got to return, without equivocation, to the pace of Africa. The Maulas have outgrown Macmillan; they are ready for something else. They mustn't be prevented from attaining that something else, because a few of them tried to anticipate history."

Godbold stood up, and smiled. "Thank you for coming along, and for listening. A captive audience, I'm afraid. . . . I shall be seeing Dinamaula this afternoon, and I value your account of him, and your judgment. I think we might say, in the White Paper, that he will remain in exile until the state of the Territory is normal and tranquil, when we will review the ban on him. Something like that. We'll see how things develop, and how he behaves here."

"He could be of great value, sir. He's in a different mood now. He hasn't been talking to the press, and I don't think he will."

They walked towards the door. "Thank you very much for the job, sir," said David.

"I won't see you again," said Godbold, and held out his hand. He walked down the corridor with David, past a marble bust of Cecil Rhodes. "Once, during or just after the American Civil War, Lincoln was asked why he did not destroy all his enemies, the men who were plotting or fighting against him. His answer was: 'I destroy my enemy when I make him my friend.' That's the only answer, in Pharamaul and a lot of other places. Make him your friend! Now go back to Pharamaul, and get to work."

WEDDINGS from Government House were so rare that no one knew quite what to expect. The proceedings in church were decorous enough: Aidan Purves-Brownrigg, the best man, produced the ring from his flowered brocade waistcoat with suitable aplomb; Sir Elliott Vere-Toombs, giving the bride away, played a monumental role. The organ thundered out the Wedding March till the old church rafters shook.

"Strolling on the spacious lawns," scribbled Miss Tilly Sproule, social editress of the *Times of Pharamaul*, "the youth and beauty — yes, and the maturity! — of Port Victoria surrendered to the

happy mood of the moment. The band re-
galed us with merry music, while the guests
partook of the lavish hospitality of their host
and hostess, Sir Elliott and Lady Vere-
Toombs (so soon to leave us, alas!), who
graciously stood *in loco parentis* to the lovely
bride.

"The receiving line stretched from the
steps of Government House to far back under
the trees. Prominent among those waiting
their turn . . ."

Lou Strogoff, the American consul, was
talking to the Samuel Loganquists. The yacht
Wander Lust was back in harbor, after a
cruise round to Lourenço Marques.

"Pretty girl," said Mrs. Loganquist. *"Very*
pretty. You know, weddings make me sad."

"Do weddings always make you sad, Mrs.
Loganquist?" asked Lou Strogoff.

"Well, mine always have."

"Honey, *please!"* said Mr. Loganquist.

Nicole, David, and Aidan met under a tree
in the center of the lawn.

"Darling, I'm dead!" said Nicole, and
gulped some champagne. "We must have
shaken a thousand hands."

"Not much longer now," said David.
"Then we can catch the Johannesburg plane."

"You know," said Aidan, "I shall miss
you two children."

"Oh, we'll be down here from time to time," said David.

"That won't be much use to me," observed Aidan. And as David
looked mystified, he went on, "If you had read your telegrams
this morning, Mr. District Officer, you would have known about
my posting to Washington."

"Oh, Aidan!" exclaimed Nicole. "How wonderful for you!" She
kissed him warmly.

"Congratulations," said David. "That's terrific."

"I've been drinking to my good fortune ever since I heard."

Nicole entwined her arm in David's, watching the people strolling to and fro, and the lengthening shadows on the lawn. Under the trees, the magnificently robed Maula servants still worked like beavers, opening, pouring, bearing trays, weaving a swift cross-pattern against the noble back cloth of Government House.

"What a lovely wedding," she said.

"It hasn't even started yet. Darling, you look ravishing. You must always wear a wedding dress."

Her eyes held his, soft and dreamy. She squeezed his arm.

"I think," he said, looking across the lawn towards a crowd of people unaccountably embarking on a square dance, "that we might start to fade out."

DAVID BRACKEN walked slowly back from the police post, across Shebiya's main square, on his way home.

He had been attending a small military ceremony — the formal lowering of colors, for the last time, at the police post, where the soldiers had been quartered. The two platoons of Lancashire Fusiliers had been stationed at Shebiya for five months; now they were on their way back to Kenya. The subaltern in charge, a keen young man who smoked a pipe and read nothing but the *Manual of Small Arms Drill,* would be coming over later for a farewell drink. After that, David would be on his own.

As he surveyed his small empire, he was content to have it so, whatever happened in the future. Though nothing in his life so far had been as exciting, as difficult, as fraught with fear and hope, as taking over the job of District Officer in this tightrope-walking corner of the world, yet, now that he had made a start, he would not have exchanged his job for any other.

The U-Maulas were still, by turns, surly, neutral, or afraid, and he himself still functioned as the sole native authority, since no candidates for the local Council of Headmen had yet come forward. But they would come, if not this year, then the next. In the meantime, the spring sowing was not far off; he had made some friends; a new mission house had been built; a produce-exchange system with Gamate had been established; and a full-width road was being cleared down to Fish Village on the coast, where — wonder of wonders — the harbor was even now being enlarged to accommodate Pharamaul's first fish-processing plant. The omens, for the most part, were good, the small future assessable.

But of course, there could be no neat ending to this story, either here in Shebiya, or anywhere else in Pharamaul; there could only be slow progress, and hard work extending over a hundred hills into the future. Such was the pace of Africa, and in the meantime, there was a garden to be cultivated, with the tools that were to hand.

There was a man coming towards him down the track, an old man in a yellow blanket and beehive hat. But for all his years he held himself proudly; and when he drew near, David saw that it was Pemboli, the headman from Fish Village, who was here to recruit labor for the work on the new harbor. That, in itself, was something fresh and hopeful; under Gotwela's hard rule, there had been perennial bad feeling between the villages.

"Well, Pemboli," said David, saluting him.

"*Jah, barena.*" Pemboli raised his hat gravely.

"All goes well?"

"*Jah, barena.*"

"The men are coming forward?"

"Slowly."

"Ask me if you need help."

"*Jah, barena.*"

"*Ahsula!*"

"*Ahsula, barena.*"

My empire, thought David wryly; what will it become, what can I make of it, where does progress lie? He recalled the proclamation recently issued by the new Governor, when he succeeded Sir Elliott Vere-Toombs at Port Victoria. His aims, declared the new Governor, a shrewd, energetic ex-soldier with a reputation for decisive action, were "to restore order, and work towards such degree of self-government for Pharamaul as Her Majesty's Government may from time to time approve."

David, struck by a familiar ring, had thumbed through the manuscript of Andrew's book on the Territory, which was now in his care. The new Governor's wording was almost identical with that used by the first Lieutenant-Governor, after the original troop landing in Pharamaul, more than a hundred years earlier.

Things moved on, but only a step at a time. It was indeed an ordained pace, and it could not be challenged. Even the murderous disorder through which they had just passed was, in the life of this fabled continent, no more than an uneasy dream, a turning-over, a muffled groaning in the sleep.

Someone else was coming towards him. This time it was Nicole. He watched her loved figure against the now familiar background of Shebiya — the dusty tracks, the thatched reed huts, the goats and the children running between them. It was the time of the evening meal; smoke from a thousand fires drifted across the sky, blunting the firm outlines, giving the whole scene a hazy dreamlike quality. He had thought that Shebiya would be a place of fear and loathing, poisoned by what he had seen there. So it had been, to start with. But Nicole had cured all that.

"Hallo, darling," he said. "What's for supper?"

"My romantic lover," she said, kissing him.

With his arm round her he turned and looked back at the way he had come. In the doorways of many huts, U-Maula men and women were standing. Some few were watching them, most were busy, intent on the evening tasks at the end of another day.

"How goes the empire?" asked Nicole, watching his face as he stared down the hill towards the police post and the bare flagpole. "Did you have a good day?"

"Not bad. Lots to do, still."

"But Shebiya *is* settling down again. So is the whole island."

"Oh yes." He pressed her side, and then swung round, looking towards a much wider horizon. "It'll be all right," he told her, "as long as we love each other."

Nicholas Monsarrat

NICHOLAS MONSARRAT was not intended by his family to be an author. Born in Liverpool, where his father was an eminent surgeon, he was sent to Winchester, then to Cambridge, where he received an honors law degree (in 1931), preparatory to entering his uncle's Nottingham law office. All seemed set for young Monsarrat to become a partner, but after eighteen months he departed for London with a half-finished novel, a typewriter, and forty pounds to his name. For six years he made a precarious living at his new trade, writing three novels and a play with scant financial success.

During the war Monsarrat served with distinction in the Royal Navy, having five years' convoy-escort duty in the Atlantic and attaining the rank of lieutenant commander. His notes during this time were the basis for four novels, among them *H. M. Corvette*. His novel *Leave Cancelled* was one of the outstanding books of 1945.

In 1946 he went to South Africa as an information officer in the Commonwealth Relations office. There, in hot, landlocked Johannesburg, he wrote of the cold Atlantic in his novel, *The Cruel Sea* (Condensed Books, Winter 1952), which became a sensational best-seller. *The Tribe That Lost Its Head,* set in tropical Africa, was written while the temperature was 10° below, in Ottawa, where from 1953 until last year Monsarrat was Director of the British Information Service.

Mr. Monsarrat now plans to devote his full time to writing. His wife, Philippa Crosby, is herself an established journalist.

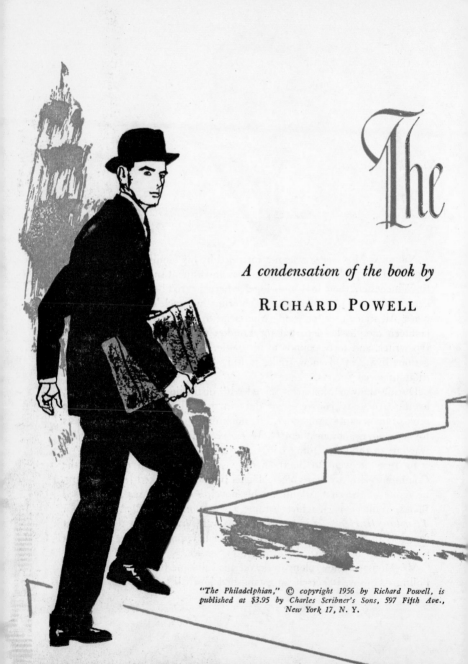

The

A condensation of the book by

RICHARD POWELL

Philadelphian

Illustrations by Noel Sickles

YOUNG Anthony Lawrence had no money, little family, no influential connections. He had only brains, charm and ambition to take him where he was determined to go.

Here, against the staid yet enigmatic background of Philadelphia's Main Line, is the always entertaining story of Anthony's progress: in school, in war, in the law, in love. Following him into the byways of his chosen profession, the reader is given a fascinating insight into Anthony's talent, his knowledge of courts and clients and the legal mind, his consummate lawyer's skill in dealing with explosive situations — traits that are to take him to the top of the Philadelphia ladder and to the unsuspected road beyond.

CHAPTER 1

IN 1924, the school Anthony Lawrence went to sold its old brick buildings in the center of Philadelphia, and joined the great migration to the suburbs. The trustees of Franklin Academy bought an estate in Wynnewood on the Main Line. The mansion on the estate had been erected in the eighteen-nineties when the castle-building urge was so common. The result had been a heap of battlements, turrets and buttresses which looked like a stone quarry turned inside out. It was just the thing for resisting either a siege in the Middle Ages or modern schoolboys.

The radical step of moving to the suburbs emboldened the trustees. They retired Doctor Luther Hay Whitney, who was getting into his seventies, and for the new headmaster they not only went outside the ministry but even outside of Philadelphia. Doctor Lowell McClintic was thirty-five, and already had a reputation in New England preparatory-school circles.

The trustees of Franklin Academy left many old furnishings and a few old ideas behind in the move to Wynnewood, but they did bring along a short strip of worn green carpet. This they placed reverently in front of the new headmaster's carved oak desk. He was a bit startled to find it there when he began his new job. It looked as out of place in his paneled office as a battered fishing cap at a Board of Directors' meeting. When he asked about it, the gaunt old head of his Latin Department, Doctor Harry Judson, said in his rumbling voice, "I should leave it there, sir, if I were you. That is where the boys stand when it is necessary for you to talk to them. They are used to that green carpet."

The new headmaster knew that discipline in a preparatory school is the result of many subtle influences. He did not move the old green carpet. When the fall term began, a wave of mischief swept through the student body, because many boys thought that with all the changes a new, free era was beginning. One by one, that fall, they met the new headmaster in his office. When they saw the old green carpet, worn to its threads by a generation of uneasy feet, something happened. They stood on the carpet, shifting unhappily from foot to foot, and said yes sir and no sir and that they would do better, sir.

In June 1929, when he was nearly fifteen, Anthony Lawrence stood on the old green carpet, facing Doctor McClintic across the oak desk. Clinky had not invited him to sit in the chair beside the desk, which was where you sat when everything was all right. Clinky let him stand on the carpet, and that meant trouble. Anthony shrugged. It didn't matter if one more person wanted to pick on him. Only why didn't Clinky start?

Not until years later did he realize that Doctor McClintic's actions were as perfectly timed as a veteran actor's, with the same keen awareness of the mood of the audience, and the same skill at moving it to tears or terror or even relief. All Anthony knew at the time was that he began by shrugging and ended by trembling. First Clinky glanced up at him, then he went on scratching away with a pen at some crackling papers. A telephone purred softly and Clinky picked it up and said brusquely, "Yes ... no ... later." The backs of Anthony's legs began aching, and he broke out in a sweat. He found himself thinking: Aw, come on, Clinky. *Please.*

Finally the man leaned back in his swivel armchair. "Well, Anthony," he said. Clinky was ready now. Or was he? He fished out his pipe. There was silence, growing slowly more agonizing, while he dipped his pipe in a tobacco pouch and carefully tamped the tobacco into the bowl. He lit the pipe and puffed several times.

This was a bit of stage business, but the headmaster, unbeknownst to Anthony, was also giving himself time to think. He had learned a good deal about Philadelphia in his years at Franklin. Moreover, he made it his business to acquaint himself with the backgrounds of his students; and since Anthony happened to be old Doctor Judson's grandson, and a scholarship boy, Doctor McClintic was fully informed about his antecedents. He found them interesting.

Anthony's great-grandmother, Margaret O'Donnell, had been an ambitious Irish immigrant girl who had landed in Philadelphia and set herself up in a dressmaker's shop. Her daughter Mary, this boy's grandmother, had taken a long step upward. She had been a teacher in the public schools, and had married Harry Judson, who came of a pleasant old family from New Jersey. There still were rumors that the marriage had cost Judson the headmastership of Franklin Academy a long time ago. However that might have been, Mary Judson had made her husband very happy.

The Judsons had had only one child, a daughter, Kate, who was Anthony's mother. She had been a beautiful girl, had gone to the right school, had made the right friends, and had got herself married to William DeWitt Lawrence, heir to his mother's horse-car millions, who had a secure position on the middle rungs of Philadelphia's social ladder. But Lawrence had been killed in an auto crash just before Anthony was born, and old Mrs. Lawrence, who had never approved of the marriage, had cut Kate and the boy off without a cent. Anthony's mother, too proud to fight for her rights, had taken him home to live in her parents' house on Spruce Street. Her grandmother, the boy's great-grandmother, had still been alive at the time.

It was quite a story, the headmaster thought. From immigrant girl to Mrs. William DeWitt Lawrence was a good many levels for three women to jump in as many generations of living in Philadelphia. Doctor McClintic smiled to himself. Three generations, and here at last was the boy that great-grandmother, grandmother and mother must always have hoped for: a boy who, given the right opportunities, could go ahead by himself, perhaps even reach the top. The headmaster puffed at his pipe a last time and peered at Anthony through an ominous blue mist of smoke.

"Well, Anthony," he said again, "I'm sorry to see you under these conditions. I've always thought you had a great deal in you.

I'd hoped I'd see you in here only to congratulate you for some fine work."

"Yes sir," Anthony muttered.

"Can you quote the motto of the Academy, Anthony?"

"Uh, yes sir. 'Mens sana in corpore sano.'"

"And it means?"

"A sound mind in a sound body, doesn't it, sir?"

"That's right. If you had translated your Caesar that well in your final exam, you would not have scored thirty-seven in it."

"I guess that means I flunked Latin?"

"I'm afraid so. Can you guess how many subjects you passed?"

He hadn't really thought of his marks because it had been unpleasant to consider what they might be. "Gee," he said, coming up with a shocking idea, "maybe I only passed one or two."

Doctor McClintic said gently, "You didn't pass any."

Not any. It was hard to take in right away.

"A sound mind in a sound body. You haven't done very well on the first part, have you?"

"No sir."

"Now about the sound body. What teams have you gone out for this year, Anthony?"

Why ask him that? Clinky must know he couldn't have made any teams, anyway. Something had happened to his body in the past year. It got tall and lanky. It went around living a life of its own, bumping into things. Last winter, in gym class, he hadn't been able to chin himself once, and in the wall climb all he had done was hang there helplessly while the other kids snickered. "Gee," he mumbled, "I couldn't make any varsity teams."

"We have junior teams, too. They didn't appeal to you?"

"Uh, no sir."

"How many voluntary work hours on the school grounds have you donated this year?"

"I guess none, sir."

Doctor McClintic leaned back, and studied him. This, as Anthony realized years later, was the start of a careful probing process, designed to break through barriers of adolescence, to find out his loyalties, and then to use those loyalties to move him in a

desired direction. "We expect a lot of our scholarship students," Doctor McClintic said. "You've let the school down badly."

What had the dumb old place ever done for him? "Yes sir," he said, without much interest.

"One of the finest members of our faculty is your grandfather. He'll take this very hard, Tony."

His grandfather. He didn't feel strongly one way or another about his grandfather, a stooped old man who wandered around home and the school, booming things in Latin. "Yes," Anthony said, "I guess Grandfather won't like it much."

"You'd probably feel badly," Doctor McClintic said, "if you had to drop back a form while all your friends moved on."

His friends. That was a laugh. What friends?

"However," Doctor McClintic went on briskly, "what we're discussing, since you are a scholarship student, is not the matter of dropping back a form but the possibility of leaving school."

That shook him a little. "If I didn't come back here, sir, where would I go?"

"You must know Central High School. It's near your home. Many people might give you a discouraging picture of it, but I don't feel that way."

Anthony frowned. Who did Clinky think he was kidding? That place was a hole. "I don't think I'd like Central," he said.

"Well, perhaps not." Doctor McClintic paused. "I don't imagine," he said gently, "that your mother would like seeing you go there, either. She's worked very hard to give you a chance to get ahead." And she's also worked hard, he thought silently, to save you a little of the social standing she won through her marriage.

Doctor Judson had once told him that when Anthony was small his mother, Kate, had conducted a wedding-present service at Wanamaker's, making use of her name of Mrs. William DeWitt Lawrence. The job must have paid fairly well, but she had given it up — doubtless because Philadelphia society did not approve of your bartering your social standing to make money. Lately, Anthony's mother seemed always to hold some modestly paid position with the Junior League or the Matinee Musical, besides working earnestly as a volunteer on charity committees. Now, Doctor Mc-

Clintic recalled, she was running the Friday Afternoon Dancing Class at the Bellevue-Stratford, with Mrs. Hoyt Phelps.

Anthony's mother had never remarried; Doctor McClintic thought he knew why. It was said that big Mike Callahan had always worshiped the ground she walked on. But though Mike was a successful contractor now, his father was only old Callahan, the Franklin Academy caretaker. Mike was second-generation Irish. Not even lace-curtain. She would have refused him for the boy's sake if for no other. Doctor McClintic drew on the pipe and peered out keenly through the swirls of smoke.

Anthony's face was twitching. Clinky didn't have to bring his mother into this. "I guess she has worked hard," he muttered.

"A couple of times in the past I've happened to meet her when I had good things to tell her about you. Her eyes really lit up then. She's very proud of you, Anthony."

She wasn't proud when he had told on the club at dancing school last winter, Anthony thought. She couldn't be proud of him now. Probably she would never be proud of him again. But that business at dancing school had begun it; he wished he didn't remember it all so clearly. Peggy Vandeventer, the most unpopular girl in the class, had threatened to withdraw — and with her mother's influence she would have taken about twenty girls with her — if he didn't rat on the club the boys had. It had meant a lot to Anthony to be in that club, because what with his grandfather on the faculty, and not being good at sports, and not having nearly the money the other kids had, he had never before really had friends at school.

Eddie Eakins had organized the club in an unused coatroom. There were eight members and they would sneak off the dance floor in rotation, to play cards and talk and drink cokes. This left not enough boys on the floor for the girls to dance with, and Peggy Vandeventer, who had spotted their system of signals, had been the girl neglected more than any other. It still hurt to remember her excited voice when she had led him off alone and said, "You're going right up to your mother and Mrs. Phelps and tell them about your club — either that or there isn't going to be any Friday Afternoon Dancing Class left, *and your mother will go broke.*"

It was awful, the way she said it, and what she said. But it was true. Even with every boy on the floor there were only two boys for every three girls and his mother had worried about withdrawals. He was trapped. "I'll tell them," he said tonelessly.

He wished now he didn't remember it. But he wished even more that he could forget what his mother had said when he had betrayed the club. "No matter what it meant to us," she had said, "you shouldn't have told on your friends."

Well, he hadn't had any friends since — Eddie Eakins had seen to that — and now, standing here on the green rug, a voice inside his head began screaming at Clinky to shut up about his mother, about everything. But the man across the desk was going on relentlessly, in a soft voice, "You've let your mother down, Anthony."

He couldn't take any more of this. He was shaking all over and there was a hot pressure behind his eyes. He wanted to throw himself in the chair beside the desk and start blubbering about the dancing class and not having any friends and the class snickering at him in the gym and everything else. But if he broke down now he was going to hate Clinky —

The man across the desk got up abruptly, walked to the window and stood there with his back turned. "Well," Clinky said in a brisk voice, "got any suggestions, Tony?"

He took a shuddering breath. "Could I go to summer school or something?" he pleaded. "You could give me exams just before school starts like you sometimes do for kids." He was talking desperately now. "Or I could ask my grandfather to help me. Oh, and my grandmother taught school once. I guess she'd help if I asked her."

"You'd have six subjects to make up. That's a lot."

"I could do it, sir. I know I could do it."

Doctor McClintic turned slowly. "I like your spirit. I'm inclined to give you a chance. But there's something else. Anthony, this past year the school paid for you, but got nothing from you in return. So to earn another chance you'd have to repay the school. You can do it by working here all summer. We're putting in a new track around the football field. A contractor has taken on the project but really just to give a couple of Penn football players he's interested

in a summer job. They'll need somebody to run errands and give
them a hand. You'd have to work here from nine until three and
study mostly at night. Your only pay would be carfare and lunch.
I'm not sure you'd want to take it on."

It would be tough, all right. But it would be like finding a long
straight path in front of you when you felt like running. "Will you
let me try?" he said quickly.

"All right," Doctor McClintic said. "You just made a sale, Tony.
Go ahead and try." Then he smiled and added, as if forced to
admit it, "By George, you might even make it, too!"

IT TURNED out to be not a bad summer at all. His grandfather
and grandmother were nice about helping him, and he got to
know them much better. His grandfather knew more Latin than
Caesar, and he could get you interested if you didn't fight it. They
all played a game at dinner asking each other questions in Latin.
The first person who gave three wrong answers had to do the
dishes, except that his grandfather wasn't allowed any wrong answers. They caught Anthony a lot at the beginning of the summer
but not so much at the end, and one wonderful night they caught
his grandfather, and they all almost died laughing.

Several of the subjects he was making up — Sacred Studies and
Math and Science — he could handle himself once he decided to
work at them, and his grandmother was good at English and
History. He had always had trouble with History, because dates
skidded around in his mind. But his grandmother fixed that. You
just got straight what was happening in Philadelphia at any given
time and then you tied in other dates with that. For example, the
French Revolution began in 1789. Well, you could remember that
they wrote the U. S. Constitution in Philadelphia in 1787, and that
the French Revolution started only two years later.

It was easy to learn Philadelphia history because you sort of
owned it yourself. His mother and grandmother took him around,
week-ends that summer, to see right where a lot of history had
been made. They even took one trip to Washington, D.C., which
was where they had moved the national government after Philadelphia had started it going properly between 1790 and 1800.

So the studying went pretty well that summer, and the work at Franklin Academy on weekdays turned out even better.

The two Penn football players who were working on the track were Joe Krakowicz and Al Horder. They were great big muscular guys who worked without their shirts and did a lot of laughing and kidding. Right from the start they began kidding with him too. That first afternoon, when three o'clock came, Joe brought out a football and threw it to Al. Anthony was starting to go home, but Joe yelled, "Hey, you Tony, stick around," and threw him a pass, so of course he stayed to pass and kick with them. After that they threw the football around every afternoon after work.

Early in July they were playing with the football when a Pierce-Arrow drove up and a man climbed out. "Hello, Joe. Hello, Al," he said. "How's everything going?"

"Fine," Al said. "Say, Mr. Callahan, here's a kid who's doing a good job of helping us. Hey, Tony, come here a minute."

Anthony had immediately recognized the man he used to call Uncle Mike. He had been edging away, hoping he wouldn't be seen. Something had happened a long time ago that had been unpleasant and upsetting. It was about Uncle Mike coming around to see his mother and her sending the big redheaded man away and then sitting down on the sofa and crying. He hadn't seen Uncle Mike since then. When Al called him again, Anthony came forward scuffling his feet and looking down at the ground.

Al said, "This is Tony Lawrence, Mr. Callahan. The school asked him to help us out."

Uncle Mike's face lighted up. "Well, Tony," he said, shoving out a big hand. "You've grown so much I wouldn't have known you. Al, I used to know this young man when he was a little kid."

Anthony grinned a little and shook hands. Uncle Mike asked how his mother was, and Anthony said she was fine. He was relieved when Uncle Mike seemed to think that covered everything and turned back to ask Joe and Al about the work. Apparently Uncle Mike was the contractor who had taken on the job.

"This is all very good," Uncle Mike said when he had been shown the track, "but what's all this throwing passes and kicking? Are you guys going out for the backfield next fall?"

Now it was Al and Joe who grinned, and scuffled their feet.

Uncle Mike turned to Anthony and said, "These two lugs are the best guards Penn has. The coaches will kill me if I let them turn themselves into lousy backs. Now look, Tony, I'm going to appoint you manager of this team. I want you to string up the school tackling dummy every afternoon so these two can get in a real workout. I'll send a charging machine around."

"It too good to last," Joe Krakowicz said gloomily, after Uncle Mike had left. "Now just work work work."

"Ah, you like it, you big Polack," Al said. "Besides, don't grumble in front of the manager."

"Ha!" Joe said, poking Anthony in the ribs. "He think you just *manage!* What you play on this school team, Tony?"

"Oh gosh, I'm not on the team. I'll only be fifteen in a couple of weeks, and I only weigh a hundred and forty-five, and — "

"Ha, we get through with you, you throw them all around," Joe said. "We teach him to play guard, huh, Al? Backfield a bunch of cheer leaders is all, Tony. You come up front with men."

"Now wait," Al said. "Tony, you might as well know they say guards are just fullbacks with their brains knocked out. If we put you on this charging machine and give you all the exercises for a lineman your muscles will get set for line work. You'll end up just a dumb guard at the bottom of the pile-up."

"I'd like to be a guard," Anthony said shyly. This was all just in fun, because of course he would never make the Academy team, but it would be nice to pretend to be what Al and Joe were.

The next day Al and Joe brought football uniforms. Old Callahan the caretaker (who was of course Uncle Mike's father, although Anthony never thought of him in that way) came up with some old shoulder pads and other stuff that fit Anthony. Practicing after work was pretty good fun. When you learned how to hit the tackling dummy just right, coming in low and hitting it with your shoulder and driving hard with short choppy steps, it didn't hurt you a bit. The charging machine had pads, and you put your shoulders against them and dug with your feet, and tried to push the machine back. Some things they practiced on each other instead of the dummy, but Al and Joe were gentle with

Anthony so they wouldn't hurt him. They practiced two-on-one charging, and showed him how to use his hands to get through two offensive linemen. They showed him how to fake other line-men out of position and how to charge low and hard to spill every-body when the interference was driving at you.

So the summer passed, and Anthony was sorry when the end of August came and Al and Joe were finishing up. It had been a swell summer but there was one angle that he didn't feel good about. It hadn't been honest to pretend to Al and Joe that he would go out for the Academy team. On the last afternoon of the job, as they were dressing, Anthony said, "I ought to tell you guys some-thing. I've just been kidding about going out for the team."

"What this you give us?" Joe growled.

"Well, gee," Anthony said, "I guess you don't realize I'm ... I'm kind of weak. I can't even chin myself."

"Oh, nuts," Joe said disgustedly. He grabbed Anthony under the arms and hoisted him up toward a pipe running below the ceiling. "Take hold the pipe," Joe said.

Anthony grabbed it and hung there miserably.

"What you wait for?" Joe said. "Go on chin."

He hated letting them see how weak he was. But he would try, anyway. He tensed his muscles. All of a sudden a startling thing happened. His body floated upward and his head bumped the ceil-ing. "I did it!" he screamed. "I did it!"

"Only one," Joe said. "Now more."

He lowered himself and tensed and went up again and down and Joe began counting slowly three ... four ... five ... and then things got a bit blurred and the next thing he knew Al was lifting him down. "You trying to kill the kid, Joe?" Al said.

"I'm all right," Anthony gasped. "I did five, didn't I?"

"Nah," Al said. "You did ten and this dumb Polack would of kept on counting till you dropped." He set Anthony on his feet and smacked him on the back and said, "You'll make it, Tony."

Years later, Anthony got around to wondering how much of that summer had been carefully planned, and by whom. It might have been his mother, or Doctor McClintic. Or Uncle Mike, picking up school news from old Mr. Callahan and moving in quietly to set the stage. It couldn't all have been coincidence. But none of the actors in the little summer drama ever let slip a hint. Certainly Joe and Al played their parts to the end, waving good-by to him as they left the locker room for the last time, and never knowing that when they were out of sight a fifteen-year-old boy sat down and cried the first happy tears of his life.

ANTHONY came on the field the first afternoon of football practice wearing the old uniform that he had worn so often during the summer. He should have been used to it but it felt strange on him now. It had been one thing to fool around with Al and Joe, knowing they weren't going to hurt you. It was very different to try out for the team. Boys from the upper forms, who looked like anybody else in the school hallways, seemed strange and menacing in their black helmets and bulky shoulder pads. He didn't think it would impress them to learn that he could chin himself ten times.

For a while, that first afternoon, they did exercises and sprints. Anthony couldn't get his body moving right. He tried to tell himself that he was nervous only because of worrying about the results of the make-up exams, which he had just finished taking. But he felt pretty good about the exams. You could usually tell how you would do by whether you got a sick feeling when you saw the questions, or were eager to start writing the answers. He had felt eager. But right now, with football coming up, he felt sick.

The head coach came up to Anthony and said, "Lawrence, you've never played football, have you?"

"Uh, no sir."

"What's your weight?"

"I gained ten pounds this summer," Anthony said. "I weigh around a hundred and fifty-five. I want to go out for guard."

"That's a new one on me," the coach said. "Somebody wants to play guard. It's a tough position, Lawrence. Let's see if you can take it. Hey, Creighton, Arnold!" he called. "Come here a minute."

The two boys trotted up. One had played guard and one had played tackle on last year's team. They didn't tower over Anthony the way they had a year ago, but they still looked awfully big.

"Lawrence here has an idea he wants to play guard," the coach said. "I want a few two-on-one charges, with him trying to get through you. Now look, Lawrence, here's what you do. . . ." The coach showed him how to get into charging position.

Creighton and Arnold were digging in solidly, and their faces seemed to turn cold and hard. Anthony crouched in front of them. Al and Joe had looked bigger but they had always grinned at him.

"One . . . two . . . three . . . Hike!" called the coach.

Something awful happened. A huge force slammed into him and left him lying on his back with his helmet jammed over his eyes. On the second try they mashed him flat and something cracked into his face and made it feel numb. He got up slowly and wiped a hand over his face. A red smear came away on his hand.

The coach took a look at him. "You have a bloody nose, Lawrence. Maybe you'd better call it for the day, hm?"

"I don't want to call it." Anthony felt better somehow. He knew what he had been doing wrong. He had been standing there letting them plow into him. He hadn't been charging at all.

Crouching, Anthony began remembering what Al and Joe had taught him. With two guys trying to take you out, you used different tricks to split them. He waited with his muscles tightening.

"One . . . two . . . three . . . Hike!"

He started a split second before Creighton and Arnold. He charged at a slight angle, ramming a shoulder into Creighton and using his hands to jar Arnold off stride, digging hard and keeping his legs churning. Thud-thud-thud and he was through them.

"Okay," the coach said. "That's it."

"Give us just one more, Coach," Arnold pleaded. "No Fifth Former can do that to us twice."

"What do you think, Lawrence?" the coach said.

"I'm all ready," Anthony said. They wouldn't like it much if he walked away now. Maybe one of those other stunts Al and Joe had taught him would work.

Anthony set himself as if he were going to try the same thing again but, just as the *Hike* signal came, he went in low and hard, under their shoulders. He came up between them with his legs giving him an explosive push and caught one on each shoulder. They went sprawling.

Anthony swung around and saw Creighton getting up slowly and Arnold with his legs doubled up into his stomach. "Gee," he said, "are you all right?"

"Just . . . my . . . wind," Arnold gasped, staggering to his feet.

Creighton slapped his back. "You're all right, Lawrence. Hey, Coach, I think you got yourself a guard here."

"Will I make the squad?" Anthony asked.

The coach grinned. "You made it when you tried again after that bloody nose."

Two days later Doctor McClintic called Anthony into the office and had him sit in the chair by the desk and said that he had passed the make-up exams, and could have his scholarship back.

"By the way," Doctor McClintic said, "I hear you gave Creighton and Arnold a lesson in charging the other day." He chuckled and added, "Wish I'd been there to see it. Keep on charging that way, Tony, and you'll do all right."

That fall, for the first time, he found himself accepted by the other kids, although Eddie Eakins and his bunch still looked through him as if he didn't exist. He played on the second team for a while and then one of the varsity guards came up with a bad knee and suddenly there he was on the varsity, playing shoulder to shoulder with Creighton and Arnold. Of course he wasn't very good, but with Creighton and Arnold keeping an eye on him in the games he didn't make any awful mistakes and he even got his letter.

THE NEXT fall he was a Sixth Former and his weight was up in the hundred and sixties. Early in preseason practice the coach took him aside. "Tony," he said, "I'm going to have to count on you a lot this year. You're the only regular I have left, from tackle to tackle. Now I want to give you a choice. I can either let you play in the line on both offense and defense, or pull you out on defense to back up the line. I'll come clean with you, Tony. I need you in the line, offense and defense. But I have to warn you, you won't look too sharp in there. You'll be carrying part of the load for the other guard and for the tackle next to you. You'll just be a guy at the bottom of a lot of piles."

"I've been under pile-ups before, Coach."

"Yeah. Now let's look at the other side of it. If I give you the line-backing job, everybody will see you on every defensive play. You're a good tackler. And the way they'll gallop through our line you'll get lots of chances to make tackles. You'll look good. I wouldn't be surprised if it got you elected captain for next season."

Anthony blinked a few times. "I'll look good but the rest of the team won't. Is that what you mean?"

"That's about the size of it."

He had never thought about being captain so it really wasn't hard to give up the idea. "Gee, Coach," he said, grinning, "I wouldn't know what to do up in the daylight. I'll go back to the bottom of the pile."

"You'll see lots of them this year," the coach said grimly. "All right, Tony, thanks."

The coach hadn't been kidding about those pile-ups. It was a rugged season, but they tied for second in their league, and after it was over the team elected Bill Klepner, a halfback, as captain for the next year. Only for a moment did Anthony think about the choice the coach had given him.

It was a different story in his Sixth Upper year. The Academy had almost the whole line back, and they were all bigger and stronger. They crunched through the league by one- and two-touchdown margins and came up to the final game with Penn Charter needing only that win for the title.

It was one of those games where nobody could get a drive going. All through the game they had two guys blocking Anthony whenever Penn Charter kicked. He wanted to get through on one of those kicks because that might be the break they needed. At the beginning of the second half he began following a set pattern on his charge whenever Penn Charter had to punt. He lined up opposite the Penn Charter guard and tackle, and charged the tackle each time. Twice he almost got through, and the blocking back guarding the alley to the kicker edged out a little farther each time to make sure he would be in the right spot to block him.

Then it was the final quarter, with the score nothing to nothing, and Penn Charter was ready to punt from its own forty. Anthony lined up again in front of the guard and tackle, but this time he went in low between them, the way he had done once with Creighton and Arnold, and came up hard and split them and churned on through. The blocking back was too far to the left, and Anthony streaked down the alley and saw the kicker's foot swing up and flung himself into the air and felt the solid chunk of the ball bouncing off his chest.

There it went, back down the field, tumbling crazily. He sprinted after it, arms pumping. In three years he had never had a chance to score. He was going to now, though. Bouncing wildly ahead of him was his personal football. It was —

Not quite his, yet. The blocking back who had missed him was roaring up from one side. Farther over was Billy Edwards, the Franklin left end, coming in like a streak. Anthony would get to the ball a step ahead of the other two. Then what? Pick it up and be tackled by the Penn Charter back? Yeah, everybody would say, Franklin had a chance to win the game but a dumb guard got there first. He had all those thoughts in a flash and then swerved and threw the hardest block of his life at the Penn Charter back. They went down, and as Anthony came out of the roll he saw Billy scooping up the ball and whizzing to the goal line. That would be the game and he was where he belonged, flat on the ground.

They kicked the point and came trotting back up the field and suddenly he realized that the Franklin stands were yelling his name. There was Doctor McClintic, yelling. There was his grandfather yelling. And there, with his mouth open in the final scream of LAWRENCE – LAWRENCE – LAWRENCE, was Eddie Eakins. Anthony grinned. He guessed it had been worth it.

CHAPTER 2

MOSTLY you knew where you stood with nearly all the masters who taught at Franklin Academy, but Mr. Glenmor, a new master, did not resemble any of the recognized types. He never got flustered. He managed to keep his classes off balance, and even the wildest boys found themselves watching for tricks that Mr. Glenmor might pull, instead of planning tricks of their own. Mr. Glenmor put on a star performance, and you were an audience rather than a class. A number of the older students, including Anthony, began to copy his drawl and to use the knowing Glenmor smile that only touched one side of his face.

On a May afternoon, Anthony sat in one of the worn leather chairs in the Masters' Room watching Mr. Glenmor read his graduation Salutatory. Mr. Glenmor had been assigned to coach him in the delivery of it. As Mr. Glenmor read Anthony's speech, a smile crept up the right side of his face. Sometimes that smile made you feel that you and he were engaged in a gay conspiracy. Sometimes it made you feel childish. Today the smile worried Anthony. "Doesn't it sound all right, sir?" he asked.

"It sounds," Mr. Glenmor said, "exactly the way Franklin Academy would want it to sound."

"Then it's all right, sir?"

"Ah," Mr. Glenmor said, with no expression at all in his voice. That was the sort of disturbing thing he did all the time. Could the school be wrong about anything? It was a disturbing thought, one he had never had before. Mr. Glenmor was a great one to give you new thoughts. "I don't think you like it," Anthony said.

"I suppose you've memorized it," Mr. Glenmor said. "Let's hear you give it, or perhaps we should say declaim it."

Anthony stood up. Under any circumstances he would have felt uncomfortable here in the sacred, tobacco-smelling Masters' Room. But it made it worse to see Mr. Glenmor studying him as if he were a bug on a pin in Science Lab. He cleared his throat.

"Centuries ago, in the age of chivalry," he said, "a young squire about to receive the honor of knighthood would await that event with mingled feelings of joy and awe."

When he had written that line, it had throbbed in his head like the sound of trumpets. Now, for some reason, it seemed to squeak.

"It was a momentous occasion," he went on. "It was the culmination of effort, of self-denying service. With some such feelings we have awaited the coming of graduation; for to us this . . . uh . . . for to us . . . how does it go from there, sir?"

Mr. Glenmor glanced at the paper. "For to us this occasion is momentous," he chanted. "It, too, marks a culmination of effort. And as the mind of the young squire was filled with great projects of knightly achievement, so, too, are the minds of us aglow with high resolve and happy anticipation." He paused and gave Anthony that side-of-the-face grin.

"Should I go on with it?" Anthony asked.

"Oh, please do."

"Um . . . oh yes. The last mile of our trail here is finished. Now, we come to the parting of the ways, where the Class of 1932 pauses for a few brief hours before it is scattered by the winds of destiny. This parting fills us with sadness. Yet — joy prevails, joy inspires the occasion, and it is in this spirit that we rejoice in your presence. Ladies and gentlemen, we bid you — welcome."

"Yes," Mr. Glenmor murmured, "I can see you doing it. With full round tones for such words as joy and rejoice. And perhaps — oh, definitely — an outflung right arm when you say welcome."

An ugly prickling crawled over Anthony's skin. Mr. Glenmor was making fun of him. "It's awful, isn't it?" he said miserably.

"It depends on the viewpoint, Tony. It's safe, sound and doesn't mean a thing. Do you know anything about knighthood?"

"Well, uh, it grew up in the age of chivalry. You had to promise to defend the weak against the strong and — "

"Medieval History, Sixth Form course in," Mr. Glenmor said, yawning. "Like all institutions for training the young, knighthood was a system for preventing independent thinking. Any time young men think independently, there is danger that they may realize they are stronger than old men. So old men develop institutions that will coax young men to play the game. In other words, kindly wait until I die, young man, before you take over."

"Gee, I see what you mean," Anthony said eagerly. "In promising to defend the weak against the strong, the young knights were really promising to protect the weak old men who ran the place against themselves, the young knights, that is."

"Anthony, I have hope for you."

A happy glow toasted his body. "Do you really, Mr. Glenmor?"

"You have a good brain. It just hasn't been used. Now let's take that phrase about great projects of achievement. . . . I'll pick a couple of your classmates at random. McKane Edwards. What's his great project of achievement?"

"Girls, I guess. That's all he ever talks about."

"And you, Tony?"

"Gosh, I guess I'm hoping for a scholarship to Princeton."

"And then what are you planning to do?"

Anthony hesitated. He knew very well what was expected of him. He had known, in a way, since he was five. Anthony's personal memories of his great-grandmother, Margaret O'Donnell, were very few, but right now he could close his eyes and see her lying propped against a pillow, looking like the thin transparent shell of a human. He had been taken into her bedroom not long before she died, and she had stared at him from faded blue eyes and said, "We in the family have kept our pride hot and bright, and you're the boy we've been waiting for. I hope you know what you have to do, Anthony."

His mother's hand had gripped his arm and he'd said, "Oh, yes, I know," just as his mother had told him to say if his great-grandmother asked him. He had had no real idea, of course, why she wanted him to say it, or what he was supposed to know and to do, but his great-grandmother had nodded and closed her eyes. Even now it was hard to put into words what was expected of him, but he knew, all right. Not even for Mr. Glenmor, however, was he going to talk about that. "I'm not sure," he said.

"Well, I won't pry. You have a lot of drive and intelligence, and all I'm interested in doing is making you think a little. Now, just for fun, let's see what kind of a Salutatory you would write, if you gave it some real honest thought. Shall we?"

This time Mr. Glenmor's smile was conspiratorial. "Yes sir!" Anthony said happily, and each time when they met after that to rehearse the real Salutatory they spent some time on the one they were doing as a joke. It was wonderful having a secret like that with Mr. Glenmor. It opened his eyes to a lot of things he had never seen before. Finally, when Mr. Glenmor suggested that it might be fun, Anthony memorized the private speech, and at their last meeting he stood up before Mr. Glenmor and recited it.

"Ladies and gentlemen," he said. "All human societies have developed ways of taming the young male before he becomes too big and strong to be handled. The various methods of taming, known in some countries as education, are always designed to produce a young man who will come into adult society without thinking of knocking over either his elders or their beliefs. If this often produces young men who go through life without thinking at all, that is regrettable but cannot be helped.

"You see before you, on this platform, the Class of 1932, about to graduate from Franklin Academy. For some years now, the school has been working to make us fit to enter your society. We have been trained to do the right thing. We will produce our share of lawyers and doctors and engineers and businessmen, and will not embarrass you by turning out to be poets or rebels.

"We know that Philadelphia is not generally recognized as the center of the universe, but we also know that this is only because of the narrow-mindedness of people who live elsewhere. We are aware that there are other parts of the United States, notably the seashore and Princeton to the eastward, the Poconos and Maine to the north — with Yale and Harvard up there someplace — Florida to the south, and a vast area called the Midwest which begins not far beyond the limits of our own Main Line.

"You can count on us to react patriotically to things like the Flag, Our Country, and Beating Penn Charter; with due gravity to words like duty, honor and property rights; to bristle at things which can be labeled radical, traitorous or bad form.

"We have adopted as our creed the words: 'What will people think?' and by that we mean what will you, our parents and friends, think. We hope that you will always think as highly of us as perhaps you do tonight. Ladies and gentlemen ... welcome."

There was a hush in the room. "Wonderful," Mr. Glenmor said softly. "Tony, I'm proud of you."

Hearing Mr. Glenmor say that was like getting your varsity letter for the first time.

"And the best thing about it," Mr. Glenmor said, "is that you worked out those ideas for yourself. And we had fun, didn't we?"

"I had a great time fooling around with it, Mr. Glenmor."

Mr. Glenmor slouched down, put the tips of his fingers together, and peered through them at Anthony. "Well," he said casually, "which one are you going to give at graduation tomorrow?"

Anthony stared at him. "You must be kidding, Mr. Glenmor," he said uneasily. "We . . . we did this as a joke."

"Perhaps we did. Truth is often treated as a joke."

"I know, but gee, Mr. Glenmor, what — "

"What would people think," Mr. Glenmor cut in, grinning up one side of his face. "Well, Tony, I'll tell you. It would be over the heads of half of your audience. Most of the others would be angry. A few might start to think clearly and honestly, just as you did. You would be doing a tremendous favor to those few, because they might never be given another chance to think."

"That . . . that makes it sound like a pretty serious thing."

"It *is* a serious thing. The choice between giving or withholding knowledge is the most important choice a man can face."

It was almost like being in church to hear Mr. Glenmor talk so solemnly. "I guess I backed into something pretty big, sir."

"Perhaps you did, Tony." Mr. Glenmor got up, and put a hand on his shoulder. "I'm not going to try to influence you," he said, with a rare both-sides-of-the-face smile. "You can give either speech. It's a very simple choice, between honesty and hypocrisy. Good luck, Tony." He walked out of the room.

Anthony slowly followed. Every once in a while, when things seemed to be going smoothly, life gave you a jagged decision to make. But as Mr. Glenmor had said, it was really a simple choice. He would of course give the new, honest Salutatory. . . .

The next night Anthony paraded into the gym with his classmates, marching solemnly and a little out of step to the music played by the Academy orchestra. They climbed to the platform and fanned out into the rows of chairs and faced the proud upturned faces below them. Anthony mouthed the words of the opening hymn but no sound came from his dry throat. After the hymn it would be his turn to give the Salutatory.

In the audience he saw his mother's shining face. She was trying, in the embarrassing way that all mothers had, to catch his glance and exchange proud smiles with him. Next to her was his grandmother, blinking as if she had trouble trying to see. They had worked awfully hard to help him get through the Academy, and the new Salutatory made fun of it. Down in the first row, with the faculty, was his grandfather. The Academy meant everything to him. He would be hurt by the new Salutatory, too.

Down there was his football coach, too. "There he was," the coach might say later, "one of our best guards, standing up there poking fun at the idea of beating Penn Charter. I don't get it."

Down there, finally, was Mr. Glenmor, catching his glance and giving him a wink. That seemed to say, as clear as anything, "It's the two of us against the world, Tony." Of course it was, too. Not many people believed in speaking or hearing the truth, but at least Mr. Glenmor would be proud of him.

The "Amen" of the hymn died away, and silence crept across the big room like a stalking tiger. Anthony walked forward on wobbly legs, the opening phrases on the tip of his tongue: "Ladies and gentlemen: All human societies have developed ways of taming the young male . . ."

He stopped in shocked surprise. Why, those weren't his words at all. They were Mr. Glenmor's words. So were all the other words and ideas in the new Salutatory. He didn't know whether the ideas were the truth or not. But if they were, they were Mr. Glenmor's truth — not Anthony's, not his family's, not the school's.

He squared his shoulders and looked out over the audience and said, "Ladies and gentlemen: Centuries ago, in the age of chivalry, a young squire about to receive the honor of knighthood would await that event with mingled feelings of joy and awe."

That had the sound of trumpets again. He went on, confidently. Toward the end he allowed himself a glance at Mr. Glenmor. There was no smile on Mr. Glenmor's face, and somehow Anthony got the idea that Mr. Glenmor was hoping he would forget the next line and go uh . . . uh . . . uh. . . . He found he didn't like Mr. Glenmor now, and he put full round tones into the words "joy" and "rejoice" as he gave the final lines: "Yet — joy prevails, joy inspires the occasion, and it is in this spirit that we rejoice in your presence. Ladies and gentlemen, we bid you — welcome." As a finishing touch, he used an outflung right arm when he said "welcome." Mr. Glenmor winced. Anthony sat down with applause rattling pleasantly around his ears.

After the ceremonies were over, Doctor McClintic drew him

aside. "Tony," he said, "I have a graduation present for you. The Princeton Club is nominating you for one of its scholarships."

Anthony tingled. "Gee," he said, "that's wonderful, sir."

"You deserve it, Tony. Oh, and before I forget it, nice work on your Salutatory. A good sound piece of writing and delivery."

"About the Salutatory," Anthony said hesitantly, "there's something I should tell you, except there's somebody else involved."

"Ah yes," Doctor McClintic said, smiling. "Mr. Glenmor told me about it. He has an excellent memory, and he recited the whole of the Salutatory which you didn't give."

"I don't understand," Anthony said. "Wasn't he taking a big chance telling you, sir? I mean, about his job here?"

Doctor McClintic got out his pipe and began slowly packing it. "Perhaps knowing the whole story will add something to your education," he said. "To start with, Mr. Glenmor knew he was not returning next year. He doesn't fit into the school. So he wasn't risking a thing by coaxing you to work on that second Salutatory. In some ways, Tony, Mr. Glenmor has a rather subtle mind. He presented the thing to me as a challenge. First, did I dare let you make the decision for yourself. Second, what would your decision be. In other words, did I dare rely on the training the school had given you, or didn't I? It was a challenge to test Mr. Glenmor's way of teaching against ours. He's an interesting person, Tony. What did you think of him?"

"I guess he's sort of a rebel, sir."

"Yes, but not of the usual type. You'd never find him leading a mob against a barricade. He'd be peering out from a doorway, thinking what idiots they were on both sides. He's like a devil who doesn't want the bother of running a hell."

"I guess this has taught me not to trust people too far unless I know them pretty well. Why ... why, if I had given that Salutatory of Mr. Glenmor's, I bet you would have called off my scholarship to Princeton."

Doctor McClintic laughed. "The thought didn't enter my head, Tony. I'll tell you a secret. Mr. Glenmor never had a chance of winning that little contest."

Anthony watched him for a moment as he moved off, wondering whether it was true that Mr. Glenmor never had a chance of winning. In his conscious mind Anthony had not made the decision until the last possible moment. But had it actually been made much earlier? Had there, in fact, never been a decision to make? He did not have the answers to those questions.

IN MANY ways, Anthony's four years at Princeton were like being buried under one long pile-up in football. His scholarship only covered tuition. He had to earn the rest by waiting on tables in Commons and doing other jobs around the campus. He didn't have any energy left over, after earning money and studying and playing scrub football, to try to be a big man on the campus.

Along with two thirds of his class he made one of the eating clubs in the spring of his sophomore year. But that was sheer luck. Each club had the right to take in one man who would get meals and membership free in return for helping to manage the club. On Monday of Bicker Week one club found it had lost both its first- and second-choice scholarship men to other clubs. In desperation, a club committee visited the head of the Student Employment Bureau and asked if there was an unbid sophomore who was presentable, intelligent, hard-working, a good mixer and in fact an all-around nice guy. The head of the Bureau brought out the records and photographs of half a dozen men.

"Isn't there anything outstanding about any of these guys?" the head of the committee asked, not at all impressed.

The head of the Bureau thought for a moment, and chuckled. "You might not believe it," he said, "but this man Lawrence has some kind of a drag with whoever runs the big deb parties in Philadelphia. He told me once he could get a dozen guys invited to most of them, but he doesn't have time to round up the right kind of guys. Does that sound outstanding to you?"

Fifteen minutes later Anthony made a club.

The committee had to take the debutante angle on faith, but it turned out very well indeed. The Friday Afternoon Dancing Class had not survived the Depression, but Mrs. Hoyt Phelps had already become established as a social counselor and she had taken Anthony's mother in as her assistant. Mrs. Hoyt Phelps did need presentable stags for dances, and she was glad to have Anthony produce some of them.

The club scholarship let Anthony give up his other jobs. And, when he became undergraduate manager in his senior year and had an assistant, he had some time he could call his own. The free time was important, because it was in December of his senior year that he became interested in Joan Dickinson.

It all started when he cut in on her at a dance at the Merion Cricket Club. She switched on a brilliant smile and gave half of it to the man she was leaving. "Good-by, Princeton," she said. Then she swung into Anthony's arms and gave him the other half of the smile and said, "Hello, Princeton."

He knew that the guy she had just left went to Penn, and the loose way she used the name of Princeton offended him. "I'm sorry," he said, "but I'm from Kansas Aggies."

"Oh dear," she said. "I just call everybody Princeton and usually that pleases everybody except Yale men. How wonderful to meet someone from Kansas Aggies! What do you take there?"

"Animal husbandry," he said. "I'm majoring in Hoof and Mouth Disease, with a minor in Stoppages of the Udder."

"That's marvelous!" she cried, looking up at him from wide brown eyes. "So many boys just go to college to use up some time. Do you have a football team at Kansas Aggies?"

"No, ma'am. We got a mighty nice milking team, though."

"You're going to have to tell me all about it," she crooned. "Why you went there, and what the boys are like and everything!"

He started inventing a wildly improbable campus and got a grim pleasure out of the way she took it all in. It was a crime the way they let these girls give all their attention to their figures and none to their brains. This slender girl was a pretty kid, with shining brown hair, but under that page-boy bob she was a refugee from the Jukes family. He didn't have time to get very far with his imaginary campus, because after a minute someone cut in. She gave Anthony the first half of the brilliant smile, and said, "Thank you, Mr. Lawrence." Anthony was almost back to the stag line before he remembered that he hadn't told her his name. He waited a few moments and then cut back in.

"Oh, goody," she said. "I bet you came back to invite me to the Senior Cornhusking Bee."

"You've been taking me for a ride," he said.

"Why, Mr. Lawrence, you were the one taking me for a ride. A hayride, I would call it."

"How do you know my name? I didn't tell you."

"Oh dear. It's a long story, and somebody will cut in soon, and you wouldn't want to take me outside on the porch because you feel that when you go to a dance you should show your appreciation to the hostess by staying on the dance floor. Right?"

This girl could tie you in knots. "Yes," he said, "that's right. But how do you know?"

"I go to Miss Moriarty's School for Delinquent Girls, and major in Mind Reading and Man Snatching."

"How about coming out on the porch and talking?"

"Just a moment while I read your mind," she said.

She stared at him, then nodded. "Okay," she said. "Your intentions are strictly conversational. Let's go."

Out on the big enclosed porch of the Club, he asked again: "Now what's this about your knowing my name and all that?"

"You've forgotten our moment of passion," she sighed. "Correction. My moment of passion. You practically snored in my face."

He wanted to grab her and shake her. "Look," he growled. "You're Joan Dickinson. You came out last June and I was in the mob scene. I've cut in on you at several dances since then and danced only a few steps with you each time. I bet we've had a minute and twenty-seven seconds together. Now what gives with this moment-of-passion line?"

She curled one shoulder forward and looked at him across it. "About the third time you cut in, I noticed that you never seemed to drink too much, and I realized that you didn't hand me the usual heavy line — you know, the one designed to break a girl into small quivering pieces in ten seconds flat. I was slightly insulted. So I dug up who you were. Then one time you cut in on me and I asked you to take me outside, and you gave me that lofty sentiment about staying on the dance floor because it was your duty to the hostess. What is this devotion of yours to dancing?"

He couldn't help laughing, and for some reason he began telling her about the time he played traitor to the club at the Friday Afternoon Dancing Class. He had never told it to anyone else, but Joan listened eagerly. It was a rather amusing story, now that he could look back on it. "So that," he said finally, "ended my career of crime."

Joan began choking, and said, "H-handkerchief, please."

He didn't like her to laugh quite so hard. He gave her a handkerchief, and said irritably, "What's so sidesplitting?"

"Nothing," she gasped. "You've got me bawling, you big idiot."

It was amazing. She really was crying. He couldn't help putting an arm around her. She snuggled up against him, trembling and sniffling, and he patted her and said please to stop crying.

She drew back at last and blew her nose and said, "I bet I look like something the cat dragged in. Oh, I could kill that girl!"

"What girl?"

"The troublemaker at that darn dancing class of yours."

"She really did me a favor," he said. "Because after that I started getting in trouble at school and — "

"Oh, shut up," she said angrily. "I can't take any more sob stories right now. You're so dumb and nice and innocent it breaks me up. I think I'd like you to kiss me."

He started to look around, to see if anybody else was on the porch, but she put her arms around his neck and said, "What do I care if somebody's looking at us?" and came up on tiptoes and kissed him. It was an odd kind of kiss, soft and quivery and faintly salty from her tears, friendly in one way and provocative in another. It scrambled his emotions badly.

After she moved away, he said huskily, "I don't think you know what you're doing to me. I've never really had a girl."

She laughed unsteadily. "You don't have to tell me — it's written all over you. I guess I'm trying to make it up to you. What are you doing this Christmas vacation?"

"Going stag to dances, the way I always do."

"No you're not. You're going to take me."

"Oh now look," he said. "Christmas vacation is just starting. You've had all your dates booked for months."

"I just lost my engagement book."

"I hate to tell you this, but I haven't got any money or a car or much of anything."

"Oh goodness," she said. "He's working his way through Princeton selling magazines. Listen: I've got a car, and who needs money going to dances?"

All of a sudden he felt very light and carefree and happy. "Miss Dickinson," he said, "may I have the pleasure of escorting you during the Christmas rat race?"

She linked an arm through his, and said gaily, "You've just argued me into it. Now you can drop me at the ladies' room, and then you and I are walking out on this party."

They found an all-night restaurant on Lancaster Pike where they sat eating scrambled eggs and buttered toast and telling each other the story of their lives. There wasn't anything complicated about Joan's, because life can be smooth for a girl who has good health, good looks, and a family with a good deal of money. She had been graduated from Baldwin School the previous June and she didn't want to go to college. She was, she said, an out-of-date creature who merely wanted to get married quickly and have four children without delay, two boys and two girls.

"I've had the names picked out for years," she said. "Arthur, Jonathan, Elaine and Betsy. But now that I've met you, I've decided you can name one of the boys and one of the girls." At the look of horror on his face she collapsed into giggles.

He realized it was all a joke, but just to be on the safe side he said casually that he would be going to Penn Law School next year, which of course meant three years more of studying and then a few more years to get started.

"Why law?" she asked.

He explained that to get anywhere in Philadelphia he would have to make money, and he didn't want to take forever making it, either. In banks, or in big corporations, you could spend twenty years getting to be assistant to the vice-president in charge of the water coolers. He didn't have the specialized skills needed for engineering or architecture. He didn't have the family connections that would push you along fast in insurance and in the investment business. He added, "Connections are important in law, but a guy can still go up fast in it if he knows his stuff, and gets a few breaks. If I have any talent at all, it's for law. I like digging up the facts about a problem, and thinking about the angles, and then figuring out an answer that fits all the rules and precedents."

"Oh, please," Joan said. "Don't ever treat me like a problem."

"In your case," he said seriously, "I don't think any rules and precedents would help me."

"Good. Just be emotional about me, please. You're planning to practice law in Philadelphia?"

"Yes, and that's another reason why I like law. A big corporation might send me anywhere. I want to stay in Philadelphia."

"I don't suppose you know Daddy's a lawyer."

"A lawyer? Dickinson? Oh yes. Dickinson and Dawes, I bet." He felt suddenly uncomfortable. Mr. Dickinson might figure that a would-be lawyer who chased Joan might be hoping to catch

Dickinson and Dawes. "I think you just became a problem," he muttered.

"I've been reading your mind again, and please don't be stuffy. Now take me home before I get to be any more of a problem."

Anthony drove Joan's car up to the Dickinsons' low, rambling house in Penn Valley, wondering if a suggestion about phoning for a taxi would sound as if he were inviting himself in.

"Tea dance tomorrow," Joan said, "at two." She started to get out of the car, then added, "Take the car with you now."

"I can't borrow your car. I —"

She leaned over and kissed him. "As long as you've got my car I know you have to come back to return it," she said calmly. She waved and went into the house.

He sat there for a moment, frowning. He didn't like the idea of driving off with her car. It gave her a little more claim on him than he wanted her to have just yet, and of course people always lifted their eyebrows when a man began sponging on a girl. But he started the car and drove home.

He was with Joan almost every day during Christmas vacation. Being an escort was very different from being a stag. You got in on the little dinners before big dances, and on opera and theater parties, and you met people in their homes rather than merely in big ballrooms. You began to be accepted as a person. Of course his acceptance was on a very special basis. After he had been going around with her for about a week, he noticed that he was not being introduced as "Mr. Lawrence" but as "This is Joan's man, Tony." It took him a while to get used to that label.

After ten days, her family began to study him carefully and to ask questions about his background. He knew they weren't satisfied with it, and he suspected that from time to time they told Joan to remember that there were other men in the world. He liked her parents, though, and he thought they had a real, if unwilling, liking for him.

He saw Joan at least once every week-end while college was in session, and had her up for Junior Prom and House Parties. She became a very necessary part of his life. He had tried to prevent that; his future relationship with her was a problem he didn't know how to solve. On the day before graduation from Princeton he found he had to solve it anyway.

He was finishing breakfast in the club when Joan walked in. There was a special light in her eyes. He had invited her for graduation but that wasn't until tomorrow. He jumped up and said, "This is a nice surprise. What brings you here?"

"I'd tell you it was somebody named Tony Lawrence," she said, "but I hate to let a man feel too sure of me."

"I couldn't. There's something elemental about you, like spring. A guy can wait for spring but he can't feel he owns it."

"How nice! I feel I've just been elected Miss Nature of 1936. Tony, I'll take a cup of coffee if you'll give me one."

They sat down and she took a couple of sips of coffee and studied him over the top of the cup. "Brace yourself," she said. "I'm going to tell you how to feel sure of me."

"Yes?" he said, beginning to feel uneasy.

"Tony, we can be in Elkton, Maryland, by one o'clock. We can get married by a justice of the peace. By five o'clock we can be back in Trenton. My bags are all packed in the car."

"Good Lord," he said slowly.

"You're supposed to fall at my feet babbling gratefully."

"Joan, there's nothing I'd rather do, but — "

"I can answer all the buts," she said. "Nothing really matters except getting married today."

"Your family will have a fit."

"Of course they will. So what? They'll get used to it."

"But marrying a guy who has no money and three years of law school ahead of him — "

"Tony, I have two hundred a month from what my grandfather left me. On top of that my family would help out. Why shouldn't they? If you want, you can look on it as a loan you'll pay back when you get on your feet, just as your scholarship to Princeton is a loan you're expected to repay when you're able."

"You make it sound too easy," he muttered. "Dammit, you've got to give me a few minutes to think."

"I don't want to give you minutes to think! I'm nineteen. You're almost twenty-two. A hundred years ago people younger than us were driving covered wagons West and starting homes. What's wrong with our having our chance while we're young?"

"Only one thing. That's no covered wagon you have parked outside. It's a 1936 Cadillac convertible."

"All right. Let's get back to 1936. Tony, after we're married my father will offer to be your preceptor in law school."

He was a bit startled that she knew about preceptors. To enter Penn Law School, you had to get a member of the Philadelphia Bar to sponsor you. Your sponsor agreed to advise you while you were in law school and to give you a job for a year or so after you finished. Tony didn't have a preceptor yet.

"I wouldn't be too sure of that," he said. "If he gets mad, you won't push him around."

"No girl with any sense tries to push a man around, not even her father. It just takes a little coaxing. And Tony, Judge Dawes has a son but Daddy hasn't. He'll end up as proud of you as if — "

Someone tapped Anthony on the shoulder, and the colored doorman said, "Gentleman to see you, Mistuh Lawrence."

Anthony looked up. Outside the dining room, in the hallway, the sunlight was glinting on steel-gray hair and a sharp profile. A pulse started thumping in Anthony's stomach. "Maybe you'd better practice up on that coaxing," he muttered. "There's your father."

Joan took out her compact and studied her face. "I suppose he found out what I planned to do," she said, "but that needn't stop us if you'll keep your head. Just remember he's a lawyer and he's going to try to win a case. And if he wins, we lose."

They went into the hallway and Joan kissed her father calmly and Anthony shook hands. Joan said, "All right, Daddy? How did I give it away?"

He smiled and patted her shoulder. "The bureau drawers in your room, honey. We're all familiar with the way you throw things this way and that when you're packing. And your Mother and I have been sort of on the lookout for something like this."

"Darn," Joan said. "You should have trained me to be neater. Just to get things straight at the start, Daddy, I'm over the age of consent. It's eighteen for girls in New Jersey."

"Spoken like the daughter of a lawyer," her father said, chuckling. "But I'm not here to play the heavy father. Merely a friendly discussion with Tony."

"Tony," Joan said, "don't believe a word of it."

Her father said, "Tony, I hope you won't mind talking it over with me. And Joan, I'd like to talk to Tony alone. You had your chance this morning. It's only fair to give me one."

"I'm not interested in being fair," Joan said. "All I'm interested in is getting married. However, I'll go up to the poolroom for half an hour. And Tony — " she blinked away dampness in her eyes " — don't forget you're up against a professional." Her voice broke on the last words, and she swung around and ran upstairs.

Years later, Anthony remembered distinctly what it was like to be up against a professional, and began to use the technique himself. A professional like Mr. Dickinson first made sure he knew everything possible about his opponent. Then he worked little tricks to put you at a psychological disadvantage. He coaxed you into a foolish move, and then acted with the smooth grace of a judo wrestler to turn your own strength against you.

Mr. Dickinson suggested going into the living room, which was empty at that hour. It was Anthony's club and ordinarily he would have felt more at home and confident in its manorial living room than would a visitor. But Mr. Dickinson reversed that situation quickly. "Do sit down, Tony," he said genially, becoming the host and making Anthony the guest. As he spoke, he sat in a big leather chair placed by itself near a window. Anthony stood for a moment, half remembering an old green carpet before the headmaster's desk at the Academy. He didn't want to lug one of the other leather chairs across the room, so he got a straight wooden chair. As a result, Mr. Dickinson was at ease in a comfortable armchair while Anthony sat squirming on a hard wooden one.

"I must apologize," Mr. Dickinson said. "I really don't usually drop everything and go chasing Joan like this."

Anthony thought, as he was intended to, that it took a remarkably thoughtful man to look at things from this angle. From all normal points of view, Mr. Dickinson had more right to be upset than Anthony. He felt obliged to explain that to Mr. Dickinson, and began floundering in a swamp of apologies.

"Oh, let's not mention that," Mr. Dickinson said. "The important thing is what is best for you and Joan. You don't have to tell me that you love her sincerely. Nor do you have to convince me that you're a fine young man. In fact, Tony, if I had a son I couldn't ask for one better than you."

This was very disarming, and at the same time it made Anthony feel uncomfortable. "Thank you, sir," he said earnestly. "I hope you'll never have to change your mind."

"I'm sure I won't, Tony. Now I suppose you and Joan have talked this morning about the problems involved."

It was difficult to talk about it to Mr. Dickinson, but he had to try. "I guess the main problem is that I'm going to law school and don't have any money," he said. "Joan thought that could be handled one way or another."

"Oh yes," Mr. Dickinson said brightly. "She has a modest income of her own. Then of course she'd expect us to help out. How did all that strike you?"

"Well, the way Joan put it, it was like my scholarship here. It would be a loan that I could repay when I got on my feet."

"You and I," Mr. Dickinson said, leaning forward confidentially, "are a lot alike, Tony. So I wonder. Did that sound just a shade too smooth and easy to you?"

"Yes sir, I guess it did. I said something to Joan about it."

"Well, Tony, let's see. Now I happen to remember the first night you had a date with Joan. She loaned you her car so you could drive home. Did you have any special reaction to that loan of the car, Tony?"

"I felt kind of funny about it. As if I didn't want to give her that much claim on me. And I felt it was sort of sponging on her."

"I knew we were alike," Mr. Dickinson said, beaming at him. "That's the reaction of a man who isn't really happy unless he's standing on his own two feet. Now then, how would you feel if, instead of the car keys, Joan tossed you an apartment for two, and new suits every few months? Would your reaction be the same?"

"I don't know. It might be different, being married."

"Or it might not be different. Right, Tony?"

"Yes sir, it might not be different."

"Now let's look at it from Joan's point of view. All of a sudden we take away the glamour. Instead of a Princeton senior taking her out on exciting dates you're a law student coming home tired from classes and then buckling down to books half the night. That's asking a debutante to make a big transition."

"Well, but look, Mr. Dickinson, don't most girls have to make that transition when they get married?"

"Indeed they do, Tony. But most of them would have a great advantage over Joan. They may have lost a carefree sweetheart, but they have gained a breadwinner. And Tony, you wouldn't even be bringing home crumbs."

"I guess it's a gamble, all right," Anthony muttered.

"You and Joan might work it out. But it might also end with one of you walking out on the other. Do you want to take that gamble with Joan's life and your own?"

"It's not the sort of gamble people ought to take," Anthony said miserably. "If I could see some other way out of it — "

"Instead of a gamble, Tony, I'd like to suggest a sure thing. I'd like to be your preceptor for law school. In your spare time, I'd like you to work as a law clerk at Dickinson and Dawes. As soon as you pass your Bar exams, I'd like you to marry Joan and join the firm. How does that sound?"

For twenty minutes, Anthony had been led slowly and carefully through a sort of Chamber of Horrors. Now, suddenly, the doors at the far end were flung open and there was sunlight and happiness. "It sounds wonderful," he said solemnly. "I only hope I can live up to the chance you're giving me."

Mr. Dickinson got up quickly: a lawyer who knew that when you won over the jury you rested your case immediately. "I couldn't feel more sure of it," he said. "I'm going to run along now, my boy. Joan's going to be a bit difficult to handle, but this is a good time to start learning how to do it. Good luck, Tony." He shook hands briskly and left.

Anthony went bounding up the stairs to the poolroom, calling for Joan. She looked up when he rushed in, and held up a hand so that he couldn't take her in his arms. "I don't like it," she said. "You're too happy."

"But Joan," he cried, "your father was wonderful. He straightened me out. Everything's going to be fine for us. It — "

"No it isn't," she said. "I was hoping you'd come up here with your face red and your jaw stuck out and mad as anything. That would have meant you'd won. What bill of goods did he sell you?"

He explained the wonderful offer her father had made, and how the other thing would have been an awful gamble with both their lives, and couldn't she see that?

"Of course I saw it," she said. "I was willing to take the gamble. Oh Tony, we had a very simple question to settle. I wanted to marry you today. Daddy didn't want me to marry you today. So Daddy won, you think you won, and I know I lost."

"I wish you wouldn't take it that way."

He walked with her out to the car, telling her earnestly how much he loved her and how hard he would work to make her proud of him. She cheered up a little, and said that of course she loved him too and maybe the three years would go quickly. But, as she started the car, Anthony noticed that her lips were moving.

"What are you saying to yourself?" he asked.

She smiled wanly. "I was just saying: Arthur, Jonathan, Elaine and Betsy. You remember those names I picked out for my four kids? I had a sudden crazy notion that I'd better repeat them a few times, so I wouldn't forget them in the next three years."

That was a strange thing, and Anthony thought about it after she drove away. He began to suspect that Mr. Dickinson had coaxed him into making a bad trade. It would have been a gamble to have married Joan immediately. But it was a much worse gamble to bet that a girl who wanted four children, and had already named them, was going to wait three years for anybody.

CHAPTER 3

LOOKING BACK later, it seemed to Anthony that graduation from college marked the end of a sort of nursery period of his life. Law school was very different from college. The law professors threw stuff at you and walked off without waiting to see if you could catch it. Also, there were changes at home.

One day, during Anthony's first year at law school, his grand-father came home from the Academy with a bad cold which gradually turned into pneumonia. For two days he lay silently in bed. Then he sat up, fighting off restraining hands, and triumphantly declaimed, *"Ave atque vale!"* With that, Harry Judson sank back and died. He would have been glad to know that his last words were spoken in Latin.

Two months later, Anthony's grandmother died one night in the parlor of the house on Spruce Street, slumping quietly in the old wing chair where for so many years she had done her embroidery. There was nothing dramatic in her passing.

The house seemed very large and empty after that, and Anthony's mother sold it and they took an apartment on Walnut Street. At about the same time Miss Rogers' Select School offered her the job of housemother. The new job took more of her time and gave her an interest in which Anthony had no part.

So, in a very brief time, his life was greatly changed. At first he had a feeling that all his ties with the past had been snapped, but eventually he realized that you did not sell your memories with a house, or bury them along with coffins. Part of his mind would always live with his great-grandmother and his grandparents in the old Spruce Street house. Whatever he did in the future would be governed to some extent by that part of his mind.

There was one other change in his life. During that first year at law school he and Joan moved slowly apart. They saw less and less of each other. For a time each of them felt guilty about it, and would apologize to the other for not having called, but as the months went by Anthony realized — and suspected that Joan did also — that the course of their romance had been firmly charted on a June day in Princeton.

However, you can see something coming and still be hurt when it arrives. He had been working as a law clerk for Mr. Dickinson in his spare time, and one day in late spring Mr. Dickinson called him into his office.

"There's something I have to report to you, Tony," he said. Then, staring out of the window, he added, "Joan is going to be married next month. She begged me to break the news to you."

Anthony felt a slow throb of pain go through his body. "Well," he said, "I suppose I've seen it coming."

"I hope you won't blame Joan," Mr. Dickinson said, and Anthony knew that Mr. Dickinson really meant not to blame him. "She wants a home of her own, and a family. It's natural enough."

"Who is she marrying, Mr. Dickinson?" Anthony asked.

"A very nice young fellow. Carter Henry, his name is." Mr. Dickinson turned and looked earnestly at him and continued, "I want you to understand, Tony, that you compare quite well with him, from my point of view. But Carter Henry is in a position to get married now. His father owns the Quaker City Battery Works, and the boy will be a vice-president in a year or so."

"I hope she'll be very happy."

"That's a mighty fine way to take it, Tony," Mr. Dickinson said warmly. "It does great credit to you. Now," he added briskly, "I want to assure you that I'm looking forward to having you join the firm after you pass your Bar exams."

Anthony thanked him, and that ended the discussion. It was clear to Anthony, however, that he had still been a child on that June day in Princeton, listening wide-eyed to the words of grown-up Mr. Dickinson. In the future he would examine the motives back of words like a bank teller studying a queer-looking bill.

A little examination now hinted that his future with Dickinson and Dawes might not be bright. Mr. Dickinson felt guilty. In time, Mr. Dickinson would begin to dislike the person who was making him feel guilty. It would be wise, Anthony thought, to begin planning for the day when that would happen.

Fortunately for his morale at that time, Anthony was enjoying every minute of law school. There was a neatness to the study of law that appealed to him. When you ran up against a problem you could go to the library and work out your answer in the light of the answers found by other men before you. Learning how to become a lawyer was much like learning how to become a Philadelphian.

Some of the students in his class — Jews fighting for the coveted title of professional man, Italians from South Philadelphia aiming at politics — were brilliant in ways he could never hope to match.

He spent some time with one of them, an Italian named Louis Donetti. They were completely unlike in background and temperament, and they were always on the opposite sides of arguments, and it was graduation time before they realized that they had actually been friends instead of enemies.

Rather to his surprise, Anthony found he could match Donetti and the others in marks if not in brilliance. In his first year he ranked in the upper tenth of his class, and was one of the few who were invited to try out for the Law Review.

He did even better in his second year, and by the end of it knew he was slated for editorship of the Law Review in his final year. When he handed in his last examination, the monitor said that the Dean wanted to see him. He reported to the Dean's secretary, who called the Dean himself to the outer office.

"Hello there, Lawrence," the Dean said. "There's a gentleman in my office I want you to meet. A Mr. Wharton, John Marshall Wharton, in fact. Of Morris, Clayton, Biddle and Wharton."

The Dean breathed those four names almost the way you might recite a psalm in church. That, of course, was quite proper. Morris, Clayton, Biddle and Wharton was one of the great law firms. But it was more than that. When you said Morris, or Clayton, or Biddle, or Wharton, you were reciting chapters of Philadelphia history. Meeting a member of the firm was rather like having the statue of William Penn atop City Hall bow gravely as you passed.

"Mr. Wharton wants to discuss a certain matter with you," the Dean said. "Let's go in, shall we?"

Mr. John Marshall Wharton was a tall slender man of about sixty, with wavy silver hair that might have looked theatrical if it had been allowed to grow an inch longer than normal. He talked pleasantly and casually to Anthony for a few minutes. Then he said, "At my time of life, many of us in the legal profession get an urge either to go on the bench or to write a book. My weakness is a desire to write a book. It will discuss the evolution of the Sherman Antitrust Act through court decisions. I need a bright young man to help me with the research."

"Yes, sir," Anthony said alertly.

"I am looking," Mr. Wharton went on, "for a law-school student who gets excellent marks, and who has had Law Review experience. The Dean tells me that you qualify."

"Thank you, sir," Anthony said, looking at the Dean.

"There are pros and cons," said Mr. Wharton. "Perhaps I don't have to go into the pros very deeply. I'll be glad to pay you fifty dollars a week. I will be at my lodge in Maine during the summer, planning the framework of the book. I would expect you to be here, digging up everything you can find on Sherman Antitrust decisions. In the fall, we would begin work on the book, which I hope to finish within a year."

"It's hard to see how the cons could outweigh the pros, sir."

Mr. Wharton said, "The main objection, of course, is that this would mean giving up a fairly good chance to be editor of the Law Review. You couldn't do both."

Anthony realized that this was a tricky decision. The editor of the Law Review could be sure of getting a bid to a good law firm. On the other hand, a few years after you got out of law school nobody would care whether or not you had been on the Law Review. But the prestige gained from helping John Marshall Wharton to write a basic textbook would last a long time. Then there was another angle: if he did a good job he might be invited to join the firm of Morris, Clayton, Biddle and Wharton.

"There is one other point that I ought to consider," Anthony said. "In my spare time I've been working as a law clerk with Dickinson and Dawes."

"I know about that," Mr. Wharton said. "You would have to give that up too. So you see," he added, with a sudden, charming smile, "I'm asking you to give up a lot. But I'm selfish enough to want the best man for the job."

It was skillful and disarming of Mr. Wharton to admit that he was being selfish. Because of course he was. He was asking Anthony to gamble a sure thing, the Law Review, against fifty dollars a week and a hope. Mr. Wharton also thought he was asking Anthony to gamble his future with Dickinson and Dawes. He said, "Would you like time to consider this?"

Two years before, Anthony had allowed himself to be frightened away from taking a gamble. That hadn't worked out well. "I don't need any more time, sir," he said. "I'd feel greatly honored to have a chance to work with you."

"Good. I'm sure that neither of us will regret the decision."

DURING the summer Anthony lived so closely with the Sherman Antitrust Act that everything else in his life began to seem faintly unreal. Mr. Wharton returned from Maine early in September and fired a machine-gun series of questions at him, designed to probe his knowledge of famous antitrust cases. When Anthony began answering, he listened for ten minutes, then laughed and held up a protesting hand. "All right," he said. "That's fine. Now we can get down to work."

At first they worked together a few evenings a week, at the Racquet Club or at Mr. Wharton's office. Then Mr. Wharton began coming in Sundays. Finally he asked Anthony to come out to his place week-ends so they could get more done. And that opened an entirely new life to Anthony.

The Wharton mansion was old Philadelphia, even though it was far out on the Main Line. The Georgian house seemed to float on its green lawns. Inside, it was filled with the amber glow of mahogany and satinwood, the bluish flames of old silver, the deep shine of Wedgwood and lusterware.

Mr. and Mrs. Wharton had no children. Mrs. Wharton was considerably younger than her husband, a slim and graceful woman, unobtrusive as a candle flame. Anthony thought she was perhaps several years younger than his mother, although in his eyes that still made her middle-aged. She might have been in her early forties. She had black hair with glints of silver, cut short and brushed back in dark wings from her temples.

Now and then, while her husband was talking at dinner about the Sherman Antitrust Act, she would find an opening for a hopeful comment about art or music, but the Sherman Antitrust Act smothered all her efforts at conversation.

More than a month went by before he ever really talked to Mrs. Wharton. Then one Sunday morning before breakfast, he decided to explore the huge library in the west wing. He was examining an early edition of *Robinson Crusoe* when Mrs. Wharton came in.

"Good morning, Mr. Lawrence," she said. "I didn't realize you were in here."

"Just admiring things," he said. "This is quite a library, isn't it?" He closed the book and replaced it.

"Yes, it is nice." As she spoke, her hand moved, apparently without conscious thought, to the copy of *Robinson Crusoe,* and turned it so that its spine faced up instead of outward. Her action reminded Anthony that the book had been turned over that way when he took it from the shelf. In fact, now that he noticed it, many of the books in the library were turned upward. "Do you mind if I'm curious?" he asked. "Why are so many of the books turned over on the shelves?"

"Well," she said, "I understand that, around 1910, John's father needed more room on the shelves. So he turned over the books he was considering giving up. But he debated about it for a few years, and then he died. Naturally no one has disturbed the arrangement."

It struck Anthony as very funny, though her tone implied that this was a solemn matter. In spite of himself, he began grinning. Mrs. Wharton looked at him in shocked surprise. Then suddenly she giggled. It was such a delightful little sound that Anthony began laughing. Mrs. Wharton started laughing too, and then in a few seconds they were both slightly hysterical.

"Oh dear, oh dear," Mrs. Wharton wailed finally, dabbing at her eyes. "I haven't laughed like that in years. All those b-books lying solemnly that way since 1910 . . ."

"It's wonderful," Anthony choked. "I'm sure it could only happen in Philadelphia."

They were just recovering when Mr. Wharton walked in, looking slightly offended. "What's so funny?"

Mrs. Wharton managed to explain in between fits of laughing, and Mr. Wharton said, "If my father thought it was a good idea I can't see what's so funny about it. I— " He stopped. The muscles of his face began working. "Come to think of it," he said, "it is ridiculous. It — " Then he looked startled, and out came a big booming laugh, and then they all began howling madly. In the middle of it Mr. Wharton gasped, "Let's put the blasted things back the way they belong," and all three of them ran around wildly standing the books up properly on end.

After it was all over they were a little abashed at having been so unrestrained. There was no talk at breakfast. Anthony pretended to study the sports section of *The Philadelphia Record*. The startling thing that had happened in the library would certainly make a change in their relationships.

The clue to what this change would be appeared early that afternoon. He and Mr. Wharton were working in the study when a knock sounded on the door and Mrs. Wharton came in.

"I've decided to take a firm stand," she said pleasantly. "John, you're working this boy too hard. Why don't you two take the afternoon off, and get some fresh air and exercise?"

"Perhaps you're right," Mr. Wharton said. "Tony, you are getting a little thin and pale. Well, what do you suggest, Carol?"

"What about riding? Do you ride, Tony?"

"I like riding," Anthony said, "but I don't suppose I'm any good. We learned to ride in R.O.T.C. at college."

"No reason why you can't take Tony out this afternoon," Mr. Wharton said. "I'd do it myself, but I'm a bit afraid of that sacroiliac of mine."

"I suppose I could," she said, looking uncertainly at Anthony.

Before the episode in the library he would have backed away from that, because Mrs. Wharton had seemed as awesome as a glacier. Now he smiled at her and said, "I'd like it."

So that afternoon they dug up riding breeches and boots of Mr. Wharton's which didn't fit him too badly, and went down to the stable. They saddled two magnificent jumpers, a chestnut and a black, and rode off at a walk on a bridle path through woods. After a while Mrs. Wharton stepped up the pace to a smooth trot and they finally came out on the edge of some rolling fields. Up ahead were meadows, low stone walls and rail fences.

"Are you game?" Mrs. Wharton called.

He had done a little jumping in the riding hall at Princeton, but always over barriers that went down if your horse hit them. He hoped the black package of dynamite under him knew more about jumping than he did. "Let's go," he shouted.

Anthony leaned forward slightly. That was all the black was waiting for. The ground blurred and the wind scraped at his face. Fifty yards ahead, Mrs. Wharton's chestnut soared over a stone wall. Anthony took a deep breath. The wall swooped at him and his black horse floated over it.

They went galloping on and on over the hunt country, until, at last, Mrs. Wharton lifted a hand and they brought the horses down to a walk.

"Oh, weren't they glorious!" she cried. "It's been so long since they've had a run. And so long since I've had one, too." She reached out a hand and touched his arm, lightly. "Tony, I'm so grateful to you. Today you've either added ten years to my life or taken ten off my age, I can't figure which."

He laughed, and looked at her curiously. She had taken off her cap, and her short black hair with its silver frosting tumbled around her face. The belt of her riding breeches accented her slim waist. For the first time he saw that she had a good figure. On an impulse, he said, "You look about eighteen."

Her cheeks, pink from the exercise, turned crimson. "I wasn't fishing," she said. "It all started with that wonderful crazy laugh this morning. Tony, have you ever felt like a piece of crystal that's vibrating nearer and nearer to the cracking point? I've been getting closer to that point for months."

There were subtleties in that which he didn't even want to understand. They were moving along toward home now, with no sound but the creak of leather and the clop of hoofs.

"I'm afraid I shocked you," she said. "Did I sound disloyal?"

"No," he said, "it wasn't that. If I was shocked, it was mainly because suddenly you became a real person."

"You weren't a real person either until today, Tony. You were a stuffed shirt, the classic bright young man."

He chuckled. "I deserve that. I bet the hours we've spent on this book have been awfully dull for you."

"I'm very much in favor of John writing the book. It merely came at the wrong time for me. Just when he was giving up all the things we used to do together, riding, trips and all that. And we haven't been able to have any children, and committees have begun boring me to death. I don't want you to think I'm disloyal. John means more to me than anybody ever could. I admit I married him for security. I was twenty-five, and he was forty-five, and my family hadn't a penny left . . . but he's a wonderful person, and it's not just the security any more."

"I'd have felt badly if you didn't care for him. He's a mighty fine guy."

"Tony, don't wait until forty-five to get married. I've never heard you mention a girl. Has there been a girl, Tony?"

He smiled faintly. "I had one, and got talked out of her."

"Who was she, and how did it happen?"

It was rather pleasant to talk this way with an older, under-standing woman, and so for the first time he found himself telling someone about his romance with Joan Dickinson. The memory of it didn't hurt badly now — it seemed just something that had happened to a college boy more than two years ago.

After that day, it became an accepted thing that he and Mrs. Wharton would ride for an hour or two every Saturday and Sunday afternoon. He enjoyed the rides not only for the exercise but also because it was a new experience, and very pleasant, to have a platonic friendship with a woman.

The winter passed smoothly, and spring came, and one Saturday night Mr. Wharton pushed aside their manuscript, walked to the open window and sniffed the air. "Dogwood and violets," he said. "I don't feel like working any more tonight. I'm going to bully you into taking a walk with me. And while I'm changing clothes, why don't you see if Carol will come?"

Anthony went out into the hall. There was music floating from the living room — the Philadelphia Orchestra's recording of "The Blue Danube." He walked to the doorway of the room, and paused in surprise. Mrs. Wharton was dancing by herself, drifting around the big room with her head thrown back and her eyes partly closed and dreamy. Anthony was about to move away, but one of her pirouettes brought them face to face. She came forward as if she had been expecting a partner and, without quite knowing how it happened, he found himself dancing with her.

For a few moments he felt embarrassed to be dancing with an

older woman. But then, slowly and shockingly, he realized that this was not an older woman at all. This was like dancing with a flame. It was becoming hard to breathe. He looked at her face and saw that her eyes were no longer dreamy. They were wide and dark and questioning, and seemed ready to accept whatever answer he wanted to give.

The music stopped. He stepped back, and forced himself to laugh and to say casually, "I'd almost forgotten how to dance. And I did forget to give you a message from Mr. Wharton. He's going for a walk and wants to know if you'd like to come."

She stared at him almost blankly for a moment, and then abruptly her glance flickered over his shoulder and she said, "I'd love a walk. Will you wait for me to change, John?"

Anthony managed to turn slowly. Mr. Wharton was standing in the doorway. "Of course I'll wait," he said. He seemed to study Anthony, and then flashed his rare and charming smile. "That was very nice to watch. I'm sorry I don't dance any more."

During the next few weeks Anthony took care not to let anything like that happen again. But he became sharply conscious of all Mrs. Wharton's actions: the click of her high heels, the tiny sharps and flats in her voice, the changing curves of her body as she moved. When they rode side by side, did her knee brush against his only by chance? If he helped her down from the saddle, did her hands remain in his a few seconds too long? Originally she had been cool and poised in whatever she did. Now, from week-end to week-end, she showed more signs of tension. She stared off into space. Her laugh was pitched too high. She rode the big chestnut horse more recklessly each time they went out, continually spurring it at a crazy dead run and not giving it a chance to time its jumps.

At last, on a Saturday in May, her timing at one of the rail fences didn't come out right. At the final moment the chestnut broke its run with a horrible stiff-legged slide and sent her in a pinwheel spin out of the saddle.

Anthony galloped up to where she had fallen, and leaped off the black. She was lying face down. Her jumping cap, its stiff crown dented, had fallen off, and her hair fanned out around her head like the petals of a black flower. He rolled her over carefully, letting her head come to rest in the crook of his arm. She was breathing, and her color looked all right. He unbuttoned the tight collar of her shirt. She sighed and took a deep breath and opened her eyes.

"Oh, Tony," she said weakly. "I was so bad, wasn't I?"

He couldn't help what happened. She looked soft and young and helpless, and he bent and kissed her. For a moment she rested in his arms. Then she arched toward him and her arms slid around his neck. Somehow he managed to recover a little sanity. He untangled himself and got up and began to help her to her feet. She looked at him, almost pouting, and said, "You don't have to treat me like a little girl who doesn't know what she's doing."

They rode home without speaking. He had a suspicion, however, that her long dark lashes sometimes hid a glance that studied him carefully. He wished he knew what to do. Lawbooks didn't tell you how to handle a situation of this type; they merely pointed out the various legal results of letting it get out of control.

When they got back to the house Mrs. Wharton went to her room to rest and he and Mr. Wharton ate dinner alone. He kept imagining that Mr. Wharton was studying him in the same secret way that Mrs. Wharton had done. Later they ended work early, because Mr. Wharton said he was tired. Anthony took the manuscript of the book to his room, but the Sherman Antitrust Act couldn't hold his attention.

His mind examined the case of Lawrence vs. Wharton from all its angles. There seemed to be only three courses of action. He could pretend to be called home, and then avoid visiting the Whartons again. However, Mr. Wharton might guess the reason for such a sudden break. So he would hurt Mr. Wharton, and of course kill

his own chances of joining Morris, Clayton, Biddle and Wharton. He would also — and this was a point to consider — hurt Mrs. Wharton. The second course of action was to follow the prompting of nature and have an affair with her; it would be a wild disorderly business that would leave three lives blowing around like waste-paper in the street. The third course involved saying loftily to Mrs. Wharton, "How then can I do this great wickedness?" A man named Joseph had used that line once with a certain Mrs. Potiphar, and it hadn't worked out at all well for him.

Then there was a light rapping at his door, and it seemed possible that Lawrence vs. Wharton might be coming up for trial. He opened the door and saw her standing there. For a moment he was quite willing to lose the case. Her hair was brushed back in clean pure lines from her face. Her lips were very red and gave him a small trembling smile. She said in a faint voice, "I thought you might be worrying about me, Tony. Were you?"

"I've been worrying about you for a couple of months."

She slipped into his room and closed the door quietly. "Tony," she said, "this is awful of me, isn't it? I couldn't help myself. Do you have to stand there looking at me like a judge?"

"I'm trying to think. I —"

"I don't want you to think!" she said with a flash of anger. She moved close and hid her face against his chest.

There was no use lecturing her on the moral and legal points involved. Women never cared much about such things; in general, they only approved rules of behavior which supported them in what they wanted to do. If he hoped to stop Mrs. Wharton without getting into the Joseph-and-Potiphar's-wife mess, he'd better find something she wanted to do that conflicted with her notion about him and which was much more important to her. Like all women, Mrs. Wharton put a high value on security. She admitted having married for it. He wondered what would happen if he asked her to trade in her security. It might be worth while to find out. It couldn't make things much worse.

"What do you want?" he said hoarsely. "Just a quick little affair? I'm not going to settle for that."

She looked up at him and pouted slightly. "Why do we have to think about that now, Tony?"

"I've got to. This can't be a hit-and-run thing with me. Will you go away with me? Tonight? For good?"

He was holding her now, and she put her hands on his chest and pushed back slightly. "Tony! You're so abrupt and hasty. There are so many things to consider."

"All we have to consider is a divorce."

"But Tony darling, we have to be civilized and think about John's position and our own. You won't be through law school until next month and then you have your Bar exams and —"

"Who cares about exams! I can do something else. We can rent a little apartment and make out somehow. I know it's asking you to give up a lot, your position and husband and home and all that. I know people will sneer at us and not understand. But — "

She put a hand against his lips. "Can't we just have tonight and then think of what's best to do?"

It was very difficult to keep his control, standing near her like that. He let himself slip down onto his knees, and stared up at her pale face and said earnestly, "I love you too much for that." He buried his face in her skirt and waited.

The seconds ticked past in a stumbling file. Then at last her hand reached down and touched his hot face. "You're such a sweet boy," she murmured. He looked up at her. There was a smile on her face: a lovely quiet smile with a hint of satisfaction in it.

"But I'm a boy, though. That's what you're thinking."

She patted his cheek. "Of course you are. And I've been silly and selfish. I've got to think of what's best for you, Tony. You have your whole life and career ahead of you, and I'm not going to wreck it. Now stand up, like a good boy, and look at me."

He got up, feeling his legs tremble as if their muscles had turned into old rubber bands. "You're so lovely," he whispered.

Her laugh was crystal. "Just knowing that you think so is enough," she said. She tilted her head and kissed him briefly and gently. "I'm sorry I've been so bad and thoughtless. I hope you'll go on being very fond of me, but keep all the rest for that wonderful girl you'll marry someday. Good night, Tony." She touched his cheek once more, and went out of the room.

He listened to the small final click of the door latch, and went to the bed and threw himself on it face down.

Two WEEKS later he and Mr. Wharton finished the manuscript of the book, and Mr. Wharton said happily, "Well, we did it, didn't we? How do you feel about the book, Tony?"

He smiled a trifle grimly. He felt nothing about the book except relief that it was finished and that he could clear out. "You've done a fine job," he told Mr. Wharton. "There isn't a law school in the country that doesn't need a book like this."

"That's very flattering, Tony. And of course you've contributed a great deal to it. Now that we're through, I'd like to express my thanks in a practical way. Perhaps the thought of joining Morris, Clayton, Biddle and Wharton has crossed your mind?"

"Well, naturally, I've thought about it," he said carefully. "But of course I realize you can take your pick of a lot of men."

"I've made my pick," Mr. Wharton said. "You're it, Tony. But I do want you to understand the conditions under which you'd join us. You'll have to make your own way. I'll do my best for you but I'm going to retire in a year or two, and then you'll be on your own in a big cold law factory. Are you willing to risk it?"

"The way I look at it," Anthony said, "is that in a big firm it's a tough climb to the top but a mighty nice view if you can get there."

"I'll watch your career with interest. Personally I think you'll end up with a mighty nice view."

"Thank you, sir. That's good to hear."

"My reason for saying that," Mr. Wharton said, studying the ceiling, "is that you have an unusual skill in dealing with people, and of course the practice of law is nine-tenths people and one-tenth law. I am not unaware of the fact that there have been certain undercurrents in our relationship. Neither you nor I, I'm sure, wish to discuss them. I merely want to say that you have handled yourself very well."

Anthony nodded gravely. Mr. Wharton, too, had an unusual skill in dealing with people.

CHAPTER 4

HE GRADUATED from law school in June of 1939, took his Bar exams in July, and learned four months later that he had passed. Meanwhile untidy things started to happen in Europe. It became evident that people like Reserve Corps Second Lieutenant Anthony J. Lawrence would not be able to concentrate on law careers very much longer. Anthony decided that, as long as he would be called to active duty in the Army sooner or later, and would just be marking time at Morris, Clayton, Biddle and Wharton, he might as well get in early. Besides, it didn't seem fair to let the Army train him for a possible war and not go as soon as he could.

He went off late in 1940, feeling slightly heroic, but when Pearl Harbor came he was on the West Coast nursing a hatch of barrage balloons near San Francisco. It was dull and lonely work. Other officers his age were going overseas. The ones who were both smart and lucky would come back with promotions and rows of fruit salad on their jackets, and when the war ended everybody would try to give them the breaks in business and they would be sitting pretty. When the war ended he would just be sitting.

As soon as you got the barrage balloons flying nicely at the ends of their cables there wasn't much to do, so he started reading Army Regulations. The Army had a regulation for everything, just as, in a way, Philadelphia did. In Philadelphia, of course, you could absorb things by example and precept, but the result was the same in both: an orderly society which seldom moved in the wrong direction and sometimes did not move at all.

Up in the Western Defense Command, a few people heard about the second lieutenant in barrage balloons who read Army Regulations for pleasure. Then someone found out that he was also a lawyer. By March of 1942 he was being detached from duty on occasion, to act as defense counsel in courts-martial held by the Defense Command.

From the Army point of view, Second Lieutenant Anthony J. Lawrence was a perfect defense counsel. He knew his ARs. He had a knack of making every officer on a court-martial feel like a Commanding General, and at the same time he won an amazing number of acquittals. This gave him a reputation not only for knowing Army Regulations but also for knowing how to get around them. By August of 1942 he was promoted to First Lieutenant and transferred to Defense Command headquarters.

Then, in October, a new Corps Commander, Major General Buckley D. "Buck" Brimmer, came boiling out of Washington on his way to the Southwest Pacific Area, snatching up a staff as he moved. He paused in The Presidio in San Francisco, raiding officers right and left. There was a bright young lawyer in the Defense Command who knew how to get around the ARs, was there?

Grab the guy. Let's go! There's a war on. Orders whipped through the mimeographs like bullets through a machine gun, and Anthony was on his way to New Guinea.

He worked quietly on the staff of Buckley's 19th Corps. Nobody had told him why he was overseas, so he was startled one day in January of 1943 to be called in for a conference with General Brimmer. The General was sitting before a wooden field table, scowling at a sheaf of papers as if they were soldiers who didn't know how to salute. He was a solid red-faced man who had once played a lot of fullback at The Point. Nobody else was in the Quonset hut except his aide, Major Thomas Strang, a lean West Pointer, Class of 1936.

"Lawrence, sir," Anthony said. "The General sent for me."

General Brimmer glanced at him. "Pull up a chair and sit down, Lawrence. You know Major Strang, my aide? Now I grabbed you back in San Francisco because somebody said you knew how to get around the ARs. I got a problem for you. What do you know about Major General Oliphant?"

For a Corps Commander to ask a first lieutenant about a division commander was like handing you a grenade with the pin out. Actually Anthony knew a lot about General Oliphant, just as he knew a lot about General Brimmer. He liked finding out all he could about people and their motives. But he thought he would move carefully, and try to hand the grenade back to the CG.

"Well, sir," he said, "General Oliphant is commander of the so-called Thunderhead Division, which got its name back in the First World War. National Guard, of course. The General is a big feed-and-grain man in his home state, and the National Guard has been his lifelong hobby. It was probably a dream come true when he found himself commanding the Thunderhead when it was mobilized. It's still about fifty percent home state in its personnel. That's about all, sir."

General Brimmer jerked a thumb at Anthony, and growled, "This guy knows a lot and says damn little."

"General, I don't trust these cautious guys," Strang said, looking in dislike at Anthony.

"It's all right," the General said. "He's walking on eggs. Lawrence, nothing I say goes beyond this room. Question. If you were in my shoes, how would you get rid of General Oliphant?"

Anthony allowed himself to grin. That was taking a liberty, but it showed he wasn't too cautious. "General," he said, "are you waiting for me to ask why you don't just relieve him from command?"

"I was waiting for it, all right," the General said. "And if you'd given me that, tomorrow you'd have been laundry officer on Snafu Island. Now go ahead. And don't worry about breaking a few of those eggs you're walking on."

"Sir, you've probably thought of all these things — but would General MacArthur ask him to do some terribly important job, like cementing our relations with the Aussies back in Brisbane?"

"Yeah, Mac did that for me, and Oliphant balked. What's your next try?"

"Sir, this New Guinea climate is very unhealthful. If General Oliphant were up here for a conference, and if your staff doctor happened to notice that he had a queer color, it would be natural to insist on an immediate physical exam. Then if he found some very serious things wrong, you'd be forced to send General Oliphant stateside to recover."

"He's onto that trick," the General said. "The son of a gun has a Mayo Clinic hot shot in his division who checks him all the time. What else you got?"

"General, you're not only making me walk on eggs, but also you're making me do it in the dark. I'd have a better chance of coming up with something if you'd give me the picture first."

"Okay, Lawrence," the General said. "Here's your picture." He thrust the pile of papers across the desk.

Anthony scanned them rapidly. "Wow!" he said.

"Yeah, wow," the General said bitterly. "I've drafted orders relieving him from duty for failure to carry out orders, failure to press home an attack, Lord knows what all. If he demands a court-martial I got the papers ready."

"General," Anthony said, "can you prove those charges?"

"I sure can. Oliphant's soft with that division of his. They're boys from his own state and he doesn't want them killed. Hell, people get killed in a war. The softer they are, the more of them get killed. Oliphant had that Lona River job to do. He didn't push home the attack because his boys were getting killed. The Aussies had to do it for us and they'll never let us forget it."

"Unfortunately, sir," Anthony said, "you won't be court-martialing General Oliphant. You'll be putting the National Guard on trial. You'll also be putting his state on trial. There are three war correspondents out here from big newspapers in his state. General Oliphant treats them like kings. They think he's wonderful."

"Oh come on, Lawrence, I know all that. I didn't call you in so we could cry on each other's shoulders."

"Sir, I'm just trying to get a clear field of fire. General Oliphant's public-relations setup is the best out here. Every time a private gets upped to Pfc, a story about it goes back to the kid's home-town paper, mentioning General Oliphant. Sir, I strongly recommend against a court-martial. General Oliphant's home state will scream murder, and the Pentagon will ask what size noose you'd like."

"Lawrence, you have now arrived at the point I'd reached just before I called you in. Okay. I don't dare get rid of him in any regulation way. Tell me how to get around the regulations."

A little less than three years ago Mrs. Wharton had backed Anthony into much the same type of corner. "General," he said, "when you've got to get rid of somebody and the usual ways won't work, you can try to trick the person into getting rid of himself."

"Yeah? How?"

"Well, sir, General Oliphant wants very much to go on commanding the Thunderhead Division. We've got to find something he wants to do even more. Have you any ideas?"

"Sure," the General growled. "He wants to be Governor of his state. He'll swap his division for that."

"Sir, why doesn't he go home and run for Governor? The state primary is this spring."

General Brimmer got up and began stamping around the hut like a bulldozer with a loose track. "That's been my only hope," he said furiously, "and nothing came of it. Here he is, a shoo-in to win, and no one has asked him to run. I've had friends of mine in Washington checking into it. Now what do you say?"

Anthony liked this big red-faced man who was clanking up and down the room. The guy was trying to do a job, and Oliphant was messing it up. He braced himself. A plan that might work had slipped into his mind, along with thoughts of what would happen if he tried it and it went wrong.

"General," he said. "We ought to start a Draft-Oliphant-for-Governor campaign."

General Brimmer stopped as if he had just run over a land mine. "You don't know what you're saying!" he gasped.

"Yes sir. I know all the regulations barring Army officers from engaging in politics."

"Um. How would you go about this, Lawrence?"

"Sir, do you think you should know? You may have to cut my throat. The less involved you are, the better."

"You serious about this?"

"Yes sir. I'll need some orders detaching me for temporary duty, sir, and top-priority travel orders."

General Brimmer turned to his aide. "Give him whatever he wants, Tom. All right, Lawrence. You're on your own."

Anthony left the hut with Major Strang. When the orders were cut, Strang handed them to him and said, "The Old Man's a great guy. If he has to cut your throat, he'll be sorry as hell about it."

"As I hang out the day's wash on Snafu Island," Anthony said, "that will be nice to remember."

He grabbed the first plane for Port Moresby on the south coast of New Guinea. It was the forward echelon of GHQ and a logical place to start looking for the men he wanted. When he reached Moresby he hunted up the Public Relations Office of GHQ and learned that one of the war correspondents from General Oliphant's state was in Brisbane and two were in Moresby. That night he hung around the PRO mess hall until he could slip into a vacant chair beside one of them, Bill Cleamer of the Menapolis *Herald.* Anthony introduced himself and started a casual conversation.

"You're new around here, aren't you?" Cleamer said.

"I'm just visiting. I'm from G-1 at the Nineteenth Corps."

"G-1, huh? That's Intelligence, isn't it?"

"No. G-1 is Personnel. G-2 is Intelligence," Anthony said.

"Oh. I don't know the Army setup very well. Not that it matters. My paper sent me here for human-interest stuff."

"We have your state's division in the Nineteenth Corps, haven't we? The Thunderhead?"

"Yeah. Great bunch. I got some swell human-interest stuff about the way the boys in the Thunderhead busted through the Japs on the Lona River. Anything cooking now up north?"

"It's kind of quiet," Anthony said. "Of course in G-1 we just deal with people, like you do, from privates right up to generals like Oliphant. In fact, a message came in from Washington last night on General Oliphant. Listen, do you think it would be right to let a guy commanding a division out of the Army so he can run for governor of a state?"

Cleamer choked suddenly on his food. Then, recovering, he said in a very casual voice, "You're talking about General Oliphant?"

"Yeah. You probably know all about it. It's that quiet little movement back in your state to draft him to run for Governor. They're keeping it under wraps because I suppose it's a touchy thing grabbing a division commander from a combat zone. You must know him well. Would he make a good Governor?"

"Come to think of it," Cleamer said, "he'd make a swell Governor. Do you think he's going to get out of the Army?"

"I wouldn't know. This message I saw, it was one of those top-level things. I guess some big shots from your state have been putting the heat on about breaking him loose to run for Governor, and the Pentagon messaged GHQ asking what they should do."

"I wonder what General Oliphant thinks about it?"

"He may not even know," Anthony said. "This wasn't a message to him. Say, I just happened to think, I shouldn't be talking about the messages we see in G-1. Still and all, I suppose you war correspondents get the inside dope on a lot of things, so anything I've said is safe with you."

"Oh, sure," Cleamer said. "Well, I got to run along and do some work. Nice to have met you, Lawrence."

After Cleamer left, Anthony waited a few minutes and then walked to the pressroom. Yes, there was Cleamer typing busily.

Now the problem was to make sure the story got through censor-

ship. Anthony knew that, in the Southwest Pacific, Public Relations censored for accuracy and general policy as well as for military security. Cleamer's story might worry the censor who got it. Anthony thought he'd better tag the Public Relations Officer himself. He asked some questions and learned that the PRO, Colonel Thompson, was Regular Army and a sharp guy. So he was a good bet to have guts enough to make the right decision.

He went into Colonel Thompson's office and introduced himself. Thompson asked what he could do for him.

Anthony said, "Colonel, if one of your censors gets a story that has some political angles in it but no military security of any kind, what would he do with it?"

"He might pass it. He might bring it to me."

"I think one of your censors is going to get a story like that pretty soon. I'm hoping it will be cleared."

Colonel Thompson was a sort of hawklike guy, and now he looked ready to pounce. "That's an interesting thing to tell me,

Lawrence," he said briskly. "Are you here just representing your-self, or somebody else?"

"In a way, just myself, Colonel."

"That would make you pretty stupid, Lawrence. You don't look stupid. What sort of orders are you carrying?"

Anthony dug out a copy of his orders. "They're a bit vague, Colonel," he said.

Thompson glanced at them. "Vague is right. They let you go anywhere in the theater for as long as you want. Mission confidential. That's quite a set of orders. Now what's the deal?"

"Colonel, the less you know about it, the better. Would it be out of line to ask you to let things ride that way, until and unless the story comes in to you?"

Thompson glared at him for a moment, then chuckled. "Lieutenant," he said, "I ought to be sending out the alarm right now for that story. But I'll take a chance. If it gets past my boys, okay. If they bring it in here, we'll see. You can wait if you like."

Anthony thanked him, and settled down to wait. Fifteen minutes went by. Twenty. Then a tall black-haired first lieutenant came in. "Got a story here I'd like you to see, Colonel," he said, holding out two typewritten pages.

Thompson read the story quickly. Finally he pushed the pages across the desk to Anthony. "This it?" he asked.

Anthony began reading the dispatch, which was written in choppy cablese. It began: "Brass here hints politicos homeward casing Oliphant governorship. Reported topmost Washington asks can fightingest division spare Lona hero . . ." Probably that would be translated into: "It was learned on high authority here today that top political leaders of the state are exploring the possibility of drafting Major General Arthur C. Oliphant, Commanding General of the Thunderhead Division, to run for Governor. The movement, it was understood, has reached the point of high-level queries from Washington as to whether General Oliphant, the hero of the Lona River battle, could be spared from the state's hard-fighting division . . ." It went on like that. Without actually saying so it gave the impression that FDR, Marshall and MacArthur were all trying to decide what would be best for the country.

"Yes sir," Anthony said, keeping his face blank. "This is it."

"Lieutenant," Thompson said, "this is one of our censors, Lieutenant John L. York, Jr. Jack, this is Lieutenant Lawrence. He's from G-1 of the Nineteenth Corps. By an odd coincidence he was here waiting to see if this story would come in."

"Hello, Lawrence," York said. Then he grinned at Thompson and said, "Bill Cleamer's out there bleeding all over my desk, trying to get this thing through."

Thompson nodded. "It'd be a big story for his paper. Look, Lawrence, would I have to hunt very far to find the high authority, the reliable source, the theater spokesman who cannot be identified, who gave this yarn to Cleamer?"

"No sir," Anthony said. "You wouldn't have to hunt very far."

"Jack," the Colonel said gravely to his censor, "if Oliphant went home, it would be a great loss to the theater. However, our loss would be the country's gain, wouldn't it, Jack?"

"Yes, Colonel. I guess we all want to make sure the hero of the Lona River gets everything that's coming to him."

The Colonel frowned. "Well then, don't bring stories in to me that any censor ought to have brains enough to pass. You do what you think is right, and you never asked for my opinion."

"Why is it always the lieutenants who have to stick their necks out?" York said disgustedly. He took the story and marched grumpily out of the room.

"Very poor discipline we have around here," Colonel Thompson said. "Well, Lawrence, anything else I can do for you?"

"Can I hang around a few days, Colonel?"

"Sure. Ask Jack York to take care of you. I left for Brisbane a couple hours ago, so I didn't even meet you. Good luck, Lawrence."

Anthony settled down to see what was going to happen. As it turned out, things moved fast and Lieutenant York grabbed copies of incoming messages and outgoing stories for him.

Cleamer took off the next morning for Thunderhead Division headquarters. That afternoon a bitter message came in from Midland City, in Oliphant's home state, for a correspondent named Johns, of the Midland City *News:* MENAPOLIS HERALD BANNERING CLEAMER STORY ON SECRET DRAFT OLIPHANT GOVERNORSHIP STOP WHY

YOU KEEPING IT SECRET TOO QUESTION MARK. Johns caught the next plane for Thunderhead Division headquarters. Next came queries from the AP and UP to their correspondents, and traffic to the Buna airstrip took another jump. Then stories began to come back from Thunderhead Division headquarters. First General Oliphant told Cleamer that it was all news to him and that his place was at the fighting front but that naturally he was honored to be considered for the state's highest office.

Then came Johns' dispatch to the Midland City *News*, beginning: "Oliphant denied ambitions governorward today exclusive interview but readiest bow popular decision . . ." Next came the AP and UP stories in which General Oliphant rather unwillingly admitted that certain quiet approaches had been made to him.

Meanwhile, far south in Brisbane, the third correspondent from General Oliphant's state — Sundstrom, of the New Oslo *Times* — had been caught off base and was furiously filing stories from GHQ. All he could get from GHQ were flat denials of any pressure from Washington to release Oliphant. But Sundstrom managed to give the impression that the pressure was growing every hour.

On the basis of messages from editors to their correspondents Anthony could guess at what was happening in General Oliphant's home state. Political leaders in the state had obviously been badly jolted by the first dispatches. A secret move had developed to draft the state's unbeatable war hero, and they had been left out of it. There was, however, one saving feature. The draft movement had been launched so secretly that nobody knew exactly who had started it! All over the state, party leaders began a wild scramble to get word to Oliphant that each was the original and most important leader of his cause.

Anthony spent a week in Moresby watching all this develop. It was an interesting lesson in practical politics and he enjoyed it. He realized, of course, that chance had stacked up a lot of firewood, and all he had done was touch a match to the right spot. He went back to his own headquarters and reported to Major Strang.

"Major," he said, "I think the show is on the road."

Strang grabbed his hand and shook it. "Lawrence," he said, "it's a smash hit. Look at this message that just came in."

Well, there it was. A week ago he had pretended that such a message existed. Now it did. FROM MARSHALL FOR MACARTHUR FOR BRIMMER. TREMENDOUS PRESSURE TO DRAFT OLIPHANT TO RUN FOR GOVERNOR OF HIS STATE. YOUR RECOMMENDATIONS DESIRED AS TO WHETHER HE CAN BE RELEASED WITHOUT DAMAGE TO WAR EFFORT.

"I hope you'll be a bit reluctant, and make General Oliphant beg for it," Anthony said.

"Indeed we will. General Brimmer is practicing a heartbreak right now."

Two weeks later, Anthony watched General Brimmer award the Distinguished Service Medal to Major General Oliphant and wish him all kinds of luck back in the States. After General Oliphant had left, Major Strang caught Anthony's arm.

"Don't run away," he said. "We have another little ceremony." He led Anthony into General Brimmer's office. In a few moments Brimmer came in and said to his aide, "All right, Tom. Read it."

Major Strang took out a paper and read: "Citation for Bronze Star Medal. First Lieutenant Anthony J. Lawrence, Army of the United States. For meritorious achievement. As an officer attached to G-1 of the Nineteenth Corps he was assigned a personnel problem of the most important nature. By his exceptional ability, broad knowledge of human nature, and sound judgment, First Lieutenant Lawrence contributed immeasurably to the success of combat operations in the Nineteenth Corps Area."

General Brimmer stepped forward and pinned the Bronze Star medal on Anthony's shirt. "Congratulations, Captain," he said.

Anthony gulped. "Did you say Captain, sir?"

"Yep. Strang has the order promoting you. Well, that winds it up. I'm only sorry about one thing. The wrong guy got the DSM."

CHAPTER 5

ANTHONY came home from Japan in October of 1945 wearing the gold oak leaves of a major, the Legion of Merit, Bronze Star, Asiatic Pacific Theater campaign ribbon with three battle stars, American Theater ribbon, World War II Victory ribbon, and the Philippines Liberation ribbon. That impressed everybody at

Morris, Clayton, Biddle and Wharton, and they gave him an honor, too. It consisted of putting his name on the right-hand side of the firm's letterhead along with the names of eleven other lawyers. This also entitled him to a modest office of his own.

All that was very nice. But the right margin of the letterhead was farther from the left than you might think. On the left side, which was irreverently called the Happy Hunting Ground, were two groups of names. First came the five senior members of the firm. Then there was a discreet white space, and the five associate members of the firm. You could leap from the right-hand side of the letterhead to the lower group on the left if you could bring in about fifty thousand dollars' worth of fees a year. From there you could jump the half inch of white space to the upper group if your name was respected in U. S. Supreme Court circles or in the best homes in Philadelphia. The latter was considered harder to achieve than the former.

Anthony didn't intend to spend the rest of his life on the wrong side of the letterhead. He had already lost five years, and now he had to move fast to make up for it. He was thirty-one, he still had to make a reputation, and make money, and find a wife who could help him to get ahead.

The first thing he needed was a big client who would give him a steady flow of profitable work, or pay him a large retainer for the right to call him when necessary. There probably weren't more than a thousand big clients in the Philadelphia area, and you couldn't go out and try to lure a client away from another firm. That was one of the worst types of "unprofessional conduct." The penalty could be disbarment, ending your legal career.

Anthony didn't have family connections that would produce a big client, and nobody was going to give him one, and he couldn't go out and fight for one. All he could do was set out his wares in the market place and wait hopefully beside them.

He spent a lot of time trying to decide what those wares should be. Lately a new field of legal work was developing. Taxes of many kinds had grown tremendously under the New Deal and during World War II. It was possible to have a very large income or big gross profits and still end up with little after taxes. The most promising legal work now was not helping clients to make money but showing them how to keep it. Lawyers were starting to specialize in one type or another of tax laws. But Anthony decided he was going to be a lawyer who knew all forms of taxation, and could use one tax to take the sting out of another.

All during 1946 he buried himself in tax laws and decisions: federal, state, county and city. And then, in December of 1946, Mrs. J. Arthur Allen walked into his office, and gave him the chance for which he had been waiting.

Anthony was one of the few members of the staff working at his desk on the morning before Christmas. The receptionist came to his office and said, "I'm awfully sorry to bother you, Mr. Lawrence. There's an elderly woman outside who seems a bit eccentric and wants to see a lawyer."

Anthony said, "What does she have on her mind?"

"Oh dear. It's something about a will she wants to make for a dog, if you can believe that. Shall I just say nobody is around?"

Anthony looked at the work he still had to do, and sighed. The visitor sounded like a screwball. However, he disliked the idea of slamming the door on her the day before Christmas. She might worry about the will all day Christmas. He said in a resigned tone, "Call me Santa Claus, and bring her in."

The girl went back to the reception desk and returned with a brisk little old lady. Philadelphia was filled with little old ladies like her. They wore dresses and hats that had been in bargain sales thirty years ago. They clutched shabby handbags. You saw them whisking in front of clanging trolleys and putting their heads down to dive through traffic. Somehow they always made it.

"How do you do?" Anthony said. "My name is Lawrence. Please sit down and tell me how I can help."

"Well," the little old lady said, "so you're a lawyer. I'm glad to see somebody is still practicing law in Philadelphia. I want a codicil added to my will. Right now. Will you do it?"

"Yes indeed. Now your name is . . ."

"I'm Mrs. J. Arthur Allen."

He printed the name slowly on a pad of paper. Was there something vaguely familiar about it? J. Arthur Allen . . .

"All right, Mrs. Allen," he said. "Suppose you tell me just what you want done."

"Well," she said, "when I got up this morning my collie — her name is Beauty and she's a lovely dog — came bounding in to say hello. And I suddenly wondered what Beauty would do if I weren't here to get up in the morning. Well, of course the servants would take care of her for a while, but after that . . ."

"Just one moment," he said, "while I make a few notes."

Servants. The servants. How many people nowadays had a plural number of servants? He scribbled on a sheet of paper as though he were making notes: "Look up the name Mrs. J. Arthur Allen in the Social Register and in Poor's Register of Directors and Executives, and bring me the answer in writing quickly."

"Now would you go on?" he said.

"I realized that I hadn't said a thing about Beauty in my will. So, really, if I died she might be sold or given to someone who wouldn't appreciate her. This may sound like a little thing to you, Mr. Lawrence, but Beauty means a lot to me."

"You're quite right," he said warmly. He slipped the note into his Out box, and pressed a button for a stenographer.

"Now I want to make sure," Mrs. Allen said, "that Beauty goes to my granddaughter, Grace, who will love her and take good care of her. So I want a codicil to my will giving Beauty to Grace. That sounds odd, doesn't it? Make sure you don't mix up those two names, young man."

Anthony chuckled, and said he'd keep them straight. The stenographer came in, and he pointed at the Out box. She took the note and left with it.

"Well, so anyway," Mrs. Allen said, "I took the train in town and walked here from the station, and do you know what, I suddenly realized I had been so upset I hadn't had any breakfast. So I went to the Automat, where they don't stick you with awful prices, and had breakfast and came back here."

"Here?" Anthony said. "You mean our office? Does a member of our firm handle your work, Mrs. Allen?"

"Oh no, no. I went to my own lawyer's office in this building. But everybody I knew was out, and they have some stupid girl at the reception desk who didn't know me and I simply wasn't getting anywhere. So I went down to the lobby and looked over the names listed on the directory board. Anybody knows you can't go very far wrong with names like Morris, Clayton, Biddle and Wharton, and I decided you could handle my codicil for me."

"Do you mind if I ask who is your lawyer?"

"Mr. Dickinson and Judge Dawes. Perhaps you know them."

"Indeed I do. I even worked there for a time, while I was a law-school student. Would you like me to call Dickinson and Dawes, and explain that you're here? You see, one lawyer isn't supposed to take another lawyer's client."

"You're not 'taking' me, young man. I came in here of my own free will, and if it worries Mr. Dickinson and Judge Dawes a little I won't mind at all. The next time that girl will know who I am."

"All right, Mrs. Allen. But you understand I'm just doing this to be helpful to Dickinson and Dawes. Now if — "

The stenographer came in and laid a note on his desk. It said: "Mrs. J. Arthur Allen is listed in the Social Register. Her home is 'White Pillars,' in Haverford. Poor's Register lists her as a director and principal owner of Allen Oil Company, of Camden."

He couldn't have been more startled if Mrs. Allen had suddenly turned into Miss America of 1946. The note didn't have to tell him that Allen Oil Company was a mighty nice piece of property. Principal owner!

"Now if," he said, "you can give me the date of your will, I'll get right at the codicil."

She fumbled in her handbag and brought out a mass of carbon copies and riffled through them. "It's June 6, 1941," she said.

"And the full name of your granddaughter, Grace?"

"Her name is Grace Shippen."

That was another jolt. You couldn't live in Philadelphia very long without hearing or reading something about Grace Shippen or seeing her photograph. She was the heiress to three fortunes. Way back, one of her ancestors had been the Peggy Shippen who married Benedict Arnold. She was an ash blonde of about twenty-five, cool and beautiful.

All this had left him a bit dizzy. "I'll call a girl and dictate the codicil," he said. He pressed the button again to call the stenographer. The telephone rang just then, and he picked it up and said, "Lawrence speaking."

"Hello, Tony," a voice said softly. "This is Logan Clayton. Hold the receiver closely to your ear so my voice won't carry." Logan Clayton was one of the five senior members of the firm.

"Right, sir."

"Tony, I hear you have quite a visitor."

"That's right, Mr. Clayton."

"You have fifty to a hundred million dollars sitting across from you. This is dynamite if it's not handled properly. There mustn't be a breath of suspicion that we are disturbing the client-lawyer relationship between Mrs. Allen and Dickinson and Dawes. Did you notify them that she is here?"

"No sir."

"Did you suggest doing so?"

"Yes sir."

"I'm glad of that. But she didn't want you to do it?"

"That's right."

"Well, to make absolutely sure that we stay in the clear, Tony, I'm going to try to locate Mr. Dickinson or Judge Dawes on the phone. If I can locate one of them, he'll break his neck to get here. Remember, Tony, the good name of Morris, Clayton, Biddle and Wharton means a lot more to us than any new client. Not that we'd have a prayer of getting Mrs. Allen. Right?"

"Right, sir."

"Good-by, then."

As he hung up the phone Anthony felt a tingle of anger. It hadn't been necessary for Logan Clayton to lecture him about professional ethics. It was all very well for Clayton to be high-minded. He had always had all the power of an important family back of him.

The stenographer had arrived by that time, and Anthony began dictating to her. "This is a codicil to a will," he said. "Ready? Be it remembered that I comma Mrs. J. Arthur Allen comma of quote White Pillars comma unquote Haverford comma — "

"Young man," Mrs. Allen broke in, "how did you know my address?"

He had been caught off base, so he might as well admit it. "I sent out a note and had you looked up," he said.

Mrs. Allen bobbed her head vigorously. "You're a smart young man," she said. "Good for you. Now you may go ahead."

"Being of sound and disposing mind comma memory and understanding comma — "

"I understand a lot more than people have ever given me credit for," Mrs. Allen said.

"I'll bet you do," Anthony said. "Now let's see. Make comma publish and declare this to be a capital C Codicil to my — "

"I like codicils," Mrs. Allen said. "It always worries Mr. Dickinson and Judge Dawes when I make another codicil. But I have a perfect right to do it if I want. Besides, it keeps my nieces and nephews and my granddaughter on their toes."

"Besides," Anthony said, grinning at her, "it's fun, isn't it?"

Mrs. Allen looked startled for a moment, and then giggled. "You know," she said, "it really is. You're the first person I've ever met who saw that."

He smiled at her. He wasn't going to be stupid enough to tell her just to drop in any old time and they would have fun with codicils. But they couldn't disbar him for an encouraging smile. "Now let's see where we are," he said. He finished dictating the codicil: ". . . in the hope and belief that said Grace Shippen will give said collie the home and affection to which the said collie is accustomed period. How's that, Mrs. Allen?"

"That's just beautiful."

"All right, then," he said to his stenographer. "Please add the usual paragraphs and bring it in for signature."

The stenographer left, and Anthony turned back to Mrs. Allen. He had come to a very big decision. He was going to try to steal Mrs. J. Arthur Allen from the firm of Dickinson and Dawes. If he made a mistake, he might find himself facing disbarment proceedings or being asked to resign from Morris, Clayton, Biddle and Wharton. He had to make it appear that he was just walking innocently along, and Mrs. J. Arthur Allen happened to fall into his pocket. If he did that, his career would be made.

What he needed first was to find a soft spot at which to aim. He had nothing to go on but the information he had picked up in studying Mrs. Allen for the past thirty minutes. He thought back. She had walked in cold weather from Suburban Station instead of taking a taxi. She had eaten breakfast at the Automat. Obviously she liked to save money. If he could, very delicately, show her ways in which Dickinson and Dawes had failed to save her money but in which he could, he would have a very strong case.

He started drawing her out in conversation, keeping alert for the opening he needed. He began by asking if Beauty was a smart collie. That sent Mrs. Allen off on a long happy monologue about Beauty's tricks and intelligence. From there, she went on to the fact that many people did not treat dogs properly. "It certainly is a good thing," Mrs. Allen said, "that we have the SPCA to protect dogs and other animals. I'm a great believer in the SPCA. I contribute a thousand dollars a year to them. I — "

He leaped at that fact like a stray hound at a bone. "Do you contribute that in cash?" he asked.

"Why, of course. How else would I contribute it?"

"I don't mean to pry, Mrs. Allen, but I assume you own quite a few shares of stock? I don't mean of Allen Oil Company, but of companies like General Electric and General Motors."

"Yes, I do, but I don't see the connection."

"Well," he said, "it's likely that there are very large capital gains in some of the shares you own. You can't sell those shares without paying a capital-gains tax. But you could give a thousand dollars worth of those shares to the SPCA without paying a penny on capital gains. The SPCA could sell the shares at full price. And you could deduct the full present market price as a charitable contribution. In other words, you wipe out a capital-gains tax liability at no cost to yourself. Have you ever thought of that?"

She cocked her head, like a bright-eyed bird studying a handout of crumbs. "I like that idea very much," she said. "Now why didn't Mr. Dickinson or Judge Dawes ever explain that to me?"

It was time to cover his tracks, fast. He said smoothly, "I'm sure they would have done so, if the subject had come up."

The girl came in then with the typed copies of the codicil, and Mrs. Allen put on her bifocals and read it word by word. "Very good," she said. She signed it, and Anthony and the stenographer witnessed it. He was about to suggest sending a copy to Dickinson and Dawes when he realized that wouldn't be necessary.

From the corridor came a familiar voice, pitched a few notes higher than usual, and breathless. Joan Dickinson's father was hurrying to the rescue of a hundred million dollars.

Mr. Dickinson came galloping into the office, and gasped, "My dear Mrs. Allen! I was so terribly upset when I heard what had happened at our office this morning with that new girl at the reception desk. We will never forgive ourselves."

Mrs. Allen peered up at him. There was a smile of mischief on her face. "Why, there's nothing to forgive yourselves for," she cooed. "I've been taken care of ever so well by this nice young man."

Mr. Dickinson looked at Anthony from glacial eyes. "Well, Tony!" he said. "It's nice to see you again. Tony and I are old friends, Mrs. Allen. In fact, I was his preceptor in law school. Tony's a fine lawyer."

Mrs. Allen said, "If he's so good, why didn't you take him into your firm?"

Anthony tried to hide a smile. "It was just one of those things," he said. "In my last year at law school I helped Mr. John Marshall Wharton with a book he was writing, and so it was natural for me to join Morris, Clayton, Biddle and Wharton. But Mr. Dickinson had been most helpful to me."

Mr. Dickinson smiled bravely, and said, "I've always regretted losing Tony. Now, this was a codicil, Mrs. Allen?"

"It's all finished," Mrs. Allen said. "Done very well, too."

Anthony said, "Naturally I was going to send a copy to you, sir."

"Yes, yes, of course. Well, Mrs. Allen, perhaps we could go down to my office and file the original in our safe with your other papers, and make sure that everything else is in order."

Mrs. Allen sighed. She had obviously enjoyed this. "Mr. Lawrence was very helpful in another way," she said. "I mentioned that I always give a thousand dollars each year to the SPCA, and he suggested using a few shares of stock instead of using cash. In order to wipe out the capital-gains tax liability."

"It just happened to come up as we talked," Anthony said. "I pointed out that you would have suggested the same thing, if the subject had ever come up between you."

"Yes, naturally," Mr. Dickinson said. "May I say, Tony, that you have not only done a fine job but also conducted yourself very well, professionally?"

"Thank you, sir."

Mrs. Allen got up slowly. "Young man," she said, "I hope you'll send a good fat bill to Mr. Dickinson for taking care of me so well. And if you get any other ideas for saving me money, I hope you'll let me know."

Mr. Dickinson held his breath. This was it, Anthony knew. He had to say exactly the right thing. He had to avoid unprofessional conduct and at the same time leave the door open a crack. He picked his words like a jeweler selecting diamonds. "Mrs. Allen, you're a client of our good friends at Dickinson and Dawes. I'm sure they give your affairs their closest attention. It would be unprofessional conduct on my part to suggest that I could do something for you that they can't." Let Mr. Dickinson and Mrs. Allen think that over. It protected him completely. And yet, if you analyzed the statement, you might find in it a hint that perhaps he *could* save money for Mrs. Allen.

"Very high-minded of you, I'm sure," Mrs. Allen said.

"Thank you, Tony," Mr. Dickinson said in a very thoughtful tone. He took Mrs. Allen's arm and led her from the room.

ANTHONY paid a Christmas call the next afternoon on the Whartons, who had taken a flattering interest in him since his return from the war. After they had talked for a while he told them casually about Mrs. Allen's visit. Mr. Wharton laughed heartily.

"I'll have to run down to the Union League for lunch tomorrow and tell that story," he said. "I think I will call it The Case of The Collie's Codicil! People will laugh themselves sick, thinking how scared Dickinson must have been. He's not very popular."

Mrs. Wharton said indignantly, "I don't think it's a laughing matter! You mean poor Tony had to let Mrs. Allen go without trying to land her? When he needs a big client so badly?"

She was as lovely as ever, Anthony thought, although now the silver had crept deeply through her hair. It seemed like a century since they had taken those wild rides together.

"My dear, you don't understand these things," her husband said. "Of course Tony closed the thing out quite firmly."

"Oh Tony, you idiot!" Mrs. Wharton said.

Mr. Wharton looked at him with a faint smile. "You don't fool me," he said. "The fact is, you baited a hook, didn't you? In fact, I believe you came out today for advice. Now confess, young man."

Anthony explained about his SPCA recommendation, and then reported how Mrs. Allen had said that he must call her up if he had any more ideas for saving her money.

"Very interesting," Mr. Wharton said. "Dickinson was there, wasn't he? What, exactly, was your reply to Mrs. Allen?"

Anthony repeated the words exactly.

"Magnificent," Mr. Wharton said.

"If there's a hook in that," Mrs. Wharton complained, "it's too small for me to see."

Her husband said, "Carol, the beauty of it is that Dickinson may make the mistake of trying to explain Tony's statement to Mrs. Allen. And if he does, she'll end up by seeing the hook in it — or at least the lure."

Anthony said, "You think I'm in the clear, then?"

"Oh, definitely, my boy." Mr. Wharton chuckled. "Your ethics are delightfully bad. But so far nobody can make a charge of unprofessional conduct stick."

"I'm also worried about my standing at the firm, if anything more develops. Logan Clayton was quite upset yesterday."

"He's an old woman," Mr. Wharton said. "All he thinks of is avoiding risks and building reputation. I'll go talk to Logan tomorrow. I think I can promise that, if you handle yourself as well in the future as you did yesterday, he'll go along."

"Grace," Mrs. Wharton murmured thoughtfully. "I think I will go see Grace Shippen."

"My dear, please stay out of this."

Mrs. Wharton protested, "Grace is on my hospital committee and I have every right to see her. She has a wonderful head for money, even better than her grandmother. I think I can make sure that Mrs. Allen will understand Tony's statement."

Mr. Wharton shrugged. "Take to the hills, men," he said. "The women have broken loose."

"I've never met Grace Shippen," Anthony said. "What is she like?"

"She's delightful," Mrs. Wharton said. "She's lovely and smart, and she's fun to be with. There's only one thing wrong with her. I don't think she has a heart. I hope you won't like her."

"If she resembles her grandmother," Anthony said, "it will be love at first sight. Mrs. Allen is wonderful."

For the next ten days Anthony spent most of his time picking up scraps of information about Mrs. Allen and the Allen Oil Company. He was able to borrow copies of the company's annual reports for the past ten years, and he dug into every recorded public fact about Mrs. Allen's finances. He would have given anything for copies of her income-tax returns, but there wasn't a chance of getting those. He did succeed, through a devious route, in getting some information about her county personal-property-tax returns.

None of this turned up any obvious ways to save her money. Not that he had expected to find any. Dickinson and Dawes was too good a firm to make any glaring errors. So he was not prepared when, a few days after New Year's, Logan Clayton asked him to come into his office. When he arrived he saw Mr. Dickinson, waiting for him with one of his most charming smiles. Years ago, those smiles had won his trust and cost him Joan Dickinson.

"Nice to see you again, Tony," Mr. Dickinson said, shaking his hand cordially. "How are you?"

"Fine, thanks. You wanted to see me, Mr. Clayton?"

Logan Clayton always acted as if his desk were a high-court bench. He nodded solemnly and said, "Yes, Tony. Sit down. Mr. Dickinson has come to us with a rather grave problem."

"It really isn't serious," Mr. Dickinson said. "In fact it has its amusing angles. It's in connection with Mrs. Allen. A charming person but impressionable. You will recall that small suggestion you made, in regard to her SPCA contribution?"

Logan Clayton said, "Before you go on, do you have any objection to the fact that Tony made that suggestion? As I understand it, the idea merely popped out in casual talk."

"Oh, no objection at all. However, the amusing thing is that Mrs. Allen has built up that tiny suggestion into a feeling that Tony could save her money in other ways."

"Surely you can talk her out of that," Anthony said smoothly.

"Tony, elderly ladies look on taxes as a personal insult. I might have talked her out of it even at that but for a few unfortunate remarks you made at the close of her visit."

Logan Clayton said, "Please choose your words carefully, Mr. Dickinson. I don't care to have any reflections on the good name of this firm. What were these alleged unfortunate remarks?"

"Mrs. Allen, in leaving, asked Tony to let her know if he got any more ideas for saving her money. Tony said, and I believe I quote exactly, 'Mrs. Allen, you're a client of our good friends at Dickinson and Dawes. It would be unprofessional conduct on my part to suggest that I could do something for you that they can't.' If you read between the lines, you'll find that leaves things wide open, although I'm sure Tony didn't intend it that way."

Logan Clayton said, "Yes, that was a weak statement, Tony. I might almost agree it could be called unfortunate."

Anthony smiled. "In reading between the lines, I'm afraid Mr. Dickinson missed one that was actually present. In the middle of that statement I also said, quote, 'I'm sure they give your affairs their closest attention,' unquote."

"Come to think of it, you did say that," Mr. Dickinson said.

"Well, my dear sir, what more do you want?" Logan Clayton complained. "Tony gave you what is almost an endorsement."

"We lawyers do haggle about words, don't we?" Mr. Dickinson said blandly. "Nonetheless and notwithstanding, Mrs. Allen did come away with a feeling that Tony implied he could save her money. May I term this regrettable?"

"You're drawing an extremely fine point," Mr. Clayton said.

"Not too fine, I trust, when the reputation of Morris, Clayton, Biddle and Wharton is concerned. You see, I can't prevent Mrs. Allen from saying that you have a bright young man who wants her business and hinted he could save money for her on taxes."

"On that basis," Logan Clayton said, "it is a bit awkward. But I don't know what we can do about it."

"Very simple," Mr. Dickinson said lightly. "All Tony has to do is write me a little note asking me to assure Mrs. Allen that he does not know of any further ways to save her money."

"I see no harm in that," Logan Clayton said, handing down a high-court decision. "How do you feel about it, Tony?"

Logan Clayton ought to tell the man to run along and handle his clients himself, Tony thought grimly. But Mr. Dickinson had shrewdly pretended that the reputation of the firm was involved, and Logan Clayton's motto was: In Morris, Clayton, Biddle and Wharton We Trust.

If he refused to write the letter, he would have to give a reason. There was only one he could give. That one involved playing Russian roulette with a revolver pressed to his head, and five of the six chambers loaded. Once again, he had been a little too innocent in dealing with Joan Dickinson's father.

"Aren't you taking quite a while to decide, Tony?" Mr. Dickinson said pleasantly.

Logan Clayton said, "Come, come, Tony."

"I don't care to write such a letter," Anthony said.

"Very interesting," Mr. Dickinson murmured.

"Please explain your attitude," Logan Clayton said.

Now for the Russian roulette. There was a chance that Mr. Dickinson might be scared off when he lifted the revolver. "Sir," he said formally, "it would be untrue to say that I don't know of any further ways to save Mrs. Allen money." After all, he was sure such ways existed somewhere in her complicated tax affairs.

"My God!" Logan Clayton said.

Now, would Mr. Dickinson back away? But Mr. Dickinson's face was flaming. He got up and pointed a trembling finger at Anthony. "You'll prove that or I'll bring charges against you! You're accusing me of incompetence."

This was interesting. Mr. Dickinson had a weakness, after all. It was his self-esteem. If you attacked that, he lost control.

"I don't say that you're incompetent," Anthony said. "I happen to be specializing in tax laws. I know more about them than you do, just as you know more about other fields of law than I."

"I won't accept that," Mr. Dickinson said furiously. "A cub lawyer telling me he knows more than I do. You're going to prove your statement or eat it."

Logan Clayton said pleadingly, "Tony, what is this way to save money for Mrs. Allen?"

Anthony said, "I don't work for Mr. Dickinson. I'm not going to tell him, and let him present it to her as his own idea. If he wants to bring charges, I'll answer him at the hearing."

"Surely we can keep this . . . this unpleasantness out of the Bar Association," Logan Clayton gasped.

Mr. Dickinson broke in. "I challenge you to repeat your statement in the presence of Mrs. J. Arthur Allen, and to prove it. With Mr. Clayton and myself as witnesses."

Mr. Dickinson was pretty far gone to make an offer like that. Of course, he didn't think Anthony could come up with anything. Even so, it was a direct invitation to solicit his client under remarkable but quite ethical conditions. "Any time," Anthony said.

"You're bluffing, Tony. And I'm going to tear you to pieces. If I can arrange it, will tomorrow morning be suitable?"

"Fine with me."

"In my office, if you don't mind."

"I do mind," Anthony said. "I won't take any action that might look as if I'm going out of my way to solicit your client. I'll see you in my office or nowhere." He wasn't going to have any tricks of lighting or placement of chairs worked on him.

"Where we meet is immaterial to me," Mr. Dickinson snapped. "Mr. Clayton, thank you for your courtesy. I will telephone you about the arrangements." He marched out of the office.

"Tony," Logan Clayton said weakly, "this is a terrible mess. That is, unless you really can back up your claim."

"Don't worry, sir," Anthony said. "We'll be all right."

He went slowly back to his office. Between now and the next morning he was going to find what he needed. He shut his office door, and got out the fat folder on Mrs. Allen's affairs.

In midafternoon Logan Clayton interrupted him and said that

the meeting was set for ten the next morning. Anthony nodded; Mr. Dickinson wasn't going to give him any extra time.

At four thirty Mrs. John Marshall Wharton telephoned, her voice husky with excitement. "Tony," she said, "Grace Shippen just phoned me. She says there's to be a showdown between you and Mr. Dickinson tomorrow at ten. Are you ready for it?"

"Oh sure," he said. That wasn't a lie. A man could be ready for his own funeral, couldn't he?

"Grace is coming, too. She's getting curious about you. Don't count on any support from her, though. Grace only cheers after there's a winner. Don't fall for her, Tony."

Lady, the corpse seldom falls for anyone. "I'll have other things on my mind," he said.

"I'll be praying for you. Good luck, Tony."

He hung up and went back to work. Later, he hurried out for a hasty dinner and returned to the office. As the hours went by he began to feel desperate. He was studying the Allen folder fact by fact but was getting nowhere. Yet there must be ways to save money for her. Few lawyers had been able to keep up with all the tax laws, especially not general corporation and estate lawyers like Dickinson and Dawes. He began playing a sort of jigsaw-puzzle game with all the facts, fitting them against each other, balancing them, and figuring the effect of one type of tax on other types.

And suddenly, there it was. One small move of his hand in weighing one tax against another, and he had it. It was like watching a breeze roll the clouds away from a distant mountain peak. There the answer was in all its simplicity and grandeur.

He was too tired to feel elated. He swept the papers into a drawer and walked slowly out of the place, not at all like a man who has just seen a limitless future opening ahead of him.

At nine the next morning he was back in his office, setting the stage for the meeting. Remembering vividly how Mr. Dickinson had worked the chair game on him, years ago at Princeton, he spent some time in selecting and placing chairs. One with a deep soft seat for Logan Clayton, so that it wouldn't be easy for him to sit up and interfere. Two armchairs with firm leather-covered seats for Mrs. Allen and Grace Shippen, so that they would be comfortable but sitting up alertly. A hard wooden chair for Mr. Dickinson, placed so that the light from the window would annoy him.

A little before ten, Logan Clayton came in and began wandering around the room. Anthony coaxed him into the deep-seated chair and spoke soothingly to him. Then the receptionist announced their visitors, and he went out to greet them. Mrs. Allen patted his hand and said she hoped he had something good to tell her. Behind her was the girl he wasn't supposed to fall for. What was all the shouting about? Grace Shippen hadn't invented the idea of being a tall cool blonde. Behind her was Mr. Dickinson, giving him a look that should have been in a scabbard. Anthony led them into the office and made sure they got the right chairs.

Mr. Dickinson started right off. "Well, Tony, are you ready to admit this has gone far enough? Sometimes the enthusiasm of youth carries a man away. I think we'd all be willing to call it off."

Logan Clayton tried to heave himself forward in the deep-seated leather chair, but Anthony cut in quickly. "Do I understand that you're giving up?" he asked pleasantly.

"I was merely giving you a chance to withdraw gracefully."

"Mr. Dickinson, you suggested this meeting. You came to me with a challenge. You have brought Mrs. Allen here. I can hardly withdraw from my own office."

"You're just juggling words, Tony," Mr. Dickinson said. "Either tell us whatever wild idea you may have dreamed up, if you've gone that far, or else admit you've been bluffing."

"Mr. Dickinson, will you tell Mrs. Allen exactly what your challenge was?"

"She already knows about your ridiculous boast."

"If I may correct one thing," Anthony said mildly, "it was not a boast. You asked me to write you a letter stating that I did not know of any further ways to save money for her. I refused. I had to refuse, because any such statement would have been untrue."

"Prove it. That's my challenge."

"Oh yes," Mrs. Allen said eagerly. "Do let's hear about it."

Anthony smiled at her. Then, perhaps by a trick of lighting, he found his attention caught by Grace Shippen. She seemed to attract a great deal of light in the room. She was dressed rather plainly:

368

dark-blue tailored suit, blue hat with a small white bow, white-gloved hands folded on her lap.

He took a deep breath. It was necessary to lead up impressively to the idea he was going to present. Lawyers have nothing to sell but their thoughts. If your thoughts seem to come too easily people tend to think they aren't worth much. So he began with a general talk on taxation.

Mr. Dickinson squirmed on his hard chair. "You're not saving anybody money with this lecture," he said.

"I'm trying to show Mrs. Allen how complicated the tax problem is," Anthony said gravely. "I wouldn't want her to think that the money-saving idea I have for her was simple to uncover, and that you should have found it, too."

"Don't condescend to me, Tony."

"What we have in Mrs. Allen's case," Anthony said, "is a large and complicated fortune harassed by large and complicated taxes. We can't wrestle blindly with those taxes and hope to win. We have to adopt the tactics of judo wrestling, and turn the strength of our opponents against themselves."

Mr. Dickinson said, "Really, Mrs. Allen, I hate to subject you to this."

"Now please don't worry about me," Mrs. Allen said, her eyes bright and happy.

Grace Shippen let a smile cross her lips. She had the calm clean features you might find in an old cameo. Some people liked that sort of perfection but it seemed rather bloodless to Anthony.

"I would like everybody to understand," he said, "that I have only publicly known facts about Mrs. Allen's affairs. We start with the generally accepted belief that Mrs. Allen owns about fifty million dollars' worth of the stock of Allen Oil Company. It may be more, it may be less, but let's work with that figure."

On the hard wooden chair, Mr. Dickinson frowned and tried to get more comfortable. He was starting to look a bit worried.

"Mrs. Allen lives in Haverford," Anthony said. "County personal-property taxes are four mills on the dollar. She pays that tax on her fifty million dollars' worth of Allen Oil Company stock. That's a tax of two hundred thousand dollars a year."

"Come on, Tony," Mr. Dickinson snapped. "Don't throw these figures around as if they mean something."

"They mean something to me," Anthony said. "I don't think she should be paying that two hundred thousand a year."

"Oh my!" Mrs. Allen gasped.

"She has to pay," Mr. Dickinson said. "It's the law."

"Assuming that she owns some General Electric stock," Anthony said, "she's not paying county personal-property taxes on it."

"You don't know the first thing about her affairs," Mr. Dickinson said. "GE owns property in Pennsylvania and does business here and pays Pennsylvania taxes as a foreign corporation. So its stock is not subject to the personal-property tax. Allen Oil Company, as you do not seem to realize, is a New Jersey company. It does no business here and pays no taxes here. So any resident of Pennsylvania who owns its stock has to pay county personal-property taxes on it."

"Quite so," Anthony said. "Now let's see if we can't change all that. Did you ever hear of a company called J. Arthur Allen, Incorporated?"

Mr. Dickinson began to sweat. He still didn't see the bonfire but he could feel the heat. "Yes, of course," he said nervously. "J. Arthur Allen, Incorporated does do business in Pennsylvania. It owns and operates tank trucks and service stations here. It buys oil and gas from Allen Oil. But it's not a part of Allen Oil."

"Allen Oil owns nearly all its stock."

"What difference does that make? It's another company!"

"But it's not just any other company," Anthony said mildly. "Allen Oil directs all its activities. It would be a simple matter for Allen Oil to take over part of the J. Arthur Allen, Incorporated operations in Pennsylvania and do business here itself. Allen Oil would then pay a proportion of the Pennsylvania tax J. Arthur Allen, Incorporated has been paying, with that proportion coming out of the same pants as before but a different pocket. And that would save Mrs. Allen two hundred thousand dollars a year, because she would no longer have to pay county personal-property taxes on her Allen Oil Company stock."

Mr. Dickinson looked badly shaken, as indeed he should. He had a lot of explaining to do, and there really wasn't a good explanation. He jumped up. "Mrs. Allen," he cried, "this is a reckless juggling act. If it had been a good step to take, the officers of Allen Oil would certainly have taken it long ago."

"They never thought of it," Anthony said. "It's not their headache if Mrs. Allen loses all that money every year."

"I don't really understand this," Mrs. Allen said breathlessly. "But it would be wonderful to save all that money." She turned to her granddaughter. "Do you understand it, Grace?"

This time a full smile moved over the girl's lips. "Yes, Grandmother. It's quite simple. Mr. Lawrence is using Pennsylvania taxes on corporations to knock out the county personal-property tax. He has just saved you two hundred thousand dollars a year."

"How wonderful!" Mrs. Allen gasped.

"My dear Mrs. Allen," Mr. Dickinson stammered. "Even if this idea does turn out to be practical, I hope you won't feel that Dickinson and Dawes have been remiss. A lucky guess that could never be repeated again should not be held against us."

"I don't know," Mrs. Allen said. "What do you think, Grace?"

The girl's face was very calm. In her low soft voice she said, "What I think is that you need a new lawyer."

There might have been a chance for Mr. Dickinson to rescue something if he had tried hard. But he lost control. He stood very straight and glared at the girl and said, "First a cub lawyer tries to tell me my business and then a girl presumes to run my client's affairs for her." He turned to Mrs. Allen. "If you agree in any way with your granddaughter's remark, Dickinson and Dawes will withdraw from the handling of your affairs."

"Well!" Mrs. Allen said irritably. "I can't help thinking Grace has a point."

"We will turn over your affairs to anyone you name," Mr. Dickinson said, and marched out of the room.

"Well!" Mrs. Allen said. "Think of him acting like that."

Let us, Anthony said to himself, stop thinking about Mr. Dickinson and start thinking about that deserving young lawyer, Anthony Lawrence. "I'm sorry you had to witness a scene like that," he said. "Now, even though I have no further right to offer you legal advice, I should point out that you ought to get someone working on this two hundred thousand dollars at once."

"Yes, of course. I need a new lawyer, don't I?"

In the depths of the deep-seated chair, Logan Clayton took a strangle hold on the problem in ethics, and said, "My dear Mrs. Allen, naturally we — "

"Mr. Lawrence is your man," Grace Shippen said quietly.

"I believe he is," Mrs. Allen said, beaming at him. "You're a bit young, but you certainly seem to know what you're doing."

"And if I may say so," Logan Clayton said, "Mr. Lawrence will have back of him the full resources and experience of Morris, Clayton, Biddle and Wharton, in the handling of your affairs."

"I'll be very proud and happy to take on the job," Anthony said. "Now, Mrs. Allen, I suggest that we call in a secretary, and you can get a letter right out to Dickinson and Dawes asking them to turn over all your legal affairs to me."

For the first time Grace Shippen's face came alive. She laughed, and delightful little crinkles fanned out from her eyes. "You don't waste any time, do you?" she said.

"Time is money," he said, grinning at her. He was starting to wonder why Mrs. Wharton had warned him against the girl.

They got the letter out, and then Anthony and Mr. Clayton escorted Mrs. Allen and her niece to the elevators. Grace Shippen lagged a bit and Anthony found himself walking beside her.

"You were very helpful," he said. "I appreciate it."

"I like a winner, Mr. Lawrence. And you're every bit as good as Carol Wharton said. She has a very high opinion of you."

"She's a wonderful person."

"Now I'm going to shock you," she said, looking at him with wide blue eyes. "Are you still in love with her?"

It took him a moment to recover. Then he laughed and said, "Do you often throw things like that at people?"

"Only when I'm interested in them."

"I'm not in love with anybody, if that's interesting."

"No strings attached to you? Then, in my shy way, I'm going to ask you to take me to dinner Saturday night."

"That's the nicest legal fee I ever collected. You live out in Haverford with Mrs. Allen, don't you? I'll pick you up there."

They caught up to the others at that moment. There was an elevator waiting, and she stepped into the car and was gone, and he had a feeling that half the light in the corridor went with her.

Mr. Clayton wasted no time. He said, "A brilliant job, Tony. I do hope, though, that you realize it was only your connection with the firm which made it possible."

"I know that, sir. I want to assure you that I'm completely loyal to the firm."

That was what Mr. Clayton wanted to hear. "We'll have to get you a more suitable office, Tony. I'm sure the other senior members will agree that you should be an associate member of the firm. Your present office is not proper for an associate."

There he went, skipping over to the Happy Hunting Ground on the left side of the letterhead. "Thank you very much, sir."

A big client. Dinner with Grace Shippen. An associate member of Morris, Clayton, Biddle and Wharton. Anything more just now?

A week later, something more did come. It was a letter in a once well-known handwriting. It said: "Dear Tony. This is a voice from the past. I have just heard about The Case of the Collie's Codicil. I think you've evened things up now with Daddy, and hooray for you. Sincerely, Joan Dickinson Henry."

CHAPTER 6

DURING much of his life Anthony had been hanging around the outskirts of Philadelphia society like an eager substitute trying to make a team. Now and then they let him come in for

a few plays, and patted him and told him he was doing fine. But
he was always sent back to the bench very soon.

After Mrs. J. Arthur Allen became his client, everything changed.
Anthony could see the change in the actions of the senior members
of the firm, asking him to play golf, or to have lunch at the
Philadelphia Club, or to come out to the house for dinner. It was
proved by the new business that came to him: wills, the executor-
ship of an estate, a retainer from an insurance company. One of
the smaller banks put out a feeler to see if he would join its Board
of Directors; Logan Clayton suggested turning it down because
there would be better openings later on.

Anthony knew, of course, that there was a lot more to his full
acceptance than merely success in business. Philadelphia society
had long ago worked out a procedure for taking in new members.
Money and power were important, but Philadelphia wanted to
know that you could produce children and grandchildren who
could handle money and power. Marrying well was part of it.
Proving that you had poise and balance and culture was part of it,
but would your children have the same qualities?

People could trace his family back for nearly a hundred years:
through his mother and her marriage; through his grandmother,
and the years Harry Judson had spent teaching Latin at Franklin
Academy; back to a young Irish girl, his great-grandmother, who
had come to Philadelphia long ago with a driving urge to better
herself. They could see the family had been moving up slowly.
Now, all Anthony had to do was march firmly down the open path
ahead. After he chose one of the very nice girls from excellent
families whom he met so easily now, the Lawrence bloodline
would be firmly established in the Philadelphia studbook.

There was only one difficulty. He didn't want one of those girls.
He wanted Grace Shippen, and he couldn't get her.

It wasn't that she didn't like him. From the start it was clear
that she liked him better than anyone else. They danced and
played tennis and rode and went to shows and argued about books
and art and music. She was a wonderful companion: laughing,
lively, interested in everything. Now and then she would kiss him
in a pleasant way. After they had known each other for several

months he asked her to marry him. She patted his cheek and said
he was the nicest person in the world but she wasn't ready to think
about marriage and, please, would he keep on asking. He kept on.
"Is it time to ask again?" he would say glumly.

"Poor Tony," she would sigh. "Or maybe I mean poor me. I
can't seem to decide."

If he had been sensible he would have traded her in for one of
the very nice girls of excellent families. He didn't know why he
had to have her. Why did people feel they had to climb Mount
Everest? Because it was there. Why did he have to have Grace
Shippen? Because she was lovely and intelligent and a good companion and the heiress to three fortunes and a symbol of the very
best in Philadelphia? Because she was there?

He knew now why Mrs. Wharton hoped he wouldn't fall for
the girl. He didn't agree, though, that she had no heart. Grace
Shippen could be explained, he believed, by the simple statement
that the things she wanted were the things she already had.

NOT LONG after running into this blank wall he took up a hobby
which was to produce remarkable and unforeseen results. It involved spending an hour, several times a week, in the magistrates'
courts in the central city. He passed the one at Twelfth and Pine
streets one morning and wandered in. It was odd; this was the
first time he had realized that the law was something more than
just a fascinating game. Because here were people — sweating,
lying, sobbing, angry people — at grips with the law. He watched
and listened, and went back to his bloodless duels with tax laws
feeling curiously alive and stimulated.

After he had been attending the hearings for a short time he
began studying criminal practice just as he had once read Army
Regulations. They gave you very little of that at law school, and
of course firms like his own shunned it. He started to understand
what was happening in the magistrates' courts, and saw that
some people were getting the better of the law and others were
getting a great deal the worst of it.

One day, before the hearings began, a woman standing near
him began crying and telling him her troubles. The landlord

had raised the rent on the two rooms where she lived with her swarm of kids. She couldn't pay that much. An eviction notice had been served on her and she had threatened to throw a pot of boiling water on the landlord and so here she was and what happened to her kids if she went to jail? Without thinking, he said, "I'm a lawyer. I'll take your case if you want."

She backed off. "I don't have no money," she said sullenly.

It took five minutes to convince her that he was on the level, which was longer than it took to win the case. Her landlord was obviously playing tag with the Rent Control regulations and her eviction notice wasn't in legal form. It took only a few sharp questions to cut the plaintiff to bits. The hardest part of the whole thing was getting away from the grateful woman afterward.

She left at last, and he was about to go back to his office when someone grabbed his arm. It took him moments to recognize the plump man in a wrinkled gray suit. Then he said, "I'll be damned — it's Louis Donetti. I haven't seen you since law school. What are you doing here?"

"Got a case coming up," Louis said. "Maybe you didn't know. I'm an assistant D.A. Hey, you went pretty good in there."

"Thanks. It was just one of those open-and-shut things."

Wise black eyes studied him from under heavy, sculptured lids. "Funny thing," Louis said. "A corporation hot shot, working the magistrates' beat. If you don't mind some more slumming, let me take you to lunch someday. I'm curious about your angle."

"Sure, fine," Anthony said. "But do I have to have an angle?"

A few days later Louis called, and Anthony explained that he couldn't make it that week but would call back later. Of course he never did. He didn't want Louis grilling him on his motives in taking the woman's case. He wasn't really sure what they had been. Any time you didn't know your own mind, Louis Donetti would make you feel you didn't have one.

He kept on visiting the magistrates' courts and found that he had become a minor celebrity there. People were beginning to ask him for help. A professional bondsman might sidle up to him and mutter, "Guy over there could use you. No dough in it, natch." The phone might ring in his office and a low voice might say,

"This is the house sergeant at Twelfth and Pine. I got kinda sorry for a kid who was picked up last night." There was nothing sensational about any of the cases, just little people in trouble.

One day a reporter questioned him about what he was doing, and he laughed and said it wasn't anything. So it was a shock the next morning to see a page-two story in his paper:

Top-Ranked Lawyer Plays Robin Hood

Anthony J. Lawrence, a big corporation lawyer, was revealed today as a modern Robin Hood who haunts the magistrates' courts ready to defend people who do not have a dime. . . .

"Oh Lord," he said. He went to his office, wondering how soon the telephone would ring. He didn't have to wonder very long.

"Hello, Tony. This is Logan Clayton. I've just seen that story about you. Quite a surprise, Tony."

"Well, sir, the basic facts are true but the conclusions — well, I don't recognize myself."

"You do come out looking a bit colorful. I've been trying to decide whether this is the sort of thing we ought to be doing."

"From my point of view, sir, it's like a surgeon doing some free work for the ward patients." That sort of professional attitude ought to appeal to Mr. Clayton.

"Not a bad way of looking at it, Tony. And, as a matter of fact, it shows that in our firm we're not untouched by the facts of life, doesn't it? I assume you wouldn't stay with anything messy."

"You're quite right, Mr. Clayton."

"Good. See you later, Tony."

Almost at once came the long rings of an outside call. It was a flat voice that said, "Hello, Robin Hood," in the rasping tone that Louis Donetti used in law school when he was disgusted. "I want to compliment you on your publicity man."

"I had nothing to do with the fool story, Louis."

"Sure. You just got caught with your halo on. You bother me, pal. I read that story and I ask myself: Is this guy running for the U. S. Senate or something? Or is he running away from himself? I want to know because I'm in that nasty thing called politics."

"You make a very simple thing sound complicated."

"You kid yourself it's simple. If this is a right guy, I tell myself, I can help him to be righter. If the guy's a phony I like taking phonies apart. They go all to pieces when the going gets rough."

"You're sort of insulting, aren't you?"

"Yeah, Tony, I mean to be. Keep fooling around, and maybe someday I'll get a chance to make you prove if you're a phony or not. So long, Robin. Don't take any wooden bowstrings."

The flurry of excitement over the newspaper story soon passed, and his life went on unchanged until a September day in 1948. That morning's paper had the usual news: the Russians were being unpleasant, Truman was kidding himself he could beat Dewey. Here was something interesting, though: John C. M. Stearnes, investment banker, killed in his home on Delancey Street by a shot from his own revolver. Police suspected murder and were hunting a mystery visitor named Howard Jones, who had been with Stearnes just before the shot was fired. What made it interesting was that Stearnes was an uncle by marriage of Grace Shippen's.

After breakfast he dropped in at the Twelfth and Pine streets police station. The cops thought he might be interested in a man they had picked up the previous night. His name was Chesley A. Gwynne, and he was charged with being drunk and disorderly, breaking and attempted entering. Anthony went into Gwynne's cell. Not many people looked good after they slept in their clothes, but this one slumped on the cot like a dirty sack filled with rubbish.

"My name's Lawrence," Anthony said. "I'm a lawyer. The boys thought maybe you could use a little help."

The man might have been good-looking once but now he had the thickened nose and reddened eyes of the steady drinker. "You better run along," he said wearily. "I'm broke."

"Your name's Gwynne, isn't it? Gwynne, now and then I take a case just for exercise. Do you mind answering a few questions?"

"They better be few. I'm tired."

"The cops said you claimed you lived in that house where you were caught breaking in, even though the man who lives there never saw you before. That's all I know. If you're too tired to tell me about it, they'll give you maybe a year and a day to rest up."

"The cops got it fouled up. What I tried to tell them was that I used to live in that house. When I took on a load last night I forgot I didn't any more, and went back there and figured I had lost my keys and tried to climb in a window."

"What's the address of this place where you lived?"

"Markley Street, near Camac. Just a little block-long street."

"I never heard of a Markley Street," Anthony said. "The place you were trying to get in was 1009 Bendix Street."

"Well, I never heard of Bendix Street."

"When did you leave the place?"

"Almost twenty years ago, I guess."

"Where do you live now?"

"I've been living in L. A. for years. Great country. Warm. The people, too. Not like the iced-up people you have here."

It was a crazy story but the guy told it straight and it sounded good. "Why did you come back here?"

"I thought I might look up some people I used to know."

"What are their names?"

"What difference do the names make? I'd have to go around asking questions to locate them after all these years."

He didn't sound so good answering that question. "When did you get in town?"

"I came in by train late yesterday afternoon. I dropped into one of those bars near the station and tied one on, and the next thing I knew the cops were grabbing me down on Markley Street."

"What's the address of the bar?"

"I can't remember."

Queer, the things he could remember exactly and the things he claimed he couldn't. "Well, I can't promise you anything. Best I can do now is get you held for a further hearing, and look into that Markley Street business. How do you feel about that?"

"What have I got to lose?" the man said, shrugging.

Anthony left the cell and entered his name as Gwynne's attorney. When the hearing came up, he asked for a further hearing the next morning. Then he went to his office and telephoned the Department of Public Works. The answer to the Markley-Bendix Street problem was simple. Anthony sent his secretary on a couple of errands, and by late afternoon had all the evidence he needed.

The next morning he went to the station house and gave Gwynne the good news. It didn't seem to make him feel any better. The man was jittery.

Anthony went into the hearing room. While he waited for his case to be called, there was a stir at the back of the room, and Louis Donetti entered with a group of people. Ten minutes went by, and the magistrate's clerk called, "Chesley A. Gwynne." The turnkey brought Gwynne out. The cop who had arrested him and the man who lived at 1009 Bendix Street testified. Gwynne pleaded guilty to being drunk and not guilty to the charges of disorderly conduct, breaking and attempted entering.

Anthony took over, and said, "Mr. Gwynne, what events led up to your presence on Bendix Street?"

"Well, I dropped into a bar and I guess I had a few too many. Anyway, I wasn't quite sure what I did after that."

"Do you live in Philadelphia?" Anthony asked.

"I live in Los Angeles. I used to live here twenty years ago."

"What was your address when you lived in Philadelphia?"

"It was 1015 Markley Street."

It was odd how nervous the guy was. He was getting worse every minute. "After you had those drinks at the bar, did any thought in regard to your former home come into your head?"

"Yes, I wanted to go there. But I forgot it was a long time since I lived there, and just thought I was going home. I got there and thought I had forgotten my keys and tried to climb in a side window. This gentleman heard me and called the police."

"You told him it was your home, and gave the address?"

"Yes, but he said he never heard of me or 1015 Markley Street. He said it was 1009 Bendix Street."

"But in fact it really was your former home?"

"That's right."

"Your Honor," Anthony said, turning to the magistrate, "I submit as evidence these two documents. Exhibit A is an affidavit from the Chief Clerk, Bureau of Engineering, Surveys and Zoning, to the effect that until 1932 there was a ten-hundred block Markley Street, which was eliminated in that year when Bendix Street was cut through. At that time, 1015 Markley Street became 1009 Bendix Street. Exhibit B is a notarized photostat of a page from a Philadelphia Telephone Directory of 1930, showing that a Mrs. J. A. Gwynne had a telephone listed under her name at 1015 Markley Street. Now, Mr. Gwynne, will you tell the court your relationship to Mrs. J. A. Gwynne?"

"Your Honor, she was my aunt."

"And you lived there with her?" Anthony asked.

"Yes, I did."

"Your Honor," Anthony said. "Mr. Gwynne pleads guilty to the charge of drunkenness, but he has already been held in jail a day and a half. The disorderly conduct was merely his shocked reaction to what he considered an interference with his right to enter his own home. As for breaking and attempted entering, there has to be an intent to break and enter. I feel hopeful that the gentleman who now lives in the house where Mr. Gwynne once lived will not want to press charges under the circumstances."

The occupant of the house said he didn't think it was necessary to prosecute. "Discharged," the magistrate said.

Anthony led Gwynne away from the stand. "Get your stuff from the house sergeant," he said. "Then we'll try to figure how to get you back to Los Angeles or wherever you're going."

Gwynne was still shaking. "That was swell, Mr. Lawrence," he said. "Yeah, I sure want to get out of this town."

Next to Anthony, Louis Donetti said in his flat voice, "Tony, it's a pleasure to watch you work. Nice, neat preparation. But your client isn't going to leave town just yet. I got a warrant here charging Chesley A. Gwynne, alias Howard Jones, with the murder of John C. M. Stearnes night before last."

"Oh my God," Gwynne said.

Louis Donetti was watching Anthony, and smiling. "Okay, Robin Hood," Louis said gently. "Shall we step aside and give you a clear path back to the Main Line? Things are about to get rough."

"How long have you been holding up that warrant?"

"Only since last night, Tony. The last place you look for a murder suspect is in jail."

"You could have called me last night or this morning."

"Well, Tony, it saved us a wee bit of trouble to have the guy swear to being Chesley A. Gwynne. On account of Chesley A. Gwynne is a first cousin of the dead man."

Anthony moved close to him and said quietly, "You're a liar. You wanted to put me in a spot."

"This is only a bad spot for a phony, pal."

Anthony looked around. The court reporters weren't close enough to pick up this quiet conversation but they would have plenty for a story. If Chesley A. Gwynne was a first cousin of the murdered man, he was also a cousin of Grace Shippen's, and probably related to several of Philadelphia's leading families. This case was going to embarrass some of the best people in town.

Louis turned abruptly away from him. "All right, fellows," he said. "Slate Gwynne and take him to the Hall."

A thin, terrified voice cut the air. "Mr. Lawrence!" Gwynne cried. "Don't walk out on me! I know this town. They'll burn me, Mr. Lawrence, and honest to God I didn't do it!"

Anthony walked over to where Gwynne was writhing in the grip of two detectives. "Now listen," he said. "Listen hard. Make no statement. Answer no questions. Don't sign a thing. They'll try to make you but they haven't any right to. Got it?"

"Sure, sure, I got it," Gwynne gasped.

"I want you to understand something. I'm a corporation and tax lawyer. I've never taken a criminal case to court."

"I'll never get anybody better, Mr. Lawrence! Will you do it?"

"Yes. I'll do it."

"Take him away," Louis said. The detectives pushed Gwynne away through the crowd. Louis smiled. "My hero. You'll look good in the newspaper stories. But this is only the start, Tony."

"Will you produce him for a hearing tomorrow morning?"

"Don't get impatient, Tony. This will heat up fast."

"Tomorrow morning, or I get right to work on a writ of habeas corpus and you won't like the statements I'll make to the papers."

Louis said in a fond tone, "I always wondered what it would be like to play for keeps against you. You're looking good in your first at bat. This thing goes nine innings, though. I'll produce Gwynne for a hearing tomorrow morning."

"Thanks."

"Maybe by tomorrow you won't feel so brash. This isn't just a little old pig in a poke you bought. This is a rattlesnake in a gunny sack. So long, hero."

ANTHONY went at once to see Logan Clayton and told him exactly what had happened. You had to give Mr. Clayton credit: he might be an old woman sometimes, but he toughened up when the worst really did happen. He listened with a sort of detached concentration, like a fighter getting the word in his corner.

Finally he said, "Well, Tony, you were the victim of a very clever job of entrapment. I assume that the papers will build you up as a colorful and romantic figure. That makes it awkward to withdraw from the case. But you could still pull out, on grounds of lack of experience in criminal practice. The average newspaper reader would accept that as an honorable thing to do."

"I'm not concerned about the average newspaper reader," Anthony said. "I'm worried about what I'll think of myself, if I quit. I'm also worried about what you would think."

"My final reaction might depend on just one point: would the interests of the defendant be hurt or helped if you backed out? You work in terms of people, Tony. My guess is that, if your heart's in it, nobody can defend Gwynne better than you can, even though you've never had any criminal-court experience."

"You haven't mentioned how this might affect the firm."

"It may be embarrassing. But as long as you do the right thing, whatever that turns out to be, the firm will back you."

"I appreciate that a great deal, sir."

Mr. Clayton sighed. "I'm afraid enormous pressures will be turned on you. Brace yourself."

Anthony went back to his office and started reading the newspapers. They gave him a lot of information he needed about Gwynne. Gwynne was forty-two years old. He was a first cousin of the dead man, John C. M. Stearnes. He was a third cousin of Grace Shippen. He was related to many important people. He had been thrown out of several prep schools. He had been expelled from college. Before he was twenty he had been arrested several times for speeding, drunkenness and brawling. By that time the papers had almost a standing line of type: "Chet Gwynne, the bad boy of Philadelphia Society, was arrested again last night for . . ."

Under a 1930 date came a much more serious story. Some valuable antiques had been stolen from the home of Mrs. J. A. Gwynne, 1015 Markley Street. Chesley A. Gwynne was arrested in New York City, trying to sell them. His aunt, Mrs. Gwynne, refused to prosecute, and the case was dropped.

At that point a curtain came down over the life of Chesley A. Gwynne, and had not lifted until September of 1948, when John C. M. Stearnes was shot with his own revolver while Gwynne was believed to be visiting him. The newspapers had learned that Gwynne had been back in Philadelphia for at least a month before the murder, living in a rooming house under the name of Howard Jones. And last June in Los Angeles he had been arrested, charged with assault and battery on a woman with whom he had been living. That case was still pending in Los Angeles.

The newspaper stories were very kind to Anthony J. Lawrence, but in the late afternoon the pressure started to be turned on. The phone rang and Grace Shippen was calling. "Oh, Tony, you poor dear," she said. "What have they done to you? Of course you're going to withdraw as soon as things cool off a little."

"I'll give it a lot of thought."

"He's a cousin of mine. It's so awful. You'll probably soon find out that the family has given him an allowance for years, on condition that he adopted another name and stayed away from the city. Tony, it will be easy for the family to get him a good lawyer."

"I'm not a good one?"

"Oh, Tony, don't be stiff-necked. I know you're tired and upset now, and I'm not going to nag at you. Good-by, darling."

"We had a date for tonight, didn't we?"

"I think you need some rest, Tony dear. Let's call it off."

"All right, Grace. I'll see you."

He hung up the phone, feeling a bit sick. A half-hour later there was a call from Mrs. J. Arthur Allen. "Hello, Anthony," she said. "You know I'm not one to beat around the bush. I hope you'll find it possible to drop this hot potato you're holding."

"Mrs. Allen, I wish I could, and still feel right about it."

"This Gwynne person is no relative of mine. I'm concerned only about Grace."

"Grace and I had a little talk and didn't get very far."

"Anthony, you're one of the nicest young men I know. In general, I'd back you to the limit. But Grace is very close to me. Think it over, will you?"

There were no more calls that afternoon. But at dinner that night, at the Racquet Club, the chairman of the board of a major bank stopped by to say hello. He chatted for a couple of minutes about this and that, mentioned in passing that old Bill Brinkerhoff was retiring from the board next year, and ended with a casual comment that it was too bad the way those newspaper fellows jazzed up stories, like that one today about Anthony. You could make anything or nothing out of that.

When you added everything up, it looked as if he risked losing his girl and his big client and his prospects for a directorship of a major bank, if he insisted on defending Chet Gwynne. They claimed Philadelphia was slow, did they? This was split-second stuff. It had taken him years to build his career up to this point. They could take his career apart in five minutes, and they were making sure that he realized it.

He went home and found that his mother had dropped in and was waiting for him with the newspapers beside her. He gave her all the other news about the case. "What do you think?" he said finally. "Am I an idiot? Should I go on with the case?"

She smiled at him. "I can't advise you, Anthony," she said. "All I can do is repeat something your great-grandmother used to say a long time ago: 'Keep your pride hot and bright, and people will respect you more for it.'"

"Thanks," Anthony said, getting up and kissing her.

THE NEXT morning Louis Donetti produced Gwynne for a hearing. Anthony asked and was granted a further hearing in two weeks so that he could investigate the facts in the case.

That afternoon he interviewed Gwynne. It was a frustrating experience. The man was covering up. Either he wouldn't talk about things or he lied. Plenty of lawyers might feel they had a right to walk out on such an uncoöperative client. But there was a reasonable doubt in Anthony's mind that Gwynne was guilty. You couldn't walk out on a guy, carrying that doubt with you.

One morning, a week after the preliminary hearing, Logan Clayton came into his office and asked if he would be available for a meeting that afternoon. Dr. Shippen Stearnes wanted to come in with his grandniece, Grace Shippen, and discuss a matter with Anthony and Logan Clayton. Mr. Clayton said, "I suppose you know he's the grand old man of the Shippen and Stearnes clans. We'll have to see them."

"It's not fair for them to start turning the heat on you and the firm as well as on me," Anthony said.

"Start turning it on?" Mr. Clayton said. "My boy, you don't know what we've had to go through these last ten days."

"It might be better if I resigned from the firm."

Logan Clayton stuck out his jaw. "We wouldn't accept it."

THE MEETING began very pleasantly. Dr. Stearnes was a wonderful erect old man of eighty-one. He was worth millions and had devoted his life to studying the effect of heredity and environment on various creatures. His mind worked as precisely as a well-tested scientific formula.

"My dear friends," he said, smiling at them, "we have all been distressed at this terrible thing, and the consequences it has brought. May I discuss them with you this afternoon?"

"We'll be glad to discuss them, sir," Logan Clayton said. "But if we are to be subjected to more pressure, this meeting will be useless. Mr. Lawrence has been doing what an honorable man should do. This firm will not let him down."

Dr. Stearnes said gently, "Let me point out that any pressure brought to bear on you was by people, acting on their own part, in the belief they had your best interests at heart. Speaking for the families involved, we have had a formal council, and you will be happy to hear that we approve completely of Mr. Lawrence's acting as Chet Gwynne's lawyer." He looked around, beaming.

"Astonishing," Mr. Clayton said in a toneless voice.

Dr. Stearnes went on, "We have decided that the best thing we can do is to stand aside and let justice take its course."

"He might go to the chair," Mr. Clayton said bluntly.

"True. And, as one who has always upheld the influence of heredity over environment, I would have to admit that the families would bear a certain stigma."

Anthony said, phrasing the question carefully, "And if, by some chance, he was acquitted . . . ?"

"I think I can promise you that we would not in that event turn our backs on Chet. As an alcoholic and a man of generally weak moral fiber, he should not be tossed willy-nilly back into the world. A small place in the country might be best for him."

"A sanitarium, you mean?"

"Not exactly, Mr. Lawrence. A place of his own, where he could potter around. Well looked after, of course."

Anthony shuddered slightly. It sounded like Eastern Penitentiary, but with nice silverware. "I'm very glad you've come to this decision," he said. "Every man has a right to be defended in court. If I didn't do it, somebody would."

"Quite so. And we are not unaware that another lawyer might approach this in a very different spirit from yours. Since no great financial rewards could be expected, another lawyer might seek his payment in headlines, with scant regard for justice."

Justice for whom? Anthony thought. Did the families Dr. Stearnes represented really have some dirty linen they didn't want washed in public? Had they been afraid that he would be able to rummage through the right bureau drawers and find it? It might be worth while to explore that subject very delicately.

"Yes," Anthony said. "It's always possible for a lawyer to twist facts, and to make good intentions seem bad."

Dr. Stearnes looked at him with approval. "Exactly. We feel confident that you will deal honestly with the facts of the case. Ah, by the way, what sort of a man is this Assistant District Attorney who will handle the prosecution?"

"Louis Donetti? Louis will play rough."

"He has been investigating the background of the case very thoroughly. In fact, more thoroughly than seems necessary."

So that was it, Anthony thought. Louis and his boys had been poking around. The families were worried.

"I suspect," Dr. Stearnes said, "that he would like to make political capital by putting the Philadelphia way of life on trial, along with Chet Gwynne."

"He can't do it by himself," Anthony said. "The defense would have to open the subject for him."

Dr. Stearnes studied him for a few moments. "That is why," he said finally, "we would like Chet defended by a lawyer who will seek justice rather than headlines."

This might be a good time to rummage through those bureau drawers. Anthony said, "Young Chet was obviously a real problem. What were the reasons why he left various prep schools?"

"Lack of study. Pranks. His late aunt — a niece of mine, by the way — was a delightful person but she did spoil the boy."

"And why was he expelled from college?"

"A girl. Pretty enough, but quite cheap. And of course she had a greedy mother. The girl was caught in his room at college. Chet wanted to marry her, but it would have been a tragic and unsuitable thing. We bought off the girl and her mother."

"Did Chet take a job after that?"

"Let me see. Yes, poor old Johnny — John C. M. Stearnes, you know — gave Chet a job in that investment-banking firm of his. It didn't work out well. Chet was starting to drink and gamble. When a few thousand dollars was missing, things pointed to Chet. So we sent him out into the country to manage a dairy farm which your father owned, Grace. We hoped that would straighten him out. But he wouldn't stay. No bright lights, you know. He returned to his aunt on Markley Street, although he was warned. Well, you know how he repaid his aunt, because the papers dug up that business of the stolen antiques. She was brokenhearted. At that point it was necessary to take a firm stand with the young man. Poor old Johnny arranged a monthly allowance, and told him to get out and stay out or the allowance would stop."

"About his parents," Anthony said. "I assume they died when he was very young. Was any money left for him?"

"Not directly. Let's see, now. Chet's father died rather young, before he could earn much money or inherit any of the family fortune, and left his modest estate to Chet's mother. When Chet's mother died, she left part of her estate for Chet's education and general upbringing. The rest went to Chet's aunt. The intention was that this should go to Chet someday, but when he turned out so badly it became obvious that the money would only be wasted, and his aunt cut him out of her will."

"Thank you," Anthony said. "That answers everything."

"I am so glad," Dr. Stearnes said. "And I'm delighted that we have managed to straighten things out. You might thank my grandniece for that. She stood up for you like a trouper. Well, that concludes my business."

"Tony," Grace said, "may I see you alone for just a moment?"

Anthony walked with Grace into his office. She waited for him to close the door. "Tony," she said in a small voice, "I was wrong to treat you that way."

"Don't worry about it."

"But I do," she murmured. She moved close to him and her arms crept around his neck. "Do you forgive me, Tony?"

"There's nothing to forgive. You acted in a very natural way."

She shivered a little. "Murder is so ugly. Tony, I felt so proud when everybody decided they could have confidence in you."

"Confidence about what?"

"Why, as Uncle Ship said, to make sure that justice is done."

"I'll do my best to make sure of it," he said, trying to keep any note of grimness out of his voice.

"I know you will, Tony." She kissed him, and left.

Two minutes later Logan Clayton walked in. His usually pink face was flaming. "I held myself in," he said. "That is the damnedest proposition one alleged gentleman ever made to another. I'm not crazy, am I, Tony? He made the proposal so gently and subtly that it's hard to pin anything down. What was your impression?"

"The same as yours," Anthony said. "Get him off without a scandal. Otherwise, let him go to the chair quietly, please."

"Is there a way to get him off without a scandal?"

"I haven't seen it."

"How about with a scandal?"

"Doctor Stearnes said a great many interesting things. From his point of view, the families acted honorably and with the best intentions. My client may not have seen it in that light."

"It's a possible line of defense, isn't it?"

"Yes, sir."

"Would you use it, Tony?"

"I can't answer that question now."

Logan Clayton shook a fist under his nose. "Let me make this clear," he said. "If your client is convicted, and if you fail to make full use of any legitimate line of defense, we'll accept that resignation you offered this morning." He stamped out of the room.

Anthony nodded. Yes, indeed, there was a real man in the firm. He didn't know whether there were two of them or not.

CHAPTER 7

H E SAT in Chet Gwynne's cell at Moyamensing Prison and studied the man. Now that Gwynne's eyes were no longer bloodshot you saw how weak and watery they were. Now that his face had lost its puffiness, it looked like soggy gray cardboard.

"How are we doing, Mr. Lawrence?" Gwynne asked. "You're going to get me off, aren't you?"

"If I can, Chet."

"Look, Mr. Lawrence, if a guy blacks out and can't remember anything, how can they prove he killed somebody?"

"By circumstantial evidence. Blacking out is no defense, unless it's insanity. Let's talk about that blackout, Chet."

"I'm not going to talk about it! That's what happened, see, and I'll tell anybody. I was drinking and don't remember."

Anthony shrugged. Deliberately or not, the man had erased part of that evening from his mind. He'd have to try something. "Let's go back a bit earlier in the evening," he said. "You were talking to Mr. Stearnes about that woman in Los Angeles who charged you with beating her up. You were telling Mr. Stearnes it was going to cost something to buy her off, and — "

"Don't pull that stuff on me," Gwynne snapped. "I never told you why I went to see Johnny. Lay off trying to trick me."

"You've got me confused with the prosecuting attorney," Anthony said. He got up slowly.

Gwynne grabbed his arm. "Don't get sore, Mr. Lawrence. It's just that I'm not used to having anybody on my side."

"My job is to put up the best defense for you I can. If you tell me something that would hurt your case, it's not my duty to bring it out in the trial. But I've got to be ready if the prosecutor brings it out."

"Yeah, I see what you mean. Well, your guess was right. That was what I was talking about to old Johnny. Five thousand bucks would square the woman in L.A."

"You had been in Philadelphia a month before that night. Why did you wait so long before asking him for the money?"

Gwynne's glance flickered around the cell. "A month, was it? Well, it took me a couple of weeks to work myself up to getting in touch with him, because he always said no more allowance if I ever came back. Then he put me off for a week or so."

Gwynne had found an answer but it wasn't a very good one.

Anthony decided to come back to that question later from another direction. "Some of your relatives have been giving me a little background about you," he said casually.

Gwynne stiffened. "Who?"

"Doctor Shippen Stearnes, for one."

"That louse."

"Chet, I've heard their side now, and I'd like to hear yours."

"What did they say?"

"You got a girl in trouble at college and were expelled. The family bought you out of the jam with the girl. John C. M. Stearnes gave you a job. You were drinking and gambling and walked off with several thousand dollars. They gave you a job running a dairy farm and you refused to do it. You carted away some valuable antiques from your aunt's house and tried to peddle them in New York and were caught. It broke her heart. Because of that, she cut you out of her will."

Chet Gwynne started trembling. Now his eyes were bright. "The devils!" he said. "The girl wasn't their kind, so the fact that I wanted to marry her didn't mean a thing to them except I was a wild kid. Sure, I'll tell you about her. I'll tell you the works."

He paced the cell, opening and clenching his fists. Anthony sat quietly. The dam was breaking, and if he didn't move or interrupt he would see how much dirty water had been backed up.

"She was a good kid," Gwynne said hoarsely. "All right, I got her in trouble and I wanted to marry her, but her mother's a scrub woman and so the family thinks it would be a worse scandal to marry her than it was to get her in trouble. I'm telling you, we'd have made a go of it if we had had the chance. But I let the family make a dirty thing of it and rub her nose in a little money.

"Then old Johnny gave me a job in his office. Yeah, I started drinking some, but I kept thinking about that girl. It got so bad I took some money from the firm and hunted her up and tried to get her back. But she's married by then and spits in my face, and won't even let me look at the kid.

"I went on a real bender and blew the money, and old Johnny kicked me out of the office and the family sent me back in the sticks to run a lousy farm. I was going nuts. I came back to my aunt's, and I didn't have any dough at all and they told her not to give me any. So I walked off with a load of antiques and got caught. You know who owned that stuff? My mother and father. Sure, everything was in my aunt's name but it was supposed to come to me. Then they really turned the screws on me. They gave me a choice of going to jail or getting out of town on a lousy hundred bucks a month. That's a choice, is it? I got out.

"I went to the West Coast and I had one hope left. I was supposed to get some money when my grandfather died and when my aunt died. The family took care of that. They made my grandfather and aunt cut me out of their wills. If I'd had any sense I'd have taken those wills to court on grounds of undue influence. Because the money was supposed to come to me. Everybody knew it. But they don't let loose any dough in families like mine to somebody who doesn't fit their holy pattern. Play ball, keep your nose clean, marry a girl they approve of, and you get all kinds of nice little things. But bust loose, like me, and they cut your throat.

"Well, that's it. They took my girl. They took away my money. Then you know what they did? Do you? Do you?" He was standing in front of Anthony, his face twisted, his voice cracking like glass. "They took away my name!" he cried. "They kicked me out and said there wasn't any Chet Gwynne any more and that my name was Howard Jones. Who's Howard Jones? He's a nothing. And that's who I've got to be from then on." He dropped onto the cot in the cell and pushed his face into the mattress. You could hardly catch his muffled words. "Of all the dirty things they did to me that was the worst. They stole my name."

It was very odd, Anthony thought. There was Gwynne hating his family and everything it stood for, but clinging to a name that meant nothing if it did not mean the family and its standards and its orderly way of life.

"Chet," Anthony said gently, "feeling the way you do, it couldn't have taken you several weeks to work up courage to go to Stearnes. When you came back to Philadelphia, you were ready to fight. What did you do in that month before Stearnes was shot?"

Gwynne lifted his head. "You're a smart cookie," he said blankly. "I'm glad you're not the prosecutor. I knew old Johnny. Next to him, stainless steel is soft. He'd have told me to get out or no more checks, if I'd gone to him cold. But I knew something else about old Johnny. He always liked women, and everybody knew it but his wife and kids. He never got in trouble. He played it nice and quiet. So I spent three weeks watching him. At the end of that time I knew everything about the latest one. So finally I dropped old Johnny a note with a few hints in it. Then I went to see him, and told him what I needed and said if I didn't get it I'd let his wife and kids know about the dame. You want to call it blackmail? Go ahead. It's a long way from murder, though."

"You must have had quite a row with him."

"I don't know what happened," Gwynne said sullenly. "I was drinking when I went to see him. But I'm not a murderer, see?"

"All right, Chet."

"Spell it out for me, Mr. Lawrence. Would all this stuff add up to a defense? If you presented it right?"

"I think it would."

"Wouldn't they squirm!" Gwynne muttered. "Wouldn't they hate to see all the skeletons dragged out of closets. I don't like the idea. But I don't like the idea of going to the chair, either."

"We'll see what turns up," Anthony said.

It might be a very good defense, he thought as he walked to his office. Juries decided murder cases, and juries were made up of people, and you could do a lot when you were dealing with people. He and Logan Clayton had seen that line of defense emerge hazily when Dr. Shippen Stearnes was telling them the families' side of the story. It was a very clear line of defense now that Gwynne had told his side. You put Gwynne on the stand and let him tell about a persecuted kid who wanted to marry a girl and was forced to leave her. You showed the kid being slowly crushed until there wasn't much left but husk, and then you showed people taking the husk of his name from him and throwing the rest of him away. And you showed that these people were not upright and honest, as they pretended to be, but that they too had stains in their lives which they had managed to conceal. Finally you showed the man who had been crushed putting up a fight in the only way he could fight, by threatening to tell about the stains.

Gentlemen of the jury, who drew out the gun? Did a man who once made a mistake and was crushed for it become maddened into grabbing it and firing? Or did the man who claimed to be righteous reach for his gun and threaten his visitor? Who meant to shoot whom? Did somebody try to commit suicide? Was there a struggle? Who knows? Who can call it murder?

It was a defense, all right. It could be a winning defense. Of course it would leave a few losers in its path. Among them would be Dr. Shippen Stearnes and Grace Shippen and their relatives. Also Morris, Clayton, Biddle and Wharton. Also Anthony J. Lawrence. Was it right for all of them to lose, just to save one man? Perhaps it was, if the truth was on Chet Gwynne's side. And that brought you back to the question: What was the truth?

AT THE further hearing two days later Louis Donetti put on the stand the policeman who had been called to the house, the medical examiner who had conducted the autopsy, and the Stearnes butler. John C. M. Stearnes had been killed by a bullet from his own .32-caliber revolver which had entered his chest from the front and passed through his heart. The bullet had been fired from close range, but it was highly unlikely that the fatal wound could have been self-inflicted. A visitor calling himself Howard Jones was in the room at the time and loudly quarreling with Mr. Stearnes, and fled afterward, probably through a French window opening onto the garden. Donetti asked the butler if he saw Howard Jones in the courtroom, and the butler pointed to Chesley A. Gwynne.

Anthony let the policeman and medical examiner go without cross-examination, but he cross-examined the butler deliberately and at length. He was careful not to give him any cause for alarm or hostility. He wanted thousands and thousands of words of testimony from the butler which he could study at leisure. Perhaps something might turn up. And if it did, he wanted the butler to be relaxed and off guard at the trial.

The butler's name was George Archibald. He was thin, and combed his hair in precise lines over a bald spot on his head. When he took the stand he looked around the crowded room and frowned slightly, as if wondering how so many people could possibly have bought their clothes at the wrong shops. He had worked for John C. M. Stearnes, he testified, for fourteen years. He had obviously been devoted to his employer, and would not willingly say anything that might discredit him.

Archibald's testimony was very damaging. On the evening of the shooting, Stearnes told him that a visitor named Howard Jones would be coming, that he was an unpleasant person, and that Archibald should stay within call in case there was any trouble. The butler admitted the visitor soon after eight p.m. and led him to the ground-floor study at the rear of the house. Stearnes was upstairs. Archibald did not like the way the visitor peered around the study; the man was badly dressed and had been drinking. Archibald checked the position of valuable things in the room, before leaving to call Stearnes, so that he would know if anything was missing when he returned.

He notified his employer, who said he would be down soon and told Archibald to offer the visitor a drink. Archibald returned to the study and asked the visitor what he would like to drink. The visitor pulled a half-empty pint bottle from the left-hand pocket of his jacket, and said that all he wanted was a glass for his own whiskey. Archibald brought a glass to him on a tray. Meanwhile, Archibald noticed that the center drawer of Mr. Stearnes' desk was slightly open, although it had been closed when he first brought the visitor into the room. In that drawer Mr. Stearnes kept his revolver. Archibald saw that something heavy was weighing down the inside pocket of the visitor's jacket. When the man leaned over to pour a drink into the glass, the jacket bulged outward and Archibald saw a gleam of metal. Archibald went back upstairs and warned his employer and asked if he should call the police. Stearnes looked thoughtful, and said that wouldn't be necessary at the moment.

Stearnes went downstairs and spent the next two hours with the visitor. Now and then Stearnes rang for Archibald. Each time it was to have Archibald carry away two empty glasses on the tray; Stearnes liked everything neat and did not care to use a glass twice without having it washed. In fact Stearnes did not even like to have emptied glasses around the room.

Not long after ten o'clock the buzzer rang again. This time Stearnes met Archibald at the door of the study, and handed him a tray with one glass on it. Stearnes said he would not need Archibald any more that evening, and closed the door of the study. Archibald went up to his room at the second floor rear. Half an hour later he heard loud and angry voices from his employer and the visitor. There was the sound of a scuffle, and a shot. He ran downstairs, opened the door of the study and found Stearnes lying on the floor with the revolver two feet away. A French window opening onto the garden in the rear of the house was open. Stearnes seemed to be dead. Archibald telephoned for the police.

That was his story, and it was bad.

In cross-examination Anthony led him back over every bit of it. Archibald made an excellent witness for the prosecution. He had a remarkable memory and was very observant. He gave an exact description of the visitor's clothes. He described the contents of the study in enormous detail. Evidently he was proud of his ability to remember details, and liked to demonstrate it. He answered many questions much more fully than was necessary.

For example, when asked how many drinks John C. M. Stearnes had during the evening, he replied, "Mr. Stearnes had three drinks while his visitor was present. I assume that he took about an ounce and a quarter each time, because that was his usual amount. He had a Scotch and soda, using Glen Murry Scotch, for his first and second drinks. For his third, he had a rather heavier-bodied Scotch, Royal Tartan, with his soda."

Anthony said, "Why do you say you assume that he took about an ounce and a quarter? You must have known exactly, since you apparently served him each time."

"No sir, I did not serve him. Mr. Stearnes kept a liquor cabinet in the study, containing a bottle of Glen Murry Scotch and one of Royal Tartan Scotch, and one bottle of Napoleon brandy."

"Mr. Archibald, if you did not pour his drinks and were not in the room, how do you know exactly what Mr. Stearnes had to drink each time?"

"I was able to check on that, sir, from the glass he had used. The aroma of the two Scotches is quite distinctive. Most good liquor has a characteristic bouquet of its own. So does bad liquor, though I hesitate to call it a bouquet. Mr. Stearnes' visitor was drinking a very raw, cheap rye. It was easy to tell which glass he had used."

"You sniffed at each glass whenever you took ones that needed to be washed from the room? Isn't that rather unusual?"

"There was a practical reason for it, sir. In that way I could keep track of which bottle Mr. Stearnes was using, and bring a new bottle if it became necessary. By the end of the evening my calculations indicated that there were four ounces of Glen Murry remaining and fifteen ounces of Royal Tartan."

"You are a connoisseur of fine liquor, Mr. Archibald?"

"Well, yes sir. To provide proper service to a gentleman like Mr. Stearnes it is necessary to have a rather wide knowledge in the fields of food, liquor, clothing, and so on."

"Do you yourself drink, Mr. Archibald?"

"To a limited extent. I permit myself two drinks a day, always in the evening, after the serving of dinner. Usually one at eight o'clock and the other at ten."

"Naturally you had two drinks on the evening in question."

"Yes sir. The first one a bit later than usual, because of the visitor, and the second at about the usual time. I do not care to gulp a drink. I prefer to relax and savor it slowly."

Anthony probed into the details of Archibald's final trip to the study in answer to the buzzer, accepting every answer politely and making no attempt to back Archibald into corners. He took two hours for his cross-examination. Then he said he was not calling any witnesses for the defense. The magistrate held Chesley A. Gwynne, alias Howard Jones, without bail for the Grand Jury.

Two weeks later the October Grand Jury brought an indictment, and Gwynne was arraigned in court and entered a plea of not guilty to the charge of murder. Louis Donetti put the case on the calendar for trial in December.

To Anthony, there was a dreamlike quality to the days that followed. On one hand, his life went on normally: tax work, corporation law, Grace Shippen. On the other hand there was the Gwynne case, seeping through his life like a dark stain. There was a new and subtle type of pressure. People kept prying at him.

What they really wanted to ask was: You're not going to drag fine names in the dirt, are you? We can trust you, can't we?

Meanwhile an odd thing was happening to Gwynne's attitude. He had adjusted himself to the prison community, and he was talking about his case, in spite of Anthony's warnings. He was getting sympathy and advice and responding to it. Every time Anthony visited him there were more signs of a change in his thinking. First Gwynne had posed as a bewildered victim of circumstance. Then he turned into a martyr. The final step was to become a man with a mission. As one who knew the dark truth about many leading people, it was his duty to bring it to light.

Prisons being what they were, Anthony knew that much of this was relayed to Louis Donetti. Louis, as Dr. Shippen Stearnes had said, wanted to put Philadelphia society on trial along with Chet Gwynne. And the big question was: How did you defend Gwynne without doing just that?

THIS WAS the second day of the trial. The Quarter Sessions courtroom was filled with people, whispering and stirring around as they waited for the judge. Chet Gwynne, seated at the defense table, said with satisfaction that the house was a sellout.

Anthony glanced around the room, and had the odd sensation that his life was starting to repeat itself. Was this really a courtroom where, in a short time, he might have to make a decision that would affect the course of his life? Or was it the gym at Franklin Academy where he was trying to decide which of two Salutatories he would give? The faces in the crowd were different, of course. Now he saw Logan Clayton and the Whartons and Grace Shippen and Dr. Shippen Stearnes. Instead of the radical master, Mr. Glenmor, who had wanted to rip apart the classic pattern of Philadelphia life, there was Louis Donetti at the prosecutor's table.

There was one link in the audience with that long-ago night. His mother was still trying to catch his glance and exchange proud smiles with him. Years ago he had been embarrassed by that. Today he smiled back at her. He wasn't at all sure, however, that today she would have any reason to be proud of him.

This was the day when he would see if the quickness of the hand

could deceive the observant eyes of George Archibald. Yesterday
Donetti had finished his direct examination of Archibald, and
today Anthony could cross-examine.

The prosecution had built a strong case. Yesterday, in addition
to testimony by the medical examiner, by the police, by the butler,
Louis Donetti had brought out his secret weapons, and they had
been deadly. Stearnes had kept the letters Gwynne had written to
him throughout the years. There were ten of them. Nine of them
wheedled, begged and whined, and Chet Gwynne squirmed as
they were read into the record. The tenth letter, written by Gwynne
a few days before the shooting, was threatening. It said:

> If you're smart you won't hang up on me next time I call. I've
> been back here more than three weeks, watching you all the time.
> Does that give you the chills? It better. I want to talk to you. I'm
> in a jam out on the coast with a woman, and I need five thousand
> bucks. It's got to be five thousand or you're going to be very sorry.

Louis Donetti's case was as strong as a hangman's knot.

The solemn jury came in and then the judge, and George Archibald was recalled to the stand and turned over to Anthony for
cross-examination. Anthony gave the man every chance to prove
how remarkable were his powers of observation and memory.
Archibald loved it; in fact, he seemed more at ease with Anthony
than he had been with Donetti. Anthony, of course, was a gentleman who dressed well and respected butlers while Donetti was a
South Philadelphia Italian in clothes dusted with cigar ashes.

Anthony devoted a lot of time to questions and answers about
the three drinks John C. M. Stearnes had taken during the evening,
and the butler's skill in identifying the type of liquor by sniffing
the glasses. He went over the details of Archibald's final trip to the
study. Not once in all the questioning did he try to trap the witness.
Up on the bench, the judge was looking puzzled. At the prosecutor's table, Donetti sat tense with suspicion.

"Now, Mr. Archibald," Anthony said mildly, "when you went
to the study on your final trip, you found the door closed?"

"That is correct," Archibald said. "I rapped twice on the door, as was my custom. Mr. Stearnes opened it about two feet and handed me the tray containing one glass."

"You did not actually see the defendant at that time?"

"No sir. His chair was not in my line of sight."

"Is it possible that the defendant could have left, and that the glass on the tray was from Mr. Stearnes' nightcap?"

"Oh no, sir. The visitor was there. I sniffed at the empty glass. The aroma was definitely that of the raw and cheap rye which the visitor had brought."

Anthony turned to his table and signaled to a man who had been sitting there quietly. The man rose and pulled a small table up close to the witness stand. He opened a brief case and placed on the table three small medicine bottles labeled A, B, C, and three plain glasses also labeled A, B and C.

"Mr. Archibald," Anthony said in a friendly tone, "I wonder if you would mind demonstrating to the jury your ability to identify various types of liquor by the aroma."

Louis Donetti leaped from his chair. "Objection!" he snapped. "A test of this type is not material or relevant."

"Your Honor," Anthony said in a hurt tone, "the witness has testified that he believes the defendant was still in the study, at the time in question, because the glass which Mr. Stearnes handed him was reeking with the fumes of the raw and cheap rye which the defendant had been drinking. I submit that it is material and relevant to allow the witness to demonstrate to the jury his ability to identify various types of liquor."

Donetti said, "Your Honor, there can be no real comparison between the witness's ability to identify types of liquor in his place of employment, and his ability to identify types of liquor under the badgering and bullying of counsel for the defense."

Perhaps Donetti realized, the moment he said it, that he should not have used the phrase "badgering and bullying." But it was too late. The tension of the courtroom exploded in laughter. Archibald permitted himself a wisp of a smile. Even the judge, pounding for order in the court, was fighting off a grin.

When order was restored, the judge said, "May I say to the prosecutor that never have I seen defense counsel treat a key prosecution witness with such remarkable consideration. Perhaps we might ask the witness if he feels badgered and bullied."

Archibald said, "Your Honor, the gentleman has been most kind and thoughtful. I have no doubt at all of my ability to give the demonstration which has been requested."

"Objection overruled," the judge said.

"Your Honor," Donetti said, "I object to the introduction as evidence of unidentified bottles containing mysterious liquids."

"Your Honor," Anthony said, "I have not introduced the contents of the bottles in evidence, nor may it be necessary to do so. But in good time I will be glad to, if it seems essential, together with the testimony of my assistant, a chemist who bought a bottle of Glen Murry Scotch, a bottle of Royal Tartan Scotch, and a bottle of cheap rye at a State liquor store, who has subjected the contents to chemical analysis, and who has had the various liquids in his possession and control ever since."

"Objection overruled," the judge said.

Anthony turned to his assistant and asked him to pour a small amount from bottle A into glass A, from bottle B into glass B, and from bottle C into glass C. While this was being done, Anthony went back to his table and waited until the pouring was completed and his assistant had returned to his seat. Everybody was looking at him now. There was a water carafe and glass on the defense table. Anthony poured himself a glassful and took a sip and walked back to the witness stand. In a forgetful way he carried the water glass with him, and then noticed it in his hand and put it on the small table containing the three liquor glasses. He picked up the glass labeled A. "Mr. Archibald," he said, "please identify the liquor in this glass by your sense of smell. I'm not going to rush you on this." He handed the glass to Archibald, who smiled happily. This would be one of the great moments of his life. He put his nose to the glass, and inhaled with delicate little sniffs.

"There's not a doubt in the world," he said. "It is definitely a cheap rye which has had a very short aging period."

"Thank you, Mr. Archibald," Anthony said, giving him an encouraging smile. "Now here is the second glass, labeled B. Please take plenty of time."

Archibald sniffed. He looked slightly puzzled. He lowered his head again and spent a long time sniffing. Gradually he began to smile. "I am ready," he said. "My delay was not due to any confusion but because you asked me to take plenty of time. This is Royal Tartan Scotch. Heavy, rich, peaty bouquet."

Anthony took the glass and said, "Thank you, Mr. Archibald." He put the glass back on the small table, without looking down, and fumbled for the third glass. "Now the third," he said, handing it to Archibald.

Archibald began to sniff. Then his head jerked up and he looked reproachfully at Anthony. "I am afraid," he said, "that you gave me your glass of water this time."

"Did I really?" Anthony said nervously. He looked around, quite flustered. "Are you sure? Did you smell it?"

"Now Mr. Lawrence," Archibald said reprovingly. "I know water when I see it. I tried to smell it and of course there was no smell at all, except perhaps a touch of the chlorine which the city puts into its water."

Anthony said quite irritably, "How could it be water? I reached down and picked up glass C and handed it to you."

"This is not labeled C," Archibald said kindly. "It is your water glass. If you will pardon me, since my throat is somewhat dry — " He lifted the glass to his mouth.

Anthony held his breath. He had not counted on this.

Suddenly Archibald choked. A strangled cry bubbled from his throat. "It's gin!" he gasped. "It's gin! You tricked me!"

Anthony grabbed the glass from Archibald's hand and, while the courtroom rang with noise, whipped out a sticker and pasted it on the glass. On the sticker was a big red D. Above the noise you could hear Louis Donetti shouting a furious objection. The judge's gavel rapped sharply and the noise died away.

"Your Honor," Donetti cried, "I move that this entire vaudeville act be stricken from the records!"

Anthony cut in sharply, "Your Honor, you had already overruled the prosecutor's objection to this test. The fact that it became more dramatic than I expected has nothing to do with its relevance."

"You tricked him!" Donetti shouted. "You filled his nose with fumes so he couldn't smell anything. You didn't give him that glass of gin by chance. You deliberately handed it to him."

"Your Honor," Anthony said mildly, "if the Assistant District Attorney wishes to testify, let him take the stand and I'll be glad to cross-examine."

The judge banged his gavel heavily. "I order the prosecutor's last remark stricken from the record. Mr. Donetti, if you have been making an objection, it has not been in a form this court recognizes. Unless you wish to make an objection in proper form, the cross-examination may proceed."

Louis Donetti flicked a glance at the jury. He said, "If your Honor please, I would like to enter on the record my contention that the ability or inability of the witness to identify gin by smell has nothing to do with his ability to identify the types of liquor which were drunk during the evening in question. I contend that the incident involving the gin is immaterial and irrelevant."

"Objection overruled," the judge said. "Cross-examination may continue."

Louis Donetti began shuffling back toward his table. He passed close to Anthony, and whispered, "Dirty pool, Tony. I knew you were laying for him."

"Hold your hat," Anthony muttered. "You haven't seen anything yet." He moved toward the witness stand. Archibald was no longer relaxed and happy. He shoved himself back in the chair as if trying to get as far away from Anthony as possible.

"Mr. Archibald," Anthony said briskly, "do you believe that the fumes from the first two glasses may have saturated your sense of smell, and therefore led you to identify gin as water?"

"I don't know," Archibald stammered. "It . . . it . . . well, perhaps. I had some difficulty in identifying the second glass, and perhaps that was because of the fumes from the first."

"You didn't tell us that at the time, Mr. Archibald. In substance, you said your delay in trying to name the contents of the second glass was not due to confusion but merely because I had asked you to take plenty of time. Is that correct?"

"Well, I suppose it is."

"You testified earlier that you generally take two drinks each evening, one usually around eight o'clock and one at about ten. You said you had your first drink a little later than usual on the night in question. You said you had your second drink at the usual time, that is, ten o'clock. Do you agree?"

Archibald had stopped giving long full answers. "Yes sir."

"You testified that you like to savor your drinks. Do you inhale their fumes as part of the enjoyable process?"

"Well, yes, I do."

"You had your second drink, by my timetable, just before making your final trip to the study. If fumes destroy your sense of smell, they had destroyed it that evening when you sniffed at the single glass which your employer handed you on the tray. Is this true?"

"Objection," Donetti said. "There has been no testimony indicating how long or short a time the sense of smell might be affected by the fumes of liquor taken previously."

"Sustained," the judge said. "Strike the question. The jury will disregard it."

Anthony was not disturbed. You could tell a jury to disregard something until you were blue in the face, but they would still remember. "Mr. Archibald," he said, "in view of the test you just took, do you now claim that the empty glass on the tray actually had held a raw and cheap rye? Please remember that this is important as indicating whether or not the defendant was in the room on the occasion of your final trip."

"I — I certainly thought it was that cheap rye," Archibald said hesitantly. "But — " He paused, seeking a way out, and thought he saw one. "But actually the defendant was in the room!" he said triumphantly. "Don't forget I heard his voice later!"

There was a slight groan from the table where Donetti sat as Anthony pounced at the witness. "Are you trying to tell the jury," he said, "that at ten minutes after ten you knew the defendant was in the study because a half-hour later you heard what you thought was his voice? How can you make a decision at ten ten based on something that happens at ten forty?"

"I see what you mean," Archibald said unhappily. "Perhaps the two events ran together a bit in my mind."

"You admit that sometimes details do run together a bit in your mind?"

"It . . . it doesn't sound very well that way."

"It certainly doesn't," Anthony said grimly. "Now, Mr. Archibald, you claim that the voice you heard was the defendant's?"

"Yes sir, I do."

"At the time you were up in your room above the study. What was between you and the voices?"

"There's the floor of my room and the ceiling below."

"A solid, well-built house?"

"Oh yes. Quite solid."

"Yet you claim to identify the defendant's voice?"

"Yes, he was shouting rather loudly."

"How many words had you heard the defendant speak, before this episode of the shouting?"

"It might have been around fifty."

"How many of those fifty words were shouted at you?"

"Why, none at all."

"Yet on the basis of fifty words spoken in a normal tone, you claim to identify angry shouts coming through the ceiling and floor of a well-built house?"

"It sounded like his voice."

"Want to make a test?" Anthony snapped.

"No sir," Archibald said, shuddering.

"Objection," Donetti growled. "The witness is in no condition to take such a test. This time perhaps it's obvious that he is being badgered and bullied."

"Sustained," the judge said.

Anthony was satisfied. The jury would remember that point, too. "Mr. Archibald," he said, "let us return to the test you took when, by your own statement, you were not at all doubtful of your ability. You saw me at my table pouring liquid from a water carafe into a glass. Did you assume anything from that?"

"Of course I did," Archibald said eagerly, seeing a chance to justify himself. "Naturally I assumed it was water."

"But your assumption was wrong, wasn't it?"

"Well, yes."

"You even went so far as to assume that you smelled the chlorine with which the water had been treated, didn't you?"

"I guess I did."

"How many wrong assumptions did you make the night Mr. Stearnes died?"

"I — I don't know what you mean."

"After the defendant arrived, you took him into the study. You claim you checked the position of every valuable object in the room. When you returned a little later, you claim that the center drawer of Mr. Stearnes' desk, where he kept his revolver, was slightly open, although you say it was closed previously. You assumed from that fact that the defendant had stolen the revolver, didn't you?"

"Oh, but there was a heavy bulge inside his jacket."

"How do you know it was a heavy bulge, rather than a bulge from a large but light object?"

"I saw a gleam of metal when he leaned forward."

"And from those tiny facts, no more significant than the sight of me pouring liquid from a water carafe, you made an assumption. In one case you assumed a stolen revolver hidden inside a coat. In the other you assumed a glass of water."

"Well, you see I thought — "

Anthony jabbed a finger at him and cried, "Mightn't the defendant have had a wallet and a pen-and-pencil set in his pocket?"

"I suppose so," Archibald said weakly. He looked ready to cry. Anthony studied him. He had backed the man into corners and slapped him around. Archibald hadn't shown any fight. Perhaps if you offered him a face-saving way to escape, he might take it.

"Now, Mr. Archibald," he said in a gentler tone, "isn't it possible that whatever mistake was made was not your fault? Isn't it possible that there was no revolver in the desk drawer? Wouldn't that seem to tie up with the fact that Mr. Stearnes did not seem very worried when you told him about the disturbed drawer?"

"Oh, yes sir," Archibald said gratefully. "That could very well be the case."

"And doesn't it seem unlikely that Mr. Stearnes would sit drinking and talking quite normally with the visitor, if he really knew the visitor had stolen his revolver?"

"Yes sir, that seems very reasonable. Or," Archibald said, with the air of a man discovering a great truth, "Mr. Stearnes could have coaxed him to give it up. Or a burglar could have crept in and caused the fight I heard. There are really a great many possibilities, aren't there, sir?"

Anthony smiled. He had given the rabbit a clear path to its burrow, and the rabbit had run. "Indeed there are," he said. "Thank you, Mr. Archibald. Let us close on the thought that there are a great many possibilities." He walked back to his table.

Gwynne leaned over and said, "You really took the guy."

Anthony nodded. He watched Donetti, looking old and tired, begin his redirect examination. He listened to Donetti trying to patch up his case. Louis didn't get anywhere. The rabbit was safe in his burrow and was not coming out. Finally Louis gave up, and told the judge that the prosecution rested. The judge said, "It is now twenty minutes of twelve. Does the defense wish to proceed with its case now, or have a recess until after lunch?"

Anthony glanced at Donetti, and saw that Louis was being nagged by an unhappy thought. Louis was right, too. Gwynne wasn't going on the stand. "Your Honor," Anthony said in a confident tone, "with cross-examination of the last witness, the case for the defense has been established. The defense rests."

Whispers scurried around the courtroom. The judge banged his gavel and said, "Court will reconvene at two o'clock."

Chet Gwynne was staring at Anthony. "What's the idea?" he said hoarsely. "When do I go on the stand?"

"You don't go on."

"What do you mean, I don't go on? That's what I've been waiting for! I have something to say about this."

"You'd better say it to another lawyer, then. This case is won! I'm not going to try to win it twice. I don't care what the jury says now. With what's on the record I could bust a guilty verdict into a million pieces on appeal. If you got another lawyer and took the stand, you'd be asking for trouble. Sure, you could bring out your sob story. But then Donetti would cut you into bits. You saw what I did to the butler. That would be a tea dance compared to what Donetti would do to you."

"But this was my chance," Gwynne said tearfully. "For once people were going to see what a dirty deal I've had."

"I'm not interested in people pitying you," Anthony said bluntly. "I'd rather have them envy you because you beat the rap. I'll see you after lunch." He got up and walked away. He felt he had been brutal, but it was the only way.

When he returned after lunch, a change had taken place in Gwynne, the man with a mission. He didn't want to change lawyers. He trusted Anthony. Anthony would get him off, wouldn't he? That was all he wanted.

Louis Donetti gave his closing argument to the jury. He did as well as he could with the threatening letter and the medical and police testimony and what he could salvage from the butler's testimony. Then he returned to his table like a groggy fighter wading back to his corner.

Anthony made his argument short and easy to remember.

"Ladies and gentlemen of the jury," he said. "There is just one question for you to decide. Is the defendant guilty of murder beyond any reasonable doubt? It is not enough for the prosecution to hint that he might have done it or that he could have done it. The prosecution has to prove absolutely that murder was committed, that the defendant committed it, and that no one else could have. You must decide whether or not the prosecution has managed to do that. All I ask you to do is to examine the facts.

"Fact one. The prosecution has made a point of what it calls a threatening letter. The prosecution would like you to believe this was a threat of murder. But is it not just as reasonable to assume that the writer was threatening suicide? Or threatening to bring discredit on his family? So all we have are several conflicting assumptions, with no proof backing any of them.

"Fact two. The alleged theft of the revolver. In cross-examination you heard the butler, George Archibald, back away from the assumption that a drawer left partly open and a bulge in a coat meant that the revolver had been stolen.

"Fact three. The single glass on the tray, which at first was assumed to mean that the defendant was still in the study. You saw a test which proved that the witness can make mistakes in identifying the contents of a glass. The prosecution has tried to dismiss this test as a vaudeville stunt. It was far more than that. It was clear, direct proof that the witness could draw false conclusions from a set of facts. From a water carafe, he assumed water. From a drawer which he thought had been opened, and from a bulge in a coat, he assumed a stolen revolver. From a glass on a tray, he assumed that the defendant was in the study.

"Fact four. From shouts heard through the floor and ceiling of a solidly built house, the witness assumed the presence of the defendant, although he admits he had only heard the defendant speak about fifty words and that none of these had been shouted. Once again an assumption.

"Ladies and gentlemen, I ask you to consider several other assumptions. Did the defendant attempt to commit suicide, and was John C. M. Stearnes accidentally shot in an attempt to prevent this? Or did Mr. Stearnes grab his gun to force the defendant to leave, and did the defendant in his turn try to protect himself and engage in a struggle during which Mr. Stearnes was shot? Or, as the key witness for the prosecution himself has suggested, did a burglar cause the fight in which John C. M. Stearnes was killed?

"These are all things which you, as reasonable people, will want to consider. I can close in no better way than by quoting the exact words of George Archibald. Quote. There are really a great many possibilities, aren't there? Unquote. Ladies and gentlemen of the jury, I ask you to find the defendant not guilty."

After that the judge gave his charge to the jury. It was clear and concise, and it didn't do the prosecution any good. The jury was out for thirty-seven minutes and came back with a verdict of not guilty. A sound made up of dozens of sighs and whispers crept through the room.

There were a number of people in court who admired legal skill, and they came up in a steady parade. Here was Logan Clayton, saying fervently, "Magnificent, Tony, magnificent. I wouldn't have thought it possible, except that once I saw you take Mr. Dickinson apart." One vote for skill.

Here were the John Marshall Whartons, smiling proudly at him. Two more votes for skill. Here was his mother, looking a little pale and weak, and very relieved that he had come out of it so well. You couldn't exactly call that a vote for skill because it was just a mother's vote for her son.

Here was Dr. Shippen Stearnes, beaming at him and saying, "My boy, our trust in you was more than justified. We are forever in your debt." Another few votes for skill.

"I appreciate that, sir," Anthony said. "Now what about . . ." He jerked his head toward Chet Gwynne, slouched in his chair like a sack whose contents were slowly draining away.

"Ah, yes," Dr. Stearnes said, with a bright smile. He touched Gwynne's shoulder. "Hello, Chet," he said gently.

The weak eyes looked up. "It . . . it's Uncle Ship, isn't it?" Gwynne said. His voice might have sounded like that years ago, as a boy who had done something wrong and had been caught at it. "I'm sorry I caused you so much trouble, Uncle Ship."

"Everything's going to be all right now, Chet," Dr. Stearnes murmured. "We want to look after you. Won't that be nice?"

Gwynne was very tired. "That will be nice," he said.

"Would you like to come along with me now, Chet?"

Gwynne got up slowly and put an arm around Dr. Stearnes' shoulders to steady himself, an old man of forty-two leaning on a younger man of eighty-one. They walked slowly from the courtroom. Anthony shivered. There was Chet Gwynne, moving off the stage of life to that quiet little place in the country.

And here, finally, was Grace, lighting up the drab courtroom like a million candle power. "Tony," she said, "I just can't get my breath. Darling, it was tremendous. Are you awfully tired? Could you come out to see me tonight? Because by then perhaps I'll have caught my breath again." Another vote for skill.

"I'll be there," he said.

She flashed him a smile and went away.

It was odd. All those votes for skill, and nobody had looked behind the skill to ask the basic question which ought to come up whenever a case has been tried . . . unless . . . He watched Louis Donetti amble toward him through the nearly deserted room. Fat, balding Louis with cigar ashes on his unpressed coat. It would be unpleasant but sort of refreshing to listen to Louis' vote.

Louis said, in that voice like a file scraping metal, "You know I'm not going to congratulate you."

"I wouldn't want you to."

"That stunt you pulled. It'll be one for the books."

"It's already in the books. Bill Fallon used it years ago in New York City. You've read about Fallon."

"Yeah. Criminal lawyer. Slick. How did he use that trick?"

"He was defending a guy accused of arson. A fireman testified he had smelled kerosene at the fire. On the stand, Fallon asked him to identify kerosene by taking some long sniffs of it. The fireman's nose and lungs got full of kerosene fumes. Fallon handed him a glass of water. Kerosene was all the fireman could smell so he called the water kerosene. Not guilty."

"You did a nice job of adapting it. Well, Tony, your Main Line friends ought to pay off good."

"You think so?"

"Sure they will, Tony. They're emperors in the last days of Rome. They're too soft to do their own fighting. You're captain of the palace guard, Tony. They got to keep you loyal. You might even get to sit on the throne someday."

"You make it sound too romantic."

"How do you feel about it, Tony?"

"I feel lousy about it, thanks," Anthony said brightly.

"Don't feel too bad," Louis said. "It's half my fault. I lost sight of the main issue. I wanted to bust the stained-glass windows and drag some of your friends out in the open, so I set up the case too tight. I tried to nail every door but one shut so you would have to use the only door left open. Well, some of the doors didn't fit good. I forced them shut. I let that butler try to prove too much. That gave you a chance to mousetrap him. I lost sight of the main issue trying to outsmart you."

"Just out of curiosity," Anthony said, "what's your idea of the main issue?"

"The issue was to try to get some justice done."

"Do you think he was guilty, Louis?"

"I don't know. I guess you don't either. That's reasonable doubt, so he goes free. Maybe a little justice sneaked in the back door on us. But we never invited it in. All we were trying to do was outsmart each other, and you won."

"You know I took a big chance, Louis. I tried that test on myself, and it worked. But there was no guarantee it would work on the butler. Magicians don't look good when their tricks flop."

Louis stared at him curiously. "And if it had flopped, you had only one chance for an acquittal. Tell me. Would you have put Gwynne on the stand, and to hell with the Main Line?"

Anthony sighed. "I wish I knew the answer," he said softly.

When he drove up to "White Pillars" in Haverford that evening, all the lanterns along the crushed-stone driveway were glowing, and every window was glittering. "White Pillars" only turned on all its lights for great events: a wedding, a birth, the end of a war. So this was quite a special evening.

Mrs. Allen came into the hallway to greet him. "I hear you're a holy terror in a courtroom, Anthony," she said happily. "I'm sorry I couldn't be there. Did you notice the lights as you drove up?"

"Of course. It's beautiful. Tonight must be a big occasion."

"You're the occasion. You're a good boy, Anthony. It's a comfort to have you around. You'll find Grace in the living room."

Anthony could sometimes tell how Grace felt by the clothes she was wearing. Tonight she wore flat-heeled sandals and a plain white dress with a flaring skirt and a tiny string of pearls. Her bright hair was pulled into a pony tail. She looked as if she were going to her first dancing class. She said in a low voice, "Hello."

He grinned and said, "Where's that older sister of yours? She's the one I came out to see."

"Don't tease me, Tony. I even feel like a child."

"Is that bad?"

"Tony, until the trial was over and I left, I hadn't realized how scared I was."

"What were you scared about?"

"Tony, I don't ever remember being scared before." She looked up at him, and blinked, and a single file of tears began coming in solemn procession from her eyes. "I was scared!" she wailed, and threw herself against him, shaking with sobs.

He had never seen her cry. It was hard to believe that all the poise and glamour could be washed away like so much lipstick, leaving a bawling child. He led her to a couch and sat beside her. She burrowed against him, and gradually the sobs faded into long quivering gasps. Her wet face lifted and her lips followed a trembling course across his cheek until they found his mouth.

He brushed her shining hair and said softly, "What was the trouble?"

She looked at him with eyes that had just opened after a bad dream. "It could have been so awful," she gasped. "If Chet had gone on the stand, he would have lied and lied, but people would have believed him and we would have been dragged in the mud. And we would have hated you, Tony, as if it were your fault that Chet had been weak and bad. And if you had kept Chet off the stand and let him be convicted we would have been relieved but then we would have despised you. And I didn't want to hate you! I didn't want to despise you! I wanted to love you! Oh, it could have been so black and nasty. Am I making sense to you?"

"Yes. You're making sense."

"But it ended up all right, didn't it, Tony?"

"Most people would think so."

She sniffled a bit, and said, "I do want to love you, Tony."

"You have too many words in that sentence. It would sound better if you just said I love you. How do you feel about that?"

She sat up and smiled. "Tony," she said, "we haven't played our question-and-answer game in months!"

"Is it time for me to ask you again? Wait till I put on my glum look and brace myself for the pat on the cheek."

"Come on, Tony. You have to ask."

"Will you marry me, Grace?"

"Yes!" she cried. "Oh yes, I will, Tony!" She threw her arms around him and clung as if she meant never to let go.

This was it, his brain told him coolly. This was Fish House Punch and scrapple and the Liberty Bell. This was Philadelphia rattling into his hands in one big jackpot. Counting himself, four generations of his family had worked to put him way up here at the absolute top. It turned out to be a rather cool and lonely place.

Long ago he had suspected that the answer to Grace Shippen lay in the simple statement that the things she wanted were the things she already had. But something had disturbed the bright and ordered pattern of her life. Chet Gwynne had come to town, and her world had seemed to be in danger. He had put her world back in order. So she would marry him. Whether she knew it or not, she was really taking out an insurance policy; but he was ready to accept her on any terms at all, because he was in love with her.

CHAPTER 8

I T TURNED out to be a very nice life. Grace was as delightful a companion as always, and willing to concede that marriage entitled a man to make love to his wife from time to time. In the first four years of their marriage she produced two healthy sons, and did it with a minimum of fuss.

They made their home at "White Pillars." Grace pointed out that her grandmother was going to leave the place to her and so it would be foolish to buy or build another home. As it happened, in the second year after their marriage Mrs. Allen began failing. Not that she ever admitted it. Her mind remained clear, and she had one great pleasure until she finally died: changing her bequests. She hoisted her codicils and flew them like battle flags in a war against fate. But one codicil she had never changed — the famous one in which she gave her old collie, Beauty, to Grace. And there was one new codicil which Anthony had not been allowed to draw up or to see. It left him five hundred thousand dollars.

At the office, getting ahead became almost easy. Of course, soon after he and Grace were married, his name moved up across that half-inch chasm on the left-hand side of the letterhead of Morris, Clayton, Biddle and Wharton. Someday it might be Morris, Clayton, Biddle and Lawrence. He became a director of one of the best banks in the city, and went on the board of a leading insurance company. When you reached that point, new clients began drifting in without any real effort on your part.

Among his new clients was an astonishing one. The man walked in unannounced one day: a huge white-haired man who brushed past the secretary like a bulldozer pushing aside a sapling. "My Lord," Anthony said, "Uncle Mike! How long has it been?"

Shaking hands with Mike Callahan was like putting your arm into a cement mixer. "It was 1929," Uncle Mike said. "Twenty-three years ago."

"That's right. I had a summer job at the Academy. A couple of boys from Penn were teaching me football." Anthony paused. "Funny I never see you around town. I hear about you, though, and I see those big Callahan Construction signs all over the place."

"Well, you and I don't walk exactly the same beat. They wouldn't like me tracking mud into the Academy of Music and the Racquet Club. I tracked some mud in here just now from a lot where I'm gonna put up an office building. I want a separate corporation for it. Thought I might get you to draw up the papers."

"That's the nicest compliment I've ever had as a lawyer."

Mike Callahan let out a grunt. "Yeah? I'll expect you to charge a nice low fee, then. Now here's the deal . . ."

After that he saw Mike Callahan quite often, and gradually much of the legal work of the Callahan Construction Company found its way to Morris, Clayton, Biddle and Wharton.

So that was the way things went. It was a smooth, successful life, although nothing about it seemed very important. Fortunately there were things to do around the city that kept him interested. The Board of Judges and the Bar Association decided to make a study of the magistrates' courts, and asked him to head the committee. A group of top businessmen formed the Greater Philadelphia Movement, and Anthony helped write the new City Charter and push it through. There were jobs in connection with City-County Consolidation and Penn Center and the new Food Distribution Center. You could work on projects like those and keep your hands clean; whatever fights you got into were on a pleasantly high level. So it was a nice life, and probably even useful.

He saw Louis Donetti often during those years. Louis was in City Council now, and swung a lot of weight in the South Philadelphia wards. If you wanted aid from Council on a civic project, Louis was a good man to know, because he played politics the way an expert plays three-cushion billiards. Anthony found him very helpful. He knew, of course, that Louis as a practical politician would expect the favors returned someday, and therefore he was not surprised when the day came.

Anthony's appointment list for that day merely carried the note: "Donetti, 11 a.m.," so he knew something was up when Louis arrived not alone but with Mike Callahan. They sat around for a few minutes telling him how well he looked. Finally Louis said, "The little matter we came about, Tony, is about me. You're not gonna get upset because your old pal Louis wants some help."

"You've got me softened up. Bring it out in the light."

Louis smiled at him like a cherub in an old Italian fresco. "Like you may have heard, I'm kinda in politics. Some of my friends," he said, looking abashed, "think I ought to run for Mayor."

"Wow," Anthony muttered.

Mike said anxiously, "What do you think of it, Tony?"

"I'd like to hear what Louis thinks of it, leaving out the stuff about being forced into it at gun point."

"You're a practical guy," Louis said, "so I'll give it to you without any gift wrapping. I'm a politician. I want to get ahead. Maybe in the old days I'd have played the game all the big boys did. Build up a machine. Grab patronage. Buy votes. Rake in graft. But that don't go nowadays. Offer them a handout? They laugh at you. They got unemployment compensation or relief. Offer them jobs? Most jobs are under Civil Service. Graft? Sure, you can still graft. But you can't be sure of staying in office and covering up. So the way to play it now is straight, see? Pass out just enough favors and jobs to keep the ward leaders sullen but quiet, and make your real play for the independent vote. That means good government. That's the Donetti platform."

Anthony grinned. "I think there's a nasty hunk of idealism hiding in that cynicism of yours."

Mike said, "What do you think of him, Tony?"

"I think he'd make a good Mayor."

"Give it to us straight," Louis said. "You think I couldn't win."

"All right. I don't think you'd have a prayer. You're a Republican. The Republican machine in this town is strictly from the junk yard. The Democrats are in office. They came in on a reform ticket. They made reforms."

"That was the last four years," Louis said. "Now reform is getting to be a dirty word around City Hall. I got nothing against Democrats. I just like a two-party system, is all."

"I couldn't agree with you more," Anthony said. "But that still doesn't elect you Mayor. Don't get sore, Louis, but outside of South Philadelphia they never heard of you."

"I worked it out the same way," Louis said. "So I figured first I would run for District Attorney, and then four years later make a pass at being Mayor."

"What we want to know," Mike said, "is will you back us up if Louis runs for D.A.? You could pull in the business crowd."

"I'm with you," Anthony said. "But I still don't think it will work."

"Yes it will," Louis said. "There's one little point we didn't mention yet. We got just the right gimmick to make it work."

"I don't believe you. What is it?"

"You'll love it," Louis crooned. "First *you* run for District Attorney. First *you* run for Mayor. Nice, huh?"

Anthony jumped up. He said angrily, "That's a hell of a way to try to trap a guy."

"If any trapping has been done," Louis said softly, "you did it to yourself, pal. You've been running for Mayor ever since you started playing that Robin Hood game in the magistrates' courts. You've been like a dame at a beach sticking her toes in the water and squealing so everybody will look at her. Well, dive in, pal, dive in!"

"What gives you crazy guys the idea I could win an election?"

"Oh Lord," Louis said. "On top of everything we have to teach him politics. You got sex appeal, pal. The little guy never forgets a big guy who goes out of his way to help him. We plug that Robin Hood angle in the right places, and you get a hundred and fifty thousand votes. We plug that work you did on the magistrates' courts and on Penn Center and the rest, and you get a hundred and fifty thousand independent votes. Mike, here, twists the arms of some of the ward leaders and you got a hundred thousand organization votes. I pull fifty thousand votes for you in South

Philly. You rate with the business and society crowd, and that gives you five thousand votes and all the dough we need. That's four hundred and fifty-five thousand votes, pal. Only seven hundred and seven thousand votes were cast in the last election for D.A. You got it made. Four years later you're a shoo-in for Mayor."

Anthony paced up and down the office, his visitors watching him. He said finally, "It was all a gag about Louis running, was it?"

"It's no gag," Louis said. "But I'm not the guy to break the hold the Democrats have on this city. You're the guy. I'll back you for D.A. and run for Council again. When you run for Mayor, I can make it as D.A. When everybody admits you've done a good job as Mayor but hates your guts for doing it, and after you've had a second term if you can take the punishment, little Louis will run for Mayor."

"You certainly make it sound attractive."

"Who wants to make it sound attractive? You'll have to get right down in the middle of the people, pal. A lot of them eat garlic and don't wash enough. We're not inviting you to join a country club. We're asking you to run a big tough city."

Anthony said, "I don't even live here. I live in Haverford."

"We know where you live," Louis said. "It doesn't matter if you do live in Haverford, because you could move back here in time."

"Grace would never move into town in a million years. You don't know what you're asking me to give up."

Louis said, "If you didn't have to give up anything, you wouldn't be worth putting up for office."

Anthony stared at the two men for a moment. "I'll have to think it over," he muttered. "I'll have to talk to Grace. How much time will you give me?"

"Until tomorrow morning," Louis said promptly.

"You turn on the heat pretty hard, don't you?"

"Listen," Louis said, "you've had your mind made up on this for years. Only you don't know which way it's made up, and neither do we. Whatever it is, you aren't gonna change it. You could find out if you thought about it for two hours, but you have a right to see your wife first. Tomorrow morning. Or call Mike any time tonight if you want."

They got up and walked out slowly, without shaking hands or giving him another glance.

H<small>E</small> <small>SAT</small> at the dinner table across from Grace, trying to find the right moment to bring up the subject. It was hard to start. There would never be a right moment to bring up this subject.

"I had a couple of visitors today," he said. "Mike Callahan and Louis Donetti. You remember Louis."

She gave a shudder. "I certainly do. A very unpleasant man."

"He's all right when you get to know him."

"You work with the strangest people in that civic work you do. Sometimes I think you do more than your share of it."

"I wonder what a person's share is. And if we do enough of it."

She smiled at him. "Poor Tony. Something's nagging at your conscience, isn't it? What did Mr. Callahan and Donetti want?"

He took a deep breath. "They want me to run for District Attorney in the next election and for Mayor four years later."

The smile balanced delicately on her lips. "How ridiculous."

"That's what I told them. But they wouldn't accept it. I ended up saying I wanted to talk to you and that I'd give them my answer by tomorrow morning."

"That was very tactful of you, Tony."

"I wasn't being tactful," he said. "I needed time to decide."

That erased the smile. "Oh, Tony," she said. "Time to decide! The whole idea is impossible and you know it."

"It's not as impossible as you think. They both believe I could win and they have some good arguments. Let me tell you why they think I ought to run." He gave her the facts and said, "So it's not ridiculous or impossible at all, don't you see?"

She had listened quietly, with no sound except a light clicking of her fingernails on the Duncan Phyfe table. "Tony darling," she said, "my remark had nothing to do with whether or not you could win. I admit you'd be a strong candidate. The thing is impossible because it simply doesn't fit into our way of life."

"We've got something pretty fine here, have we?"

"Oh really, Tony! You're not going to begin questioning the way we live? Would you even for a moment consider trading this for politics? Letting your name be bandied around? Moving into the city with all its dirt and noise and crime? And can you see me campaigning for you on street corners!" She laughed pleasantly and rose from the table. "I'm going to round up the children and see they get started for bed."

She smiled at him and went out of the room, a slim straight goddess, at home in her temple and very sure of herself. He sighed, and got up and went into the living room. It was a very pleasant way of life, of course. Neat and hygienic, insulated against rude noises. A lovely wife and two swell kids and a blue-chip career. Grace had strong arguments on her side. The trouble was that she hadn't argued with him. She had coolly taken the decision out of his hands. He was going to talk to her some more about it.

He finished the *Evening Bulletin*. It was odd that Grace was taking so long with the kids. He went upstairs and looked in at the boys. Grace wasn't there and the kids were asleep. He walked down the hallway and saw light showing under the door of her dressing room. He rapped and called, and she told him to come in. She was sitting in her peignoir at the dressing table with her back to him. As he entered she turned.

"Tony," she said, in an oddly husky voice, "I have been thinking. I was going to call you in a few minutes."

"Were you?"

"I wasn't fair to you when we were talking at dinner. I realized that afterward. I just brushed it all aside, didn't I?"

"You were a little rough," he said. His hands touched her gleaming hair and traced the curve of her neck.

"You deserve better than that from me," she said, trembling under his hands. She got up quickly, and turned and moved close to him. "Tony," she went on tensely, "you know I'd never tag along with you into politics. You know that, don't you? It would mean a separation, Tony. I'd stay here and keep the boys, and you'd have to go your way alone. But I'm not going to let that happen. I want to keep you. Do you know why?"

"I'm not sure I do."

"Tony, can't you stop thinking for at least a few minutes?"

He ran his hands along her shoulders. He didn't want his emotions to get out of control but it was not easy to keep them in line. He gathered her into his arms. She was no longer a cool goddess, she was watching him with wide questioning eyes.

"Tony," she whispered, "something has happened to me tonight. Tony, after seven years of being married, would it be silly for me to tell you that I'm in love with you?"

He didn't answer.

"It makes a difference, doesn't it? You couldn't leave me now, could you?"

He bent to kiss her. It was strange to find her lips so warm and yielding. "Yes, it makes a difference," he said. "It makes it just that much harder to decide. I'm going downstairs and think it over."

Behind him, as he closed the door to the room, he heard the weeping start.

HE CAME downstairs slowly, with the pulse of blood hammering inside his skull like a rivet gun.

He went into the library and lowered himself into the desk chair. The pounding in his head made him dizzy, and for a moment his thoughts whirled like autumn leaves in a gale. He had to work hard to sweep them into neat piles. His name was Anthony Judson Lawrence and he was forty-two years old. He had come here to make a decision. He had made a number of important decisions in his life, but this one would be the most important of all.

When you were a lawyer you did not make snap decisions. You looked up the law and the precedents that bore on the case. He would do that now. There were ninety-nine years of precedents to be studied. He had been building his whole life on them, and adding new ones to the record. He unlocked a drawer of the desk and took out a photograph in an old German-silver frame.

There they were, the three wonderful and rather frightening women who had created many of those precedents. His great-grandmother and grandmother were standing behind a chair. His mother was seated on it with a baby on her lap. The three women were staring at the baby, who was looking up with wide eyes as if asking what they wanted of him. The baby's name was Anthony Judson Lawrence.

As he studied the photograph now he could feel the blood of the three women pulsing through his body and their ideas marching through his head. He knew what their hopes and beliefs had been. But he didn't know why they had clung to certain hopes and followed certain beliefs. It was like reading a judge's decision, and knowing you ought to abide by it, without having a chance to look at the testimony that came before. He wished he could have read the testimony of their lives, because it would have helped him now.

However, he could read the testimony of his own life. A dozen times he had been faced by the need to make an important decision. What he had done, each time, had been to a great extent decided for him by the lives and hopes and beliefs of the three women in the photograph. So he could learn something about them, and about himself, by going to the record of those decisions.

He took each one out of its filing place in his mind and examined it carefully. There was a long line of them; some had been hard to make, some rather easy, some painful to remember, some that made him feel fairly good. What made each of them important was that a different decision could have changed the course of his life. He put them in question form and examined the moral problem that each contained:

Should a teen-age kid sell out his gang to help his mother?

Should a boy who is unhappy at school try once more to make a go of it, just to please his family?

Should you give up a chance to star in football because the coach says it will help the team?

Which Salutatory are you going to give — the brilliant and radical one, or the dull safe one?

Should you ask a girl to put off marrying you and having the babies she wants badly, because you don't think it's right to let somebody else support you?

Will you let passion outweigh the rules of conduct and lead you into an affair with a married woman?

Will you stick your neck out for a general who doesn't mean a thing personally to you, merely because he's doing a good job and needs to be helped out of a jam?

Are you willing, because you want to get ahead fast, to try to steal a big client from another lawyer, when you know that the slightest mistake will wreck the career you want?

Will you agree to defend a bum named Chet Gwynne, although that too may wreck your career?

Will you carry your defense of Gwynne to the absolute limit, and put your own class of society on trial?

Well, he had made a decision in all those cases, except the last one. He had managed to find a side exit and avoid making that decision. But right now, tonight, that decision was back again, in only slightly different form. Will a man who has everything he has struggled to win pick a different way of life? It was harder to decide, because he had just found out he had won a final thing which he had wanted. Grace was in love with him.

But was he really facing a different way of life in the career Mike Callahan and Louis Donetti had mapped out for him? When you came right down to it, wouldn't it be the same way of life he had always followed — one of risk, struggle and great rewards for himself, yet with an opportunity for giving help to others? In fact, Anthony thought, it would be the logical next step in his growth.

Suddenly Anthony knew that he didn't have to make a decision after all. It had been pieced together for him over the long slow years. The decision was there waiting for him, already made.

He lifted the telephone and dialed a number. After a minute the growl of Mike Callahan rumbled across the wires. "Yeah?"

"This is Tony."

"Yeah, I knew when I picked up the phone."

"I'm with you, Mike."

There was a rather long silence.

Anthony said, "Did you hear me?"

"Yeah," Mike said, more hoarsely than usual. "I heard you." He paused and then said, "Thanks for calling, Tony. Louis and I will drop in on you tomorrow. Good night."

"Good night," Anthony said, and slowly hung up the phone.

A light footstep sounded at the doorway, and Grace came in. Her face looked pale. "I heard your telephone call," she said. "I've been sitting outside the door for two hours, waiting for you to make it. I knew you were going to make it, and what you were going to say."

"You know me fairly well, don't you?"

She walked to the window and parted the curtains and stared out. "You can see the glow of the city from here, can't you?" she said. "It's not the sort of view most people think of, when they talk of the lights of a city. They're thinking about diamonds on black velvet. All you can see from here is just a big dirty glow, made up of tiny particles of dust and fog that pick up the shine of electricity. It's hard to believe that anybody can have a love affair with a city. And yet some people do."

He didn't know what was in her mind, so he didn't answer.

She turned and pulled the curtains shut behind her. "Where will we live, Tony?" she said, going toward him. "Are there still some good addresses left in town?"

Richard Powell

THE AUTHOR of *The Philadelphian* comes from a long line of Philadelphians himself. Born in the Quaker City in 1908, Richard Powell went to work as a police reporter on the *Philadelphia Evening Ledger* after his graduation from Princeton in 1930, and tried to eke out a meager salary by writing on the side. Not a line sold, he says, until suddenly, in June 1936, three leading magazines each bought a story.

In 1940 Mr. Powell joined N. W. Ayer & Son, a leading advertising agency, leaving two years later to become a first lieutenant in Army Public Relations. Later he served in the Southwest Pacific as a lieutenant colonel on General MacArthur's staff. Even during his war service he managed to produce three adventure-mystery novels.

After a period of postwar free-lancing, Mr. Powell returned to N. W. Ayer, where he is now a vice-president. He lives with his wife and two children in Merion Station, Pennsylvania.

A Family

A condensation of the book by

John O'Hara

Illustrations by Robert Fawcett

Party

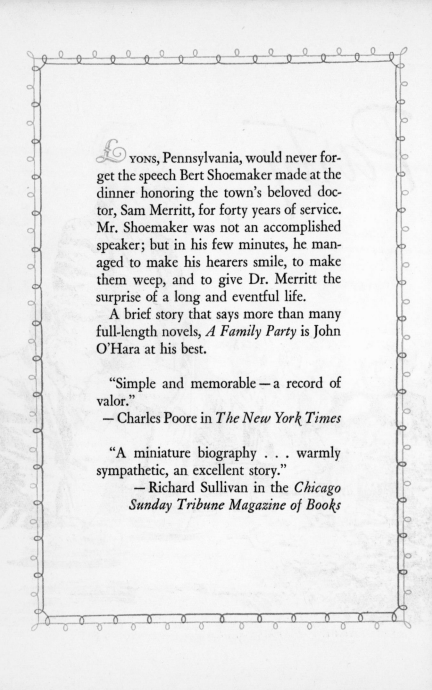

$\mathcal{L}$YONS, Pennsylvania, would never forget the speech Bert Shoemaker made at the dinner honoring the town's beloved doctor, Sam Merritt, for forty years of service. Mr. Shoemaker was not an accomplished speaker; but in his few minutes, he managed to make his hearers smile, to make them weep, and to give Dr. Merritt the surprise of a long and eventful life.

A brief story that says more than many full-length novels, *A Family Party* is John O'Hara at his best.

"Simple and memorable — a record of valor."
— Charles Poore in *The New York Times*

"A miniature biography . . . warmly sympathetic, an excellent story."
— Richard Sullivan in the *Chicago Sunday Tribune Magazine of Books*

The following is a stenographic report of an address by Mr. Albert W. Shoemaker, president of the Shoemaker Printing Company and former editor and publisher of the Lyons Republican, *at a dinner in honor of Dr. Samuel G. Merritt. The dinner, which took place on September 17, 1955, in the main dining room of the Lyons Hotel, Lyons, Pennsylvania, commemorated the forty years of Dr. Merritt's service to Lyons and surrounding communities and to wish him well upon his retirement from active practice of his profession.*

The affair was sponsored jointly by the Lyons Rotary Club, Kiwanis, Lions, Junior Chamber of Commerce, Patriotic Order Sons of America, Knights of Columbus, Benevolent & Protective Order of Elks, Ancient Order of Hibernians, Knights of Pythias, Ministerial Association, Holy Name Society, Veterans of Foreign Wars, American Legion, Lyons Gun Club, Merchants Association, Boy Scouts of America, Order of the Eastern Star, American Red Cross, Daughters of Isabella, Delphian Society, United Mine Workers of America, and the Nesquehela County Medical Society.

More than two hundred persons, including many prominent in business, labor, industry and the professions, were present at the dinner. The invocation was by the Reverend Father Alexis P. Smirnolinski, pastor of St. Boniface R.C. Church, after which the toastmaster, Mr. Cyril V. Longenecker, introduced several leading out-of-town visitors, who were called upon for brief remarks. They were followed by the address by Mr. Shoemaker, who was the principal speaker of the evening.

The benediction was asked by the Reverend Eustace Muhlenberg Fry, rector of the Lyons Methodist Episcopal Church. Music was provided by the Lyons High School Orchestra under the leadership of Miss Charline K. Smith, B.M.

MR. TOASTMASTER, Distinguished Guests, Reverend Members of the Clergy, and Ladies and Gentlemen:

Back in February, when a few of us old-timers accidentally discovered that we had in our midst a man who had held the same job for close on to forty years, that seemed such a remarkable accomplishment in these days that a few of us decided we ought to do something about it. This town of ours used to be an important railroad center, before they put in the buses and before the business of mining coal was all shot to — well, a certain place that I understand they have all the coal they need, if the reverend clergy will pardon me.

I mention the railroads because when they were prosperous, one of the greatest honors a man could have was the watch that the railroad company gave a man when he retired. I used to sometimes wonder why they gave a railroader a watch when he retired instead of when he started out, but of course the railroads used to do a lot of things I could never understand, but that's not saying I don't wish we still had them with us. But as I was saying, it was an honor when the company gave a man a watch, and the reason why a man was so proud of his watch was because it meant something. It represented something.

What did it represent? It represented that a man had given thirty or forty years of faithful service to his company and to his community, out in all kinds of weather, often performing his duties at the risk of his very life. Railroading was hard work and not only hard work physically. A man had to keep on his toes. If you wanted to go from brakeman to fireman or fireman to engineman, you had to study the rules and pass difficult examinations that if you ever saw the examination for fireman, I wonder how many college graduates could pass it today.

Well, ladies and gentlemen, the more we thought of it the more we decided that we had in our midst a friend of ours who had held a job for forty years, and while he wasn't a brakeman on the railroad, or an engineman, still he had been serving his community that long, and he was entitled to some recognition. Of course you all know who I am talking about, so I guess I can take the liberty of saying that this old friend of ours, he held his job for forty years. Sure he did. Why? Nobody could fire him.

But seriously, if you want to look at it that way, I'm wrong, because to put it another way, there wasn't a man or woman in Lyons or nearby communities that couldn't fire him. But nobody ever did that I know of, so we had to give him credit for keeping his job for forty years with more bosses than anybody I can think of. Not to take anything away from those of you who worked on the railroads, but this friend of ours was every bit as important as any engineman or fireman, and I'm sure some of you will agree with me that maybe he was a little more important. I could look around this room right now and see the faces of some former railroaders that wouldn't be here tonight if it hadn't been for the friend we are honoring this evening.

And I guess anybody that's old enough can remember how desperately he worked the night of the Short Mountain wreck. That was the time when an 1800-type locomotive ran away and plowed into the Bug loaded with a hundred and eighty miners on their way home from work. For the benefit of the younger ones present, the Bug was the name they gave to the train that took the miners up to Short Mountain and Outerbridge Colliery. They killed fourteen miners not counting members of the crew, and when I was in the Army in France in 1918 I still never saw anything to compare with that rear car of the Bug. I don't want to turn your stomachs with a description of the carnage that evening.

I was reporting on my father's newspaper, the good old Lyons *Republican* that I unfortunately couldn't keep its head above water after 1929, and when we heard there was a wreck up on Short Mountain my father sent me up there to cover it, and all I can tell you is that I wish it had been my day off. We got the word just about as soon as anybody because we used to publish the *Republican* in the building where Hartman's Garage is now, right across from the old freight station, and somebody mentioned it to my father and they were making up a train to go up there to the scene of the wreck. They had young boys going around to the doctors' offices and trying to get miners that had first-aid experience and any National Guard men that could be of assistance.

We only had the three doctors in town then and I remember thinking when I got on the train, they had two of the doctors, but I didn't see Sam Merritt. "Where is Sam Merritt?" I asked myself. Well, I could have saved my breath, because when we reached the scene of the wreck, Sam was there already. But I'll tell you this much. At first I couldn't recognize him. And I'll leave it to your imagination what his face was covered with that I couldn't recognize him. How did Sam happen to be the first there? The first doctor? Well, it's a good question, and I'm not taking anything from the other doctors we had then or since, but I never knew a man like Sam Merritt for being there when he was needed.

Well, I took a look at Sam and he took a look at me, and then he put me to work. There was nobody standing around that night, taking notes. He worked us all so hard that we hardly got any chance to show any signs of weakness. We got help from Johnsville, and also from Singerstown and Mountain View, and by the time it was dark, some of the doctors and nurses from Gibbsville and Fort Penn, but the commander in chief was Sam Merritt, and we'll never know how many miners had their lives saved because Sam was on the scene so quickly after it happened.

Later on, weeks later, I happened to think of that and I asked Sam, I said, "How did you happen to get there so soon the evening of the wreck?" And do you know what his answer was? His answer was typical, I mean typical of how a doctor can never call his time his own. He said he had a new 16-gauge, a Fox I remember it was, 16-gauge Fox in the back of his tin Lizzie and he'd been meaning for days to take it out and fire a few rounds just to get the feel of it, and this particular day he decided that he'd put it off long enough and he was going to fire that gun no matter whose baby didn't get delivered or who got the croup.

So he took the back road out by Schwarzwald's and was looking for a place to stop and get in a little shooting and suddenly he heard the crash. It was suppertime almost, but he had no trouble locating the crash because the boiler blew up and the rear car caught fire. Right away he guessed what happened. Back went the new gun and Sam drove as near as he could to the scene of the wreck and went the rest on foot. And just to show you that the world isn't full of men like Sam Merritt, somebody stole the gun from the back of the Ford. While he was tending to the injured and dying, somebody went up to his car and stole the shotgun out of the back seat of the car and he never laid eyes on it again.

Well, maybe some of you good people are wondering a little about this speech of mine, if you can call it a speech, so I guess I better tell you how it all happened. I think everybody, or at least everybody from town, all know that Sam Merritt is my best friend and has been since we were boys together. As boys we weren't too close. We didn't get along very well. I never thought much of him and he never thought much of me, but there weren't so many boys the same age, so there was only the four or five white boys and two colored that played together then, and Sam and I were in that bunch. We all used to go out the Glen swimming, or get chased off coal cars and empty freights, and sometimes get caught stealing apples out of Mrs. Fiddler's orchard. Halloween we used to take gates off people's fences, or chalk up their sidewalks — where there were sidewalks — or barns, if they didn't have any sidewalks.

Lyons was a great deal different then than it is now, when we were boys. When we were boys they didn't have any radio or television and Sol Pollock hadn't even started up his movie house. You could count the automobiles on the fingers of one hand, and the hose company had a hand pumper that we also pulled by hand, or the firemen did. We just ran along after them.

Oh, there were a great many things we have now that we didn't have then, but I can tell you a few things we had then that we don't have now and one of them is trees. You wouldn't know it now, but almost every house in Lyons had its tree in front of it, and sometimes two, and I know in our back yard we had four apple trees and two oxheart cherry trees and two or maybe three sickle pears and a grape arbor. All I have to do is shut my eyes and remember how Lyons looked thirty, forty years ago when we still had trees.

Now instead of trees we have parking meters on Main Street and Market Street and very few trees anywheres else.

But I started to tell you good people how I happened to be making this speech this evening. I didn't ask to do it, I guarantee you that. But when we began talking among ourselves about giving a banquet in honor of Sam Merritt we had several discussions about asking somebody prominent like the Governor or maybe some famous doctor or somebody like that. But the more we thought of it the more we wanted to make it what you might call a family party. You won't find anybody here tonight that's a stranger to Sam Merritt. We're all either his friends or related to him, and that includes those from out of town that you heard earlier this evening.

We could have got the Governor to come here this evening, but we decided that if we got somebody like the Governor it would make it a different kind of a party. Sam Merritt was never much for show and I doubt if he would have permitted us to hold this dinner if it got too elaborate. In fact he said so.

Well, you can't have a party like this without there being a speaker, and the more we went ahead with the preparations the more I noticed that they didn't say anything about who the speaker was going to be. Then finally about two weeks ago I brought it up at a meeting of the committee and the other fellows looked at each other and laughed and I think it was Reese Evans said to me, "Bert, you're it."

"Me?" I said.

"That's right. You. Bert Shoemaker."

"But the dinner's only about two weeks off," I said. I said, "I can't go to work and prepare a speech in two weeks."

"We know that," said Reese. "That's why we didn't tell you before. We don't want a speech. All we want you to do is stand up on your two feet and kind of reminisce about Sam. You're his best friend and you know him better than anybody else and you won't spill all over with sentimental hogwash."

"That you can be sure of," I said. "Because if I did the first person to leave the room would be Samuel G. Merritt, M.D." So that's how I happened to get picked as the speaker. They allowed me to write down a few notes that I could refer to in case I got stuck for something to say, but that's all. I have these notes here, and just let me hold them up for you to see and you'll readily understand that I wasn't allowed to do much preparation.

So far I haven't referred to my notes but I think I ought to start touching on some of the highlights and I notice I have written down here the word *Family*. People don't seem to care so much about family any more, and that being the case, I wouldn't be surprised if half the people in this room, especially the younger ones, don't know a great deal about Sam's family history.

For their benefit, Sam was born right here in Lyons in the year 1887. His father was Isaac Merritt and Isaac was born here too. The family originally came here from Connecticut by way of York State, and I understand the road they have called the Merritt Parkway was named after some family connection, although you'll have to verify that with Sam as that's only my impression. But that's what the stock was. New England. Then in 1883 Sam's father married Miss Frieda Langendorf, and the Langendorfs are an old Lyons family, which most of you know. The Langendorfs built the first trolley line here and I guess there wasn't much accomplished around here that the Langendorfs didn't have something to do with.

Sam was the second son of that union. He had an older brother,

Isaac Junior, known as Boo for some reason I couldn't fathom. Boo received an appointment to the United States Naval Academy at Annapolis, Maryland, and he was in his third year there doing extremely well when he contracted spinal meningitis and passed away at the age of twenty. He was the tallest of the Merritt family and some said he grew too fast. That may be, but I can tell you all the girls fell for him when he came home on vacation in his Annapolis midshipman's uniform. In those days we used to have a dance at Christmas at the Odd Fellows Hall and the rest of us weren't in it when Boo was around.

Boo passing away was very hard on Sam not only because they were very close for two brothers about the same age, but also Sam had the responsibility of being the oldest of the Merritt children. There was Victoria, now Mrs. J. J. Singer, and Dorothy, Mrs. D. W. Schleicher, of Johnsville, both ladies it is my pleasure to see here tonight observing the affair in honor of their older brother. Then there was Oscar Merritt, Sam's younger brother, who passed away at the age of six of typhoid, so I guess you couldn't call him a responsibility when Boo died, although naturally Mr. and Mrs. Merritt must have thought back to their early loss when Boo died, and that was a sort of a responsibility for Sam, too.

I often think it was Boo that decided Sam to become a doctor. When he passed away, that is. Up to then I don't remember Sam ever saying much about being a doctor. When we were young boys together I would have said Sam would grow up to be a carpenter. Carpenter and builder. In those days a master carpenter could build a house and all the help he needed was an apprentice. By the time Sam was fourteen or fifteen years of age, he was the handiest with tools in our bunch, and one summer when he was fifteen or sixteen, he put in new shelves and bins and one counter in his father's store. He did it all by himself.

Today I guess Sam has the best amateur carpentry shop in town down in the cellar of his house, and a lot of us here tonight have articles of furniture that Sam made in his own shop, just for pleasure. Very fine workmanship, too. Not only articles of furniture but also the gavel they use at Rotary, that was made by Sam. The pulpit at the M.E. church, that was made by Sam, not to mention countless cigar humidors and things for the ladies to keep their sewing in.

I often heard Sam say he could make more cash money as a carpenter than as a doctor, because people pay their carpenter before they pay their doctor, but I promised I wouldn't say anything about that because I don't think anybody'd have the nerve to show their face here if they owed Sam for an unpaid bill. I wouldn't think of mentioning that, because I don't think anybody'd drive here in a nice new sedan if they still owed Sam for medical attention a year or two ago. So I won't say anything about that.

Nobody has to make excuses for not paying Sam the money they owe him, because Sam makes up their excuses himself. I remember saying to him some years ago, I said I noticed that a certain family were sending their son away to college and they seemed to forget they owed Sam over eight hundred dollars. "Well," said Sam, "eight hundred dollars will only pay for one semester and if the boy's no good and flunks out at the end of the one semester, that'll be a heartache for the parents. And if the boy finishes and makes a good showing, I'll get some satisfaction out of knowing that I helped put him through." That's the kind of story that everybody here can tell about Sam Merritt.

I used to try to persuade him to leave his money at home when he went out on his calls because if he had twenty-five dollars in his pocket when he went out, that was no guarantee that he was going to have twenty-five when he got home.

"At least don't give away more than you earn in a day," I used to say to him. But Sam would take a look at some poor family and how they were living, or existing, and before he got home that evening he'd have an order of groceries and meat and clothes for the children on their way to the poor family.

I guess if there's one man here tonight that knows more about this than I do it's Reverend Smirnolinski, because he had more poor people in his parish than the other denominations. If you want to know what the Irish think of Sam Merritt you ought to take a look at some of the embroidery tablecloths and napkins the Sisters made for the Merritt family. And don't think that makes Sam any the less a good Methodist, because it doesn't. Sam's a good

Mason and I don't have to say any more on that subject because I just got the signal to pipe down, but I think you get my meaning.

I was saying a minute ago that when he was a young fellow in his teens, I didn't think Sam Merritt would ever be a doctor. Take high school. In botany he was all right, but when he had biology Sam would turn green when he had to dissect a frog. As far as any of us know, there was never a doctor in the Merritt or the Langendorf family, and the nearest thing to it was I understand the Merritt store did a thriving business in Peruna. That was a medicine that you didn't need a prescription for and it cured all your aches and pains. Some people took Peruna that wouldn't permit you to mention the name of Old Overholt, but the one made you feel just as good as the other.

One summer Sam got a job tending the soda fountain at Brown's but he didn't learn anything about medicine that summer. I had the same job another summer and we used to close at half past nine, but it was always near eleven before I got home by the time I got finished washing the soda glasses and ice-cream dishes and packing down those cans with ice and mixing syrup for the next day. Nobody had time to learn anything on that job. Except how smart old Doc Brown was, hiring a young fellow that thought he was going to gorge himself on ice cream and paying him two dollars a week and working him so hard he didn't even have time to eat up the profits.

But I'm not up here to pay compliments to old Doc Brown and his business ability. You wanted somebody to take a cinder out of your eye, Doc was as efficient at that as any professional man. Or, a little indigestion, Doc would give you a glass of soda water, or somebody'd faint and they'd be revived in Doc Brown's drugstore. In fact, Brown's drugstore in those days was the closest we had to a hospital here in Lyons. The collieries had shacks where injured men would be taken and put in bed till it was time to move them to the hospital in Fort Penn. But if someone got hurt anywhere near Doc Brown's drugstore, that's where they'd take him. And when Sam finally did go away to medical college, when he came home for vacation he always used to sit and talk to Doc Brown in those two big easy chairs Doc had in the back of the drugstore.

Doc would sit there in one of those big easy chairs and without getting up he could see who was in the store. I guess a lot of people used to wonder how Doc Brown would know they were in the store. Well, I'll tell you. He had a peephole. There was a row of medicine bottles on a shelf that stood between the store proper and the back room. Well, there was an empty place in that row of bottles and from where he sat Doc could see through that vacant place and watch the people come in the front door.

One time when I was about fourteen years old, I went in the store and Doc was in the back and I didn't think he heard me. So I helped myself to two Philadelphia Hand-Mades and stuck them in my pocket. Then I called out, "Anybody here?" and Doc came out and waited on me. I guess I was getting something for my mother or father, and whatever it was, I said to charge it, and Doc said to me, "Want me to put the cigars on the bill or will you pay for them yourself? Since when did your father start smoking cigars?"

Well, I guess Doc Brown and Sam Merritt had many an interesting chat after Sam started going to medical college. I noticed since then that other Lyons boys that studied medicine used to drop in and loaf around at Doc Brown's till they got started building up a practice, although in a town like Lyons there was always plenty of work for a doctor if he didn't care when he got paid. I guess that's the same everywhere, not only Lyons.

The established men, they got so much a year being company doctor at one of the collieries, and so much for various lodges, and usually the Protestant doctors got all the Protestants and the Catholic doctor got all the Catholics, and one of the older doctors would get the Reading Railway and the other would get the Pennsy. What was left for the young fellow just starting out was pretty slim pickings and some of it we don't have to talk about in mixed company. I know this much, that in 1915, when Sam Merritt hung out his shingle, I was getting eighteen a week working for my father on the old *Republican* and Sam was Dr. Samuel G. Merritt, I was a married man with a wife and daughter and Sam didn't feel he could afford to get married yet. Of course I didn't have to have my own tin Lizzie and buy surgical instruments and things like that.

Perhaps it would be fitting here if I went back to what I was saying about Boo Merritt and how when he passed away it decided Sam to be a doctor. Up to then Sam wouldn't even help out if a mare was having a colt, and I told you how he felt about dissecting. I'll tell you this much too. Sam Merritt the first time he ever saw a real operation fainted. He told me that himself. That was at the Jefferson Medical College in Philadelphia and he just keeled over. Well, a man that wanted to be a doctor that bad must have had some underlying reason for it, and according to the way I look at it, Sam was so incensed over what happened to Boo that he began to wonder or say to himself, "If I can prevent that, it's my job to prevent it."

Well, I don't think Sam said it in so many words. But if you look at Sam's whole career as a doctor and as a man, I never saw anybody like Sam for wanting to right a wrong. I don't say Sam resolved to find a cure for spinal meningitis, nothing like that. But Boo passing away just showed Sam that there was a way he could right wrongs and make it his lifework.

Sam began having long talks with Dr. George Steever, and there is a man that ought to be here tonight to give us the full story of how Sam finally made his decision, because if it hadn't of been for Dr. George Steever, in my opinion Sam never would have gone to medical college. They gave Dr. Steever a celebration years ago when he retired to St. Petersburg, Florida, and this party is for Sam Merritt. But it wouldn't be complete if I didn't mention the late Dr. George Steever. He used to let Sam go along with him on his calls and that way Sam got a firsthand look at what it would be like to be a doctor, and of course we have to give Dr. Steever credit for recognizing Sam's ability. Or maybe not ability, because Sam didn't have any ability then, but Dr. Steever had the insight to realize that Sam would make a good doctor and helped him get into medical college and also convinced Mr. Isaac Merritt that it was worth going to all that expense. I just remembered now that I made a note of Dr. Steever and here I mentioned him without consulting my notes.

Well, since I took a look at my notes I might as well take a good look and see what I have down here. *Hobbies.* I guess if you didn't know it before you know it now, that Sam always liked to go gunning. That was one hobby. I wouldn't be surprised if Sam brought down as many as fifteen deer in the space of thirty years.

Sam hardly ever took a real vacation but there was one day he kept sacred and that was the opening day of the hunting season, even if all he went out for was pheasant. If he ever came back with an empty pouch I never heard of it, because Sam was a very good shot with gun or rifle. He had a lot of patience. I don't mean that the way you took it. I meant the other kind of patience, not p-a-t-i-e-n-t-s. If Sam was convinced there was deer in a certain locality, he'd stand there like a statue till he got a shot at the animal. Sam could stand there with a chew of tobacco in his mouth and never move a muscle. Maybe I shouldn't have said that about chewing tobacco. But Sam chewed all his life and half the time I wouldn't know if he had a chew in or not. Most people didn't know he even chewed. Well, I guess that about covers gunning.

Carpentry I already spoke of. This do-it-yourself craze you hear so much about nowadays, Sam was ahead of the public by forty years. Other hobbies I won't mention because a Methodist isn't supposed to play cards. Well, anybody that ever played bridge or poker with a certain friend of ours, he didn't violate any religious scruples with the kind of bridge and poker he played. All I can say is that if Methodists aren't supposed to play bridge or poker, this friend of ours played like a Methodist.

Maybe the true test of how fond we are of this man is that any-body that even speaks to him, let alone attends a banquet for him, must be very fond of him after being his partner at a game of bridge. They tell the famous story of the fellow that was playing bridge one time and after he got set five tricks doubled and re-doubled and vulnerable, his partner said to him, "Herman, when did you learn to play bridge? Don't just say today, say what time today." That fits our friend to the letter.

Earlier in this talk, or remarks, or whatever you wish to call them, I spoke of Sam Merritt's service to the community. In my opinion it would have been enough just to have Sam Merritt attending to our aches and pains, great or small, and carrying us through our illnesses, major or minor. The majority of us here tonight have felt the touch of his hand on our pulse or had him tell us to say "Ah." We all felt better for having Sam in charge because we had the confidence that with Sam there beside us and looking after us, we had more than a doctor there. We had the instinctive feeling that here was a man that the thing he wanted most in the world was for us to get well, and if there was anything in his power, he'd see to it that we did.

I look around and see a lot of you nodding in agreement. Yes, so many of us have shared that experience in our acquaintance with Sam. Speaking from personal experience, he saved my life on two separate occasions. Once when I had pneumonia and the other time was when we were both about twenty and out swimming at the Glen I got cramps, and it was Sam that not only pulled me out but brought me to. Some of us are walking around with both legs or have the use of both hands that if it hadn't of been for Sam's care we would have been minus a limb. In all our memories as long as we live we'll all have some reason to be grateful to Sam Merritt. And it ought to be a great satisfaction to Sam, although the kind of man Sam is, I don't even think he gives that a thought. He would only consider that he had done his duty according to the oath of I am sorry to say I can't recall the name of the famous Greek person that made up the oath that all doctors are supposed to take.

But as though that were not sufficient to make an indelible impression on the history of our community, let us not, my friends, overlook his service to the community as a whole and not merely to individuals. For Samuel G. Merritt made a contribution to this community that to the best of my knowledge is not generally known.

Now I see our friend frowning at me because he is beginning to suspect the nature of what I am about to tell you and he would vastly prefer that I maintain silence on the subject. But this is a family party in which I see nobody here that does not belong here. Therefore in spite of the silent protest of our guest of honor, I consider it my duty at least once and for all to relate to you the true story of a service which he rendered the community.

Sam, you're just going to have to sit there and let me talk, so stop making faces at me.

Back in the middle of the nineteen twenties, and all the years preceding, if somebody from Lyons had to have a major operation or hospital care, they had their choice of two hospitals. The person could go to Gibbsville, thirty-five miles away, or they could go to Fort Penn, a distance of forty-four miles. In the old days when I was a boy the only ambulance we had was owned by the colliery and it was drawn by mules. If a miner got badly hurt in the mines they would bring him first to the first-aid shack and then put him in the ambulance and put him in the baggage car of the Pennsy train, the morning one or the evening one, and I don't have to tell you that half the time by the time the train was ready to leave, the injured man was beyond all assistance on this earth.

Later on the collieries had an automobile ambulance, but even that wasn't much of an improvement in bad weather. The roads from here to Gibbsville were usually drifted, or that old Winton would get engine trouble and there they'd be stuck halfway between here and Gibbsville till somebody came along and pulled them out. From here to Fort Penn was better, but not all that better.

Well, then came the great influenza epidemic of 1918 and the people around here were dying like flies. Odd Fellows Hall was turned into an emergency hospital and so was the Moose Hall. Sam and our other doctors used to work till they dropped and then they'd have a cup of coffee and start working some more. But all those conditions convinced Sam that we needed a hospital here in Lyons. So that was when Sam began his one-man campaign to raise funds for a hospital here.

You know what the first thing he did was? He put up all his savings, a little over $14,000, mortgaged his house for another ten, got his mother to donate a thousand, and he was in business. In other words, he was able to go around to people and say he had raised $25,000 toward a new hospital for Lyons.

But the lowest estimate he could get for a small hospital, completely equipped but with nothing fancy, was $300,000. So he went to his sisters and got between them another five thousand, and that way he was able to tell people that ten percent of the cost was already raised. He didn't bother to tell anybody that all the money had been raised inside his own family, mostly by Sam himself. Some of you easily remember what a campaign he put on. First he started with his friends, and he bled us dry, but Sam made it seem like a pleasure to dig down and give till it hurt and then give some more, as they used to say. The other two doctors in town put up five thousand apiece and more credit to them, because it was a lot of money in those days.

Of course everywhere Sam went to collect money or pledges, everybody said what about the coal companies? Why don't you get the money from them? But Sam said he was more anxious to have it a community enterprise first and save the coal companies for big contributions later, when more than half the money was raised. The same with the Union. Sam felt that if Lyons raised most of the money, the Union and the operators would be practically forced into putting up the balance.

Well, Sam was doing fine, pleading and persuading and badgering. All the town churches had euchres and bake sales and sold chances on this or that, and Rotary and Kiwanis and the fraternal organizations all chipped in, and Sam realized one day that he had in money and pledges just a little over $200,000. Now was the time to go to the coal companies and the Union!

Then the ax fell.

The day before he was going to call on the coal companies the miners went out on strike. That turned out to be a strike lasting from the first of September, '25, to the twelfth of February, '26. What a winter that was. Men standing around with nothing to do and no colliery whistles sounding in the hills, everybody short on rations or going to soup kitchens, and merchants wondering if they'd be able to stay open much longer. And who was the most unpopular man in Lyons? Not the superintendent, not the district leader of the Union. No, the most unpopular man was Sam Merritt, because he held onto the cash he had collected. He knew if he gave it back it would be twice as hard to collect again and he held onto it in two special accounts at the two town banks.

I am proud to confess that I gave one fellow a punch in the jaw right in the middle of Main Street when he hinted that the strike didn't worry Sam Merritt with all that money in the bank. And there was a lot of that kind of talk that I didn't hear firsthand or I would have had to give a few more socks in the jaw. I happened to know that the only meat Sam had in the house during the whole month of December was some venison he shot, and likewise he only had enough heat in the house to warm the first floor where the office was. A lot of people went to that office that didn't have much wrong with them but only wanted to keep warm.

Well, the strike was settled on Lincoln's Birthday and Sam and I had a little drink of schnapps to celebrate the occasion and he said he was going back to work. "Back to work?" I said.

"Back collecting for the hospital," he said. And so he did. Inside a week he was around getting a few pledges, then he tackled the coal companies. He got twenty thousand apiece from the two independents, but then when he went and called on the Nesquehela he got nothing but a cold stare.

"Why not?" he said.

"We have other plans," they said.

"Well, let me in on the plans. I've raised most of the money. It's all in the town banks. Every penny accounted for. It didn't cost a cent to collect the money, but we can't start to build without your contribution. We need seventy-five thousand," Sam pleaded.

"We have other plans," was all they'd say.

Then about two days later Sam had a visitor. Call him Dr. Blank. He's a blank as far as I'm concerned. He came into Sam's office and said, "Doctor, we've been hearing a lot about your little hospital, or at least your plans for a little hospital."

Sam said yes, and to go ahead. "Well," the other doctor said, "we've been having the same idea up in Johnsville."

"Oh, you have, have you? When did you first get your idea?"

"Well, when we got the idea doesn't make any difference. The point is we've raised some money too because we want the hospital to be in Johnsville."

"Why not Lyons? We've worked on this for a year," said Sam.

"Yes, but you've gone as far as you can without the contribution from Nesquehela."

"That's true," said Sam. "Why don't you come in with us and we'll have a Lyons-Johnsville hospital. We can go ahead without Nesquehela."

"Ah, but we have Nesquehela, and we want the hospital for Johnsville."

Sam picked up the phone and called the super and asked if it was true that Nesquehela was backing Johnsville. Yes, he was told, it was true. "And I suppose Dr. Blank is to be superintendent of the new Johnsville Hospital?" said Sam. Yes, that was true.

"All right, Doctor, you'll hear from me," said Sam.

I don't know what must have gone on in Sam's mind the next few hours, but I know that he sat down and wrote a letter that we printed and sent to every single person and organization that had contributed to the Lyons Hospital campaign. I could quote you the whole letter but what's the use. It explained what had happened, that Johnsville was also planning a hospital and had been promised the Nesquehela contribution, without which Lyons could not start to build. He then urged all who had contributed to the Lyons hospital to authorize him to turn the contribution over to Johnsville, because it would mean a much bigger and better-equipped institution, and after all Johnsville was only eight miles away.

Sam worded that letter so carefully that most people were convinced that it was their duty to turn the money over to Johnsville, and over eighty-five percent of them did. And this is something that nobody ever knew before tonight — namely, that included in the money that Johnsville got was the $30,000 that Sam raised inside his own family.

That's the kind of man we honor here tonight.

Now I hope Sam forgives me for telling that story. I know he won't hold it against me, because if Sam was the kind of a man that held things against people, that story never would have happened and I wouldn't be telling it tonight. I know this much: I would not have forgiven myself if I hadn't come out with the true facts on why Johnsville has a hospital and Lyons doesn't. And I could tell by the way you good people applauded that many of you were hearing it for the first time, and that does my heart good. I don't know of a better story that illustrates the bigness of Sam Merritt, a bigger man than his own personal, professional disappointment, bigger than envy, bigger than mere personal pride. No one would have blamed Sam for getting out of the hospital deal and withdrawing his support, no one would have been disappointed in Sam. But I'll tell you, my friends, I think we would have been surprised if he had acted in any other way. . . .

And now I come to the part of Sam's life that we all make the mistake of pretending it did not exist and therefore, in my opinion, make it worse than it really is. This is a family party and every person in this room is a member of a family and every family has its family secrets. Or so we think, that they are secrets. Yet I say with no hesitation that there is not a man or woman here this evening who has not at some time during the course of the evening said to himself or herself, "How sad that Alice cannot be with us tonight."

You look at me, some of you, as if to say, "Haven't you got sense enough to avoid certain topics? Do you have to speak of Alice tonight of all nights?" I say to you in reply, to pretend to ignore the subject of Alice would be hypocritical to the nth degree. And worse than that, if I got up here and talked about Sam without talking about Alice would be as wrong as if I did not mention Dr. George Steever and the part he played in Sam's medical career, or the sadness that came to Sam when his brother Boo died. And worst of all, I would be cruelly unfair to Alice herself. Yes, unfair to Alice.

I know what is going on in some minds, but I do not agree. We have now been here since half past seven, a good three hours, and yet I have not heard anyone mention Alice by name. Why? Alice is not dead. We all know that. But if I don't risk the displeasure and disapproval of a few, this evening would pass without mentioning her and it would be as though Alice had never existed. And how dishonest and false that would be.

Do some of you think that by not mentioning Alice I would be sparing Sam? If you do, then you don't know the man as I know him. For there is never a minute of the day when Alice is not in his thoughts. And believe me, my friends, if we ignored Alice tonight, I don't think we would earn Sam's gratitude. I know Sam Merritt and I know that when he finally went home tonight, after he turned out the light and was alone with his thoughts and mulling over the events of the evening, I know that he would wish that someone, someone had found the words to express some appreciation for the one person, the one person who more than anybody else in the world was responsible for the position that Sam Merritt occupies in our community and in our hearts.

They have a saying that they use nowadays and like so many sayings, they think it's a new one. But it isn't. We used to say it when we were young fellows and girls. It is the expression "going steady." Young people were going steady forty, fifty years ago. It is that long ago that Sam Merritt began going steady with Alice Connor. In fact, Sam started going steady with Alice when he was in high and she was still in grammar because they had the three years' difference in their ages. Some parents, like today, did not approve of their daughters going steady so early and Mr. and Mrs. Connor were among them. But with Alice it was Sam or nobody and it was the same with Sam. Mr. and Mrs. Connor had nothing against Sam, but they naturally didn't want her to get serious when they were only in high school. Therefore they had a talk with Sam and in a friendly way they told him that they thought Alice should be given the chance to get better acquainted with other boys.

But they soon found out that their daughter had no interest in other boys. Luckily they were sensible people and accepted the verdict but they would not allow the young couple to become engaged until Sam finished medical college. Then it was delayed because Sam was interning at a hospital in Philadelphia and then delayed some more while he was getting started. They finally felt they were in a position to get married and I was given the honor of being best man. Now I don't believe there's anybody in this room that would be such a damn fool as to think that I would say anything that would injure Sam Merritt. I was his best man, he was my best man, and next to my own wife Lou there was never a girl that I revered more than Alice Connor.

They got married and the early years of struggle were happy ones because they were practically the one person. Alice didn't take the training course to be a nurse, but she learned it all. She learned bookkeeping in high, so she was able to keep Sam's books for him. In addition she did all the housework herself and when Sam began doing a little better financially and tried to persuade her to get a hired girl, she said she would rather use the money for a new car, or office furniture, or for the new additions to the family. Unfortunately, both times they were expecting, they lost both babies. One died at birth and the other was premature.

Alice was terribly disappointed when the babies did not live but it did not deter her from going right on working to assist Sam in his professional career. But without realizing it, her strength must have been more seriously affected than anyone realized, and soon after that she began to show signs that after the second baby she had not made a complete recovery. She was subject to depression and after a time Sam took her to the best doctors in Fort Penn and they examined her and recommended a complete rest in a private hospital near Fort Penn.

When she came home she was all right for a while, but the old trouble returned and once again Sam accompanied her to Fort Penn. Only a few of their closest friends knew about her condition at the time. We used the excuse that Alice was having a series of operations. The second time she came home from the private hospital Sam brought a trained nurse back and we all made believe that the nurse was there to help Sam in the office, but then I guess the truth got to be known publicly when what we all know happened. One of her moods of depression and she jumped out of the second-story window. Broke both her legs, one arm.

We all know about it. It happened in broad daylight, people walking in the street. I never saw the use of any secrecy after that. As long as there was a chance of recovery, yes. But by the next day it was no more a secret in Lyons than if the borough hall caught fire and burned down. We didn't run anything in the *Republican* about it, but I often thought since then that it would have been better for all concerned if we had. Maybe we would have put a stop to all the idle rumors that circulated.

Well, that was a long time ago, a long time ago. Some twenty-five years, and a little more. We're all getting on. What Alice looks like today, I don't know. But what I do know is how I prefer to think of her, slender, light-brown hair, devoted to the only man she ever cared for, working with him, encouraging him until she was no longer able to. Now they have operations that they can cure the kind of illness Alice had, but they didn't have them then and they don't advise it now.

Well, I've brought it out in the open and it isn't a happy story, of course, but would anybody be any the happier if I didn't mention the only woman that Sam ever loved, the woman that loved him? That helped him when he needed help most? Friends, I don't think anybody, Alice or Sam, or anybody, was hurt by any of this, and maybe somebody was even helped.

In fact, I can be sure of that. I don't have to say maybe. Because I have the honor to announce — to you, Sam, because everybody else in this room knows it — that those here tonight have raised the sum of $20,000 for the maternity ward of the Johnsville Hospital, to be known as the Alice C. Merritt Ward. And I take great pleasure in handing you this check, on this engraved silver platter. I will read the engraving:

Presented to
Samuel G. Merritt, M.D.,
at a Family Party in Honor of
His First Forty Years of Service
To His Community.

I thank you.

John O'Hara

THE SHARP reality in John O'Hara's stories and novels is due, in part, to the fact that he has not written from an ivory tower. The son of a Pottsville, Pa., doctor, he had to go to work, on his father's death, at an early age: he held jobs as boat steward, soda clerk, railroad freight clerk and gas-meter reader. Finally, he landed a job as secretary to columnist Heywood Broun, and this led him into newspaper reporting.

Mr. O'Hara's first novel, *Appointment in Samarra,* was one of the smash hits of 1934 and brought him immediate fame. (It is included today in the Modern Library series of classics.) Since then, in addition to numerous screenwriting and magazine assignments, he has produced a dozen novels and volumes of short stories, including the best-selling *Butterfield 8, Pal Joey* (which became a prizewinning Broadway musical), *A Rage to Live* and *Ten North Frederick,* winner of the 1955 National Book Award for fiction.

Married, and the father of one daughter, Mr. O'Hara makes his home in Princeton, New Jersey.

STOPOVER

Illustrations by Tom Hill

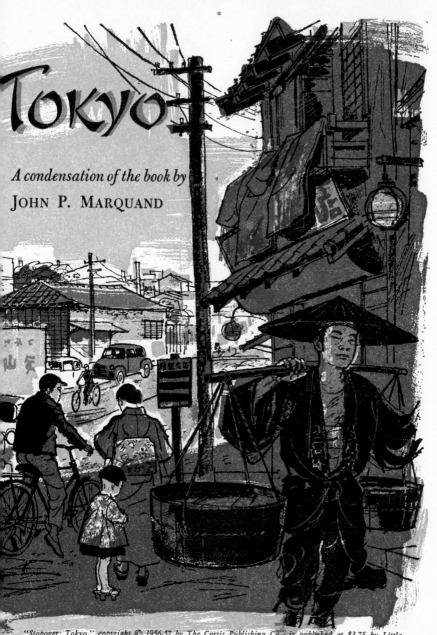

Tokyo

A condensation of the book by

JOHN P. MARQUAND

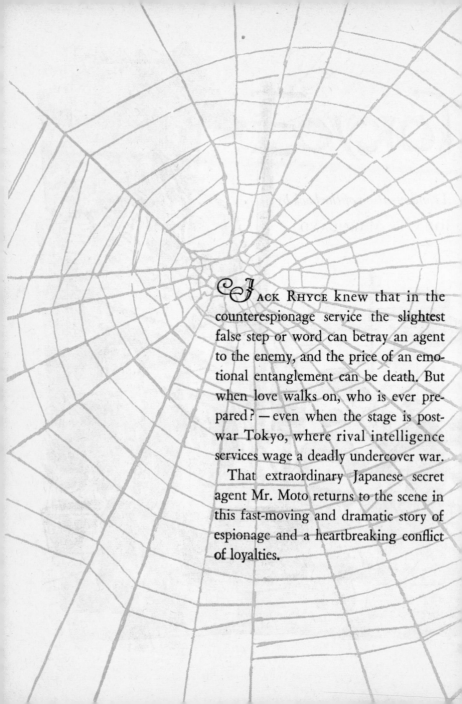

JACK RHYCE knew that in the counterespionage service the slightest false step or word can betray an agent to the enemy, and the price of an emotional entanglement can be death. But when love walks on, who is ever prepared? — even when the stage is postwar Tokyo, where rival intelligence services wage a deadly undercover war.

That extraordinary Japanese secret agent Mr. Moto returns to the scene in this fast-moving and dramatic story of espionage and a heartbreaking conflict of loyalties.

ACK RHYCE had not expected to see the Russians in San Francisco. The word in Washington had been that the celebration of the tenth anniversary of the United Nations would be over and that Mr. Molotov and his delegation would have left the city, several hours before Rhyce's arrival; but no one could have notified him of the change of plans without creating undue attention. The Russians were just leaving the Mark Hopkins Hotel when he arrived by taxi from the airport. There was hardly time for him to get his bags out before the driver was shooed away by a police escort.

"What's going on?" he asked the bellboy.

"It's the Russians," the bellboy said. "Mr. Molotov has been having a cocktail here with Secretary Dulles."

It would have looked conspicuous if he had moved backward. It was better to stand quietly and watch. The guards were grouping themselves around the leading limousine, heavy, stocky men with potatolike faces. He was sure two of them were officers high up in the secret police. He could only hope that the recognition was not mutual; not that there would have been any great harm in it. Nothing could have been more natural than that he should be in San Francisco at this particular time.

"The one with the glasses is Mr. Molotov," the bellboy said.

Jack Rhyce had not seen Mr. Molotov since they had once exchanged amenities over caviar and vodka, at the end of the war, when Jack had been traveling with one of the American missions.

"Young man," Mr. Molotov had said, "let us touch glasses in token of a lasting friendship between our two countries."

"This is a great honor, sir," Jack Rhyce had answered.

"No, no. You and I are both men."

"Yes, Excellency, and all men are brothers."

"You speak Russian not badly," Mr. Molotov had said.

Jack Rhyce instantly realized that by showing off his Russian he had called attention to himself. His chief had spoken to him very roughly about it afterward.

"Just get it through your head," the Chief had said, "that boys like you aren't supposed to be heard at all. Never try to be conspicuous. Never."

Mr. Molotov, beaming, waved to the crowd. Then the car door closed. The Russian party was gone. There was no way to discover whether any of them recognized him or not. He would have felt easier if he had not encountered them just when he was on the point of flying to Japan.

Twice during the war he had been to the Mark Hopkins Hotel, but only to ascend in the elevator to that popular cocktail room known as the Top of the Mark. He had been with the paratroopers, never dreaming that anyone would select him for what he was now doing, but even then his memory had been excellent. Consequently, he had the general layout of the hotel straight.

The Chief had once told him, never chaffer long at a hotel reception desk, and as rapidly as possible get up to your room. He printed his name in block letters on the registration card.

"The name is Rhyce," he said. "John O. Rhyce, from Washington, D.C. I don't suppose you have any letters for me? Or telegrams or messages?" He spoke in a gentle, cultivated voice with an accent difficult to identify.

"No messages, Mr. Rhyce," the clerk said, "but we do have your reservation. Room 515."

It was a pleasant, airy room which looked toward the Bay. As soon as the bellboy left, Jack started on a routine tour of inspection. No transom; the door lock sound; no balconies or closely adjoining windows; no air shaft in the bathroom. It was five o'clock in the afternoon, ample time in which to make a final appraisal of his personal effects before dinner.

First he examined his passport. Unlike several others that he had carried, it told his true history except for his occupation — height five feet eleven, hair light brown, eyes blue, no distinguishing marks or features. His place of birth was Lincoln, Nebraska, his date of birth was January 13, 1920. A good deal of thought had been given to his photograph, and the result was that it only vaguely resembled him. There was no disguising his high broad forehead, or the arch of his eyebrows, or the firmness of his jaw, but if he changed his expression he could repudiate the whole document.

Next, he turned to his brief case. The proper odds and ends and letters in a brief case could be of the utmost value. One never could be too careful with cover details.

The latest advices were that Japan was getting hot again and there was bound to be increased interest in any strange American. He expected and hoped that someone would go through his personal effects, and the sooner the better. The main point was to demonstrate early in the game that he was harmless, with nothing to conceal.

He put his brief case on the writing table and drew out its contents, placing the items in a neat row. The New Testament he had felt was too obvious by itself, and he had added a small volume of the sayings of Buddha. Both these volumes were well worn, with many cogent passages annotated in his own writing. He was satisfied with the way everything looked. The letters had been well handled, his fingerprints on them proved it. The letters indicating his family background gave him particular pleasure. One was from Omaha, Nebraska. Not only the words but the handwriting revealed the writer's character.

Dear, darling Bunny:

I am so pleased and proud that this wonderful chance has come to you after so many years of working so hard for other people. I know you don't know much about the Japanese, but we both know their hearts are in the right place. And your personality that inspires trust in everyone will get through to them, I know, in spite of all the barriers of race and creed. I would be worried about the Oriental women that you are going to meet over there if I did not have a mother's knowledge of a devoted son. Send me a post card every day, and happy landings.

Mumsie

After all, there could be little sinister about a mother's boy.

The second letter was written in a girlish hand on the stationery of the Department of Sociology of Goucher College.

Dear Jackie:

I'm going to miss you terribly. But seriously, sweetie, I think it's a grand thing that you are going away to new countries for a while, to study how other people live — not that I want you to get interested in any girls there. But seriously, sweetie, although I don't like to be a "bore," I think the time has come for you to make up your mind. This doesn't mean I don't love you dearly, but a girl can't wait all the time for any man, can she? And this has been going on ever since we met at your Senior Prom — remember? I know your mother is a darling, but honestly, I don't feel that she need interfere with a happy marriage. And so as you wing your way over the ocean, I hope . . .

Jack Rhyce did not read the rest of it, because he was familiar with the contents. The letter had been composed, though not hand-written, by an elderly spinster who specialized in cover work.

Then there were the letters of introduction to representatives of an institution known as the Asia Friendship League, which had branches in Japan and other countries. There was nothing wrong with this part of the cover. The organization had been conceived by public-spirited citizens and, at least in its Washington head-quarters, had no employes with subversive records.

Connecting him with the Asia Friendship League had been the Chief's idea. The Chief had known the man who had given the money to form the League, a Texas oil millionaire named Gus Tremaine. Jack now had a letter on the League's letterhead:

ASIA FRIENDSHIP LEAGUE
NATIONAL HEADQUARTERS
WASHINGTON, D.C.

Dear Mr. Rhyce:

It is a real delight to hear from Mr. Gus Tremaine that he has com-missioned you to make a survey of our work in the Orient, and to write a general report for him. You will find that in this show we have all our cards on the table and nothing up our sleeves. The main ideal behind our organization, endorsed by all the fine people whose names you see on the left margin of this letter, is in one word — good will. A lot of people out in the Pacific area need a lot of help but not handouts that smack of colonialism. Our concept is simply to help folks to help themselves. And on your travels you'll find out what a swell, alert team of truly dedicated folks we have in Tokyo, Seoul, Hong Kong and Saigon.

Looking forward to helping you in any way I can, in what I predict will be for you a real eye-opening adventure —

Cordially yours,
Chas. K. Harrington

This letter also interested Jack Rhyce. As soon as he had received it, he had asked to see the Chief.

"Well," the Chief said, "what's so funny about it?"

"I didn't say it sounded funny. I said I thought it sounded phony. This Friendship League setup sounds a little too good to be true."

"You say it sounds phony, but I'm afraid you think it's funny too. Please don't think it is, because I'd like to have you come back alive from Tokyo." The Chief looked hard at Jack and smiled in a frigid way. Jack understood that his briefing was about to start.

"Of course it sounds like a front organization," he said, "but as far as we can see, this one is harmless, although Bill Gibson has not reported on it yet. Anyway, Chas. K. Harrington is harmless, but he isn't funny. People like Harrington *aren't* funny. Please don't underrate them, Buster. They're usually narrow and dogmatic — but they have a certain idealism. Never underestimate the do-gooders. As a class, they've made us a lot of trouble in the last thirty years. You see, your cover is a do-gooder and you've got to understand the species. The thing to keep in mind is that this individual you're going to represent is a distinctly modern type. Do-goodism in its purest form is new in the world. Maybe it's our greatest hope, but it's also our biggest danger."

"You mean certain people and ideologies take advantage of it?"

"You're smart today, Buster," the Chief said. "Do-gooders are unrealistic. They don't think. They feel. The same used to be true of you, but I trust you're getting over it."

"How do you mean — it used to be true with me?" Jack asked.

"Do you remember," the Chief asked, "that damn-fool remark you made to Molotov about all men being brothers? I nearly sent you back to the Army after that. Here's another letter for you, Buster." He opened the top drawer of his desk and pulled out a photostat of a letter dated a week before from Amarillo, Texas.

Dear Mr. Harrington [he read]:

I've been kind of out of touch with our project, the Asia Friendship League, but I've heard a lot about the fine things you're doing out there, and I feel right gratified, to use a Texas phrase. Now just in order to keep myself up to date, I am commissioning a young friend of mine, for whom I can vouch in every way because we've rode the range together, to make a survey for me of everything you're doing.

The name is Jack Rhyce — a good American, by the way. Feel free to tell him anything, because, honestly, he's a prince. Here are a few facts. Jack graduated from Oberlin College in 1941. He has a fine religious background, but is at the same time a real he-man. He played right tackle for Oberlin and also commenced interesting himself in civic and welfare projects. During summer vacations, he was counselor for the YMCA boys' camp at Lincoln, Nebraska, and helped out in the organization of the Tiny Tim Football League. During the war he served in the paratroopers until wounded. After this he did desk work for various services in Washington, and since then has stayed in Government, traveling the world for Point Four and things like that.

I've been lucky enough to shanghai him out of Washington because Cupid has entered into the picture in the shape of a very lovely little trick who is working in the Department of Sociology at Goucher College, whose name is Helena Jacoby. What with his lovely mother, whom he's never let down, and this Cupid deal, Jack needs a little more dough.

Well, that's the story, Harrington. Give him the red-carpet treatment all the way and so, *hasta mañana*.

Gus Tremaine

The strength of the letter was that its main facts were provable. He had been to Oberlin. He had played right tackle. He had been a YMCA camp director, and his parents did entertain strong religious convictions. He had been a paratrooper until the Chief had run into him at Walter Reed Hospital. Since the war he had served in Washington.

"How do you like it?" the Chief asked. "It ought to be good, because I spent two nights over it, personally."

"It looks pretty good, sir," Jack said, "but it might help if you were to tell me just why you've selected me for this spot, and what I'm supposed to do when I get to Japan."

"Question Number One: You're going out to the East because you've never operated out there. Europeans, and especially Americans, stand out like sore thumbs in the East. Everybody knows your income and your girl friend. Even the rickshaw pullers know whether you are a spy or not. Orientals are experts about people, and that's why we are working so hard on your cover, but it won't help indefinitely. They find out everything eventually."

"What about Sorge?" Jack asked. "He lasted quite a while."

He was speaking of one of the greatest men in the profession — the German Sorge who, in the guise of a newspaper correspondent, ran the Russian spy ring, and for years had given Moscow accurate intelligence regarding Japan. He had been a foreigner in a highly suspicious country, he had been watched by a highly organized secret police, and yet it had been a long while before the Japanese caught up with him.

"Exactly. Sorge had a good cover. But the Japs got him in the end, and made him sing."

They were both silent for a few seconds.

"All right," the Chief said. "Question Number Two: You're going out to assist Gibson. He's got the wind up, and he doesn't scare easy. He thinks the Commies are planning a political assassination, and anti-American demonstrations in Tokyo. Gibson says a new personality is running things. An American, he thinks." The Chief's voice dropped to a lower note. "All we can do is to sketch this character. He's a new mind in the apparatus. There's been a sudden marked change in Japan, according to Gibson. There's more anti-Americanism, more pro-Communism. There's more and better Red literature in the bookshops. It's Gibson's notion that all this is the prelude to large-scale disturbances."

"It sounds like the usual Moscow technique," Jack Rhyce said.

"Actually, it's gayer. The atmosphere of the whole town is predominantly American. Maybe they think America is good because we won the war. You hardly see a kimono in Tokyo any more. Go to a ball game — and you might think you were back at home. The girls wear American dresses and the men are in business suits. They like everything American. That's the point. They don't fall for anything Russian. And this new propaganda has an American touch. It's damn clever, and it's dangerous. Frankly, I wouldn't say that Japan is very firmly in the camp of the freedom-loving nations, and Gibson thinks there's a hell of a better chance of the country's going Communist now than there was six months ago."

"I hope you're going to tell me what's been dug up," Jack Rhyce said. "I have personal reasons for being curious."

"Oh, yes," the Chief said. "As far as we can make out, none of our people has seen this individual. However, there is reason to believe that he has been to Japan several times. We think his cover name is Ben Bushman. The man who is really masterminding things is Skirov, who comes to Tokyo to meet Ben. Gibson thinks there's a meeting due pretty soon."

Skirov had been on the Moscow first team for a long while.

"He's been improving in the last few years like rare old wine," the Chief said, "and he's slippery as an eel. Am I right in remembering that you've seen Skirov?"

"I'm sorry, sir, I missed him if he was at any of those parties in Moscow, but I have him clear in my mind. I've examined his photographs."

"I suppose it's too much to think you'll run into Skirov," the Chief said, "but if you should, don't forget the sky's the limit. There's just a hope that this new one — Big Ben — may lead you to him, but I doubt it. Skirov never sticks his neck out. That's why your main mission is Big Ben. I want him located and taped."

"There's no personal description of him yet, is there?"

"Nothing definite," the Chief said. "He may be big and it looks as though he were energetic, and therefore young. I'd say he was college-educated. He must have been in the East for a while, because our bet is that he has a smattering of Japanese. He must have a vigorous, engaging personality, be quite a ball of fire in fact. There's one thing that I'm pretty sure of. Big Ben has been in show business."

"What makes you go for that one, sir?" Jack asked.

"The Communist drama groups in Japan. You know how the Communists have always used drama to make their points. Now, according to Gibson, these productions have been jazzed up. Pretty girls are singing blues, there's soft-shoe and tap dancing, and American-type strippers."

"He sounds like someone in the Hollywood crowd."

"It could be," the Chief answered. "But for my money, Ben has been around the live stage. I rather think that he was in one of those musical-comedy road companies that travel around the country."

"What do we do if we find him?" Jack asked.

The Chief laughed, one of his rare laughs.

"You know my motto. Always do it with velvet gloves — when possible. I wouldn't want to hurt Big Ben if it isn't necessary, but we don't want a political assassination or anti-American demonstrations either. Bill Gibson will give you the line to take. Of course, if you run into Skirov that will change the picture. Also, if you stir things up, it may be that the whole Skirov apparatus will get ugly. I want you to take two weeks off at the Farm to study the material, and every afternoon you're to have a workout with the boys. Right through the whole curriculum."

"It isn't necessary," Jack said. "I know those things."

"It won't hurt to have a refresher course," the Chief said. "From now on you're a do-gooder. And do-gooders don't carry rods. I want you to be good if you have to rough it up with people. I'm most anxious for you to come back alive, Jack."

Chapter 2

ONE OF the troubles with working in the office was that you could have no life of your own because you knew too much, and the moment might arise when you forgot what was classified or what was not. You always had to appear to be normal; in no respect could you seem peculiar or conspicuous. Sometimes you hardly knew who you were, after months in foreign parts.

The Chief had once told Jack Rhyce that he had only one handicap: he was too good-looking. But for once his athletic build, his guileless face, and his irrepressible interest in everything were helpful to his cover. As he sat in his bedroom in the Mark Hopkins, checking over his brief case, he had almost forgotten who he was.

He examined the odds and ends that had seemingly fallen there by mistake — those bits that gave more veracity than any letters could, and all revealed character: the paper of matches from an inexpensive and very respectable hotel in midtown New York; theater-ticket stubs to a matinee; a memorandum of telephone numbers of persons to whom Chas. K. Harrington had referred him. He was examining these when his telephone rang.

THERE WAS no reason why the jangling of the bell should have run through his nerves like an electric shock. It must have been that sight of the Russians, and also the fact that no one knew he was in San Francisco. He watched the telephone for a time without lifting it, but the bell continued ringing. Whoever was calling the room must have been very sure that he was there. He finally picked up the instrument. "Hello," he said.

He was startled when a girl's voice answered.

"Hello" — the voice had a slightly husky quality, and sounded young and seductive. "Is this Mr. John Rhyce?"

"Yes," he answered.

"Gosh, I'm glad I contacted you, Mr. Rhyce. I was afraid you might have left your room. This is Ruth — Ruth Bogart."

"Oh, yes" — he cudgeled his brains. He was good with names and faces; but he could not place Ruth Bogart.

"Don't you know who I am?" she asked.

"Why, no," he said, and he laughed. "I don't, to be quite frank, but then perhaps I'm not the Rhyce you're looking for. My name is spelled with a *y*."

"Oh, dear, didn't Mr. Harrington tell you? I'm one of the Asia League girls, and we're going on the same plane tomorrow."

"Why, no," he said. "Mr. Harrington didn't tell me."

"Oh, dear," she said. "Charlie is so absent-minded."

There was a slight pause while his mind moved rapidly. There were a number of possibilities in this call, and the most important one was that it might have originated with the Russians.

"Well, it's very kind of you to give me a ring," he said, "especially when you must have many acquaintances in the city, Miss Bogart."

"No," she said, "I haven't, and it's awfully lonely in a strange city, isn't it?" If it weren't for the implacable self-confidence of American women, he would have thought the approach was crude. "I'm stopping at the Mark, too, and Charles did suggest I call you. I was hoping if you weren't too busy we might have dinner. There's a place called Fisherman's Wharf, I understand, where they have divine sea food. My room is 312."

"Why, that sounds swell," Jack said. "I could certainly do with some sea food. I'll knock at 312 in just a jiffy."

It was much better to see what was going on than not. It was the oldest game in the world, to lure someone away so that his room could be searched, and a girl was conventionally the shill. He very much hoped he was correct in this suspicion, because the sooner he was placed the better. The only doubt he harbored was how dumb he ought to be. Should he put his brief case in the upper drawer of the bureau, or should he leave it in sight? He tossed it carelessly on the bed, closed the room door noisily behind him.

One of the oldest tricks was also the ambush, the alluring call on the telephone, the welcoming inward opening of the door, and the blow on the base of the skull. A great deal of thought had been given at the Farm to the right way of entering a room. He rose to the balls of his feet, rapped briskly on the door of Room 312 with his left hand, his right low at his side, shoulders forward, knees bent, but only slightly.

"Oh," a voice said. "Just a moment, please."

He moved closer to the door and touched the knob with his left hand in order to be fully prepared when it turned. As the door opened inward, he moved with it. You had an opportunity to advance or retreat, as long as you were moving with the door. He entered the room almost on tiptoe, knees still bent. It was a duplicate of his own, and the bathroom door was closed. He had a glimpse of two matched suitcases. A girl stood by the door.

She was very pretty. He would have estimated her age at not over twenty-five. Her height was five feet six, hair dark brown, eyes gray green. Her face was longish with a mouth that showed character. She wore a dark dress of heavy silk, and she held a red leather handbag.

"Why, Mr. Rhyce," she smiled, "I didn't know you'd come rushing down quite so rapidly."

He smiled back in the overcordial manner that anyone might use when meeting an attractive girl. The color in her cheeks was natural, and she had only a touch of lipstick. He had grown adept, long ago, in spotting persons engaged in his line of work. There was something about them — an overalertness, or an impression of strain — but her personality baffled him.

"I guess I hurried down faster than was polite," he said, "because it was such a pleasure to hear a friendly voice. I'm surprised that Charlie didn't say anything about you, because, without wanting to be forward, I don't see how you could possibly skip anyone's mind."

"Why, Mr. Rhyce," she said, "what cute things you say."

Her looks, and the word cute, were like a tag in a museum case, although the possibility remained that she, too, had a cover.

"It is a real pleasure, making your acquaintance, Miss Bogart," Jack Rhyce said, "and it will be fun exploring San Francisco with you. I'm especially glad you mentioned Fisherman's Wharf, and after that we might visit Chinatown."

"I think dinner would be lovely," she said, "but I'm afraid I'll have to beg off on Chinatown, although it sounds awfully romantic. I'm a little woozy, because I've just flown in from Chicago, and we have an early start tomorrow."

In the elevator she opened her red leather bag and took out a gold compact. She looked at herself critically in the little mirror. It was the correct technique for examining the elevator operator.

"Oh, I forgot to powder my nose," she said.

Her nose did not need powder, and he told her so.

"Well, anyway," she said, "this is a very exciting hotel. I had the good fortune to have a glimpse of Mr. Molotov this afternoon."

"Did you?" Jack Rhyce said heartily. "I had that good fortune, myself. I was just getting in from the airport."

"I thought he was cute," she said. "I was surprised. I thought he was just an old teddy bear, didn't you?"

"Well," Jack Rhyce said, "not exactly a teddy bear."

He kept wishing he could place her. The business with the compact mirror still disturbed him.

As he sat beside her in the taxi, she took out her compact again. Then she snapped her bag shut, and put her hand over his, where it rested on the seat. He was startled. "It is so romantic, isn't it," she said, "to see the sun setting over the Golden Gate?"

"Yes," he said. "It is going to be a lovely sunset."

Her fingers were pressing on the back of his hand, first long, and then short, the continental code.

Being followed, he read: *orange-and-black taxi.*

He was not disturbed by the news that she had given him. What did disturb him was his inability to place the girl.

Okay, he signaled back. *So what?*

Have message from Chief, she signaled back.

He drew his hand away. There were plenty of people in the outfit whom he did not know, since the cardinal principle in conducting such an operation was to have an individual know as few others as possible. He still could not be sure of her.

"Driver," he asked, "what is the best place for sea food at Fisherman's Wharf?"

"A lot of newcomers here sort of go for Fisherman's Grotto."

Jack Rhyce studied the back of the driver's head. He turned to the girl beside him. "Do you think we'd better try it?"

"I think it would be lovely," she said. "I always love to dine in new places. And we have so much to talk about."

"Yes," Jack said, "and I can't tell you how pleased I am that we will be traveling together."

"They hurried things up back East just so we could. Mr. Tremaine said I might as well go with you, since you've traveled so much. He's a lovely old man, isn't he? Just a regular teddy bear."

"I never thought of him in that category, exactly."

"You don't seem to think of anybody as teddy bears."

"Well, frankly, no, I haven't — not for a good many years," Jack Rhyce said. "And maybe it's just as well."

"Oh, dear, I hope you're not going to be a dim-view artist. I didn't think you would be, from what I heard at Goucher."

"Where?" he asked.

"Why, Goucher College, of course. Helena and I room together. In fact, frequently we're mistaken for each other."

"Now that you mention it," Jack Rhyce said, "I can see you look like Helena."

"I've heard so much about you," she said, "that I almost called you Jackie. What's the latest news of your mother?"

There was no time to answer because the taxi had stopped at Fisherman's Wharf. Jack Rhyce was out and beside the driver as quickly as he could manage it. An orange-and-black cab had stopped behind them, and a slender man in his sixties got out. It was close to sunset, but Fisherman's Wharf was well equipped with artificial illumination. It was not the sort of place to finger anyone. The elderly man from the cab lingered outside Fisherman's Grotto, examining some abalone shells. There was no immediate danger, Jack thought, but he would have felt safer if he had not met the Russians.

"Helena says you always call your mother 'Mumsie,' " the girl said, as they went into the restaurant.

"Oh, yes," he said, and he laughed in an embarrassed way. "It's a holdover from childhood."

He was reasonably sure by now that she was the girl at Goucher College who had transcribed the "Dear Jackie" letter. Still, he needed to make a further check before he accepted her.

He smiled and nodded to the headwaiter. "I believe it's the season for Dungeness crabs," he said to her, "and if you've never tried one, they are a most rewarding experience."

Her smile was exaggeratedly gay and provocative; she was telling him that they should be absorbed in each other and oblivious to what went on around them. As he threw himself into the make-believe, it assumed the quality of a genuine boy-meets-girl scene. The bored look of the waiter as he handed him the menu proved that the audience believed.

The most harmless thing in the world, the Chief was accustomed to say in one of his lectures on cover, was a young couple falling in love. It was clear from the way she looked at him that she, too, could have heard that lecture. It was a problem to appear completely engrossed in her, and at the same time to examine the man two tables behind. He looked like a bank clerk of retirement age, and he made no apparent effort to hear what they were saying, showing that his job was only to keep them in sight.

"You can't blame me for being surprised when you called," Jack said. "No one gave me the least inkling that you'd be coming along." He laughed with embarrassment. "I hope this doesn't mean they're losing faith in me."

"Oh, no," she answered quickly, "it was only that it suddenly occurred to Mr. Tremaine that your job might be bigger than he thought, and that you might need some help."

"I'm very glad you're coming," he said.

"So am I, because I love to travel, and it's hard for a girl to travel alone. After I graduated I was with an insurance firm in London. I love London. I always feel at home when I can hear Big Ben."

Jack raised his wineglass. It reflected the old man two tables behind him.

"You know, I've been told you can hear Big Ben striking right in Tokyo, over the BBC — that is, when Radio Moscow doesn't interfere. I wonder if we'll hear Big Ben when we get to Tokyo?"

"I think we will," she said, "almost right away."

She had told him almost everything. "I love to be in strange places and see strange people, don't you?" she asked.

"Yes," he answered. "I often play a little game with myself wondering who people are."

"You can't ever tell, can you? There's a little old man, all sort of worn and threadbare, just behind you, and he keeps looking at us, as if he were lonely. I wonder what he's been doing all his life."

Jack laughed as though she had said something highly amusing. "Whatever he's done, he's kept alive," he said.

"They say," she said, "that San Francisco is the gateway to the Orient. And it's true, isn't it? Because there's an Oriental here. I can't tell whether he's Chinese or Japanese."

"Where?" Jack asked, and his voice had an edge to it.

"Over there near that case with the queer fish on ice."

A young Japanese, whom he had not noticed, had entered Fisherman's Grotto.

"Oh," he said, "yes. I'd put him down for Japanese, and Nisei. It's funny, I didn't see him come in." It was safe, in his opinion, to discount the Japanese.

The old man behind them must have paid his check, because he rose as Jack signaled to the waiter, pausing, as he passed their table, to light a thin black cigar, and to glance at his wrist watch. The waiter arrived with their check just as the stranger went out the door. Jack had a bill ready.

"Thanks," he said, "and keep the change."

The lights were on outside and there was still daylight in the sky. Their shadow called a taxicab. "He was a dear old man, wasn't he?" Ruth Bogart said. "I wonder where he's going now."

"Home. He's finished work, I think," and he linked his arm through hers affectionately, partly from relief, and partly because of cover. "The whole thing was only a check on our baggage," he told her softly.

The shadow's glance at the watch confirmed the theory. They were to be watched for a time so that a warning could be given in case they returned too soon — and now the time was up.

"I think there's light enough," he said, "if you'd care to look at Alcatraz through the telescope."

"That would be lovely," she said, and then she giggled, "as long as we don't get any nearer."

"That's one place where we probably won't end up," he said. Then he put a coin in the slot for the telescope and added, "We can talk at the hotel. I think we're in the clear now."

"Why, it's fascinating," she said. "Hurry and take a look, before we have to spend another dime."

He had been careless, because he thought they were in the clear. When he heard a step behind him, he almost whirled around instead of turning slowly.

"Sir, I beg your pardon, but would you like to see Chinatown?"

It was the young Japanese from the restaurant.

"No, thanks," Jack said, "not tonight."

The Japanese, he saw, was in his early twenties. His neat, dark suit, his shirt open at the neck and his hair in a crew cut gave him the appearance of a college student.

"There are many interesting things to see in Chinatown."

"I know," Jack Rhyce said, "but not tonight, thanks."

He had not thought until then that there might be something wrong with the picture. The young man's hands were at his sides. There was no indication of a forward motion, and nothing in the face, eyes, shoulders, or the set of the feet indicated trouble. Nevertheless, he did not move away.

"Excuse me, sir," he said. "Would you mind if I ask you another question?"

"Why, no, not at all. Go ahead and ask it, son."

After all, he was a do-gooder who liked kids.

"I was so near your table that I overheard some words you said to the lady. It was accident — I did not mean to be intrusive."

Jack laughed good-naturedly. He felt a slight tingling at the base of his skull. "Why, that's all right, son," he said. "There's nothing I should mind having you overhear. What was it?"

"Well, you see, I'm Japanese, sir," he said.

"And I can see that you're American, too," Jack said heartily. "My guess is you were born right here in California."

"That is so, sir, and I'm a graduate of Cal. Tech."

"Well, well. Congratulations. That's a great school."

"I was interested in what you were saying," the boy said, "because I have relatives in Japan. May I introduce myself? My name is Nichi Naguchi. They called me Nick at college."

"Well, well," Jack said. "This is a real pleasure, Nick. My name's Jack Rhyce, and this is Miss Bogart."

It was hard to tell if the meeting was offbeat. After all, people were more breezy and friendly on the West Coast than the East.

"Well, don't hold back on us, Nick," Jack said. "What was it you heard us say that caught your attention?"

"Might I ask if you are going to Japan? You were saying you hoped to hear Big Ben strike in Tokyo, over the BBC."

The tingling at the base of Jack's skull grew more pronounced. "Why, certainly," he said. "We're flying out tomorrow. Miss Bogart and I happen to be working for the Asia Friendship League."

He watched for some revealing sign, but the boy only looked reassured, and began to speak more eagerly.

"May I ask if you will need a guide when you get to Tokyo? The Japanese language is difficult for Americans sometimes." He laughed nervously. "I know a very good guide. My uncle. His English is very good. He is also fond of Americans, knows all about Japan — everything. He can answer all questions."

"That's quite a recommendation," Jack said, and he laughed. "Do you suppose he knows Big Ben?"

It was dangerous, but now and then you had to play a card.

"Big Ben?" the boy repeated.

Jack laughed again. "Didn't you get it, Nick? The clock that you heard us talking about, the one that strikes."

He could read nothing in the boy's face.

"Oh, yes," the boy said, "I forgot. If you would like, I can give you my uncle's address. I can write it on a card."

"Why, sure," Jack said. "I'll give him a buzz if I need him."

The boy handed the card to Jack. "Good-by, sir," he said, "and good-by, Miss Bogart, and good luck, and a very happy trip."

The wharf was more crowded now. No one seemed to take any interest in them, but it was safer, in case there was anybody who cared, to be happy about each other.

"Well," he said, "that was quite a little human experience, wasn't it?" He put the card in his wallet.

"Nichi Naguchi," she said. "They have funny names, don't they? It was cute of him, thinking of his uncle. Let's stroll around and look at the fishing boats before we go back to the hotel."

Undoubtedly she was as anxious to get back to the hotel as he, but it was never wise to hurry.

THE ELEVATOR boy who took them to the third floor only looked bored when Jack said, "I'll just see you to your door."

"It isn't really necessary, Jack," she said, "but it's sweet of you to think of it."

When she took her room key from her handbag, he snatched it from her playfully, and there was a merry little scuffle in the corridor, just in case anyone might be interested.

"Now really, Jack," she said, "now please try to behave."

When he turned the key in the door he approved of the way she covered him and watched the hall, and kept the correct distance behind him when he entered the darkened room. The second the door was closed behind them he pointed to the closed bathroom door. She opened it, turned on the light, and pulled open the closet door.

"Okay," she whispered. "Lord, I'm tired of being a Salvation Army lass!"

"Just a minute," he said gently, "before you get so frank. Would you mind writing a few words on the back of this envelope? I'll just take a look at your handbag while you're writing."

"You don't miss any tricks, do you?" she said.

"I try not to," he answered. "Hurry, please."

"What do you want me to write?" she asked.

"Anything. Write 'I'll do my best to be a good coöperative girl if I go with you on this trip.'"

When she handed him back the envelope he read: *I don't like people who have to be so careful and, as I said, it has been a boring evening*. Her writing was the same as the Helena Jacoby letter in his brief case.

"I'm sorry," he said, "if you think I'm disagreeable, but I had to make up my mind about you. Let's check the luggage."

Her matched suitcases were lying one on top of the other, with a small brief case on top. She unzipped the brief case while he sat on the edge of the bed watching her, aware for the first time that he was feeling tired. All of her gaucheness was gone. Even before she looked up and nodded, he knew that the baggage had been searched.

"It must have been a woman or a ribbon clerk," she whispered. "They folded the nylons back beautifully."

"Brief-case contents?" he whispered.

"All through everything. They had it out all over the writing table."

"Careless of them," he said.

"Clever of me," she whispered, "for being dainty and using lots of dusting powder. See where they brushed it off?"

"Gloves," he said. "They dusted with them before they put them on."

"Smart as a whip, aren't you, Buster?" she said.

"You bet," he said. "What makes you call me Buster?"

"The Chief calls you that."

"Right," he said. "Now — what's the story?"

"Gibson asked for both of us. Skirov's coming over to meet Big Ben. It's definite."

They both stopped and listened. Someone was walking down the corridor with jaunty, heavy footsteps, and they heard a man's voice singing softly:

> *"For every day is ladies' day with me.*
> *I'm quite at their disposal all the while!"*

The song was from *The Red Mill,* the old Victor Herbert musical comedy that had been revived recently. They were both silent until the steps and the voice died away.

"Any identification of Big Ben?" he asked.

"Nothing new. The Chief still likes show business."

"Well," he whispered, "things don't look too bad for us, now they've gone through the bags."

"I know, but what about that Jap?"

"I'd like to get a check on him, but I think it wiser not to signal Washington. Don't you?"

They looked at each other, and nodded. From now on, any communication with the Bureau might ruin everything.

"I guess that's that," he said. "I wish I'd met you before I took on this cover. I hate to be such a pratfall all day long."

"Oh, well," she said, "it won't be as bad as all that. Breakfast downstairs at seven thirty, what? Good night, Buster."

"Good night," he said, and he put his hands on her shoulders. "Don't worry. We'll get through all right."

"I've given up worrying long ago," she said.

Chapter 3

B Y THE time he and Ruth left Honolulu for Tokyo Jack Rhyce
was positive that they were in the clear. After a number of
years' experience, there was a sense of malaise when you were
being watched. You could not put your finger on any one thing,
but finally you could depend implicitly upon that feeling of im-
balance. There had been none of that feeling in Honolulu. He felt
that he was exactly what he was supposed to be, a muscular do-
gooder, full of good will toward the world. The cover he had
assumed had finally blended with his own personality.

The passengers on the plane were a Hawaiian-Japanese couple,
a Dutch businessman, two British businessmen, and thirty members
of a world-tour group. They all became congenial, flying across
the Pacific at nineteen thousand feet. They began singing songs,
and Jack Rhyce threw himself into the spirit of it. He had a good
baritone. As far as he could remember later, Ruth and he broke
away from cover only once. It was when the merriment had died
down and he took the sayings of Buddha from his brief case.

"This fellow Buddha," he said, "is a little difficult, due to his
antiquity and his foreign way of life, but a lot of it fits right in with
today. Would you like me to read you a little of it, Ruth?"

"Oh, shut up," she said, "and let me go to sleep."

On the whole he could not blame her. They were silent for half
an hour. "Jack," she said, "I'm sorry. When we set down at Wake,
can't we get away for twenty minutes and be ourselves?"

"Why, yes," he said. "I think that would be a wonderful idea,
but it will be dark at Wake — just before dawn."

"All right," she said, "in the dark then. In fact, it would look
better. We're supposed to be in love, aren't we?"

"Yes," he said, "and you've been wonderful about it."

"Oh, shut up," she said again, "and let me go to sleep."

SHE WAS still asleep hours later when the plane was letting down.
He put his hand on her arm to awaken her, and she gave a start

and looked around as though she did not know where she was. He had experienced the same confusion more than once. And this was dangerous. "Wake Island," he said, "in about ten minutes."

"I was having a bad dream. I thought you were someone else."

"Just take it easy," he told her.

At Wake there was a change of crew, and passengers could go to the resthouse for early morning refreshment. There was no checkup on anyone, and no reason at all why he and Ruth Bogart should not walk anywhere on that small island.

"Lord," she said, "it's lonely."

"Yes," he said, "it's lonely all right." But he was surprised that she should be impressed by it, because nothing was more lonely than the existence of anyone who was in the business.

They walked up a road, illuminated by dim electric lights, with ugly Nissen huts and Army shacks on either side. "We may as well take a look at the lagoon," he said. "It's getting light. That crowd in the plane — did you think any of them seemed offbeat?"

"I had some ideas about the thin Englishman, but I'll clear him now."

"He'll do," he said. "I think we're still in the clear."

"You're not worried about that Jap in San Francisco? You don't think he was trying to tell us something?"

"It doesn't seem to hold water. Let's forget him for now."

"I wish I could forget him and everything else. After a while you don't know what you are."

"I know what you mean. Maybe chameleons feel that way."

"We might have a nice time together, mightn't we," she said, "if we weren't all mixed up in this?"

"I'm not sure I would know how. I'm a chameleon now. I might turn green and yellow and not know I was doing it."

"How long have you been in?" she asked.

"Long enough to forget what it's like outside. About ten years."

"I'm newer than that."

"Yes," he said, "of course. What were you doing outside?"

"College, majoring in Romance languages. I met the Chief at a cocktail party in New York. Let's skip it, shall we?"

They walked for a while without speaking, through the moist

hot dark. In a few minutes, there would be a glow of sunrise, and the colors of sand and sea would be unbelievably beautiful.

"It seems queer to me," he said, "that they haven't picked Big Ben out by now. I never knew anyone in show business who doesn't try to push into the front row, and I never knew one who could keep his mouth shut for long."

He felt almost happy, walking with his partner. In the distance he could hear the noise of the island generating plant, and then he heard another sound. She must have heard it too, because she put her hand on his arm, and they both stood still.

"Someone singing," she said. "San Francisco. Remember?"

Of course he remembered the footsteps outside the hotel door, and that snatch of outmoded song. Now in the dark a man was singing another song from *The Red Mill*. His voice was excellent. It sounded carefree and full of the joy of living.

"*...in old New York!*" The words came incongruously through the darkness. "*The peach-crop's always fine!*"

They stood motionless on the road, listening. It was the kind of long shot that might possibly have a meaning.

"It comes from over by the lagoon," he told the girl. "Let's move over that way." The song continued as they walked.

> "*They're sweet and fair and on the square!*
> *The maids of Manhattan for mine!*"

There was light enough to see the lagoon, by now.

"From *The Red Mill*," Jack Rhyce said, in a loud and hearty voice. "It sounds like home, doesn't it? Do you remember the rest of it, Ruth dear?"

"Why, no, Jack," she said. "Not that old song. Do you?"

"It goes like this: *You cannot see in gay Paree, in London or in Cork! The queens you'll meet on any street in old New York.*"

It seemed very natural when he heard a voice call back: "Hey, let's do it again, whoever you are. *In old New York! In old New York! ...*"

A man in khaki swimming trunks was walking toward them. His yellow hair was dripping sea water, and he had a towel over his shoulder. He was very large — two inches taller than Jack, and a good twenty pounds heavier. He was beautifully built. He had heavy sandy eyebrows, greenish eyes, and a large mobile mouth.

There was occasionally a time when you could be sure of something, beyond any reasonable doubt. Such a moment of utter conviction was with Jack now. He felt his heart beat with a quick, savage triumph. It was one of those moments that made all the drudgery worth while. It was just as though someone were whispering in his ear, "There he is, there he is." As sure as fate, he was looking at Big Ben.

Even in that moment of revelation, he contrived to keep his balance. He found himself joining in the song without a quaver, and he put his arm around Ruth. When he paused to catch his breath, the big man raised his hand like an orchestra leader.

"Now we're hitting it," he said. "Come on, let's give it the works. You take the lead, I'll follow."

"Well, it's nice to meet another Red Miller," Jack Rhyce answered, "especially on a rock like this. All right, here we go. Come on and join in, Ruth. *You cannot see in gay Paree . . .*"

He knew that he was talking to Big Ben, although he still had to prove it, and his main hope was that Big Ben did not have intuition, too. The man's size was impressive. In spite of all Jack had learned at the Farm, he was not sure how things would come out if they reached a showdown.

"Say, that was good," the big man said. As far as Jack Rhyce could see, his smile was friendly, and his eyes showed no suspicion. "You're not joining this flying installation here, are you?"

Jack laughed. "If you'll excuse my insulting such a lovely piece of real estate — thank goodness, no. We're just passengers out for a stroll, and heading west in about an hour."

"Oh," the big man said, "you mean Flight Five-zero-one."

"Yes, I think that's the number," Jack said. "Five-oh-one."

Even the clumsy use of numerals could help with cover. They were just tourists.

"That's too bad," the big man said. "I'd hoped you were on some crew so we could think up some more old songs. You've got to think up something when you lay off on this rock. Let's see. There's a

world-tour group, isn't there, on Flight Five-zero-one? There was
something about it, seems to me, at Operations."

His voice was gentle and lazy, with a drawl that might have
belonged either to the Tidewater country or to the Southwest. But
Jack was interested in more than the voice. Big Ben had over-
stepped. It was doubtful whether a world-tour group would be
mentioned in Operations.

"That's right," Jack said, "but we don't happen to be in the
party. Miss Bogart and I work for the Asia Friendship League."

"Well, it's too bad you're not staying on," the big man said,
"because you both look like nice folks. We air-line folk get lonely.
And now we're just ships that pass in the night."

"That's a very nice way of putting it," Jack said, "but it's a
pleasure even to have made such a short acquaintance. I suppose
we really ought to be getting back to that resthouse."

"Well, so long, folks," the big man said, "and don't let those
Japs give you wooden nickels."

"So long," Jack said, "and many happy landings."

They turned and walked back toward the airstrip. For a while
he felt that the big man was watching them.

"Turn and wave to him," he said to Ruth.

"He's gone," she said. "Do you think he is the same man that was
singing in the hall?"

"I think so."

"Do you think he knew that we were in that room?"

Jack sighed. You couldn't think of everything.

"That's a sixty-four-dollar question," he said, "but I shouldn't
be surprised if we knew the answer someday."

No matter how you met a situation, it was impossible to do everything right. He did his best to follow the maxims of the business,
one of which was to disturb nothing unless it was absolutely
necessary. He had only a hunch to act on, yet, if his hunch was
right, they had Big Ben. The man was an air-line employe at Wake
Island, he was as safe as a book in the reference library. The question was: *Did their man know who they were?* If so it would be
best to break out of cover at once and communicate with Washington. Afterward Jack could never convince himself that he had not

moved properly at Wake, but doubts still plagued him even after the plane had taken off.

"I might go up forward and have a chat with the crew," he said, "in a purely social way."

"I wouldn't, if I were you, Jack," she told him. "It could get back to Wake that you were asking."

Of course she was perfectly right.

"Did you notice his hands? The way he kept his fingers half closed — they frightened me."

He did not tell her that he had been wondering what he could possibly do if Big Ben were to get him by the throat. "He looks very able," he said, "very first-class." He was thinking of the ease of motion which showed that mind and body moved contentedly together. "Well," he said, "let's wait until we see Gibson."

"WE ARE now approaching the coast of Japan," the steward said over the loudspeaker. "The sacred mountain of Fujiyama is visible off the left wing."

The Japanese were realists. Their representations of Fujiyama on textiles and on porcelains were exactly like that cinder-coned volcano. All the beauties and the difficulties of Japan were starkly obvious as one approached the coast by air. The sharp folds of the mountains showed why only a fifth of the land was suitable for agriculture. Jack could see the bright green of the rice paddies, the lighter green of bamboo and the darker shades of giant fir trees. The fishing boats off the coast added a last touch to the broad picture of the Japanese struggle for existence.

Japan's army was gone, and its navy, but not its national will to live. During the Occupation, the Japanese had displayed a disturbing absence of rancor, a good-natured acceptance of reality, almost a polite regret for any inconveniences they might have caused. They had been picking up the Tokyo wreckage, smiling cheerfully in the depth of their misfortunes. Now the new air terminal, shining with glass and plastics, was handsomer than any in New York.

The time, he saw, was quarter to twelve. Ruth's face looked drawn, which was not surprising, because pursuing the sun across the Pacific was a tiring process.

"We may as well get a taxi to the hotel," he said. "Nobody around here seems interested in us."

"I hope you're right," she said. "I don't want to go into an act right now. I'm tired."

He wished that he was feeling more alert himself because it was hard to trust decisions made under the strain of fatigue. He noticed that the main concourse at the airport was not crowded, except for hotel and travel agents and friends of passengers who had come to meet the plane. The faces were Japanese, but the women were dressed in the same style that one might see in New York and the men wore neat dark business suits. Only a few generations, Jack was thinking, lay between the grotesque shadows of the double-sworded samurai, who had once roamed the streets of Tokyo as symbols of feudalism, and this entirely Western scene.

"Taxicab?" Jack said to a porter.

The porter shook his head. "All people go in big limousine."

"No, no," Jack answered. "The lady and me — taxicab."

He was so anxious to make his point that he was not aware that anyone had been watching until a small, middle-aged Japanese, dressed in a business suit of an unpleasant purplish-blue color and wearing very yellow tan shoes, stepped toward him.

"Excuse me, sir," he said. His hair was grayish and close-clipped, and he bowed in the manner of an older generation. "Do I speak to Mr. Rhyce?"

Jack wished that his mind were moving faster.

"Why, yes," he said, "I'm Mr. Rhyce."

The Japanese smiled, and Jack Rhyce saw that his upper incisor teeth were gold-covered. "May I introduce myself?" His voice was high, and slightly monotonous. He gave a nervous laugh, and his hands moved with astonishing rapidity as he snatched a wallet from inside his coat and whipped a card out of it.

"Why, thanks." The thing to do was to take the card slowly, to exhibit no alertness or suspicion.

"*I. A. Moto,*" he read aloud from the card. "Well, let's see — that name rings a bell somewhere. . . . Yes, I've got it now." He pulled out his own wallet and produced the card he had been given at Fisherman's Wharf. "Your nephew gave me your name in San

Francisco. Well, this is a real surprise." He turned to Ruth Bogart, smiling with fatuous enthusiasm. "You remember that nice Japanese boy on Fisherman's Wharf who told us about his uncle who might show us around the city?"

"Why, yes," Ruth said. "He must have sent a cable. What a lovely thing to do."

"Yes," Mr. Moto said, "my nephew. He sent a cable."

"Well," Jack said. "It's a pleasure to meet you, Mr. Moto, and a mighty nice surprise, just when I was trying to tell the porter that I wanted a taxicab to take us to the Imperial Hotel."

"We can get a taxicab downstairs," Mr. Moto said. "This way, please."

"This is mighty kind of you," Jack said. "This young lady and I are pretty tired. If you could just get us a taxi and tell the driver Imperial Hotel — then suppose you come around at, say, six o'clock, and we can talk over what you can show us in Tokyo."

Mr. Moto looked delighted. "Thank you so very much. I will call at six o'clock."

Once in the taxi, Jack and Ruth were silent for a few moments.

"So this is Tokyo," Ruth said finally. "I must say it isn't as romantic as I thought it was going to be."

She was right. Tokyo lay sprawling over a large area, divided by a muddy river and canals — a dusty, smoky city that sweltered in the summer and shivered in the winter. Except for the areas contiguous to the Imperial Palace, all districts were jumbled together like a deck of cards thrown on a table. He remembered a paragraph about Tokyo in a prewar guidebook. It was fortunate, the book had said, that most of the dwellings in Tokyo were of fragile frame construction, with paper windows, because they caught fire so easily, thus making better city planning possible when they were rebuilt. There had been ample opportunity to rebuild Tokyo. During the war the modern business district in the vicinity of the Palace was about all that had withstood the bombing, yet Tokyo was rebuilt in the same disorder as before, and with the same flimsiness. The shops were back again, wide open to the street, displaying dried fish, vegetables, bolts of cloth, earthen and enamel ware. You could buy anything from raw tuna fish to a whole gamut of Western-style goods in the great department stores along the Ginza.

Tokyo was itself again, but there were signs advertising American tooth paste and American cosmetics, and the streets were as full of motor traffic as any American city. Japanese and English cycles, motorbikes, pedicabs, small three-wheeled private cars, heavy-duty Japanese trucks, small shiny Japanese cars that competed with the German Volkswagen, American cars, French and English and Italian motors — everything, including rickshaws and hand-pushed barrows. But the Chief had been right. Where had the kimonos gone? And where were the wooden clogs called getas?

There was only a suspicion, among all that modernity, of something older, only an occasional, fleeting glimpse through a gateway of a dwarfed tree, or a pool or a rock garden. Nevertheless, most of old Japan still lay behind those perishable façades, and Jack Rhyce sensed that there was a peculiar peace there. Once they had reached home, the Japanese women, in their New York cotton dresses and their high-heeled shoes, and the Japanese schoolgirls, in their navy-blue skirts and white middy blouses, and the men in their business suits would move magically into another kind of life.

The shoes would be left outside. There would be straw matting underfoot. European clothes would be hung away, and there would be kimonos. There would be cushions beside low tables, a charcoal brazier and tea, and *suchi* made of raw fish and rice, and a porcelain jar of hot sake surrounded by minute cups. The old conventions still lay just behind the modern curtain.

"You'll see the Imperial Palace grounds in just a minute," Jack said. "We're reaching the handsomest part of Tokyo now."

"You know so many interesting facts," she said. "I would have boned up on this, too, but I didn't know I was coming."

The Palace grounds of Japan's Emperor were guarded by a moat and behind it by a grim, sloping, dry-masonry wall of black lava rock. The walls and moat were at least a thousand years old, and the etiquette and spiritual qualities that they protected were vastly older. A part of the Palace had been destroyed by bombs, but the Emperor was still residing among the trees and gardens. Across the street the skyscraper buildings of banks and insurance companies and the modern Nikatsu Hotel made a dramatic contrast.

They were driving up to the Imperial now, and he heard her exclaim when she saw that low structure of yellowish volcanic stone, with its strange windows and angles. It was a maze of terraces, loggias, turrets, inner gardens, glassed-in corridors and roof gardens. Although it was designed by an American, it must have once represented the quintessence of Japanese aspirations.

Chapter 4

H E COULD not tell whether he was surprised or relieved when he found that their rooms on the third floor had a connecting door. "You can take either room you like," he said. "I'd go to sleep if I were you. Knock on the door if you want anything."

There was a Lilliputian quality about the rooms and everything inside them. His bathtub was too small. He had to bend his knees to reach the washbasin. He went through the wardrobe, looked behind the mirror and over every inch of the wall. He took off his coat and shoes and opened the door for a glance at the corridor, but there was no one there. On the whole he approved of the rooms. They looked over the fantastic porte-cochere and the driveway, thus affording a view of all the hotel traffic. The walls were thick, so that it would be possible to talk freely if voices were kept low, and all the locks were sound.

He knew the number he wanted, but he did not give it to the operator. "I want to speak to Mr. William Gibson," he said, and he spelled the name slowly, "at the Osaka Importing Company. If he asks who's calling, say it is Mr. John Rhyce," and he spelled his name and put down the telephone.

The sun of late June shone hot and strong on the lotus pool in front of the porte-cochere, and he stood at the small window looking at the pink and yellow lotus flowers while he waited for his call. He did not turn when he heard the door connecting the two rooms open, because he knew the sound of her step.

"Is everything all right in your place?" he asked.

"Everything's okay. So you knew this door was unlocked?"

"Yes," he said. "Gibson must have wanted it that way."

"Well, let's keep it open," she said. "Do you like the way things are going?"

"Not with that Jap meeting us at the plane. He looked to me as though he were in the business. When he reached into his pocket to take his wallet out, I almost thought he was going for a gun. You don't move that way without training."

"So you're feeling jumpy, too, are you?"

"It's the trip," he answered. "I'll feel clearer just as soon as I get a little shut-eye. I'm just contacting Gibson. They ought to call back any minute now. How about a drink?"

Just then the telephone rang. There was no mistaking Bill Gibson's voice. Jack went into his act again.

"Say, Bill," he said, "guess who this is? Jack Rhyce."

"Why, *Jack*," Bill answered. There was no one who could throw himself into a game better than Bill. "Where did you drop from, you old buzzard, and what are you doing in Tokyo?"

"I'm over here to write a report for the Asia Friendship League.

And who do you think I've got with me, to help out? Ruth Bogart. You remember Ruth, don't you? Why don't you drop everything, and come on up, Bill?"

"There's nothing I'd rather do in the world, but right at the minute things are pretty busy in the office."

"Oh, now Bill, can't you let things drop for just half an hour?"

"Oh, all right," Bill said. "You always did have a bad influence on me, Jack." His laugh had the proper tolerant affection, but his final remark struck Jack Rhyce as disconcerting. "Leave your door unlocked," he said.

Ruth Bogart was standing close beside Jack.

"Why did he ask you to leave the door unlocked?" she asked.

"I guess because he wants to get in in a hurry."

"Maybe I'm not going to have a nap after all."

"It could be possible, but how about that drink?" He pulled a flask from the bottom of his bag.

The worst thing in the world for anyone in the business was to develop any dependence on alcohol, but he was sure that the whiskey was good for them, under the circumstances. It was one of those few opportunities afforded them to be natural. They sat smiling at each other when they were not watching the door.

"Here's looking at you," she said. "Jack, are you carrying a gun?"

"Absolutely not. Are you?"

"I have one of those fountain pens in my handbag."

"Well, never mind it now," he said. "I suppose you've been told that you're a very pretty girl."

"I've been told, but I'm glad you mentioned it. And now may I make a remark about you, as long as we're being personal?"

"Why, yes," he said, "anything at all."

"I keep wondering what sort of a person you really are. I mean, what you're like when you're being yourself."

He felt depressed at her question.

"You know," he said, "I'm really beginning to forget what I used to be. That's the trouble with this business, isn't it?"

"Yes," she said. "I wish we could have met on the outside. Have you ever thought of getting out of all this? What would you do if you ever did?"

"I'd get a canoe and some canned goods and a tent. I'd paddle up through the lakes in Ontario until I got about a hundred miles from anywhere, and then I'd pitch the tent. And when I wasn't asleep I'd sit in the sun, doing absolutely nothing — "

The door opened. His mind was jerked from northern Ontario, and he realized he never should have been thinking of it. He was not surprised at the manner in which Bill Gibson entered the room, having seen Bill move fast before, although he had never understood how it could be done with excess weight and a sagging waistline. Bill looked the part he had played for years in Tokyo — a middle-aged American businessman who drank too much before lunch, who fell asleep at the bridge table in the evening, who talked too much, and who had amorous proclivities which he could never suppress when he should. He was wearing a washable business suit. His jowls were heavy, his black hair was brushed back in a pompadour and he wore horn-rimmed spectacles.

"Hi," he said, and he nodded to Ruth. "Lock the door, kid. I'm sorry to barge in this way, but I've had a hunch for the last few days that I'm hot as a pistol, and I don't want to be seen." He sat down on the edge of the bed. "I'll have a drink," he said. "These rooms are all right to talk in. What's the emergency, Buster? I thought I was to call you, and not you me."

Jack Rhyce realized that he was being rebuked.

"That's right. I took the liberty, Bill. It's about Big Ben. I have a feeling we've seen him."

He started with San Francisco and the steps outside the door, and the singing of the tune, and then the other tune at Wake.

"When I heard that voice, it linked up with that song in the hall. It wouldn't have given me a jolt if it had not been from the same show."

Bill Gibson sipped his drink. "Well, describe him."

Jack complied. "He was damn big, and a beautiful build," he concluded. "I'd hate to tangle with him."

"How did he react?" Bill Gibson asked.

"Friendly. Maybe a little too friendly. He thought Ruth and I were new air-line personnel, and then he asked if we were passengers on a world cruise. He indicated he had read about the cruise group on Operations teletype. That's the one wrong move he made. My hunch would be that he picked it up in San Francisco the night he was singing 'Every Day Is Ladies' Day With Me.'"

"Ruth dear," Bill said, "would you look out the window in a nice careful way and see if there's an old beat-up Chevrolet out there? Dark-green coupe, left front fender pretty well mashed in, and the door missing a handle." Gibson sipped his drink. "So he's on a plane crew?"

Jack nodded. "And I'll bet he's only a few hours out of here right now," he said.

"There isn't any Chevrolet outside yet," Ruth said.

"Well, thanks, sweetie," Bill Gibson said. "Keep on looking, will you? That Chevvy's been like Mary's little lamb to me the last few days. . . . Did you check up on him at Wake?"

"No, it was a big temptation, but it might have been a giveaway."

"Maybe you've got something, Buster," Bill said. "It's the first good lead on him I've seen for quite a while."

Sometimes it was hard for Jack to realize that Bill's mind and techniques were among the best in the office. His face looked bloated and his eyes rheumy and dull, but he was not missing anything as Jack told about the encounter with the Russians, about the old bank clerk at the table, and about the Japanese who mentioned Big Ben. "Cripes, Jack," he said, "this thing is closing in."

"And that isn't all. There was this other one at the airport."

"Let's see his card." Bill held out his hand. "Moto isn't a Japanese name," he said. "It's only a suffix to a name, like Yamamoto, or Mikimoto, who puts pearls in the oysters — and maybe there'll be some Mikimoto pearls for you, Ruth dear, if you happen to see that Chevrolet." He finished his drink. "Well, kids, it looks as if we're going to get some action. Would you guess this Moto boy was in touch with Wake?"

"The thought has crossed my mind, Bill," Jack said.

"This has been very interesting, kids, because it ties up with some other stuff that's just come in. Big Ben is around, all right. I've a lot of things to do, and I can't brief you now. We've got to get together somewhere. Now here's what I want — "

He stood up. It was amazing how quickly he could pull himself off the bed, fat abdomen, jowls and everything. "I want you two to take tomorrow to get your cover sweetened with this Asia Friendship League. I also want you to make fools of yourselves about each other. The day after tomorrow, you're going to a resort hotel in the mountains. It's a real off-the-record honeymoon retreat, and no one will notice you if you just keep interested in each other. I'll be up there Saturday night. You'll see me at the bar at six o'clock, but don't pay any attention to me. Go to the dance that night and have a good time. My room will be in a cottage called Chrysanthemum Rest. It's near the ballroom. Around ten o'clock, leave the ballroom as if you were going out in the dark to smooch. There'll be so much noise and music, no one will hear us talking, or care. Have you got it?"

"This hotel," Jack said, "where is it, and how do I get there?"

"In Myanoshita." Bill scribbled in his notebook, and tore out a page. "The Army used it during the Occupation. Officers and their wives spend the week-ends there, and young men and their girl friends. It's a comfortable and friendly place."

"Why don't you give us the whole fill-in now?" Jack said.

"There's not time. But I'll tell you this, it's dangerous as hell. They are planning a political assassination — "

He did not complete his sentence because Ruth said, "A Chevrolet with a dented fender is driving up."

"Let me know what whoever gets out looks like, but tell me later. Good luck. You've got everything?"

"Yes, Bill," Jack said. "We'll be seeing you."

He was gone so quietly that the closing of the door hardly made a sound.

"Only one man in the Chevrolet," Ruth said. "He's getting out. Thirty-five or six, sunglasses, brown hair, balding at temples. Height five feet ten. Weight maybe one seventy. Pale face, professorial type. Aloha shirt with goldfish on it. Trousers white silk. Shoes, white buckskin trimmed with brown leather. He's entering the hotel. He seems American and harmless-looking."

"Right," Jack said. "You'd better go and lie down for a bit, Ruth." His hand firmly on her elbow, he gently propelled her into the other room.

"Hadn't we better talk things over? Bill looked upset."

"You take a nap first," he answered. "I'm afraid we're going to have a lot of time to talk things over."

She kicked off her shoes, and tossed herself inelegantly on the bed, indicating there was not much reason for reticence when you were in the business.

He believed that she was already asleep when he closed the door to the adjoining room, and he envied her. One of them must stay awake. The Chevrolet outside was disturbing. He was wondering whether it would be wise to stray down and take a closer look at it when someone knocked on the door.

The necessity for being alert again was difficult to face. He walked to the door and opened it with a few technical precautions. He was too tired for further shocks, but he had to face another. Standing outside in the narrow corridor was the man whom Ruth had described. There was no mistaking the shirt, the silk trousers, the white buckskin shoes trimmed with tan, the brown hair receding at the temples. He had the look which Jack had begun to associate with hundreds of individuals sent out by the Government to work on helpful projects — the eager and self-satisfied expression of someone who knew he knew the answers.

"Hello," the man said, and he had a warm, hail-fellow voice. "You're Mr. Rhyce, aren't you?"

Jack smiled. "The name is Rhyce. I'm just off the plane."

"Well, it's a real pleasure to welcome you to Tokyo," the man said. "My name's Harry Pender, running the shop here for Asia Friendship. Chas. Harrington wired you were coming in today. It's fine to have you aboard."

"Well, Harry Pender," Jack said, "this is mighty kind of you to look me up so promptly. I was on the point of taking a little snooze, but come on in. You've waked me up already."

It was true that Harry Pender had waked him up. Why was it he had not called on the house telephone? How long had he been outside in the hall? If the Chevrolet with the battered fender had been following Bill Gibson, how *about* the Asia Friendship League? Jack Rhyce wished that the Chief were there to know that it was not harmless.

"I won't take a minute of your time," Harry Pender said. "I should have met you at the airport, but we're going to have a conference of Japanese writers tomorrow, and I've been unusually busy as a consequence."

"You mustn't have me on your mind," Jack said. "I'm just here to look things over and do this report. I'd like to sit in on that writers' conference with you."

Mr. Pender nodded. "The whole place is open to you. Nothing up our sleeves or anything like that." He laughed heartily. "And I don't know any way in which you can get the spirit of what we're up to here more than by sitting in at the table with some of our Japanese writers. They're lovable people, the Japanese."

"How do you mean — lovable?" Jack Rhyce asked.

"You'll get their spirit, given time. They're basically only a bunch of mixed-up kids, but lovable at heart. You'll see."

Jack Rhyce nodded in a respectful, sympathetic manner.

"I suppose I'm prejudiced in my point of view about the Japanese," he said. "I was in the Pacific during the war."

"I know the superb record that you made with the paratroopers in Burma. I wish I might have been with you, but I had to serve in a more sheltered branch — the USO — due to being in the Four F category."

"Oh," Jack Rhyce said, "so you were in the USO?"

He could have kicked himself the moment he had said it. The USO and Big Ben might come together somewhere and he never should have betrayed interest. He thought there was a sharpening in Mr. Pender's brown eyes.

"It used to hurt at times," Mr. Pender said, "not to be able to be up forward with you boys, but we did our best in our small way. I was in a singing troupe. We called our group the Song Caravan, and they were a fine dedicated bunch — boys and girls with a smattering of experience from the summer theaters and whatnot." His glance traveled about the room with a casualness which could have been overelaborate. "Oh, by the way, the young lady who was coming over to assist you — is there anything I can do for her? What is her name? It's gone out of my head."

"Ruth Bogart," Jack said. "She's asleep, I think."

"Bring her over to the office tomorrow. The more the merrier." He held out his hand. His muscle tone was excellent. "Well, so long. Half past nine tomorrow? You have the address?"

"Oh, yes," Jack said, "and thanks for dropping in."

After Mr. Pender had left, he stood by his window watching the parked Chevrolet. In two and a half minutes Mr. Pender had reached it — approximately the time it should have taken him to walk down the staircases, across the lobby and out the front door. Jack turned from the window and very gently opened the door of Ruth's room. She was wide awake.

"I'm sorry if we've kept you awake," he said. "It was the man in the Aloha shirt."

She smiled at him. "You didn't keep me awake. I went down and took a look at the car."

"That was a very good girl, provided you got away with it."

"I think I did. I'm pretty good with cars. There was nothing except a gun in the glove compartment. A Beretta, all loaded."

It was interesting that anyone in Mr. Pender's position should have been carrying an Italian officer's pistol.

"And now," she said, "go away and let me sleep, and you'd better, too. I think things are going to be quiet for a while."

It was exasperating to discover the desire for sleep had left him. He stretched out on his bed and tried to relax. He was full of the old malaise that told him that a net was closing. The elderly man in the San Francisco restaurant and the Nisei Japanese boy were parts of it, and so was the middle-aged Japanese named Moto. Pender was another strand of the net, and there was the fact that Bill Gibson was on the run. The net was closing on Bill, but it might be, Jack thought, that he and Ruth were still out of it. He was almost positive that Mr. Pender had accepted them.

Mr. Moto was due to call at six and until six there was nothing to do but rest. Then he realized he had forgotten something, and he pushed open the adjoining door. Ruth was asleep. The tenseness about her mouth had relaxed. She had a half-cheerful, half-expectant look. She was a very pretty girl now that she was asleep, the way she would have looked on the outside, and he was sure that her dreams had taken her there. He was sorry to bring her back into the business. "Sorry," he said. "Just one thing, Ruth."

You could tell that she had been at the Farm from the way she awakened. Her right hand moved toward her handbag.

"This Moto who's calling at six," he said. "I think he'll ring the house telephone and not barge up like Pender. The bell will wake you. Get up and listen, and keep that fountain pen handy. It might just be we'll have to use it."

"I'd have covered you anyway. Now go relax or you'll be fidgety when he comes, and leave the door open. I need company."

He could not sleep when he lay down. The truth had begun to dawn on him that his old resilience and iron were wearing thin. The girl's face that looked so young and happy in sleep had disturbed him. He began thinking, just when he should not have, of the outside. If he had stayed on the outside he would undoubtedly be married by now. He would have had a home and children, and he would have been a decent man — warmhearted and genuine — not a suspicious, machine-tooled robot who had been through too much, a man who had played under so many covers that it was becoming impossible to guess what he could have been.

There had always been people like himself who could not adjust to civil life after the violences of war. There had been some wonderful moments and triumphs, of course, and the satisfaction of knowing that in ten years he had made a place for himself in a highly exacting profession. But in the end, what was there of real value? Very little, and little of which to be proud. He was a spy, or a secret agent, if you cared for a politer word, trained to be a sneak, and if necessary a betrayer; trained to run from danger and let his best friend get it, if it helped the business; to kill or be killed inconspicuously; to die with his mouth shut, in the dark. There was only one loyalty — loyalty to the business.

He raised himself on his elbow. The whiskey flask was in his bag and the glasses were on the table. He could see the traces of Ruth Bogart's lipstick on her glass. She should have been more careful. Drinking was dangerous in the business — it was far safer to indulge in bitter thoughts.

The telephone awakened him. He heard Ruth close the adjoining door before he was on his feet. He had slept heavily, something that should never happen in the field. "Hello," he said. "Jack Rhyce speaking."

The time on his wrist watch was six to the dot. He was feeling hungry, and also rested. He was on the beam again.

"Please." It was Mr. Moto. "I hope I did not awaken you."

"Oh, it's you, is it?" Jack Rhyce said. "Do I sound sleepy?"

"Just a little in your voice, Mr. Rhyce."

The man downstairs was a smart Jap, and when they were, it was hard to find anything smarter. "Well, as a matter of fact," Jack said, "I have been having a little shut-eye. But come on right up."

There was time to tie his shoes, and put on his seersucker coat. Then his heart gave a startled jump. He had forgotten the three glasses on the table, but as he moved toward them he saw that only two were there, one with lipstick smears. Ruth must have been in when he was asleep, and he felt ashamed. He should have thought of the two glasses himself — one of them with lipstick.

The tap on the door was gentle and discreet. He felt a species of nervousness. He knew too much about Japan, yet he must not show it. Japanese were sensitive.

"Well, well," he said, "step right in. You're on the dot, I see."

Mr. Moto's features were finely chiseled. His hands were slender and graceful. In native dress, he would have been a fine figure of a samurai, and it was possible that his family had held that feudal rank. But the hideous purplish-blue business suit ruined this romantic picture, and so did the light-tan shoes. Mr. Moto was a figure of low comedy. Then a startling idea came to Jack: that he and Mr. Moto might both be impersonating clumsy people. The hissing intake of Mr. Moto's breath was too loud and too comic.

"So nice of you to receive me," Mr. Moto said. "You have enjoyed your sleep, I hope."

"Yes, sir," Jack Rhyce said. "I had a real nice shut-eye and I feel the better for it, Mr. — excuse me. I forget your name."

"Moto," Mr. Moto said. He laughed politely.

"I hope you'll excuse it, Mr. Moto. Japanese names are tough for me. And I suppose Rhyce is hard for you."

"Oh, no. R is easy in Japan. We have trouble when we pronounce your letter rell. See — I cannot say it."

It was hard for Jack Rhyce to decide whether or not **Mr. Moto** was having deliberate trouble with his *l's*.

"It takes all kinds to make a world, doesn't it?" Jack said. "You know, I'm kind of hungry after that plane ride. I wonder if we could get some bacon and eggs and tea. Maybe you can make the room boy understand in Japanese better than I can in English."

"Oh, yes. I shall call room service. Everything is up to date at the Imperial Hote-ru. Excuse me when I cannot say the *l*."

Mr. Moto had slipped, and Jack was sure that he was unaware of it. He had pronounced the letter *l*. When he picked up the telephone and asked for room service in Japanese, his accent was crisp and educated. His posture was very good, showing that he had done his tour of military duty. When he gave the order, he asked for bacon and eggs and coffee — not tea.

"Everything will be right up," Mr. Moto said. "Chop-chop, as they say in China. Ha-ha."

"That's mighty kind of you," Jack said. "Sit down, won't you please? And I hope the food comes up chop-chop. I could certainly do with a cup of coffee."

He could have bitten off his tongue the moment he mentioned coffee, but there was nothing to do but go ahead, without showing embarrassment.

"You've come at just the right time, Mr. Moto," he said. "I'm here to do a report for the Asia Friendship League. I'll need somebody like you to show me around."

Mr. Moto's glance had turned toward the glasses on the table; Jack had a feeling that tension had relaxed when he saw them. You could discount a good deal of potential menace in a man if you saw a glass with lipstick smears in his bedroom.

"The Asia Friendship League is known to me," Mr. Moto said, "and Mr. Pender, its new head, is such a good man."

"So you know Mr. Pender? I've had a talk with him: he's going to show me around the shop tomorrow, but Saturday and Sunday I shall need a little rest and relaxation. You know — all work and no play makes Jack a dull boy." He smiled fatuously.

"There are lots of amusements in Tokyo," Mr. Moto said. "I would be so happy to show geisha girls or anything, Mr. Rhyce."

"That would be swell sometime later, but this Saturday and Sunday I was thinking of taking a spin into the country. I've heard that during the Occupation the Army took over a hotel up in the mountains. In Mio — Mio — "

"Oh," Mr. Moto said, "Miyanoshita. Very nice."

Jack Rhyce gave Mr. Moto a man-to-man look.

"I thought if you could rent me a good car and a driver, I might go there, and well — you know, take a girl along."

"Oh, yes," Mr. Moto said. "I can drive. I can get a good car for you, and very nice girl."

"That's the spirit. I had a hunch when I saw you at the airport that you'd be broad-minded. You supply the car, and I'll supply the young lady. Be here at nine o'clock on Saturday morning."

"Oh, yes," Mr. Moto said, "and we can see Kamakura, the Daibutsu Buddha — many other things."

There was a knock on the door. It was a waiter with bacon and eggs and coffee. Mr. Moto rose and bowed. "Nine, Saturday," he said. "Big, fine American car. You will be satisfied, I am sure, and thank you very much, Mr. Rhyce."

It had been a long while since Jack Rhyce had been so unsure of his cover work. That slip of his worried him. His expression must have disturbed Ruth when he called her to come in.

"What's bothering you?" she asked.

"The coffee," he answered, and he told her.

"Well, it's over now," she said. "I didn't know you knew a word of Japanese. I thought you'd never been in Japan."

"Frankly," he said, "I did live in Japan from age zero to five. Japanese servants are devoted to kids, and I was speaking the language all the time. My father was a missionary."

"Why didn't you lose your Japanese when you went back home?"

"My father wanted me to keep it up," he said. "You see — don't laugh — he wanted me to be a missionary, too. My fluency came back to me during the war, at language school." He stopped. "By the way, thanks for doing that about the glasses."

"Don't mention it," she said. "You can't be a mastermind all the time, you know. Did he notice?"

"Oh, yes, he noticed. I'm afraid he's very smart. I don't know where he fits in — not to mention this man Pender in the Chevrolet." As Jack told her about Harry Pender the outlines of her face hardened. Her eyes were still very pretty, but they hardened, too.

"We're still in the clear with Pender, I think," Jack said, "or I think he wouldn't have told about that USO singing caravan. But we're running into something."

"Yes," she said, "but let's not take it too big."

"Just what do you mean?" he asked.

"We're teamed up on this, and you're running the show, of course," she said. "I like the way you work, but one thing about you makes me nervous. You try to think of everything, and no one can. Why not try to think of one or two things tonight, and put the rest out of your head?"

"All right," he said. "Name the one or two things."

"I'll name one. How about thinking about me for a while?" When she smiled at him his nerves were not on edge any longer.

"I mean," she said, "let's try to be friends. I think it would help the cover if we found out a little more about each other. Aren't you curious about me? Guess what I was outside."

He was surprised, because girls in the business seldom cared to talk about their pasts. It was a safe bet they all had them or they would not have been in the business. He honestly preferred to take her as she was, without knowing any more.

"Why, yes," he said, "I could make an educated guess about you, but I don't know that you'd like it."

"You're such a pro, aren't you? You know everything."

He was sorry to detect an undertone of antagonism in what she said. It was better, when working with a woman, to keep things on an impersonal basis, and not to quarrel; but the strain of the day had told on him, too. "I'm sorry if I've displeased you," he said. "Of course I don't know everything, but I've been acquainted with a lot of girls in the business. I've often had to check their backgrounds. I've made a guess about you already."

Her face flushed. "So you think I'm just another tramp," she said.

"No. There's no cause to lose your temper, Ruth."

"I'm not losing my temper," she answered. "Tell me what you think you know about me, and I'll tell you if you're right."

"All right, if you want the professor to give you an analysis — in the first place, you're not in the tramp class, and you never will be. You have too much background and character."

"That's nice to know," she answered. "Go ahead, what else?"

"Most girls in your position," he said, "tell the same story. All of them are born of wealthy parents, then along came a business failure, or an undesirable marriage. The undesirable marriage is usually correct — but in your case the rest of it is true. You come from an excellent background. You were brought up in a large American city, but I can't tell you which, from your accent."

"Go ahead," she said. "What else?"

"You also spent a lot of your time, while you were growing up, in the country. You schooled and jumped horses once."

"What made you make that guess?" she asked.

"Your posture, but mainly your hands. You have beautiful hands. They are riding hands."

"All right," she said. "You hit that one. Go ahead."

"I'd guess that you're an only child. You went to college, and I'll bet it was nearer to Bryn Mawr than Goucher. You fell in love, and the boy friend left you flat."

"What makes you say that?" she asked.

"From the way you act with a man. You don't trust men. Then you met the Chief. He found that you were a natural at the business. You were rattling around loose, and that's about all."

"Just how did you happen to see my file?" she asked. "I thought those things were confidential."

"No file," he said. "I've just been watching you."

She was looking at him with a new respect. Suddenly she smiled, and he knew that they were friends.

"You make me feel naked," she said. "Actually we owned a place in Virginia. In fact, I own it still."

"Now, listen, you don't have to tell me anything. It's dangerous."

"You're always careful, aren't you?" she said in an exasperated way. "How do you mean — dangerous?"

"When you get talking this way you get interested. It's dangerous to get interested in anyone in the business, Ruth. You might have to ditch me, or I might have to ditch you, tomorrow."

His hand rested on her shoulder, and she had not moved away, and he was right that it was dangerous. He knew all the rules about women and emotional involvement. He knew that he was coming very close to breaking several of them, but he had never realized that the prospect could be so pleasant. He felt he was himself again, exactly as he had been on the outside. Caution was gone when he looked at her.

Chapter 5

A GREAT deal of the business was very dull, but that ensuing Friday was one of the most irksome that Jack Rhyce could remember. To fall into the mood of the dedicated people in the Friendship office, and still not miss a trick, demanded every bit of his patience.

It was a time to be very, very careful. It was a time to be naive and to convey emphatically the utter harmlessness of himself and Ruth Bogart. It was also a time to show a picture of their growing attachment.

The Asia Friendship League occupied half the floor of a postwar office building in the neighborhood of the Ginza. Mr. Pender had a truly beautiful office, furnished with new Japanese furniture that had been adapted to the European fashion. The furniture had been designed right in the Friendship League; a lot of leading Japanese artists and merchants had been consulted, Mr. Pender explained. This was just a small example of what the Asia Friendship League was up to. There was a group in the office, studying the new Japanese films. Then there was the sports group. And this afternoon there would be a panel discussion on writing, in the conference auditorium.

Then there was Harry Pender's pet project, the Friendly Pen Pals. Jack's interest quickened.

"It's an idea of my own," Harry said, "and I hope you'll play it up big in your report, Jack. It just came over me — why not get Japanese kids in school and the universities to swap ideas and news with their own age groups back home, and set up a translation post right here in the League? It would be exactly the cultural interchange we're looking for."

Jack Rhyce nodded slowly. He was wondering how he had over-looked Harry Pender in his research back in the states and he could not see how the Chief had overlooked him either. Pen Pals could form the basis of an excellent message center.

It was late in the afternoon when he picked up another piece of information that interested him.

"You see," Harry was saying, "this job is a real challenge to me, Jack. I was running our settlement house at Pnompenh not six weeks ago — and along came the news that the League board had selected me for Tokyo. It's a big jump."

"Pnompenh," Jack Rhyce said slowly. "I don't think I've ever heard of Pnompenh."

"I don't blame you," Harry Pender said. "It's in Cambodia, and not many people get there now."

It was also an excellent place from which to communicate with China. Jack glanced at his wrist watch.

"This has been a very fascinating day, Harry," he said. "But now maybe Ruth and I had better call things off until Monday, or else we'll lose perspective. We can get a taxi, can't we?"

"Oh, don't do that," Harry said. "Why don't we all go to a real Japanese restaurant for supper, and see the night life?"

Jack shook his head. "Let's make it sometime next week. I think Ruth's still tired from the trip. Aren't you, Ruth?"

"Well, yes," she said. "I am a little, Jack."

"I'll just take her for a walk along the Ginza."

"Well — " Mr. Pender smiled broadly " — have fun, kids, but come back to school on Monday."

The heat on the street outside made them catch their breath.

"I noticed quite a lot today," Ruth said. "We'd better be careful."

"That's why we're walking down the Ginza," he said. "If any-one's tailing us . . . I agree, we'll have to be damn careful."

EVERY large city in the world was bound to have a characteristic street or square, and it seemed to Jack Rhyce that the Ginza was the most vital of them all; it best expressed the spirit of the people who had made it. It was not a beautiful street, any more than Broadway was beautiful. It was tawdry, but gay. There were huge department stores, and smaller shops filled with garish Japanese goods. There were motion-picture houses displaying the latest Hollywood films as well as Japanese-made pictures. There were beer halls, cabarets and billboards, jewelry and cultured pearls. The Ginza was a reflection of the indomitable spirit of a people anxious to be in the front rank of what was perhaps erroneously known as progress. The startling vigor of Japan was reflected in the burgeoning of manufactured goods, from plastic toys to electric refrigerators. And where was Japan going to sell this glittering output? This was one of the world's new, restive questions.

"I wouldn't say we had a tail on us, would you?" Ruth said after a while.

"No. Between us we should have spotted one by now."

"Then let's go back to the hotel and have a drink in the bar. You can make eyes at me in front of the bar boys just to build the cover, darling — just to build the cover."

"We'll go there pretty soon," he said, "but there's one place I'd like to take you first. From what I've heard about it, I think perhaps we can pick up some ideas there."

Along the Ginza it was simple enough to find a taxi driver who could speak a little English.

"Street with all the bookstores," Jack said.

"For heaven's sake, why bookstores?" she said.

"I want to see," he said, "what people are reading in Japan."

The book district in Tokyo extended for block after block. The wide-open doorways leading to the brightly lighted interiors displayed stacks of new paper-backed editions, translations from all over the world, and the classical literature of Japan. Most of the bookstores were filled with customers. No one interrupted Ruth or Jack as they moved from shop to shop. The displays of periodicals were what interested him most, particularly the large numbers that dealt with Russia and Red China. These were crude but effective projections of American formats. Except for some scurrilous pictures of Uncle Sam and heavily armed gentlemen with dollar signs on their waistcoats who whipped starving workers into factories, everyone was happy in the pictures. Fat Chinese peasants were smilingly learning to read. Soldiers carrying the Freedom Flag of the Hammer and Sickle gave candy to children.

"You see," he said, "how it rounds out the picture?"

"Yes," she said, taking his arm and pressing it urgently. "But we shouldn't have come here. Buy some cheap American magazine and let's get out."

"We're in the clear," he said as they stood on the curb waving to a taxi. "There was nothing queer in any of those shops."

"We were. We were the only foreigners and everyone remembers foreigners. Where would you keep a lookout for new operators? Put yourself in their position, Jack."

He felt mortified that he had not thought of her point himself. Too many small mistakes added up to something fatal.

"There are some people looking at us," she said.

"But, darling," he said, and he laughed loudly. Then he put his arm through hers. At least he could leave the impression of dalliance if anyone was watching. "Honey," he said, "I'll get you a nice cool drink in that nice cool bar. Frankly, I can't wait."

The bar of the Imperial Hotel was aggressively modern and so over-air-conditioned that Jack felt for a moment that they were inside a refrigerator. Nearly all the tables were filled, mostly with rather weary-looking Europeans. There was nothing professional about anyone there, nothing technically disturbing. It was becoming easier and easier to appear conspicuously interested in Ruth Bogart.

"What would you like, sweet?" he asked.

"Scotch on the rocks, darling," she said.

They gazed at each other fatuously, and then they began to laugh, and it was the first time in several weeks that he had been genuinely amused. He was happy, and happiness was such a rare sensation that he was suspicious of it, but it made the whole day worth while.

"You know," he said, "I think you're a pretty clever girl. In fact, maybe you are smarter than I am. You were right about those bookstores."

"I like to have you wrong sometimes," she said. "It shows that maybe you are human."

"Believe me, it's better not to be."

She smiled at him, ironically, but very pleasantly.

"You remind me of a poem of Whittier's," she said, "about the boy and the girl at the schoolhouse. *'I'm sorry that I spelt the word: I hate to go above you, Because,' — the brown eyes lower fell — 'Because, you see, I love you!'* "

"Yes," he said, "but I don't like what comes later. *Dear girl! the grasses on her grave Have forty years been growing.*"

"I don't like that either," she said, "and I wish you hadn't brought it up."

But even so, nothing changed his mood.

"You know," he said, "I don't see why we shouldn't have a nice time going there tomorrow."

"Please," she said, "please let's, Jack."

JACK RHYCE stood beneath the porte-cochere of the Imperial Hotel. Mr. Moto had done very well with the car. It was a vintage Buick limousine, with the chauffeur's seat separated by glass from the owner's.

"Thirty thousand yen for week-end," Mr. Moto said. "Me, automobile, and glass for privacy. It is not too expensive, I hope."

"Oh, no," Jack Rhyce said, "not for this once."

There was one good thing about the business. Money was never an obstacle, and nobody audited expense accounts if you happened to get home. "All right," he said, "let's go." The mood of the afternoon before was still with him, and he felt no sensation of tenseness or discomfort.

Jack Rhyce knew that he would never forget the motor ride to Myanoshita. It was one of those periods of unalloyed beauty. It was dangerous to feel as he was beginning to about the girl beside him, but as he looked back over that long day he could not experience a single qualm of regret. There was nothing that he or she could have done until they made contact with Bill Gibson at the hotel that night. Besides, all they did was part of the cover.

It was part of the cover to be conscious of her nearness and to hope that the car would soon take another curve so that she would lean against him. The way a draft of air blew a wisp of hair across her forehead was beautiful, and so was the austere perfection of her profile when softened by a smile, and so were the quick gestures of her strong but delicate hands.

"It's just as though we were on the outside," he said.

"Yes," she answered, "and please let's keep it that way." And she did not move away when he took her hand.

EXCEPT for the heavy traffic on the roads, the disruptions of the machine age were gone once they reached the country. The thatched farmhouses, the jade green of the rice plants reflected in the shallow water of the checkerboard squares of the paddies, the bamboo windbreaks, the farmers in their huge straw hats meticulously tending each rice shoot, the jagged mountains in the background were part of an eternal picture of a way of life that could survive all change.

There was a fortuneteller who had his concession on the path leading to one of the shrines at Kamakura, an emaciated elderly man who smiled and beckoned to Jack and Ruth. On a stand near him was a miniature red-lacquer temple with three small black-and-yellow birds perched in front of it. The fortuneteller whipped from his pocket a typewritten explanation.

"Give any bird a fifty-yen folded note," Jack read. *"Bird will drop it in the cashbox, fly to temple door, ring bell, enter temple, get fortune on folded paper and bring back same."*

"It might be worth fifty yen," Jack said.

"Yes," she said, "but let me pay for it. I want it to be my fortune." She handed the old man a folded note. He held it in front of one of the birds, and the bird took it in its beak and dropped it in a tiny money chest.

"Come on, Joe," the old man chanted, "come on, Joe."

That act of fortunetelling must have dated back to temple necromancy, but the words were new, telling their tale of lonely American soldiers on leave, back at home now, or dead perhaps in Korea.

The tiny black-and-yellow bird cocked its head and its beady

eye was remarkably intelligent. It fluttered from its perch to tiny
steps that led to the temple porch. It pushed a small bell smartly
with its beak, and the bell tinkled. Then the bird disappeared
inside the temple and emerged carrying a folded bit of paper. It
fluttered back to its perch, and Ruth took the paper from its beak.

"Don't be afraid to read it," Jack said. "They're bound to have
only good fortunes here."

She glanced at the words and handed it to him.

"Once you were unhappy," he read, *"but you are happy now."*

"That's true, you know," she said. "Absolutely true. And you're
happy too, aren't you? I mean for just now?"

"Oh, yes," he said. "I'm happy."

"There's only one catch," she said. "It says I'm happy now but
it doesn't say how long, and I want it to be long-term. Would you
like it long-term?"

"Yes," he said. "You couldn't possibly know how much I want
it that way."

They both knew that the moment would be transient, but a
weight was lifted from him. He felt a grateful relief that he was
alive. Then he heard a footstep behind them and he was back from
the outside to the inside, turning slowly and accurately on his heel.

He did not know that Mr. Moto had followed them until then,
nor was there any way of telling how long Mr. Moto had been
behind them or what he might have heard. There was nothing
harder, Jack Rhyce was thinking, than to tread softly on a graveled
walk, and only that single footstep had attracted his attention.

"Oh, hello," he said. "Have we been staying here too long?"

"No," Mr. Moto said, "but there is still a great distance to go."

"All right," Jack said. He put a slight edge to his words because
he wanted to make it clear that he had not approved of that gentle
approach. "Go on back to the car. We'll be with you in a minute."

"You're right about his being in the business," Ruth said when
Mr. Moto moved away. "Do you think he knows what we are?"

"Let's not worry right now," he said. "We'll know better when
we see Bill tonight. Let's still try to be happy."

There were long cool shadows across the road as they began
to climb into the hills. They would be at the hotel at about six.

Jack had heard there were hot springs at the hotel, and a swimming pool. The rooms were comfortable, he told her, and the food and service very good.

"But I'd rather stay at a Japanese inn," he said. "I'll take you to one sometime."

"I'd like it," she said, but he knew she was thinking of something else. "Jack, will you promise me something?"

"Promise what?" he asked.

"If we get out of this, let's try to live on the outside. And promise me you'll get out of the business if I don't come back."

"Have you got a hunch about something, Ruth?"

"No," she said, "no. But I'd like to have you promise, Jack."

"Let's talk about it later, but I'm glad you like me that much."

"Yes, I like you that much," she said.*

Chapter 6

THE TOWN was on a slope of the winding road that led to the sacred Mount Fuji. The hot springs and the scenery had made it a resort for a great many years, patronized by the old nobility and wealthy people from Tokyo. The hotel had been designed as a concession to European tastes, long before the war; time, plus the imagination of its proprietors, had given it an exotic Eurasian charm. Its grounds on the mountain slope were watered by rills from natural springs that made a merry sound of running water. The hotel gardens were very beautiful. The Japanese had ancient ways with plants and flowers which were different from those of other gardeners. Everything, even if seemingly wild, was actually in order, even down to the arrangements of wind- and water-worn rocks.

The hotel had been designed as a place for a happy holiday. Built on the side of a hill, it had a profusion of halls, staircases, outside galleries and connection ells that had English names with an Oriental lilt — Plum Blossom Cottage, Cozy Nook, Peach Bloom.

The day was still warm but the air was cooler than it had been in Tokyo. Mr. Moto was speaking authoritatively to the Japanese concierge, and Jack was contented to hear him say that his passengers were good people who would appreciate attention.

"I will take the car," Mr. Moto said, "but I will call later for orders and to see if all is right."

"You don't have to until tomorrow," Jack told him. "It's been a very fine day, and thanks a lot."

There was plenty of time before dark to stroll about the grounds and to locate the cottage called Chrysanthemum Rest, where Bill Gibson would be staying.

Ruth and he followed the boy and their bags, passing through an arcade lined with display cases of silks, lacquer, ivories and porcelains. As they climbed a flight of stairs to the upper level of the hotel, he realized that, in spite of years of practice in many places, the ground plan of this rambling building was too much for him, and he greatly disliked the sensation of not being oriented.

When the boy opened the door to a spacious double bedroom, Jack encountered in himself an embarrassment that made him very formal. He gave a liberal tip and spoke enthusiastically as the boy backed out, bowing.

"This is a nice room, isn't it, dear?" he asked. "I think I'd better take the bed by the doorway, don't you?" It did not help his uneasiness to find that she was laughing at him. "And if you want to bathe or anything," he said, "I'll go out and stroll around."

"For heaven's sake," she said, "don't take it so seriously, even if your father was a missionary. I'm going to take a bath. Do you snore, darling?"

"You ought to know I don't; not in this business, Ruth."

"The more we forget the business while we're here, the better," she said. "Darling, aren't you going to give me a kiss?"

She raised her voice when she asked that question.

"I've been waiting for this for hours," he said.

"Oh, darling," she said, and then she whispered, "there's someone in the hall outside. We have the privacy of goldfish in this room."

His first instinct was to tiptoe to the door and snatch it open, but she held him and shook her head. "No, no," she whispered, "maybe it isn't anything, but I think this place is spooky, Jack."

She was right about the room. There was a transom above the door and he especially disliked transoms. Two windows at the foot of the twin beds looked over the carefully tended grounds at the rear of the hotel. The third window, a ground-glass one in the bathroom, opened on the corridor, and a sound of footsteps made a rhythmic beat along the corridor's jute carpet.

"I seem to be losing my grip," he said, "what with one thing or another."

It was a mistake, he realized, to have said such a thing. He believed in holding a positive thought; as soon as one became worried and overanxious, accidents occurred. He stepped to the open windows, examined the shades and curtains and then made a thorough inventory of the bedroom. The Japanese prints on the wall seemed surprisingly good; the curtains were of heavy cotton, green and yellow with a bamboo motif. Whoever had decorated the room had good taste. But there was one disturbing feature. The lock on the door was an old contraption which any trained operator could pick in a matter of seconds.

Ruth turned on the bathtub taps and the running water made a cheerful sound.

"I suppose we'll have to look nice but informal," she said, "if we're going to that dance." She was taking out clothing from her neatly packed bag. "I'll wear my light-green silk."

"Better put on the dark green or a dark blue if you have it," he told her. "Remember, we are going outside the hotel."

"Right. I forgot. I wonder whether Gibson's here yet."

"That's his problem," he told her. "I'm going out to walk around while you take your bath."

"You don't have to, you know," she said.

She was hanging things in the closet as though they were going to stay for an indefinite period. The voices of the hotel guests came gaily through the open windows. Then in the distance someone began whistling a tune that made Jack look at Ruth Bogart. Their faces assumed the old watchful look. Jack hummed, along with the whistling, *"You cannot see in gay Paree, in London or in Cork! The queens you'll meet on any street in old New York!"*

"Well, well," he said softly, "our old favorite, isn't it?"

"It's no favorite of mine," she said. "I told you this place was spooky."

"Well," he said, "go ahead and take your bath. I'd better go down there and see what I can see."

She shook her head. "I'm not going to stay here alone. I'll go right down with you. Frankly, that song frightens me."

They walked arm in arm up the hill past the swimming pool and tennis courts, almost deserted now. They wandered heedlessly past Chrysanthemum Rest — a small cottage, not much more than a hundred and fifty feet from the ballroom ell. Bill Gibson could not have picked a better place for a private conversation because, as he had said, the noise of the orchestra would drown out anything else. Then they stopped at the fish pond and watched children feeding bread crumbs to the giant goldfish.

"You know," she said, "I wouldn't mind being a fish myself, right now. No wonder they live a hundred years."

"Don't wish that, sweet," he said, loudly enough so that everyone could hear. "Just compromise and be a mermaid."

"All right, if you say so," she answered, "you old sea dog, you."

"Just don't overplay," he whispered to her amorously.

"All right," she said, and she laughed.

There was reassurance in her laughter; it meant that, like him, she had noticed nothing out of the ordinary.

"Let's go to the Main Bar," he said. "There may be something new there."

THE MAIN BAR was on the hotel's lower level. Its decoration derived from foreign influence close to the turn of the century. Its comfortable chairs and tables were not crowded too closely together. A dozen happy couples were at the tables in small groups, and several unaccompanied men were seated at the bar.

He beckoned to a waiter. "Gin and tonic, dear?"

They had selected a table in a far corner from which the whole room was visible.

"Scotch and water," she answered. "Everybody here looks very cool and comfortable, and I can't locate any types."

"Don't try too hard. Don't forget we're in love." He leaned

back and sipped his drink. If it had not been for that tune, he would have believed that the place was wholly antiseptic.

"That's right," she said. "I've got to keep remembering. You look handsomer than you did yesterday, but I'd like it if you could get your seersucker suit pressed."

"It makes me look informal, feeble and good-natured," he told her. "Nobody cares what happens to a man in a seersucker suit."

"I care," she said. "Oh, Jack! Look across the room."

His glance followed hers to the entrance by the bar. Bill Gibson had entered the room, and there was no mistaking what he was — a tired, middle-aged American exporter from Tokyo out for a good time over the week-end. He sauntered in an aimless way about the room, just as a lonely man with a few drinks would. He walked close by the table where Jack and Ruth Bogart sat, and for a second Jack thought he might be giving some sort of signal, but nothing in Bill's expression changed as he passed the table. He ambled to the bar, hoisted himself on one of the stools, calling happily: "Scotch and soda, and make it a double, boy-san."

"Listen," Ruth said, "school's out now, isn't it? Can't we please go up and get a bath?"

"You go ahead," Jack said. "Maybe I ought to stick around here for a few minutes."

"No. All those corridors . . . I won't go up there alone."

"Now, listen. I don't think there's a cough in a carload here." And then he checked himself, and his voice dropped to a whisper. "Fasten your seat belt, and for heaven's sake let's be natural."

She was a good girl, back in the act again. She had glanced for a fraction of a second at the doorway to the bar, long enough to see what he had seen. There was no mistaking the sandy hair, the clear-eyed glance, the lazily swinging arms, and the characteristic half bend of the fingers of the man who had just entered. Big Ben was wearing khaki trousers, Army issue, and an Aloha shirt.

"You look awfully sweet tonight, honey," Jack said.

He saw Bill Gibson at the bar tossing off his double Scotch and soda. Bill had the description and he never missed anything. He and Jack Rhyce must have shared the same consternation, and also the same exalted sense you had when the game was getting hot — because anything might happen now.

As Big Ben stood by the door, Jack saw that he had recognized them. He could feel it in the nerves of his neck. Honest pleasure rippled over Big Ben's face, and he waved to them.

Jack beckoned, at the same time lifting his glass. "Darling," he said loudly, "look who's coming over! Ships that pass in the night!"

Big Ben sauntered toward them. Jack did not like to think that the physical sensation he experienced was one of fear; it was rather a state of intense watchfulness that set all his perceptions at concert pitch. He pushed back his chair and stood up, smiling.

"Well, hello, troops," Big Ben said.

"Why, hello yourself," Jack Rhyce said. "If it isn't our sweet singer from Wake. Remember, Ruth?"

"I certainly do remember." Ruth smiled invitingly. "It was so terribly romantic, and you had such a lovely voice."

"Gee, thanks," Big Ben said. "It was quite a surprise to me to hear the boy friend answer right back from nowhere."

"Take a chair and take the weight off your feet," Jack said. "We certainly owe you a drink. It ought to be a double for a boy as big as you."

"You're not such a peewee yourself, fella." Big Ben smiled. "I'll bet you played football in your time."

"Well, you win, Mr. Holmes, I played right half for Oberlin. Where did you play?"

"Oh, shucks," Big Ben said. "I was never in the big time like that. I played for a jerkwater Southern Baptist college." His words trailed off apologetically, and then he gave his order to the waiter.

Jack had never watched or listened more carefully, but he could detect no flaw. He and Ruth were accepted for what they appeared to be. He was so sure of this that he had to fight down a sense of elation.

"Seriously," he said, "this is a real pleasure, meeting you. I suppose we ought to introduce ourselves. My name's Jack Rhyce, and this is Ruth Bogart. We're out here to make a survey for the Asia Friendship League."

"Say, it's a pleasure to meet you two nice people again. My name's

Ben Bushman. Flight engineer, at the present time. Our crew lays over at Tokyo about ten days out of every month, and Bushman comes up here for relaxation." He chuckled. "Just the way Jack Rhyce and Ruth Bogart have come up to study Asia Friendship. Am I right, or am I right?"

"Well, now, I don't exactly know how to answer that one," Jack said. He laughed self-consciously, and so did Ruth.

"But you must admit it is a friendly place here, Mr. Bushman," she said, and smiled at him dazzlingly.

"Now, now, honey," Big Ben said. "You call me Ben, and just remember, any time if two isn't company and three isn't a crowd, look around for me, will you? We might sing some old songs."

"Why, that will be splendid, Ben," Ruth said. "Jack loves old songs, too. But if he gets preachy or tiresome, I'll know where to turn, and two will still be company, won't it?"

"Oh, now, Ruth," Jack said. He wished that her flirtatiousness did not sound so genuine. "I'm not as bad as all that, am I? But she's right, Ben. I do like a song fest sometimes."

"Maybe we can have one tonight," Big Ben said. "Just drop into the bar later, say, eleven — that is, if you haven't something better to do." He slapped Jack affectionately on the shoulder and stood up. "See you later, I hope. And now I've got to be gittin'."

Jack drew a deep breath as he watched Big Ben leave. The man's walk was the loose-jointed, perfectly coördinated gait of the highly proficient athlete. He sauntered past the bar, shoulders squared and arms swinging easily. Bill Gibson had surely seen him now. Things were moving so fast that everything at any moment might pour itself into a barrel and go over Niagara Falls.

"It was all so natural, wasn't it?" Ruth said, and her words echoed what Jack had been thinking.

That conversation with Big Ben had been interwoven with threads of truth. Football at Oberlin, song fests because both of them honestly loved to sing, and even his growing interest in Ruth Bogart had all contributed to honesty. That bit about the small-time Southern Baptist college must have been true; its hidden tones had been touching in their frankness. There must have been some sort of social frustration there, similar to what everyone faced in adolescence and to which most people learned to adjust, but which Big Ben could not handle yet. There was a quality in his voice and gait that told its own story.

He felt her hand on his arm. "Darling, you've got to talk to me," she said. "What have you been thinking about, Jack?"

"You ought to know. About You-Know-Who, and you needn't have given him such a big glad eye."

They were leaning toward each other, ostensibly absorbed in each other's words, and they had waited long enough in the bar. Jack signaled to a waiter, and paid the check.

They were just another happy couple as they walked hand in hand to their room in the ell called Cozy Nook.

"You know, darling," he told her, "I was just thinking of another one of those *Red Mill* songs."

"Oh, sing it now, dear," she said, "softly, just for me."

He drew her closer to him.

> *"Not that you are fair, dear,*
> *Not that you are true,*
> *Not your golden hair, dear,*
> *Not your eyes of blue . . ."*

He stopped and laughed. "It doesn't fit, does it? Your hair is dark, dear, and your eyes are grayish green."

"Never mind," she said. "I approve of the general scheme. Go ahead and finish it."

> *"When we ask the reason,*
> *Words are all too few!*
> *So I know I love you, dear,*
> *Because you're you."*

"I wish to goodness," she said, and her voice had a catch in it, "that I could be me again."

They had reached their room, and he was pulling the clumsy key from his pocket. "Why, say," he said in a bemused tone, "it's unlocked. I thought I'd locked it. Didn't you think I had, honey?"

"Yes, I kind of thought so." And then she giggled. "But I did have other things on my mind."

"I'm losing my memory in my old age," he said.

They laughed like college freshmen. Then they opened the door, using the standard Farm precautions.

Mr. Moto was standing in the center of the room. Jack was not entirely surprised, but he hoped that he acted surprised. "How the hell did you get in here?" he asked, assuming the badgering tone of an honest American dealing with a wily Oriental.

"So sorry," Mr. Moto said. His hands shook with artificial agitation. "The door was unlocked. So sorry."

The door had not been unlocked, and it was a safe assumption that Mr. Moto knew he knew it. The only solution was to raise one's voice a hectoring octave higher.

"And if the door was unlocked — so what?" Jack Rhyce said. "Does that mean you should walk inside?"

"Excuse, but the door was wide open. More better, I thought, to wait for your return. Then things would not be stolen."

"That's funny," Jack said in a more reasonable tone. "I thought I'd locked that door. Anyway, you had your handbag with you, didn't you, sweet?"

"Yes," Ruth said. "I think it was very thoughtful of Mr. Moto to wait for us."

Mr. Moto was becoming an annoyingly loose end to the problem.

"Of course I'm grateful to him too, sweet," Jack said. "I was only sort of startled, seeing him here. Excuse it, Mr. Moto. What did you want to see me for?"

Mr. Moto bobbed his head and rubbed his hands together.

"First, may I ask you if all is right here, and proper?"

"Everything is swell, thanks," Jack answered.

"And your wishes for tomorrow?" Mr. Moto asked. "Might I suggest a picnic and a ride toward the base of Mount Fuji?"

If it wasn't one problem, it was another. He should have rented a car and driven it himself, but now his mobility was controlled by the Japanese in front of him.

"I tell you what," he said. "You be waiting outside at seven o'clock in the morning, then we'll decide what we want to do." He smiled at Mr. Moto. "Forgive anything I said about your being in the room. I'll see the door's locked next time."

He stood close to the door listening to the sound of Mr. Moto's footsteps retreating down the hall. Ruth made a quick check of the suitcases. She shook her head as a signal that nothing had been disturbed. He moved to the window and drew the curtains.

"Turn on the water in the tub," he whispered.

"Oh, Jack," she called as she turned the water on, "hasn't it been a wonderful day, darling?"

She moved close to him and rested her head on his shoulder, and he was glad to put his arms around her. He had seldom felt so grateful for companionship.

"It's really started now," she said.

"Yes," he said, "it's moving. What do you know about Skirov?"

"Skirov . . ." she repeated vaguely.

"The Russian who's running the Communist show here. The Chief briefed you on him, didn't he?"

"Oh, yes. I was thinking about the Jap and the big goon down in the bar. I saw Skirov in Vienna once."

"Then you can tell me if I have his description straight. Middle forties, five feet five, one hundred twelve, thin, agile, delicate hands and feet, Mongoloid features."

"Yes," she said, "that's he."

"All right, what about Moto? Is he Skirov playing a Jap?"

It had been one of those swift inspirations which he had learned to suspect, but, if he were right, they might be able to end the show that night, because they would have worked out the whole scheme of the apparatus. He had never been so desperately anxious to end a mission, not so much because of himself as because of her.

Her forehead was wrinkled and she gazed straight ahead. He was aware of her nearness and her beauty, which annoyed him because his mind should have been concentrated on abstractions. Finally she looked up at him.

"I guess I was wrong in thinking that big handsome boys like you are dumb. I like your thought. I wish I could buy it."

"Maybe it's more reasonable than it sounds," he said. "They looked us over in San Francisco. They think we're absolutely pure.

Then what could be better than using us as a cover? Skirov and Big Ben want to meet. What's better than having Skirov as a Japanese chauffeur? That explains his being in the room — just to make a final check."

"It's too easy, darling. Life isn't made that way."

Her criticism confirmed his own inner dread. She was right. Nothing ever came easy in the business.

"Besides, Jack," she said, "he simply isn't Skirov."

"You don't know Japs as well as I do," he answered. "This one's like something on the stage."

"Perhaps he's trying to hide his rank or education, but he isn't Skirov."

"Well, if he isn't," Jack Rhyce asked, "who is he?"

"He's in the business, all right, but he isn't Moscow-trained. You know how that Moscow school sticks out all over them. Skirov is a Moscow boy. Now unzip my dress, will you? I'm going to have that bath, but I'll leave the door open, if you have any more ideas."

He had a number of ideas as he sat in an easy chair near the window and listened to her splashing in the tub, but he had learned long ago that it was folly to spread ideas around. He was already getting the structure of the story so clearly that a question of policy was beginning to arise. Should the apparatus be smashed, or should it be left alone in the hope of locating Skirov? Bill Gibson would make the decision.

He wished that he did not have to see Bill that night. The dangers of the meeting had measurably increased with Big Ben on the scene. However, the importance of an immediate meeting had increased correspondingly.

"Jack," she called, "I thought you were going to tell me some new ideas."

"You know that's bad technique," he said.

"Yes," she said, "I know." She was out of the bathroom, brushing her hair with brisk, almost savage strokes. She was wearing an oldish cotton print robe.

"I'll buy you a kimono tomorrow," he said. "You'd look well in a kimono, green and blue."

"Thanks," she said. "I'm sorry about the thing I have on."

He began taking things from his suitcase, putting his brushes and toilet articles on the tall dresser, laying his blue suit carefully over the foot of the bed and his black shoes with their composition soles on the floor beneath it. Both he and she were neat as pins, as you were bound to be in the business.

"I was thinking about Big Ben," he said. "From the way he looked at you I think you could take him."

"Yes, I know I can," she answered.

"It makes me mad, but maybe it would be a good thing for tonight. I want Ben's mind off things for about an hour. He mustn't worry where I am, and only be glad I'm not where he is. You do it and I'll see Gibson." Her face grew stiff and wooden. "Are you afraid of him, Ruth?" he asked gently.

"No, but I hated the way he looked at me, and you'd have to be mighty convincing with a man like that."

It was what she was there for, and they both knew it, but he felt his face redden. "I didn't mean anything serious," he said. "Just a walk, or a ride up the mountain in his car."

She smiled. "It's nice to know you're human occasionally. I'm glad the proposition doesn't appeal to you personally, but I don't think it would be a good one, anyway. Don't you see it would tell him right away that there was something wrong with us? It would look better if I simply let him know he was attractive to me — and made him want to get me away from you."

She moved closer to him and put her hands on his shoulders.

"Now listen," he said, "I'm ashamed I made that proposition, but it was business, Ruth."

Her grip on his shoulders tightened. "Just get it through your head that I want to stay with you tonight. I don't want to see you get a knife in your back," she said.

"It's going to be harder for two to get up to Gibson's cottage."

"Jack," she said, and she moved closer to him, "I'm frightened. Ben scares me, on your account more than mine. But I promise I won't let you down."

He bent over and kissed her. Even as he did so he knew that he was being very foolish. "All right," he said, "put on a dark dress, and let's go down to dinner."

Chapter 7

THERE WERE a great many couples on the hotel dance floor at shortly before ten o'clock that night, following the uninspired rhythms of the Japanese orchestra, which did its best to follow the American tradition.

She was a light and beautiful dancer, much better than he, but they were both of them good enough to be disturbingly outstanding. "Don't do anything fancy," he told her. "Just dance in a mediocre way. You're too good-looking as it is."

"That's what I thought about you when I saw you first," she said. "You're too good-looking for the business."

"I wish he were here so we could keep an eye on him," Jack said. "We've been dancing about half an hour, haven't we?"

"Yes," she said. "Don't you like it?"

"I would under other circumstances, but Bill's going to get nervous pretty soon. I wonder where the Big Boy is."

He felt her shiver. "I wish you'd get him off your mind. Hold me closer. We're supposed to be in love."

It was another quarter hour before he saw Big Ben. He had stepped in from the grounds outside. He wore a charcoal flannel suit, black shoes and a dark tie.

He felt her shiver again. "If he cuts in," she said, "cut back soon. Please, Jack."

"All right," he said, "but don't discourage him."

Big Ben's glance roved over the dancers. Jack noticed that he pulled his coat straight, then he took a handkerchief and passed it over his forehead, though he had not been dancing. He made a gesture with his hands as though he were ridding them of dust.

"He sees us now," she said. "He's coming over."

A second later he slapped Jack on the shoulder. "Hello, Oberlin."

"Why, hello, Alabama Baptist U."

Big Ben's laugh was easy and infectious.

"Your guessing cap's on crooked, boy," he said. "Not Alabama, Mississippi. And now may I relieve you of your lovely burden?"

"You mean you want to dance with my girl? All right, but only for a little while."

"Oh, now," Ruth said, "don't act jealous, Jack. I'd love to dance with Ben just as long as he wants." She gave Big Ben one of her dazzling smiles.

Jack Rhyce walked to an open doorway and watched them. Like many large men, Big Ben danced very well. It was a sordid matter, standing there watching Ruth and the big man dancing. Seeing them dance was like watching the merging of two different worlds, a world of grace and refinement with another of ruthless force. He saw Ruth's lips move in some smiling remark. He saw Big Ben answer, and he did not care to guess what they had said.

HE LOOKED into the night. The cottage called Chrysanthemum Rest was completely visible. Though its shades and curtains were drawn, its rooms were lighted, as was the path that led toward it from one of the hotel verandas. But if one were to follow another path up toward the greenhouses, there would be shadow and concealment. A glance at his wrist watch told him it was time — 10:20 — for Ruth and him to walk into the shadowy grounds together. He moved across to where she was dancing with Big Ben.

"Okay, Baptist," Jack said, "the half is over."

"Aw, gee, coach," Big Ben said, "nobody's even blown the whistle. How about us all meeting in the bar in a while? I'm going there right now to drown my frustrations, honey."

Ruth Bogart giggled. "We'll be there, won't we, darling?"

Jack put his arm around her. "We'll see you down there, Ben."

"We'll dance a few minutes," Ruth said, "and then I want to go out and get a breath of fresh air. It's awfully hot in here."

Big Ben laughed uproariously. "You didn't want fresh air when I asked you three minutes ago, honey. Well, no hard feelings. So long, troops."

They danced for a minute or two without speaking.

"He's gone," Jack said, "and he hasn't gone outside, either."

"That's so," she said. "I don't believe he's on to us at all."

"What makes you say that?" Jack asked her.

"If you want to know — from his very clumsy efforts with me."

"It could be that we're barking up the wrong tree," Jack said. "It could be that he's just a lonely soul. . . ."

"It could be," she said. "But there was one queer thing. He hadn't been dancing but he was all in a glow, wringing wet with perspiration. Did you notice him dust his hands and wipe his forehead when he came in? Whatever he was doing, he was exercising."

"Well, he's gone now. Let's go out and look at the moon."

THEY WALKED toward the greenhouses, talking softly. A number of other couples were wandering about the grounds. While they walked they examined Chrysanthemum Rest from all angles. There was a clump of bamboo by its door, which was the only cover near it. Jack was sure that he had missed nothing. He could swear that Chrysanthemum Rest was clear. They sat for a while on a bench in the shadow of an old cryptomeria.

"Does it look all right to you?" he asked.

"There's only one offbeat thing. We've been out here for fifteen minutes, and no one's moved inside the house. Not a shadow against the curtains — nothing. Perhaps he isn't there."

"He wants it to look as if he weren't. He's a smart operator."

The danger that someone might notice them entering Chrysanthemum Rest was a calculated risk which the bamboo thicket by the door would minimize. The door would be unlocked. There would only be the crucial second when they crossed the threshold. Nevertheless, he delayed for a while. He wished that he could be sure that Big Ben was in the bar.

"Come on. Let's go," he said. His arm tightened around her waist. "Follow me quick," he whispered.

They were inside the house in a twinkling; the door was closed behind them without a sound and without a fingerprint on its knob. They were in a small entrance hall. An open door showed a lighted room, furnished with wicker easy chairs and a couch. There was a Chinese rug on the floor and gay Japanese prints decorated the walls. The room, to Jack Rhyce's surprise, was empty. He could detect no sound except the blare of the dance music. He gestured to Ruth and they moved along the wall so that their shadows would not show on the drawn curtains.

"Bill," he whispered. Later, he never could recall what it was that made him sure that he would not be answered.

The bedroom door was open. The lights were on there, too. He tiptoed to the doorway with Ruth behind him. Bill Gibson, in a pair of Shantung-silk pajamas, lay beneath the covers of his bed, eyes closed, head resting on his pillow, his clothes neatly folded on a chair. A glass, a half-empty bottle of whiskey and a pill bottle stood under the lamp on the bedside table. His restful posture gave every indication that he was asleep, but he was not breathing. Bill Gibson was stone dead.

Jack felt in his pocket and drew on a pair of gloves. "Better go through his suitcase, Ruth," he whispered. But he knew there would not be anything they wanted.

While she moved noiselessly about the room, he stood gazing at the body of Bill Gibson, trying to estimate this new situation. Now that Bill was dead, a whole new line of action was required. He was still in the grip of shock, but he was able to see that he was looking at a professional, almost a classic job of elimination. The only trouble was that, for the job to have been perfect, Bill should have been discovered in the morning, and doubtless that had been the intention. This was encouraging; it showed that no one knew that Bill was there for a meeting and that he and Ruth Bogart were not suspected yet.

The job was one that had obviously required meticulous planning. It also betrayed an anxiety to keep things quiet which was understandable to anyone in the business, where violent ways of taking out a man always offered embarrassing complications. The danger of complication here was very small indeed. Jack did not believe that a doctor called in the morning would, with the evidence before him, make more than a perfunctory examination; no doubt if a more thorough examination should be made this contingency would have been provided for. He picked up the pill bottle, which still held three yellow capsules, a very pretty touch when added to the cork which had fallen to the floor. A drunken man had accidentally taken an overdose of sleeping pills. Jack had no doubt that a lethal dose was safely in the stomach. There were several ways to make reluctant people swallow.

Jack set down the pill bottle and sniffed at Bill Gibson's lips. There was the requisite odor of whiskey. It had been applied over-liberally to the lips, but no one would have noticed in the morning. Like every killing in the business, this one had its signature, and it was ridiculously easy to decipher once you knew it was a killing. The job presupposed enormous and expert strength. It had required someone who could take care of Bill Gibson as gently and effortlessly as a nurse might handle a baby, and Bill was no weakling. He touched Bill's hand. The body was still warm. He slipped his hand under the head. The mark of a hypodermic was barely visible in the hair at the base of the neck. If one had not known exactly where to look, the mark could easily have gone unnoticed.

Ruth Bogart was looking at him from across the room.

"Ben was here all right," he said. "I wish I could have the privilege of polishing off that rat. I thought a lot of Bill."

"Yes, so did I," she said.

But when you were gone you were gone, in this game. His attention turned to the neatly folded clothes. Bill must have planned to meet them in pajamas and a dressing gown. A burgundy silk dressing gown hung from a hook on the bathroom door. There was a slight tear at the right elbow, the silk was scuffed and a few tiny hairs of blue woolen lint were mingled with the fabric. It was pile from the Chinese carpet in the living room.

Ruth Bogart had finished with Bill's baggage and with the contents of his pockets. She shook her head. "Where did it happen?" she asked.

"The living room. He must have grabbed Bill right by the door."

He walked gingerly to the living room and she followed him. Of course there had been a struggle. Big Ben had been all of a glow, and he hadn't been dancing. The signs had been eliminated, yet the impersonal orderliness of the room told its own story of rearrangement. He could reconstruct what had happened as though it were going on now before his eyes — Big Ben in a noise-less bound, towering over Bill, the jolt in the solar plexus that knocked out the wind. Big Ben's arms wrapped around the smaller man's gasping body ... the fighting for breath ... the expert hands lowering the struggling man to the floor. . . .

"When you danced with him," he said to Ruth Bogart, "was there anything in his coat?"

"I think so," she said.

It would have been the hypodermic.

"They don't know about us yet," he said, "or they wouldn't have pulled it this way. We'd better get out of here, and brace yourself. There's one thing more that's going to be tough tonight."

"What else?" she asked, and he saw that her nerves were shaken.

"We've got to go and meet that rat in the bar, and we'd better be in the mood for it, because he's a smart Joe. Kiss me. Put some lipstick on my cheek. He's got to know we've been out in the garden making love."

No matter what happened in the business you had to go on with the show. You learned how to dish it out and to take it, too. When they left the small building, Jack's arm was around her, and they stopped and kissed shamelessly underneath a light on the path. Their abandon had a quality that was partially genuine.

"You're adorable," he said loudly.

"Darling," she said, "not *here*. Everyone will see us."

Their words and actions were only a shadow on his deeper thoughts. He did not have ice water in his veins any more than she, and he had not recovered from the impact of Bill Gibson's pseudo-quiet death. In his imagination he could see Big Ben pinning Bill down, gasping and helpless. The scene in Chrysanthemum Rest was playing on his emotions, which wasn't right. He felt Ruth shiver, and he shook her in a rough playful way.

"Pull yourself together," he said. "The show's on the road."

"All right," she said. "So it's on the road, and stop being a space cadet."

He straightened his blue coat and felt his belt. He might not be carrying a weapon but a properly fixed belt was a good substitute. He wished that he could slash his belt across Big Ben's face just once. Twice would be better — twice and Big Ben's closest relative wouldn't know him.

THE ATMOSPHERE in the Main Bar had changed since he and Ruth Bogart had been there last. There was no doubt any longer that the patrons — aside from their Japanese girl friends — realized that they were far from home. Their loneliness had begun drawing them together, so that an undercurrent of companionship in misery formed the motif for the now crowded bar. A sea of smoke and voices washed like a wave over Jack and Ruth.

"Why, look — there's Big Ben, just where he said he'd be." He leaned down until her hair brushed his cheek. "Remember, he doesn't know who we are," he whispered. "Just hold that thought, sweet, and give me another kiss."

"Oh, Jack," Ruth said, "Ben's got a man with a squeeze-box with him."

Big Ben stood in the middle of a noisy group near the center of the room, and a man with an accordion was with him.

"Jack," she whispered, "he's changed his shirt." He had been wearing a white shirt at the dance, but now his shirt was blue.

"That's right," Jack said. "He's been having a busy evening, sweet. Wave to him. He's seen us now."

"Hi, Ben," she called.

"Why, sweetness!" Big Ben shook his finger at her. "Say, whatever have you been doing to Oberlin?"

Ruth glanced at Jack's face. She gave a stifled scream.

"Oh, Jack," she said. "I'm sorry. They told me in the States that it wouldn't come off, darling."

Jack Rhyce grinned self-consciously, then he pulled out a handkerchief, wiped his cheeks and lips and shook his head.

"This isn't the States, dear. Maybe nothing's kissproof in Japan."

It was a pretty good line, considering, and the laugh that greeted it confirmed his impression. A man with lipstick on him couldn't help but be a nice guy. There was no sharpness in Big Ben's glance.

"Say, boy," Big Ben said. "Let's do a song for the crowd."

Ruth gave him a playful push. "Go ahead, Jack," she said. "You can sing just as well as he can."

"Well, let me have a double Scotch first," he said, "so I can half-way catch up with things."

He tossed off the drink when it was handed to him. Big Ben was holding a half-empty highball glass. He was cold sober, but he was abnormally elated. It was the sort of elation that came after

emergence from danger. He was happy, and he must have felt
completely safe.

"Well, I feel better now," Jack said.

Big Ben patted his shoulder affectionately; in return Jack Rhyce
gave him an affectionate punch on the chest — just two big boys
roughhousing. There was no softness in Big Ben's mid-section.

"Say," Big Ben said, "how about a little harmonizing? How
about 'Every Day Is Ladies' Day With Me'?"

"Why that old chestnut? Why is it you have this yen for *The Red
Mill?*" Jack asked.

Big Ben drew his hand across his eyes. "It's a kind of theme song
with me. Will you sing it with me if I tell you why?"

His invitation, which included a group around them, had a professional tone. He was a born master of ceremonies.

"Why, sure," Jack said, "if it's a good yarn."

"Aw, shucks, it isn't much of a one — just kid stuff." His voice
was eager and appealing. "It was senior year in this Baptist college
down South. . . .There was this banker in town — the local rich
guy — and he had this pretty daughter. Well, my folks were poor,
in the missionary business actually, and I was sort of shy back
then. For two years I used to walk past her house most every night,
without daring to knock on the door, and then comes senior year.
That autumn when I'd sort of built up my ego by playing football,
I walked up the front stoop and rang the bell, and there she was all
alone, and she asked me to come inside. Well, she asked me if I
liked hearing music on the phonograph. It was one of those kind
you wind with a crank, and she put on this *Red Mill* record, and
held my hand, and then — well, we kinda got to loving each other
with that old *Red Mill* playing." Big Ben's voice grew softer. "Then
her old man came in, and he kicked me out, and I never saw her
again, but that's how I remember *The Red Mill.*"

He had held his audience, and there were sympathetic murmurs
applauding his tale of young frustration. Something had happened
then, and *The Red Mill* was its monument and the music of youth
was always the best music.

"Well," Big Ben said, "stand up here, Jack. Let's show 'em.
Strike up the band. 'Every Day Is Ladies' Day With Me.'"

Bill Gibson was dead at Chrysanthemum Rest. Their arms were draped over each other's shoulders as they sang, and applause came from all over the bar when they had finished.

"Say, Jack," Big Ben said, "if we only had straw hats and canes, we could soft-shoe it, couldn't we?"

"We don't need hats and canes," Jack Rhyce said.

"Why, we don't sure enough," Big Ben said. "Come on."

It wasn't a bad show. Jack Rhyce had to admit that they both had an unusual gift of comic interpolation. He was tempted to join in the laughter of the crowd as he watched Big Ben slip deliberately and recover himself. His impulse to laugh died when he saw Ruth Bogart's expression as she watched them. An instant later he picked out Mr. Moto. He was standing near the street entrance of the bar. When the dance was over, Jack looked toward the spot where the Japanese had been standing, but he was gone.

"Well, folks," Jack Rhyce said, "it's been nice seeing you. Come on, Ruth. Let's say good night."

They had done what was necessary, and the clock showed it was ten minutes to twelve. He could tell from the tight grip of her

hand when they walked toward the Cozy Nook ell that her nervous resistance was wearing thin.

"Jack — " she said, as they closed the door of their room.

"Just a minute before you say anything," he told her. "Just let me wash the touch of that goon off me first. I'm sorry, Ruth."

When he came back she said, "You've washed the lipstick off and now you won't have anything to remember me by. Please unzip the back of my dress. I don't know why people sell unzippable dresses."

"Maybe they do it to get girls into trouble," he said.

"Jack," she said, "don't you think it would look better if we turned out the lights? We don't know who's watching."

"Just get it into your head no one's watching. We're out of this as of now."

"But it won't be long," she said. "And it would be better if you did turn out the lights. I must look like hell. I feel like it anyway."

"So do I. We haven't exactly been playing charades tonight."

He turned out the lights, except the one in the bathroom.

"Jack," she said, "I don't know anything about Bill Gibson's setup here, do you?"

"No," he answered, "and we won't, now Bill's dead."

"What are we going to do?"

It was the question he had been asking himself, because he was left with no contacts, unless he communicated with home, and that was far too dangerous.

"Maybe we'll think of something in the morning," he said.

"Come here. Come closer. I want to ask you something. Why did they kill Bill?" she whispered.

"Because he knew something they didn't want passed on."

"But what did he know?" she asked.

"We've got to try to find out, come morning."

"Jack," she said, "wasn't it awful?" He felt her arms steal around his neck, and she buried her face against his shoulder.

"Go ahead and cry," he said. "I don't blame you, Ruth."

"I'm not going to cry, but I'm glad you're here."

"I wish you weren't," he said.

"Oh, Jack," she said, "I don't think that's very polite."

"It's too dangerous here," he said. "Let's face it. I love you, Ruth — and I'm not pretending."

"I'd almost given up hoping that you'd ever say it."

"Well, I have. But it's a fool thing for anyone like me to say."

It was bad for business to fall in love, but there they were, alone together with their secrets, miles from any help except what they could give each other.

Later it was easy enough to tell himself that no one should rely on convictions that had no solid foundation of fact — except that his belief that they were in the clear did have its foundation: Bill Gibson would not have been killed in the way he had if anyone had suspected who Jack Rhyce and Ruth Bogart were. But still, Jack realized, he should have been more alert. The trouble was, there had been so much on his mind that he had yielded to the temptation of blacking out the whole problem for a few hours that night, which had been inexcusable. You always paid for it, but he never dreamed that he would pay so soon.

Chapter 8

THE HOUR when he was awakened must have been shortly after two. The callers were expert operators. The first he knew of anything wrong was when they switched on the ceiling lights. In the instant his sight was adjusting to the light, he was on his feet.

"Please, Mr. Rhyce, no noise, please."

Mr. Moto and two stocky Japanese in blue serge suits were in the bedroom.

Ruth Bogart, in her twin bed next the wall, reached for her handbag, but the man nearest to her knocked it from her hand.

"Quiet, please," Mr. Moto said. His English had become impeccable. "Get dressed, please, Mr. Rhyce. The man here will hand you your clothes." Mr. Moto smiled politely. "He was a valet for a member of your Cabinet in Washington — before the war, of course."

The loquaciousness disturbed Jack Rhyce because it indicated Mr. Moto's belief that he held the cards. He wished he was not barefoot in pajamas, and he also wished he could keep down his rising anger.

"I'll give you and your chumps just ten seconds to clear out of here," he said, "or I'll throw you out, right through that window."

Mr. Moto raised his hand in a placating gesture.

"Please," he said, "make no disturbance, Mr. Rhyce, or I shall be obliged to call for the police."

"How's that again, you little yellow rat?"

"Please do not be insulting," Mr. Moto said, "though I can understand how you feel, Mr. Rhyce. I mentioned the police."

"So you're a cop, are you?"

Mr. Moto shook his head. "I am just what you are, Mr. Rhyce, and you and I do not want cops. I only want a quiet talk with you."

"Go ahead, you yellow rat. Call in your police."

He had made the Japanese angry, which was a useless luxury.

"I do not understand," Mr. Moto said. "You must be an intelligent man to have been sent here, and your work was very good last evening — but not the police, Mr. Rhyce. I should have to tell them that you and the lady had murdered Mr. Gibson."

"Well, well, so that's the picture, is it? All right, tell your valet to hand me my pants and a clean white shirt." He pulled on his trousers over his pajamas. The first surprise was leaving him. He pointed to his shoes and socks, and when they were handed to him he stole a glance at Ruth Bogart. Her face was white.

"Please, may I repeat, you did it very well?" Mr. Moto said. "So neat with the pills, so nice with the needle. No reason to tell the police."

Jack pulled a shirt over his head, tightened his belt carefully.

"Not the belt, please," Mr. Moto said. "I should rather hear Big Ben strike only over the BBC."

He heard Ruth Bogart draw in her breath.

"So you've got me down for Big Ben?" Jack said.

"Yes," Mr. Moto said. "Your coat, please, Mr. Rhyce. We will leave quietly. Miss Bogart will stay here. She will understand that it will do no good to make trouble. I shall drive her back to Tokyo in the morning."

"You don't know what you're doing," Ruth began.

It was not the time to break security; indeed it was a question whether they would have been believed. Jack smiled at her and shook his head. "I don't think there's much you can do, Ruth," he said, "the way the ball is bouncing."

"But, Jack," she said, "they're going to — "

"Let's not be mind readers," he said.

"It is so true," Mr. Moto said, "what you say about the ball bouncing. One day it is you. One day it is me. The young lady is not important. I can give you my assurance that I will see her off for home from the airport tomorrow." He picked up her handbag and tossed it to one of the men. "I shall give this back also tomorrow."

Jack said, "Do you mind if I ask you one question?"

"If it is short. The sooner we leave the better, Mr. Rhyce."

"What makes you think I killed that man?"

"Because he knew too much. We're going where we can have a quiet talk, and I think you will tell us what he knew before we are finished. Moscow does not know all the tricks."

"You ought to know I'm not a graduate from there. Well, as long as I have your word about Miss Bogart — "

"I never do anything unnecessary. Why should she come to harm? Are you ready now, Mr. Rhyce?"

"Jack — " Ruth began. Her voice was dangerously loud.

"Don't, Ruth," he said " — but it's been nice to have known you. Come on, let's go."

They walked in a compact, softly stepping group down a flight of stairs and out into the night. It was dark and very still. A car was parked on the hotel drive. "You will sit in the front with me, please," Mr. Moto said. "The men will be in the back. One of them will have you covered. He is a good man with a pistol."

Jack got into the car. Mr. Moto took the wheel. The place where they went was not far from the hotel. It was a substantially built Japanese house surrounded by a high wall.

"You will step out quietly, please," Mr. Moto said.

"Tell that goon of yours to take his hand off me," Jack said. "I can still get out of a car."

A light burning above the doorway showed the platform where

one sat to remove one's shoes, but there was no neat row of shoes such as one might have seen if the house had been occupied. One of the men opened the front door, at the same time switching on the lights in the entrance hall.

"The man will not touch you," Mr. Moto said. "Walk behind me into the house, please."

There was a distance of about six paces of gravel driveway between the car and the hallway of the house. Mr. Moto walked ahead of him, not bothering to look back, but the man walking behind was overanxious. He was too close, as Jack could tell from the sound of his steps. If you held a gun at someone's back, one of the first principles was to keep a decent interval.

Jack whirled on the ball of his right foot. He had the man's wrist in his left hand and the barrel of the pistol diverted to the ground in the split second before he brought his fist across to the jaw with all the momentum of his body behind it. The pistol exploded at the same moment. Then the hand that held it relaxed, and Jack Rhyce had the weapon — from its size and weight, another Beretta. Mr. Moto turned and Jack spoke.

"Shall we leave it the way it is?" he said. "I told you I didn't want that man crowding me — and tell the other one to stop."

Mr. Moto gave a curt order. "I am so sorry he annoyed you," he said. "He was very clumsy."

"Just overanxious. Let's not you and me get overanxious. I'll get you anyway before you and the other one get me."

They stood motionless for seconds that seemed to last for a long while.

"Yes," Mr. Moto said. "Yes, and what do you suggest?"

"You tell that friend of yours behind you," Jack Rhyce said, "to come over here and help his friend. He's coming to, now. I don't like being treated this way, Mr. Moto."

"Yes," Mr. Moto said, "yes?"

"You tell your two people to keep out of the way," Jack said, "and I'll go into that house with you. I want to talk to you as much as you want to talk to me. I'm not Big Ben, and I didn't kill Bill Gibson. Frankly, he was my boss."

"You are not Big Ben?" There was doubt in Mr. Moto's voice.

"You're damned well right I'm not. I'm on the American team. Gibson came up here to meet me. He was dead when we got to the cottage, and I want to know what he knew as much as you do."

"You may put the pistol of the clumsy man in your pocket, Mr. Rhyce," Mr. Moto said. "If you gave it to him now he would kill himself for shame, but I am grateful to him for his clumsiness. You would have shot it out with me if you had been Big Ben."

"Yes," Jack Rhyce said. "That's exactly the point I've been trying to make. Here, take the gun." He tossed the pistol on the driveway.

"Thank you," Mr. Moto said. "I am very mortified that I should be so mistaken. Excuse me, please."

"That's all right. It's too bad we didn't know sooner we were after the same boy."

"It was so very stupid of me," Mr. Moto said again. "So you were after Big Ben, too?"

"Yes," Jack said, and everything was easy now. "That's what I was sent over from the States for. Gibson wanted help."

The man on the ground groaned and struggled to his knees. Jack pulled him to his feet. "Out like a light, weren't you?" He slapped him affectionately on the back. "Never mind. We're pals now."

Mr. Moto laughed. "His English is not good. Tell him in Japanese."

"I apologize for your discomfort," Jack said in Japanese. "So it was the tea and the coffee back there at the hotel that gave me away on the language, was it?"

"Oh, no," Mr. Moto said. "Earlier, Mr. Rhyce. In Burma, we had your name on file. Japanese linguist, born in Japan."

"The word always was that you people had good intelligence, but I didn't know you were working so hard at it now."

"Oh, not so hard," Mr. Moto said, "with shortness of funds and the misfortunes. Poor Japan. We would not have made a mistake such as I made tonight, before the war."

"It's a tough life, all right," Jack Rhyce said. "It's beginning to get me down these days."

"Get you down? I wish so much I could visit your great country more often. I cannot keep up with the idiom now. Before everything was so unhappy, I was over once a year at least. Even when

my duties were in Paris and London I endeavored to spend a week
or two of observation in New York.... In old New York the peach-
crop's always fine, isn't it, Mr. Rhyce?"

"I wish I knew where you picked that one up," Jack said.

"A song from *The Red Mill* was sung in the third-floor corridor
of the Mark Hopkins Hotel in San Francisco," Mr. Moto answered,
"the evening before you left, Mr. Rhyce."

"You Japs get things twisted. I didn't sing the song."

"So sorry I have been so very stupid," Mr. Moto said. "This house
is loaned, for a purpose which I am so glad is now not necessary,
by a very kind Japanese nobleman. Come in, please, and my associates will warm us some sake."

The furnishings of the entrance hall gave forth a musty odor,
from age and disuse; but they were elaborate, designed to impress
the European guest. The hall carpet was crimson, sprinkled with
fleurs-de-lis; the wallpaper artificial cordovan leather; the mirror
bad Victorian; and the chairs golden oak, upholstered with red
plush. The European section of such houses was usually as ugly
and uncomfortable as its Japanese counterpart was beautiful.

Mr. Moto must have read Jack's thoughts.

"We used to try so hard," he said. "Poor Japan. The chairs are
equally hideous in the parlor, but Americans like chairs."

Several lighted table lamps in the parlor revealed oil paintings
of English cattle, and upholstered easy chairs. There was a European fireplace with a coal grate, in which a fire glowed in spite
of the hot night. On the coffee table were knotted strings and
leather thongs and a pair of handcuffs. "Well, well," Jack said, "so
you were fixing to have a singing school."

Mr. Moto laughed. "So nice a way you have of saying funny
things." He called an order in angry Japanese. "Take these away
and bring the sake and cigarettes. Please sit down, Mr. Rhyce."

Jack Rhyce sat down in one of the easy chairs. The sake came
immediately, in a jar with a glaze that looked like celadon.

"Beautiful," Jack Rhyce said, nodding at the jar.

"You appreciate it? I am so pleased. It has been in the Baron's
family for many hundred years. The Baron would be pleased to
present it to you. He is my cousin. You enjoy the wine?"

"I do," Jack Rhyce said. "It's nice and hot."

"To happy peace between the United States and poor Japan," Mr. Moto said. "Very foolish men made the war. Ha-ha. Nearly all of them are dead."

Jack drank and held out his cup for more.

"Judging from my short stay here," he said, "it looks to me as though Japan is going to make out pretty well."

"I am glad you think so. It is very lovely to talk to an intelligent American again who is engaged in my own line of work. Let me see. There were once such nice men in your Intelligence in Washington. Do you remember Colonel Bryson? I was so sorry he broke his neck in Vienna. Then there was Mr. Makepeace. What has become of him, I wonder?" Mr. Moto was checking on Jack's background, and Jack was relieved he could come up with an answer.

"He was in Prague six years ago, but since then he has not been heard from."

"So too bad so many lovely people cannot live forever. Some more wine, Mr. Rhyce?"

"Thanks, I could do with a little more," Jack said.

Mr. Moto gestured to one of the men.

"Poor Japan. We never can understand how you Westerners can drink so much and not lose your wits. That turn on the right foot was very beautiful. I could admire it even when I did not know what might follow. But I did know that the move was not Russian."

"They'll be pleased to know that, back home."

"Please, I hope you will treat my errors kindly. I did not have the benefit of records because ours were destroyed in the bombing. Therefore, I can only rely on memory — but you were in Japan until the age of five. You were in Japanese-language school in Colorado, because one of my own young men taught you and reported you as far above the average. Please do not make a mental note. Your Counterintelligence found him out. Then you were in Combat Intelligence in Burma. You were in Moscow in 1946, and you made a remark to Mr. Molotov in Russian. You said all men are brothers."

Jack Rhyce winced. It was growing clearer every minute why Mr. Moto should have confused him with Big Ben.

"Then there was an alert in my echelon, just as there must have been in yours. Orders to look for a new personality, an American. The name — Big Ben. Popular. Someone on your stage. Look out for this American — Big Ben, with the singing voice and with the weakness for singing a song from *Red Mill*. Imagine my joy to hear of you from San Francisco. So pleased when I saw you at the airport. So pleased about the Friendship League, which we have watched with interest. So pleased about your week-end excursion, where Mr. Gibson was going. So pleased when you and the pretty Miss Bogart entered Chrysanthemum Rest — and then to find you are American Intelligence is difficult. I should have kept an open mind, but you will admit that everything did fit."

"Don't blame yourself too much," Jack Rhyce said. "Anyway, you're not Russian. I've been worried about that."

"Nationalist Japan Party, Mr. Rhyce. Pro-Emperor, anti-Communist. So much trouble — poor Japan. But when the typhoon ceases, back will spring the bamboo."

"Are Nationalists anti-American these days?" Jack asked.

Mr. Moto shook his head. "Not now. The United States is so very useful. So silly to shoot Santa Claus. You see, I'm being very frank, because I hope that we will be temporary partners. There are groups here anxious to arouse feeling against America. And the plain Japanese man can change so quickly."

He paused and Jack had a moment to speculate on Mr. Moto's background. He came from the old aristocracy. He must have been educated abroad, probably in an Eastern American university.

"The Left Wing has been growing very dangerously lately," Mr. Moto said. "At the moment we are as anxious as you are to uphold American prestige, and I am willing to pool information."

Jack appeared to hesitate, even though the man seated opposite must have known that he had no choice.

"I don't see why we shouldn't do business, but I had no briefing from Mr. Gibson, you understand. That was to have occurred up here. He only told me that he was being followed."

He did not blame Mr. Moto for looking discouraged. It was time to hurry on and show that he had some value.

"Still, Mr. Gibson sent us back a few facts," he went on. "Big

Ben has been meeting a Russian agent named Skirov at intervals. Do you know Skirov?"

Mr. Moto's features sharpened. "An *après-guerre* Russian, well trained, and very dangerous. We have tried very hard to find him."

"We rate him above Big Ben," Jack Rhyce said. "I've never seen him, but we have a photograph and description. It might amuse you to know that when I found you in our room I had a hunch that you might be Skirov."

"So funny how often people confuse things when they get fixed ideas. What other information did Mr. Gibson send back home?"

"Bill believed that there was a meeting between Skirov and Big Ben coming up. He had learned something new, but he did not have time to tell me."

Mr. Moto lighted a cigarette. "Perhaps I know somewhat more than you about what was troubling Mr. Gibson. I am sorry that you do not know your apparatus here. I was hoping we could have profitable exchange of facts."

"You mean you won't tell me any more because you don't think I know anything worth while?"

"Yes," Mr. Moto said, "so sorry, Mr. Rhyce."

It was clear to Jack that he could achieve nothing unless he had coöperation. There was a risk, but it was a necessary one.

"Okay," he said. "Suppose I told you I've found Big Ben. Suppose I could finger him for you . . . then would you tell me what you think was on my boss's mind?"

The Japanese gave a violent start. "You mean he's in Japan now?"

"You tell me what Big Ben and Skirov are going to do," Jack said, "and I'll tell you who Big Ben is. What's so important about this Skirov meeting?"

"We are still trying to discover. Mr. Gibson knew — otherwise he would still be living. Our information is that they are planning some coup with political repercussions that would adversely affect your country. I think there will be political murder and afterward public demonstrations."

"Who's going to get murdered?" Jack Rhyce asked.

"It would be a murder that would be ascribed to United States imperialism; one of a liberal politician. We do not know who, but we think we know the date — three days from now."

Bill Gibson must have known the date as well. Jack was trying to put together the details of that hurried call on the day of their arrival, the Chevrolet with the Beretta in the glove compartment, and the Asia Friendship League.

"Do you know a man named Harry Pender," Jack Rhyce said, "who is heading the Asia Friendship League now? He was transferred recently from Cambodia, I think."

Mr. Moto raised his eyebrows. "You spent the day with Mr. Pender before you drove here, Mr. Rhyce."

"That's right. Have you any information on him?"

"He is a very naughty man," Mr. Moto said. "His alias is Harry Wise. Hank is his cover name in the apparatus."

Jack Rhyce nodded. That name meant quite a lot.

"Moscow has been moving their first team in here, in the last two weeks," Mr. Moto said. "But now I wish to hear from you. Where is Big Ben, Mr. Rhyce?"

"Haven't you guessed? He was right there with me in the bar, and you saw us do that dance together. He's a flight engineer on an American air line."

Mr. Moto slapped his hand against his forehead. "Oh, dear me," he said. "Excuse me, Mr. Rhyce. This is very serious. I've been so very stupid. We must leave here right away."

"Well," Jack Rhyce said, "I'm glad it rings a bell with you."

"Ha-ha," Mr. Moto said, "yes, it rings a bell. It would be funny if I were not so ashamed. He said he was United States Intelligence, last night, after you sang the song. He told me you were Big Ben. I can make no excuse for my carelessness, Mr. Rhyce, except that I was so sure of you."

"How's that?" Jack responded incredulously.

Mr. Moto hesitated as though he did not like what he was about to say. "You were so much more intelligent, so much more of a trained agent, so much more dangerous — while he, if you will excuse me, was so immature, so harmless, like so many of your government officials. But please believe I was astute enough to recognize my error when you took my man's gun away."

Never to underestimate an adversary was a motto of the business. Had Big Ben learned through some fluke who the couple in Cozy Nook were, and had he taken that method to knock them out of the game? This was unbelievable in Jack's judgment. Big Ben had shown no professional interest in them while they had been in the bar, but something had occurred later to cause a change. His glance must have picked out Mr. Moto's face in the crowd and instantly recognized him as a Japanese agent. Mr. Moto had spelled danger, and Big Ben had conceived the smoke screen that permitted escape. He must have suspected that Mr. Moto had come to the hotel to make contact with Bill Gibson. While they were still doing that soft-shoe dance Big Ben must have been fairly certain that Mr. Moto would visit Chrysanthemum Rest. Being in the business himself, Mr. Moto would know that it was murder. Big Ben had been obliged to move quickly.

"Let's get our lines straight," Jack said. "You saw us go into that cottage. Then you went into the cottage yourself. When did you get to the bar?"

"When you and he were dancing," Mr. Moto said.

"He'll be halfway to Tokyo by now. I suggest that we drive back in the morning, and I'll see Pender first thing Monday. The name is Ben Bushman. You can check him at the hotel."

"Yes. And what is it that Mr. Gibson knew that makes him dead tonight? I hope in another day to have the full details."

"And you'll let me know?" Jack Rhyce said.

"Yes," Mr. Moto said, "with pleasure, Mr. Rhyce."

"I'll appreciate it," Jack Rhyce said. "Maybe you wouldn't mind walking back with me until you can point out the hotel."

"Yes," Mr. Moto said, "we should be moving before it grows too light. There is only one thing more I have to say. If you'll excuse me, there may be much trouble, in which case it might be just as well if you did not tell Miss Bogart what we have been saying."

"I agree with you. She won't be useful here any longer. Suppose we send her home on Monday?"

"With so much pleasure," Mr. Moto said. "She is a very lovely lady. And now we should start back."

It was still dark outside but a refreshing coolness in the air told the hour almost as accurately as a watch. In half an hour the sky would begin to lighten and the stars would disappear.

"A very lovely dawn," Mr. Moto said. "I shall let you proceed alone. A lovely time for a walk if one has difficulty with sleeping. That is what I should say to the hallboy if you should see him. He will be interested to see you returning. He also is in what you call the business, Mr. Rhyce."

The hotel was dark, except for the lights in the corridors and along the drive. A path led through a garden of ponds and tiny cascades bordered with dwarf pines and maple, to the upper terrace. He was halfway across it when he saw Ruth, and he knew she had been watching as he walked up the drive.

"Jack," she whispered.

"Why, sweetness," he said, "were you looking for me? I went out for a little stroll. I thought you were sound asleep."

"I wish you'd told me, dear," she answered. "It did make me frightened to wake up all alone. Are you all right?"

"Oh, yes, dear. I'm sorry I frightened you, but let's forget about it now, and sneak upstairs."

They walked up the stairs of the Cozy Nook ell without another word until they were inside their room. From the way she clung to him he knew she had been afraid for him. It all went to show how unwise it was for two people in the business to become emotionally involved. His concern for her threatened to throw other factors out of balance, but there was nothing he could do about it.

"It's all right," he said. "There wasn't any trouble."

"Did you have to tell them who we were?" she asked.

"Oh, I had to tell them this and that."

"Did you find out what Bill Gibson knew?"

"No," he answered, "not exactly."

"Jack," she whispered, "why aren't you telling me the truth?"

"Because from now on it's safer to keep you in the dark."

"I don't care whether it's safe or not," she said. "I want to stay in this with you."

He was moved by her wish. "Thanks," he answered, "but the thing's moved far enough so that you're not necessary here any more. I want you to be back in Washington ready to meet me at the airport when I get there. It would be common sense even if I had not lost my head about you, Ruth."

Yet if he had not cared about her, it was possible that he might have still thought her useful. Anyone as attractive as she, and as good an operator, always did have uses.

"This shouldn't have happened with you and me," he said. "It was all a great mistake — professionally speaking, Ruth."

"I'm not going back," she said. "You're going to want me around when you know what I know."

"It's got to be awfully good," he said.

"It is. I know how to get Big Ben. What do you think of that?"

"You mean you've seen our boy again?" he asked.

She giggled in that annoying way that she used so well as cover.

"Am I going home on the first plane?" she asked.

"Go ahead," he answered, "and tell me about our boy."

"Well, it was this way. After you left with those people I didn't know exactly what to do. I know you told me to stay here, but I felt I had to do something, and so I went downstairs and out to the driveway, and who do you think I saw?"

"All right, you saw Big Ben. What was he doing?"

"He had come out of the hotel with one of those big Army Valpaks. He was putting it in the back of a car."

"A dark-green Chevrolet coupe with a dented fender?"

"Yes," she said. "Naturally."

"They haven't got much of a car pool, have they? But then, they didn't know we'd spotted it. Was he in a hurry?"

"No, he was perfectly natural," she said. "I didn't think we ought to let him go away like that, so I walked out into the driveway and said hello."

"Was he surprised? How did he act?"

"Natural. He didn't seem surprised at all. He said, 'Why, hi, there. Are you looking for the boy friend?' And I said, 'Yes. A sort of funny thing happened. A Japanese knocked on the door a while ago and asked him to step out for a minute, and he hasn't come back, and I'm wondering where he is.'"

She had said all the right things. She knew her business.

"He laughed," she went on. "He said, 'It was only a little joke I played, honey. He'll be coming back all right. I was just coming up to knock on your door as soon as I'd stowed this bag.'

"I asked him if he honestly meant that he had got you out of the way on purpose and he said, 'It was just a gag. But I'm crazy about you, honey, and what you need is a real man and not one of those do-gooders.' How do you like that one, darling?"

"I don't like it. What did you tell him then?"

"I said I was beginning to like him, too, and I said that you were always so prim and proper, and that I liked people with a real sense of humor. I said I wished he wasn't leaving so soon. It was important to play up to him, wasn't it?"

"Yes," he said. "How much did you play up?"

"Not so very much," she said. "Only when he held me in his arms I kept thinking of Bill Gibson, and wondering where you were. It was darned unpleasant."

It helped him only a little to tell himself that of course she had to do what she had done.

"For just a second I thought he was going to take his bag out of that Chevrolet and stay," she said. "But there was something that made him know he had to go in a hurry. He kept saying, 'Gosh, I wish it wasn't fixed so that I had to leave.'" She gave a perfect imitation of his accent. "He said, 'Honey, this mustn't be good-by. Call me as soon as you get to the city.' Then he wrote down a telephone number and gave it to me. If he wasn't there I was to leave my name and he'd call me back."

"Good going," he said. "I can use that number."

"Oh, no, you can't, because I've torn it up. Besides, he'll know my voice. When you want him, I'm the only one who can talk to him, Jack. And now let's stop being so businesslike. Lord, I wish we were on the outside."

They were a long way from the outside.

"We could have a cabin by a lake," she said. "I'm a pretty good cook, and you could fish or make snowshoes or whatever they do in the woods."

"Yes," he said, "but we'd better talk about it later."

"We could travel," she said. "Think what it would be like if we

went to London, and didn't have to check in anywhere, or be
startled when we saw one of those familiar faces — if we could just
be ourselves, having a quiet breakfast and reading the papers, without having to watch for anything."

"Without a fountain pen in your handbag, dear," he said.

"That reminds me, what happened to my handbag, Jack?"
Her question broke the illusion.

"Moto has it," he said. "He'll bring it in the morning. We're
going to pull out of here for Tokyo first thing after breakfast."

"To do what?" she asked.

"Just what we did before," he said. "The Friendship League, Mr.
Harry Pender, all that sort of thing."

"Aren't you going to tell me anything?"

"No," he said. "What you don't know won't hurt you."

"Is it as tough as all that?"

"Never mind," he said.

"I don't," she said, "as long as it means you like me."

"That's the trouble," he said. "I like you."

"Then let's talk about the outside some more," she said. "There
are all sorts of things I'd like to tell you — about when I was a girl
at school, about parties, about all sorts of things. Jack, it's time
we got to know each other in an outside way."

"I know," he said. "Later — there isn't time right now."

There was never time to think about yourself when you were in
the business. He wished he could keep her out of it, but it was
too late now, after what she had told him. He wished to heaven
that he did not have the feeling that time was running out.

Chapter 9

AFTER they returned to the Imperial Hotel on Sunday afternoon,
he left Ruth in her room. He told her to sit quietly and to
read a good book, and he and Mr. Moto left the hotel together in
the Buick. He was the foreigner who needed a guide and, if anyone was listening, they had heard him ask to be taken to the Mei-ji
Museum. Mr. Moto and he were able to say a good deal by the time

they had parked the car in front of the building that housed the pictures illustrating the reign of Japan's greatest Emperor. The hour was so late that the place was closed.

"I know the guardians," Mr. Moto said. "They will put on the lights, and while I telephone you may enjoy the pictures. I think I can do everything from here very safely."

It was a question of Moto's getting the latest news and so Jack walked alone up the marble staircase to the two great galleries. He must have examined the pictures for more than half an hour before Mr. Moto joined him.

"Skirov is believed to be here, but cannot be traced," he said. "There is much activity. Large quantities of banners have been made saying 'Down with American Imperialism' and 'Avenge the People's Martyr.' We will have more definite news by tomorrow, I hope. Some of our best people are working on it. They have found the lodging of your Mr. Ben, but he has not returned."

"Miss Bogart can get him if necessary," Jack Rhyce said.

They did not speak again until they were in the Buick.

"Will it be a large demonstration?" Jack asked.

Mr. Moto nodded.

"Simultaneous outbreaks in different quarters. The street fighters are being given special training. It will be ugly, I am afraid. A great deal can be accomplished by assassination."

"Depending on whom you assassinate," Jack Rhyce said. "You told me they were going to take out a left-wing liberal. Can you name some prospects?"

"Oh, yes," Mr. Moto said. "Eight, perhaps ten possibilities. I wish so very much Mr. Gibson were alive. Are you sure you know no one else in his apparatus?"

"I told you I didn't. Don't you trust me?"

"Yes, as much as you trust me, I'm afraid. I am not anti-American. I hope that you are not anti-Japanese, Mr. Rhyce."

"Not at the minute. I'm anti-Communist right now."

Mr. Moto cleared his throat. "Would you object," he asked, "if my people were to question Big Ben?"

"Not if it's necessary, but I'd rather have him followed. He can lead us to what we want just as easily that way."

"If we cannot trace him tonight," Mr. Moto said, "I am very much afraid we should use Miss Bogart to find him."

"All right," Jack said.

"From now on, there will be a car and driver in your name, outside of your hotel. He will take you to me at any hour. And please take care of Miss Bogart. She may be so very useful tomorrow."

Jack Rhyce nodded. The net was around Big Ben, and a European was too conspicuous in the Orient to hide for very long. His number was nearly up.

Jack arrived at the Asia Friendship League offices at half past ten next morning to find Harry Pender seated in his office. The light from the window glinted cheerfully on his spectacles as he waved a welcoming hand.

"Come in, Jack," he said. "Are you ready to pick my brains?"

"I'm all set and raring to go, Harry," Jack said.

He was embarrassed that he had not placed Harry Pender until Mr. Moto had explained him, but, after all, he had only seen the face in a group photograph. The man before him was certainly the individual known as Harry Wise, a former American college instructor who had been holding a Communist card since the late 1930's, but with no record of activity. He looked older than his photograph and, since he had not been heard from for some time, he must have been behind the Curtain.

"It sure is nice to see you back," Harry Pender said. "I see in the Japan *Times* that one of our fellow countrymen took too many sleeping pills up there. I hope it didn't spoil your fun."

"There was a little mix-up with the Japanese authorities," Jack said, "but it didn't amount to anything. We left yesterday morning and drove around seeing the sights. I sort of wanted to get the feel of the country."

"That's very wise. A first impression has a lot of value. By the way, where's Ruth Bogart?"

The question indicated unnecessary curiosity. "She wasn't feeling well this morning," Jack answered. "Nothing serious."

"Too bad. Do you want me to send one of my girls over?"

"Oh, no, she's going to be all right. I just told her to take it easy.

Well, let's get down to business. You must have some pretty big policy problems, Harry."

Mr. Pender took off his glasses and allowed them to swing like a pendulum between his fingers. He raised his eyebrows inquiringly.

"I mean, for instance," Jack said, "problems of personnel. I was just wondering, well, whether you had any trouble with Communists or anything like that." He had intended to bring out the subject with flat-footed innocence, and from the tolerant way Harry laughed he was rather sure he had.

"Excuse me for laughing, Jack," Harry said, "but that question is characteristic of the point of view that everyone brings here from the States. Why, there's hardly a Communist in Japan — but you will find varieties of liberals. From my observation, democracy has a permanent foothold in Japan."

"Well, it's mighty nice to hear you say so, Harry. I'm glad, too, if there's a healthy liberal party here."

"You'll find liberalism here in the best sense of the word," Harry said, "and the leaders are highly dedicated people. I want you to get to know some, Jack. I want you to get this Communism bias thoroughly washed out of your hair."

"It's curious how distance distorts facts. Back in the States we hardly hear about Japanese Progressives. Who are some of them?"

He hoped that his interest appeared genuine. Harry Pender's eyes were fixed on him.

"There's Hata and Iwara, and Yamashita and Nichiwara," Harry said.

"Who's the best of them, would you say?"

"Every one of them has quite a following, but Noshimura Hata is head and shoulders above the rest. I'll see that you meet him sometime."

"It would be a real pleasure, provided he lives around here."

"He does, as a matter of fact," Harry said, "in an attractive house with a beautiful garden. He's an Oxford graduate, a member of a wealthy family, and a philanthropist."

"Oh," Jack said, "then he can speak English."

Perhaps he should not have pursued the subject so long. His

attention was riveted on Harry's swinging glasses. The motion had been accelerated, and there was always betrayal in unconscious gesture. It was time to drop all show of interest in Hata.

"Preconceived opinions are always off the beam, aren't they?" he said. "I had no idea that the Japanese would be so enthusiastic about sports, for instance."

"Sports have a leading priority with us," Harry answered. "Nothing pulls people together so much as meeting on a playing field...."

At least they were away from liberalism. It was necessary to sit there for an hour or more mouthing platitudes. It was ironic to think that Harry Pender and he were each talking for the other's benefit. Did Mr. Pender believe he was impressing him? And did his own guilelessness seem real to Mr. Pender?

It was quarter of twelve when he pushed back his chair. "Harry," he said, "it's been swell of you to give me so much of your time."

"How about a bite of lunch? Not more than five minutes away from here is the best beef-sukiyaki restaurant in the world."

"There's nothing I'd like better, and please give me a rain check," Jack said. "But I'd better go back to the hotel and see how Ruth is. How would lunch tomorrow be? Because I'll be right back here, making a nuisance of myself with another batch of questions."

SHE WAS in her room, reading Terry's *Japanese Empire.*

"Has anything happened here?" he asked.

"Yes," she said. "One thing. Big Ben telephoned."

He tried to forget about her as a person when she told him that. Nothing must interfere with the business. "What did he want?"

"He wanted to make a date for five this afternoon. I told him I wasn't sure I could get away. I said I'd call back at three."

"That's my girl. I think the time has come to pick him up, Ruth. It's a good thing you're along, all right."

"Thank you, sir. How did you get on with Pender?"

"I wish I knew," he said. "He worries me a little. I think I'd better see the Japs again, right off."

"Aren't you going to cut me in on anything?" she asked.

"Only about Big Ben," he said. "Don't ask for any more."

"Jack — be careful. Don't be too sure of yourself."

Frankly, he wished he felt more assured.

He had not been under the porte-cochere for half a minute before the car and the driver that Mr. Moto had indicated the day before appeared. The meeting place was the back room of a curio shop.

Mr. Moto sat at a table with a telephone in front of him, drinking tea. "No more news than yesterday," he said. "So sorry. And how is Mr. Pender?"

"He knows a lot about liberal politicians. I've been doing some thinking this morning."

"I hope so much that you will tell me the results."

"I think we'd better pick up Big Ben," Jack Rhyce said. "I'm sorry. I hate to break up an apparatus."

"No one has seen him. He is hiding very carefully."

"Not so carefully," Jack said. "I think we're overrating our boy. He called Miss Bogart this morning. He wants to make a date with her. She said she'd call him back at three."

Mr. Moto shook his head. "I do not like it," he said. "It does not sound correct. I wish Miss Bogart would give us the telephone number. We could have traced it by this time."

"I told you she wouldn't, and I decided not to put pressure on her. The fact is she may be highly useful in picking up Big Ben. She'll call him any time we want."

"If we knew the telephone number," Mr. Moto said, "we could be watching and take him when he receives the call."

"I don't think our chances would be good. He's a professional — he would be on the lookout. We're safer to let Miss Bogart make a date with him."

Mr. Moto nodded slowly. "I am inclined to agree with you. Miss Bogart is a very intelligent girl who has had training in handling these matters. I shall come to the hotel at a quarter before three."

"Trace the call, then, if you want, but let's catch him where he's waiting for Miss Bogart. It will be safer that way. And I want to be along when you pick him up — just out of interest, Mr. Moto."

JACK RHYCE had played a part in several similar actions in America and Europe. The details seldom varied. Find your man and keep him at a given spot. Get the group distributed. Have the car ready. Close in simultaneously from all sides. If properly executed, there would hardly be a ripple of a struggle. Often pedestrians ten feet away did not notice the group around the victim, trussed and pinioned, being half pushed, half carried to the waiting car. Even if things did not move quite as planned, a well-placed blow at the back of the skull could solve the difficulty. Big Ben was a big man, but he could be handled. Jack Rhyce was certain that there would be no trouble if he were in the party.

By the time he and Mr. Moto reached the hotel, the preliminary preparations were in hand; the equipment immediately necessary was packed in Mr. Moto's brief case. When Ruth saw it she smiled a thin, Mona Lisa smile. Jack had never seen her looking prettier.

"So you boys need me, do you?" she said. "All right, rig up the telephone."

Mr. Moto took the wire-tapping instruments out of his brief case and attached them. He handed Jack Rhyce a pair of earphones.

"It is three o'clock," Ruth said. "Perhaps — if you are ready — I'd better make the call?"

"No," Jack said. "Let him sweat it out for ten minutes."

He never forgot that interval of waiting, or how happy Ruth looked. "Jack," she said, "you're glad I'm along now, aren't you?"

"Yes," he answered, "at the moment, Ruth."

"It's nice to know I'm useful, under the proper circumstances," she said. "Maybe that's all any woman wants."

"Excuse the question," Mr. Moto said. "Do you carry a black-jack, Mr. Rhyce?"

"No, I haven't one with me."

Mr. Moto reached inside his brief case. "If you will permit, it will be a pleasure to present you with this one. It may be useful."

Jack balanced the instrument expertly in his hand before he slipped it into his back pocket.

"Thanks," he said. "I'll do my best to be neat and clean."

"I'm sure," Mr. Moto said. "And now perhaps Miss Bogart should call. Let us not have the gentleman too discouraged."

She gave the number, and there followed a moment of suspense until they heard the answering voice. There was no doubt in the world that it was Big Ben.

"Gosh, honey," he said, and his voice was plaintive, "I've been settin' here. I mighty near thought it was a brush-off."

"Oh, Ben, I'm sorry, but I couldn't call until I was alone."

"You mean he's hanging around you now?" Big Ben asked.

"Ben, I told you I was tired of him, and he's gone now."

"Well, don't forget you're my girl now, honey. How about around six tonight?"

She glanced questioningly at Mr. Moto.

"Why, that would be lovely, Ben," she said. "Will you call for me at the hotel?"

There was a silence on the other end of the wire.

"Why, honey," he said, "I had some trouble there, last time I was in Tokyo. The folks there don't like me too much. How about going down to the Ginza and meeting me outside the Cimaroon beer hall? It's a GI place, with good food and singing and everything. I'll be waiting by the front entrance, come six o'clock."

"But, Ben dear, I don't know this town."

"I'm going to see personally that you're going to know it and love it before you're through, honey," he said. "It's no trouble to get there. Any taxi driver can take you to the Cimaroon."

"Well, then you be right outside," she said. "It's spooky being in a place where you don't know the language or anything. Are you sure you'll be there, Ben dear?"

"Sure as hell isn't freezing. Don't forget — the Cimaroon."

The conversation was over.

"How did I do?" she asked.

"You did fine," he said. "Don't you think so, Moto?"

Mr. Moto was dismantling the wire-tapping device. "It is not for me to analyze the Western mind, but he gave me the impression that he wanted so very greatly to see Miss Bogart. The Cimaroon is a suitable place for him to select. It should not be difficult to take him quickly if he is waiting on the sidewalk. I must be leaving now to make arrangements. The car and driver will take you there, Mr. Rhyce. May I ask you to arrive at half past five?"

"Let's make it five fifteen," Jack said. "These Joes have second thoughts, and get careful and early sometimes."

"And what about me?" Ruth asked. "Am I going with you?"

"Certainly not," Jack said quickly. "There won't be any need, Ruth."

"If he doesn't see me, he may not show," she said.

It seemed safe to discount that possibility. Jack was experiencing a feeling almost of peace. As far as he could see, the Japan assignment was drawing to a close. If the ending was not wholly satisfactory, it was effective. His main mission had been Big Ben. He took the blackjack from his hip pocket, tossed it in the air and caught it.

"You'll only be in the way if there's any kind of hassel," he said. "He's a big boy, and he may muss things up."

"I think Mr. Rhyce is correct," Mr. Moto said. "I am most grateful to you, Miss Bogart, and it would be so nice if I could pay you my respects when this is over. Perhaps a Japanese supper tonight just with me and Mr. Rhyce. At five fifteen, then, Mr. Rhyce, and thank you very much."

The feeling that everything was over persisted after Mr. Moto had gone — the easing of tensions he had experienced before when a job was almost finished, and everything was in the groove.

"I feel pretty good on the whole," he said to her. "When we get him, we can move out of here and head for home."

Her expression brightened. "It can't be soon enough for me. And why can't we start being ourselves when we get on that plane?"

"I don't see why we can't from there on in," he answered.

"What do you mean?" she asked. "From there on in?"

"A lot of things," he said, "and we ought to be able to start discussing them as soon as I get back here."

"Do you mean you still love me?" she asked.

"It's unprofessional, but I do," he said. "Come to think of it, I wouldn't have missed any of this."

"Jack," she said, "what's going to happen to him?"

"He's not our problem. The Japs will take him over. We might have gone further into this if Bill Gibson hadn't died, but I think it's time now to stop this show."

"It's sticky, letting the Japs take him," she said. "I wish you and I weren't in it. You're too nice for it, and maybe I am, too."

"I wouldn't be surprised," he told her, "but let's put our minds on pulling out of here tomorrow, Ruth."

The interval before his departure for the Cimaroon always remained in his memory as a domestic sort of scene.

"If you want something to do while I'm out you might start packing," he said.

"Jack," she said, "don't you think you ought to wear something heavier and darker than that seersucker coat?"

"I don't think so. This won't be night work."

"I wish you were carrying a gun. Wouldn't you like to borrow my fountain-pen gadget?"

"I can do fine with this jack," he said.

"You ought not to wear crepe-soled shoes," she said. "You might slip. I don't know whether you ever knew Bobby Burke. He slipped making a swing at Oscar Ertz — you know, the Czech — just outside the Gare du Nord in Paris. He had a knife in him before he could recover."

"These shoes are skidproof. No, I never did know Bob, but I've heard plenty about him. Ought I to be jealous?"

"Darling," she said, "you won't ever need to be jealous. Now let me take a look at you. You look awfully handsome."

"So do you," he said. It was time to be going, but he did not want to leave her.

"Jack, if you do hit him, follow through. Let him have it all. He's an awfully big man. Now you'd better kiss me good-by. I don't want you to be late."

"Don't forget Moto's coming to take us to dinner when we get back," he said. "I wish we were going alone. We haven't had much fun here, what with one thing and another."

"Oh," she said, "there'll be lots of other times. Take care, Jack, please take care."

He had a final glimpse of her before he closed the door. She was standing, smiling, very straight and neat, and looking very happy.

THE TASTE of the American GI was responsible for most of the innovations along the Ginza. They reflected the immaturities of youth — naturally enough, since the age average was low in the

American armed forces. In fact, Jack Rhyce thought the Cimaroon offered everything that he would have wanted when he was an undergraduate at Oberlin — air-conditioning, cold beer on draft, an enormous gaudy bar, a jazz orchestra, a Japanese torch singer, and dozens of tables with pretty Japanese hostesses.

At 5:15 the Cimaroon was already full. The brash notes of the orchestra, the high voice of the singer and the chatter of the patrons would be an excellent background for a shot, if a shot were necessary. It could easily be minutes before anyone would know what had happened. He checked the entrances and exits. These were limited to a wide entrance on the street, and two doors in back leading to service quarters.

Mr. Moto was waiting at a wall table, facing the door. He waved to Jack. "Beer, of course?" he said. "Everyone is posted."

"Have you looked for him all through this building?"

"Oh, yes," Mr. Moto said. "No sign."

"I'm just wondering whether he will be hiding until he sees her. Maybe we were wrong in not having her drive up."

Mr. Moto thought for a few moments. "It is not too late," he said. "We might call her, from the manager's office."

The office was a cubbyhole only a few paces from where they were sitting, and it was startlingly silent, once they had closed the door. She answered almost immediately.

"Ruth, we've got a second thought," he said. "Maybe you'd better take a taxi and come here at six o'clock. Get out and stand by the main entrance."

"Okay," she said. "It's nice that great minds think alike sometimes. I'll be there."

He felt a momentary qualm as they returned to the table, because he disliked revising a plan on such short notice. Any revision always presented a new set of factors. Yet he had not the slightest premonition that he had made an error until it was six o'clock and there was no sign of Ruth outside the Cimaroon.

"There is traffic," Mr. Moto said. "Do not let it upset you for five more minutes, Mr. Rhyce."

He had believed that experience had made him immune to sudden reverses — but he had not felt a shock of helpless panic for years comparable to what he experienced then. Everyone went wrong sometime, he said to himself, and this was it for him.

"I'd better telephone and see if she's left," he said.

When he reached the manager's office and gave the number, his hands shook. He had never in his life wished for anything so vehemently as that he might hear her voice, but there was no answer. She had gone. Outside the office he was startled at the sight of his own face, reflected from one of the wall mirrors.

"I think they've double-crossed us," he said.

Mr. Moto looked grave. "Wait. We gain nothing by hurrying. Remember that you made her wait ten minutes, only not to appear too prompt. She may be doing this — and remember one thing more."

"What's that?"

"I am to blame as much as you are, Mr. Rhyce. And what is it they say in America? The show must go on."

He did not like the appraising look in Mr. Moto's eyes. After all, he was representing the Intelligence of his country. "Damn it," he said. "Don't you tell me how to behave." He stood up. "I'm going back to the hotel. It's the place to start from, isn't it?"

"Yes, that will be the proper procedure," Mr. Moto said. "I shall go with you. They have won this game. He was brighter than we thought him."

It was accepted practice on any battlefield to draw opponents to one spot, and then to strike in another. They sat in rigid silence until they were slowed by the traffic at the Zimbashi station.

"I'm so very sorry," Mr. Moto said.

The remark jangled against the raw edges of Jack's nerves.

"To hell with it," he said. "Do you think they got her in the room or outside?"

"It would be the room, I think," Mr. Moto answered.

He was relieved by that opinion because, if true, his asking her to join them was not responsible for what had happened. The car turned in the drive of the Imperial Hotel, and the lotus pool and the low building looked as ugly as his thoughts.

"Let us not appear too worried," Mr. Moto said. "I shall ask a question or two and join you in your room. I think we had better set up the telephone again, because they will be making contact with you, allowing only time for your return from the Cimaroon. Why else would they have caught her, Mr. Rhyce?"

What had come over him not to have thought of it before? He should have taken suitable precautions. He had been drawn off as easily as though he had been the third team. What had happened that had made them able to outguess him? At some point something had occurred to give away the show. It might have been that night in the Main Bar, or it might have been that morning in the office of Harry Pender. Some detail had gone wrong, and it was futile to guess what it might have been. Play as safe as possible all across the board was another maxim of the business, and he had disobeyed it by not having her room guarded. Neither his mind nor hers had been on their work. They had been thinking about the outside.

He never forgot the appearance of her room. Everything was exactly as he had anticipated. The lock of the door had been forced by an instrument that had made it give immediately. The only sign of struggle was an overturned suitcase that had fallen from the bed to the floor. Her handbag was gone. There was the faint scent of the perfume she used, and the bottle was still on her dressing table beside her gold-backed comb and brush. He picked up the brush and gazed at the initials on the back, R.B. She had started packing, and her dresses and lingerie that had fallen from the overturned suitcase still showed signs of careful folding. Mr. Moto came in while he was holding one of her dresses. Jack Rhyce laid it down gently.

"They were not seen to leave," Mr. Moto said, "but then, no one was watching. We should have taken measures, but the conversation on the telephone sounded so very true. I am so sorry. I am also very much ashamed."

"You and me both," Jack Rhyce said. "Sorry and ashamed."

Mr. Moto, having adjusted the broken lock so that the door would close, opened his brief case.

"The telephone," he said. "We must both listen, I think."

"I don't see why you're so sure they'll call," Jack said.

"Please, it is inevitable. They would not have taken her otherwise. I am having the call traced, but I fear it will not help. They are so very clever. They know you are in love with her, Mr. Rhyce."

The words came out brutally in the ravaged room, and Jack felt his face grow brick red, but he had no right to be angry because of his stupidity.

"It was a mistake," he said. "We both knew it."

"Please, I am not criticizing," Mr. Moto said. "It may be a mistake, but sometimes one cannot help them, Mr. Rhyce."

It was infuriating to have something which should have belonged only to him and her tossed out in the open to be used as a point in a game. Mr. Moto's voice was silkily smooth.

"I do not wish to offend," he said. "I only speak because I think you should be ready. I think they will be prepared to make you an interesting proposal, Mr. Rhyce."

Jack gave a start. "What sort?" he asked.

"I do not know, but I think you have come close to finding something that worries them, Mr. Rhyce."

Mr. Moto's words aroused a suspicion in Jack Rhyce that gripped him with icy fingers. He cleared his throat.

"Do you think they're going to propose a swap?" he asked.

"I believe they will offer to bring Miss Bogart safely back if you will agree to leave here."

Jack felt a spasm in the pit of his stomach and his heart was beating faster. Mr. Moto was watching him carefully. He resented the detached critical manner and the air of academic curiosity. Mr. Moto was weighing him in an Oriental balance.

"You will have to make a decision as to whether to leave or to stay," he said, "and I am so very much afraid I cannot help you, Mr. Rhyce."

"Damn you," he said, and the sound of his voice warned him that he must compose himself, "you don't have to help me."

Mr. Moto watched him without moving a muscle. Just then the telephone rang. The small bell had a mocking sound. Mr. Moto slipped the earphones over his head.

When Jack picked up the phone he was steadier. "Hello," he said. His voice was even and agreeable. He was playing the old game of wits.

"Hello." He recognized the voice on the other end of the line immediately. "That's you, isn't it, Jack?"

"Indeed it is," he said affably.

"This is Harry Pender. You recognize my voice, don't you?"

"Well, well, Harry. It's nice of you to give me a ring. I sure do recognize your voice. I'd know it anywhere."

"Okay, Jack. Then let's cut out the monkey business. You and I won't have to do our clowning from now on in."

"Thanks. That's a big relief. What's on your mind?"

"We've got Ruth Bogart here. I thought you'd like to know."

Though he had anticipated it, he found it hard to control himself, and the instant while he struggled for calmness could not have been lost on Mr. Pender. "Thanks for letting me know," he said. "I was beginning to be worried about her."

There was a good-natured laugh on the other end of the wire.

"We thought you might be. Well, take it easy, Jack. She's right here, and we wish you were, too. She's happy and comfortable as of now. I'll let you speak to her in a minute."

"Why, thanks," Jack said, "thanks a lot."

He heard Harry laugh again. "You know who I am, don't you, Jack? I mean you've got me taped by now?"

"Yes," Jack said, "I've got a pretty good idea."

Harry Pender's laugh was excited. He was obviously on edge.

"I may as well admit," he said, "that I was pretty dumb regarding you. All of us were. In fact, we never got wise to you until lunchtime today. Nice going, Jack."

"Thanks for the compliment," he said.

"When I heard you'd been looking at the bookshops, I admit, I should have taken the news more seriously. Maybe you'd still be fooling me, if it hadn't been for a guy who just blew in here, by the name of Skirov. Remember him, Jack?"

"I can't say that I remember him exactly. I don't think I ever saw him, but I'm sure I'd recognize him."

"Well, he remembers you, boy. He saw you in Moscow back in '46. He was a waiter at one of those big parties, and passed you caviar. Just as soon as I described you he clicked. You were talking to Molotov. You were saying all men are brothers."

Never try to be conspicuous, the Chief had said.

"Let's cut out the hamming and get to the point," Jack said.

"All right, Jack." Harry spoke soothingly. "We didn't want Bill Gibson around, and we don't want you, either. Do you get my drift?"

"Is it a threat or a promise, Harry?"

"It's neither. It's a firm offer that we're making."

His eyes encountered Mr. Moto's half-inquisitive, half-blank stare. He felt as though a cord were being drawn tight about his head. Anybody in the business could have told what was coming.

"Go ahead and make it," he said. "I've got an open mind."

It came in mild, insinuating tones.

"You're fond of Ruth, aren't you, Jack? You wouldn't want to have her go through any kind of drill, would you? She wouldn't be much fun to see afterward, would she? And you know, they do keep alive — surprisingly often — don't you, Jack?"

Jack Rhyce tried to laugh. It would have been shameful if he had betrayed his pain. "I understand your build-up. Why don't you get to the point?" he said.

"Don't get mad," Harry Pender said. "The point is, we're busy, and we don't want you monkeying around. We want you out of here. How does that sound, Jack?"

He felt his heart beat faster. "If you want it straight," he said, "I don't like this town much, or the folks in it, including you."

"Now you're talking. I had an idea we could get together, Jack. You'd like to have Ruth back at the hotel tonight, safe and sound, and you know what I mean by safe and sound, don't you? If not, there's a pal of yours named Big Ben who might explain. Would you like to talk with Ben, Jack?"

He could hear Big Ben singing at the other end of the wire. He was singing "Every Day Is Ladies' Day With Me." Jack Rhyce put his hand to his forehead. His face had grown damp, but he kept his voice steady.

"Let's cut out the technique," he said. "Consider you've scared hell out of me. Yes, I'd like Ruth back safe and sound. So what's the proposition?"

"It's easy." Harry Pender's voice was warm and enthusiastic.

"Half an hour from now Ruth will be knocking at your door. There's a night flight leaving for Honolulu at eleven, and we have two tickets for you free. Merely pack your bags, and shut up and go to the airport. How do you like that, Jack?"

"It sounds wonderful," he said. "And how do I know we'll ever get to the airport, Harry?"

"You've got to trust us for that, just the way we're going to trust you. Give me your word — you communicate with no one from the minute you set down that telephone, and Ruth will be back with you in half an hour, with a boy from our office to expedite your passage. How does it sound? Would you like to speak to Ruth?"

"Yes," he said. There was a pause. He was trying to think of some way out. Then he heard her voice, and it was excruciating agony to hear it. Her voice was faint and level.

"Hello, Jack."

"Ruth," he asked, "are you all right?"

"I'm all right, Jack," she said, "but don't do it. Don't — " Her voice was choked off in a stifled gasp that ended in a scream.

Mr. Moto was watching him. Jack could not tell whether his expression was one of sympathy or surprise. He knew that his own expression had revealed pain. Harry was back on the wire.

"Will you take the proposition, or won't you?"

"Suppose I don't?" Jack Rhyce asked.

"We'll handle you anyway. Give us twenty minutes and Ruth will tell us what you know. Won't you, Ruth?"

Jack felt a wave of nausea sweep over him, and he set down the telephone. There was one thing certain — she did not know enough. He sank down in a chair, drew out a handkerchief and mopped his forehead. The telephone rang again.

"Let it ring," he said. For a moment he felt as though he were going to be sick. "Take those damn earphones off. Excuse me. I'll be all right in a minute." He felt his shoulders move convulsively and he hid his face in his hands.

"That is quite all right," Mr. Moto said. "Would you like a little whiskey, Mr. Rhyce?"

Jack shook his head.

"You didn't think I'd do it, did you?" he said.

"No, I did not. Please be easier in your mind, for you did what you should have, Mr. Rhyce."

"How in hell can I be easy in my mind," he said, "when we should have put a guard here?"

"It is something that we will regret always — you more than I," Mr. Moto said. "But in life we cannot relive regrets."

"That's right," Jack said. "I'm all right now."

He was far from all right. He knew he would never be the man he had been an hour before. There were certain things that could haunt one always, but he had to keep moving ahead, and try to make what was happening to Ruth to some extent worth while.

His training had not left him. He had learned long ago not to forget words or pauses on a telephone.

"Pender said a boy from the office, didn't he?" Jack Rhyce said. "That was a slip, I think."

"I'm not quite sure that I follow you," Mr. Moto answered.

Jack's mind was moving forward to another fact.

"We know that Skirov is in town," he said. "That's another mistake of Pender's. Maybe we can connect with him now. Anyway, there's no use hanging around here."

"No," Mr. Moto answered. "We must go to where the call came from. They will have gone, but there may be traces."

"I wouldn't do that," Jack said. His mind was moving forward out of the nightmare of self-incrimination that had entangled it. He remembered the accelerated swing of the glasses in Mr. Pender's hand that morning when he had pursued the subject of liberal politicians.

All that Intelligence consisted of was finding facts, evaluating them and fitting them together, and there were times when you had to leave the path of painfully accumulated evidence to play a hunch. All he had was a hunch. He was prepared to play it because it was better to move than to do nothing.

"Did you ever hear of a man named Noshimura Hata?" he said.

"Oh, yes, I know Mr. Hata. Where did you hear of him, please?"

"In Mr. Pender's office, this morning. Pender said he was head and shoulders above any other politician in the liberal party, and afterward I think he was sorry he had said it."

"So — ?" Mr. Moto said. "Tell me what you think."

"I think they were going to kill Mr. Hata tomorrow — but now I think they will do it tonight, now that I didn't take their offer. I'd get him out of his house, if I were you. I'd be delighted to wait there for whoever is coming to do the job, and I'll bet it will be Big Ben."

Mr. Moto was on his feet.

"I think that is a very nice suggestion, Mr. Rhyce. Let me have the telephone."

"It's only a guess, you know," Jack Rhyce said.

"Yes, but one must always guess," Mr. Moto answered. "I shall be there with you to wait for whoever may be coming."

Jack Rhyce had a friendlier feeling for Mr. Moto than any he had previously experienced.

Mr. Moto spoke over the telephone in Japanese. Jack stood for a moment listening. As he listened, his anguish, which had been dulled for the last few minutes, returned. He knew that it would be with him always. He walked to the overturned suitcase and replaced the tumbled-out clothing. He picked up the comb and brush and perfume bottle, and put them in the suitcase. He touched his lips to the back of the brush, and he did not care whether Mr. Moto saw him or not. He closed the suitcase and snapped the lock, and knew that he was doing all he ever could for Ruth Bogart.

Chapter 10

AGAIN it was the old matter of waiting. Again, it was the trap or ambush. But this time there was a feeling of promise in the air. Jack knew as sure as fate that things were going to work that night. If you sacrificed enough you were bound to get something in return, and the only thing that he wanted just then was to see the job through, and meet Big Ben in the process. He had paid enough for the privilege. For the rest of his natural life he had given up peace of mind. Even though she had told him to go ahead — and her voice and her scream would echo in his memory always — he would wonder whether duty had been worth it. Ever

afterward his ingenuity would work on plans that might have saved her and still have achieved what they were there for.

As it turned out later, the prognosis was correct that the plan for assassination would look like an American job. The only thing that gave Jack a shock was the wallet subsequently discovered on the premises: it purported to be his, and contained excellently forged identity papers. They had said that they would handle him, and they had meant it.

The house and grounds of the Hata family stood in one of Tokyo's most desirable districts, on land not far from the palace grounds. Mr. Hata had been carried to a safe spot before Mr. Moto and he made their appearance, and the servants had been replaced

by agents. Rigorous precautions were taken in case the house was watched; the usual household routine was followed faithfully. The operation had been planned with a smoothness that impressed Jack Rhyce.

It was half past eight once he and Mr. Moto were inside the house. Mr. Hata's retiring hour was ten.

"First he walks through the garden," Mr. Moto said, "having put on the kimono and recited Buddhist prayers. I shall be Mr. Hata, and you may watch me from the house. We must be very careful, but I do not think the killing will be in the garden."

The austere charm of that house formed a violent contrast to Jack Rhyce's thoughts. The sparseness of its furnishings, the bare space of its walls gave a balanced beauty to its interior. There were no furnishings except the bedding prepared for the night, a black lacquer headrest, a low table and a scroll painting in a niche with an arrangement of flowers beneath it. The outer wall was formed of sliding glass panels which had been pushed back so that the back garden was a projection of the room itself. The garden was small, but assiduous art gave the illusion of its being a Japanese countryside. The lawn was a plain, the carefully twisted pines and small deciduous trees that bordered it were wind-swept forests. The eroded stones were mountains. The garden spelled peace, but it did not give Jack peace of mind.

The business had taught him the patience of a fisherman or a hunter, who could be alerted at any second. The business demanded an endurance that raised the watcher beyond self, to a realm where personal consideration meant nothing. He had not been restless, but his thoughts were beyond control. He was back again looking at the suitcase that had tumbled on the floor. He tortured himself with what might have been, with how she had looked on that long drive to the mountains, with what she had said when they were at Wake, and finally with the knowledge that everything was ended. He could not think of what was happening to her now, or speculate on whether she was alive or dead. It was best to know that it was absolutely ended.

He was waiting in a corner of the sleeping room when Mr. Moto stepped through the windows from the garden. In the air there was a telepathic sense of something already moving.

"When the garden lights go out," Mr. Moto said, "I shall ask you to step outside, and stand by the corner of the house. I shall rest on the bed. I think he will approach through the garden. When he is near enough you may move on him, but please wait until he is near, for we do not wish shooting."

"Don't worry. I have only the jack you gave me."

"It is so much better," Mr. Moto said. "There are others here who will take the further steps if necessary. If he enters this garden or this house, I do not think he will get away."

"That's fine with me. There's only one thing I want."

"Yes?" Mr. Moto said. "What is that, Mr. Rhyce?"

"Let me handle him. I want him to know I'm here."

"It will be a pleasure," Mr. Moto said, "if he comes through the garden and not through the house, when he will be my responsibility, Mr. Rhyce."

"Even so, I'd like him to know I'm here."

He had learned how to take cover as skillfully as any jungle fighter. When the lights were out he blended into the shadows by the angle of the house so completely that he was a part of the shrubbery. The night was as warm as a Burmese rain forest, but drier, and the glow of the city's lights was reflected in the sky. The grounds and the house were silent in spite of the sounds of the great city that rose all around them. A stirring of the bushes near the driveway revealed the presence of one of the guards and Jack Rhyce could hear a whisper of breeze in the pine trees.

The approach was made with such care and deliberation that Jack Rhyce had heard the first sound fully ten minutes before Big Ben slipped through the bushes at the far end of the garden and began his walk across the lawn toward the bedroom ell. He moved with a noiseless confidence which showed he was familiar with the house and grounds. Once he was on the lawn the background of the trees and shrubbery, combined with the lights reflected in the sky, made him stand out clearly. He wore a seersucker suit. He would have been an easy target for a pistol with a silencer, Jack Rhyce was thinking, and he was glad that the idea had not crossed Mr. Moto's mind. He wanted Big Ben to know that he was there.

Ben was drawing nearer, lazily, gracefully. When he was a few yards from the house he reached in his side pocket, drew out a knife and switched open the blade carelessly. Jack Rhyce coughed gently, but loudly enough to hold the other motionless. Then before Big Ben could move, he was on top of him and his blackjack had struck the knife out of the hand holding it. Big Ben took a step backward; he must have known in that second that he could not get away. Jack Rhyce spoke softly.

"It's me, Ben. It's Jack."

"Hello, you gumshoe artist. That girl of yours was pretty good, but she didn't last for long." He laughed.

The words robbed Jack Rhyce of his judgment. He had told himself long ago that it would be unsafe to close with Big Ben, yet that was what he did; and before he could get a wrestling hold, Ben had him by the throat. The thought flashed through him that his neck would be broken in seconds. He was in luck to be close enough to bring up his knee before Big Ben moved clear, but he had to strike again before the hold relaxed. There was a vicious moment when they rolled together on the ground. He could feel Ben's thumbs groping for his eyes. He rolled free and was on his feet while Big Ben was still on hands and knees. He delivered a kick to the side of the bleeding head, and Big Ben rolled over on his face. Then he felt arms holding him, and he heard Mr. Moto speak.

"That is enough, Mr. Rhyce. You can leave him to the others now. It would be so much nicer if you were not killing. Perhaps you would feel unhappy about it later. Americans are such sentimental people."

"He's not half dead," he said.

"No," Mr. Moto answered, "but my men are very conscientious."

The thing was over and now Jack had to move on. "All right," he said. "That's one down. Now let's go and get Skirov."

He heard the sharp intake of Mr. Moto's breath. "But where is Skirov?"

Although it was only a hunch, it was based on a line of reasoning. Skirov, who always kept in the background, would be in a quiet place where he would not be likely to be under surveillance. He would be in communication, but removed from the center of trouble.

"It's only a guess," Jack Rhyce said. "I believe he's in Pender's office in the Asia Friendship League."

"And what makes you think that?" Mr. Moto asked.

"Do you remember Pender on the telephone? He was too damned elated. He was talking about a boy from the office seeing us off for the airport. I think he made a slip when he used the word 'office.'"

"It would be a pleasure to try," Mr. Moto said. "I think, Mr. Rhyce, that you are a very clever man."

Chapter 11

"So he jumped out the window?" the Chief asked.

"Yes, sir," Jack Rhyce answered. "Eight stories, from Mr. Pender's office in the Asia Friendship League."

"You're sure he was Skirov?" the Chief asked.

"Yes, sir. His fingerprints checked with Mr. Moto's records. I have them with me, sir."

"Moto," the Chief said. "That's not a name. It's a suffix."

"Yes," Jack answered. "That's what Bill Gibson told me."

Less than forty-eight hours previously he had been in Tokyo, and now he had the feeling experienced by other air passengers, that some part of him had been left behind, and this illusion was sharper than it had ever been before. After other trips, the Chief's office had seemed like a threshold to rest and safety; but now it extended no such welcome.

"Gibson," the Chief said. "That's a tough one. It's no fun hearing that people you've trained and been fond of are gone. It's no fun because you can't do anything except send out more. Maybe you'll face it yourself sometime. I'm not going to hold down this desk forever, Buster."

At another time, the open hint that he was in line would have awakened a thrill of pleasure. "I don't think Bill had a hard time, sir," he said. "I'm afraid it was different for Miss Bogart."

The Chief picked up a pencil and tapped it softly on his desk. "I've often wished this business were not coeducational," he said, "but then the score more than makes the trip pay off. We can scratch Skirov and Big Ben, but what's your evidence on Pender?"

"The word of Mr. Moto, and there was a piece in the paper just before I left that Pender was run over by a truck in Tokyo."

"It's a queer thing," the Chief said. "I used to be something of a specialist on the prewar Orient, but I never heard of this Moto."

"You might have missed him because he was abroad. From what he said, he would have been some sort of embassy attaché. I can fill out the description and get it in the works."

"Yes," the Chief said. "We ought to get more of a line on him. I'd almost like to hop a plane and go over and take a look at him."

"I think you'd find it hard to come up with him, sir. I don't think he'd have appeared at all if he hadn't set me down for Big Ben."

He was no longer being two things at once, as he sat in the Chief's office. He was not a do-gooder, enamored of an American girl whose profile he could not forget, whose hands were strong and delicate, whose loyalty and humor were impeccable.

"He sounds like a right guy," the Chief said.

"I'd say he's from the nobility or in the high-officer class, and educated in America. But I'll get it all down on my report."

"Well," the Chief said, "that's enough for a quick runover. Are there any other loose ends?"

"That's all, sir, except for disposing of Miss Bogart's personal effects. They're outside now."

"I'll attend to them," the Chief said. "That's one of the tough things about where I sit, Jack."

"By the way, sir, I suppose Ruth Bogart is a cover name?"

"The Ruth's real, the Bogart isn't. If I were you, I'd only be inquisitive when you're asked to be, Buster."

He appreciated the Chief's reproof, but also he resented it.

"When you've been in the business ten years," he said, "and have all your personality knocked out of you on the road, even so sometimes you can't help being interested if you have to throw in with someone for a while. Occasionally, you can't help being human."

From where he sat the Chief had frequently had to deal with temperament. He understood better than most psychiatrists the inevitable results of long repressions. "You're looking tired, Jack. I know you've had it rough," he said, "but I know you, and it's nothing that a couple of weeks off and some sleep won't fix."

His diagnosis could have been correct some weeks ago, but it was not right now. Something had happened the moment Jack Rhyce had seen the empty room in the Imperial Hotel in Tokyo.

"Even if I rest up," he said, "I'm afraid I'll still stay human, Chief. I won't be the old smooth-running machine again."

The Chief smiled tolerantly. "Listen, Buster," he said, "you're in no shape to analyze yourself. What you need is a shot in the arm and sleep. Never mind putting anything in the works until tomorrow afternoon."

"Very well, sir," Jack said, and he pushed back his chair. "Only one thing else. I'd appreciate it if you could see your way clear to giving me her photograph."

The Chief raised his eyebrows and let his pencil drop to the desk, and the minute disorderly sound was an adequate measure of his surprise.

"So that's the way it was?" he said. "I'm sorry for you, son."

Jack Rhyce was glad that the thing was in the open for once, and it would only be for once. "That's the way it was," he said. "We fell in love like a couple of kids. We both knew it was a damn-fool thing to do, but it didn't spoil the operation, Chief."

"She wouldn't have wanted it to," the Chief said. "She was a very good girl, Jack."

"She wanted me to go ahead," he said. "She told me to, over the telephone. Anyway, we couldn't have found her in time."

"You didn't tell me she spoke to you," the Chief said.

"I left it out," Jack answered. "Maybe I should have this time. It's something that belongs to her and me. As I was saying, sometimes you can't help being human, Chief."

He was talking too much and he despised self-pity.

"I'll tell you all about her someday," the Chief said, "but I don't believe now is quite the time."

"If it's just the same to you, I'd rather not know any more about her, except what belonged to us. I admit it wasn't very much."

He stood up. He had not intended to speak his mind, but that brief talk about her had crystallized his thoughts.

"We didn't have many opportunities to talk, but we both decided that we'd go back to the outside when we came home. She isn't here, but I'm going, anyway, sir."

"Now, wait," the Chief began, "this is all on the spur of the moment. Is it anything I said that made you come up with this?"

"No, sir. But I'm going to hand in my resignation."

"Now, Jack, you can't do that. You're the best man in the office. You're in line to follow me here. You'd be like a fish out of water, on the outside."

He was aware that what the Chief said was true. He had intended to think it over, but instead it was done already.

"I've got reasons, sir," he said.

"All right," the Chief said. "Just name the reasons."

Jack Rhyce squared his shoulders.

"After what happened over there I could never be the man I used to be. Being with her made me too human, Chief, and when you get too human you get fallible, and when you get to thinking about the outside you get forgetful. Part of me's back there. I've lost something, and I'll never get it back."

The Chief was also on his feet. "You're talking off the top of your head," he said.

"You may be right, sir, but she wanted me on the outside. She asked me to promise."

"Jack," the Chief said, "you're going through what everyone in the outfit goes through periodically. Something chips off you every time you go through anything, but you're the kind it only makes sharper. I'll make you a bet: in a week or so you'll want to stay in the business on account of her. I just want two promises from you. Don't say anything to anyone about this talk, and don't make a decision until you've had two weeks away somewhere."

"All right," Jack said, "if that's the way you want it."

He felt closer to her, now that he had spoken, than he had since she had gone. He knew as sure as fate that he was not coming back.

John P. Marquand

Two WEEKS after John P. Marquand graduated from Harvard in 1915, he joined the Boston *Transcript* as a reporter. His brief career in journalism, and even briefer one as an advertising copy writer, terminated in 1921 when *The Saturday Evening Post* bought a short story of his, the second he had written. This sale marked the beginning of a long and fruitful association with that magazine, the first publisher of his "Mr. Moto" stories.

While periodically recording Mr. Moto's adventures Mr. Marquand was establishing his reputation as the foremost satirist of the New England social scene. In this field his first entry was *The Late George Apley*, which won the Pulitzer Prize for 1937, followed by *Wickford Point, H. M. Pulham, Esq.*, and half a dozen other best-selling novels.

Several of Mr. Marquand's novels and stories have been made into movies, and two of them — *The Late George Apley* and *Point of No Return* — were successful Broadway productions. *Melville Goodwin, USA*, a penetrating study of a general's life and ambitions, appeared in the Winter 1952 volume of Condensed Books.

Mr. Marquand's home is at Newburyport, Massachusetts, where his family has lived for over a century.